For Reference

Y0-CVG-412

Not to be taken from this room

MAGILL'S LITERARY ANNUAL 2024

Essay-Reviews of 150 Outstanding Books Published in the United States During 2023

With an Annotated List of Titles

Volume II
M-Z
Indexes

Edited by
Jennifer Sawtelle

SALEM PRESS
A Division of EBSCO Information Services, Inc.
Ipswich, Massachusetts

GREY HOUSE PUBLISHING

Cover photo: Leonardo Cendamo/Getty Images

Copyright © 2024, by Salem Press, a Division of EBSCO Information Services, Inc. All rights in this book are reserved. No part of this work may be used or reproduced in any manner whatsoever or transmitted in any form or by any means, electronic or mechanical, including photocopy, recording, or any information storage and retrieval system, without written permission from the copyright owner. For permissions requests, contact permissions@ebscohost.com.

Magill's Literary Annual, 2024, published by Grey House Publishing, Inc., Amenia, NY, under exclusive license from EBSCO Information Services, Inc.

For information contact Grey House Publishing/Salem Press, 4919 Route 22, PO Box 56, Amenia, NY 12501.

∞ The paper used in these volumes conforms to the American National Standard for Permanence of Paper for Printed Library Materials, Z39.48-1992 (R2009).

Publisher's Cataloging-In-Publication Data
(Prepared by The Donohue Group, Inc.)

Names: Magill, Frank N. (Frank Northen), 1907-1997, editor. | Wilson, John D., editor. | Kellman, Steven G., 1947- editor. | Goodhue, Emily, editor. | Poranski, Colin D., editor. | Akre, Matthew, editor. | Spires, Kendal, editor. | Toth, Gabriela, editor. | Sawtelle, Jennifer, editor.

Title: Magill's literary annual.

Description: <1977->: [Pasadena, Calif.] : Salem Press | <2015->: Ipswich, Massachusetts : Salem Press, a division of EBSCO Information Services, Inc. ; Amenia, NY : Grey House Publishing | Essay-reviews of ... outstanding books published in the United States during the previous year. | "With an annotated list of titles." | Editor: 1977- , F.N. Magill; <2010-2014>, John D. Wilson and Steven G. Kellman; <2015>, Emily Goodhue and Colin D. Poranski; <2016>, Matthew Akre, Kendal Spires, and Gabriela Toth; <2017->, Jennifer Sawtelle. | Includes bibliographical references and index.

Identifiers: ISSN: 0163-3058

Subjects: LCSH: Books--Reviews--Periodicals. | United States--Imprints--Book reviews--Periodicals. | Literature, Modern--21st century--History and criticism--Periodicals. | Literature, Modern--20th century--History and criticism--Periodicals.

Classification: LCC PN44 .M333 | DDC 028.1--dc23

FIRST PRINTING
PRINTED IN THE UNITED STATES OF AMERICA

CONTENTS

Complete Annotated List of Contents vii

A Man of Two Faces—*Viet Thanh Nguyen* 357
Master Slave Husband Wife—*Ilyon Woo* 362
Monica—*Daniel Clowes* 367
Monsters—*Claire Dederer* 372
Monstrous—*Sarah Myer* 376
More Than a Dream—*Yohuru Williams and Michael G. Long* 381
The Most Secret Memory of Men—*Mohamed Mbougar Sarr* 386
Mott Street—*Ava Chin* 391

Nearer My Freedom—*Monica Edinger and Lesley Younge* 396
No One Prayed Over Their Graves—*Khaled Khalifa* 401
North Woods—*Daniel Mason* 406

Old God's Time—*Sebastian Barry* 411
Ordinary Notes—*Christina Sharpe* 416
Our Migrant Souls—*Héctor Tobar* 421
Owner of a Lonely Heart—*Beth Nguyen* 425

Parachute Kids—*Betty C. Tang* 429
The Parrot and the Igloo—*David Lipsky* 433
Pineapple Street—*Jenny Jackson* 438
Pomegranate—*Helen Elaine Lee* 443
Poverty, by America—*Matthew Desmond* 447
Promise Boys—*Nick Brooks* 452
Promises of Gold—*José Olivarez* 457
Prophet Song—*Paul Lynch* 461

Quietly Hostile—*Samantha Irby* 466

The Rediscovery of America—*Ned Blackhawk* 470
Remember Us—*Jacqueline Woodson* 475
Roaming—*Jillian Tamaki and Mariko Tamaki* 479
Roman Stories—*Jhumpa Lahiri* 484
Rough Sleepers—*Tracy Kidder* 489

Saints of the Household—*Ari Tison* 494
Saying It Loud—*Mark Whitaker* 498
Silver Nitrate—*Silvia Moreno-Garcia* 503
Simon Sort of Says—*Erin Bow* 507

The Six—*Loren Grush* 512
The Slip—*Prudence Peiffer*. 517
Small Mercies—*Dennis Lehane* 522
Soil—*Camille T. Dungy*. 527
A Spell of Good Things—*Ayọ̀bámi Adébáyọ̀*. 531
Starling House—*Alix E. Harrow* 536
A Stranger in Your Own City—*Ghaith Abdul-Ahad* 541
suddenly we—*Evie Shockley* 546
Symphony of Secrets—*Brendan Slocumb* 550

Temple Folk—*Aaliyah Bilal* 555
Tenacious Beasts—*Christopher J. Preston*. 559
The Terraformers—*Annalee Newitz*. 564
Thin Skin—*Jenn Shapland* 569
This Other Eden—*Paul Harding* 574
Thunderclap—*Laura Cumming*. 578
Tom Lake—*Ann Patchett*. 583
Tremor—*Teju Cole* 588
The 272—*Rachel L. Swarns* 592

Valiant Women—*Lena S. Andrews* 597
The Vaster Wilds—*Lauren Groff* 602
Vera Wong's Unsolicited Advice for Murderers—*Jesse Q. Sutanto* 607
Victory City—*Salman Rushdie*. 611

The Wager—*David Grann* 616
Warrior Girl Unearthed—*Angeline Boulley*. 621
We Are All So Good At Smiling—*Amber McBride* 625
Wednesday's Child—*Yiyun Li* 629
Wellness—*Nathan Hill* 634
Western Lane—*Chetna Maroo* 639
Weyward—*Emilia Hart*. 643
Whalefall—*Daniel Kraus*. 648
What an Owl Knows—*Jennifer Ackerman* 652
When Crack Was King—*Donovan X. Ramsey* 657
White Cat, Black Dog—*Kelly Link*. 661
The Wind Knows My Name—*Isabel Allende* 665
The Windeby Puzzle—*Lois Lowry* 670
Witness—*Jamel Brinkley*. 674
Women We Buried, Women We Burned—*Rachel Louise Snyder* 679
The Words That Remain—*Stênio Gardel*. 684
The World—*Simon Sebag Montefiore* 689

CONTENTS

Yellowface—*Rebecca F. Kuang* 694
You Have to Be Prepared to Die Before You Can Begin to Live—*Paul Kix* . . . 699
You: The Story—*Ruta Sepetys* 703

Category Index 709
Title Index 713

COMPLETE ANNOTATED LIST OF CONTENTS

VOLUME I

Above Ground. 1
  Clint Smith's second poetry collection explores the joys and anxieties of raising young children in a world full of contradictions and injustices.

The Adventures of Amina al-Sirafi 5
  The Adventures of Amina al-Sirafi is a thrilling tale of a legendary pirate wrenched from retirement to complete a challenging quest. While encountering mystical places and creatures, she seeks redemption and confronts the ambitions she buried for her family.

After the Funeral and Other Stories. 10
  Tessa Hadley's fourth short story collection explores the daily lives, hidden regrets, and life changes of various people living in England and Wales from the 1970s to the present day.

Age of Vice 15
  Set in India around the turn of the twenty-first century, Age of Vice is a captivating novel following the infamous Wadia family and the bystanders caught in the crossfire of their grandiose yet immoral actions.

All the Sinners Bleed 20
  Investigating a shooting at the local high school in his rural Virginia county, Sheriff Titus Crown discovers a deeper web of crime that puts him on the track of a serial killer. However, his investigation is complicated by the racial strife and other tensions that permeate every aspect of life in the community.

American Ramble: A Walk of Memory and Renewal. 25
  American Ramble: A Walk of Memory and Renewal is a meditative travelogue that recounts the author's experience of walking 330 miles from his home on Capitol Hill in Washington, DC, to Manhattan, exploring the nation's past and present along the way.

An Amerikan Family: The Shakurs and the Nation They Created 30
  Santi Elijah Holley's carefully researched book traces the Shakurs, a family bonded by their commitment to the struggle for Black liberation, across multiple generations, highlighting their goals, triumphs, and tragedies.

The Art Thief: A True Story of Love, Crime, and a Dangerous Obsession 35
    In The Art Thief: A True Story of Love, Crime, and a Dangerous Obsession, *Michael Finkel recounts the crimes of French art thief Stéphane Breitwieser and the events surrounding his arrests and imprisonment.*

August Wilson: A Life 40
    August Wilson: A Life *is the first book-length biography of the influential American playwright. The book traces Wilson's family from the moment of emancipation after the Civil War through Wilson's death in 2005, with its principal focus on the playwright's career and major theatrical works.*

The Bee Sting 45
    In The Bee Sting, *Irish author Paul Murray tells the story of a family on the brink of collapse.*

The Berry Pickers 50
    A Mi'kmaq family is exposed to tragedy after tragedy over nearly a half-century, starting with the disappearance of four-year-old Ruthie while her family picks blueberries in a field in Maine. Intertwined with their tale are chapters narrated by Norma, a girl who struggles with an overprotective mother as well as the feeling that all is not right with her family.

Beyond the Door of No Return 55
    David Diop's historical novel imagines the secret life of eighteenth century French botanist Michel Adanson in order to shine a light on a dark chapter in Europe's colonial history.

Big 60
    Vashti Harrison's award-winning picture book tells the story of a young girl attempting to come to terms with her body.

Big Tree 64
    Spanning millennia, the children's novel Big Tree *tells the tale of two sycamore seeds. Through Brian Selznick's thoughtful words and illustrations, the vast history of the natural world and how it connects to humankind is revealed.*

Biography of X 68
    Catherine Lacey's fourth novel, Biography of X, *is an ambitious project that encompasses biography, reportage, alternative history, politics, opinion, mystery, and adventure in the course of describing the life of a multitalented yet enigmatic woman.*

COMPLETE ANNOTATED LIST OF CONTENTS

Birnam Wood 73
   Eleanor Catton's third novel, the suspenseful Birnam Wood, *pits a motley crew of New Zealand guerrilla gardeners against a ruthless American billionaire in an effort to protect precious natural resources.*

Blackouts 78
   Justin Torres's experimental novel unfolds as a conversation between a young man and his older, dying friend as the latter passes along his incomplete life's work, a project based around a real-life 1941 study of homosexuality. The result is a complex, lyrical narrative that blends rich fictional lives with historical documents to examine the complexity of queer experience.

Bright Young Women 83
   Bright Young Women, *a novel by suspense writer Jessica Knoll, tells the story of one of America's most famous serial killers from the victims' point of view. Featuring an intricately built plotline and carefully constructed characters, the novel gives the women the last word in the final murderous spree of Ted Bundy.*

Chain-Gang All-Stars 88
   In Chain-Gang All-Stars, *Nana Kwame Adjei-Brenyah, the author of the acclaimed 2018 short story collection Friday Black, imagines a dystopian future in which American prisoners vie to win their freedom by participating in gladiatorial fight-to-the-death battles on a popular reality television show.*

Cobalt Red: How the Blood of the Congo Powers Our Lives 93
   In Cobalt Red, *prizewinning author and activist Siddarth Kara presents a searing depiction of the inhumane working conditions faced by cobalt miners in the Democratic Republic of the Congo. Kara demonstrates that the modern world economy is dependent upon a resource mined by people who are being treated like slaves.*

A Council of Dolls 98
   A Council of Dolls, *by bestselling author Mona Susan Power, is a sweeping historical novel following three separate generations of young Indigenous girls that focuses on the ways in which seemingly inanimate objects—their worn yet beloved dolls—help the young women survive discrimination and persecution.*

The Covenant of Water 103
   In this epic novel of twentieth-century India, the story of a family in Kerala that suffers from a mysterious medical condition causing the drowning deaths of at least one family member in each generation intertwines with that of a young Scottish doctor who joins the Indian Medical Services.

The Crane Husband 108
    Kelly Barnhill's short novel uses the device of a reimagined fairy tale to tell the story of a teenage girl dealing with familial abuse.

Crook Manifesto 113
    Part crime novel and part social history, Crook Manifesto, *Colson Whitehead's sprawling and ambitious sequel to Harlem Shuffle (2021) continues the tragicomic misadventures of furniture store owner and ex-fence Ray Carney, who, in a triptych of stories, encounters a wide cast of characters in corruption-riddled 1970s New York City.*

A Day of Fallen Night. 118
    Set five centuries before the events of the 2019 novel The Priory of the Orange Tree, A Day of Fallen Night *chronicles its protagonists' efforts to combat a dire threat that has emerged from the volcano known as the Dreadmount.*

The Deadline 123
    The Deadline *collects an array of essays by award-winning historian and columnist Jill Lepore, covering a wide range of topics including politics, law, and literature.*

The Devil of the Provinces 128
    Juan Cárdenas's short novel The Devil of the Provinces *is a twist on the classic crime novel that pursues the question of whether returning home again is ever truly possible.*

The Diaspora Sonnets. 132
    In The Diaspora Sonnets, *award-winning poet Oliver de la Paz uses deft and rich formal invention to convey a family's search for home and belonging as members of the Filipino diaspora in the United States*

Don't Fear the Reaper. 136
    A sequel to the hugely successful horror novel My Heart Is a Chainsaw, Don't Fear the Reaper *continues the story of protagonist Jade Daniels, a rebellious young woman who must outthink a murderer as he embarks on a spree of revenge killings.*

Dust Child. 140
    Nguyễn Phan Quế Mai's second novel, Dust Child *(2023), focuses on the hidden casualties of the Vietnam War: lost children left behind, the result of temporary relationships between vulnerable people, and aggressive American soldiers.*

COMPLETE ANNOTATED LIST OF CONTENTS

The End of Drum-Time 144
    Hanna Pylväinen's historical novel tells the story of a mixed community of Sámi people and Christian settlers living in northern Scandinavia amid religious awakening and creeping colonialism in the nineteenth century.

The Exceptions: Nancy Hopkins, MIT, and the Fight for Women in Science . . 149
    In The Exceptions: Nancy Hopkins, MIT, and the Fight for Women in Science, Kate Zernike chronicles the life and career of molecular biologist Hopkins and explores the role she and fifteen other women played in exposing systemic discrimination at the Massachusetts Institute of Technology.

Family Lore 155
    In Family Lore, Flor, the second eldest of the Marte sisters, has a special gift: she can accurately predict when and where someone will die. When Flor mysteriously decides to host her own living wake, the story explores its characters' struggles in the days leading up to it in a tale that weaves present-day New York City with flashbacks to the Martes' upbringing in the Dominican Republic.

Family Style: Memories of an American from Vietnam 160
    In his graphic memoir Family Style, Thien Pham describes his journey from Vietnam to the United States as a youth and his gradual acculturation as an American citizen. Pham organizes his book in chapters featuring different kinds of foods, both Vietnamese and American. This culinary theme underscores the importance of family and community to his story.

The Ferryman 165
    On a seemingly utopian tropical island in the far-distant future, privileged Prosperans enjoy the benefits of health, wealth, and happiness until they are retired and returned to society with their youth restored and their memories wiped.

A Fever in the Heartland: The Ku Klux Klan's Plot to Take Over America,
    and the Woman Who Stopped Them 169
    Journalist Timothy Egan details the rise to power in the 1920s of the Ku Klux Klan in the Midwest under the leadership of D. C. Stephenson, and the events surrounding the death of Madge Oberholtzer that led to his swift fall from power.

Fire Weather: A True Story from a Hotter World 174
    In Fire Weather: A True Story from a Hotter World, John Vaillant investigates both the causes and effects of the massive wildfire that devastated the community of Fort McMurray in Alberta, Canada, in May 2016.

A First Time for Everything 179
    In this graphic memoir aimed at middle-grade readers, author and illustrator Dan Santat chronicles his thirteen-year-old self's formative trip to Europe in 1989.

Flee North: A Forgotten Hero and the Fight for Freedom
in Slavery's Borderland 184
    Flee North: A Forgotten Hero and the Fight for Freedom in Slavery's Borderland *recounts the life and accomplishments of Thomas Smallwood, a formerly enslaved man who helped hundreds of enslaved people escape via the Underground Railroad and published scathing accounts of how he outwitted slavecatchers, slave traders, and police officers.*

The Fraud 189
    Award-winning British author Zadie Smith's first historical novel, The Fraud, *is a groundbreaking chronicle of social and racial tension in Victorian England, populated by characters both real and fictional.*

From From 194
    Award-winning poet Monica Youn's collection From From *employs a wide range of forms and techniques to explore themes of anti-Asian racism, misogyny, desire, fear, and language.*

From Unincorporated Territory [åmot] 198
    From unincorporated territory [åmot], the fifth volume of Craig Santos Perez's ongoing poetry series, considers how poetry and storytelling can heal the compounded trauma of colonialism, militarism, and environmental injustice endured by his CHamoru people on Guam.

The Future. 202
    Unsettling and thrilling in equal measure, British author Naomi Alderman's dystopian novel The Future *follows an unlikely group of friends working to defeat a common corporate enemy while saving the world from the apocalypse.*

Ghost of the Orphanage: A Story of Mysterious Deaths, a Conspiracy of Silence,
and a Search for Justice 206
    Ghosts of the Orphanage *traces Christine Kenneally's historical research into orphanages of the early twentieth century. The author shares stories of abuse, illness, emotional upheaval, and even torture and death from across the globe in homes where children were supposed to be protected, mostly by Catholic nuns and priests.*

The Great Displacement: Climate Change and the Next American Migration . . 211
    Journalist Jake Bittle profiles Americans who have been forced to move due to climate-related disasters and considers the future migrations that will reshape US demographics.

COMPLETE ANNOTATED LIST OF CONTENTS

Greek Lessons. 216
 Greek Lessons *(2023), the fourth novel of South Korean author Han Kang to be translated to English, was first published in South Korea in 2011 and presents the attempts of two lonely, flawed characters to communicate with one another.*

The Half Known Life: In Search of Paradise 221
 Told through a series of essays divided into three sections, Pico Iyer's The Half Known Life *explores how people around the world use spirituality to find deeper meaning in their lives.*

Happiness Falls. 226
 Framed against the backdrop of the COVID-19 pandemic, Happiness Falls *follows a family torn apart by the disappearance of their father. As the investigation brings more questions than answers, they are forced to reconsider their perceptions of success, happiness, and each other.*

The Hard Parts: A Memoir of Courage and Triumph 231
 In this gripping, inspirational, and deeply personal memoir, Oksana Masters recounts her lifetime journey of survival and triumph, overcoming horrific conditions at a Ukrainian orphanage and severe physical disabilities to become one of the most decorated Paralympic athletes of all time.

The Heaven & Earth Grocery Store. 236
 James McBride's The Heaven & Earth Grocery Store *weaves realities about race and class into the plot through depictions of characters' lived experiences as they earn their livelihoods, seek justice, and uphold family and community ties against a backdrop of endemic anti-Black and anti-Jewish discrimination.*

Hell Bent 241
 In the second installment of Leigh Bardugo's dark academia fantasy series for adults, street-smart heroine Galaxy Stern, a wheelwalker who gains strength and knowledge from ghosts, battles the demons of hell to save the soul of her mentor, Darlington.

Hello Beautiful 246
 Hello Beautiful *examines the complex dynamics of familial love and estrangement by chronicling the relationships between four sisters over the course of three decades.*

The Hive and the Honey 250
 The Hive and the Honey *is a collection of short stories about the Korean diaspora that span hundreds of years and multiple continents.*

Holler, Child..254
    LaToya Watkins's short story collection brings to vivid life the stories of a handful of African American women and men living in Texas who experience trauma, pain, and racism.

The House of Doors..258
    Tan Twan Eng's third Booker Prize–nominated novel, The House of Doors, *concerns events in Penang, Malaya, surrounding visits by author W. Somerset Maugham and Chinese revolutionary Sun Yat Sen.*

A House With Good Bones...263
    A House With Good Bones *is a Southern gothic horror novel from Hugo Award–winning author Ursula Vernon, writing as T. Kingfisher. In it, archaeoentomologist Sam Montgomery returns to her childhood home in rural North Carolina, where she is puzzled by the absence of insects, her mother's strange behavior, and other unsettling phenomena. As she tries to solve these mysteries she must reckon with her family's past.*

How to Sell a Haunted House...267
    How to Sell a Haunted House *is a horror-comedy novel by Grady Hendrix that examines the impact of generational trauma on families.*

Hula..271
    Chronicling the lives of multiple generations of women in a Native Hawaiian family from the Big Island, Hula *is both a classic coming-of-age tale and a depiction of the enduring trauma that Western colonialism continues to have on Hawaii.*

I Have Some Questions for You.......................................276
    An astute critique of true crime and the inherent misogyny baked into contemporary culture, Rebecca Makkai's I Have Some Questions for You *is the story of a woman returning to the boarding school of her adolescence, and becoming entangled in a mysterious murder that took place when she was a student.*

I Saw Death Coming: A History of Terror and Survival in the
    War against Reconstruction......................................281
    Williams chronicles the stories of Southern Black families who were terrorized by bands of White vigilantes for daring to exercise their newly acquired civil rights during the years immediately following the American Civil War.

Imogen, Obviously...286
    Becky Albertalli's novel Imogen, Obviously *is a coming-of-age story focused on friendship, family, and first love. The young adult novel presents a cast of relatable and endearing characters who show what it means to support and love each other through the trials that come with discovering one's sexuality and identity.*

COMPLETE ANNOTATED LIST OF CONTENTS

Impossible Escape: A True Story of Survival and Heroism in Nazi Europe . . . 291
    In this meticulously researched nonfiction thriller, Sheinkin chronicles the remarkable Holocaust survival story of Rudolf Vrba, who, with fellow prisoner Alfred Wetzler in 1944, escaped from the Nazis' notorious Auschwitz concentration camp and became one of the most famous whistleblowers during World War II. Lending added perspective to the book is the parallel story of Vrba's friend and future wife Gerta Sidonová, who similarly overcomes great odds while hiding in Hungary.

In the Lives of Puppets 296
    In the Lives of Puppets *tells the story of a young human who must travel to the City of Electric Dreams to save his android father from the collective Authority, learning challenging truths about himself and his companions along the way.*

Into the Light 301
    Mark Oshiro's young adult novel Into the Light *follows the journey of an unhoused teenager as he searches for his sister who has fallen victim to a dangerous religious group.*

King: A Life 306
    In the National Book Award-nominated King: A Life *(2023), biographer Jonathan Eig uses new sources and interviews to provide readers with an updated understanding of who civil rights icon Martin Luther King Jr. really was.*

Lady Tan's Circle of Women 311
    Lisa See's 2023 novel draws on real-life events to tell the story of a female doctor who successfully navigates the rigid class and gender structures of Ming Dynasty China over many decades.

Land of Milk and Honey 316
    In a dystopian near-future where Earth is engulfed in smog, Land of Milk and Honey *tells the story of a young chef recruited to serve the residents of a secluded mountaintop colony. Through the depictions of culinary abundance, wealth disparity, and scientific innovation, the novel grapples with the ethical quandary of indulgence in a dying world.*

The Last Animal 321
    The Last Animal *tells the story of a teenager, her sister, and their mother as they navigate grief and attempt to bring the woolly mammoth back from extinction.*

The Last Tale of the Flower Bride 325
    In The Last Tale of the Flower Bride, *the husband of wealthy heiress Indigo Maxwell-Casteñada seeks to uncover the truth about her long-missing childhood friend, Azure, while also reckoning with his own memories of the past.*

Let Us Descend 330
    Let Us Descend *follows an African American teenager enslaved in the antebellum South as her separation from loved ones after being sold becomes a journey into hell.*

The Librarianist 334
    The Librarianist *is a moving tale of a retired librarian, an examination of one introvert's life and the people who pass through it, marked by melancholy but also tinged with humor.*

Liliana's Invincible Summer: A Sister's Search for Justice. 339
    Cristina Rivera Garza's hybrid nonfiction book follows her efforts to both bring justice to her sister, who was murdered by her boyfriend in 1990, and to recreate her sister's life.

Lone Women 343
    Victor LaValle's novel uses elements of speculative fiction, horror, and the western genres to probe previously underexplored corners of American history and to craft a compelling drama of self- and community-empowerment.

Loot 347
    At the heart of Tania James's historical novel Loot *is a life-sized automaton of a tiger eating a soldier of the British East India Company. The tiger was fabricated by a French artisan and an Indian woodcarver for Tipu Sultan, the warlike ruler of the Indian state of Mysore and an inveterate opponent of the British.*

The Lost Year: A Survival Story of the Ukrainian Famine 352
    While helping his hundred-year-old great-grandmother during the COVID-19 pandemic, thirteen-year-old Matthew discovers the long-hidden history of the Holodomor, Joseph Stalin's planned famine in Soviet Ukraine. This middle-grade novel, a National Book Award finalist, connects the twin tragedies of the COVID epidemic and the Holodomor to confront the past in a rapidly changing world.

VOLUME II

A Man of Two Faces: A Memoir, A History, A Memorial 357
    In his eccentric but stimulating memoir A Man of Two Faces, *Viet Thanh Nguyen presents a politically charged explanation of his life and work, including an analysis of his experiences as a Vietnamese American in a White-dominated culture and a wrenching recovery of memories about his parents.*

Master Slave Husband Wife: An Epic Journey from Slavery to Freedom 362
    Master Slave Husband Wife *is the story of Ellen and William Craft, enslaved in Georgia, who escaped to freedom by disguising themselves as a wealthy, ailing young man and an enslaved valet, and of the lives they made for themselves as free people.*

COMPLETE ANNOTATED LIST OF CONTENTS

Monica 367
    In the graphic novel Monica, *distinguished cartoonist and writer Daniel Clowes presents a compelling tale of a woman's quest to find her parents, an endeavor that eventually takes on cosmic significance. In a series of sometimes subtly interrelated chapters, Clowes evokes various genres from the history of comic books, ranging from military comics to cosmic horror.*

Monsters: A Fan's Dilemma. 372
    Claire Dederer's memoir/criticism hybrid Monsters: A Fan's Dilemma *attempts to reconcile fandom with moral code by examining such artists as Ernest Hemingway, Virginia Woolf, and Roman Polanski, among others.*

Monstrous: A Transracial Adoption Story. 376
    In this graphic memoir, Sarah Myer recounts their childhood struggles with feelings of abandonment and incidents of racism as they explore their gender identity and develop a passion for art and anime.

More Than a Dream: The Radical March on Washington for Jobs and Freedom . . 381
    Historians Yohuru Williams and Michael G. Long offer middle-grade readers an in-depth look at the making of the 1963 March on Washington for Jobs and Freedom, an iconic episode in the civil rights movement.

The Most Secret Memory of Men. 386
    Mohamed Mbougar Sarr's genre-defying novel, The Most Secret Memory of Men, *follows a rising Senegalese novelist solving the mystery of another novelist while simultaneously immersing himself in the African French literary scene.*

Mott Street: A Chinese American Family's Story of Exclusion
    and Homecoming 391
    Ava Chin's Mott Street: A Chinese American Family's Story of Exclusion and Homecoming *examines the lives of the author's key ancestors, many of whom resided at the same apartment building in New York City's Chinatown.*

Nearer My Freedom: The Interesting Life of Olaudah Equiano by Himself . . . 396
    Educators Monica Edinger and Lesley Younge reshape Olaudah Equiano's classic eighteenth-century slave narrative into a work of found verse for contemporary young adult readers.

No One Prayed Over Their Graves 401
    A poetic novel spanning several decades, No One Prayed Over Their Graves *follows two childhood friends and their descendants as they seek to find purpose among strife in early twentieth-century Aleppo, Syria.*

North Woods 406
    Daniel Mason offers a sweeping vision of life in western Massachusetts and a commentary on the relationship between humans and the environment through the interlocking stories of several generations of families who inhabit a cabin set in the deep woods.

Old God's Time 411
    In the novel Old God's Time, *police officer Tom Kettle emerges from retirement to investigate a case from his past, reckon with the magnitude of his personal losses, and separate reality from fiction.*

Ordinary Notes 416
    Ordinary Notes *is Christina Sharpe's depiction of the love, joy, triumph, labor, pain, and tragedy that marks everyday Black life under the White supremacist regime of the United States. As the title suggests, the work collects notes composed by the author—fragments of memoir, personal reflection, critical theory, literature, and archival documents—blended with art images, artifacts of public history and personal life, and the author's photographs.*

Our Migrant Souls: A Meditation on Race and the Meanings and
    Myths of "Latino" 421
    Pulitzer Prize–winning journalist Héctor Tobar explores what it means to be Latino in twenty-first-century American culture with his essay collection Our Migrant Souls. *Through careful self-examination and a curiosity about the experiences of others, Tobar creates a moving tapestry that questions the foundation of modern ideas about race and culture.*

Owner of a Lonely Heart 425
    Beth Nguyen's second memoir chronicles the complicated relationship she and her mother share after being separated following the author's birth. Gravitating around the events of the Fall of Saigon in 1975, the memoir traces the fallout and trauma that accompanied her family's upheaval from the lives they knew before immigrating to the United States as refugees.

Parachute Kids 429
    After traveling to the US from Taiwan under the unknowing guise of a family vacation to Disney Land, Feng-Li and her two older siblings are left to take care of themselves in Betty C. Tang's graphic novel Parachute Kids. *Filled with poignant moments,* Parachute Kids *is a story about resilience and bravery in the face of uncertainty.*

The Parrot and the Igloo: Climate and the Science of Denial. 433
    The Parrot and the Igloo *offers a deep dive, over more than two centuries, into three types of figures central to human civilization's ability to engage with climate*

COMPLETE ANNOTATED LIST OF CONTENTS

change: the inventors, the scientists, and the deniers. Author David Lipsky explores several such figures to make a clarifying determination of the role played by a small group of deniers in obfuscating, attacking, and crippling positive change.

Pineapple Street. 438
The fictional story of a wealthy New York City family, Pineapple Street *provides witty yet humanizing insight into the lives of the one percent, including their attitudes toward marriage, the factors that motivate them, and how they interact with those outside of their social circles.*

Pomegranate. 443
Helen Elaine Lee's groundbreaking novel about incarceration, healing, and self-actualization is a stark condemnation of the US prison system, a spotlight on the exploitation of Black women and their bodies, and, finally, an inspiring road to beauty and recovery in spite of these seemingly insurmountable challenges.

Poverty, by America. 447
In Poverty, by America, *sociologist Matthew Desmond lays out the systemic sources of entrenched poverty in the United States and, without assigning blame to one political party or the other, describes ways Americans of means can become "poverty abolitionists" for the betterment of the entire country.*

Promise Boys 452
This young-adult novel about three charter-school students suspected in the murder of their principal is as much a portrait of systemic racism in the American school system as it is a page-turning, unpredictable mystery.

Promises of Gold 457
Drawing on his background as the son of Mexican immigrants, José Olivarez employs colloquial speech and a range of poetic forms to explore the Chicano experience.

Prophet Song 461
In a future Ireland in which the elected government is sliding into totalitarianism and civil unrest is brewing, microbiologist Eilish attempts to care for her children and aging father as she watches the situation spiral increasingly out of control.

Quietly Hostile 466
Quietly Hostile *is the fourth collection of autobiographical essays by humorist Samantha Irby.*

The Rediscovery of America: Native Peoples and the Unmaking
of U.S. History. 470
In The Rediscovery of America: Native Peoples and the Unmaking of U.S. History, *historian Ned Blackhawk retells five hundred years of postcolonial history to illustrate the fundamental role that Indigenous peoples have played in shaping the nation that the United States would eventually become.*

Remember Us. 475
Jacqueline Woodson's lyrical middle grade novel tells the story of a girl growing up in 1970s Brooklyn while dealing with a number of trying circumstances.

Roaming. 479
Cousins Jillian Tamaki and Mariko Tamaki bring to brilliant life an event that touches most young peoples' lives: traveling with friends for the first time. Set in New York City in 2009, Roaming *follows the adventures of childhood friends Dani and Zoe, and Dani's new college friend Fiona and explores how relationships shift and evolve with age.*

Roman Stories. 484
Jhumpa Lahiri's Roman Stories *is a return to the writer's celebrated form: the short story. Set in the Eternal City, the stories that make up this collection explore many paths of life, including those of locals, expats, immigrants, and tourists. The rich backdrop of Rome lends each story an additional element of drama and atmosphere.*

Rough Sleepers: Dr. Jim O'Connell's Urgent Mission to Bring Healing
to Homeless People 489
Rough Sleepers *explores the storied career of Dr. Jim O'Connell, a Harvard Medical School graduate who founded Boston Health Care for the Homeless and led the program for almost forty years. Paired with the history of O'Connell's career, Tracy Kidder presents vivid descriptions of unhoused patients, giving the reader intimate and unromanticized portraits of these complex individuals and their life stories.*

Saints of the Household. 494
Saints of the Household *is a young adult novel about two teenaged brothers born of a Bribri mother and a father of Nordic descent. Told in alternating voices, the book follows the two as they navigate life in a small Minnesota town in the aftermath of a violent incident.*

Saying It Loud: 1966—The Year Black Power Challenged the
Civil Rights Movement 498
In chapters organized chronologically around core dates and events throughout 1966, Mark Whitaker traces the competing origins of the Black Power movement

COMPLETE ANNOTATED LIST OF CONTENTS

in Saying It Loud. *The book seeks to set an accurate historical course between contradictory first-person accounts and inflammatory journalistic coverage. Saying It Loud also probes the origins of the movement in intersection and conflict with the civil rights movement.*

Silver Nitrate 503
   Following a pair of film industry workers neglected by the business they love, Silvia Moreno-Garcia's novel Silver Nitrate *is both an homage to classic horror films and a chilling tale of the real occult terror that might be lurking nearby.*

Simon Sort of Says 507
   A heart-wrenching yet hopeful middle-grade novel, Simon Sort of Says *follows a young boy who moves to a deliberately isolated town in order to escape the past trauma of a school shooting, only to find that you can never completely evade the past, even in the most remote of places.*

The Six: The Untold Story of America's First Women Astronauts 512
   In The Six, *science journalist Loren Grush chronicles the experiences, struggles, and accomplishments of the first six American women to ever go to space.*

The Slip: The New York City Street That Changed Art Forever 517
   Art historian Prudence Peiffer chronicles the lives of a group of artists who lived in the same New York City neighborhood during the 1950s and '60s, revealing a unique perspective on the postwar American art scene.

Small Mercies 522
   Set against the backdrop of the South Boston riots protesting school busing, Small Mercies *is at once a taut crime novel and a harrowing study of a fractious time in American history.*

Soil: The Story of a Black Mother's Garden 527
   Camille T. Dungy's memoir Soil: The Story of a Black Mother's Garden *connects societal issues such as racism, sexism, and climate change denial to the loving labor that goes into tending to a garden and family. Vivid scenes from Dungy's "prairie project" combine with careful examinations of historical wrongs to culminate in a surprising and exciting read.*

A Spell of Good Things 531
   In Ayòbámi Adébáyọ̀'s second novel, a local election entangles the fate of two Nigerian families from very different social classes.

Starling House 536
   Opal, a high school dropout and sole caretaker of her younger brother, Jasper, is plagued by nightmares involving Starling House—*a sinister place shrouded in*

mystery and the subject of many ghost stories. When she accepts a cleaning job from the house's warden, Opal is drawn into a real-life nightmare that threatens to tear apart not just her own life, but that of all the residents of the small coal town of Eden, Kentucky.

A Stranger in Your Own City: Travels in the Middle East's Long War 541
  Journalist Ghaith Abdul-Ahad chronicles the modern history of conflict, occupation, corruption, and war in Iraq—a history that resulted in a severely fragmented Baghdad, leaving the author to feel like an outsider in the city in which he was born.

suddenly we 546
  Evie Shockley's poetry collection suddenly we, a 2023 National Book Award finalist, seeks to understand what it means to exist in the world, today and in the past. Poems in the collection focus on the struggles and triumphs of historic characters, like Ida B. Wells, as placed alongside more exploratory pieces with an eye on the pandemic and post-pandemic life.

Symphony of Secrets 550
  Interspersed between 1920s and present-day Manhattan, Symphony of Secrets explores the enduring power of music connecting individuals across centuries, and the troubling erasure of diverse voices within the industry.

Temple Folk 555
  Aaliyah Bilal's debut short story collection, Temple Folk, explores the lives of Black Muslims in the United States through carefully written stories that expose both the good and the bad experienced by members of the Nation of Islam community.

Tenacious Beasts: Wildlife Recoveries That Change How We Think about Animals 559
  In Tenacious Beasts: Wildlife Recoveries That Change How We Think about Animals, Christopher J. Preston discusses efforts to increase the populations of select animal species and the lessons that can be learned from such resurgences.

The Terraformers 564
  With a plot spanning more than a thousand years in a distant future, Annalee Newitz's ambitious novel The Terraformers (2023) explores complex ethical challenges facing inhabitants of a planet purpose-built to be a paradise, offering both highly imaginative worldbuilding and insightful social commentary.

Thin Skin 569
  Thin Skin is a collection of essays about different topics, including racism, environmental concerns, late-stage capitalism, and post–Roe v. Wade motherhood that have come to define life in the 2020s.

COMPLETE ANNOTATED LIST OF CONTENTS

Weyward 643
Despite living in three very different time periods and worlds, three women are tied together through a powerful family connection to the natural world in this intricate novel. All three protagonists search for peace and enlightenment as they navigate womanhood, face trauma, and find themselves.

Whalefall 648
While scuba diving off the Californian coast to find his father's remains, seventeen-year-old Jay Gardiner is swallowed by a sperm whale and has only an hour left of oxygen to escape in this thrilling work of fiction by Daniel Kraus.

What an Owl Knows: The New Science of the World's Most Enigmatic Birds . . 652
In What an Owl Knows: The New Science of the World's Most Enigmatic Birds, *Jennifer Ackerman explores contemporary research into the capabilities, biology, and behavior of the world's many owl species.*

When Crack Was King: A People's History of a Misunderstood Era. 657
Alternating the in-depth stories of four individuals with historical and political background, journalist Donovan X. Ramsey paints a multifaceted portrait of the US crack epidemic of the 1980s and 1990s.

White Cat, Black Dog. 661
In the short story collection White Cat, Black Dog, *acclaimed writer Kelly Link puts a modern, genre-blending spin on seven classic fairy tales.*

The Wind Knows My Name 665
Isabel Allende's continent and generation spanning novel The Wind Knows My Name *explores the trauma of child separation, from the horrors of the lead up to World War II to US border policies that saw thousands of children taken from their parents.*

The Windeby Puzzle: History and Story 670
In The Windeby Puzzle, *a unique blend of historical facts and fictional imaginings, Lowry enchants and educates young readers about teenage life during the Iron Age and the existence of bog people.*

Witness 674
In this insightful collection of ten short stories, Jamel Brinkley explores the inherent tension that exists between observation and action in life.

Women We Buried, Women We Burned 679
Rachel Louise Snyder's fourth book, Women We Buried, Women We Burned *(2023), tells how she became a journalist, activist, and author, and why she began specializing in reporting about domestic abuse and violence.*

The Words That Remain 684
    Stênio Gardel's debut novel employ shifting narrative voices and a scrambled chronology to tell the powerful story of a Brazilian man's coming to terms with his sexuality.

The World: A Family History of Humanity. 689
    The World: A Family History of Humanity *approaches the history of human civilization through the lens of lineages and dynasties, following power families across the globe from ca. 2613 BCE into the twenty-first century CE in a massive, yet concise, twenty-three-act tome.*

Yellowface. 694
    Yellowface *is a dark, thrilling satire about competition, greed, privilege, cultural appropriation, and tokenism in the publishing industry. It is the fifth book by Poppy War trilogy author R. F. Kuang.*

You Have to Be Prepared to Die Before You Can Begin to Live: Ten Weeks in
    Birmingham That Changed America 699
    Paul Kix provides an in-depth look at a pivotal ten-week period in which civil rights leaders staged an operation in segregated Birmingham, Alabama, in 1963.

You: The Story: A Writer's Guide to Craft through Memory. 703
    In You: The Story; A Writer's Guide to Craft through Memory, *best-selling novelist Ruta Sepetys introduces aspiring writers to the valuable creative inspiration they can glean from their own lives, from the lives of the people around them, and from history.*

A Man of Two Faces
A Memoir, A History, A Memorial

Author: Viet Thanh Nguyen (b. 1971)
Publisher: Grove Press (New York).
 380 pp.
Type of work: Memoir
Time: 1971–present
Locales: Vietnam; United States

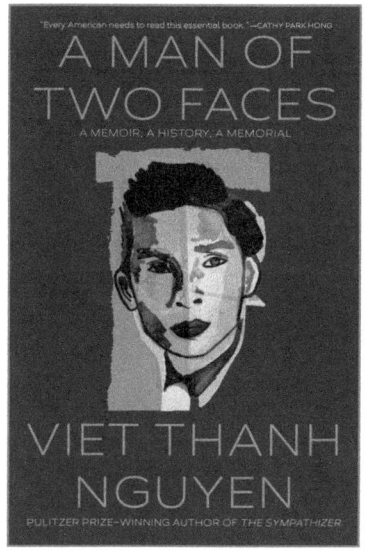

In his eccentric but stimulating memoir A Man of Two Faces, *Viet Thanh Nguyen presents a politically charged explanation of his life and work, including an analysis of his experiences as a Vietnamese American in a White-dominated culture and a wrenching recovery of memories about his parents.*

Principal personages

VIET THANH NGUYEN, the author and narrator
MÁ, his mother
BA, his father
TUNG, his brother
"J", his first girlfriend
LAN DUONG, his wife

Vietnamese American author Viet Thanh Nguyen burst onto the literary scene with a bang in 2015. His first novel, *The Sympathizer* (2015), was a brilliantly dark and complex tale of espionage and betrayal set during and after the Vietnam War, during which communist North Vietnam fought South Vietnam—a country ostensibly democratic and backed by the United States. Written in the grand spy novel tradition of earlier pioneers such as Joseph Conrad, Graham Greene, and John Le Carré, the style and the subject matter of *The Sympathizer* won it universal acclaim, culminating in a Pulitzer Prize for fiction. Nguyen followed up this triumph with *The Refugees* (2017), a collection of short stories, and *The Committed* (2021), a sequel to *The Sympathizer* that further traced the career of his first novel's antihero. For his 2023 memoir, *A Man of Two Faces: A Memoir, A History, A Memorial*, Nguyen shifted away from fiction to tell the story of his own life and family.

By any normal measure, Nguyen's is an exemplary American success story. Looked at from the outside, this tale of accomplishment is all the sweeter because Nguyen is an immigrant, the son of Vietnamese refugees. Nguyen enjoyed a successful career in academia before experiencing a rare level of critical acclaim and commercial success as a fiction writer. Yet, as *A Man of Two Faces* reveals, Nguyen is not fully at ease with this mainstream acceptance. He balks at becoming a poster boy for the

Viet Thanh Nguyen

American dream. In his own words, he is an "ingrate." In this regard, Nguyen is very like the unnamed protagonist of *The Sympathizer*, a communist double agent for the North Vietnamese embedded on the staff of a South Vietnamese general who later follows his ostensible boss into exile in the United States to continue spying on anti-communist Vietnamese refugees. After relocating to the US, the equivocal perspective of the narrator's character deepens; while remaining loyal to his duties as a double agent, he enjoys the material benefits of American life. Acutely conscious as both a spy and a Vietnamese refugee of his doubled otherness in America, the main character of *The Sympathizer* is unable to wholeheartedly assume an undivided faith in one side or the other. Hopelessly alienated, even as he murders and betrays a number of other refugees, he is a perpetual sympathizer with the opposition and continually at war with himself.

A Man of Two Faces clearly demonstrates that there was a metaphorically autobiographical dimension to this character. Nguyen was only four when his family fled Vietnam as the North Vietnamese stormed the Southern capital of Saigon in 1975 and brought the Vietnam War to a sudden, dramatic conclusion. His family relocated to the US as refugees; as a result Nguyen grew up in a very different world than the one that produced his parents. His cultural understanding of Vietnam came through a language that he grasped only imperfectly, the food his parents prepared, and the older Vietnamese he met who were sentimentally attached to a lost cause that meant nothing to him. Nguyen, for his part, was enveloped in 1980s US pop culture. A youthful viewing of Francis Ford Coppola's *Apocalypse Now* (1979), a spectacular reimaging of Joseph Conrad's *Heart of Darkness* (1899) set during the Vietnam War, made a huge impression on him and left Nguyen wondering which side he was supposed to be rooting for. This helped spark Nguyen's lifelong fascination with American depictions of the Vietnam War, which eventually resulted in a scholarly book entitled *Nothing Ever Dies: Vietnam and the Memory of War* (2016), which was nominated for the National Book Award. It also inspired an increasingly ambivalent attitude toward the land in which he grew up. Nguyen became intensely conscious of the almost complete absence of Asian voices in American popular culture, and the largely stereotypical representations of Asians in American movies and television.

As he relays in his memoir, Nguyen's increasing discontent came to fruition when he attended the University of California, Berkeley, and enthusiastically embraced its established tradition of student activism. Radicalized by a course in Asian American history, he helped lead protests calling for more Asian representation on campus and even took part in an occupation of the administration building and chancellor's office. His studies at the university also gave Nguyen a critical vocabulary to express the concerns causing him disquiet. There, and subsequently in graduate school, he was exposed to the full panoply of what he calls "a new language: Theory" and made it his own. Nguyen immersed himself in a number of philosophical and intellectual traditions, including Marxism and poststructuralism. Nguyen's romance with "Theory" no doubt informed aspects of *The Sympathizer*, but he kept it in check. He was less successful in doing so with *The Committed*, where his Communist spy turned 1980s drug dealer is anachronistically intersectional in his musings on class, women, and race.

It is clear from *A Man of Two Faces* that this theoretical outlook still informs Nguyen's worldview. Nguyen indulges himself with frequent editorializing on a variety of contemporary topics, including immigration, the 2016 election of US president Donald Trump, and the 2020 murder of George Floyd by a Minneapolis police officer. Nguyen's distaste for Trump is so clear that he conspicuously blacks out Trump's name. Nguyen makes other stylistic choices to emphasize his politics; for example, he persistently refers to America as "AMERICA™"—his term for the United States and its capitalist ideals. Readers' tolerance of these aspects of the memoir will vary, likely depending upon their political convictions. Such broad editorializing at the expense of a considered argument may resonate with those who share Nguyen's political convictions, but it is a pity that it might drive away an audience that would benefit from his acute observations. At one point he declares himself skeptical of all orthodoxies; this is not at all evident in a book that seems determined to reflect the heavily left-leaning worldview of a university faculty lounge. Immersion in academic theory may also explain the peculiar construction of *A Man of Two Faces*; Nguyen dispenses with traditional paragraphing and typography and instead mimics a polemical stream of consciousness, playfully experimenting with the faces of his pages for effect. While visually intriguing, this could also prove distracting for some readers.

Nguyen is too capable a writer and too subtle a psychologist to completely surrender to rhetoric. The emotional heart of his memoir is a riveting and wrenching tribute to his parents, Má and Ba. While Nguyen had discussed his family's story in the past, this memoir offers him the first chance to do so at length in print form. Nguyen's parents were born in the north of Vietnam; like hundreds of thousands of other Vietnamese Catholics, they moved south after the country was split into a communist North and a noncommunist South in 1954, following Vietnam's successful war of independence against France. Nguyen's parents settled in South Vietnam's Central Highlands. They were religiously devout and firmly anti-communist as North and South Vietnam fought each other throughout the 1960s and into the 1970s. When the North Vietnamese launched their successful, war-ending final offensive in 1975, Ba was in Saigon, the Southern capital, on business. Má left an adopted teenage daughter in charge of their house while she headed to Saigon with their two sons, including Nguyen, to look for Ba. Má and Ba would not see their daughter again for many years.

In real life, Nguyen can only recall flashes of memory from these early years in Vietnam and his family's dramatic escape, though he draws on stories from his parents and older brother, Tung, to flesh out this narrative in his memoir. After a tumultuous period as refugees in Pennsylvania, where bureaucratic complications briefly separated the family, his parents settled with their two sons in San Jose, California, where they joined a growing community of Vietnamese expatriates. There, they opened a Vietnamese grocery store in downtown San Jose and became the sort of hardworking and patriotic immigrants that sometimes exasperates Nguyen in his mode as critic of "AMERICA™." Má and Ba worked very hard, spending long hours at their grocery store, yet they soon established a comfortable home and enjoyed a middle-class lifestyle. While the family lived in relative comfort, Nguyen describes how occasional moments of terror disturbed the family's domestic tranquility; for example, one time, a thief shot Má and Ba at their store. Despite this, the couple raised two successful sons. Tung, Nguyen's older brother, became valedictorian of his high school class, attended Harvard University, and went to medical school, while Nguyen followed his own path to becoming a university professor and writer.

Much of Nguyen's book revolves around his ambivalent, complex relationship with his parents. On the one hand, they clearly loved him in their traditional Vietnamese way, and never objected to his voluminous reading, even driving him to the library every week as he loaded up with books. Yet he grew distant from them as he began to question the world around him, a shift the memoir describes in detail. Although he dutifully attended Catholic school and weekly Mass, he inwardly abandoned his parents' faith. Most dramatically, he defied Má and Ba's expectation that he date Catholic Vietnamese girls, secretly entering into a relationship with "J," who was Catholic but from a Filipino family. More traumatic was Nguyen's grappling with the deteriorating mental and physical health of his mother. Má, as Nguyen reveals, had suffered numerous mental health crises during her time in the US, dating back to the family's brief stint in Pennsylvania. As a young man, Nguyen blamed himself and feared that this was a consequence of Má discovering the truth of his relationship with "J." While she enjoyed periods of recovery, Má's mental health issues became more debilitating in 2005, and she continued to struggle enormously with her mental health until her death in 2018. While reflecting on his mother's life and eventual death, Nguyen wonders if she was a belated casualty of war and hints at the lasting trauma that impacted an entire generation of Vietnamese people.

A Man of Two Faces was well received upon its publication, and it was longlisted for the National Book Award for nonfiction. In a representative review for the *Chicago Review of Books*, Joe Stanek complimented the memoir's "lyricism" and highlighted Nguyen's "adept family memorialization," though Stanek also felt that the "immensity of ideas" contained in the memoir's political commentary "threaten[ed] to distract from" the book's family history. Lisa Ko, who reviewed *A Man of Two Faces* for the *Washington Post*, praised the memoir as "sharp and affecting . . . a weapon, a lamentation." While noting the book's serious subject matter, Ko complimented Nguyen's "playfulness," including his experimental formatting and "sardonic humor." Like other critics, Ko felt that Nguyen's loving yet sharp-edged depiction of his parents' physical and spiritual journey from Vietnam to the United States was the book's strongest feature; indeed, it is this delicate balance between political tract and family history that makes *A Man of Two Faces* a fascinating if sometimes difficult book.

Author Biography
Viet Thanh Nguyen began his career in academia and taught for many years at the University of Southern California in Los Angeles. His nonfiction books include *Race and Resistance: Literature and Politics in Asian America* (2002), and *Nothing Ever Dies: Vietnam and The Memory of War* (2016). His works of fiction include *The Sympathizer* (2015), which won a Pulitzer Prize; *The Refugees* (2017); and *The Committed* (2021).

Daniel P. Murphy

Review Sources
Christenson, Lauren. "Pieces of a Man: Viet Thanh Nguyen Blends Polemic and Family History in a Fragmentary Memoir." Review of *A Man of Two Faces*, by Viet Thanh Nguyen. *The New York Times Book Review*, 19 Nov. 2023, www.nytimes.com/2023/10/03/books/viet-thanh-nguyen-man-of-two-faces.html. Accessed 16 Feb. 2024.

Ko, Lisa. "Nguyen's *A Man of Two Faces* Tackles War, Colonization, Death and More, but Still Manages to Be Playful." Review of *A Man of Two Faces*, by Viet Thanh Nguyen. *The Washington Post*, 5 Oct. 2023, www.washingtonpost.com/books/2023/10/05/viet-thanh-nguyen-memoir-sympathizer/. Accessed 16 Feb. 2024.

Review of *A Man of Two Faces*, by Viet Thanh Nguyen. *Publishers Weekly*, 6 Oct. 2023, www.publishersweekly.com/9780802160508. Accessed 16 Feb. 2024.

Stanek, Joe. "Double Vision and Self-Deception in *A Man of Two Faces.*" Review of *A Man of Two Faces*, by Viet Thanh Nguyen. *The Chicago Review of Books*, 5 Oct. 2023, chireviewofbooks.com/2023/10/05/double-vision-and-self-deception-in-a-man-of-two-faces/. Accessed 16 Feb. 2024.

Master Slave Husband Wife
An Epic Journey from Slavery to Freedom

Author: Ilyon Woo
Publisher: Simon and Schuster (New York). 416 pp.
Type of work: Biography, history
Time: 1848–60
Locales: Macon, Georgia; Boston, Massachusetts; other locations along the east coast of the US; Halifax, Nova Scotia; and Liverpool, England

Courtesy Simon & Schuster

Master Slave Husband Wife is the story of Ellen and William Craft, enslaved in Georgia, who escaped to freedom by disguising themselves as a wealthy, ailing young man and an enslaved valet, and of the lives they made for themselves as free people.

Principal personages

ELLEN CRAFT, an enslaved woman who passes as a White man to escape enslavement
WILLIAM CRAFT, her husband who passes as her enslaved valet
JAMES SMITH, her father, a White businessman and enslaver of her mother
ROBERT COLLINS, her enslaver
WILLIAM WELLS BROWN, an abolitionist and friend of the Crafts
DANIEL WEBSTER, American congressman and author of the compromise that led to the Fugitive Slave Act of 1850
LEWIS HAYDEN, a Black leader who hid and assisted the Crafts in their escape

Master Slave Husband Wife: An Epic Journey from Slavery to Freedom is the second work of narrative nonfiction by Ilyon Woo. In many interviews about the book and its remarkable protagonists, Ellen and William Craft, Woo touched on two important questions that continue to vex American society. First, how do we teach, write, and learn about the experiences of individuals who were enslaved, and second, how does the legacy of slavery inform the character of the United States itself? Woo asks, as many readers will, why she had never heard of the Crafts, whose escape from slavery in the Deep South in 1848 was only the beginning of a story marked by bravery, hope, and peril. Part of the reason for this, she concludes, is that their story is not a linear tale with a pat ending. Rather, their story, particularly its end, is complicated, and as with many Black lives, records are often absent or incomplete. Luckily for Woo, as well as for readers, much of the Crafts' escape and subsequent activism is well recorded, both in their own narrative, *Running a Thousand Miles for Freedom* (1860), and in the abolitionist press of the day. Woo invests additional research and attention to locate Ellen

Ilyon Woo

Craft at the center of the story despite the fact that she lived at a time when she was expected to defer to her husband and other men, at least in public.

Master Slave Husband Wife begins with two very useful elements: a map of the Crafts' travels and an "Overture," which sets the political, cultural, and international stage upon which the Crafts will appear in 1848. Indeed, one of the defining characteristics of this story is how it played out in the public eye—the Crafts became lecture-circuit celebrities who widely publicized their escape. But first, they must survive a harrowing journey from Macon, Georgia, where they are both enslaved, to Philadelphia, Pennsylvania.

Ellen Craft was born enslaved in Clinton, Georgia. Her mother was enslaved by her White father, James Smith, a businessman and planter. It is likely that Ellen's light skin and resemblance to her father was an unpleasant reminder to Smith's wife of the sexual proclivities of her husband, whose advances Ellen's mother would have been unable to rebuff. In any case, Ellen was given to the Smiths' daughter, her half-sister Eliza, upon Eliza's marriage in 1837 to Robert Collins, who lived in Macon, Georgia. Ellen and Eliza Smith had grown up together, and Ellen was a trusted and intimate member of the household, valued for her ability to sew and responsible for the care of the children.

Ellen met William Craft, an enslaved craftsman who was able to earn some wages on the side, in Macon. The two shared the sadly familiar legacy of traumatic separation from family members, as both had been separated from their mothers. William had also been separated from his siblings, including a sister sold away as a child. Given these experiences, their desire to marry, with its attendant hope for children, only felt possible to the Crafts if they could escape to freedom and ensure that their family would not be torn apart.

Ellen and William planned their escape for months, knowing that if they failed, it could cost them their lives. It would certainly have meant the end of their relationship and the positions of relative privilege they held. Woo traces the changing narrative about whose idea it was to escape, another lens on the shifting dynamics between Ellen and William that also reveals the gendered expectations of both abolitionists and enslavers—later, most people could only believe that William had convinced Ellen to undertake something so daring. Ellen, a talented seamstress, fashions an outfit for a young man of wealth. Fitted with a jacket, baggy trousers, a white silk shirt, and a double-story silk hat, she is able to appear convincingly male. Dark glasses and poultices on her face complete the disguise, transforming her into "Mr. Johnson," while a bandaged hand in a sling provides a plausible reason for her inability to sign required documents along the way. As an enslaved woman, Ellen was prohibited by law from knowing how to read and write. Thus the moments when she is pressed to sign travel documents prove to be extremely perilous.

With darker-skinned William acting as the disguised Ellen's attentive enslaved valet, the couple set off from Macon by train to Savannah and by steamship to Charleston, South Carolina, and beyond. Woo provides a detailed record of their escape in the first half of the book, rendered almost unbearably suspenseful, even though it is revealed at the outset that the couple was successful. At every stop, the reader is confronted not only with the peril William and Ellen face but also with the institutions that support and enforce the enslavement they are fleeing. In Savannah, Woo masterfully describes the site of the largest sale of enslaved people in American history, and the heaviness of a city that has witnessed so much suffering that the trees seem bowed from the weight of it. When the pair move on to Charleston, there are slave markets on every corner, a sight so shocking to foreigners that the city would soon force the trade indoors to protect its commercial reputation.

Woo punctuates the experience of the Crafts as they move through cities marked by the terrible trappings of slavery with descriptions of other instances of rebellion, uprising, and escape, from Nat Turner's 1831 rebellion in Virginia to the 1848 attempted escape of nearly eighty enslaved people on *The Pearl*, a schooner sailing from Washington, DC. The Crafts were part of a long tradition of those who sought self-emancipation against almost impossible odds. It is only because of a series of lucky breaks, and because Ellen had carefully studied her White enslavers and neighbors, enabling her to play to class and gender expectations, that the couple was able to avoid detection and recapture.

The Crafts' four-day journey from enslavement across the Mason-Dixon Line to Philadelphia and freedom, while entirely captivating and breathlessly rendered, is just the beginning of an equally perilous tale. The Crafts make their way from Philadelphia to Boston, honing their skills as darlings of the abolitionist stage, a role that Ellen appears to embrace but then cedes to her husband, her voice becoming more difficult, though not impossible, to hear in the historical record. Woo, a careful researcher, is able to skillfully narrate between the lines, finding meaning in Ellen's silence as well as in her voice. The author never defaults to the louder voices in the room, working to keep Ellen central to the story even as she fades from public view. It is a compelling reminder that good research can also rely on context, deep reading of scant evidence, and empathy.

Despite making it to freedom in the North, the Crafts become targets under the Fugitive Slave Act of 1850. The figures who wrought the act as a hard-fought political compromise are described in detail, their complex motivations rendered understandable, if not forgivable. Noted statesman Daniel Webster, in particular, becomes a powerful example of the danger of compromising moral principles for political expediency. In Boston, the Crafts are hunted again, this time defended and assisted by a fierce cadre of allies and abolitionists. However, when Ellen's enslaver, Robert Collins, hires bounty hunters to recapture the couple and it becomes clear that the attempts to capture them will not stop, they are forced to flee, this time across the Atlantic to England.

It is in England where William Craft publishes their narrative, *Running a Thousand Miles for Freedom*, with Ellen's name conspicuously absent from the author credit. Woo is careful to point to moments where Ellen cedes the stage to her husband, but her reasons for doing so are myriad and not entirely clear: perhaps it is because of Ellen's discomfort with being advertised as a "white slave," or perhaps it is because of public expectations of her role as a married woman. It may also be because of a sense of privacy, or because she focused her energy on raising their children—they would have six—or a combination of all those factors. What is clear is that Ellen and William remained partners as they moved back to the United States together, returning to Georgia, after the end of the Civil War.

The last, fast-moving chapter of the book covers the complex and chaotic period after their return to the United States. The Crafts open a school, weather accusations of impropriety and financial reversals together, and steadily fade from the record. Ellen's death remains a mystery. The way she lived in the years immediately following her escape is so richly rendered by Woo as to make these final unknowable details bittersweet. In the end, she was buried under a Georgia tree, her journey a circle.

Reviews of *Master Slave Husband Wife* were overwhelmingly positive. Kitty Kelley of the *Washington Independent Review of Books* remarked that it "hits all the marks of a masterpiece: unforgettable characters, stirring conflicts, breathtaking courage, and a pulsating plot wrapped around an unforgivable sin." W. Caleb McDaniel, the reviewer for the *New York Times*, praised Woo's compelling, detailed writing, noting her "cinematic eye" and that "she excels at setting scenes." Likewise, writing for the *Wall Street Journal*, Priscilla M. Jensen commended her attention to research, explaining that the narrative "admirably resists oversimplifying the motives and characters of its antagonists as well as its heroes," which is in part accomplished through Woo's extensive "research that extends and contextualizes the Crafts' story." Woo resists trite explanations and is careful to offer multiple viewpoints of moments where records contradict each other, or where the narrative may be bent to serve a social or political cause. Indeed, Woo noted in interviews that every description and line of dialogue in the book comes directly from a primary source.

Most importantly, Woo never lets Ellen slip away as she moves in and out of the public eye. One of the most poignantly described scenes, a searing indictment of American slavery, shows Ellen and William with a mixed-race group in 1851 at the Great Exhibition at London's Crystal Palace, unfurling a poster of an enslaved person in chains staring up at an American flag. Then, in an act of defiance, the group walks together, silently, challenging the world to define them as anything but friends and allies. Ellen Craft, in silence, is front and center.

Author Biography

Ilyon Woo is the author of *The Great Divorce: A Nineteenth-Century Mother's Extraordinary Fight Against Her Husband, the Shakers, and Her Times* (2010). She has written for numerous national publications, including the *New York Times* and the *Wall Street Journal*.

Bethany Groff Dorau

Review Sources

Hoyle, Arthur. Review of *Master Slave Husband Wife*, by Ilyon Woo. *New York Journal of Books*, 17 Jan. 2023, www.nyjournalofbooks.com/book-review/master-slave-husband-wife. Accessed 22 Nov. 2023.

Jensen, Priscilla M. "'Master Slave Husband Wife' Review: To Freedom Together." Review of *Master Slave Husband Wife*, by Ilyon Woo. *The Wall Street Journal*, 5 Mar. 2023, www.wsj.com/articles/master-slave-husband-wife-review-to-freedom-together-5bb97afa. Accessed 22 Nov. 2023.

Kelley, Kitty. Review of *Master Slave Husband Wife*, by Ilyon Woo. *Washington Independent Review of Books*, 7 Feb. 2023, www.washingtonindependentreviewofbooks.com/index.php/bookreview/master-slave-husband-wife-an-epic-journey-from-slavery-to-freedom. Accessed 22 Nov. 2023.

Review of *Master Slave Husband Wife*, by Ilyon Woo. *Kirkus Reviews*, 19 Oct. 2022, www.kirkusreviews.com/book-reviews/ilyon-woo/master-slave-husband-wife/. Accessed 22 Jan. 2024.

McDaniel, W. Caleb. "Fleeing Slavery in a Top Hat and Cravat." Review of *Master Slave Husband Wife*, by Ilyon Woo. *The New York Times*, 15 Jan. 2023, www.nytimes.com/2023/01/15/books/review/master-slave-husband-wife-ilyon-woo.html. Accessed 22 Nov. 2023.

Monica

Author: Daniel Clowes (b. 1961)
Publisher: Fantagraphics (Seattle, WA).
  Illustrated. 106 pp.
Type of work: Graphic novel
Time: 1960s to the present
Locales: Vietnam; California; Texas

In the graphic novel Monica, *distinguished cartoonist and writer Daniel Clowes presents a compelling tale of a woman's quest to find her parents, an endeavor that eventually takes on cosmic significance. In a series of sometimes subtly interrelated chapters, Clowes evokes various genres from the history of comic books, ranging from military comics to cosmic horror.*

Courtesy Fantagraphics; ©Brian Molyneaux

Principal characters
MONICA, the eponymous protagonist
PENNY, her mother, an artist
MOMMA, her grandmother
POPPA, her grandfather
HEATHER, her employer, a celebrity
V. LAMONTE FLOWERS, the head of a cult called "The Way"
STAN, a nice man Monica meets when she is retired
JOHNNY, Penny's fiancée, a Vietnam War veteran
LEONARD KRUGG, one of Penny's lovers, an artist

The publication of Daniel Clowes' graphic novel *Monica* was a highly anticipated event for many comic lovers. This oversized, brilliantly colored, and handsomely produced book was the author's first new work since the release of *Patience* in 2016. Perhaps best known for his 1997 graphic novel *Ghost World*, Clowes is a legend among fans of alternative comic books. He burst on the scene in the 1980s and established his reputation with the groundbreaking comic *Eightball* (1989–97), going on to win numerous honors including multiple Ignatz Awards, seven Eisner Awards, thirteen Harvey Awards, and a 2011 PEN Award for Outstanding Body of Work in Graphic Literature. Clowes also distinguished himself as a screenwriter, earning an Academy Award nomination for the 2001 film adaptation of *Ghost World*.

Throughout his writing career, Clowes has focused on themes of loneliness, abandonment, and alienation. These are all on full display in *Monica*, a tale that reads like an offbeat, existential episode of *The Twilight Zone*, only in comic book form. Throughout, Clowes upends expectations and blurs genres. The tone of the story ranges

Daniel Clowes

from gritty realism to creepily psychedelic horror. Connoisseurs of the weird will revel in both the intricate narrative and the inventive, often visually stunning illustrations.

Though his medium is the comic book, Clowes does not write for children. *Monica* is an uncompromisingly adult story. And despite the sharply defined clarity and bright colors of its graphics, this is an exceedingly dark work. Its imagery includes depictions of full-frontally nude men, bare-breasted women, and grotesque manifestations of death. Its characters wrestle with loss, mortality, and the haunting implacability of what for them remain inexplicable fates. Many of its themes are driven by Clowes personal experience entering his seventh decade of life. As an "In Memoriam" at its opening acknowledges, this is a book written by a man who grieves the accelerating departures of family members and friends. For all its narrative extravagances, an elegiac quality haunts *Monica*. It is apparent that Clowes, like his title character, has looked back upon and assessed his personal history, and has used this story to explore what is important and meaningful in life.

Indeed, the concepts of history and life, both in their general and personal connotations, figure prominently in *Monica*. The title pages feature an ominous landscape of molten lava bubbling in rocky pools next to a blood-red sea, while overhead lightning bursts from roiling dark clouds and a hail of meteorites plummet towards the ground. Presumably this is an evocation of a primeval earth. The copyright pages offer more familiar images, a series of comic-strip frames featuring snapshots of first terrestrial and then human evolution. These include protozoa swimming in the primordial soup, early amphibious vertebrates climbing onto land from the sea, a T-Rex dominating the dinosaur world, the asteroid explosion that ended the reign of the dinosaurs, grassy plains and forests teeming with mammals, the emergence of humans, the rise of civilization in ancient Egypt, the crucifixion of Jesus Christ, the medieval Black Death, the arrival of Europeans in the Americas, William Shakespeare's Hamlet, the Industrial Revolution, the American Civil War, the trenches of World War I, Adolf Hitler and World War II, the explosion of the atomic bomb, Little Richard and rock 'n' roll, Sputnik and the exploration of space, the assassination of President John F. Kennedy, and, finally, *The Beverly Hillbillies*. These images are notably Western and American-centric, perhaps reflecting that Clowes' protagonist Monica is born in the United States at the point when *The Beverly Hillbillies* was a top-rated television series. Such a kaleidoscopic opening may also facetiously imply that the development of the world and Western and American civilization has culminated in Monica. As one begins the book this potted and ironically pretentious history of the world may seem unfathomable. By the end, it makes a grim sort of teleological sense.

The main narrative of *Monica* is rooted in a particular historical milieu, though the title character does not become a sort of Forrest Gump bumping into famous figures or moments over the course of several decades. Monica is literally a child of the 1960s, and this becomes a thematic thread through the story, as she attempts to unravel the true story of her origins. The book begins in Vietnam, with a soldier named Johnny, doomed to be jilted by Monica's mother Penny, discussing war and the good life with one of his comrades. Penny is portrayed as a quintessential product of the decade's upending of traditional patriarchal sexual manners and mores; early in the book her consciousness is raised by a support group of putatively liberated women. Clowes accurately captures the groovy fashion and attitudes of this period. However, his painstaking attention to detail is clinically dutiful; there is nothing there of the sentimental nostalgia so often seen in books and movies looking back at the era of flower power. Instead, Monica's story ends up becoming a powerful critique of the irresponsibility and excesses of the sixties countercultural movement.

For Clowes, the freedom asserted by those who took Timothy Leary's advice to "Turn on, tune in, drop out" could also foster the hedonism that quickly devolved into the moral solipsism of what Tom Wolfe called the "Me Decade" in the 1970s. This judgment does not appear to be the result of a measured conservative argument. It is more visceral and bound up with Penny's inability to settle down and above all her eventual decision to abandon Monica. Notably, this part of the story also in some ways reflects Clowes's own backstory. Although the circumstances were different, Clowes as a child also experienced the fallout of the sexual revolution when his mother left their family to be with another man. Born at the tail end of the baby boom in 1961, Clowes writes as a man who came of age in the 1970s, with memories of the upheaval of the sixties but from the perspective of a child. When it comes to the world of the protesters and hippies who so captured the attention of posterity, he displays the unillusioned perspective of a skeptical younger brother. For Clowes there is nothing romantic or noble about Penny's rebellion; it is a microcosmic expression of a macrocosmic societal dysfunction. Any rhetoric of emancipation and self-expression on her part is negated by Monica's life-long scars.

Clowes's implication that the experiments of the sixties ended in failure manifests in his depiction of a cult called The Way. Like Charles Manson's notorious clan, the fictional group is simultaneously crazy and dangerous. Unlike the Manson family, however, it survives into the twenty-first century, headquartered in a small California town called Boondale. Having learned that Penny was once involved with the cult's founder, Monica infiltrates their run-down compound hoping to get news of her mother. The depiction of the superannuated hipsters clinging to The Way after so many pointless years is a damning commentary on the millennial aspirations of the Age of Aquarius.

Monica would arguably be a notable work simply as an intriguing and powerful commentary on the dark side of the 1960s and the price of self-indulgence for an individual and those in that person's orbit. Clowes accomplishes that, but he does not stop there. The book soon ventures beyond social observation and enters the realm of cosmic horror, as Monica pursues her quest to unravel the mysteries surrounding her parents and her tale of personal trauma turns apocalyptic. Cosmic horror is a variant of supernatural and science fiction that portrays human beings and the wider world as prey to vast, unknowable, and inherently dangerous forces. H. P. Lovecraft pioneered the subgenre in the 1920s and 1930s, self-consciously repudiating traditional bogymen rooted in Judeo-Christion cosmology in favor of new terrors fit for a post–World War I modernist universe in which, as philosopher Friedrich Nietzsche proclaimed, God was dead. In the Lovecraftian oeuvre, human beings are threatened by supernatural beings who are utterly indifferent to them, who crush them the way humans might obliviously squash ants while walking down a sidewalk. Clowes brilliantly captures the disorienting eeriness of incomprehensible dangers while expertly mimicking the macabre style of classic horror comics like *Tales from the Crypt* (1950–55) and *The Haunt of Fear* (1950–54).

Monica's life subtly takes on an eschatological significance as she attempts to understand how she came to be. Clowes interrupts her story with two thematically interrelated episodes: an adventure of a young man named William who comes home to find his town in the thrall of ghastly rites, and an account of a hard-boiled private detective gradually coming to the realization that people are behaving very strangely. In between these episodes, Monica relates her own weird tale of being abandoned by those she loves. She never knew her father and was still a young girl when she was left at the door of her grandparents' house by Penny, who then disappeared. Her grandfather, Poppa, died when she was at camp. Then as, a junior in college, Monica was abandoned again when her grandmother, Momma, died.

While seeking peace and solace at her grandparents' summer cottage, Monica is astounded when Poppa starts speaking to her through an old radio. At first horrified by this, she soon finds this aural visitation comforting. After a few months Poppa's voice fades away, and Monica buries the radio. This strange interlude becomes a baffling memory that Monica explains away as symptomatic of a subsequent mental breakdown. Its significance and that of the other supernatural elements of the book achieve focus in a shocking and enigmatic ending. Here Clowes satisfyingly blends the tropes of pulp fiction with symbolic profundity.

Established fans of Clowes will surely find *Monica* well worth the long wait since his last book. Readers who are new to the author will also likely be inspired to delve further into his work. The book was widely acclaimed, winning the Fauve D'Or at the Angouleme Comics Festival in 2024 and listed as one of the best graphic novels of 2023 by the *New York Times*, the *New Yorker*, the *Guardian*, and *Forbes*, among other publications. Many reviewers offered glowing praise. For example, writing for *Booklist*, Sarah Hunter called it "a hauntingly precise and compellingly strange study of the human struggle to reconcile a decentered past with a path forward" in a starred review. Tom Batten also gave it a starred review for *Library Journal*, lauding the novel as "an emotionally resonant and unforgettable opus." As such plaudits suggest, *Monica* is a must-read for anyone receptive to sophisticated creepiness.

Author Biography
Daniel Clowes is an acclaimed cartoonist and graphic novelist who has won numerous awards. His work includes the comic series *Eightball* (1989–97) and the graphic novels *Like a Velvet Glove Cast in Iron* (1993), *Pussey!* (1995), *Ghost World* (1997), *David Boring* (2000), *Ice Haven* (2005), *Wilson* (2010), *Mister Wonderful* (2011), *The Death-Ray* (2011), and *Patience* (2016).

Daniel P. Murphy

Review Sources
Baker, R.C. "Daniel Clowes's *Monica* Goes to Hell and Finds It Is Us." Review of *Monica*, by Daniel Clowes. *The Village Voice*, 14 Dec. 2023, www.villagevoice.com/daniel-clowess-monica-goes-to-hell-and-finds-it-is-us/. Accessed 14 Feb. 2024.

Batten, Tom. Review of *Monica*, by Daniel Clowes. *Library Journal*, Aug. 2023, p. 85. *Literary Reference Center Plus*, search.ebscohost.com/login.aspx?direct=true&db=lkh&AN=164978910&site=lrc-plus. Accessed 14 Feb. 2024.

Brogan, James. "Daniel Clowes Sheds Cynicism and Embraces Maturity." Review of *Monica*, by Daniel Clowes. *The Washington Post*, 16 Oct. 2023, www.washingtonpost.com/books/2023/10/16/daniel-clowes-monica-graphic-novel-review/. Accessed 14 Feb. 2024.

Cooke, Rachel. "Pitch-Perfect Portraits of an Ever Scarier US." Review of *Monica*, by Daniel Clowes. *The Guardian*, 9 Oct. 2023, www.theguardian.com/books/2023/oct/09/monica-by-daniel-clowes-review-pitch-perfect-portraits-of-an-ever-scarier-us. Accessed 14 Feb. 2024.

Diaz, Junot. "Daniel Clowes Dreams of the Apocalypse." Review of *Monica*, by Daniel Clowes. *The New York Times*, 2 Oct. 2023, www.nytimes.com/2023/10/02/books/review/daniel-clowes-monica.html. Accessed 14 Feb. 2024.

Hunter, Sarah. Review of *Monica*, by Daniel Clowes. *Booklist*, 15 Sept. 2023, p. 38. *Literary Reference Center Plus*, search.ebscohost.com/login.aspx?direct=true&db=lkh&AN=171870988&site=lrc-plus. Accessed 14 Feb. 2024.

Mouly, Francoise. "*Monica*: A Guided Tour Through Daniel Clowes's Mind and Library." Review of *Monica*, by Daniel Clowes. *The New Yorker*, 28 Aug. 2023, www.newyorker.com/culture/culture-desk/monica-a-guided-tour-through-daniel-clowess-mind-and-library. Accessed 14 Feb. 2024.

Monsters
A Fan's Dilemma

Author: Claire Dederer
Publisher: Knopf. New York. 288 pp.
Type of work: Memoir, criticism
Time: Present day
Locales: Seattle, Washington; New York, New York

Claire Dederer's memoir/criticism hybrid Monsters: A Fan's Dilemma *attempts to reconcile fandom with moral code by examining such artists as Ernest Hemingway, Virginia Woolf, and Roman Polanski, among others.*

Claire Dederer's *Monsters: A Fan's Dilemma* (2023) combines the traditions of memoir and criticism to create a book both unique and often challenging. Other books fall within this genre, including Geoff Dyer's *Out of Sheer Rage* (1997), in which his attempt to write a biography of D. H. Lawrence ultimately fails, causing him to write about that failure instead; Ada Calhoun's *Also a Poet: Frank O'Hara, My Father, and Me*, (2022) a work about Calhoun's father, the critic Peter Schjeldahl; and Wayne Koestenbaum's *The Queen's Throat: Opera, Homosexuality, and the Mystery of Desire* (1993), an energetic and deeply researched memoir-heavy work about the obsession many fans feel about opera. With *Monsters*, Dederer similarly mines the personal and the cultural, exploring the controversial aspects of the artists she loves most. Her lens is feminine, maternal, and journalistic: Dederer, a life-long lover of music, film, and art, is attempting to raise two kind and thoughtful teenagers while reflecting often about her time working as a critic in a male-dominated field. She also writes from the lens of the eternal fan, albeit one who has been let down by some of the artists whose work meant the most to her in her personal and professional life.

Monsters opens with an admission of guilt: though Dederer knows that some of the artists she loves have done reprehensible things, she cannot seem to stop admiring their work. In the book's foreword, Dederer tells the reader that she dove back into the films of filmmaker Roman Polanski, whom she loves, for a project and tries to reconcile his violent past in which he was indicted over the alleged drugging and raping of a thirteen-year-old girl in 1977 with her own admiration of his work. Dederer further complicates this with her feelings for filmmaker Woody Allen, whose films she has loved for much of her life. However, when she considers Allen's own complicated past—allegations of sexual abuse by his daughter Dylan Farrow—she has trouble reconciling the work with the man, specifically his film *Manhattan* (1979). Thus began

Claire Dederer

the long project of Dederer's *Monsters*, which was sprung from a viral essay first published by the *Paris Review*. Covering other artists including Ernest Hemingway, Pablo Picasso, Joni Mitchell, and Doris Lessing, Dederer fuses criticism with her own personal experiences to ask what one does with the monstrous side of great artists?

The results of Dederer's investigation are at times quite interesting. One could argue that each chapter operates as its own contained essay in many ways: frequently, Dederer thoroughly investigates an artist by the chapter's close. However, touchstones like Allen show up frequently throughout the work, with the filmmaker being the subject of the book's first chapter. From this starting point Dederer begins to weave into her writing the political climate of the country along with her own experiences of sexism within the field of writing. Choosing to focus on Allen's film *Manhattan* in this first chapter titled "Roll Call," she also provides a basis for her arguments about the other men (and women) discussed in the following pages. She cites specifically the *Access Hollywood* tapes that came out came out ahead of the 2016 presidential elections in which then-candidate Donald Trump speaks frankly about sexually assaulting women as a famous man. Dederer moves from the tapes to the #MeToo movement, which went mainstream the following year after decades of existence on a much smaller scale. Suddenly, in part because of the internet, the bad deeds of famous men were front and center and women were using social media platforms to tell their own stories of assault.

However, not all of the men in *Monsters* have been publicly scrutinized or condemned the same way as Allen or Polanski. Dederer spends considerable time discussing Pablo Picasso's troubled history with women, detailing how he regularly mistreated and abandoned women in his life. She calls into question the long-held belief that men who are "geniuses" must allow that energy to move through them, and that it often results in considerable damage to those around them. But, somehow, Picasso, and other similar male artists, have been excused from the public cancellation that other men have endured. Dederer recalls taking her two teenage children to an exhibit in Seattle focused on Picasso's work through the lens of the women who were destroyed along the course of his career. She notes that by the exhibit's end, she and her children could barely stomach looking at the art. And yet, it endures.

Some of the book's more interesting criticism concerns artists who have touched Dederer's life most personally, namely the composer Richard Wagner and writer Raymond Carver. When focused on Wagner, whose antisemitic views are well documented and whose music was used by the Nazis for propaganda during WWII, she does so through the lens of a BBC series hosted by actor and comedian Stephen Fry, who is himself a fan of the composer's music but also disdains what he stands for, that she watched with her father. It is these familial connections that make fandom for some of these men difficult for her, and Wagner is no different. The Wagner chapter, titled "The Anti-Semite, the Racist, and the Problem of Time," calls into question the liberal ideal that people and society get better with time as people gain more knowledge and experience. "Everyone used to be such a jerk. This is an easy and natural thing to think," Dederer writes, acknowledging that as she is "writing the autobiography of the audience" which is further complicated by the passage of time. In some cases, like writer Virginia Woolf, Dederer notes that many are not aware of the antisemitism she held during her lifetime. Meanwhile, Wagner's views are well understood and even Fry himself wishes he could go back in time to tell him not to write one vitriolic essay he published anonymously. Dederer argues that it is not the passage of time that is the issue here, but public sentiment and the complexity of people's bigotry.

While much of Dederer's work in *Monsters* is clear and moves towards a complicated, but necessary thesis, her writing about women artists lacks clarity. Chapters on Doris Lessing, who abandoned two of her children in Africa when she traveled to London with only her small son in tow to become a writer, and Joni Mitchell, who gave up a baby for adoption at in her twenties to pursue a music career, rely heavily on mainstream and gendered ideas about what a woman should be. Dederer's seeming bias that women should be mothers is given away in her words, with a repeated appeal that abandoning children is the worst thing a woman can do, and the most monstrous. The comparison of Lessing, who later housed writer Jenny Diski as a teenager during trying years, to abusive men like Picasso rings false. Her writing on Mitchell, who chose adoption and to live life as a single woman to pursue her music, further exposes Dederer's bias. She compares Mitchell to fellow singer Carole King, who raised a family while building a career, clearly believing King to be the more morally sound of the two. These chapters, unfortunately, fall amid an exciting run of writing within the book. However, *Monsters* ends on a high note with chapters discussing Raymond Carver, in which Dederer shares surprising information about herself, and Miles Davis, whose work Dederer closes out the book with, as she attempts to find a satisfying summation to her argument.

Monsters was a national bestseller and appeared on many publications' best-books-of-the-year lists, including the *New York Times* and the *New Yorker*. It was widely hailed by critics with only a few outlets delivering mixed or negative reviews. For the *New Yorker*, author Melissa Febos wrote, "Through the act of writing, Dederer confronts herself, the figures she cannot excise from her own lineage, like Roman Polanski, and also the ones she gets to choose, like Pearl Cleage. The result is a work of deep thought and self-scrutiny that honors the impossibility of the book's mission." The book received a starred review in *Publishers Weekly*, whose anonymous reviewer stated, "There are no easy answers, but Dederer's candid appraisal of her own relationship with troubling artists and the lucidity with which she explores what it means to love their work open fresh ways of thinking about problematic artists. Contemplative and willing to tackle the hard questions head on, this pulls no punches." For the *Baffler*, Rhian Sasseen took a more critical position, writing, "Does the artist have a political obligation? I think so. But Dederer's embrace of vague terminology at the end of *Monsters* obscures both the actual political capabilities and emotional impacts of art. Neither a demon nor a monster, art turns into that other cultural fixation of our era: therapy."

Author Biography
Claire Dederer is writer and critic. She is the author of the bestselling memoirs *Poser: My Life in Twenty-Three Yoga Poses* (2010) and *Love and Trouble* (2017). Her writing has appeared in *the New York Times*, *the Atlantic*, *Vogue*, *Slate*, *the Nation*, and *New York* magazine.

Melynda Fuller

Review Sources
Arieff, Allison. "Review: What Do We Do with the Art of Monstrous Men?" Review of *Monsters: A Fan's Dilemma*, by Claire Dederer. *Datebook*, 4 Aug. 2023, datebook.sfchronicle.com/books/monsters-fan-dilemma-dederer-review-17800138. Accessed 21 Dec. 2023.

Cooke, Rachel. "Monsters: A Fan's Dilemma by Claire Dederer Review – What's Your Cancellation Policy?" *The Guardian*, 7 May 2023, www.theguardian.com/books/2023/may/07/monsters-a-fans-dilemma-by-claire-dederer-review-whats-your-cancellation-policy. Accessed 21 Dec. 2023.

Febos, Melissa. "Can You Love the Art and Hate the Monster?" Review of *Monsters: A Fan's Dilemma*, by Claire Dederer. *The New Yorker*, 24 May 2023, www.newyorker.com/books/under-review/can-you-love-the-art-and-hate-the-artist. Accessed 21 Dec. 2023.

Jacobs, Alexandra. "Face to Face with Culture's 'Monsters.'" Review of *Monsters: A Fan's Dilemma*, by Claire Dederer. *The New York Times*, 23 Apr. 2023, www.nytimes.com/2023/04/23/books/monsters-review-claire-dederer.html. Accessed 21 Dec. 2023.

Kipnis, Laura. "The Problem with Art by 'Monsters.'" Review of *Monsters: A Fan's Dilemma*, by Claire Dederer. *The New Republic*, 5 May 2023, newrepublic.com/article/172433/problem-art-monsters. Accessed 21 Dec. 2023.

Review of *Monsters: A Fan's Dilemma*, by Claire Dederer. *Publishers Weekly*, 27 Jan. 2023, www.publishersweekly.com/9780525655114. Accessed 18 Dec. 2023.

Sasseen, Rhian. "Of Monsters and Men." Review of *Monsters: A Fan's Dilemma*, by Claire Dederer. *The Baffler*, 20 Apr. 2023, thebaffler.com/latest/of-monsters-and-men-sasseen. Accessed 21 Dec. 2023.

Monstrous
A Transracial Adoption Story

Author: Sarah Myer (b. 1986)
Publisher: First Second (New York). Illustrated. 272 pp.
Type of work: Graphic nonfiction
Time: ca. 1986 to the early 2000s
Locale: Rural northern Maryland

In this graphic memoir, Sarah Myer recounts their childhood struggles with feelings of abandonment and incidents of racism as they explore their gender identity and develop a passion for art and anime.

Principal personages
SARAH MYER, the author, who was adopted from South Korea and has a passion for drawing and anime
MARY ANN MYER, their adoptive mother
STEVE MYER, their adoptive father
ELIZABETH "LIZ" MYER, also known as Lizzy, their older sister, also was adopted from South Korea

Author Sarah Myer was a child who stood out in their rural neighborhood for their indomitable energy and artistic talent, but they also struggled with feelings of self-doubt, abandonment, and anger. Born in South Korea in 1986, Myer was placed for adoption by their birth parents and then adopted by US citizens Steve and Mary Ann Myer of Maryland. This was the second adoption for the Myer family, who had adopted the author's older sister, Liz, also from South Korea, a year and a half earlier. Myer focused their memoir on their relationship with their adopted parents and recounted their experiences growing up as an Asian American child in an overwhelmingly White community. Myer's adopted parents never concealed the facts of the adoption, though there was little information to share beyond Myer's birth parents' occupations in the fishing industry and a tiny pair of shoes Myer's foster mother included. This lack of information about the reasons Myer's was put up for adoption resulted in their feelings of abandonment and worthlessness, feelings that plagued them for many years. The Myers were patient with their second child's exuberant personality and supportive of their endeavors, particularly in art, but despite receiving love and support at home, Myers struggled with feelings of inadequacy, bullying at school, and overt racism, which the school administration did not appear to take seriously or act to ameliorate. Thus, Myer's graphic memoir, which covers their childhood and young adulthood,

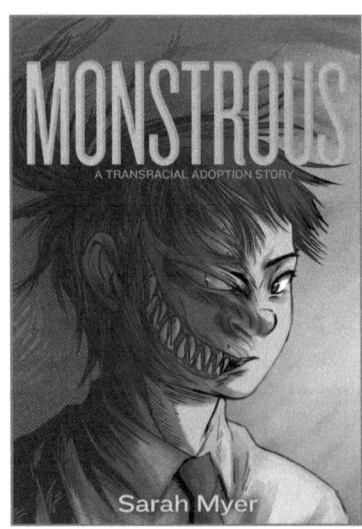

Sarah Myer

explores their honest reflections of their personal struggles and triumphs, made vivid through their beautifully expressive art work.

One consistent theme throughout the memoir is that Myer felt like an outsider. They did not feel as though they fit in, mostly in their community and at school but also sometimes within their family. Myer and their sister, Liz, are very different personalities, and while Liz was well-liked by her peers, did well in school, and seemed not to draw racist attacks, Myer had problems in all those areas. Where Liz was quiet and did not draw attention to herself, Myer did just the opposite. They were an energetic child who appeared to exhibit symptoms of attention deficit disorder (ADD), so staying focused on a task was a challenge, particularly at school.

Myer also had a passion for art and fantasy at a very early age, but even as their art drew praise, it ostracized them in other ways. For example, Myer had a particular love for the Teenage Mutant Ninja Turtles, which was a popular cartoon from the late 1980s through the 1990s. Myer drew these characters well and enjoyed inventing role-playing games with them, yet the boys in their class, who were also Ninja Turtle fans, did not always appreciate a girl joining their play group, and Myer was often ignored or banished. Myer did not fit in with the girl groups either because the girls generally wanted to play games with traditional gender roles, such as "house" or "princesses," rather than the fantasy scenarios of mermaids and Ninja Turtles that Myer preferred.

These incidents intensified throughout Myer's school experience. In middle school and high school, students admired their drawings but did not necessarily include them in their social groups, and the covertly racist remarks of their childhood escalated into more blatant racial slurs in middle school. Myer also felt like an outsider because they were exploring their gender identity and chose more masculine dress, such as button-down shirts and ties, as depicted on the memoir's cover. As a consequence of their forceful personality, androgynous gender expression, and difficulties grappling with racist incidents, Myer struggled with friendship and fitting in and constantly questioned their place in the world.

Another significant theme in the memoir is the way Myer depicts their anger, the result of their feelings of abandonment by their birth parents and their continued status as an outsider. The first indications of anger are depicted through the title of the memoir, *Monstrous*, and the cover art. On the cover, Myer created a self-portrait head shot that is half human and half monster. The monster is drawn with huge, sharp teeth along the side of their face and a large, oblong, animalistic golden eye with a black slit for a pupil, reminiscent of a snake or dragon. The other side of the face has normal human features, signifying, overall, a persona that is half human and half monster.

This half-human, half-monster self suggests Myer's inner struggle to recognize and own their anger rather than hide it or pretend it does not exist. The title, too, connects Myer's "monstrous" self to their adoption and their background as a South Korean with the subtitle, "A Transracial Adoption Story."

While numerous factors drive Myer's anger, their race and adoption are singled out as the most compelling. The mere facts that Myer is South Korean by birth and adopted do not in themselves make them monstrous, but it is their feelings of abandonment from the adoption and their community's and school's unyielding racist comments that lead them to feel like an outsider, resulting in an anger Myer did not fully understand until they were an adult. Myer describes their anger with honesty and integrity. Often, when Myer was confronted with racist slurs and bullying for their art or forceful personality, they did not know what to do with those feelings and acted out in angry, sometimes violent, ways. Myer fully owns the inappropriate ways they acted out in anger, and their reflections on this issue may help others understand and take more positive action to control their own anger issues. As Myer's anger builds, their physical responses escalate from stomping on preschool peers' toys when they are not allowed to play, to hurling a ball at an elementary school classmate during gym and then punching another for a racist remark, to kicking a so-called friend, Calvin, who is treating them badly with racist teasing in middle school.

To make matters worse, Myer's teachers, in general, ignored racist and homophobic slurs said against Myer rather than punishing those who made them. In elementary school, for example, Myer's classmate, Zoe, repeatedly calls Myer a racist slur. When Myer responds by calling Zoe a "flat brain," Zoe tells the teacher what Myer called her, and the teacher criticizes and punishes Myer for name calling. When Myer tries to defend themselves, reporting that Zoe's use of the slur, the teacher responds, "That's no excuse." The teacher does not even reprimand Zoe, and Myer reflects, "I knew the drill by then." Myer's reflection indicates that this kind of teacher response to slurs has been repeated many times in Myer's school experience. Racist incidents like these persist through high school, and Myer's anger and acting out also escalate, until they have more of an understanding of why they are acting out and they decide, "I'd have to be the one to give myself the life I wanted." Myer's ability to tell the stories of their childhood alongside their affecting and informative reflections as an adult, make the memoir especially poignant.

In terms of structure, Myer often makes a distinction between the childhood event they are recounting and their adult reflection of that experience, using speech bubbles for dialogue and rectangular boxes or floating text for storytelling and reflection. In preschool, for example, Myer depicts themselves as an energetic youth very invested in their own artwork, and they wanted to be identified as the *best* artist, not just a good artist. When they are praised for a drawing by the teacher with, "Oh, that's very nice, Sarah. Everyone's doing a fantastic job," Myer responds with "Especially ME!" Myer also includes a reflection rectangle underneath with, "To be fair, I didn't always make it EASY to like me." Drawing brings Myer positive attention for their exceptional skills, and being acknowledged as "the best" is important to them, especially in light of all the identity questioning and negative feelings they are experiencing.

Through all their struggles, Myer's art distracts them from their torments and inspires passion for a better, creative life. Myer pairs this love of art and drawing with a love for anime, a type of television and film animation originating from Japan. Myer particularly likes the anime television shows *Sailor Moon* and *Pokémon*, and despite being ridiculed and teased about it at school, Myer continues to be inspired by it, often styling her hair and dressing as Ash Ketchum, a male Pokémon trainer who aspires to become a Pokémon master. In 2000, Myer also convinces their father to take them to an anime convention in Baltimore, and it is there that a new world opens for them. They find like-minded people who enjoy drawing and anime, and they even see people selling anime-inspired art there, which Myer will do on subsequent visits. Myer's father is especially supportive of their participation in anime and their developing interest in cosplay, or designing costumes and dressing as a character. His support is especially helpful in allowing Myer to pursue a more satisfying life and career. Myer also uses anime and cosplay as a way to explore their gender identity, so what appears in childhood to be an interest and talent in art develops into an important outlet for artistic and gender expression. The final portion of the memoir highlights Myer's exploration of this and various other artistic outlets and chronicles their rocky journey toward self-acceptance and genuine friendship later on in high school.

Most book review journals have given *Monstrous: A Transracial Adoption Story* starred reviews, noting both its depth of storytelling and expressive artwork. *School Library Journal* listed it among the Best Graphic Novels of 2023, citing the book's "dynamic" visuals. *Kirkus* noted that the graphic memoir was "immersive and engrossing: a beautifully depicted emotional journey," and most reviews praised Myer's ability to portray artistically and describe in words their feelings when confronted with racism and bullying and then reflect upon them in hindsight with true understanding. They appreciated how Myer was able to shift years of anger at mistreatment by classmates, teachers, and their community, which caused tremendous self-doubt in their abilities, into a career that was emotionally fulfilling. Renee Scott, writing for *School Library Journal*, made special note of Myer's artwork, writing, "How each feeling is detailed in *Monstrous* was extraordinarily done. The vivid colors and detail that Myer uses to tell their story will make an impact on the reader, as it did me." Myer is especially adept at depicting the emotions of their childhood self through facial expressions and bodily movements. They capture both the curiosity, mischievousness, and sadness of their younger self and the anger, disappointment, and moments of pride in their teenage and young-adult years. Ultimately, Myer triumphs over their anger and fears and, through *Monstrous: A Transracial Adoption Story*, provides inspiration to those confronting the same obstacles and looking for a way to move forward.

Author Biography

Sarah Myer is a comics creator, illustrator, and art educator. *Monstrous: A Transracial Adoption Story*, their first graphic memoir, received best-of-2023 honors from *Booklist*, the *Boston Globe*, *Bulletin of the Center for Children's Books*, *Kirkus*, the *New*

York Public Library, *School Library Journal*, and many more. Myer is also the author of *Maker Comics: Create a Costume!* (2019).

Marybeth Rua-Larsen

Review Sources
Review of *Monstrous: A Transracial Adoption Story*, by Sarah Myer. *Kirkus Reviews*, 28 Mar. 2023, www.kirkusreviews.com/book-reviews/sarah-myer/monstrous-myer/. Accessed 8 Nov. 2023.
Review of *Monstrous: A Transracial Adoption Story* by Sarah Myer. *Publishers Weekly*, 20 Apr. 2023, www.publishersweekly.com/9781250268792. Accessed 8 Nov. 2023.
Scott, Renee. "Monstrous: A Transracial Adoption Story: Review." Review of *Monstrous: A Transracial Adoption Story* by Sarah Myer. *School Library Journal*, 24 Aug. 2023, goodcomicsforkids.slj.com/2023/08/24/monstrous-a-transracial-adoption-story-review. Accessed 8 Nov. 2023.

More Than a Dream
The Radical March on Washington for Jobs and Freedom

Authors: Yohuru Williams and Michael G. Long
Publisher: Farrar, Straus and Giroux (New York). Illustrated. 272 pp.
Type of work: History
Time: 1963
Locale: Washington, DC

Historians Yohuru Williams and Michael G. Long offer middle-grade readers an in-depth look at the making of the 1963 March on Washington for Jobs and Freedom, an iconic episode in the civil rights movement.

Principal personages
BAYARD RUSTIN, the openly gay civil rights leader who became the driving force behind the march
A. PHILIP RANDOLPH, a labor leader and director of the march
JOHN LEWIS, a civil rights activist, director of the Student Nonviolent Coordinating Committee (SNCC) and future congressman
MARTIN LUTHER KING JR., minister and civil rights leader who delivered his famous "I Have a Dream" speech at the march
ANNA ARNOLD HEDGEMAN, an activist who fought for women's inclusion in the march

As its title suggests, *More Than a Dream: The Radical March on Washington for Jobs and Freedom* is a nuanced account of one of the most famous protest marches of all time, emphasizing the complexity and radical nature of an event that is often reduced to its most iconic element: Martin Luther King Jr.'s "I Have a Dream" speech. Aiming at young readers, authors Yohuru Williams and Michael G. Long provide a thoroughly researched and engaging look at the planning and undertaking of the 1963 March on Washington. Importantly, they do so without shying away from tackling difficult issues, from the overt racism faced by Black activists to the conflicts within the civil rights movement itself. Interweaving information gleaned from an array of primary and secondary sources, the authors give readers a chance to learn the march's full backstory—the good, the bad, and the ugly—and form their own opinions about its impact and what might have been done differently.

This book is not the first joint venture for Williams and Long; they previously collaborated on *Call Him Jack: The Story of Jackie Robinson, Black Freedom Fighter* (2022), another social justice-themed history book for middle-grade audiences. Both works fit into the broader collection of literature for young readers examining the mid-twentieth century civil rights movement. Other notable examples include Russell Freedman's *Freedom Walkers: The Story of the Montgomery Bus Boycott* (2006) and the memoir *Students on Strike: Jim Crow, Civil Rights, Brown, and Me* (2007) by John A. Stokes. Within this genre, there are already numerous books about the famous 1963 March on Washington, from basic histories to more creative presentations

Michael G. Long

such as *The Story of the Civil Rights March on Washington for Jobs and Freedom in Photographs* (2014) by David Aretha and the poetry collection *Voices from the March on Washington* (2014) by J. Patrick Lewis and George Ella Lyon. There are also many works about King's "I Have a Dream" speech specifically, including a 2012 book version of King's words illustrated by Kadir Nelson.

Despite this crowded field, *More Than a Dream* sets itself apart as a worthy new addition. This is largely due to Williams and Long's willingness to go beyond the well-known highlights of the 1963 March on Washington and dig into the details—both the inspiring and the challenging ones. For instance, they highlight the role of activist Bayard Rustin, who was crucial in organizing the march but was forced to operate mostly behind the scenes because he was openly gay, and therefore never received the same cultural recognition as many of his peers. While many other accounts, especially for young readers, simply portray the march as a glorious success story of the civil rights movement, Williams and Long devote careful attention to serious points of contention among the organizers. These include disagreement between those who wanted to make sure the march was a peaceful protest and those who desired a more militant demand for equal rights, as well as the ways women were sidelined throughout event. There are also reminders that the march had an urgent socioeconomic agenda, not just a hopeful vision of the future. With this approach, the authors ensure that *More Than a Dream* is indeed about much more than just the "I Have a Dream" speech.

In many ways, Rustin becomes the central character in the story of the March on Washington. On the first page of the first chapter, the authors begin to explain why he is a little-known figure in the popular imagination of the march, especially compared to King. Rustin and King had been close allies in the late 1950s and attempted to organize a major civil rights march in 1960. However, prominent Black politician Adam Clayton Powell Jr. opposed that plan and threatened to insinuate that Rustin and King were a couple. King therefore canceled the planned protest and distanced himself from Rustin to protect his reputation. Williams and Long include a newspaper clipping of Rustin's 1953 arrest on a morals charge, which further helps underline the deeply homophobic reality of the era.

Rustin nevertheless remained active in the early 1960s, and soon he and A. Philip Randolph of the Brotherhood of Sleeping Car Porters labor union began formulating plans for another protest event in Washington, DC. The idea caught on with many other leaders of the civil rights movement, including the so-called Big Six, the heads of six influential organizations who were lobbying Congress and President John F. Kennedy for a civil rights bill. However, the Big Six—Randolph, King, Roy Wilkins, Whitney

Young, James Farmer, and John Lewis—did not see eye-to-eye on every issue, which extended to the question of who would lead the protest. Though Rustin was eminently qualified to continue what he had started, others felt that his sexual orientation and ties to Communism would generate backlash. In particular, Wilkins was vehemently opposed to naming Rustin director of the event. As a compromise, Randolph officially took the position but named Rustin as deputy director. Rustin subsequently handled most of the logistical organizing while Randolph served as the figurehead.

Throughout the book, which is divided into five chronological sections covering the planning and carrying out of the march, Williams and Long continue to squarely show the divisiveness that lingered behind the scenes. The tension between moderate and radical participants is a key focus. This is especially apparent after the Big Six becomes the Big Ten with the addition of four White leaders (Walter Reuther of the United Automobile Workers union, Joachim Prinz of the American Jewish Conference, Mathew Ahmann of the National Catholic Conference for Interracial Justice, and Eugene Carson Blake formerly of the National Council of Churches). These four pushed for what they considered more inflammatory language to be struck from proposed speeches, with the aim of keeping the event as peaceful as possible and broadening its appeal. The speech prepared by John Lewis, director of the Student Nonviolent Coordinating Committee (SNCC), in particular was heavily edited to tone down its criticism of the Kennedy administration's proposed civil rights bill as being too weak.

Another piece of the march's backstory that rarely gets told is the role that women played in organizing it—perhaps because women were given very little stage time during the event itself. Williams and Long are careful to include as many of the women involved as possible. They introduce everyone from Patricia Worthy, who answered the phones at the march's Harlem headquarters, to Anna Arnold Hedgeman, the only woman on the march's administrative committee. Hedgeman, along with Dorothy Height, the leader of the National Council of Negro Women, fought hard to add women to the program held at the march's destination point, the Lincoln Memorial. In the end, however, although a vast number of women showed up to march, they were restricted from the most prominent positions. While performers like Marion Anderson, Mahalia Jackson, and Camilla Williams were invited to sing, the only women speakers were given short shrift, allowed only brief remarks prepared by staffers.

Despite these controversies, the Lincoln Memorial program is undeniably the most famous part of the March on Washington, and indeed one of the most iconic events of the entire civil rights movement. Williams and Long showcase the many powerful moments from the event in the fifth and final part of the book. And though the authors deliberately avoid letting King's "I Have a Dream" speech dominate their narrative, they do ultimately give King his due. The iconic speech has its own backstory, which includes the fact that many parts of it were recycled from previous appearances. Williams and Long highlight the fact that Randolph introduced King as *the* moral leader of the nation, implying that he alone deserves that title over Kennedy or any other figure. They also quote several people in the audience who were awestruck by King's elocution, such as an anonymous man, who remarked "He handles words as if he invented them."

As it lays out its fascinating story, *More Than a Dream*'s main text is supplemented with numerous additional materials. Williams and Long excel at choosing insightful photos and other images, as well as quotes, to add extra meaning and emphasis. Besides the newspaper clipping covering Rustin's arrest, snippets from contemporary media include other news articles, political cartoons, and fliers for march fundraising. Sidebars are also used liberally throughout to offer even further information. In the case of "The Dream" chapter, for example, a gray box headlined "The Three Lives of the Dream Speech" shows how public attitudes toward King and the speech evolved over the years, including backlash following his criticism of the US involvement in the Vietnam War. Sidebars are also used to offer questions to consider. In this way, young readers are guided to analyze the information provided and draw conclusions for themselves.

More Than a Dream was not widely reviewed by major publications, but the limited critical coverage was very positive. *Kirkus Reviews* called the book "coherent, compellingly passionate, rich in sometimes-startling and consistently well-founded insights." of what was arguably the biggest event in the civil rights movement. Similarly, in a starred review for *School Library Journal*, Kate Rao touted its "remarkable blend of primary resources, firsthand accounts, and thought-provoking questions" that "provide a vivid glimpse into history." Writing for Common Sense Media, Lucinda Dyer echoed such praise while cautioning that the book does contain racist and homophobic language—a fact that the authors also address in an introductory note, arguing that "we think it's important for readers to know—and feel—the words that white people used when trying to hurt Black Americans." In recognition of its comprehensive look at a vital historic event, *More Than a Dream* was longlisted for the National Book Award for Young People's Literature. Anyone looking for a vivid yet accessible introduction to civil rights history will surely find it valuable.

Author Biography

Yohuru Williams is a historian and the founding director of the Racial Justice Initiative at the University of St. Thomas. He is the author of several books, including *Black Politics / White Power* (2000), *Teaching US History Beyond the Textbook* (2008), and *Rethinking the Black Freedom Movement* (2015).

Michael G. Long is a historian with a focus on civil rights, nonviolent protest, and gender and sexuality. His books include *Martin Luther King Jr., Homosexuality, and the Early Gay Rights Movement* (2012) and *Troublemaker for Justice: The Story of Bayard Rustin, the Man Behind the March on Washington* (2019; with Jacqueline Houtman and Walter Naegle).

Diana C. Coe

Review Sources

Dyer, Lucinda. Review of *More Than a Dream: The Radical March on Washington for Jobs and Freedom*, by Yohuru Williams and Michael G. Long. *Common Sense Media*, www.commonsensemedia.org/book-reviews/more-than-a-dream-the-radical-march-on-washington-for-jobs-and-freedom. Accessed 8 Nov. 2023.

Review of *More Than a Dream: The Radical March on Washington for Jobs and Freedom*, by Yohuru Williams and Michael G. Long. *Kirkus Reviews*, 8 June 2023, www.kirkusreviews.com/book-reviews/yohuru-williams/more-than-a-dream/. Accessed 8 Nov. 2023.

Rao, Kate. Review of *More Than a Dream: The Radical March on Washington for Jobs and Freedom*, by Yohuru Williams and Michael G. Long. *School Library Journal*, 18 Aug. 2023, www.slj.com/review/more-than-a-dream-the-radical-march-on-washington-for-jobs-and-freedom. Accessed 9 Nov. 2023.

The Most Secret Memory of Men

Author: Mohamed Mbougar Sarr
First published: *La plus sècrete mémoire des hommes*, 2021, in France
Translator: Lara Vergnaud
Publisher: Other Press (New York). 496 pp.
Type of work: Novel
Time: 1930s; 2018
Locale: Paris, France; Dakar, Senegal

Mohamed Mbougar Sarr's genre-defying novel, The Most Secret Memory of Men, *follows a rising Senegalese novelist solving the mystery of another novelist while simultaneously immersing himself in the African French literary scene.*

Principal characters
DIÉGANE LATYR FAYE, a Senegalese novelist gradually earning recognition in Paris
T. C. ELIMANE, a Senegalese author from the 1930s who vanished after being embroiled in a scandal
SIGA D., a writer harboring many secrets
AÏDA, a flighty photojournalist with whom Diégane forms a close relationship

Postcolonial African literature, a famously broad and amorphous category, is inherently difficult to categorize. The term could refer to anything from *Things Fall Apart* (1958), Nigerian author Chinua Achebe's famous indictment of European imperialism, to the existential works of Egyptian novelist Naguib Mahfouz. When it comes to distinguishing itself from other literatures, the work of African authors is perhaps subject to greater challenges, and higher standards, than its counterparts. One such obstacle was faced by the Malian author Yambo Ouologuem, who won the respected French literary award, the Prix Renaudot, for his gorily imaginative 1968 epic *Le devoir de violence* (*Bound to Violence*). At first, Ouologuem was hailed for his book's gritty and honest condemnation of both the patronizing exoticism of Africans by the French, and the manipulative romanticizing of sub-Saharan Africa by corrupt African rulers. Yet soon after, Ouologuem was accused of plagiarizing certain passages from several Western authors, including the British novelist Graham Greene. Ouologuem left France in disgrace and returned to Mali, where he lived a reclusive lifestyle until his death in 2017.

Ouologuem's rise, fall, and departure from the public eye leave much room for inevitable theories to arise. Was he happy, did he re-embrace his beginnings, or continue longing for European fame? Paris-based Senegalese writer Mohamed Mbougar

Mohamed Mbougar Sarr (Courtesy ©DR)

Sarr's novel, *La plus secrete mémoire des hommes* (2021), is heavily inspired in part by Ouologuem's story, and attempts to solve the mystery of what may have happened to the earlier writer following his literary scandal, and why it matters for the future of French African literature. Translated from the French as *The Most Secret Memory of Men* by Tunisian American translator Lara Vergnaud in 2023, the novel ambitiously takes on many of the concerns plaguing modern postcolonial writers: the pretentiousness of Western literary establishments, the sometimes-clumsy friendships between writers with little in common besides their foreignness, the demand for "exotic" African writing from the French public, and many more.

Sarr's previous work has been equally biting, mercilessly critical of both Europe and his native Senegal. His first novel, *Terre ceinte* (2015), translated as *Brotherhood* (2021), won multiple prestigious awards for its depiction of an imagined African city occupied by violent Islamists, and whose residents subsequently form an underground resistance to chronicle the siege. Two years later, Sarr came out with *Silence du choeur* (2017), about a tense encounter between Italian nationalists and a group of African migrants. Sarr followed this with perhaps his most controversial novel to date, in 2018, *De purs hommes*, about a Senegalese professor who develops conflicted feelings about the country's intolerance towards male same-sex relationships, and eventually finds his own reputation endangered, along with his life. *De purs hommes* earned Sarr a great deal of renown in France and the Western world but was widely criticized by the Senegalese press and religious leaders, though he also received the National Order of the Lion from the president of Senegal.

The Most Secret Memory of Men is narrated from the point of view of Diégane Latyr Faye, a young Senegalese novelist leading an unstable, unpredictable life in Paris. A former academic, he has since moved into a more bohemian world and published one largely unsuccessful novel. Despite his few prospects and his lack of meaningful connection—his girlfriend has recently left him—Diégane refuses to go back to Dakar, instead spending his days with members of the "African Ghetto," a group of artists of African origin, struggling to make their mark in the French industry.

Despite the many women available for and interested in possible love affairs, the anxious Diégane has trouble finding his footing in amorous relationships. However, following an awkward encounter with an older woman, the writer Siga D., she presents Diégane with a book called *The Labyrinth of Humanity*, by an author named T. C. Elimane. The book was published during the 1930s, and was supposedly hugely successful at first. Yet following a scandal similar to the real-life events of Ouologuem's

Lucas, Julian. "Absence Africaine: A Prix Goncourt–Winning Novel about a Quest to Unearth a Literary Legend." Review of *The Most Secret Memory of Men*, by Mohamed Mbougar Sarr, translated by Lara Vergnaud. *The New Yorker*, 11 Sept. 2023, www.newyorker.com/magazine/2023/09/18/the-most-secret-memory-of-men-mohamed-mbougar-sarr-book-review. Accessed 16 Feb. 2024.

Review of *The Most Secret Memory of Men*, by Mohamed Mbougar Sarr, translated by Lara Vergnaud. *Kirkus Reviews*, 26 Aug. 2023, www.kirkusreviews.com/book-reviews/mohamed-mbougar-sarr/most-secret-memory-men/. Accessed 16 Feb. 2024.

Mott Street
A Chinese American Family's Story of Exclusion and Homecoming

Author: Ava Chin (b. 1970)
Publisher: Penguin Press (New York). Illustrated. 400 pp.
Type of work: Memoir, history
Time: 1800s to the present
Locales: China; San Francisco; Seattle; New York City

Ava Chin's Mott Street: A Chinese American Family's Story of Exclusion and Homecoming *examines the lives of the author's key ancestors, many of whom resided at the same apartment building in New York City's Chinatown.*

Principal characters

AVA CHIN, the author and narrator
WONG YUAN SON, her maternal great-great-grandfather
ROSE MAI DOSHIM, her maternal grandmother
GENE KAI FEI WONG, her maternal grandfather
CHIN ON, her paternal great-grandfather
STANLEY CHIN, her father
LAURA WONG, her mother
DEK FOON, also known as Ng Dek Foon, her maternal great-great-uncle
ELVA LISK FOON, Dek Foon's wife

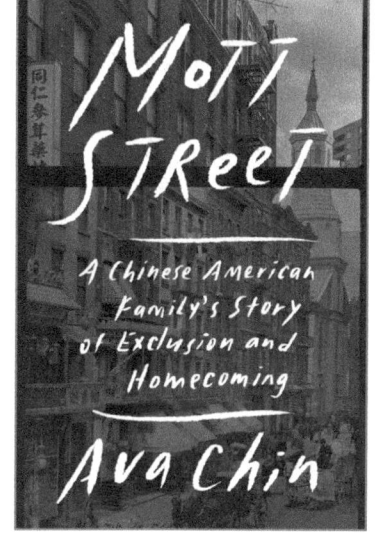

As author Ava Chin notes, though she was born in the United States and grew up in Flushing, Queens, in New York City, she is descended from a lineage that can be traced back to China's Yellow Emperor Huangdi (ca. 2697–2597 BCE) on her mother's side. Tracing this lineage, and especially her family's eventual move to the United States, provides the heart of her book Mott Street: A Chinese American Family's Story of Exclusion and Homecoming. Combining elements of memoir, biography, genealogical research, and history, the work is at once both epic in scope and deeply personal. Its illumination of both the challenges and triumphs faced by Chin's family over the centuries provides rich insight into the Chinese American experience in general.

Among Chin's other illustrious ancestors was Wong Yue, a scholar during the tenth-century Song dynasty, whose three wives each produced seven sons. The Wong, Ng, and Chin family lines she descended from (as shown in a useful introductory family tree that helps identify the many members mentioned) originated around the communities of Tong Yun Gai and Toisan in the Pearl River Delta region in Guangdong

Ava Chin (Courtesy Penguin Random House and Ava Chin; ©Tommy Kha)

Province, China. The area, as Chin details, features three major rivers, "a maze of canals and streams, and a semi-tropical climate" that "provided a year-long growing season." The Pearl River was also infamous for cycles of widespread flooding, followed by years of devastating drought. It was because of such climatic uncertainties that the author's ancestors began leaving China to seek their fortunes elsewhere, particularly in the United States.

One of the first to seize the opportunity was Chin's great-great-grandfather Wong Yuan Son (born ca. 1849). As a teenager Yuan Son traveled across the Pacific Ocean to California, in the wake of the Gold Rush of the late 1840s and early 1850s. Chinese immigrants formed enclaves in major American cities, beginning in San Francisco in 1848; within twenty-five years, there were many so-called Chinatowns across the country. Yuan Son, along with thousands of other immigrating Chinese men, found work on the transcontinental railroad because, unlike many White workers, they were willing to perform the difficult, dangerous, low-paid labor that the railroad companies deemed necessary to clear the rugged land across the Sierra Nevada Mountains. The Central Pacific Railroad began laying track for the Western portion of the railway in 1863, during the Civil War, while the Union Pacific (dominated by Irish workers) moved west from Omaha, Nebraska. Within two years, 90 percent of the western workers were Chinese. Scores of these workers died during construction of the transcontinental railroad, which was completed in 1869.

Following completion of the project Yuan Son moved to southern Idaho, where the population was nearly 30 percent Chinese. He established a gambling parlor and dry goods store near Boise. The businesses thrived until the Panic of 1873, a global depression that adversely affected the national economy into the 1880s. Coinciding with the depression was another wave of immigration, which—despite the heroic work of Chinese laborers on the transcontinental railroad—generated vicious, violent anti-Asian sentiment and spurred legislation focused on banning Asians from entering the United States. The Page Act (1875) barred Asian laborers and sex workers. Under the influence of White labor organizations (such as the Workingmen's Party Order of Caucasians, Caucasian League, and the Knights of Labor) that advocated for Chinese expulsion, federal legislators passed the Chinese Exclusion Act in 1882. For more than sixty years the Page Act not only blocked further immigration of Chinese laborers, but also denied their rights to become US citizens. After Yuan Son was driven from his home in Idaho by an angry White mob—following similar incidents staged against Chinese residents in many California towns—he moved to New York City.

Another of the author's notable ancestors, Dek Foon, was the uncle of Ava Chin's grandmother Rose Mai Doshim. An English-speaker who served as an interpreter, he immigrated to San Francisco and later set up a hand laundry. By 1886, he had moved to New York City and in partnership with other Chinese immigrants offered local advertising, personal banking, and translators for various purposes. After the Geary Act—requiring Chinese immigrants to be interviewed and registered with the government, and to carry identification with photo at all times or risk deportation—was passed in 1892, Dek Foon joined civil rights champion and orator Wong Chin Foo and others to form the Chinese Equal Rights League and launched one of the first Chinese-language newspapers in the city. Ten years later, he would marry a White woman, Elva Lisk, who was born intersex. In China, meanwhile, there was great resentment over the tightened Exclusion provisions, in addition to anger toward Western nations over the Opium Wars, which sowed the seeds for the Boxer Rebellion in 1899, and resulted in the murder of Chrisian missionaries across the country.

Throughout the late nineteenth and early twentieth centuries, Ava Chin's forebears continued to enter the United States and gravitate toward New York City where, after 1915, many lived in an apartment building at 37 Mott Street in Chinatown. The author's paternal great-grandfather, Chin On, for example, entered the country from Canada. Chin On's older brother Hing, a worker at a fish cannery near Seattle, relocated to New York after winning travel money in a large gambling wager. In New York, the Chin brothers were invited to join a society of business owners, the On Leong tong. The Chins subsequently operated a gambling parlor, tea parlor, opium den, and brothel in Newark, New Jersey, and Chin On invested in a Broadway nightclub, Palais d'Or. Such enterprises supplemented their main business of importing silk items, porcelain, and teas that they supplied to their own establishments as well as to department stores like Macy's and Wanamaker's.

Mott Street is rich in detail grounded in Chin's meticulous research, conducted over decades. She began the project for a personal reason: she wanted to know more about Stanley Chin, her father, who deserted his family when she was a child. Ironically, in the 1990s she found him living and working just blocks away in the same neighborhood. As Chin learned more about her family members and the impact of the discriminatory Chinese Exclusion Act and its permutations (the act was finally repealed in 1943 by President Franklin Roosevelt), she expanded her investigation. She traveled around the country to interview those who had known her family members and their history. She visited her family's ancestral village in Toisan in 1994 and located the gravesite of Yuan Son. She traveled to Utah in 2019 to witness the celebration of the 150th anniversary of the transcontinental railroad. She and her family toured the old detention center at Angel Island in San Francisco Bay, where incoming Chinese immigrants were interrogated, and pored over existing records. She visited the Foon family plot at Woodlawn Cemetery in the Bronx.

Not unexpectedly, the author concludes that the long-lived Exclusion Act has been partially responsible for twenty-first-century anti-Asian sentiment in the United States. She asks, "What happens when a young country closes its doors against a nationality, and then a 'race,' and *an entire continent* to which your family once belonged?"

She then suggests that it leads to negative outcomes, "not the least of which is a perpetual 'otherness,' a cloud of unwarranted suspicion and a rejection of innovations and achievements by a significant portion of the population." Chin also argues that the Exclusion Act left the United States "open to the kind of inequality and perpetuation of violence that can be stoked by political figures during times of economic strife and geopolitical posturing."

Critical reception of Mott Street was largely positive, though reviews were mixed. Dwight Garner, writing for the New York Times, described Chin's work as "sensitive, ambitious, well-reported, heavily peopled yet curiously remote. . . . It's a book that has everything going for it except that intangible spark that crisp and confident storytelling throws off. The air is a bit still in this book, as if one is walking behind the docent on a long museum tour." In a review for the Washington Post Rhoda Feng agreed, to a point, writing that "Chin writes with a Proustian flourish," and praising the "highly readable narrative of the various ways that her predecessors managed to make a new life for themselves in an often inhospitable country." Feng, however, called Mott Street "less successful when it awkwardly strains for a kind of grandiloquent universality," with rhetorical flourishes that "threaten to undercut the personal force of the book." She wished that "Chin had lavished more attention on the lives of her immediate ancestors . . . as well as her own upbringing as an Asian American."

Despite such criticisms, most reviewers found much to commend. In the Los Angeles Review of Books Megan Vered praised Chin for her ability to probe "the plight of four generations of her ancestors with the tenacity of a historian, the fine brush of an accomplished artist, and the sensitivity of one who openly communicates with the dead." Leland Cheuk, writing for the San Francisco Chronicle found Mott Street to be "admirable and deeply researched," and zeroed in on the book's major theme, which "shines a harsh and unforgiving light on this country's legacy of racist politics." Like many critics, Cheuk found the book highly resonant in the contemporary sociopolitical landscape, suggesting that it "is an important read for those interested in learning about the origins of some of today's most hard-line immigration proposals in America."

Author Biography
An associate professor at the City University of New York, Ava Chin published the award-winning *Eating Wildly: Foraging for Life, Love, and the Perfect Meal* (2014). Her writing has appeared in such publications as the *New York Times*, the *Village Voice*, the *Los Angeles Times*, and the *Washington Post*.

Jack Ewing

Review Sources
Cheuk, Leland. "Review: History of Generations Is Reflected in Chinese American Author's Own Family in America." Review of *Mott Street: A Chinese American Family's Story of Exclusion and Homecoming*, by Ava Chin. San Francisco Chronicle, 4 Aug. 2023, datebook.sfchronicle.com/books/review-history-chinese-american-experience-u-s-17917099. Accessed 29 Dec. 2023.

Feng, Rhoda. "Unlocking the Mysteries of One Family's Past." Review of *Mott Street: A Chinese American Family's Story of Exclusion and Homecoming*, by Ava Chin. The Washington Post, 27 Apr. 2023, www.washingtonpost.com/books/2023/04/27/ava-chin-mott-street-review/. Accessed 29 Dec. 2023.

Garner, Dwight. "'Mott Street' Chronicles 4 Generations of Chinese American Life." Review of *Mott Street: A Chinese American Family's Story of Exclusion and Homecoming*, by Ava Chin. The New York Times, 24 Apr. 2023, www.nytimes.com/2023/04/24/books/ava-chin-mott-street.html. Accessed 29 Dec. 2023.

Review of *Mott Street: A Chinese American Family's Story of Exclusion and Homecoming*, by Ava Chin. *Kirkus Reviews*, 23 Feb. 2023, www.kirkusreviews.com/book-reviews/ava-chin/mott-street/. Accessed 29 Dec. 2023.

Review of *Mott Street: A Chinese American Family's Story of Exclusion and Homecoming*, by Ava Chin. *Publishers Weekly*, 16 Mar. 2023, www.publishersweekly.com/9780525557371. Accessed 29 Dec. 2023.

Newsham, Gavin. "This Chinese-American Family Has Lived on Mott Street for 5 Generations." Review of *Mott Street,* by Ava Chin. *New York Post*, 17 Apr. 2023, nypost.com/2023/04/15/this-chinese-american-family-has-lived-at-37-mott-street-for-5-generations/. Accessed 29 Dec. 2023.

Vered, Megan. "Echoes of Her Ancestors: On Ava Chin's *Mott Street*." Review of *Mott Street: A Chinese American Family's Story of Exclusion and Homecoming*, by Ava Chin. *Los Angeles Review of Books*, 4 May 2023, lareviewofbooks.org/article/echoes-of-her-ancestors-on-ava-chins-new-memoir-mott-street/. Accessed 29 Dec. 2023.

Nearer My Freedom
The Interesting Life of Olaudah Equiano by Himself

Authors: Monica Edinger and Lesley Younge
Publisher: Zest Books (Minneapolis). 216 pp.
Type of work: Biography; history; poetry
Time: Eighteenth century
Locales: Various

Educators Monica Edinger and Lesley Younge reshape Olaudah Equiano's classic eighteenth-century slave narrative into a work of found verse for contemporary young adult readers.

Principal personages
OLAUDAH EQUIANO, a writer, abolitionist, and formerly enslaved person
MICHAEL HENRY PASCAL, a British naval officer
ROBERT KING, an American merchant
CHARLES IRVING, a Scottish naval surgeon and inventor

The most famous, and widely read, slave narratives, such as *Narrative of the Life of Frederick Douglass* (1845) by Frederick Douglass, an icon of the abolitionist movement, and *Incidents in the Life of a Slave Girl* (1861), by Harriet Jacobs, follow a general pattern. Written by enslaved people primarily in the United States but also elsewhere in the world, these accounts trace the journey of the writer from slavery to freedom, addressing the horrors they experienced while enslaved, the ingenuity of their education and escape, and the necessity of abolishing slavery.

By the time the literary tradition of slave narratives emerged, the transatlantic slave trade was a long-lasting, varied, and widespread global enterprise that enriched White American and European merchants at the expense of Africans who were kidnapped, enslaved, and sold to enslavers around the world to sustain this lucrative business. In a 1789 memoir, *The Interesting Narrative of the Life of Olaudah Equiano, or Gustavus Vassa, The African, Written by Himself*, a formerly enslaved man named Olaudah Equiano gives the reader a picture of this wider reach and of his own somewhat morally compromised role in the slave trade, in addition to narrating his own complex and globetrotting story. Kidnapped from his home village in what is now Nigeria, Equiano, who was also known as Gustavus Vassa throughout his life, was enslaved and sold to a British naval officer, followed by two other enslavers, and was eventually able to buy his freedom after years of enslaved labor, primarily on naval ships. Once free, Equiano

Monica Edinger

worked in a variety of jobs, including several stints as a sailor, often finding himself uncomfortably involved in the slave trade. Eventually, Equiano embraced Christianity and became a prominent abolitionist in England, where he died in 1797.

In their 2023 book *Nearer My Freedom: The Interesting Life of Olaudah Equiano by Himself*, educators and authors Monica Edinger and Lesley Younge bring Equiano's story and words to a new audience. In their introduction, they explain why they chose Equiano's narrative, instead of the more straightforward and morally clear writings of authors like Douglass. "Slavery is—and has always been—a global industry that creates wealth for generations of traders, consumers, and enslavers around the world," they write. "Many would like to forget or erase this uncomfortable fact, yet the truth persists." In opting to recreate Equiano's story, Edinger and Younge choose to present to their audience, young-adult readers, the complicated and global nature of slavery. While virtually everyone recognizes the universal evil of slavery, not everyone realizes the ways it compromised everyone it touched, even formerly enslaved people.

To bring Equiano's story to their audience, Edinger and Younge use the best tool at their disposal: the man's own words. The writers' method in creating *Nearer My Freedom* was to cull selected words, phrases, and sentences from Equiano's narrative and arrange them in verse form. Over the course of two hundred pages, these words unfold to chronicle the most important events in Equiano's life as well as his thoughts on these events. As the authors explain in an afterword, in creating their "series of found-verse poems," Edinger and Younge essentially remixed Equiano's words, picking out his "most glittering gems of phrasing and description" and arranging them into lines of verse. The authors did not add any of their own words into the main text, relying solely on Equiano's text. Their only direct commentary comes in a series of historical sidebars that recur throughout the book and provide the reader with some much-needed background information.

In using Equiano's words as the basis for a found poem, the authors generally maintain the order of the words as they originally appear and tell his story in a manner that is as straightforward as possible. In an example of their methodology, which is provided in the book's afterword, they provide a side-by-side comparison of a passage of original text from Equiano's narrative and the poem they created from the text. While some words are reordered, most of the poetic effect from this section comes from the selection and isolation of individual lines. In the sample the authors give, Equiano describes his painful separation from his sister. The authors take the second half of the final sentence in the original passage, eliminate unnecessary words, and

Lesley Younge
Courtesy Lerner Books

recreate the remaining words as two lines arranged in their own stanza. The effect is simple, stark, and effective: "She was torn from me and carried away. / I was left in a state not to be described."

In other instances, Edinger and Younge use a less subtle and more obviously poetic arrangement of Equiano's words, also to powerful effect. For example, in one of the book's most harrowing passages, Equiano finds himself chained aboard a slave ship as it sails through the notorious Middle Passage, an Atlantic Ocean route through which enslaved people were transported from Africa to the Americas under horrific conditions. After a relatively prosaic section in which Equiano describes the cruel treatments inflicted on the enslaved people on the ship by the White crew, Edinger and Younge follow up by crafting a list poem out of Equiano's words that consists of a simple catalog of nouns (and one adjective) that describe the horrors. Each word occupies a single line. The list begins with "Filth / Stench / Pestilential / Shrieks," and continues on until, at the bottom of the page, after a line break, the passage ends with the phrase, "A Scene of Horror." Later, when Equiano is taken to a plantation in Virginia and given a new name, Edinger and Younge use a similarly artful arrangement, in this case a parallel construction, to convey Equiano's feelings. With one exception, every line in the section begins with the word "now" and the section ends with a mournful plea: "Now I wished for death."

Nearer My Freedom is divided into two sections, the first dealing with Equiano's time as an enslaved man and the second with his time as a free man. In both periods, Equiano traveled widely and experienced an array of adventures. While Equiano underwent some extreme horrors, he also experienced some thrilling expeditions, such as a treacherous journey to the Arctic in search of a passage to India. These adventures, especially when he was a free man, often involved him in some morally compromised situations. For example, after Equiano purchased his own freedom, he occasionally took employment on slave ships and even as an overseer of enslaved laborers on a sugar plantation on the Mosquito Coast in Central America.

Equiano's role in continuing to prop up the slave trade, as well as earlier remarks he makes about the benevolent nature of some of his masters, create a complexity and a moral uncertainty in the original text, an uncertainty the authors preserve in their adapted work. Edinger and Younge do not shy away from including these passages or addressing them in the sections of historical context they insert amidst the text. They understand that slavery, at that time, was a far-reaching, insidious political and economic institution, one that compromised everyone who came into contact with it, including Equiano himself. Nonetheless, the authors are unafraid to offer their own opinion on his assumptions. Although they understand that Equiano had a goal in mind in describing some of his enslavers as benevolent while writing his book—specifically, that of encouraging enslavers to treat enslaved people better by appealing to their better nature—Edinger and Younge do note that "even the most 'benevolent' enslaver deprived people of basic human rights." Similarly, in evaluating Equiano's employment as an overseer, they note that while he felt he was doing right by the enslaved people under his supervision, this was no excuse. "Although he saw himself as a compassionate overseer," Edinger and Younge write, "he was still participating in slavery."

Eventually, Equiano embraced the Christian religion and turned his attention more fully to the abolitionist cause. He no longer sought employment that propped up the slave trade and began writing and agitating for the emancipation of all enslaved people. In the end, Equiano proved to be an influential voice for abolition and his efforts were rewarded, although unfortunately not until after his death. In 1807, a decade after Equiano died, British Parliament officially put an end to their international slave trade, the same year a similar ban passed in the United States. In 1833, Parliament passed the Slavery Abolition Act, officially ending the practice of slavery in most parts of the British Empire. However, slavery was not formally abolished in the United States until the ratification of the Thirteenth Amendment in December 1865, shortly after the end of the US Civil War (1861–65).

Centuries after its publication, Equiano's autobiography continues to fascinate, not only because of his adventures and its vivid evocation of the horrors of slavery, but because of the insight it provides into the breadth and scope of the global slave trade. Although Equiano was often complicit in this slave trade, he eventually became a staunch abolitionist and an inspiring figure in this international movement. In bringing his words to a contemporary audience, Edinger and Younge provide readers a chance not only to see this fascinating figure in a new light, but also to contemplate both the horrors and the unsolvable contradictions of the global slave empire at its height.

Although not widely reviewed, *Nearer My Freedom* received considerable praise from the outlets that covered it. In a starred review for *Publishers Weekly*, the anonymous reviewer found that the book offered an excellent introduction to Equiano's writing for younger readers, "without losing the source text's emotional heft." These sentiments were echoed by an anonymous reviewer for *Kirkus*, who also gave the book a starred review. According to the *Kirkus* reviewer, Edinger and Younge's "highly successful adaptation" is "exceptionally readable as well as informative" and provided a great perspective on an important, if occasionally troubling, eighteenth-century figure. Contributing yet another starred review for *School Library Journal*, Karen T. Bilton strongly recommended the book, noting that "this important and unique work introduces this pivotal man to a new audience and will make for interesting classroom discussions."

As all these reviewers noted, Edinger and Younge open up a meaningful dialogue about a difficult subject by making Equiano's words not only accessible, but enthralling, to students and casual readers alike. The history of slavery does not always break down into easily digestible, good-versus-evil narratives, and Edinger and Younge allow the reader to grasp that uncomfortable truth in all its complexity.

Author Biography
Monica Edinger is an author of books for children and young adults as well as a retired classroom teacher. Her 2013 book *Africa Is My Home: A Child of the Amistad* won the Children's Africana Book Award.

Lesley Younge is a writer and middle school educator. Her 2023 picture book, *A-Train Allen*, was the Own Voices, Own Stories Grand Prize Winner from Sleeping Bear Press.

Andrew Schenker

Review Sources
Bilton, Karen T. "Nearer My Freedom: The Interesting Life of Olaudah Equiano by Himself." Review of *Nearer My Freedom*, by Monica Edinger and Lesley Younge. *School Library Journal*, 1 Apr. 2023, www.slj.com/review/nearer-my-freedom-the-interesting-life-of-olaudah-equiano-by-himself. Accessed 11 Dec. 2023.

Review of *Nearer My Freedom*, by Monica Edinger and Lesley Younge. *Kirkus Reviews*, www.kirkusreviews.com/book-reviews/monica-edinger/nearer-my-freedom/. Accessed 11 Dec. 2023.

Review of *Nearer My Freedom*, by Monica Edinger and Lesley Younge *Publishers Weekly*, www.publishersweekly.com/9781728464077. Accessed 12 Dec. 2023.

No One Prayed Over Their Graves

Author: Khaled Khalifa (1964–2023)
First published: *Lam yusalli 'alayhim ahad*, 2019, in Lebanon
Translated from the Arabic by Leri Price
Publisher: Farrar, Straus and Giroux (New York). 416 pp.
Type of work: Novel
Time: 1881–1951
Locales: Aleppo, Syria, and various surrounding villages, including the fictional town of Hosh Hanna

A poetic novel spanning several decades, No One Prayed Over Their Graves *follows two childhood friends and their descendants as they seek to find purpose among strife in early twentieth-century Aleppo, Syria.*

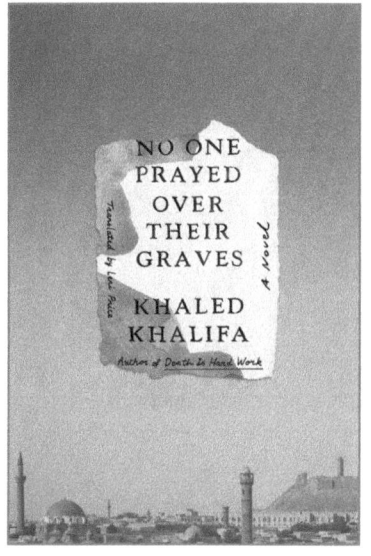

Principal characters

HANNA GREGOROS, the novel's protagonist, a pleasure-seeker turned puritan
ZAKARIYA BAYAZIDI, his lifelong best friend and business associate
SOUAD BAYAZIDI, his lost love, Zakariya's sister
MARIANA NASSAR, his devoted follower
AISHA BAYAZIDI, his close friend later in life, Zakariya's daughter
WILLIAM BAYAZIDI, Zakariya's son, Aisha's twin
SHAMS AL-SABAH, his favored sex-worker, who assumes leadership of his infamous citadel

No One Prayed Over Their Graves is the enchanting sixth and final novel from Syrian author Khaled Khalifa. It is a fitting installment to his prior works, which both celebrate and criticize Syria's rich and complex history. Khalifa was born in Syria and remained in the country throughout its volatility during the Syrian War that began in 2011, writing from his residence in Damascus until his death in October 2023. He was an author, screenwriter, and poet, and each of his six novels was banned by the Syrian government. His efforts to not only examine his country's history but also depict the lasting impact of violence and tragedy on individuals are embodied throughout his writing. Equally conveyed, however, is his tangible affection for his homeland, seen in his descriptions of Aleppo as a thriving city of abundance, culture, and diversity.

No One Prayed Over Their Graves chronicles the lives of the inseparable Hanna Gregoros and Zakariya Bayazidi, beginning with their childhood in Aleppo in the late 1800s. Hanna, orphaned following a brutal attack on his family, is informally adopted by the Bayazidis, a well-regarded, wealthy family in Aleppo, headed by the meticulous accountant Ahmed and his mystical sister Amina. The young Zakariya and Hanna quickly befriend William Eisa and Azar ibn Hayyim Istanbouli, becoming a blended group of Jewish, Muslim, and Christian adolescents and a public nuisance to the residents of Aleppo. The foursome frequents the local brothel, intoxicated by women and alcohol, and instigate knife fights with their peers. Among their immoral activities, they also share wholesome moments with Zakariya's sister, Souad, whose willful nature and alluring beauty capture Hanna's attention.

When the boys' tomfoolery becomes too sinful for Aleppo to tolerate, Zakariya and Hanna flee for their safety and find sanctuary in Venice, Italy. The duo, under the guise of a fabricated backstory, drink in the extravagance of the city and learn their penchant for frivolity and splendor. While Hanna is engulfed in various women and fine goods, Zakariya discovers his passion and a keen eye for expensive horses, deciding to devote his life to the trade. During this time, the pair concocts an idea that will cause their names to live in infamy for decades. They design their own town, called Hosh Hanna, complete with grand stables for Zakariya's herd, vast fields for farming, and a citadel erected for pleasure, filled with elegant prostitutes and fine goods, where every night is a celebration of indulgence. The building is a haven for extravagance, with an elaborate stage for those who wish to commit suicide at the altar of pleasure.

Though Hanna engages in relationships with several women, he aches for Souad, fantasizing about her self-assurance, fierce loyalty, and creative vision. She represents the safety and lightheartedness of his childhood in Aleppo, a vision of innocence that has since disappeared. Having lost his mother at a young age, Hanna consistently grapples with his relationship with women throughout the novel. He is confused by his concurrent lust and desperate need for a proxy mother figure in his life. This is exemplified by his affection for Souad, who is both a source of passion and security for Hanna. Yet when given the opportunity to share his true feelings with her, he remains silent and slinks away in shame back to Hosh Hanna. A man familiar with extremes, Hanna expresses, "At times he felt like he could kill himself for her, but at others he felt like an abominable coward." Her confidence, comfort, and beauty render Hanna completely confounded. As the novel unfolds, he finds himself desperately searching for a semblance of the simultaneous love and security that Souad imbued in his life.

Because Hanna cannot articulate his love for Souad, their relationship disintegrates, tarnishing their pure memories from childhood. As time passes, Hanna and Zakariya are soon both happily married with young sons. Yet becoming family men does not deter the two from visiting their citadel and engaging in their typical debauchery. In 1907, they return from one such visit to discover Hosh Hanna has been devastated by

Khaled Khalifa

Courtesy Farrar, Straus and Giroux; ©Yamam Al Shaar

a raging flood, which has taken the lives of their sons and Hanna's wife. The tragedy irrevocably changes Zakariya and Hanna. Gone are the desires to succumb to the flesh, and the two must struggle to recover from unspeakable loss and find meaning in life once again. Having spent much of their lives indulging in luxuries, Hanna and Zakariya seek repentance for their prior selfish ways. Zakariya attempts to recover peace through supporting his closest companions, including his anguished wife, Shaha, and Hanna, who has become an emaciated recluse since losing his family. In his despair and search for purpose, Hanna devolves into a deep reflection of his life choices. He attempts to find solace through religion, unearthing a buried church and completing a pilgrimage with his devoted admirer, Mariana. Despite being declared a saint, Hanna remains unsatisfied and instead turns to earthly asceticism. He focuses on the beauty of nature, including the flowers across his land and the creatures in the river. Hanna admires its endless ebb and flow of birth and death, finding it provides comfort for the tragedies that have befallen him and his companions.

As Hanna and Zakariya grow older and reckon with the tragedy of the flood, the novel shifts from their perspectives and becomes an anthology of stories about their friends and descendants. Khalifa flits through time and place, returning to Hanna and Zakariya's childhood, then back to the present as the pair ages. Each vignette is remarkably distinct and charming, encompassing familiar themes, such as forbidden love and quests for glory, set against the backdrop of religious and political turmoil in Aleppo. Khalifa alternates timelines and perspectives to allow each character to tell of the tragedies and joys they have endured. Though at times disjointed, the author's narrative construction is both intimate and grandiose, with each tale resulting in a stirring conclusion of epiphany and heartbreak. Further, Khalifa dives into each anecdote with such fervor and sensory detail that any momentary disorientation at the new setting and focal character is quickly forgotten. At the same time, the author takes care to continuously return to Hanna and Zakariya, whether it be a fleeting mention or a more in-depth presence in these extraneous stories. The effect is a deftly woven, sprawling portrayal of the diverse religions, social classes, and families in Aleppine society and a simultaneous chronicling of Hanna and Zakariya's lives well into their twilight years.

At its core, *No One Prayed Over Their Graves* is a novel about storytelling, demonstrated by the characters' firsthand accounts of their experiences and the tales others spin about them. Aleppo is a small city brimming with gossips eager to exchange fables about its inhabitants. At times, Khalifa is quite literal in his expression of storytelling, specifically through Mariana, the Christian zealot obsessed with curating the myth of Hanna's sainthood and controlling the narrative surrounding him. More subtle, however, are the techniques Khalifa used to craft his novel, which is ultimately a collection of anecdotes about Hanna and the Bayazidi family in Aleppo. While the beginning of the novel establishes Hanna and Zakariya as the protagonists and regales their early years up to the devastating flood in Hosh Hanna, the second half concocts their lives through small vignettes. Throughout the book, Khalifa intertwines his theme of curating one's legacy through stories, first introduced with Hanna and Zakariya's grand plan of the citadel, then repeated with each minor character seeking a purpose. The varying accounts from Zakariya's twins, Aisha and William, and other

Aleppo residents flow smoothly from one person to another so seamlessly it is at times indiscernible that Khalifa has shifted to another perspective.

While Khalifa's lyrical prose paints a vivid portrait of Aleppo, *No One Prayed Over Their Graves* is nearly devoid of lengthy descriptions, facts, or tangible dates to establish the historical setting across the decades. Twentieth-century Syria has a complex history of religious and political upheaval, yet Khalifa remains singularly fixated on his character studies and allows these humble vignettes to touch on the larger societal conflicts of the time. It is through these individual stories, compiled to create the greater anthology of Hanna and Zakariya's lives, that Khalifa demonstrates his intention in writing *No One Prayed Over Their Graves*. It is a book about perseverance and love but also unspeakable violence and loss, much of which he has witnessed firsthand in his home country of Syria. Each romantic anecdote ends in sadness, due to individuals' actions and the turbulent circumstances in which they find themselves. As characters are subjected to natural disasters and religious persecution, Khalifa fixates entirely on their perceptions while war and famine are waged in the background. For instance, when Maryam, who escaped the Armenian genocide at the hands of the Ottoman Empire in the early 1900s, marries a wealthy Turkish man for security, she reflects on her decisions and concludes, "Survival is a journey through a trackless wilderness, and its pain cannot be calculated, any more than it can be summarized or spoken about lightly." Through these accounts, the central characters must combat the frustrating futility of their actions in a tempestuous society and strive to establish meaning in their lives through love and friendship.

For *No One Prayed Over Their Graves*, Khalifa was praised for his skillful focus on individuals enduring the conflicts that shaped modern Syria, specifically presenting the tales of minor characters through entertaining story arcs. As Sarah Cypher described in her 2023 review for the *Washington Post*, "Through the lens of a few central families, the story cycles through motifs that repeat across generations: wandering men, the paradise of the natural world, and varieties of corporeal and mystical love." Reviewers often mentioned the book's construction, with some praising Khalifa's poetic prose and others critiquing its dense inclusion of characters and constantly shifting perspectives. The anonymous reviewer for *Publishers Weekly*, for instance, called the novel "a lyrical if laborious story." While some found the intricacies to be arduous, Marcel Theroux, writing in the *Guardian*, concluded that "readers who persist will be rewarded by a series of moving revelations," and further elaborated to say the novel "takes on the burden of granting all of its characters the blessing of a final prayer." Overall, *No One Prayed Over Their Graves* is a notable final addition to Khalifa's literary oeuvre, serving as an exemplary culmination of the author's dedication to celebrating the rich tapestry of Aleppine culture while brazenly sharing the religious and political turmoil of his homeland.

Author Biography

Khaled Khalifa was an acclaimed Syrian author of six novels, including *Death Is Hard Work* (2019), which was a finalist for the 2019 National Book Award. He was also the recipient of the Naguib Mahfouz Medal for Literature, distinguishing him as one of the most prominent Arabic writers of the twenty-first century.

Leri Price is a translator of contemporary Arabic literature. She was a finalist for the National Book Award for Translated Literature in 2019 and 2021.

Annie Schwartz

Review Sources

Cypher, Sarah. "A Catastrophic Flood Alters a City—and a Lifelong Friendship." Review of *No One Prayed Over Their Graves*, by Khaled Khalifa. *The Washington Post*, 18 July 2023, www.washingtonpost.com/books/2023/07/18/review-khaled-khalifa-prayed-graves. Accessed 3 Jan. 2024.

Garner, Dwight. "After a Great Flood, a Struggle between Faith and Reason." Review of *No One Prayed Over Their Graves*, by Khaled Khalifa. *The New York Times*, 17 July 2023, www.nytimes.com/2023/07/17/books/review/khaled-khalifa-no-one-prayed-over-their-graves.html. Accessed 3 Jan. 2024.

Review of *No One Prayed Over Their Graves*, by Khaled Khalifa. *Publishers Weekly*, 18 Apr. 2023, www.publishersweekly.com/9780374601928. Accessed 3 Jan. 2024.

Theroux, Marcel. "No One Prayed Over Their Graves by Khaled Khalifa—a Syrian Epic." Review of *No One Prayed Over Their Graves*, by Khaled Khalifa. *The Guardian*, 26 July 2023, www.theguardian.com/books/2023/jul/26/no-one-prayed-over-their-graves-by-khaled-khalifa-a-syrian-epic. Accessed 3 Jan. 2024.

North Woods

Author: Daniel Mason (b. ca. 1976)
Publisher: Random House (New York).
  Illustrated. 384 pp.
Type of work: Novel
Time: Early 1600s–2020s
Locale: Rural western Massachusetts

Daniel Mason offers a sweeping vision of life in western Massachusetts and a commentary on the relationship between humans and the environment through the interlocking stories of several generations of families who inhabit a cabin set in the deep woods.

Principal characters

CHARLES OSGOOD, an apple grower who first builds the yellow house in the 1760s
ALICE OSGOOD, his spinster daughter, who manages the house after his death
MARY OSGOOD, his other spinster daughter, who manages the house after his death
WILLIAM HENRY TEALE, a landscape painter who inhabits the house in the 1830s
KARL FARNSWORTH, the owner of the house in the early twentieth century, who uses it as a hunting lodge
EMILY FARNSWORTH, Karl's wife, who is visited by ghosts
ANASTASIA ROSSI, a.k.a. Edith Simmons, a medium who conducts a séance for the Farnsworths
LILLIAN FARNSWORTH, Karl and Emily's daughter
ROBERT, the Farnsworths' grandson, Lillian's son inhabits the house in the early 1900s
MORRIS LAKEMAN, an amateur historian and retired accountant, who moves into the house in the early twenty-first century
NORA, a botanical researcher, who investigates the abandoned house in the twenty-first century

While Daniel Mason's novel *North Woods* (2023) may be classified as historical fiction, this "brave and original book," as Alice Jolly called it for the *Guardian*, is much more than a fictional chronicle of the generations of people who live on a secluded piece of land in western Massachusetts. *North Woods* is a novel about families and family relationships, sibling rivalry, ambition, forbidden love, psychological distress—and about natural disasters, climate change, and the slow but inevitable changes to the landscape brought about by forces of nature over which humans have little control. The text is a pastiche of journals, letters, ballads, psychiatrist's notes, true-crime reporting, and

Daniel Mason

transcriptions of formal speeches, as well as more conventional methods of narration, such as first-person omniscient accounts. No one character is treated extensively; rather, Mason employs a slice-of-life technique to highlight the fate of several generations of people whose lives are inextricably intertwined with a homestead that is built, expanded, modified, and eventually left to decay by generations of its inhabitants, and whose history affects (sometimes in strange ways) future generations of inhabitants.

The novel begins at the time of the arrival of European settlers in the region that became New England, with brief vignettes about Puritan and Indigenous inhabitants in the early 1600s. The first major section is set in the mid-eighteenth century. Charles Osgood, recently discharged from the British Army, evades efforts by his well-meaning family to treat him for insanity because he is fixated on raising apples. He flees to western Massachusetts, where, after discovering a wild apple tree with delicious fruit, establishes an orchard to raise apples the family names the Osgood Wonder. Osgood builds a modest home in the woods—"lemon yellow, with white shutters on the windows and a tall black door"—for himself and his twin daughters, Mary and Alice, who assist him in managing the orchard until he departs to rejoin the British Army, which is fighting a group of rebellious colonists. There follows a section focused on the life of the daughters. Their devotion to each other and to their father's legacy is threatened when Mary becomes envious of her sister, who attracts numerous suitors, while Mary receives none. The sisters' macabre deaths add an element of mystery that carries through to future sections of the novel. Subsequent vignettes describe how various owners of the Osgood property expand the house and how changes in the economics of the region affect the prosperity of its various residents. Among the most extensive of these is the story of a landscape artist, William Henry Teale, who lives with his family in the old Osgood house. His intense friendship with a prominent poet, hinted at being gay, causes his wife to leave him.

Another major episode involves the Farnsworths, who purchase the yellow house and surrounding property early in the twentieth century from the estate of an Osgood heir. Karl Farnsworth, a successful business magnate, intends to turn the house into a high-end hunting lodge for distinguished guests. His wife, Emily, is plagued by "voices," and to allay her fears, Mr. Farnsworth enlists the aid of a celebrated medium, Madame Anastasia Rossi. Unfortunately, Rossi cannot convince Mrs. Farnsworth that she is hallucinating because Rossi too comes to feel the presence of these spirits. Some years later, Morris Lakeman, an amateur historian, attempts to solve a long-rumored mystery associated with the deaths of Mary and Alice and the concurrent disappearance of a government agent sent to collect taxes from them; unfortunately, Lakeman cannot get anyone to listen to his theories, and he ends up reading to himself a paper he has prepared to document his startling discoveries.

A quarter of the narrative focuses on the lives of the Farnsworths' daughter, Lillian, and her children, Robert and Helen. Lillian grows increasingly concerned about the mental health of Robert, who is under the care of a psychiatrist because he shows signs of schizophrenia. Robert's mother and his therapist are vexed by his constant wandering through the woods—to "stitch" together rifts in the fabric of the countryside, he says, which has been rent by spirits that are harrowing him. Robert eventually disappears. Lillian's efforts to bring her son home place her in danger when a prisoner comes to the yellow house to rob her; she escapes when the prisoner is suddenly killed thanks to a seemingly supernatural act. Robert eventually returns home but never rids himself of the voices that drive him to pace the woods. In settling his affairs after his death, his sister, Helen, finds numerous films Robert has made to document the spirits that have haunted him.

In the final vignette, Nora, a postdoctoral student, travels to the region to find sites for ecological work. Driving too fast, she crashes her car near the yellow house, which is now abandoned. Exploring the area after the accident, she muses on the history of the region, speculating about what might have occurred here to the people and the habitat over centuries. In her reverie, Nora expresses a major theme of the novel: "To understand the world as something other than a tale of loss is to see it as a tale of change."

One of the most striking features of *North Woods* is Mason's employment of multiple narrative techniques. While this methodology may seem confusing at first, readers carefully attuned to the point-of-view in each section will find great satisfaction in discovering how the way a story is presented affects one's attitude toward both the narrator and other characters in the story. Charles Osgood's tale, for example, is presented in the form of a journal for his daughters, in which he writes to explain how he came to create the orchard. The story of Teale is reported through letters to his lover. Robert's apparent schizophrenia is described in the notes of the attending psychiatrist, who is eager to convince Robert's mother that her son should be lobotomized. The brief scientific treatises interspersed throughout the novel give a dispassionate account of the changes in the environment, contrasted with the more biased narratives of people intent on adapting the natural environment to their own ends. The importance of perspective becomes evident when the story of Mary and Alice's death, first told from Mary's viewpoint, is recast as a series of true-crime reports that sensationalize what is clearly a tragic occurrence.

Though it may seem that each section of the novel ends tragically, comic elements abound, as Mason pokes fun at people's vainglory and their doomed attempts to understand both the present and the past. For example, through the character of Madame Rossi, who comes to western Massachusetts to help communicate with the spirits tormenting Mrs. Farnsworth, Mason gently satirizes the gullibility of so many Americans in the early twentieth century who put their trust in these charlatans. There is no question about the fraudulent nature of Rossi's practice, as this portion of the novel is related through the perspective of Rossi (a.k.a. Edith Simmons), who has assumed the foreign-sounding name as a means of adding an air of mystery and credibility to her performance in leading séances. Mason also indicts the academic community, whose members ignore Lakeman's extensive historical research simply because the retiree lacks an advanced degree. Mason's ribald account of beetle copulation that leads to the proliferation of a species that devastates the forest further reveals that he is a master of dark humor. Additionally, when juxtaposed against the valiant efforts of generations of people to improve the yellow house and surrounding property, the vignette becomes a wry commentary on humans' ability to control the environment.

Despite the almost hyper-realistic quality of Mason's text, with its lengthy scientific descriptions of natural processes and its focus on the psychology of its principal characters, there is a supernatural element as well. For instance, Mary and Alice appear to later generations, and the "voices" Robert hears and tries to film are the ancestors who inhabit the land. As Jolly observed, "No character in [this] novel is ever entirely dead."

Reviewers trying to describe this quirky yet eminently satisfying novel pointed out similarities to such distinguished nineteenth- and twentieth-century authors as Nathaniel Hawthorne, Edgar Allan Poe, Flannery O'Connor, Henry David Thoreau, and E. L. Doctorow. That list could likely be expanded further, as Mason seems to be able to adopt the techniques of earlier writers without becoming a slavish imitator. One constant among reviewers was the high praise *North Woods* garnered. Alexis Burling, writing in the *San Francisco Chronicle*, praised Mason for constructing "this curiosity-piquing cocktail of mystery and wonderment" with "equal parts whimsy and aplomb." *New York Times* reviewer Rand Richards Cooper, acknowledging that some readers might be put off by the "piecemeal structure" of the novel, ultimately found *North Woods* "captivating" and praised Mason's "blending of the comic and the sublime" by "deftly toggling between the macro and the micro." Reflecting on the theme of change as the only constant, Ron Charles observed in his review for the *Washington Post* that the novel "projects that revelatory vision so powerfully that you can't help but feel the book evolve in your hands."

Principally through its narrative methodology, *North Woods* raises additional questions: How do we come to understand the past? Can we really know it? Why should we want to? Most importantly, do individual human lives really matter? To these, Mason offers no definitive responses, leaving it to his readers to develop their own answers.

Author Biography

Daniel Mason is a physician and the author of several novels, including *The Piano Tuner* (2002) and *The Winter Soldier* (2018), and a short story collection, *A Registry of My Passage upon the Earth* (2020), which was a finalist for the Pulitzer Prize. Among his awards are a Guggenheim Fellowship, the Joyce Carol Oates Prize, and a National Endowment for the Arts Fellowship.

Laurence W. Mazzeno

Review Sources

Burling, Alexis. "Review: Haunting New Novel Traces the Households of a Cottage over Four Centuries." Review of *North Woods*, by Daniel Mason. *San Francisco Chronicle*, 12 Sept. 2023, datebook.sfchronicle.com/books/review-daniel-mason-s-haunting-new-novel-18351069. Accessed 7 Jan. 2024.

Charles, Ron. "Let 'North Woods' Be Your Next Book Club Pick." Review of *North Woods*, by Daniel Mason. *The Washington Post*, 13 Sept. 2023. www.washingtonpost.com/books/2023/09/13/daniel-mason-north-woods-book-review/. Accessed 7 Jan. 2024.

Cooper, Rand Richards. "The Story of a House and Its Occupants over 3 Centuries." Review of *North Woods*, by Daniel Mason. *The New York Times*, 19 Sept. 2023. www.nytimes.com/2023/09/19/books/review/daniel-mason-north-woods.html. Accessed 7 Jan. 2024.

Jolly, Alice. "North Woods by Daniel Mason Review—An Epic of American Lives." Review of *North Woods*, by Daniel Mason. *The Guardian*, 16 Sept. 2023. www.theguardian/com/books/2023/sep/16/north-woods-by-daniel-mason-review-an-epic-of-american-lives. Accessed 7 Jan. 2024.

Sacks, Sam. "Fiction: 'North Woods' by Daniel Mason." Review of *North Woods*, by Daniel Mason. *The Wall Street Journal*, 13 Oct. 2023. www.wsj.com/arts-culture/books/fiction-north-woods-by-daniel-mason-c933fb0c. Accessed 7 Jan. 2024.

Old God's Time

Author: Sebastian Barry (b. 1955)
First published: *Old God's Time*, 2023, in United Kingdom
Publisher: Viking (New York). 272 pp.
Type of work: Novel
Time: The present, with flashbacks to earlier decades
Locale: Ireland

In the novel Old God's Time, *police officer Tom Kettle emerges from retirement to investigate a case from his past, reckon with the magnitude of his personal losses, and separate reality from fiction.*

Principal characters

TOM KETTLE, a retired Irish police officer
JUNE KETTLE, his deceased wife
WINNIE KETTLE, his daughter
MR. TOMELTY, his landlord
JACK FLEMING, his former boss on the police force
FATHER JOSEPH BYRNE, a priest whom he investigates
FATHER THADDEUS MATTHEWS, a priest killed under suspicious circumstances

Sebastian Barry's eleventh novel, *Old God's Time*, is a stunning investigation into the nature of guilt, memory, time, and reality itself. The book opens like a prototypical detective novel: retired Irish police officer Tom Kettle is visited by two young detectives who have a question about one of his old cases. Tom has just spent nine months living in solitude by the sea—a period of time that is pointedly compared to a term of pregnancy—and has begun to make peace with the death of his wife and the end of his career. The visit of the detectives, and their reopening of a case involving a pair of predatory priests, throws Tom back onto unwelcome thoughts of his traumatic past. The child of an unwed mother, Tom was raised in an orphanage where he was sexually abused by the Christian Brothers who ran the place. After returning from military service as a sniper in Malaya, Tom made a place for himself in respectable society as a police officer with the Garda Síochána, Ireland's national police service. He married June, a young woman who, like him, had grown up in an abusive orphanage, and together they raised a son and daughter. But when Tom, early in his career, investigates a pair of priests who have a connection to their childhoods, his and June's past and present collide. The couple must choose between maintaining the stable middle-class life they have forged for themselves, or risking it all to avenge themselves against one of the men who abused them. One of the most compelling aspects of the novel is

Sebastian Barry (Courtesy Penguin Random House)

the process by which Tom excavates his long-repressed past, and faces the magnitude of his and June's actions. The detective is, ultimately, the subject of his own enquiry.

Described in this way, the novel seems both like the stuff of classic detective fiction and like a meditation on the legacy of abuse that the Catholic Church wrought upon generations of Irish people. Barry's interest, however, goes beyond the mechanics of a police procedural and beyond a reckoning with his country's past. In this book, he seems to be investigating the nature of reality itself. Early in the novel, for example, Tom looks up from a conversation with his landlord, Mr. Tomelty, to see a remarkable sight: "In the corner of the room stood a unicorn, with a silver horn, or possibly white gold, raising its delicate right hoof, and innocently staring out through quiet eyes. Mr. Tomelty and his missis made no reference to it. It was just there, verifiably." The unicorn might be merely a figment of Tom's imagination. Yet for the reader, it recalls the novel's epigraph, drawn from the Bible's Book of Job: "Will the unicorn be willing to serve thee?" The vision, then, has an authorial stamp to it: the unicorn is not merely a hallucination, but an integral part of the novel. Tom Kettle, by extension, is another Job, a good and faithful man whom God has made to suffer grievously. Indeed, the unicorn is only one of many beings in Tom's world that may not actually exist; he routinely has conversations and encounters with people whom we later realize are imagined figures or ghosts. Perhaps the most poignant of these apparitions is Tom's daughter Winnie, who at times appears to be alive—a solicitous visitor checking up on her aging father—and at other times is long dead of a heroin overdose. Tom's understanding of this phenomenon waxes and wanes: even after Winnie tells him that she lies buried in their old hometown, Tom quickly drifts back into thinking of her as being alive. His understanding of the past is equally elusive. The reader intuits that Tom, and perhaps June, had something to do with the death of one of the priests, but it will take the whole novel before Tom can look squarely at his role in the case.

Although Tom cannot separate past from present and reality from fantasy, *Old God's Time* is not the story of a man who is losing his mind. Rather, it is Barry's novel itself, and perhaps of all fiction, that is unstable. The appearance of the epigrammatic unicorn is only one of many times that Barry draws attention to the metafictional nature of his story. In one remarkable scene, Tom returns to Dublin to help reopen the case of the dead priest, Father Matthews, and is given a hero's welcome at his old police station. He engages in witty banter with his former boss, Fleming; is reunited with the detectives who had paid him a visit; and meets the young woman who has replaced him as a detective—who, of course, makes him think of Winnie. Just as the novel seems to have found its gear as a police procedural, the scene dissolves: "Oh, but suddenly, or gradually, or in a blur, clearing slowly, or was it quickly, there was no chair. There was no Fleming. Tom was waking. . . . On one of the benches in St. Stephen's Green." To find that this reunion was merely a dream signals a devastating loss of the community and comradery that Tom clearly pines for. In the hands of a lesser writer, this kind of imaginary sequence would feel like a cheap trick. For Barry's reader, it is a deft reminder that what they may accept as reality is entirely an artifice. Though readers might be tempted to accept the verities of the detective genre, and to watch Tom happily slip into the groove of a familiar and satisfying plotline, Barry continuously destabilizes the reader's grasp of reality. Genre itself becomes one of many ways that Barry interrogates the nature of reality and representation.

The instability of the novel's fictional world may be meant to express something about the unstable nature of history, trauma, and loss. It is not merely Tom Kettle, but Ireland itself that must confront its traumatic past and understand that, for decades or centuries, it had been sold a fiction. It was only in the 1990s that the magnitude of church abuse was fully revealed, and Barry is one of a generation of Irish authors who are grappling with what this collective national trauma means for the country's past, present, and future. In a sense, the nation must tell a new story about itself. The case of Father Byrne and Father Mathews, therefore, stands as a metonymy for all of the abuses that members of the church perpetrated or covered up. For Tom, it is a thread that, when pulled on, entangles the fabric of his childhood, adulthood, and old age. Though he remembers investigating abuse allegations against Father Byrne—a case he was eventually pressured to drop—Tom seems to have suppressed his memories of being the investigating office in the case of the Byrne's housemate, Father Matthews, who was murdered on a hike in the mountains. When Fleming reminds him of his role in the case, Tom has a visceral reaction:

> It was the pain of trying to remember that coiled about his throat, or he thought it must be, because Tom was struggling to breath easily. The shock of being told something he did not remember but instantly did as soon as it was put to him. It was the most extraordinary out-of-body experience.

Again and again, Tom's trauma returns to confront him, forcing on him a reckoning with his own past and that of his family and country. For author and protagonist alike, the past and the present seem to exist side-by-side; when Tom takes a train ride to Dublin, for example, he sees the sea, "rinsed and silver, rattling the little pegs of memory," and thinks, "you can hold nothing in its place now, two thousand known years, back to Romans and Vikings and God knows who." It is not just Tom's flat, but the whole island that is peopled by ghosts of the past. In his long view of history, his struggles to overcome past trauma, and his fleeting moments of joy and contentment, Tom becomes a stand-in for his generation.

As the novel moves toward its conclusion, Tom finds himself swept up in a new case, protecting the son of his upstairs neighbor from her murderous, sexually predatory husband. On one level, this final plot line skillfully fuses together so many other elements of the novel, calling on Tom to put to good use the skills he developed as a sniper in Malaya, to stand up for the kind of child he once was, and to set wrongs right again. He will put down the mantle of victim or avenger, and finally become what both the priests and the Garda had always promised to be: a guardian. Yet the novel has trained its reader to ask whether the upstairs neighbor and her son are fact or fantasy, and whether this final moment of catharsis is one last fiction playing out in Tom's mind and on Barry's page. Perhaps the path to redemption and grace does not require such a heroic journey; perhaps it is to be found not in a climactic future, but in making peace with one's past and present.

Critics have praised *Old God's Time* as one of the prolific Barry's strongest and most absorbing novels. Writing for *NPR*, Michael Shaub calls it 'a relentlessly bleak, stunning novel about how the effects of violence and abuse can reverberate for years and across generations.' Shaub praises Barry's 'wonderful' prose and concludes that he is 'clearly one of the best Irish writers working today.' Many critics praised Barry's deft reworking and expansion of the detective genre. In his review for the *New York Times*, Andrew Miller notes that what opens as 'that darling of the genre, the cold-case review' becomes something else as 'the sideways sliding of [Kettle's] mind, and a constant deferment of the revelations we expect' move the book into the realm of the fantastic. Miller concludes that this instability about such basic questions as which characters are real and which are imagined give the novel 'a kind of shimmer and motility some will find attractive . . . and others a source of frustration.' Writing for the *Guardian*, Declan Ryan likewise argues that Barry's novel is a 'woozy rendering of unstable memories and the difficulty in telling your story as it disappears 'into old God's time', as well as a tribute to enduring love and its ability to light up the dark." Giles Harvey, in a piece in the *New Yorker*, singles out Barry's "exquisite prose," as offering up "a great demotic aria to existence, which, for all its grief and abjection, he sees as something full of grace."

Old God's Time is a stunning meditation not just on the nature of a family and a nation's trauma, but on the very nature of existence itself.

Author Biography

Born in Dublin in 1955, Sebastian Barry is the award-winning author of eight novels and more than a dozen plays. His novels *A Long Long Way* (2005) and *The Secret Scripture* (2008) were shortlisted for the Booker Prize, while *Days Without End* (2016), *On Canaan's Side* (2011), and *Old God's Time* (2023) were longlisted for it. He was the Laureate for Irish Fiction from 2018 to 2021.

Matthew J. Bolton

Review Sources

Harvey, Giles. "The Accursed Brilliance of Sebastian Barry." Review of *Old God's Time*, by Sebastian Barry. *The New Yorker*, 20 Mar. 2023, www.newyorker.com/magazine/2023/03/27/old-gods-time-book-review-sebastian-barry. Accessed 15 Oct. 2023.

Miller, Andrew. "Once a Detective, Always a Detective." Review of *Old God's Time*, by Sebastian Barry. *The New York Times*, 21 Mar. 2023, www.nytimes.com/2023/03/21/books/review/sebastian-barry-old-gods-time.html. Accessed 15 Oct. 2023

Ryan, Declan. "*Old God's Time* by Sebastian Barry Review: A Cop You Can't Trust." Review of *Old God's Time*, by Sebastian Barry. *The Guardian*, 27 Feb. 2023, www.theguardian.com/books/2023/feb/27/old-gods-time-by-sebastian-barry-review-a-cop-you-cant-trust. Accessed 15 Oct. 2023

Schaub, Michael. "In *Old God's Time*, Sebastian Barry Stresses the Long Effects of Violence and Abuse." Review of *Old God's Time*, by Sebastian Barry. *NPR*, 22 Mar. 2023, www.npr.org/2023/03/22/1163042950/old-gods-time-sebastian-barry-book-stresses-effects-of-abuse. Accessed 15 Oct. 2023

Ordinary Notes

Author: Christina Sharpe (b. 1965)
Publisher: Farrar, Straus and Giroux (New York). Illustrated. 392 pp.
Type of work: Memoir, history, current affairs

Ordinary Notes *is Christina Sharpe's depiction of the love, joy, triumph, labor, pain, and tragedy that marks everyday Black life under the White supremacist regime of the United States. As the title suggests, the work collects notes composed by the author—fragments of memoir, personal reflection, critical theory, literature, and archival documents—blended with art images, artifacts of public history and personal life, and the author's photographs.*

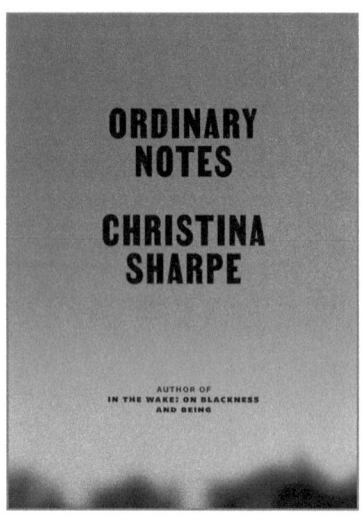

Principal personages
IDA WRIGHT SHARPE, the author's mother
STEPHEN, one of her older brothers
CHRISTOPHER, one of her older brothers
IDAMARIE, one of her older sisters

Ordinary Notes is the latest of Christina Sharpe's three major works that illustrate, each in its own way, the continued racialized subjugation and brutality normalized in the aftermath of the long enslavement of Black people. All three books—*Monstrous Intimacies: Making Post-Slavery Subjects* (2010), *In the Wake: On Blackness and Being* (2016), and now *Ordinary Notes*—argue that Black people as a subjugated group have had to contend with the ever-present threat, if not the actuality, of many forms of abuses wrought by systemic White domination, as they have created lives and found ways to be as free as possible over the centuries within a roiling and unrelenting context of anti-Blackness. Sharpe is part of a long-standing and growing community of scholars and artists whose works are unequivocal in resisting whitewashed distortions of racial history and the anti-Black context of contemporary Black life. Many of these scholars and artists are referenced in *Ordinary Notes*.

The legacy of Toni Morrison figures prominently in *Ordinary Notes*, with quotes and excerpts throughout the text and a particularly evocative reference to Morrison's Pulitzer Prize–winning masterpiece, *Beloved* (1987), appearing as the second note of the book. Sharpe's inclusion of a photo of her well-worn paperback copy of *Beloved* in Note 211 denotes the significance of Morrison's influence on Sharpe's thinking and her work. She writes of *Beloved* as one of the books that "changed what I thought a

Christina Sharpe

novel that took slavery and the enslaved as its subject could do and how it could animate those enslaved people who did and did not survive its hold."

In the opening pages, Sharpe provides a list of definitions for the word "note," which in itself is a note to the reader to think broadly about the term and to look for how the book will explore language and connect elements of different modes of expression. The list includes definitions such as "to notice or observe with care," "a symbol, character, or mark used in writing," "a brief record of facts, topics, or thoughts written down as an aid to memory," "tone, call, sound." The notes are organized into eight sections and vary in length, some consisting only of a single sentence, while others are pages long. The notes reveal contemporary Black life as it is lived in the turbulent wake of slavery through the author's own lived experience, her scholarship, and her ancestral Black ways of seeing and knowing.

Ordinary Notes stands in contrast to Sharpe's earlier works, most obviously in form but also in its deeply personal nature. Sharpe describes the book, a collection of 248 numbered notes, as a love letter to her deceased mother, Ida Wright Sharpe, from whom the author says she received her gifts for observation and discernment as well as the ability to see and create beauty and tenderness amid the harshest realities of living. In Note 10, she writes, "My mother wanted me to build a life that was nourishing and Black." The deep attention, tenderness, encouragement, and care with which Ida Wright Sharpe loved her daughter reverberates vibrantly throughout this book and lends the work notes of gentleness, love, and generosity.

Observing her mother's way of living within difficult circumstances in which she would focus on beauty—flowers from her garden, literature and the arts, dress and personal adornment, Sharpe came to think of beauty and tenderness as freedom methodologies, a kind of design theory for the realization of joy and inspiration in a world intent on the destruction of Black life. Sharpe refers to such methodologies as "Black notes" that "refuse altogether to accede to those logics that simultaneously de/re and unhuman Black people." Black notes are expressions of care in various tones, colors, pitches, and symbols that light up the imagination about living Black life in freedom. They are necessary because, as Sharpe explains, we live in a regime of White supremacy and anti-Blackness and "its effects are made to be felt through all kinds of systems: most visibly, in policing and mass criminalization; less observably, but no less potently, in education and art." Black notes save Black lives by igniting possibilities of freedom.

In Note 189, subtitled "Life," Sharpe gives ample space for thoughts of sixteen other writers who sound Black notes on the topic of Black life. Kimberly Nichele

Brown writes of Black life being a process of moving ahead while looking backward, "navigating the contradictions," and remaining on guard. Lorgia Garcìa Peña thinks of Black life as rebellion and an "affirmation of possibility through collective, ancestral, radical joy." Phoebe Boswell speaks of Black life as a "loving practice," an idea similar to Sharpe's recollections of her mother's freedom methodologies.

Sharpe returns repeatedly to the concept of care practiced among Black people. The warnings and instructions that Black parents give to their children to take care of them in the face of White authority are Black notes. Sharpe cites Dionne Brand, Saidiya Hartman, and Canisia Lubrin, Black scholars, writers, and artists whose works sound Black notes in their determined resistance to White supremacy and open up space and new vocabularies for discourse about Black life as an entity of its own, a creative project made of Black energies, intellect, and care. Black notes from across a sweeping array of expressive forms affirm, validate, and inform Black experience regarding the destructive workings of Whiteness but simultaneously light a path to an enriching and enlivened Blackness as a way of living. Note 209 speaks of imagination as "an engine of Black life."

Some Black notes are imperceptible to the White power structure, but those that are heard can ignite White fear and rage. They are received as so objectionable, so illogical, and so threatening to the social order as to trigger violent correctives such as police action and, more broadly, institutional, legislative, and juridical responses affecting Black access to safety, freedoms, resources, and life itself. Sharpe is direct and descriptive in her notes about anti-Black violence, state-sponsored and otherwise, and how the knowledge of that violence as an ever-present threat can affect the way Black people move through the world in the ordinary course of their everyday lives. One simply stated and plaintive note reads, "It is hard sometimes to step into the world when you know, really know, the viciousness of white people."

In her note discussing a national culture that fails to acknowledge historic and contemporary anti-Black injustices baked into all US social, governmental, and economic systems, Sharpe refers to Whiteness as an "innocence-making machine" that makes White disavowal of anti-Blackness possible and logical. Note 217 states, "The machinery of whiteness constantly deploys violence—and in a mirror-register, constantly manufactures wonder, surprise, and innocence in relation to that violence."

About halfway through the book, Sharpe describes another of her projects, a "dictionary of untranslatable blackness" that would answer a question she poses in Note 164 about how an encyclopedic dictionary of significant philosophical concepts that "began from Black" would sound, how it would differ from extant cultural dictionaries that begin and end in Whiteness. The twenty or so notes that follow Note 164 feature quotes and excerpts from the works of a long list of writers, poets, and artists (beginning from Black) about concepts including grace, property, spectacle, memory, and abstraction, among many others. This section of the book is particularly compelling not only because it introduces the reader to an idea whose time has come—claiming the right of Black people to record Black experiences in Black terms in a major publishable volume—but also because the reader encounters such a wide range of Black thought that is exciting, thought-provoking, confrontational, and original.

Ordinary Notes has been met with enthusiastic praise by critics, many of whom were particularly appreciative of the numbered-note format of the book for the expansiveness it allows the author to traverse complex and starkly varied terrain and expressive styles. A *Kirkus* review described the form as a "collagelike structure" and an "original celebration of American Blackness," noting how the images of Black life in the book connect to the prose. Similarly, Jennifer Szalai in a *New York Times* review commented favorably on Sharpe's assemblage of so many different artifacts, observations, and literary references that bring Black life to the foreground. She described the fragmentation as Sharpe's way "to propose and to elaborate, eddying back and forth between cruelty and care, sorrow and joy." Erica Cardwell, in a *Brooklyn Rail* review of *Ordinary Notes*, valued what she referred to as the "fragments, jump cuts, glimmers, vignettes, [and] blackout text" for the way they take apart and examine the everydayness of racism in the Black experience. Megin Jimenez wrote of Sharpe's form in the *Chicago Review of Books* as a "kaleidoscope of styles and tones" and suggested that the form allows Sharpe to be as vulnerable or as detached as she deems appropriate, given what she intends to communicate about the topic at hand and reveal about herself in relation to it.

Some reviewers have commented less on the book's form and more on its focus on anti-Blackness as a foundational and persistent element of American culture that simultaneously sustains and destabilizes the national culture. The *Boston Globe* review by Walton Muyumba characterized Sharpe's work as "preoccupied with the West's foundation in spectacles of violent Black death, photographic/pictorial representations of Black experience, and philosophies of Black freedom, especially those conceived by literary artists and critics." Indeed, Sharpe's work is a necessary Black note in response to such spectacles. Muyumba concluded by declaring the book a practice by which to guide a commitment to Black freedom.

Near the end of the book, in the final notes, Sharpe poses a critical question, leaving readers to consider their own adjacency to the precarity of Black life: "What is required of us now? In this long time of our undoing?"

Author Biography

Christina Sharpe is an American-born scholar who studies literature, art, history, and culture of the Black diaspora. *Ordinary Notes*, her third book, was awarded Canada's largest prize for nonfiction by the Hilary Weston Writers Trust in 2023 and shortlisted for the 2023 National Book Award.

RoAnne Elliott, MA

Review Sources

Cardwell, Erica. "Christina Sharpe's *Ordinary Notes*." Review of *Ordinary Notes*, by Christina Sharpe. *The Brooklyn Rail*, July/Aug. 2023, brooklynrail.org/2023/07/art_books/Christina-Sharpes-Ordinary-Notes. Accessed 15 Nov. 2023.

Jimenez, Megin. "Seeing through the Kaleidoscope of *Ordinary Notes*." Review of *Ordinary Notes*, by Christina Sharpe. *The Chicago Review of Books*, 5 May 2023, chireviewofbooks.com/2023/05/05/ordinary-notes-christina-sharpe. Accessed 20 Nov. 2023.

Muyumba, Walton. "In *Ordinary Notes*, Christina Sharpe Reflects on a Black Freedom Grounded in Beauty and Possibility despite White Supremacist Violence and Degradation." Review of *Ordinary Notes*, by Christina Sharpe. *Boston Globe*, 27 Apr. 2023, www.bostonglobe.com/2023/04/27/arts/ordinary-notes-christina-sharpe-reflects-black-freedom-grounded-beauty-possibility-despite-white-supremacist-violence-degradation. Accessed 20 Dec. 2021.

Review of *Ordinary Notes*, by Christina Sharpe. "An Exquisitely Original Celebration of American Blackness." *Kirkus Reviews*, 25 Apr. 2023, www.kirkusreviews.com/book-reviews/christina-sharpe/ordinary-notes. Accessed 28 Nov. 2023.

Szalai, Jennifer. "In *Ordinary Notes*, a Radical Reading of Black Life." Review of *Ordinary Notes*, by Christina Sharpe. *The New York Times*, 19 Apr. 2023, www.nytimes.com/2023/04/19/books/review/ordinary-notes-christina-sharpe.html. Accessed 15 Nov. 2023.

Our Migrant Souls
A Meditation on Race and the Meanings and Myths of "Latino"

Author: Héctor Tobar (b. ca.1960s)
Publisher: MCD (New York). 256 pp.
Type of work: Essays
Time: 2000s–2020s, with some historical context
Locales: United States, Mexico, Guatemala

Pulitzer Prize–winning journalist Héctor Tobar explores what it means to be Latino in twenty-first-century American culture with his essay collection Our Migrant Souls. *Through careful self-examination and a curiosity about the experiences of others, Tobar creates a moving tapestry that questions the foundation of modern ideas about race and culture.*

At the heart of Héctor Tobar's essay collection *Our Migrant Souls: A Meditation on Race and the Meanings and Myths of "Latino"* (2023) is an analysis and deconstruction of the modern idea of race and how it has come to be used by and against groups of people. For example, Tobar, who is a Pulitzer Prize–winning journalist among other literary accolades, meditates on the idea that many people still believe that race is a biological concept; that people of different skin tones are somehow fundamentally different from each other. Looking at the idea of race through historical and sociological lenses, Tobar begins to unpack troubling ideas about race and how they have been used to create the image of Latinos in modern American culture. Tobar, as a frequent contributor to the *New York Times*' opinion section, has the ability to aptly and professionally interrogate mainstream viewpoints, a skill that serves him well in essay form. While less personal than, perhaps, Joan Didion in her early tomes like *Slouching Towards Bethlehem* (1968) and *The White Album* (1979), Tobar's work in *Our Migrant Souls* stands within that tradition of using a personal-political lens to exorcise a deep injustice in American culture.

Our Migrant Souls is divided into two sections, "Our Country" and "Our Journeys Home," each filled with a slew of essays on that topic. Loosely connecting the collection is Tobar's own origin story and connection to both the term *Latino* and the modern immigrant experience. He uses the story of his parents—two young people living in Guatemala who got married after getting pregnant and moved to Los Angeles, where Tobar's mother gave birth to him—to carry the collection through to its impactful conclusion. Sprinkled through each of the collection's essays are also stories from his many students, who each share their own memories, complications, and traumas related to being a migrant in the twenty-first-century US. Tobar does not shy away from implicating his native United States from its role in creating the immigrant crisis, either, and frequently uses important (and perhaps little-known) pieces of Central and South American history to show how the US came to play a pivotal role in the crisis. In clear, concise language, Tobar makes a poignant impact with each fact and anecdote he neatly stacks on the last.

Tobar opens *Our Migrant Souls* with a prologue speaking directly to his readers, namely those who might identify as Latino or Latinx, and his students. He writes, "'Ethnicity' and 'race' are sold to us as boxes containing our skin tones and our surnames, but the truth about you, about us, will not fit in any box. You have the labels 'undocumented' and 'Mexican' and 'Cubana' attached to you, and yet English is your mother tongue and your favorite band is the Smiths," before going on to dissect the many other ways in which those who are labeled Latino are lumped together using sweeping generalizations. He places these ideas alongside the realization that most, if not all, of the people he is speaking to have experienced racism in their lives and have been subjected to violent words and real-life setbacks because of the labels placed on them by society. But the prologue also provides Tobar with a way to imagine the successful trajectories of Latino people, the very real paths many of his readers and their family members have taken as both documented and undocumented citizens of the US. The heartfelt touch Tobar brings to the collection's opening sets the tone for the remainder of the work, bringing the reader into the warmth of his writing and thinking, even when tackling difficult subjects.

Tobar's personal connection to the lives of the people he writes about is extracted in a slow and meaningful way throughout the collection. The reader learns his parents' history early on; that they left Guatemala for Los Angeles before he was born, settling in West Hollywood where they soon lost interest in each other and ventured out to create their own lives in the city as young twenty-somethings. The way Tobar is able to view his young parents from his present-day perch brings empathy to his position as a son, and he frequently revisits his mother's life in Los Angeles after his parents' divorce, when she was raising him and putting together a life of her own all at once. Tobar's mother becomes an anchor of sorts to the collection when she appears in its second section, when Tobar travels back to Guatemala to meet family. He reminds the reader of the importance of family, especially within Guatemalan culture, and uses this moment to reflect on the pain that immigrant laws have created for those separated by arbitrary international borders.

These separations become the keystone to the book's second part. Story after story appears in which undocumented immigrants, unwilling to leave behind a well-built life in the US, could not to return to their countries of origin to see family members before death. Tobar shares one such story to great effect. In the collection's final essay "Home," he recounts a cross-country trip he undertook to uncover what it means to be Latino across the United States. He begins by driving north from Los Angeles to Oregon before driving down along the coast and border, eventually ending up in Pennsylvania, where he visits the daughter of a woman he knows from Guatemala. The daughter, Claudia, is undocumented and has raised four children in Harrisburg, where she was able to buy a house with her husband. When Tobar reaches her home, Claudia tells him that since they last saw each other, her mother, Loty, had died after a decline. Because of Claudia's undocumented status, she was unable to visit Loty before she died, as Claudia's adult children decided that they needed her here, in the US, and would not risk her becoming stuck in Guatemala. Tobar addresses the pain experienced by Claudia and her family, but also writes of Claudia's resilience, as she and so many others face these difficult and life-altering decisions based on the attitudes of international governments. Tobar writes of many others who have also been separated from loved ones, able to only connect with a phone call as a parent or sibling lay dying in their home country, and the complications these feelings create for so many.

Our Migrant Souls was well received by critics and was awarded the 2023 *Kirkus Prize* for Nonfiction. Ahead of publication, both *Publishers Weekly* and the *Kirkus Reviews* gave the collection a starred review. The anonymous reviewer for the *Kirkus Reviews* wrote, "Tobar's travels and meditations are altogether provocative and thoroughly well thought through, his account sharply observed and elegantly written," while *Publishers Weekly*'s critic called the collection "lyrical and uncompromising." For the *New York Times*, critic Francisco Cantú wrote, "there is power in the refrain of Tobar's direct address, which gives his writing the feel of warm advice dispensed to youngsters grappling with a sense of self." For the *Atlantic*, writer Geraldo L. Cadava notes that Tobar's *Our Migrant Souls* is even more personal than some of his unflinching novels, including *The Last Great Road Bum* (2020) and *The Tattooed Soldier* (1998). He writes, "For the writer Héctor Tobar, *latinidad*, which means something like Latino-ness,' or the condition of being Latino, is both sweeping and particular." Writing for *BookPage*, Eric A. Ponce called *Our Migrant Souls* "one of the most important pieces of Latino nonfiction in several decades." Ponce continued, "Tobar's blend of philosophy, narrative and history puts him on the same level as literary giants such as Eduardo Galeano and James Baldwin. Turning the last page of this book, you will feel the weight of history on your shoulders—yet it is an uplifting experience."

Throughout the collection, Tobar meets the paradoxes and absurdities of so many individuals from so many different backgrounds being boxed into a collection of labels with an unwillingness to validate such labels. He does this while considering what might lay in wait for marginalized groups in the US, including the ever-growing population of those experiencing homelessness who face more and more discrimination with each passing year. At the collection's conclusion, Tobar makes clear that what is most important as people are sacrificed to capitalism, politics, and war is to maintain a sense of humanity and self and to continue to interrogate the labels thrust upon the vulnerable and marginalized across within and across national borders.

Author Biography
Héctor Tobar is a Pulitzer Prize–winning journalist and author of the *New York Times* bestselling book *Deep Down Dark* (2014), as well as *The Barbarian Nurses* (2011), and *Translation Nation* (2005), among others. His writing has appeared in the *New Yorker*, the *Los Angeles Times*, the *New York Times*, *Best American Short Stories*, and *Slate*.

Melynda Fuller

Review Sources
Cadava, Geraldo L. "The Fundamental Paradox of *Latinidad*." Review of *Our Migrant Souls A Meditation on Race and the Meanings and Myths of "Latino,"* by Héctor Tobar. *The Atlantic*, 16 June 2023, www.theatlantic.com/books/archive/2023/06/on-migrant-souls-hector-tobar-book-latinidad/674425/. Accessed 23 Jan. 2024.

Cantú, Francisco. "Who or What Is 'Latino'? Héctor Tobar Considers a Term's Many Meanings." Review of *Our Migrant Souls A Meditation on Race and the Meanings and Myths of "Latino,"* by Héctor Tobar. *The New York Times*, 9 May 2023, www.nytimes.com/2023/05/09/books/review/our-migrant-souls-hector-tobar.html. Accessed 23 Jan. 2024.

Martinez, Monique. Review of *Our Migrant Souls A Meditation on Race and the Meanings and Myths of "Latino,"* by Héctor Tobar. *Library Journal*, 1 Apr. 2023, www.libraryjournal.com/review/our-migrant-souls-a-meditation-on-race-and-the-meanings-and-myths-of-latino-1796405. Accessed 23 Jan. 2024.

Ponce, Eric A. Review of *Our Migrant Souls A Meditation on Race and the Meanings and Myths of "Latino,"* by Héctor Tobar. *BookPage*, 2 May 2023, www.bookpage.com/reviews/our-migrant-souls-hector-tobar-book-review/. Accessed 23 Jan. 2024.

Review of *Our Migrant Souls A Meditation on Race and the Meanings and Myths of "Latino,"* by Héctor Tobar. *Kirkus Reviews*, 9 May 2023, www.kirkusreviews.com/book-reviews/hector-tobar/our-migrant-souls/. Accessed 23 Jan. 2024.

Review of *Our Migrant Souls A Meditation on Race and the Meanings and Myths of "Latino,"* by Héctor Tobar. *Publisher's Weekly*, 17 Feb. 2023, www.publishersweekly.com/9780374609900. Accessed 23 Jan. 2024.

Owner of a Lonely Heart

Author: Beth Nguyen (b. 1974)
Publisher: Scribner (New York). 256 pp.
Type of work: Memoir
Time: 1970s–present
Locales: Saigon (now Ho Chi Minh City), Vietnam; Grand Rapids, Michigan; Boston, Massachusetts; Chicago, Illinois; New York, New York

Beth Nguyen's second memoir chronicles the complicated relationship she and her mother share after being separated following the author's birth. Gravitating around the events of the Fall of Saigon in 1975, the memoir traces the fallout and trauma that accompanied her family's upheaval from the lives they knew before immigrating to the United States as refugees.

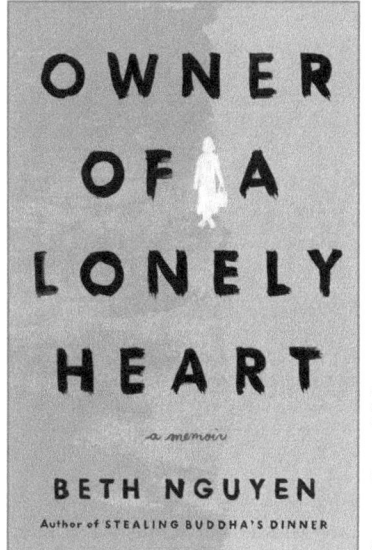

Principal personages

BETH NGUYEN, a.k.a. Bich Minh Nguyen, the narrator, who moved from Vietnam to Michigan shortly after her birth
ANH, her older sister
NOI, her grandmother; a surrogate mother and caretaker to the entire family
BICH'S FATHER, her custodial parent, who fled the country with her and her uncles and relocated to Michigan
BICH'S BIOLOGICAL MOTHER, her noncustodial parent, who was separated from the family by their move to Michigan; later a refugee living in Boston, Massachusetts
BICH'S STEPMOTHER, her primary mother figure; a woman of Mexican descent
CELIA, her boyfriend's mother; a wealthy, White woman

Vietnamese American author Beth Nguyen, who previously published works under her given name of Bich Minh Nguyen, has drawn prodigiously from her past experiences to create her art. In matters both painful and enlightening, Nguyen understands the urgency of examining one's life in an effort to make sense of its challenges and connect to others. In her 2007 memoir, *Stealing Buddha's Dinner*, the author explores her coming-of-age years in Grand Rapids, Michigan, as a teenage girl of Vietnamese heritage living in a mostly White suburb and grappling with the pressure to embrace American culture to fit in with her community. In that work, which won the PEN/Jerard Award and was named a best book of the year by the *Chicago Tribune*, readers were introduced to Nguyen's grandmother Noi, as well as the allure of American food, which feels exotic and exciting to Nguyen's teenage self. As Nguyen experiences the

Beth Nguyen

pains of adolescence, she also feels pulled to ever-present, ever-marketed food items such as Kit Kats, Pringles, and Jell-O. Exploring questions of assimilation and belonging, *Stealing Buddha's Dinner* laid the groundwork for Nguyen's 2023 memoir, *Owner of a Lonely Heart*.

Similarly, Nguyen's latest memoir is built on contradictions and struggles. While Nguyen establishes herself as someone who has often felt out of sync with the world around her and quite lonely as a result, she comes from a home that is crowded with many people, including her father and sister, grandmother, stepmother, and a rotating cast of uncles and cousins who sometimes need shelter while establishing themselves in the United States. Mothers are at the center of Nguyen's narrative: the biological mother she has known for less than twenty-four hours in person during her adult life, though they have been a presence in each other's lives for decades; the Mexican woman her father married after immigrating to the United States with her and her sister, Anh, around the time of the Fall of Saigon in 1975; her grandmother Noi, who was a pillar of strength and calm for the entire family, caring for the young girls and creating an oasis from the chaos of their home inside her small bedroom; and finally, Celia, the mother of Nguyen's White high school boyfriend, who introduced Nguyen to a different version of American culture than the author has experienced during her young life in her adopted country. These women form the backbone of Nguyen's memoir, offering the writer opportunities to explore the ramifications of personal and political history, racism, and the difficult task of building an adult life for oneself through trial and error. Nguyen's narrative uses the backdrops of 1980s Grand Rapids, Michigan, a summer program in Boston, and her adult life in New York, Illinois, and California to illustrate her development into an adult who cannot help but wonder about the life she might have missed through separation from her biological mother.

While the timeframe of *Owner of a Lonely Heart* spans the author's life from the point of her birth in 1974 to her fifties, when she finds herself raising two young boys of her own, the memoir is decidedly concerned with a few brief moments from early in Nguyen's life. The most important is when the author, too young to remember, was taken by her father and grandmother to a point for evacuees ahead of Saigon's fall in 1975 when the city was taken over by North Vietnamese forces. Her family had fought against the communist cause in Saigon until it was deemed too dangerous for them to remain in the country. The decision to flee Vietnam, made before she could even speak or walk, would thus determine the rest of Nguyen's life. Moreover, it was especially poignant because her mother was not made aware of the family's plans. At the time, her mother, who lived an active life in Vietnam, was no longer partnered with Nguyen's father, living across the river from her two small children who were being raised by the author's paternal grandmother, Noi. The story is told that one day Nguyen's mother walked to the house where her children once lived only to find it empty. When she later met with Nguyen and the subject of the children's disappearance comes up, all she can tell her daughter is that she "cried and cried" upon learning they had left for the United States. Yet this moment is pivotal to the lives of both Nguyen and her mother, neither of whom was ever able to establish a true bond. Furthermore, the repetition of this moment throughout Nguyen's story makes its impact clear—illustrating how much was lost by all parties and how impossible they find it to reestablish any semblance of a relationship in the United States. Nguyen was only a baby when this fissure occurred between mother and daughter, but she learned at the age of ten that her mother had relocated to the United States as well.

The author would not reunite with her mother until the age of nineteen, however, at which point she visited her biological mother's home in Boston for the first time. Nguyen establishes the distance between mother and daughter by carefully describing each subsequent visit to her. She tells the reader that she has never called her "mother" and instead often tries to call her by no name at all, while her biological mother refers to herself as "Mommy." Each visit to her "Boston mother's" home was very brief, and sometimes her mother did not even show up, which Nguyen recounts matter-of-factly rather than with resentment. Other times, Nguyen would bring her two young sons and describes simple scenes from her apartment, such as on one visit when Nguyen recalls a blanket laid out across the floor hosting a handful of odds and ends, keeping her children captivated during their short visit. She also encountered her biological mother's Chinese boyfriend, who was constantly on his phone and spoke little English or Vietnamese. Nguyen felt and extended warmth to this man but found him to be another puzzling piece of her mother, who had established a new family of her own, thereby creating an extended family for Nguyen and her sister, though Anh was mostly uninterested in establishing a relationship with this side of the family.

Nguyen juxtaposes the passages in which she describes the handful of visits she makes to Boston with descriptions of the homes she and her sister grow up in with her father, stepmother, grandmother, and stepsiblings. She makes clear the alienation she feels in her life as a refugee in America, even in those homes created for her to thrive in. However, just as her youth is a minefield of longing and confusion, her parents' home becomes a place of inclusion and entertainment when she is older.

In addition to exploring her relationships with the various mother figures in her life, Nguyen also details the relationship with her father. He was often distant and quick-to-anger, though he had a softer side as well, such as when he recounted stories from his youth in Vietnam, riding motorcycles and fishing. Nguyen comes to understand that her father, too, had a difficult time finding his place in a new country with two young girls to raise.

Owner of a Lonely Heart was well received by critics and was named a best book of 2023 by *Time*, NPR, and *BookPage*, among other outlets. As the reviewer for *Kirkus Reviews* wrote, the book is "a quietly moving memoir that grapples with what it means to be a mother, a daughter, a refugee, an American." Critic Sara Austin, writing for the

New York Times, praised the memoir's "deeply ruminative and therapeutically self-indulgent" characteristics, as well as Nguyen's ability to show "vividly how the refugee experience imprints on a person." However, some critics found fault with Nguyen's prose, such as the anonymous reviewer for *Publishers Weekly* who wrote, "The portrait that emerges of this mother-daughter relationship is fascinating yet somewhat blurry, as Nguyen works through what little information she has about her mother on the page." That reviewer found Nguyen's strengths lay in the chapters that focus on "observations about race and class born of her immigrant experience." Mai Tran summed up many reviewers' assessments of the memoir in her review for the *Brooklyn Rail*, writing, "Nguyen is a confident and reliable protagonist even when running up against painful memories, providing readers with enough distance as to almost be objective." She further noted that "Nguyen has made a journey of facing her origins and contending with the limitations of American narratives, and we are lucky to be invited along the way."

Author Information

Beth Nguyen was the author of the memoir *Stealing Buddha's Dinner* (2007), which won the PEN/Jerard Award, as well as the novels *Short Girls* (2009), recipient of an American Book Award, and *Pioneer Girl* (2014). Her writing has appeared in the *New Yorker*, *Paris Review*, *New York Times*, and *Atlantic*, among others.

Melynda Fuller

Review Sources

Austin, Sara. "A Mother Reckons with Questions from Her Childhood." Review of *Owner of a Lonely Heart*, by Beth Nguyen. *The New York Times*, 1 July 2023, www.nytimes.com/2023/07/01/books/review/owner-of-a-lonely-heart-beth-nguyen.html. Accessed 22 Feb. 2024.

Cook, Mattie. Review of *Owner of a Lonely Heart*, by Beth Nguyen. *Library Journal*, 1 June 2023, www.libraryjournal.com/review/owner-of-a-lonely-heart-a-memoir-1798179. Accessed 22 Feb. 2024.

Review of *Owner of a Lonely Heart*, by Beth Nguyen. *Kirkus Reviews*, 12 Apr. 2023, www.kirkusreviews.com/book-reviews/beth-nguyen/owner-of-a-lonely-heart/. Accessed 22 Feb. 2024.

Review of *Owner of a Lonely Heart*, by Beth Nguyen. *Publishers Weekly*, 12 May 2023, www.publishersweekly.com/9781982196349. Accessed 22 Feb. 2024.

Spindel, Barbara. "The Fall of Saigon Split Families Apart. Hers Was among Them." Review of *Owner of a Lonely Heart*, by Beth Nguyen. *The Christian Science Monitor*, 12 Sept. 2023, www.csmonitor.com/Books/Book-Reviews/2023/0912/The-fall-of-Saigon-split-families-apart.-Hers-was-among-them. Accessed 22 Feb. 2024.

Tran, Mai. "Beth Nguyen's *Owner of a Lonely Heart*." Review of *Owner of a Lonely Heart*, by Beth Nguyen. *The Brooklyn Rail*, brooklynrail.org/2023/07/books/Beth-Nguyens-Owner-of-a-Lonely-Heart. Accessed 22 Feb. 2024.

Parachute Kids

Author: Betty C. Tang
Illustrator: Betty C. Tang
Publisher: Graphix (New York). 288 pp.
Type of work: Graphic novel
Time: 1981
Locale: California

After traveling to the US from Taiwan under the unknowing guise of a family vacation to Disney Land, Feng-Li and her two older siblings are left to take care of themselves in Betty C. Tang's graphic novel Parachute Kids. *Filled with poignant moments,* Parachute Kids *is a story about resilience and bravery in the face of uncertainty.*

Principal characters

FENG-LI, the protagonist, a fifth grader and the youngest of the Lin siblings
KE-GANG, her older brother, the middle sibling
JIA-XI, her older sister, the eldest sibling
MA, their mother, who has a thirty-day visitor's visa to stay in the US
BA, their father, a pro-bono lawyer in Taiwan
AUNT AND UNCLE TIAN, family friends who help to take care of the Lin siblings after their parents leave
OLIVIA, the Tian's fourteen-year-old daughter, a friend to the Lins with a crush on Ke-Gang

No two immigration stories are alike, but some have similar beginnings. For bestselling author and illustrator Betty C. Tang, her story began in the way so many other children's have; by arriving in the United States under the guardianship of extended family or family friends already settled in the country, without the parents who have sent their children on in the hope of a bright future. Through the years, these children have come to be called "parachute kids," because they are dropped off in their new country by parents who return to their country of origin. Tang's story took her from her home in Taiwan to California, where she continues to live today. Thousands of other kids still arrive in the US in this fashion. Tang's graphic novel, also called *Parachute Kids* (2023), is a book designed to help those children who may be experiencing a confusing time as they adjust to life in the US, but also a story intended to make others aware of what these newly arrived children experience as they navigate life on their own. Though not autobiographical—Tang addresses this in the backmatter of the novel, providing pictures of herself newly arrived on the West Coast at the age of ten—the author was able to lean on her real-life adventures to create a story that feels both specific and universal.

Parachute Kids opens with the Lin family arriving in California after a long flight from Taiwan. The family of five—Ma and Ba, younger daughter Feng-Li, middle child and son Ke-Gang, and older daughter Jia-Xi, the eldest sibling—are excited about the trip ahead during which they will see sights like Disney Land, the La Brea Tar Pits, and the Hollywood Sign. As they prepare to leave the airport, an immigration official stops them, an officer citing a lack of hyphen in their names. They are quickly ushered on by another officer who accuses the former of being too literal. This initial hang-up is an ominous note for the family, whose youngest members do not realize they will be staying in the US without the support of their parents. The Lins stay with family friends the Tians, who immigrated years earlier and are established in California. Their daughter Olivia, who is fourteen, has become quickly Americanized, no longer using the honorary "aunt" and "uncle" customary with older family friends in addition to relatives. After the sightseeing and excitement of those first days in the California, the Lin parents tell their kids what is really happening—they will be staying in California while their father returns to Taiwan immediately and their mother at the end of her thirty-day visitors' visa. As the children learn how to set up a home and take care of each other and themselves while living as undocumented citizens in the US, they also discover the pleasures and pitfalls of life in their new country.

Some stories lend themselves particularly well to the graphic novel form. Alison Bechdel's *Fun Home: A Family Tragicomic* (2006) was wildly successful in portraying the life of a young lesbian growing up in small-town Pennsylvania as she learned about who she was and wanted to be. Bechdel's technique of photographing herself in each pose struck by her drawn characters added an element of authenticity that brought them to life. *Persepolis: The Story of a Childhood* (2003), a coming-of-age story about a girl growing up during and after the Islamic Revolution in Iran by Marjane Satrapi, used stark black and white illustrations to make the story of its heroic main character accessible to a wide range of readers. *Parachute Kids* falls within this tradition of using poignant and impactful illustrations to make the inner and outer life of its young protagonist, Feng-Li, come alive.

Introducing the life of a cast of characters experiencing a language barrier among other issues is one way Tang allows her comic-book-style story to do some of the heavier lifting. Her characters communicate in a variety of effective ways. Each of the children has readily recognizable facial expressions that let the reader peer into their inner lives. For example, as the children are adjusting to the news that they will be staying in the US, Feng-Li goes to her Ke-Gang's room to share her popsicle—pineapple, her favorite—with him. It is a touching move by a young, but knowing, child who understands that her brother is having a particularly difficult time accepting the news. The interactions between the two during this scene are made more poignant by the way Tang presents the pair. Ke-Gang, after giving his younger sister a hard time, shoots her a shy-but-sincere glance, a glance of familial love that is made all the more powerful by Tang's illustration skills. Feng-Li's strong personality comes out in other scenes with silly expressions when she is trying to capture the attention of her siblings and expressions of shock when she has hurt herself—feelings or body. Jia-Xi is drawn in close resemblance to her own mother, reminding the reader that she has been placed in the role of caregiver while her parents are away.

Another way in which the graphic novel form lends itself well the Tang's story is allowing for her words to appear in one language—English—while her characters communicate in their both native language and English. Tang accomplishes this by placing the dialogue in two differently colored bubbles: yellow for their native language and white for conversations in English. While this is somewhat difficult to follow at first—there is no signal that this is what Tang is attempting to do—when the reader realizes the format the path to discover and the model itself are both surprising and enjoyable. The reader, for a moment, experiences some of the disorientation Tang's characters are feeling.

Tang also addresses the racism each character experiences in their daily lives in heartfelt and heartbreaking ways. Feng-Li, who cannot speak or read much English, is not as aware of what the kids are saying to or about her, but the reader is able to read and see their racism through each illustrated frame. Meanwhile, Feng-Li's older siblings experience cruelty from their peers in the halls of their high school, with her older brother nearly getting into a physical fight while trying to defend his sister. This leads to trouble for him a few days later.

Not everything in *Parachute Kids* relates directly to living an immigrant experience in a new country, though. The Lin kids go through many experiences that are relatable to any child their age. For example, Feng-Li covets an "Intendo" game system at the toy store that she will stop at little to get. She hopes that by owning the in-demand game the kids around her will start to be curious about her and offer friendship. Ke-Gang joins a questionable group of boys at school who are fellow parachute kids from China, and he immediately falls into their bad habits, which his sisters worry will land him in trouble like he did back in Taiwan. He is also in the midst of exploring and discovering his sexuality, which causes him anxiety in both his home culture and the US. Jia-Xi struggles to balance studying for the SATs with taking care of her siblings—she is devoted to her family but is not a natural at caring for them like her parents, nor can she be—and slowly making new friends at school. Expectedly, the lives of these three plucky kids begin to unravel as they fall into situations that are difficult for one small family of children to tackle. However, the way in which they stick together during those times is intensely heartwarming and leads to a sense of confidence for the three.

Parachute Kids was very well received by critics, receiving an advance starred review from *Kirkus Reviews*. The publication's anonymous reviewer called the book, "Emotionally moving and beautifully executed." The reviewer stated, "The development of the characters and their relationships is convincing and balanced, and the siblings' respective experiences are relatable for anyone who has tried to fit in somewhere. This empathic story centers a less widely recognized community and thoughtfully presents a distinct facet of immigration." *Parachute Kids* also received starred reviews from *School Library Journal* and the *Horn Book*. Jerry Dear for *Horn Book* wrote, "Tang weaves themes of family, racial stereotyping, cultural adaptation, sacrifice, peer pressure, sexuality, bullying, and survival into a poignant and triumphant story of perseverance and resilience, presenting a remarkably honest depiction of an Asian American immigrant experience." Likewise, *Publishers Weekly*'s critic wrote, "Tang balances humor and heart with the difficult realities of what parachute kids may face." Signifying such an accomplishment, *Parachute Kids* was longlisted for the 2023 National Book Award for Young People's Literature and was named to multiple "Best Books of 2023" lists.

Author Biography
Betty C. Tang is a bestselling illustrator and author of children's books. She is the illustrator of the *Jacky Ha-Ha* series written by James Patterson and Chris Grabenstein and *The Worry Balloon* (2023) by Mónica Mancillas. Tang has also worked for such animation studios as Dreamworks Animation and Disney TV.

Melynda Fuller

Review Sources
Dear, Jerry. Review of *Parachute Kids*, by Betty C. Tang. *The Horn Book*, 27 June 2023, www.hbook.com/story/review-of-parachute-kids-may23. Accessed 14 Nov. 2023.

Review of *Parachute Kids*, by Betty C. Tang. *Kirkus Reviews*, 24 Jan. 2023, www.kirkusreviews.com/book-reviews/betty-c-tang/parachute-kids/. Accessed 14 Nov. 2023.

Review of *Parachute Kids*, by Betty C. Tang. *Publishers Weekly*, 2 Feb. 2023, www.publishersweekly.com/9781338832693. Accessed 14 Nov. 2023.

The Parrot and the Igloo
Climate and the Science of Denial

Author: David Lipsky (b. 1965)
Publisher: W. W. Norton (New York). 496 pp.
Type of work: Environment, science
Time: Nineteenth century to the twenty-first century
Locale: Worldwide

The Parrot and the Igloo offers a deep dive, over more than two centuries, into three types of figures central to human civilization's ability to engage with climate change: the inventors, the scientists, and the deniers. Author David Lipsky explores several such figures to make a clarifying determination of the role played by a small group of deniers in obfuscating, attacking, and crippling positive change.

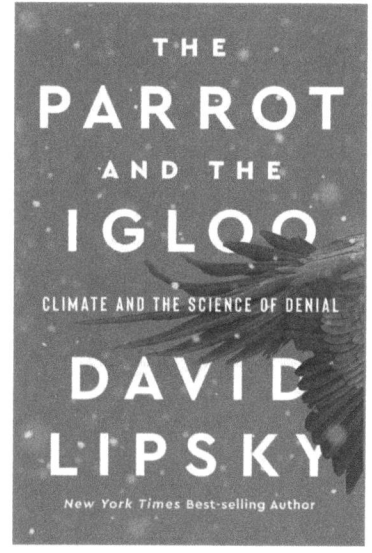

Principal personages

SVANTE ARRHENIUS, scientist who published warnings about the greenhouse effect beginning in 1896
THOMAS EDISON, inventor of a practical incandescent light bulb
AL GORE, vice president of the United States from 1993 to 2001 and climate activist
JIM HANSEN, long-serving National Aeronautics and Space Administration (NASA) scientist who led a sustained and public campaign for climate action
STEVE MCINTYRE, Canadian climate change denier
LORD CHRISTOPHER MONCKTON, a British leader in climate change denial
SAMUEL MORSE, a prominent figure in the development of the electric telegraph
ARTHUR ROBINSON, founder of the Oregon Institute of Science and Medicine and a leader in climate change denialism
FREDERICK SEITZ, a physicist who became a prominent voice for climate change denial
S. FRED SINGER, a prominent voice for climate change denial
NIKOLA TESLA, inventor recognized for his innovations with AC current
JOHN TYNDALL, scientist who studied carbon dioxide and its ability to absorb heat

Veteran writer David Lipsky's 2023 book *The Parrot and the Igloo: Climate and the Science of Denial* presents the story of climate science and its denial, from the late nineteenth century until the present day. The volume is organized into five sections: a preface and an epilogue bookend the volume, with three hefty parts in between.

David Lipsky

Courtesy W. W. Norton; ©Mark Seliger Studio

The three parts are dedicated to three different categories of actors in the development of climate science and its denial: inventors, scientists, and deniers. In the preface, Lipsky invites the reader to move through the three parts in any order they select. Despite the author's invitation to explore at will, the order in which these parts are read would doubtless have a non-neutral impact on the reader's introduction to the issues in play. Roughly, the sections of the volume are chronological, though they do interweave periods at times. The inventors introduced in part 1, primarily Samuel Morse, Thomas Edison, and Nikola Tesla, are historical figures whose technological innovations set key parts of the human impact on global climate in motion. Part 2, dedicated to scientists, also takes a long historical view. It introduces crucial early voices in the area of climate science, including Svante Arrhenius and John Tyndall, whose work in the nineteenth and early twentieth centuries laid the foundation for advocacy on the subject. In his accessible explanation of the layout of the book in the preface, Lipsky refers to these individuals as "the people who realized there might be a problem." The third part, deniers, is the most modern in focus. Its narrative centers on the corporate and political interests that built a force for opposition research against the essential facts of climate change. Lipsky deftly illustrates how this narrative of skepticism and even outright falsehoods rose particularly in postwar America, with pivotal moments in the 1980s and 1990s. The epilogue brings these issues to the contemporary context, laying bare how a small cadre of aging deniers still manages to paralyze the messaging and effectiveness of climate science with the larger public. While readers will find that each part is self-contained enough to begin at any point, the general chronological organization of the volume does enforce the logic to read parts one through three in order.

Though dealing with a serious topic, Lipsky adopts a conversational, humorous, and journalistic narrative style that remains engaging throughout the volume. This set of stylistic choices is important to the impact of *The Parrot and the Igloo* on readers. As is always the case with publications focused on climate change, Lipsky's topic is heavy reading conceptually and emotionally. His use of humor helps to counter some of the negative weight of the reading material. Similarly, he paints vivid characterizations of the numerous individuals introduced throughout the book, such that they come to life with clarity as either heroes or villains in the science of climate change. Unfortunately, the book leaves little practical hope that human civilization will manage to reverse course and save the planet from the worst impending impacts of climate change. All the evidence over more than a century of history points toward the consistent wins in the camp of climate deniers. The real work of positive change would be politically challenging to enact and cause industry and economic disruptions that powerful corporations continue to oppose. Thus, as Lipsky demonstrates, inertia and special interests favor the denier camp, even as their messaging is a smoke and mirrors game with no true scientific merit. In practical terms, the only hope Lipsky can offer the reader is the embrace of hero and villain tropes that leave a hope, even if faint, that eventually the scale must tip toward the forces of good.

As other reviewers have noted, the history of climate science that Lipsky presents builds on the work of previous scholars, as does its critical focus on why this urgent issue has gotten so little public traction. Lipsky mentions numerous such previous studies throughout the text, allowing the unfamiliar reader ample guidance in reading further. The special focus of this study, and what will likely be its lasting contribution, lies in the close scrutiny of the elusive personas that have fueled the denier camp. Lipsky also traces how each denier has gained great financial rewards from corporations by fueling climate science denial, producing solid figures and evidence that erode plausible deniability of the connection.

The author's investigation narrows in on a small but effectively malicious group of leading client deniers who are unlikely to be household names to most readers: Steve Mcintyre, Mark Mills, Lord Christopher Monckton, Arthur Robinson, Frederick Seitz, and S. Fred Singer. These six individuals, Lipsky compellingly illustrates, have had an outsized and long-lasting impact on the public understanding of climate science despite, for the most part, having limited to no scientific training. Lipsky emphasizes that the denier camp has always been small; virtually all scientists in relevant fields of expertise support the facts of climate change. Yet, corporations and special interest groups such as Philip Morris have used individuals with questionable reputations, no moral scruples, a hunger for wealth or other interests, and/or a grudge to feed to advance such fallacies as a need for further scientific research to prove the essential truths of climate science and/or to convey a smoke screen of denial regarding attempts to communicate the scientific climate truths to the general public. In the cases of denial actors such as Mcintyre and Monckton, the internet and conservative media outlets have enabled deniers to mete out vast damage with even less scrutiny to their credentials. Mcintyre's appearance in the epilogue brings disheartening contemporary awareness to the issues. From a computer in his residence, readers learn, a single aging retiree can dismantle the careers and public reputations of leading scientists through vitriolic internet attacks and constant demands for the fulfillment of freedom of information requests. Lipsky consistently presents the deniers as money grubbers who are actually few in number. His account leaves the reader to wonder why it has been so hard to defeat such a small group.

The climate scientists offer the heroic foils to Lipsky's motley cast of deniers, while the inventors are the inquisitive catalysts who, often unwittingly, set the cycle of climate change in motion. While the inventors are well known, the climate scientists are an unsung set of intellectual leaders who, like the deniers, are mostly not household names. Best known, and only touched on lightly, is Al Gore, whose influence weaves in and out of the book. While Gore's influence was made possible by his political service, it is valuable to encounter the significance of a few university science classes on

Gore's climate activism later in life. The most poignant figure in the book is certainly NASA's Jim Hansen, a scientist who, motivated by a feeling of responsibility to his future grandchildren, sought for four decades to bring the truth about climate change to the American public. Hansen spoke publicly, valiantly, and truthfully about climate science despite extreme political pressure to do otherwise. He offered extensive testimony on Capitol Hill, despite attempts to force his silence. Yet, when he retired, he did so in a world that continued to turn a blind eye to the warnings.

With its many strengths, the book also has crucial weaknesses. So many individuals appear in and out of Lipsky's narrative that it can be difficult to follow all the threads, despite his active and engaging writing style. It may seem counterintuitive, therefore, to note any absences from this book. Still, the structure of inventors, scientists, and deniers leaves certain key characters in the wings. Although they appear frequently throughout the text, politicians, corporate leaders, lobbyists, journalists, and lawyers do not receive the same level of focus—yet their influences and culpability are visible throughout. Perhaps the inventors, scientists, and deniers structure can also explain the relative sidelining of women and people from marginalized groups from the narrative, save for one female Philip Morris employee numbering among the villains. It seems like a missed opportunity to confine climate science, and its denial, to such a homogenous demographic in terms of race and gender. Lipsky also condemns inaction by both Republican and Democratic leaders at the highest levels. While the critique is justified, as is underlined by his rich research into the individuals driving climate science denial, the blame is not equal across the parties. Lipsky's attempt to be fair by spreading the blame does little to support and motivate those who work for positive change against daunting opposition politics. He frequently uses the refrain that climate science has "bad timing" in politics, yet this construct at some points avoids reckoning with the strong culpability of the Republican party's consistent, damaging stance in favor of corporations and against climate science.

Reviewers have noted the ambition, breadth, and humor Lipsky brings to "the hideous history of climate-change denialism and the vile people who still traffic in it today," as Christopher Lancette wrote for the *Washington Independent Review of Books*. While noting the overlapping information of *The Parrot and the Igloo* and other heavy-hitting cultural studies of climate change, reviews have also highlighted two principal contributions brought by Lipsky. First, Lipsky's complex narrative highlights the importance of powerful and consistent messaging to the public's understanding of the climate crisis. He reveals that a small cadre of denialists have dominated the discourse for decades, consistently beating scientists and climate-concerned politicians. Second, Lipsky's deep dive into the history and world of climate deniers clarifies the connection to "corporate deniers" who have fueled and funded the effort against climate action. Chief among these culprits in Lipsky's narrative is Philip Morris, which spurred denialism while fighting to protect corporate profits it derived from cigarette purchases.

Author Biography

David Lipsky is an award-winning author. In addition to *The Parrot and the Igloo* and other works of nonfiction, he has also written a novel and a collection of short stories. His work has featured in a variety of publication and he has taught at New York University.

Julia A. Sienkewicz, PhD

Review Sources

Lancette, Christopher. Review of *The Parrot and the Igloo: Climate and the Science of Denial*, by David Lipsky. *Washington Independent Review of Books*, 24 July 2023, www.washingtonindependentreviewofbooks.com/index.php/bookreview/the-parrot-and-the-igloo-climate-and-the-science-of-denial. Accessed 6 Oct. 2023.

Nathans-Kelly, Steve. Review of *The Parrot and the Igloo: Climate and the Science of Denial*, by David Lipsky. *New York Journal of Books*, www.nyjournalofbooks.com/book-review/parrot-and-igloo-climate. Accessed 6 Oct. 2023.

Schlanger, Zoë. "A Global Warming Book for the Streaming Age." Review of *The Parrot and the Igloo: Climate and the Science of Denial*, by David Lipsky. *The New York Times*, 10 July 2023, www.nytimes.com/2023/07/10/books/review/the-parrot-and-the-igloo-david-lipsky.html. Accessed 6 Oct. 2023.

Shribman, David. "David Lipsky's *The Parrot and the Igloo* Details the Forces behind Climate Change Denial." Review of *The Parrot and the Igloo: Climate and the Science of Denial*, by David Lipsky. *The Boston Globe*, 6 July 2023, www.bostonglobe.com/2023/07/06/arts/david-lipskys-parrot-igloo-details-forces-behind-decades-climate-change-denial/. Accessed 6 Oct. 2023.

Pineapple Street

Author: Jenny Jackson (b. 1979)
Publisher: Pamela Dorman Books (New York). 320 pp.
Type of work: Novel
Time: Present day
Locale: Brooklyn Heights, New York

The fictional story of a wealthy New York City family, Pineapple Street *provides witty yet humanizing insight into the lives of the one percent, including their attitudes toward marriage, the factors that motivate them, and how they interact with those outside of their social circles.*

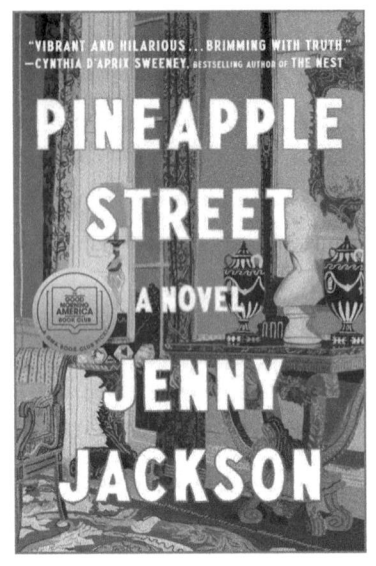

Principal characters
DARLEY, the elder daughter in the Stockton family, a stay-at-home mother
GEORGIANA, the younger daughter in the Stockton family, who works at a nonprofit
CORD, the sole Stockton son, who works in the family real-estate business
SASHA, Cord's wife, who hails from a blue-collar Rhode Island family
MALCOLM, Darley's husband, a Korean American aviation expert
CHIP, the Stockton patriarch, a real-estate mogul whose wealth can be traced back generations
TILDA, the Stockton matriarch

In 2023, Jenny Jackson, a longtime editor and publishing industry executive, made her debut attempt at a novel of her own. The result, *Pineapple Street*, quickly proved her worth in making the switch from editor to writer. Landing on multiple bestseller lists, the novel was chosen by the popular morning show *Good Morning America* as a GMA Book Club pick and was deemed one of the best books of the year by such outlets as the *New York Times*, *Time*, *USA Today*, and National Public Radio. Perhaps even more impressive, *Pineapple Street* earned Jackson comparisons to famed writers like Edith Wharton and Henry James, whose chronicles of the wealthy in earlier eras rival Jackson's ability to accurately capture details of life among the moneyed families of New York City. (As a *Kirkus* reviewer asserted of Jackson, "She knows her party themes, her tennis clubs, her silent auctions, and her WASP family dynamics.")

Though the story is fiction, the titular Pineapple Street is a real avenue located in Brooklyn Heights, a picturesque neighborhood renowned for its Gothic revival brownstones, leafy streets, waterfront promenade, and frozen-in-time charm. It is one of the neighborhood's so-called "fruit streets," which run parallel to each other not far from the waterfront and which were originally named after prominent local families.

Pineapple Street / JACKSON

Jenny Jackson

Courtesy Penguin Random House; ©Sarah Shatz

Sometime in the nineteenth century, according to some historians, an aristocratic resident named Lady Middagh, who hailed from one of the first European families to settle there, decided that practice to be pretentious and took it upon herself to affix new signs in the middle of the night. (Interestingly enough, she allowed Middagh Street's sign to remain intact.) Other historians believe that the streets were named by the Hicks Brothers, local landowners who made their fortunes marketing exotic fruits. Whatever the origin story, the fruit streets delineate an exceptionally exclusive section of the city and a fitting place for the fictional Stockton family to call home.

The family home—almost a character in its own right—is a stately four-story limestone, "a massive, formal palace," as one of its current inhabitants, Sasha, describes it. Sasha is married to Cord, the sole son of the Stockton family, fittingly named by the author, perhaps, for the intense bond he shares with his parents and sisters. In addition to Sasha, the story is told predominantly through the eyes of the two younger women in the Stockton family: Darley and Georgiana. The family matriarch, Tilda, functions largely to satirize a particular subset of society women, concerned mainly with fashion, tennis, and designing over-the-top "tablescapes" for themed gatherings.

Jackson presents Sasha as a kind of foil to her sisters-in-law. Unlike Darley and Georgiana, who refer to Sasha behind her back as a gold digger and roll their eyes when she makes innocent social gaffes, Sasha comes from a blue-collar family that includes a boisterous cadre of cousins with a history of committing petty crimes. Sasha has always found them a source of shame, but it strikes her one day, while listening to the Stocktons delightedly relate the criminal antics of some of their ancestors, that what is considered charmingly roguish behavior on the part of the wealthy is simply "trashy" when people like her family are concerned. It is one of many examples the author reveals about how the rich are, indeed, just like other people—despite what F. Scott Fitzgerald famously asserted; the only difference seems to be in how they are perceived and what they are allowed to get away with.

Like Sasha, Malcolm is an "outsider," connected to the family only through his marriage to Darley. He is set apart from the clan not by money, however—his salary as an aviation investment expert is generous—but because he is of Korean descent, one of the novel's only characters of color. When he loses his job after being blamed for the mistakes of an impetuous White coworker, the couple keeps the news secret from the rest of the family, fearing that it will taint the relative esteem in which Malcolm is held. Aside from the projected emotional fallout of Malcolm's dismissal, there are very practical repercussions: Darley, secure in the knowledge that Malcolm could support her and their children, had forfeited her inheritance when she married because she did not want Malcolm to feel forced to sign the prenuptial agreement her parents insisted upon. Thus, it seems likely that with private school tuitions looming and housing costs astronomical (Cord and Sasha have been given use of the Pineapple Street abode), she will have to approach Chip and Tilda for money.

That impending crisis is an occasion for soul-searching on Darley's part: has she been able to remain cavalier about money only when an adequate amount was flowing in? What sacrifices would she be willing to make if it truly became necessary? Has she made the right choice in becoming a stay-at-home parent rather than putting her own pricey degree to work?

The most intense soul-searching in the book is done by Georgiana, however, who is portrayed in the book's early chapters as a spoiled and vapid twenty-something, working a low-level job at a nonprofit mainly to keep busy between parties. After she falls in love with an older coworker, she discovers he is married but continues the affair nonetheless, and later, faces even greater challenges. Georgiana evolves throughout the novel, however, becoming inspired by an old school friend named Curtis to interrogate the source of her family's wealth and consider divesting herself of her portion. (For Curtis, the decision is more obvious; his family has amassed its fortune in the munitions industry.)

The Stockton family business, though not as seemingly sordid as guns, has had serious detrimental effects on society, and the novel—perhaps unexpectedly in a book that some reviewers characterized variously as "hysterical" or "a romp"—takes time to explore this theme. Chip deals in New York real estate, buying up property in neighborhoods inhabited by people of color, the financially disadvantaged, and recent immigrants and pushing them out to make room for wealthier residents. While Brooklyn Heights itself has long been a bastion of Old Money, *Pineapple Street* is still a novel about gentrification and the ways it enriches the few (like the Stocktons) at the expense of the many. In an astute review for the *Washington Post*, Susan Coll touched on the role of the Stocktons' dutiful and ever-present housekeeper, Berta, who leaves each day to take the subway home to her own family, wondering "how this novel might look through Berta's lens."

To this point, readers might look to Jackson's epigraph, a quote from the *New York Times*, that upon reflection seems somewhat chilling: "Millennials will be the recipients of the largest generational shift of assets in American history—the Great Wealth Transfer, as finance types call it. Tens of trillions of dollars are expected to pass between generations in just the next decade." Meaning, of course, that the Stockton heirs will be able to comfortably enjoy their status for the foreseeable future. As much as they've been entertaining company for three-hundred-plus pages (and however much we admire their evolution and character strengths), that also means others, every bit as admirable and deserving if not more so, will be locked within financially disadvantaged classes, as generational wealth has a chilling effect on social mobility, according to many economists.

Reviewers almost universally found something to admire in Jackson's debut. "It's no small thing to ask a reader in 2023 to empathize with characters who are not only exceedingly wealthy but *generationally* exceedingly wealthy," Jean Hanff Korelitz wrote for the *New York Times*. "This is the challenge Jenny Jackson has set herself, and not only does she succeed in getting us not to loathe the Stocktons . . . but she even succeeds in persuading us to love them." (Korelitz tempers this statement by saying readers might in fact only love them "a little bit against our will.") Coll, as well, acknowledged the warring emotions the fictional Stocktons might ignite in readers belonging to the 99 percent. "Fans of well-observed foibles will have a ball," she wrote, while warning that "class warriors might look elsewhere."

In a review for the *Guardian,* Christobel Kent examined why so many readers feel fascinated by the lives of the immensely wealthy. "Since F. Scott Fitzgerald first described the view from a West Egg mansion, the lives of the American 1% have been of keen interest to the rest of us; whether we love them, love to hate them or want to know where they buy their shoes," Kent wrote. "This, then, is the train to which Jenny Jackson's entertaining debut novel *Pineapple Street* hitches its wagon." Comparing Jackson's "smart and clever, minutely observed" work to that of Edith Wharton, Kent further noted, "From the cars they drive to the delis they favour, the granular detail of the Stocktons' lives is happily catalogued." Even so, the reviewer also warned, "It can sometimes feel as if we are drowning, like Sasha, in possessions and signifiers of affluence." Whatever a reader's attitudes toward the ultra-wealthy—fascination, envy, or disgust—*Pineapple Street* proves to be an engaging and worthwhile read. While it may be too early to know whether Jackson will eventually take a place next to Wharton, James, or Fitzgerald, readers eagerly awaited her sophomore effort.

Author Biography
Jenny Jackson graduated from Williams College in 2001 and worked briefly at a nonprofit before deciding on a book-related career and completing the Columbia Publishing Course. She steadily rose from an editorial assistant post at Vintage to a position as vice president and executive editor at Alfred A. Knopf. *Pineapple Street* was her debut novel.

Mari Rich

Review Sources
Coll, Susan. "'Pineapple Street' Gets Laughs from Tensions among the 1 Percent." Review of *Pineapple Street*, by Jenny Jackson. *The Washington Post*, 7 Mar. 2023, www.washingtonpost.com/books/2023/03/07/pineapple-street-jenny-jackson/. Accessed 18 Dec. 2023.

Kent, Christobel. "Pineapple Street by Jenny Jackson Review—Smart Debut about Wealthy New Yorkers." Review of *Pineapple Street*, by Jenny Jackson. *The Guardian*, 6 Apr. 2023, www.theguardian.com/books/2023/apr/06/pineapple-street-by-jenny-jackson-review-smart-debut-about-wealthy-new-yorkers. Accessed 18 Dec. 2023.

Korelitz, Jean Hanff. "Big Money, Big Houses and Big Problems in Brooklyn Heights." Review of *Pineapple Street*, by Jenny Jackson. *The New York Times*, 3 Mar. 2023, www.nytimes.com/2023/03/03/books/review/pineapple-street-jenny-jackson.html. Accessed 18 Dec. 2023.

Review of *Pineapple Street*, by Jenny Jackson. *Kirkus Reviews*, 13 Dec. 2022, www.kirkusreviews.com/book-reviews/jenny-jackson/pineapple-street/. Accessed 18 Dec. 2023.

Pomegranate

Author: Helen Elaine Lee
Publisher: Atria Books (New York). 352 pp.
Type of work: Novel
Time: 1990s–present day
Locale: New England

Helen Elaine Lee's groundbreaking novel about incarceration, healing, and self-actualization is a stark condemnation of the US prison system, a spotlight on the exploitation of Black women and their bodies, and, finally, an inspiring road to beauty and recovery in spite of these seemingly insurmountable challenges.

Principal characters

RANITA, a woman formerly addicted to drugs who has recently completed a prison sentence and is hoping to regain both custody of her two children and her own personal autonomy

MAXINE, her lover in prison, an academic-minded woman and continual source of hope for Ranita

JASPER, the late father of her children, a man with whom Ranita had a fraught relationship

MAMA, her severe, demanding mother, who appears in her childhood memories

DADDY, her affectionate father, with whom she was especially close, and whose death she continues to grieve

In the annals of postmodern African American literature, one of the most revered authors is likely Toni Morrison, whose novels such as *Sula* (1973) and *Beloved* (1987) are famous for their narrative tension, gothic atmosphere, and chilling revelations of the horrors of slavery and its generational traumas. *Beloved* is set in the decades following the emancipation of enslaved African Americans and exposes the terrible memories and the dire effects on their psyches resulting from the legacy of American slavery. Replete with ghosts, violence, and plot twists, it is considered by some to be the classic American horror novel.

Other authors approach the topics of systemic racism and African American trauma in a very different way. Helen Elaine Lee is one such writer; her novel *Pomegranate* (2023) specializes in quieter, character-driven prose. Lee's first novel in nearly twenty years, *Pomegranate* follows a woman coming to terms with her life and herself after her release from prison, and through this lens, examines the ways in which

Helen Elaine Lee
Courtesy Simon & Schuster; ©Mark Ostow

Black women continue to be dehumanized and exploited, particularly within the incarceration system.

With respect to incarceration rates, the United States is notorious. Home to the largest number of prisoners in the world, the US prison population is characterized by significant racial disparities in which African Americans are over-represented in correctional facilities across the nation. This disparity has led many researchers to examine the ways in which Black women specifically are affected by American prisons, both as prisoners and as support systems for other prisoners. These women, whether serving time in prison or advocating for those who do, are often subject to abuse, violence, humiliation, and condescension, a kind of inferior treatment whose origins many activists and journalists trace all the way back to White supremacy and slavery.

The protagonist of *Pomegranate* is one such woman, whose prison time, its aftermath, and the struggles that led to her incarceration in the first place, have lasting impacts on both her and her family, particularly her female relatives. Ranita Atwater is a thirty-six-year-old woman finishing a four-year sentence at the Oak Hills correctional facility for opioid possession after experiencing addiction to alcohol and drugs. By the time she is released, Ranita has been "short," or sober, for four years, and hopes to recover custody of her two children, Amara and Theo, who have been living with their great-aunt. Through all of this, Ranita must also confront and relive her own most personal memories from her childhood, her relationship with her children's father, and every other step that led her onto the violent roller coaster of addiction and eventual, painful recovery. The reader experiences these nonlinear flashbacks along with her, albeit through a detached, third-person perspective, while the events of the "present-day"—her release from prison and everything that occurs after—are narrated in Ranita's own voice.

On her first evening as a free woman, staying with her aunt Jessie, she finds it nearly impossible to eat Jessie's food or even interact with the other woman, jarred by the contrast between what she left behind and the plentiful offerings now before her. This is only one of the many lasting psychological effects of her time in prison. During her incarceration, Ranita has experienced firsthand the systemic racism built into the prison institution, the sense of being packed away from society and constantly viewed as a potential threat. "In prison... you're just breathing flesh that can house contraband, and cause violence, and run," she recalls at one point. When Ranita first arrives at the facility, she undergoes the first of many humiliating strip-searches, during which she finds herself being exposed and handled like an object by desensitized guards whose cruelty is in their apathy. She meets many other women who "got short," were released, and immediately returned to their old habits and came straight back to Oak Hills, depicting a system that seems almost deliberately warped to bring about such vicious cycles, particularly for Black women. Meanwhile, on a more personal level, Ranita misses the freedom of literature. While she finds the same pleasure in novels while "inside" as she did prior to her arrest, she wistfully compares the limited selection of the prison library to the greater comforts of the public branch.

Yet even with Ranita's freedom comes inevitable nostalgia for those still inside. When Ranita finishes her sentence and re-emerges in the "outside" world, she must leave behind Maxine, another prisoner who became Ranita's friend and romantic partner. Maxine had developed a reputation among the other women for being something of a scholar, constantly reading books about law and race theory. In a moment that does in fact contain multiple references to Toni Morrison, Maxine and Ranita first bond over a conversation about books, where each reveals the reasons she finds comfort in nonfiction and fiction, respectively. Eventually, Maxine herself becomes something of a muse to Ranita, long after Ranita has left Oak Hills.

As Ranita struggles to remain sober through recovery meetings and therapy, working towards financial independence while preparing to defend her fitness to be a mother to her children, her life's memories, both early and recent, continue to reveal themselves to the reader. Ranita seems to view these recollections as belonging to previous lives, from which her current self feels profoundly disconnected, despite how much she might grieve for the many other people who appear in these memories, and whom she has since lost. We learn how she met the father of her children, Jasper, a photographer and eventually, Ranita's gateway to opiates. We watch her, this time under the influence of a different man, discover the inescapable pull of heroin. We see her growing up in Boston, the only child of middle-class parents: a mother perpetually critical of Ranita's hair and body (a continual theme throughout the text in relation to Black women), and a deeply caring father who passed away while Ranita was in prison. Ranita's is not an epic, action-filled story led by a virtuous heroine, but rather the quiet tale of an ordinary woman who has made mistakes, and who, like many in her position, discovers moments of beauty even in suffering.

The title of Lee's novel appears to reflect a metaphor recurrent throughout the book, of a fruit whose existence Ranita first discovers on her thirteenth birthday following her mother's death. Her father introduces the curious fruit to her as a sort of late birthday gift, and Ranita is awed by the "chambers filled with winding layers of ruby-red jewels." Throughout the novel, Ranita's own experiences are compared to a pomegranate, with Ranita herself saying "I try and see myself as filled with ruby seeds. Everything I've lived, the things I've been and done . . . what's been done to me . . . and for me. The all of it, it's in me." The pomegranate becomes a symbol of hope for Ranita, who is struck by the beauty of the unassuming fruit.

Reviews of *Pomegranate* have been overwhelmingly positive, filled with high praise for Lee's frank representation of Ranita's struggles and her joys. Neither shying away from nor sensationalizing Ranita's experience, Lee offers readers a respectful glimpse into the life of a queer Black woman formerly addicted to drugs—all qualities which are central to but do not exclusively define Lee's protagonist. She also emphasizes the role of strong women in Ranita's life; her aunts, her lover, other fellow prisoners, people who have witnessed firsthand the ripple effects of a skewed and unfair system and are doing all they can to selflessly keep their families and communities from disintegrating in the aftermath.

Pomegranate has received the acclaim of various bestselling fellow authors, including Jaqueline Woodson, Tayari Jones, and Jennifer Haigh. A review in *Kirkus* applauded Lee's unhurried, personal depiction of a woman whose "freedom. . . is shackled to her past," adding, "The novel's slower moments are like a pomegranate's dull skin before it breaks to reveal a cache of jewels." Writer Zachary Houle for *Medium* appreciated Lee's stripped-back prose and her ability to write about serious themes in what is nonetheless a light and hopeful tone and summed the novel up as "an appealing effort by a skilled wordsmith." Meanwhile, Jacqueline Alnes for *Electric Literature* applauded Lee's skilled illustration of the "intentional cruelty" of the US prison complex, and the ripple effects of trauma—without rendering this trauma as an inescapable cage. *Publishers Weekly* deemed the book "irresistible" in a starred review and praised how "Lee balances the painful details of Ranita's reality with genuine, persistent hope for new beginnings." In spite of the many obstacles Ranita faces, Lee makes it clear that Ranita has the strength to withstand and perhaps even overcome the struggles of her many lives.

Author Biography

Prior to *Pomegranate*, Helen Elaine Lee published two novels, *The Serpent's Gift* (1995) and *Water Marked* (1999). Her short stories and essays have appeared in numerous journals and publications, including the *New York Times Book Review*, the *Best African American Fiction 2009*, and *Callaloo*. A professor of comparative media studies and writing at MIT, she has served on the board of PEN New England for a decade and has played a key role in affiliated organizations and initiatives, including the implementation of a creative writing program in a Massachusetts men's prison. An essay recounting Lee's experience at the prison was published in 2013 by the *New York Times*.

Maya Greenberg

Review Sources

Houle, Zachary. "Book Review: *Pomegranate* by Helen Elaine Lee." *Medium*, 13 Mar. 2023, zachary-houle.medium.com/book-review-pomegranate-by-helen-elaine-lee-833fcecb4b67. Accessed 24 Jan. 2024.

Review of *Pomegranate*, by Helen Elaine Lee. *Kirkus Reviews*, 1 Mar. 2023, www.kirkusreviews.com/book-reviews/helen-elaine-lee/pomegranate-lee/. Accessed 24 Jan. 2024.

Review of *Pomegranate*, by Helen Elaine Lee. *Publishers Weekly*, 13 Feb. 2023, p. 42. *Literary Reference Center Plus*, search.ebscohost.com/login.aspx?direct=true&db=lkh&AN=161840274&site=lrc-pluswww. Accessed 24 Jan. 2024.

Poverty, by America

Author: Matthew Desmond
Publisher: Crown (New York). 284 pp.
Type of work: Current affairs; economics; sociology
Time: Present
Locale: United States

In Poverty, by America, *sociologist Matthew Desmond lays out the systemic sources of entrenched poverty in the United States and, without assigning blame to one political party or the other, describes ways Americans of means can become "poverty abolitionists" for the betterment of the entire country.*

Principal personages
CRYSTAL MAYBERRY, an impoverished resident of Milwaukee, Wisconsin
HEATHER MCGHEE, author
JULIO PAYES, an immigrant from Guatemala and permanent United States resident
ELIZABETH WARREN, Democratic United States senator and advocate of wealth tax

Matthew Desmond's *Poverty, by America* (2023) attempts to explain the ways in which ordinary Americans, particularly those in the middle, upper middle, and upper classes, help perpetuate poverty in the United States. In writing this work, Desmond hoped to increase his readers' awareness of, and personal commitment to combatting, the endemic challenge of poverty in the United States. In Desmond's view, as well as in the view of many other scholars in his field, poverty is a vector for every major issue in American society. Poverty, he writes, "is connected to every social problem we care about—crime, health, education, housing—and its persistence in American life means that millions of families are denied safety and security and dignity in one of the richest nations in the history of the world."

Poverty, by America follows Desmond's *Evicted: Poverty and Profit in the American City* (2016), which won the Pulitzer Prize and used an embedded and case-study methodology in order to personalize the story of how eviction helps drive poverty and homelessness in the US. *Poverty, by America*, in contrast, deliberately steps away from the intimate stories of individuals suffering the indignities of poverty and takes a broader, more systemic view of the issue. At different points in his career, Desmond argued that books like *Evicted* were valuable because they helped humanize poverty, but did not go far enough in identifying causes or pointing toward solutions.

Consequently, Desmond intended *Poverty, by America* to examine the role played by a different population—in his words, "we the secure, the insured, the housed, the

Matthew Desmond

college educated, the protected, the lucky"—in perpetuating poverty. While Desmond, as a successful scholar, professor, and author, writes from the perspective of the secure "we," in the prologue he shares that his interest in poverty and inequality grew from his childhood experience of living at the edge of poverty and losing his childhood home to foreclosure. Speaking from his secure current position at the heights of academia, Desmond uses his own story as an explanation of his intellectual journey, but it is also a reminder that many promising young futures are limited or permanently sidelined due to poverty. With 12.4 percent of children in the US, or 9 million children, living in poverty in 2022, the year before the book's publication, this issue is undoubtedly one of national concern.

Poverty, by America had an unusual development process. As discussed in the author's acknowledgements, *Poverty, by America* is authored by Desmond, but its lead researcher was Jacob Haas at Princeton University's Eviction Lab, a sociology institute for which Desmond served as founding director. The book's manuscript was the result of a team of at least ten other named staff at the Eviction Lab, who Desmond credits with "organizing book workshops, synthesizing research, and . . . long weeks of fact-checking". While drawing on Desmond's many years of experience with researching poverty in America, the book, in many ways, offers the group vision of a social policy think tank housed at an Ivy league university—a fact that explains a great deal about the voice, tone, and method of the book.

In the prologue, Desmond proposes the concept that average readers must become "poverty abolitionists," a movement that he sees, alongside policy change and political action, as part of the three-pronged solution to eliminating poverty in the US. Desmond aims to inspire and unify readers around the mantle of poverty abolition in the hope that true social and political change might emerge from such consciousness. In Desmond's view, society has positioned many Americans as "unwitting enemies of the poor;" he argues that the prosperity of these more affluent Americans is based on a social bargain in which "some lives are made small so that others may grow." By articulating this point, Desmond hopes that readers will renounce this flawed framework and seek greater social equity.

Desmond's concept of poverty abolitionism is a founding principle of the text and drew significant attention and commentary from critics who reviewed the work. However, he only mentions the concept in passing throughout most of the book. Readers interested in exploring the framework of poverty abolitionism in greater depth will get relatively minimal guidance and will find most direct discussion of the concept in the prologue, chapter nine, and the epilogue.

Despite the complexity of the issues it tackles and the arguments it makes, *Poverty, by America* is not particularly long. It is divided into a prologue, epilogue, and nine chapters. This deliberate brevity seems designed to pique the interest of an educated reader who might be inclined to care about equity in society but is not a research expert in the field. (However, in order to convince experts and assert the veracity of his research, Desmond includes rich and extensive footnotes). The first two chapters define the depth and complexity of poverty as an issue and offer a historical overview of why the US failed to significantly reduce the percentage of Americans living in poverty between the late 1960s and early 2020s.

These opening chapters are followed by four chapters, each of which has a title that starts with the phrase "How We." Each chapter focuses on one aspect of the social structures in place that bolster opportunity for the wealthiest members of society (typically White, educated, homeowners) while exploiting the poorest members of American society. The topics Desmond explores include the negative consequences of the gig economy, the financial penalties paid by the poor who receive inferior services at a higher cost, the systematic limitation of opportunities available to poor people seeking employment, and other ways in which economic systems in the US discriminate against the poor. These chapters are packed with data Desmond draws on to illuminate how, in his view, certain structures in US society function to keep some individuals trapped in poverty—and permit others to backslide into poverty through illness or other unexpected setback—while bolstering or even increasing the wealth of others.

Though Desmond's arguments are likely to be of particular interest to readers with liberal views and may frustrate some readers with more conservative economic views, the author's writing takes a politically evenhanded tone. When he recounts getting into a public argument with an economist over the viability of a wealth tax plan proposed by US senator Elizabeth Warren, a Massachusetts Democrat, he is careful to underline his belief that neither Republicans nor Democrats in the US have been effective or perfect in their solutions to combat poverty in the US. Rather than taking a clear side, he appeals to readers of all political persuasions; while he argues that these readers are implicated in systemic poverty in the US, he also believes that they can contribute to the solution.

In the final three chapters of the book, Desmond shifts from outlining problems to offering solutions. While the data-based "How We" chapters may be the most memorable to many readers, the solutions chapters lay out some of the book's most meaningful points. The title of the first of these chapters, "Invest in Ending Poverty," lays out a call to fund efforts to reduce or end poverty. Specifically, Desmond estimates the amount of money needed to abolish poverty entirely: $177 billion. He then offers several different approaches to thinking about how to find and redistribute that money, while being careful not to get bogged down in too many details; he also takes care to demonstrate the viability of these financial solutions. Indeed, while $177 billion may sound like a staggering sum, one of the pieces of evidence that Desmond offers up to back his claim is an analysis that suggests $175 billion could be recuperated simply by collecting unpaid federal income taxes from US households in the top 1 percent of earners.

The second solutions chapter is entitled, "Empower the Poor." Centered on the premise that "choice is the antidote for exploitation," Desmond focuses on issues that would help individual Americans have greater ability to make choices about their employment, their place of residence, their financial institutions, and their family planning, and the author offers those interested in addressing poverty a menu of policies, initiatives, and principles that could guide such work. In particular, Desmond encourages readers to vote with their wallets, with the goal of making corporate and political antipoverty at least as visible as climate justice and sustainability campaigns.

The final solutions chapter, "Tear Down the Walls," is dedicated to explaining how to dismantle the barriers separating high-income, high-opportunity individuals from their low-income, low-opportunity counterparts. While Desmond claims that integrating these disparate groups is both possible and desirable, he also concedes that many individuals fear integration across economic lines due to what he calls the "scarcity diversion"—the idea that the limited nature of resources encourages violence, corruption, and villainizing others. Instead, he suggests that people in the US need to recognize that the country has enough resources to go around. Investing in the solutions of the preceding chapters, Desmond argues, might cause some financial pain and social disruptions during the process of rebalancing opportunities, but he feels it would ultimately lead to wider prosperity and greater freedom, since the opportunities available to one class of individuals would not depend on the oppression of others.

Poverty, by America was quickly received as a significant book when it was published in 2023 and became a bestseller, even as its avoidance of direct political judgment and party allegiance attracted some critique. Margaret Talbot, in a review for the *New Yorker*, described the book's "moral force" as "a gut punch." Noting how the book was "packed with revelations," Talbot gave Desmond credit for thoroughly outlining systemic poverty in the US and offering solutions, including the enlistment of average people in the fight to dismantle poverty. Alec MacGillis, writing for the *New York Times*, listed a few concerns about the structure and framework of the book, though also downplayed these concerns as "minor quibbles" compared to the book's larger goal of motivating readers to action and raising awareness of how all people in the US are "immiserated by poverty." While appreciative of the book's scale, many reviewers did voice at least some discontent with Desmond's decision to take a big picture, rather than personal, approach to storytelling and also questioned his decision to not lay out a single framework of policy and legislation through which his poverty solutions could be rolled out. Still, most of these same reviewers praised Desmond's willingness to provoke change through the presentation of uncomfortable truths.

Author Biography

Matthew Desmond served as the founding director of the Eviction Lab at Princeton University, where he also worked as a sociology professor. Desmond also wrote numerous works of nonfiction, including *On the Fireline: Living and Dying with Wildland Firefighters* (2007) and *Evicted: Poverty and Profit in the American City* (2016).

His work received numerous awards and honors, including the Pulitzer Prize, the National Book Critics Circle Award, and a MacArthur Fellowship.

Julia A. Sienkewicz, PhD

Review Sources

Gleason, Paul W. "How to Be a Poverty Abolitionist: On Matthew Desmond's 'Poverty, by America." Review of *Poverty, by America*, by Matthew Desmond. *Los Angeles Review of Books,*, 21 Mar. 2023, lareviewofbooks.org/article/how-to-be-a-poverty-abolitionist-on-matthew-desmonds-poverty-by-america/. Accessed 17 Dec. 2023.

Lenkowsky, Leslie. "'Poverty, by America' Review: Poverty Is Your Fault." Review of *Poverty, by America*, by Matthew Desmond. *The Wall Street Journal*, 16 Apr. 2023,www.wsj.com/articles/poverty-by-america-review-poverty-is-your-fault-84701c75. Accessed 17 Dec. 2023.

MacGillis, Alec. "In Matthew Desmond's 'Poverty, by America,' the Culprit Is Us." Review of *Poverty, by America*, by Matthew Desmond. *The New York Times*, 13 Mar. 2023, www.nytimes.com/2023/03/13/books/review/poverty-by-america-matthew-desmond.html. Accessed 17 Dec. 2023.

Moyn, Samuel. "Poverty, By America by Matthew Desmond Review—How the Rich Keep the Poor Down." Review of *Poverty, by America*, by Matthew Desmond. *The Guardian*, 22 Mar. 2023, www.theguardian.com/books/2023/mar/22/poverty-by-america-by-matthew-desmond-review-how-the-rich-keep-the-poor-down. Accessed 17 Dec.2023.

Press, Eyal. "The One Cause of Poverty That's Never Considered." Review of *Poverty, by America*, by Matthew Desmond. *The Atlantic*, 21 Mar. 2023, www.theatlantic.com/books/archive/2023/03/poverty-by-america-book-matthew-desmond/673453/. Accessed 17 Dec. 2023.

Talbot, Margaret. "How America Manufactures Poverty." Review of *Poverty, by America*, by Matthew Desmond. *The New Yorker*, 13 Mar. 2023, www.newyorker.com/magazine/2023/03/20/matthew-desmond-poverty-by-america-book-review. Accessed 17 Dec. 2023.

Promise Boys

Author: Nick Brooks (b. 1989)
Publisher: Henry Holt (New York). 304 pp.
Type of work: Novel
Time: Present day
Locale: Washington, DC

This young-adult novel about three charter-school students suspected in the murder of their principal is as much a portrait of systemic racism in the American school system as it is a page-turning, unpredictable mystery.

Principal characters

J. B. Williamson, a.k.a. Jabari, a quiet teenager at Urban Promise Prep School who often chafes against the school's rigid atmosphere
Trey Jackson, a basketball player and class clown at Urban Promise
Ramón Zambrano, an Urban Promise student with a passion for culinary arts
Kenneth Moore, the infamously draconian principle of Urban Promise, who is found murdered at the novel's opening

A notoriously austere principal is found murdered at the well-regarded prep school he founded. Three students immediately become prime suspects, as they were each spotted in intense arguments with him right before his death and appear to be linked to the scene of the crime. As various other members of the school community and surrounding neighborhoods weigh their own suspicions and assumptions surrounding the murder, the three boys must cooperate among themselves as they fight to prove their innocence. This is the basic conceit of the novel *Promise Boys* (2023), author and filmmaker Nick Brooks's young-adult fiction debut. But Brooks takes what might have simply been an intriguing twist on the classic murder-mystery premise and delves deeper, using the suspenseful plot to set up a sharp examination of the emotional and mental and physical toll of systemic racism, particularly within the American educational and criminal justice systems. The result is a timely, complex, yet highly accessible work that explores the myriad misguided ways in which adults in positions of authority use rigorous discipline to acclimate younger generations to an often-inhospitable world.

Promise Boys is set primarily at Urban Promise Prep School, a prestigious, competitive all-boys charter school in Washington, DC, with a strong reputation for helping kids from disadvantaged backgrounds get into college. The novel begins with a breaking news report: Urban Promise's founder and principal, Kenneth Moore, described

Nick Brooks

as "a beloved member of the community," was discovered shot to death at the school. Brooks then uses a nonlinear narrative told from multiple points of view to probe events before and after Moore's death. The book is divided into three parts, each made up of numerous brief chapters, ranging in length from just a few lines to a few pages. Some chapters are written as police interrogation transcripts or news clippings, while others are first-person monologues from students, school staff, and other community members. This wide assortment of perspectives evokes a sense of a true-crime documentary filled with witness testimony. Yet three characters quickly rise to the forefront, both from their own viewpoints and in the eyes of others: J. B. Williamson, Trey Jackson, and Ramón Zambrano—the three students who become the prime suspects in the murder investigation.

Tall and quiet, J. B has high academic potential and is usually well-behaved, but under the surface he has little tolerance for the strict level of discipline enforced at Urban Promise. His greatest dream is to be accepted into a good college and get out of the tough neighborhood he grew up in, though he has also been working up the courage to pursue a relationship with a girl from another school nearby. The murder, however, throws a significant wrench in his plans. J. B. was widely seen having a tense altercation with Principal Moore hours before the killing, earning him his first-ever afterschool detention, which in turn placed him near the scene of the crime. Even more incriminatingly, he was seen covered in blood soon after Moore's body was found. Several witnesses note that despite his usual reserved demeanor, J. B. was known to occasionally flash explosive anger, which leads some to assume he must be guilty.

In many ways, Trey seems like J. B.'s exact opposite. A class clown and occasional bully, he is almost always in trouble. He cares more about becoming a star basketball player than getting a passing grade or making a good impression. But his carefree façade hides a fraught home life with his harsh Uncle T, a former soldier whose model of discipline echoes Principal Moore's. Trey, too, was seen in a threatening interaction with Principal Moore and given detention, which some observers are quick to see as a potential motive. Furthermore, the school resource officer overseeing the detention notes that Trey went to the bathroom and disappeared during the exact time of the murder. Other circumstantial evidence also builds against Trey, like the fact that his uncle's gun was recently stolen and could be the murder weapon.

The third key suspect, Ramón, is a regular in detention for wisecracking and other small offenses but generally regarded as a good-natured kid. He covertly makes cash on the side selling his grandmother's Salvadoran pastries, a first step on the path to his dream of one day opening a restaurant. This passion has helped him stay relatively focused on school despite steady pressure from his cousin César to join his gang, Dioses del Humo. Like the others, Ramón is sent to detention for a spat with Principal Moore, giving him a possible motive and proximity to the murder, and other details emerge that seem to point to his involvement in the crime. Notably, as the school resource officer's narrative reveals early on, Ramón's hairbrush was found near Moore's body.

The novel's multiple-narrator approach allows Brooks to gradually reveal the full complexity of the three main characters while steadily building suspense. While all three boys assert their innocence, the reader must sort through clues and opinions that alternately support or undermine their claims. At times, the idea that one or all of them may have been provoked into killing Moore begins to seem like a distinct possibility—which highlights Brooks's biting commentary on the way stereotypes, misguided good intentions, and other forces can combine to warp society's perception of young men of color and risk creating a self-fulfilling prophecy of violence. Throughout, the rich characterization ensures that the three protagonists emerge as fully lifelike, sympathetic, but unmistakably flawed figures.

Initially, J. B., Trey, and Ramón are not friends. But as it becomes clear that they must clear their names or go to prison, the three boys are forced to cooperate with each other, doing their own detective work to figure out who actually committed the gruesome crime. As the teenagers embark on a road to the truth with a number of shocking twists along the way, they also discover a great deal about their school, their wider community, and themselves, revealing that the situation around them is not as simple as they might think.

While the gripping, fast-paced plot may be what first draws readers into *Promise Boys*, the incisive social commentary ensures that it remains thought-provoking even after the last page has been turned. Once again, Brooks's skill at developing realistic, memorable characters proves crucial here, as this helps his broader theme of racial injustice and the educational system come into personal focus rather than remain abstract concepts. Importantly, the nuanced characterization extends well beyond J. B., Trey, and Ramón; even many of the minor figures feel well-drawn as their varying perspectives illuminate the complex social issues that intersect to create systemic discrimination.

Perhaps most notable among the supporting cast is Principal Moore himself, whose own flaws quickly begin to come to light and play a central role in Brooks's overarching social message. The strict principal is portrayed as someone with good intentions that have turned problematic in practice, a concept that Brooks imbues with appropriate complexity. As a Black man, Moore was no stranger to systemic racism in his own life and made it his calling to uplift teenage boys in preparation for survival in a violently unjust society. As a result, in a disciplinary system he named the Moore Method, he emphasized treating his students as men, rather than the children that they truly still are. At Urban Promise, students must conduct themselves with military precision or face harsh punishment. The school's anthem, which J. B. recalls being forced to memorize from the moment he enrolled, is a literal "promise" to be "responsible for our futures," drilling into the students from an early age that no one else in the world will have their best interests at heart. As the school's dean puts it, the Urban Promise faculty are "in the business of building men, not coddling boys."

While not unsympathetic to the societal conditions that have shaped Moore's mindset, Brooks stresses how this approach only compounds the challenges facing the young people it aims to help. For example, the interweaving perspectives show how an oppressive, all-male environment can promote toxic masculinity, a problem that has been ignored at Urban Promise. As Nurse Robin, virtually the only female employee at the school, notes early on, Moore seems to care more about keeping up appearances of strength than actually encouraging healthy development. The failings of the Moore Method are clear in the fact that the punishments for small infractions, such as a missing tie or talking back to a teacher, are far more severe than those for engaging in misogynistic behavior. As the murder mystery deepens, hints appear that Moore's authoritarian streak may have roots in unaddressed emotional or psychological issues not so unlike the rebellious attitudes he attempts to squash in his students, further underlining the idea that he is unwittingly playing into a vicious cycle of systemic inequality.

Promise Boys had an extremely favorable reception in the press, earning recognition as an honoree for the Boston Globe-Horn Book Awards and as a best book of the year by several outlets. Many critics praised both its original, effective spin on the mystery genre and its powerful social commentary. For example, Angeline Boulley, writing for the *New York Times*, listed it among a crop of strong young-adult novels examining hot-button contemporary social issues and called it a "compelling story about the perils of prejudgments." (Boulley also recommended the audiobook version, which features a full cast of voice actors.) The critic for *Kirkus Reviews* commended the novel's "masterful use of multiple points of view from both the main protagonists and secondary characters," calling the result "breathtakingly complex and intriguing." Many reviewers also emphasized how Brooks successfully develops three-dimensional characters, with utterly realistic and relatable flaws, anxieties, and secret hopes.

Promise Boys opens with a quote from teacher and educational critic John Taylor Gatto's essay "Why Schools Don't Educate," which includes the line: "The truth is that schools don't really teach anything except how to obey orders." In the end, Brooks's novel is an examination of this idea in the context of twenty-first-century racial justice concerns, using the power of fiction to show how deep-rooted problems remain relevant. By conveying this serious message through a thrilling mystery, *Promise Boys* will connect with many readers and possibly help counteract the systemic obstacles it documents.

Author Biography

Nick Brooks is the author of the middle-grade novels *Nothing Interesting Ever Happens to Ethan Fairmont* (2022) and *Too Many Interesting Things Are Happening to Ethan Fairmont* (2023). As a filmmaker, he earned honors including the George Lucas Scholar Award. He is also a rapper under the moniker Ben Kenobe.

Maya Greenberg

Review Sources

Boulley, Angeline. "6 Thought-Provoking YA Thrillers That Tackle Social Issues." Review of *Promise Boys*, by Nick Brooks, et al. *The New York Times*, 26 July 2023, www.nytimes.com/2023/07/26/books/review/young-adult-social-thrillers.html. Accessed 13 Dec. 2023.

Harris, Monique. Review of *Promise Boys*, by Nick Brooks. *The Horn Book*, 17 Feb. 2023, www.hbook.com/story/review-of-promise-boys-jan23. Accessed 5 Feb. 2024.

Kamela, Mary. Review of *Promise Boys*, by Nick Brooks. *School Library Journal*, 1 Feb. 2023, www.slj.com/review/promise-boys. Accessed 5 Feb. 2024.

Review of *Promise Boys*, by Nick Brooks. *Kirkus Reviews*, 15 Nov. 2022, www.kirkusreviews.com/book-reviews/nick-brooks/promise-boys/. Accessed 5 Feb. 2024.

Promises of Gold

Author: José Olivarez
Publisher: Holt Paperbacks (New York). 320 pp.
Translated from the Spanish by David Ruano González
Type of work: Poetry
Time: Present day

Drawing on his background as the son of Mexican immigrants, José Olivarez employs colloquial speech and a range of poetic forms to explore the Chicano experience.

José Olivarez is a poet whose work draws on many aspects of his life. The son of Mexican immigrants who had a working-class upbringing in the Chicago area, Olivarez went on to attend Harvard University and become an award-winning writer. His work, including the 2018 poetry collection *Citizen Illegal*, details life in his Mexican American community, his sense of displacement at existing in the larger world, and the love and connection he feels for his family and friends. Adopting a conversational poetry style that occasionally draws on slang and Spanish phrases, Olivarez's work resonates forcefully with readers, while still retaining a lyrical flair and a penchant for surprising turns of phrase.

In the author's note at the beginning of his 2023 collection, *Promises of Gold*, Olivarez tells readers that his initial desire in writing the book was to compose a collection of love poems for his friends. That goal got sidetracked, he notes, both because of the state of the world and because of Olivarez's own sensibility. "But because I am who I am & because we live in the world that we live in," he notes, "I wrote this instead." As Olivarez goes on to explain, he is referring specifically to the COVID-19 pandemic which was in full force as he wrote most of the poems in the book and which exacerbated the other ills of the world that had long been raging. As he writes, COVID-19 "has laid bare all the *other* pandemics that we've been living throughout our whole lives," a list that includes "capitalism," "the police state," "colonialism," and "toxic masculinity." Being someone concerned deeply with these issues, Olivarez could not simply write the "book of love poems for the homies" that he had originally intended to create.

The result of this thwarted desire is a book that contains a number of poems that illustrate the poet's attempts to express love to his friends and family, most of which usually end with him doing it indirectly. For example, in the poem "Nate Calls Me Soft," the poet describes both his relationship with a friend and the code of masculinity

José Olivarez

that dictates that relationship. "If we were better at being honest," the poem begins, "maybe it wouldn't take a bottle / of something strong to make us talk / straight." In many of the poems in the book, the male characters can only express themselves more intimately if they have been drinking, a state of affairs set up by these first lines. Next the poet recalls a time when he and his friend used to drive around to different open mic poetry nights and begins to tear up. "If I confess that the memory alone / makes the corner of my eye itch," the poet wonders, "would you call me soft?" In the hypermasculine world of the poet and his friends, the answer to this question is "yes," because to feel emotion is to be thought "soft." The poem ends with the poet wanting to break through this façade of manliness. "Maybe the next time i see you," he writes, "I'll slap away the dap, pull you in close, / & tell you under the ordinary streetlights / how much I love you." Even this wish for direct intimacy proves to be too much, as the poet goes on to end his poem with one final line that falls back into the language of macho banter.

This masculine reserve also dictates the poet's relationship with his family. Olivarez includes several poems about his parents. As he portrays them, his mother is a devout Catholic while his father is typical of other men in the book, an emotionally guarded man who enjoys drinking. In one poem entitled "Regret or My Dad Says Love," he offers a sympathetic consideration of his father and his life. Establishing the theme of regret in both the title and the first line of the poem, the poet then goes on to recall a time when he was in Mexico with his father. They go to a bar and the poet has a vision of his father living an alternate life, one where he is not bound to a family and was free to "flirt . . . with the whole bar." Instead, the poet tells us, he had to be back home by midnight because the poet's younger brother got sick. "To be a dad is to be bossed / at work & bossed at home," the poet muses sympathetically, reflecting on the less glamorous forms of love that fathers are required to show, such as changing a dirty diaper. While his father might not have communicated his feelings directly to his family, the poet concludes, he showed it through his actions. "My dad rarely said love," he writes, "but he always left the bar."

Because Olivarez grew up in a working class Mexican American family, he is especially attuned to issues of class, particularly as he went on to Harvard and then out into the wider world. Many of his poems are explicitly about the disjunctions he has felt because of this clash of classes. For example, in the poem entitled, "Wealth," he reflects on his college experience. At the beginning of the poem, he mentions how his friends back home joked with him that he was only going to Harvard to mow the lawns, a reference to offensive stereotypes about Mexican Americans. He thought it was funny until his roommates, presumably White, made a similar joke, handing him a broom. He goes on to relate how when someone calls out his name, José, the only people who turn around besides him are janitors, line cooks, waitstaff, and landscapers. The second part of the poem reflects on Olivarez's own poetic practice, a theme common throughout the book. In considering his practice, the poet ultimately affirms a connection with an imagined landscaper named José since they are both "trying to make beauty grow. From soil / covering bones. barely. Under the surface." In the poet's case these bones are metaphorical, representing a legacy of repressed violence, and in asserting his desire to make beauty out of ugly historical experience, Olivarez offers up an encapsulation of his poetic mission.

Although many of Olivarez's poems are written in a conversational, even jocular, tone, other of his poems are more abstract or fantastical. In another poem about class entitled "Upward Mobility," Olivarez ends what had been a relatively straightforward verse with a startling, surreal image. The poem begins with an image of a boy "dancing to avoid the fluttering / of roaches" while he brushes his teeth. The middle section of the poem consists of a series of lines that proceed by parallel construction. Each line begins with the phrase "& one eye on." As the boy brushes his teeth, the poet then lists all the things he watches, which begins with concrete objects such as the bugs and his teeth and then gives way to abstract concepts such as "time" and "the future." After invoking "the future," the poet then obliges by fast forwarding the poem into a time "years later." In this future, people joke about the poem's speaker having "poor people teeth." When they do so, he undergoes a transformation. "His head will shed its skin," the poet writes, "to reveal five thousand eyes the size / of cockroach hearts." This surreal image takes the poem full circle back to the beginning when the boy tried to dodge roaches. Although the reader is not meant to take this transformation literally, it is nonetheless a statement of the power of imagination, of poetry, to examine long-lasting experiences and themes that can be difficult to describe. Throughout *Promises of Gold*, Olivarez draws on the full range of his experience and poetic techniques to not only paint a vivid portrait of Mexican American life, but to assert the power of poetry to make sense of the world and empower the powerless.

Promises of Gold received critical acclaim and was considered for several awards. Most notably the collection was longlisted for the prestigious National Book Award for Poetry. Critics found much to praise about the book. For example, Diego Báez, writing for the *Poetry Foundation*, found that the poems in the book "play with entertaining contradictions as they explore desire and fulfillment in the speaker's complicated relationships with countries and cultures." He was impressed as well by the various ways that Olivarez uses repetition, in ways both humorous and serious.

These sentiments were echoed by Angelica Flores of *New City Lit*. Flores praised the conversational nature of Olivarez's poems and how they were thus accessible to a wide range of readers. She also enjoyed the whimsical and clever touches that Olivarez employed. She was especially impressed by the poems dealing with the author's childhood and his experience as a college student.

The *Poetry Question* also had much to praise about *Promises of Gold*. The website's review lauded the collection as "an unflinching exploration of pandemics, family and healing," while offering special praise to Olivarez's poems dealing with family and unspoken love. The reviewer felt that Olivarez was particularly "masterful at writing from a place of vulnerability, exposing his flaws without ever leaning into self-deprecation."

A collection with a wide array of strengths, *Promises of Gold* inspired different critics to find different things to praise. Accessible, yet thought-provoking, Olivarez's collection has the range and approachability to speak to a wide range of readers, whether or not they share the poet's specific background. A powerful look at the first-generation American experience, as well as an exploration of class, family, and friendship, *Promises of Gold* fulfills Olivarez's original goal of writing a book of love letters to his friends, while always acknowledging the hard realities that complicate that love.

Author Biography

José Olivarez is the author of two books of poetry, 2018's *Citizen Illegal*, which was a finalist for the PEN/Jean Stein Award, and 2023's *Promises of Gold*. His work has been featured in numerous outlets including the *New York Times* and the *Paris Review*.

David Ruano González is a poet and translator.

Andrew Schenker

Review Sources

Báez, Diego. Review of *Promises of Gold*, by José Olivarez, translated by David Ruano González. *Poetry Foundation*, www.poetryfoundation.org/harriet-books/reviews/159478/promises-of-gold. Accessed 11 Oct. 2023.

Flores, Angelica. "Childhood Memories." Review of *Promises of Gold*, by José Olivarez, translated by David Ruano González. *New City Lit*, 6 Mar. 2023, lit.newcity.com/2023/03/06/childhood-memories-a-review-of-promises-of-gold-by-jose-olivarez/. Accessed 11 Oct. 2023.

Review of *Promises of Gold*, by José Olivarez, translated by David Ruano González. *The Poetry Question*, 13 Apr. 2023, thepoetryquestion.com/2023/04/13/review-promises-of-gold-by-jose-olivarez-henry-holt-and-company/. Accessed 11 Oct 2023.

Prophet Song

Author: Paul Lynch (b. 1977)
Publisher: Atlantic Monthly (New York). 320 pp.
Type of work: Novel
Time: Near future
Locale: Dublin, Ireland

In a future Ireland in which the elected government is sliding into totalitarianism and civil unrest is brewing, microbiologist Eilish attempts to care for her children and aging father as she watches the situation spiral increasingly out of control.

Principal characters
EILISH STACK, a woman trying to hold her family together in a dystopian Ireland
MARK, her eldest son, age sixteen
BAILEY, her middle son
MOLLY, her daughter
BEN, her youngest son, an infant
SIMON, her father, who has dementia

Prophet Song is a work of literary speculative fiction taking place in a near future in which a fascist political party has come to power in the Republic of Ireland. The protagonist, Eilish, is an ordinary woman who struggles—and mostly fails—to keep her family safe amid the worsening social conditions. The author, Paul Lynch, stated that the book was inspired by the Syrian Civil War, and was in part an attempt to address the lack of empathy from Europeans toward Syrian refugees by exploring the possibility of similar events taking place within Europe. Though Lynch claimed that he did not intend to address the real-life rise of far-right parties and politicians in the Western world when he began work on the novel in 2019, the book has often been called "prescient" for its depiction of where such trends might lead. Lynch, already an award-winning author, released *Prophet Song* to widespread acclaim, and it won the 2023 Booker Prize, among other honors.

The novel begins with Eilish's husband Larry, a trade unionist who has protested the repressive government, being pursued by the new organization of secret police, the Garda National Services Bureau (GNSB). At first, neither Eilish nor Larry is concerned—surely Larry cannot be arrested for protesting when "there are still constitutional rights in this country," as Eilish says. But ultimately the GNSB does find an excuse to detain him. Eilish tries to petition for his release, but it is soon clear, at least to the reader, that the GNSB has disposed of him.

Paul Lynch

Eilish, however, remains in denial, convinced both that Larry will return and that the right-wing government will not remain in power long. She focuses on caring for her elderly father, Simon, who is struggling with dementia, as well as her four children, Mark, Bailey, Molly, and Ben. During the periods when Simon is lucid enough to understand what is happening in the country, he begs Eilish to leave the country, but she will not. Simon is stubborn in his own right, insisting on remaining in his own home rather than moving in with Eilish. The distance between them puts additional strain on Eilish and feels greater and greater to her as society crumbles around them and the streets become more dangerous.

Simon, when lucid, is perhaps the most insightful character in the novel when it comes to the political situation. Lynch uses his character to convey many key social themes and warnings against the complacency represented by Eilish. At one point, for example, Simon notes that the news media have been overtaken by "the Big Lie"—a reference to a political technique involving the consistent repetition of an extreme, untrue statement. "If you change ownership of the institutions then you can change ownership of the facts, you can alter the structure of belief," Simon explains; "if you say one thing is another thing and you say it enough times, then it must be so, and if you keep saying it over and over people accept it as true." Such warnings are echoed elsewhere, too. Though Eilish continually resists accepting them, they seem to seep into her subconscious; in a dream, a malevolent police inspector mocks her faith in the system, saying "you believe in rights that don't exist, the rights you speak of cannot be verified, they are a fiction decreed by the state."

As the country falls apart, Eilish and her family face a series of increasing hardships and difficult choices. Mark is called up for mandatory military service against the armed rebels that have begun to rise against the government; instead he flees and joins the rebels himself. Molly's mental health seriously deteriorates, and she stops eating. Bailey is injured when the government bombs the rebels, and Eilish must risk death in crossing a forbidden area to reach the hospital to which he has been taken.

For much of the book, Eilish is torn between fear and the growing desire to resist. Still, she often takes refuge in denial even as reality becomes more insistent and harder to avoid. And all the while, she must also deal with the mundane aspects of motherhood—making sure her children are fed and clothed and that they get to school on time. The difficulties of this are, of course, compounded by the fact that she is suddenly a single parent.

Prophet Song has a relatively straightforward plot, but its weighty, complex themes are reinforced by Lynch's unusual prose style. Much of the novel is composed of breathless run-on sentences, sometimes lasting over a page, and it lacks normal paragraph breaks and quotation marks. While the narrative centers on Eilish's point of view, there are frequent shifts between deeply internal and somewhat more distanced perspectives. In one relatively short example that gives a sense of the style, Eilish's reaction to the GNSB's first visit to her home is described thus: "This feeling now that something has come into the house, she wants to put the baby down, she wants to stand and think, seeing how it stood with the two men and came into the hallway of its own accord, something formless yet felt." The relentlessly flowing, lyrical style creates a sense of inexorable forward momentum, reflecting the country's uncontrollable slide into dystopia. The prose overwhelms the reader, just as the events of the novel overwhelm the protagonist. Things seem to be happening too fast for Eilish to grasp; she has barely come to terms with one disaster before the next overtakes her.

Prophet Song received mostly positive reviews. Many critics focused on the timeliness of the novel and the impact that reviewers felt it could have on the reader. For example, writing for the *Guardian*, Aimée Walsh called it "a crucial book for our current times" and "a literary manifesto for empathy . . . that should be placed into the hands of policymakers everywhere." In a review for the *Washington Post*, Ron Charles wrote that the novel is "so contaminated with plausibility that it's impossible not to feel poisoned by swelling panic" and that it "rips away that easy condescension" with which people tend to view refugees. Justine Jordan, also for the *Guardian*, called *Prophet Song* "a novel written to jolt the reader awake to truths we mostly cannot bear to admit."

Reviewers also noted the effectiveness of the distinctive prose style in evoking a feeling of tension and putting the reader into Eilish's mindset. Kristen Martin, writing for NPR, praised the book's "winding, dread-filled sentences," suggesting that "Lynch's style mimics the unfolding of Eilish's confrontation with her country's inexorable drift into totalitarian rule and civil war, and what she must do to keep her family together." Similarly, Charles wrote that "with no paragraph breaks to cling to, every page feels as slippery as the damp walls of a torture chamber." In a review for the *New York Times*, Benjamin Markovits also felt that the lack of quotation marks and other stylistic decisions, though often confusing from a basic reading perspective, resonated with the book's themes, suggesting "that there's no real difference on the page between a thing said and a thing thought—You can feel the paranoia creeping in. Thinking is as bad as saying; saying is as futile as thinking."

Though *Prophet Song* was widely acclaimed, a few reviewers did offer criticisms. Most notably, some took issue with the fact that the beliefs and policies of the book's fictional right-wing party and the circumstances that led to their rise to power are left vague. As Markovits wrote in his otherwise largely positive review, "the political crisis here is a kind of blank; it has no history." For example, despite Simon's mention of "the Big Lie" being constantly repeated in the media, it is never stated what the lie actually is—that is, how exactly the government has been distorting the truth to justify the extreme measures they have been taking. The reader is told early on that the government has declared a state of emergency, but what the emergency is supposed to be, whether real or fabricated, remains unmentioned. This makes it somewhat unclear why many of Eilish's coworkers and neighbors are going along with the party; the reader has no insight into what fears or dissatisfactions the government is exploiting to keep them nodding along with each new loss of freedoms. Markovits argued that the vagueness of the setup turns the nationalist party members into a "mindless destructive force" that in turn gives the book a sense of "preaching to the choir," and perhaps implies that the readers only have to worry about being victims of such a movement, not enablers.

Even Markovits tempered that criticism, however, recognizing that exploring the whys and hows of a totalitarian government's ascent is not the book's primary concern. "*Prophet Song* is less interested in 'Could it happen here?' than in the follow-up 'Would you know when to leave?'" he wrote, concluding that, despite his initial misgivings, he found the book "persuasive." Along the same lines, Martin suggested that "the lesson for readers is not necessarily to wake up to signs of totalitarianism knocking at our doors, but to empathize with those for whom it has already called."

Regardless of what some may consider to be gaps in its narrative, *Prophet Song* is a unique book that vividly evokes the experience of a woman dealing with her society's rapid descent into repression and violence. Its effort to promote empathy for refugees and the opportunity it provides for citizens of Western democracies to consider the potential fragility of their society also add to its significance. It is in some ways emblematic of key political anxieties of the late 2010s and early 2020s, asking whether democracies can survive if one party stops playing by the rules, whether relatively privileged citizens might fail to notice what is happening until it is too late, and, most of all, how to cope once everything has fallen apart.

Author Biography

Paul Lynch is the author of four previous novels: *Red Sky in Morning* (2013), *The Black Snow* (2014), *Grace* (2017), and *Beyond the Sea* (2019). *Grace* earned multiple honors, including Kerry Group Irish Book of the Year 2018 and shortlisting for the William Saroyan International Prize for Writing. *Beyond the Sea* won the Prix Gens de Mers 2022.

Emma Joyce

Review Sources

Charles, Ron. "Booker Prize Winner *Prophet Song* Is a Prophetic Masterpiece." Review of *Prophet Song*, by Paul Lynch. *The Washington Post*, 27 Nov. 2023, www.washingtonpost.com/books/2023/11/27/booker-winner-prophet-song. Accessed 12 Feb. 2024.

Jordan, Justine. "Paul Lynch's Timely Booker Winner Is a Novel Written to Jolt the Reader Awake." Review of *Prophet Song*, by Paul Lynch. *The Guardian*, 26 Nov. 2023, www.theguardian.com/books/2023/nov/26/prophet-song-paul-lynch-booker-prize-winning-novel-ireland-fascist-control. Accessed 12 Feb. 2024.

Markovits, Benjamin. "Life Descends into Chaos in This Year's Booker Prize Winner." Review of *Prophet Song*, by Paul Lynch. *The New York Times*, 1 Dec. 2023, www.nytimes.com/2023/12/01/books/review/paul-lynch-prophet-song.html. Accessed 12 Feb. 2024.

Martin, Kristen. "In Booker-Winning *Prophet Song*, the World Ends Slowly and Then All at Once." Review of *Prophet Song*, by Paul Lynch. *NPR*, 11 Dec. 2023, www.npr.org/2023/12/11/1218053727/book-review-paul-lynch-booker-prize-winning-prophet-song. Accessed 12 Feb. 2024.

Walsh, Aimée. "*Prophet Song* by Paul Lynch Review – A Tale of Dublin's Descent into Dystopia Is Crucial Reading." *The Guardian*, 3 Sept. 2023, www.theguardian.com/books/2023/sep/03/prophet-song-by-paul-lynch-review-a-tale-of-dublins-descent-into-dystopia-is-crucial-reading. Accessed 12 Feb. 2024.

Quietly Hostile

Author: Samantha Irby (b. 1980)
Publisher: Vintage Books (New York). 304 pp.
Type of work: Essays
Time: 1980s through the present day
Locales: Chicago, Illinois; Kalamazoo, Michigan

Quietly Hostile *is the fourth collection of autobiographical essays by humorist Samantha Irby.*

Principal personages
SAMANTHA IRBY, the author, a humorist, essayist, and television writer
KIRSTEN, her wife
CEDRIC, her estranged half-brother

As a writer, Samantha Irby is known for her acerbic wit and unfiltered honesty—a writing style that reflects her background as part of the generation that broke through to the mainstream by blogging in the aughts. Like *Jezebel* and *xoJane*, Irby's blog was revolutionary at the time for how it challenged the airbrushed ideas of womanhood that magazines had long been selling. The blog also helped land Irby a book deal, which resulted in her debut, *Meaty* (2013)—a collection of memoirist essays about her misadventures as a self-proclaimed "fat" Black woman with Crohn's disease. Since then, Irby has published several other essay collections, including *We Are Never Meeting in Real Life* (2017) and *Wow, No Thank You* (2020), which have earned her both critical acclaim and a cult following.

Although a lot has changed in Irby's life and the world at large thanks to the COVID-19 pandemic that began in 2020, her 2023 book *Quietly Hostile* maintains the same sharp, confident writing style and humor that she built her career upon. Longtime fans will feel like they are picking up where they left off with an old friend as these essays, like her previous ones, function as a successful blend of personal anecdotes, social commentary, thoughts, and opinions. In the book's first essay, for example, Irby states that the only advice she has for anyone is to defend their tastes against the smug opinions of others by loudly declaring, "I like it!" She then continues to explain the effectiveness of this statement by providing hilarious scenarios in which it can be used against critical people who are trying to take away the joy of others.

In many ways, Irby's "I like it!" advice reflects the underlying sentiment behind the book's title. While not a unifying theme, as all of the book's essays are stand-alone and eclectic, Irby's depiction of herself as a "quietly hostile" person stuck in a hellish

Samantha Irby

world filled with terrible people is a reoccurring one. This is to say that the anecdotes she recalls throughout the book's essays always feel different and surprising, but her perspective as a frustrated person so stuck behind polite Midwestern manners that she avoids confrontation at all costs remains the same.

A large part of what makes Irby such a fun author to read is the specific way that she expresses her frustrations at the ridiculous situations and people she encounters in her life. In a lesser writer's hands, this could come across as overly snarky or passive aggressive, but Irby makes herself as much a part of the joke as whatever it is she is writing about. Furthermore, her self-deprecating humor never feels as though she is punching down on herself. She writes about the silliness of her thoughts, fears, and decisions while also recognizing the realness of the anxiety and depression that underly them. It is a unique comedic sensibility that is best captured in *Quietly Hostile*'s earliest pages, where she dedicates the book to Zoloft.

Indeed, by reading *Quietly Hostile*, people who are new to Irby will quickly discover her talent for finding humor even in life's darkest moments. This tendency is perhaps most evident in the book's best essay, "O Brother, Where Art Thou?," in which she writes about how, when she was eighteen years old, her mother was taken off of life support because the complications of her multiple sclerosis had become too advanced. Despite this being one of the most tragic moments in her life, Irby still manages to find the comedy of the situation—reflecting on how "weird" it must have been for other kids to have to pick her up at a hospice nursing home to go out for activities such as seeing a movie, the petty squabbling between her and her sisters when they had to take turns saying goodbye, and the outrageousness of her mother's last words to her. Later, she admits how liberating it is to have dead parents while questioning whether it is "bad" that she does not miss them at all.

Irby's dedication to maintaining her unique sense of humor in *Quietly Hostile* is a testament to how she has successfully subverted the contemporary publishing trend that encourages writers to plumb the depths of their pain and trauma to create shocking, tragic content for their readers. Like her previous books, *Quietly Hostile* is more interested in talking about life's tragedies in a way that does not aim to exploit Irby's pain for profit but rather to make people more comfortable to talk about issues typically perceived as taboo. Beyond the way she writes about her parents, this authorial tendency is most evident in the way that she writes about her health struggles with Crohn's disease. Several of the book's essays are scatological in both their theme and humor as Irby attempts to normalize conversations about gastrointestinal issues and, in turn, challenge the sense of shame that many people with them have. It is a quest that she herself acknowledges seems somewhat futile, as she has been trying to make a television series about her life with Crohn's for years without luck.

It is important to note that *Quietly Hostile* is not exclusively a work of gallows humor about life's hardships, as many of the essays explore more lighthearted, slice-of-life topics. "I Like to Get High at Night and Think about Whales," for example, is a two-page meditation on her favorite bedtime ritual. In the hilarious "David Matthews's Greatest Romantic Hits," Irby writes about how she is a huge fan of the essay's titular band before going through fourteen of her favorite songs by them—writing a funny blurb about each of these songs, describing what it is about and why she thinks it is so good. In "We Used to Get Dressed Up to Go to Red Lobster," she links multiple disparate moments from her life together with memories of experiences she has had at different chain restaurants. The list-like format shared by these particular essays provides the book with a more casual, blog-like tone and subsequently makes for easy reading.

However, an argument can be made that some of the book's best essays are the ones that provide readers with glimpses into her familial life. In "My Firstborn Dog," she recounts how she and her wife, Kirsten, adopted their problematic mutt Abe before diving into all of the various problems he has. Because Kirsten is mostly a background character in *Quietly Hostile* as Irby, who is bisexual, prefers to write about and humorize her past sexual and romantic experiences with men, "My Firstborn Dog" comes across as a rare treat by providing readers with insight into how they operate as a married couple. Meanwhile, "O Brother, Where Art Thou?" offers context as to how Irby became the writer and person she is today. In addition to describing her mother's death, the essay explores the different familial forces that led her to become estranged from her sisters and her half-brother, Cedric. While Irby can make writing about any topic entertaining and insightful, the ones that involve the people closest to her, like "O Brother Where Art Thou?," are just slightly more satiating.

Critical reception of *Quietly Hostile* has been predominantly positive, with most reviews agreeing that the book continues the winning formula of her previous work. Jason Heller touched on this in his NPR review when he wrote, "Calling *Quietly Hostile* a collection of essays is a bit limiting. These 17 pieces are more like essays crossed with stand-up bits, and that punchline-driven rhythm serves the book spectacularly well." Similarly, the anonymous reviewer for *Publishers Weekly* commented on the overall effectiveness of her writing style, concluding that, "Bouncing between irreverence and poignancy, this keeps the laughs coming while serving up intimate personal reflection and entertaining cultural commentary. Irby's fans will be glad to find her in top form."

It is important to note that *Quietly Hostile* is not without flaws. For example, the essay "Superfan!!!!!!!" involves Irby writing about the social media backlash that she has experienced as a writer on HBO's *And Just Like That* before launching into a breakdown of how she would rewrite specific episodes of the original show, *Sex and the City*, episode by episode. While "Superfan!!!!!!!" boasts a lot of Irby's trademark witty opinions, it is also quite long when compared to the other essays and subsequently begins to feel like it is dragging on after a while. Many critics commented on the shortcomings of this essay in their reviews, including Nneka McGuire, who wrote for the *Washington Post* that it "is a laborious treatise that even a SATC fan (but maybe not a superfan) might find grueling." Similarly, *Kirkus Reviews* recommended the book to readers but also warned that "some of the essays carry on too long, bogging readers down in repetitive detail."

Although it is true that one or two of *Quietly Hostile*'s essays lose momentum because of their length, readers will still be entertained by them overall as they still have many of the other unique qualities that make Irby's writing so great. Of course, not everyone will enjoy these qualities, as her sense of humor is quite specific and comedy is subjective. However, many will still be able to relate to the contemporary issues she writes about, especially when it comes to how people are in the world today as they have been shaped by the internet and social media. Similarly, there is a certain quirky but universal quality to her anecdotes about aging, eating, and marriage.

Ultimately, *Quietly Hostile* is further proof that Irby is one of the best essayists of her generation whose talent for the medium may only be rivaled by David Sedaris. Her willingness to discuss taboo matters in a frank, funny way is refreshing, and her perspective as a bisexual Black woman feels much overdue. Those who read *Quietly Hostile* will likely find it to be an enjoyable addition to Irby's other essay collections while also hoping that it is not her last.

Author Biography

Samantha Irby is a humorist, essayist, and screenwriter. In addition to the television shows *Shrill* on Hulu and *Work in Progress* on Showtime, she has also written for the HBO series *And Just Like That*. Her essay collections include *Meaty* (2013), *We Are Never Meeting in Real Life* (2017), *Wow, No Thank You* (2020), and *Quietly Hostile* (2023).

Emily E. Turner

Review Sources

Heller, Jason. "In *Quietly Hostile*, Samantha Irby Trains a Cynical Eye Inward." Review of *Quietly Hostile*, by Samantha Irby. *NPR*, 15 May 2023, www.npr.org/2023/05/15/1175717333/quietly-hostile-essays-samantha-irby-book-review. Accessed 8 Aug. 2023.

McGuire, Nneka. "Samantha Irby Is Not Quiet, Never Mind the Title of Her New Book." Review of *Quietly Hostile*, by Samantha Irby. *The Washington Post*, 26 May 2023, www.washingtonpost.com/books/2023/05/26/samantha-irby-quietly-hostile-review/. Accessed 8 Aug. 2023.

Review of *Quietly Hostile*, by Samantha Irby. *Kirkus Reviews*, 24 Jan. 2023, www.kirkusreviews.com/book-reviews/samantha-irby/quietly-hostile/. Accessed 8 Aug. 2023.

Review of *Quietly Hostile*, by Samantha Irby. *Publishers Weekly*, 13 Mar. 2023, www.publishersweekly.com/9780593315699. Accessed 8 Aug. 2023.

The Rediscovery of America
Native Peoples and the Unmaking of U.S. History

Author: Ned Blackhawk
Publisher: Yale University Press (New Haven). 616 pp.
Type of work: History
Time: 1500s–2000s
Locale: North America

In The Rediscovery of America: Native Peoples and the Unmaking of U.S. History, *historian Ned Blackhawk retells five hundred years of postcolonial history to illustrate the fundamental role that Indigenous peoples have played in shaping the nation that the United States would eventually become.*

Principal personages
TISQUANTUM, a Pawtuxet man who was captured by the British, became an interpreter, traveled between North America and Europe several times, and helped the Plymouth colony survive
PONTIAC, the Odawa leader who led a pivotal rebellion against the British in 1763
LAURA CORNELIUS KELLOGG, an Oneida leader and cofounder of the Society of American Indians
HENRY ROE CLOUD, a twentieth-century Ho-Chunk activist who helped improve Indigenous rights
ELIZABETH BENDER CLOUD, an Ojibwe activist who helped earn Indigenous people like herself and her husband the right to self-government

In recent years, the movement to expand the myopic scope of American history has started to enter the mainstream. Deviating from the long-held tradition of celebrating European colonialism and White male figures like Christopher Columbus and the Founding Fathers, a new wave of literature has emerged that aims to undo the centuries-long erasure of communities of color and their significance to American history. Many of the books at the forefront of this movement thus far have focused on the role that African Americans have played within the nation as evidenced by Daina Ramey Berry and Kali Nicole Gross's *A Black Women's History of the United States* (2020), Isabel Wilkerson's *Caste: The Origins of Our Discontents* (2020), and editors Caitlin Roper, Ilena Silverman, and Jake Silverstein's *The 1619 Project: A New Origin Story* (2021). With *The Rediscovery of America: Native Peoples and the Unmaking of U.S. History* (2023), historian and Yale professor Ned Blackhawk aims to fill another

Ned Blackhawk

fundamental gap that has been missing from the country's narrative by examining the impact of Indigenous peoples on America's sociopolitical evolution.

Central to *The Rediscovery of America* is the argument that to truly understand America, it is necessary to consider it through the perspective of those who predate the colonization of America. To accomplish this, Blackhawk retells such familiar Eurocentric chapters of history as the Revolutionary War, the Civil War, and westward expansion from an Indigenous perspective. This quickly proves to be a transformational framework as even making slight changes to the language used to tell American history dramatically changes how it is understood. Instead of telling the story of the "discovery" of America, for example, Blackhawk refers to it as the first "encounter" between Indigenous peoples and Europeans. In turn, the former term's insinuation that European colonizers were somehow heroic or geniuses by stumbling upon foreign land disappears. Blackhawk explains the logic behind the book's approach to telling American history in its introduction, stating, "Rather than seeing U.S. and Native American history as separate or disaggregated, this project envisions them as interrelated. It underscores the mutually constitutive nature of each; the two are and remain interwoven."

The Rediscovery of America is broken into two parts, each comprising six chapters. Part 1 begins in the late fifteenth century when Indigenous peoples and Europeans first encountered each other. It goes on to examine how early America was shaped over the next few centuries primarily through violence between Spanish, English, Dutch, and French colonizers and the hundreds of Indigenous communities living in what became the United States. Some of the details that Blackhawk covers in these early chapters may feel familiar to readers as he details the way in which the Europeans' violence and diseases killed millions of Indigenous people while others were forced into labor or European dominion. However, another narrative also emerges from his research—one that upends the previously accepted idea that Indigenous peoples were helpless victims against the colonizers.

More specifically, Blackhawk explains that the Europeans' intention of taking over America was never a predetermined success. Many Indigenous communities succeeded in enacting myriad forms of resistance, whether it was turning different colonizers against each other or building prosperous trading economies with them. Some became marauders, while others ousted their invaders altogether, as in the Pueblo Revolt of 1680, which Blackhawk argues can be interpreted as the real first American Revolution. After four generations of occupation, the Pueblo people drove the Spanish out of their communities and ended their sovereignty over the region, which included taxes and labor drafts. One of the biggest testaments to the strength of Indigenous resistance that the book reveals is the fact that Indigenous peoples successfully maintained control over most the country's interior until the 1800s and were even able to achieve population regrowth after the initial wave of sixteenth-century death brought on by European violence and disease. With the twentieth century came more legal and political forms of resistance as Indigenous activists like Henry Roe Cloud succeeded in getting the federal government to pass the Indian Reorganization Act of 1934, part of a series of legislation commonly known as the Indian New Deal, which marked a reversal in US policy that allowed for Indigenous self-government, land rights, and cultural autonomy while also providing new economic opportunities.

Indeed, *The Rediscovery of America* succeeds in rewriting the long-held Eurocentric idea that Indigenous peoples were a hopeless match for the European colonizers. However, it also does not shy away from detailing the horrors that were inflicted upon them by White settlers. The book uses a great amount of detail to ensure that readers understand how hundreds of thousands of Indigenous people were enslaved, raped, and/or brutally murdered during the sixteenth and seventeenth centuries. During the Civil War, Indigenous peoples were hunted by federally funded militias and vigilantes with the blessing of President Abraham Lincoln while others were forced to serve in the Confederacy. In the late nineteenth century, the US government furthered its efforts to diminish Indigenous autonomy and culture through assimilation programs that took thousands of children away from their families and forced them into distant boarding schools, where they were forced to give up their attire and hairstyles, language, and religion. As the book's chronologically organized chapters reveal, these themes of injustice, betrayal, and suffering at the hands of White America continued throughout the twentieth century.

Despite the disturbing events that it discusses, *The Rediscovery of America* never expresses despair. This is thanks both to Blackhawk's academic style of writing and to when he chooses to end his coverage of American history. The book's final chapters focus on how the federal government of the 1950s and '60s enacted "termination" policies that sought to end the rights that Indigenous peoples had won with the Indian New Deal and strip them of their tribal citizenship, more or less leaving them taxpaying US citizens like any other. Thanks to the Indigenous activists of the Red Power movement of the 1960s and '70s, however, they were able to reclaim these rights. The book's depiction of this "termination to self-determination" journey proves to be a hopeful, empowering note to conclude on.

Ultimately, where *The Rediscovery of America* is most compelling is in its explanation of how American Indians directly and indirectly shaped some of the most formative events in the nation's history. For example, in 1763, a confederation of Indigenous peoples from different communities, organized by the Odawa leader Pontiac, sought to protect their rights over land in the Great Lakes region by launching a war against the British. After two years of fighting, the British concluded further conflict was too expensive and agreed to peace terms that prohibited any more of its subjects settling on Indigenous peoples' land. This angered the colonists and subsequently fortified the growing movement for American Independence. Another fascinating example the book uses to illustrate the Indigenous impact on modern America can be found in the 1787 creation of the Constitution. Rather than allow the thirteen states try manage "Indian affairs" on their own, as was the Articles of Confederation had, the Framers of the Constitution recognized that a more centralized source of power was necessary to maintain control over Indigenous peoples who had been making westward expansion difficult. This ultimately led to the formation of the US system of federal government.

Reception of *The Rediscovery of America* has been somewhat mixed, though mostly positive. Negative criticisms have primarily been directed at the book's ambitious scope, with some critics arguing that this caused problems with organization and the time Blackhawk spent on certain topics. Alan Taylor complained in his review for the *New York Times*, "In the early chapters Blackhawk's book lacks cohesion and flow, looping back and forth in time with much repetition as he considers the first three centuries after Columbus." The first few chapters of *The Rediscovery of America* do read less smoothly than the rest of the book, as Blackhawk attempts to provide truncated accounts of as many of the early encounters between different groups of Europeans and Indigenous peoples as possible. These chapters may also come across as weaker than the rest of the book because they cover more familiar history as the stories of conquistadors and the so-called Age of Discovery have been part of the curriculum of American history for some time. Even when told from a new perspective, this time in history does not come across as a revelation.

The rest of *The Rediscovery of America*, however, does feel revelatory in an exciting way. Many critics were quick to point this out, as evidenced by the unsigned writeup in *Kirkus Reviews*, which stated that the book provides "a well-reasoned challenge for future American historians to keep Native peoples on center stage." Similarly, the *Publishers Weekly* reviewer wrote, "Striking a masterful balance between the big picture and crystal-clear snapshots of key people and events, this is a vital new understanding of American history." It is perhaps no wonder then that *The Rediscovery of America* won the 2023 National Book Award for Nonfiction.

The Rediscovery of America may not be a light read, but it is a necessary and welcome one that will educate anyone interested in better understanding the United States and the Indigenous peoples who have intersected with it. Many readers will be pleased by both what the book adds to the existing literature on the subject and how it has paved the way for more books like it to come. This sentiment defined Kathleen DuVal's review for the *Wall Street Journal*, in which she wrote, "Like Pekka Hämäläinen's 'Indigenous Continent' (2022) and Daniel K. Richter's 'Facing East from Indian Country' (2001), the comprehensive coverage of 'The Rediscovery of America' makes it a useful book to read alongside or even instead of a textbook, or as a supplement for readers interested in broad overviews of U.S. history."

Author Biography

Dr. Ned Blackhawk (Te-Moak Tribe of Western Shoshone) is the Howard R. Lamar Professor of History and American Studies at Yale University. His book *Violence over the Land: Indians and Empires in the Early American West* (2006) earned him several prizes, including the Frederick Jackson Turner Prize from the Organization of American Historians.

Emily E. Turner

Review Sources

DuVal, Kathleen. "'The Rediscovery of America' Review: A History of Violence." Review of *The Rediscovery of America: Native Peoples and the Unmaking of U.S. History*, by Ned Blackhawk. *The Wall Street Journal*, 30 June 2023, www.wsj.com/articles/the-rediscovery-of-america-review-a-history-of-violence-81d014a7. Accessed 14 Nov. 2023.

Review of *The Rediscovery of America: Native Peoples and the Unmaking of U.S. History*, by Ned Blackhawk. *Kirkus Reviews*, 11 Jan. 2023, www.kirkusreviews.com/book-reviews/ned-blackhawk/the-rediscovery-of-america-native. Accessed 10 Nov. 2023.

Review of *The Rediscovery of America: Native Peoples and the Unmaking of U.S. History*, by Ned Blackhawk. *Publishers Weekly*, 27 Jan. 2023, www.publishersweekly.com/9780300244052. Accessed 10 Nov. 2023.

Taylor, Alan. "Retelling U.S. History with Native Americans at the Center." Review of *The Rediscovery of America: Native Peoples and the Unmaking of U.S. History*, by Ned Blackhawk. *The New York Times*, 23 Apr. 2023, www.nytimes.com/2023/04/23/books/review/the-rediscovery-of-america-ned-blackhawk.html. Accessed 10 Nov. 2023.

Remember Us

Author: Jacqueline Woodson (b. 1963)
Publisher: Nancy Paulsen Books (New York). 178 pp.
Type of work: Novel
Time: 1970s
Locale: New York City

Jacqueline Woodson's lyrical middle grade novel tells the story of a girl growing up in 1970s Brooklyn while dealing with a number of trying circumstances.

Principal characters
SAGE DURHAM, an adolescent girl living in Brooklyn, New York
SAGE'S MOTHER
FREDDY, Sage's friend
JACOB, a boy from Sage's neighborhood

American writer Jacqueline Woodson grew up in the Bushwick section of Brooklyn, New York, in the 1970s and 1980s, after moving there from South Carolina with her mother. Over the course of dozens of books, most written for children and young adults, she drew on her experiences growing up in that neighborhood, as well as other aspects of her life, to share her story with readers and highlight different aspects of the African American experience. For example, in her 2014 book *Brown Girl Dreaming*, written for younger readers, Woodson created one of her most autobiographical works yet. Written in poetic form, this memoir-in-verse tells the powerful story of the young Jacqueline as she deals with the different displacements in her life and attempts to figure out her place in a world that is not always welcoming. The book was a popular and commercial success, winning both the National Book Award and the Newbery Honor, among other prizes.

In *Remember Us* (2023), Woodson revisits the Brooklyn of her youth, narrowing her focus to tell the story of an adolescent girl over the course of a single summer. Although based in part on the author's own experiences, *Remember Us* is, unlike *Brown Girl Dreaming*, a novel, centered on the fictional character of Sage Durham. *Remember Us* is written in prose, also unlike *Brown Girl Dreaming*, but it is a lyrical prose that often takes on the feel of poetry. The book is narrated episodically, with each short chapter delivering another snippet of Sage's life, often a brief memory or reflection. Within each chapter, the paragraphs are typically short and contain little bursts of detail, rather than dense accumulations of information. The effect of this style is to mimic the process of remembrance, as the book is narrated by an older Sage as she looks back on this defining summer of her childhood. In memory, the past is often episodic and lyrical, and Woodson's style brings this impression powerfully to the page.

Remember Us takes place against a specific historical backdrop Woodson experienced firsthand. During the 1970s, the neighborhood of Bushwick, Brooklyn, then a largely impoverished area with a large Black community, experienced a wave of fires, some of which were attributable to arson. Because many houses were made of wood and many landlords did not properly attend to their properties, the effects of these fires could be devastating. Since many houses were connected to each other, if one were to catch on fire, then its neighbors would often go up in flames as well. The result was that many people in the neighborhood lost everything they owned and, in a number of cases, even their lives. In *Remember Us*, Sage reads a newspaper article about the fires which refers to their neighborhood as "the matchbox," something that Woodson, in her author's note at the end of the book, confirmed she recalled from her own childhood.

Jacqueline Woodson

Courtesy Penguin Random House; ©John D. and Catherine T. MacArthur Foundation

This background creates an atmosphere of fear that runs throughout the book. Sage sleeps with emergency supplies at the foot of her bed in case her house catches on fire and she needs to leave in the middle of the night. She hears sirens every day and lives with a constant low-level tension. Throughout the book, Sage's mother is saving up money, trying to raise enough to buy a house in a different neighborhood, one that is safer from fires. Complicating Sage's feelings about the fire epidemic is the fact that her beloved father was a firefighter who died on the job. She often reflects back on her father throughout the book.

Despite the difficult circumstances created by the fires, Woodson still presents Sage as just an ordinary child trying to enjoy her summer. Woodson captures this strange divide between constant threat and youthful fun expertly in one scene where she depicts the children of the neighborhood scavenging for "treasure" in the aftermath of a fire. As the kids look in the rubble for any salvageable thing to play with, Woodson shows the ways that children will always find ways to have innocent fun even in the midst of tragedy.

For Sage, though, things are not always so simple. On top of the loss of her father and the constant threat of fires, Sage is struggling to figure out her identity. A tomboy and basketball lover, she spends her days on the local courts, where she is a better player than the boys in neighborhood. All of her friends are boys, including Freddy, who moves to the neighborhood at the beginning of the book and quickly becomes Sage's best friend. She struggles with the sense that she is not a "real girl" according to the standards of that time and place and that she is not acting according to society's expectations.

These feelings are given external voice during a harrowing scene when, one day, Sage is shooting hoops by herself in the park when an older boy comes by. He begins threatening her, asking her what "kind of girl" she is because she is playing basketball and is not dressed like most girls. His threats escalate, with him threatening to punch her in the face and even insinuating that he might sexually assault her. In the end, he steals her basketball and walks off. Although Sage never sees him again, the incident has a profound effect on her—not only was her safety threatened, but his questioning of her gender identity echoed doubts that she had already had. After the incident, Sage stays at home and does not go to the basketball courts for several weeks.

Woodson's book is a searching portrait of youthful self-questioning, as well as a vivid portrayal of a neighborhood in a specific time and place. It is also a tender portrait of young friendship, as Woodson places the bond between Sage and her new friend Freddy at the heart of the book. The two children implicitly understand each other and both share similar family situations as well, as they are both only children. In addition, they share a sense of loss, Sage because of her father's death and Freddy because he had to leave his old neighborhood in the Bronx to move to Bushwick. "Sometimes Freddy's eyes got such a sadness around the edges that they looked like they'd gone back to someplace before," Sage narrates. "They became different eyes. Still blue-gray but . . . different." They share their feelings for each other in warm but subtle ways that Woodson expertly spells out with just a few words. Freddy reveals that his family moved to Bushwick to escape the Bronx's similar fire epidemic, but that his dad did not know about the fire problem in Bushwick before he planned the move. Upon learning this Sage moves closer to Freddy, touching his shoulder with hers. "I'm glad your dad didn't know about the other stuff," she says, affirming her friendship for Freddy, who simply nods and replies, "Yeah. Me too."

Befitting the title, Woodson's book is also very concerned with the theme of memory; the narrator, reflecting back from a later point in life, often muses on the question of remembrance. As Sage muses late in the book, "there are empty spaces in memory. Long days like blank pages." This book then, for both the narrator and Woodson, is an attempt to recapture memory, to piece together the events and feelings of an important summer in Sage's life. Even as a child Sage is aware of the power of memory as she pores over pictures of her father and tries to keep his memory alive. Woodson vividly evokes the way that memory is often a longing for the past and it is this understanding that imbues her book with an aching sense of melancholy. Although Sage's life as a child was difficult in many ways, it was also filled with moments of happiness, and to recall that long-gone happy moment is inherently bittersweet. Much of the power of Woodson's book comes from this evocation of the past, in the life of Sage, in the life of Woodson herself, and in the life of her neighborhood, which changed beyond recognition in the decades after Woodson grew up there. "I am wondering now," Woodson writes late in the book, "who else remembers that year of fires? Who else remembers the Bushwick we once lived in? Who else remembers us?" Woodson remembers and communicates these memories powerfully to her readers.

Remember Us received extremely positive reviews from critics. The reviewer for *Kirkus Reviews* captured the general consensus when they declared, "Woodson has crafted a beautifully lyrical narrative of change, healing, and growth," noting that "her ability to evoke time and place is masterful; every word feels perfectly chosen." Writing for the *New York Times*, David Barclay Moore echoed these sentiments. He was particularly impressed by how Woodson captures both the horrific background of the fire epidemic and the moving, "elegiac" story of Sage that Woodson "conjures" from the "ashes" of tragedy.

Writing for the *School Library Journal*, Shelley M. Diaz was even more effusive in her praise. Among the elements of the book Diaz especially appreciated were Woodson's economy of language, her ability to be wistful and lyrical without being overly nostalgic, and her handling of both Sage's narrative and the wider events in Bushwick at that time. She concluded by calling it a "truly masterly work." As Diaz pointed out, throughout *Remember Us*, Woodson deftly juggles numerous opposed elements to craft a perfectly balanced book. Combining the historical with the personal, the prosaic with the lyrical, the nostalgic with a dose of tough-minded reality, Woodson achieves a rich, powerful, coming-of-age story that takes a hard look back at a transformative and challenging era in her community's history.

Author Biography
Jacqueline Woodson authored dozens of children's and young adult books, as well as several books for adults. She received numerous awards for her work, including a Guggenheim Fellowship and a MacArthur Fellowship. Her 2014 novel *Brown Girl Dreaming* won the National Book Award.

Andrew Schenker

Review Sources
Diaz, Shelley M. Review of *Remember Us*, by Jacqueline Woodson. *School Library Journal*, 1 Aug. 2023, www.slj.com/review/remember-us. Accessed 30 Oct. 2023.
Moore, David Barclay. "Jacqueline Woodson and Amber McBride Look Backward to Look Forward." Review of *Remember Us*, by Jacqueline Woodson, and *Gone Wolf*, by Amber McBride. *The New York Times*, 18 Oct. 2023, www.nytimes.com/2023/10/18/books/review/jacqueline-woodson-remember-us-amber-mcbride-gone-wolf.html. Accessed 30 Oct. 2023.
Review of *Remember Us*, by Jacqueline Woodson. *Kirkus Reviews*, 25 July 2023, www.kirkusreviews.com/book-reviews/jacqueline-woodson/remember-us/. Accessed 30 Oct. 2023.
Review of *Remember Us*, by Jacqueline Woodson. *Publishers Weekly*, 10 Aug. 2023, www.publishersweekly.com/978-0-399-54546-7. Accessed 20 Dec. 2023.

Roaming

Authors: Jillian Tamaki (b. ca. 1980) and Mariko Tamaki (b. 1975)
Publisher: Drawn and Quarterly (Montreal, Quebec). 444 pp.
Type of work: Graphic novel
Time: March 2009
Locale: New York, New York

Cousins Jillian Tamaki and Mariko Tamaki bring to brilliant life an event that touches most young peoples' lives: traveling with friends for the first time. Set in New York City in 2009, Roaming *follows the adventures of childhood friends Dani and Zoe, and Dani's new college friend Fiona and explores how relationships shift and evolve with age.*

Principal characters

DANI, a straightlaced first-year college art student
ZOE, her nerdy best friend, an outgoing, androgynous first-year neuroscience student
FIONA, her new friend from college, a pompous art student

Taking a first trip with friends as a young adult can be a right-of-passage. Whether that trip is by car (the classic road trip), by plane, or by train, it is common for those involved to discover new things about themselves but, more complicatedly, about their travel companions and new friendships. Cousins Jillian Tamaki and Mariko Tamaki—who previously collaborated on two award-winning young-adult graphic novels—take on that formative trip in their first collaboration for adults, *Roaming*. Turning a fresh eye on a well-known story line, the cousins enlist the best of their form to make both characters and location come alive.

Roaming is an immersive experience, opening in arrivals at Newark airport, where Zoe is waiting for her childhood friend Dani to arrive. Dani soon appears along with her new friend Fiona. The trio—all traveling from Canada, where they raised and currently attend college—have planned five action-filled days in New York City, a location Dani and Zoe have dreamt of visiting since they were children. The story plays out linearly, following the trio as they find their hostel, use fake IDs to buy drinks in an average New York City pub, eat huge slices of pizza for the first time, and experience the emotional turmoil that frequently accompanies travel.

As Dani, Zoe, and Fiona begin to find a rhythm to their time in the city, friendship alliances are tested. Zoe, who has adopted an androgynous look since going to college, has caught Fiona's attention, and Fiona wastes no time cuddling up to her new love interest. Meanwhile, Dani tries to keep her trip on track, striving to see the tourist sites

Jillian Tamaki

she has always dreamt of: the Metropolitan Museum of Art, the Statue of Liberty, Ground Zero, Central Park, the Brooklyn Bridge, and Coney Island. Fiona, who has fashioned herself as an in-the-know, been-there-done-that type early on the story, sneers at many of Dani's ideas, throwing off anything she deems too touristy and often falling back on the fact that her brother lives in Brooklyn. By story's end, the trio will deal with fractured expectations, hurt feelings, and the exhilaration that comes with experiencing New York City for the first time as a young person.

What is most interesting and exciting about *Roaming* is its storytellers' ability to perfectly convey the complexities of friendship while always keeping their vacation destination in the forefront of the action. Dani's and Zoe's characters are immediately recognizable to those readers who maintained childhood friendships upon entering college. For example, when Dani and Zoe first reunite in the Newark airport terminal, the world appears to freeze around them as they scream and hug, shouting each other's names upon first sighting. Their anticipation of the meeting is perfectly executed through panels that show Zoe patiently watching the escalator she expects Dani to come down. Four panels in all are spent allowing Zoe to scan the escalator, until finally the reader is introduced to Dani, unaware that her friend is watching her come down. These moments of reality that most readers would be able to relate provide a slower, and deeper, way to experience the story. The longtime friends waste no time falling back into comfortable company, as Dani takes in Zoe's new hairstyle—Zoe's college roommate has shaved her head, giving her a brand-new appearance and presence—but she quickly acknowledges what a bold, good look this is for her.

In this first scene, Fiona is also established as the cool outsider. She coos that, despite never having met Zoe before, she, too, thinks the new haircut is great. The three move from the airport terminal to the train that will take them to Manhattan's Penn Station. During the ride, Fiona makes quips whenever Dani says something Fiona believes to be too obvious and, when Zoe askes about her work as an artist, says she works in fiber but might switch to video. These off-hand comments and reserved delivery, combined with her blond curls and over-the-top attire, are a stark contrast to Dani, who is dressed in plain overalls and a peacoat.

Roaming's color palette is likewise expertly used. The Tamakis are known for creating poignant worlds with minimal color palates in their work, and this offering is no different. (Jillian is responsible for the artwork here, while both collaborated on the script.) Sticking closely to periwinkle, beigey peach, and black, the illustrations are vivid without being overwhelming. The minimalist approach equally allows the story

Mariko Tamaki

to unfold, as well as the hectic nature of the city, with what seems like little effort. Dark black lines appear bolder against the pastel colors and frequently stand in for the bustle of the city where words would not suffice. This works well as the trio visits landmarks around the city, but also as they pass the more ambient sights, such as store fronts and people enjoying time in the park. Splashes of color fill in the façades, giving everything a dreamlike quality, as if the reader can already feel the nostalgia these characters might someday have for this vacation early in their lives. The minimalist approach also lends itself well to a story that is fast paced in many ways, as the trio experience ups and down over the course of their visit. Each day is separated by a two-page spread that relates to their trip in some fashion. For example, Day 1 features a plane crossing the pages in the sky, while Day 5 features soft ocean waves presaging a visit to Coney Island.

The climax of the story involves a break between Dani and Zoe, heavily involving Fiona, in which each character is forced to question who she really is and how she wants to present herself as a friend. During this sequence, Dani takes herself on a solo day around the city to many of the tourist sites she had missed during the earlier part of the week. When she and Zoe reunite, the Tamakis take the opportunity to show us the pair in an earlier iteration of themselves, albeit still living in some sort of imagined present, thus providing important insight into their relationship and who they used to be to each other. It is a bittersweet moment in which each character begins to understand that no matter how much they might mean to each other, change is inevitable and they will face difficult situations like this in the future—maybe even between themselves.

As *Roaming* winds down to its quiet conclusion, each of the three characters have emerged changed, some bonds deepened and some broken following the tests they have been through. As the bustle of the city begins to fade into the background, the reader can feel the sudden new future these young characters have found themselves in and will likely be unsurprised by how much can happen to three young adults in five days' time.

Roaming was widely hailed by critics. Ahead of the book's publication, *Publishers Weekly*'s anonymous reviewer especially applauded its dialogue, stating, "For all the big emotions laid bare in the narrative, and all its wonderfully rendered teenage dialogue riddled with pseudo-profundities, the script (by Mariko and Jillian) plays out subtle and naturalistically spare. Readers, especially ones who've already come of age, will recognize the life-changing shifts and signals even when the characters don't." The outlet gave the book a starred review, as did *Library Journal*, whose reviewer Tom

Batten stated, "Rather than being bogged down in pensive navel-gazing or melodrama, the novel emphasizes the exhilaration of youth; how exhilarating it is to be young, to be in love, to explore new places and aspects of yourself, and to experience each emotion, good or bad, so very intensely." For *NPR*, reviewer Julie Depenbrock noted that *Roaming*, which was nominated for a GLAAD Media Award, falls into the tradition of other popular LGBTQ graphic novels, including Alison Bechdel's *Fun Home*, Maia Kobabe's *Gender Queer*, and Alice Oseman's *Heartstopper*, writing, "There's a magic to *Roaming*. And it's not just in the gorgeous illustrations, but the story itself." Depenbrock appreciated how the work foregrounds the experiences of Asian-descended and LGBTQ youths, "experimenting with love, sex, identity and ambition."

Guardian critic Rachel Cooke was particularly interested in the way illustrator Jillian Tamaki portrayed New York as a character in the story. Cooke opined, "Somehow, Tamaki captures the misery *and* the magic, her strips full of movement and life even as her colours bring to mind those of old Polaroids. Here in pale pink and grey blue is the spring break we've all had at least once: we felt big, we felt small, we lived on cheap noodles and adrenaline."

Author Biography

Cartoonist and illustrator Jillian Tamaki is the author of six prior graphic novels, including *SuperMutant Magic Academy* (2015) and *Boundless* (2017), each recipients of the prestigious Eisner Award. She has also authored and illustrated several picture books. With her cousin Mariko Tamaki, she previously collaborated on the YA graphic novels *Skim* (2008) and *This One Summer* (2014). For the latter, they won the Governor General's Award, Printz Honors, and Caldecott Honors, in addition to the Eisner Award for Best Graphic Album—New.

Playwright, author, and comic-book writer Mariko Tamaki also created the acclaimed young-adult (YA) graphic novel *Laura Dean Keeps Breaking Up with Me* (2019) with Rosemary Valero-O'Connell. She has received the Eisner Award for Best Writer, Printz Honors, an Ignatz Award, and GLAAD Media Awards. She curates Surely Books, an LGBTQIA imprint with Abrams.

Melynda Fuller

Review Sources

Cooke, Rachel. "*Roaming* by Jillian Tamaki and Mariko Tamaki Review—a Blissful Ode to Female Friendship and New York." *The Guardian*, 18 Sept. 2023, www.theguardian.com/books/2023/sep/18/roaming-by-jillian-tamaki-and-mariko-tamaki-review-a-blissful-ode-to-female-friendship-and-new-york. Accessed 18 Jan. 2024.

Depenbrock, Julie. "Love, Identity and Ambition Take Center Stage in *Roaming*." Review of *Roaming*, by Jillian Tamaki and Mariko Tamaki. *NPR*, 18 Sept. 2023, www.npr.org/2023/09/18/1200101308/lbook-review-jillian-tamaki-mariko-tamaki-graphic-novel-roaming. Accessed 18 Jan. 2024.

Review of *Roaming*, by Jillian Tamaki and Mariko Tamaki. *Kirkus Reviews*, 12 Sept. 2023, www.kirkusreviews.com/book-reviews/jillian-tamaki/roaming. Accessed 18 Jan. 2024.

Review of *Roaming*, by Jillian Tamaki and Mariko Tamaki. *Library Journal*, www.libraryjournal.com/review/roaming-1798323. Accessed 18 Jan. 2024.

Review of *Roaming*, by Jillian Tamaki and Mariko Tamaki. *Publishers Weekly*, www.publishersweekly.com/9781770464339. Accessed 18 Jan. 2024.

Velentzas, Irene. Review of *Roaming*, by Jillian Tamaki and Mariko Tamaki. *The Comics Journal*, 12 Sept. 2023, www.tcj.com/reviews/roaming. Accessed 18 Jan. 2024.

Roman Stories

Author: Jhumpa Lahiri (b. 1967)
First published: *Racconti romani*, 2022, in Italy
Translated from the Italian by Jhumpa Lahiri and Todd Portnowitz
Publisher: Knopf (New York). 224 pp.
Type of work: Short fiction
Time: Present day
Locales: Rome, Italy; United States

Jhumpa Lahiri's Roman Stories *is a return to the writer's celebrated form: the short story. Set in the Eternal City, the stories that make up this collection explore many paths of life, including those of locals, expats, immigrants, and tourists. The rich backdrop of Rome lends each story an additional element of drama and atmosphere.*

In 2012, Bengali American writer Jhumpa Lahiri moved her family to Rome so that she could immerse herself in the Italian language, giving up speaking and reading in English for many years. In 2015 she announced that she had shifted to writing only in Italian and released a book about her linguistic journey, which was subsequently translated to English as *In Other Words* (2016). Her first novel in Italian followed in 2018, and Lahiri released her own English translation of that work as *Whereabouts* in 2021. Lahiri is perhaps best known for short fiction, however, and her first story collection since her shift to Italian was originally published in 2022 as *Racconti romani*. The English version, *Roman Stories*, features six stories translated by Lahiri herself and three translated by Todd Portnowitz, all of which, as the title suggests, focus on characters in and around the author's adopted home city.

Like many of Lahiri's other works, *Roman Stories* is concerned with issues of both belonging and alienation. Its characters are lonely, sometimes mourning, often longing for a different reality, and frequently revisiting the past. Several of the collection's narrators come from unnamed cultures simply described as being located "on the other side of the world." Others look with bewilderment at the city in which they were born and raised, wondering where they fit into it in adulthood, but unable to imagine a life elsewhere. The common thread is that each of the collection's narrators have been ensnared by Rome, and not always unhappily.

Roman Stories is prefaced with quotes from the Ancient Roman writers Livy and Ovid, each reflecting a city in seemingly constant upheaval, with Ovid speaking of the gates of Janus lying unblocked and Livy writing of a city growing with hope for the future. The collection is divided into three sections. Parts 1 and 3 include four stories

Jhumpa Lahiri

each. Part 2's "The Steps" acts as a centerpiece, a forty-plus-page compilation of vignettes, with six numbered sections titled "The Mother," "The Widow," "The Expat Wife," "The Girl," "Two Brothers," and "The Screenwriter." In many ways, part 2 provides a primer on the characters who show up in the collection's other stories, many also unnamed and identifiable only in societal labels, personality, and physical characteristics.

The opening story, "The Boundary," sets up one of the major juxtapositions of the collection: wealthy city-dwellers versus struggling immigrants. A teenage girl whose family is from another part of the world is living on an estate outside Rome where she and her parents take care of the farm of a wealthy landowner who lives abroad. Her family came to the estate from the city after they were shaken by a tragic incident in which her father, a flower seller, was the target of a racist attack. Since then, she has been taking care of visiting families who rent the farmhouse on the estate for a week or two during the summer. The story is told from the teenager's perspective as she watches the family of four who have taken over the house for the week. She watches the husband and two children leave for the beach—after asking her in detail how to get there—while the mother lounges outside in a bathing suit, writing pensively in a journal. She observes the two children collect crickets and keep them as pets in a jar, feeding them tomatoes before the insects die the next day. She studies the family's friends who come from the city for an evening to celebrate a birthday, with the children bringing her and her father a slice of the cake. The stark disparity between the vacationing renters and the lot of the protagonist and her family haunts the rest of the collection.

Two stories appearing the third part of the collection particularly echo this feeling. "The Delivery" and "Notes" each feature women from unnamed faraway countries. The reader learns that they and their families do not look like the people they care for. Each story is set in motion by a traumatic event. In "The Delivery," a young woman works for the *signora*, a wealthy architect who lives in Rome but is often out of town. While walking to pick up a package for the *signora* one day, the young woman is shot with an air pistol by two boys on a motorbike. The story alternates between the experiences of the young woman and one of the boys who was involved.

Similarly, "Notes" features a "widow from another continent" who works at a tailor's shop and lives alone after her twin sons, both emergency medical technicians, have moved away. To make some extra money and spend more of her time away from home she begins to work at the elementary school her sons attended years before. While there, she begins to receive sinister messages from an unknown source. Whoever the culprit is, they clearly do not want her at the school and she must deal with feelings of rejection, despair, and anger. A curious childhood habit creeps back in as she processes her experiences, taking her story full circle. Like the narrator of "The Boundary," the women in "The Delivery" and "Notes" remain nameless and relatively faceless, but the pressure of their world is carried through in Lahiri's sober, clear prose. With the actions of those around them laid bare in crisp writing, there is nowhere for the intent behind those actions to hide.

Lahiri showcases similar deft crispness in other stories. Take, for example, "P's Parties," in which a middle-aged writer finds himself smitten with an unknown woman after they share a brief conversation at one of the titular parties. Like so many of Lahiri's characters, this man is dealing with a feeling of profound loneliness, in this case following the departure of his son to the US. The man becomes obsessed with seeing this woman again, often staring and embarrassing himself when he encounters her. A final awkward moment between the two upends the stability of his life and reminds the reader of the embarrassment many people experience in moments of desperation.

A lengthy marriage and memories of first love feature in "The Procession," a story about a married couple who travel to Rome for a six-week holiday to celebrate the fiftieth birthday of the wife, a biology professor who had spent time in the city when she was younger. Her husband, a law professor, has never been to Rome, and she is eager to bring him to the titular Procession of the Virgin, which she remembers fondly. Over the course of the story, Lahiri renders the tenderness and comfortable familiarity of their marriage as well as their grief over a shared loss. Similarly, a decades-long marriage, memory, love, and grief are also the focus of the collection's finale, "Dante Alighieri." That story follows a middle-aged expat from the US who is dealing with her fading marriage to a man she still loves while reliving a painful memory of first love.

The substantial overlap in theme and characterization across the collection might seem to risk the stories becoming repetitious, but in the hands of Lahiri the effect is instead to remind the reader of the universal emotions that connect everyone, whether joy or grief, love or loneliness. At the same time, she does not strive for simple summations of the human condition, but instead is willing to look at the difficult parts of life—such as violence against those who are struggling to build a better world for themselves, or the loss of children and spouses—and turn those pieces into something powerful. The shared setting of Rome, a place that is at once ancient and modern, traditional and cosmopolitan, also reinforces these themes. While it is sometimes difficult to find a foothold in the city's majesty, Lahiri does a great job of describing the contemporary atmosphere. Yet her deep understanding of her characters and the lives they have been thrown into would arguably make for compelling reading no matter the setting.

Roman Stories was widely hailed by critics, earning starred reviews in *Publishers Weekly* and *Kirkus Reviews* and a place on best book of the year list from several other outlets. The anonymous reviewer for *Publishers Weekly* wrote of the collection, "Throughout, Lahiri's luminous prose captures a side of Rome often ignored. . . . These unembroidered yet potent stories shine." The critic for *Kirkus Reviews* offered similar praise, stating, "Filled with intelligence and sorrow, these sharply drawn glimpses of Roman lives create an impressively unified effect." In a review for the *New York Times*, Lily Meyer called the work "melancholy yet electric." Meyer also commended Lahiri's collaboration with her co-translator, writing, "The fluid transitions between Lahiri's and Portnowitz's translations elevate *Roman Stories* from a grouping of individual tales to a deeply moving whole. By putting many kinds of foreignness together, Lahiri shows that they all belong." Yagnishsing Dawoor, writing for the *Guardian*, noted Lahiri's representation of immigrants and the violence inflicted upon them in Rome. "Lahiri has never been particularly political as a writer. . . . Yet across the pages of this book one senses the quiet fury of an author who, appalled and disheartened by the situation of immigrants in Italy, finally seems to have wed her pen and her politics." The collection was also well-received by critics at *Vogue*, the *Wall Street Journal*, and other publications.

Author Biography
Acclaimed author and translator Jhumpa Lahiri is perhaps best known for *The Interpreter of Maladies*, which won the 2000 Pulitzer Prize for Fiction; *The Namesake* (2003), a New York Times Notable Book; the New York Times Best Seller *Unaccustomed Earth* (2008); and *The Lowland* (2013), which was was shortlisted for the Man Booker Prize and the National Book Award for Fiction. She received a 2002 Guggenheim Fellowship, among many other honors.

Todd Portnowitz is an award-winning poet, essayist, and translator. His prior prose translations include *Long Live Latin* (2019), by Nicola Gardini; *The Greatest Invention* (2022), by Silvia Ferrara; and *In Search of Amrit Kaur* (2023), by Livia Manera Sambuy. He has also translated the poetry collections *Midnight in Spoleto* (2018), by Paolo Valesio; *Go Tell It to the Emperor: The Selected Poems of Pierluigi Cappello* (2019); and *Methods* (2023), by Lorenzo Carlucci.

Melynda Fuller

Review Sources
Dawoor, Yagnishsing. "*Roman Stories* by Jhumpa Lahiri Review – Outsiders in Italy." *The Guardian*, 19 Oct. 2023, www.theguardian.com/books/2023/oct/19/roman-stories-by-jhumpa-lahiri-review-outsiders-in-italy. Accessed 1 Feb. 2024.

McAlpin, Heller. "In Jhumpa Lahiri's *Roman Stories*, Many Characters Are Caught between Two Worlds." Review of *Roman Stories*, by Jhumpa Lahiri. *NPR*, 10 Oct. 2023, www.npr.org/2023/10/10/1204820880/jhumpa-lahiri-book-short-stories-roman-stories. Accessed 1 Feb. 2024.

Meyer, Lily. "Jhumpa Lahiri Translates the Varieties of Strangeness." Review of *Roman Stories*, by Jhumpa Lahiri. *The New York Times*, 6 Oct. 2023, www.nytimes.com/2023/10/06/books/review/jhumpa-lahiri-roman-stories.html. Accessed 1 Feb. 2024.

Mujumdar, Vika. "Jhumpa Lahiri's *Roman Stories*." Review of *Roman Stories*, by Jhumpa Lahiri. *The Brooklyn Rail*, 27 Sept. 2023, brooklynrail.org/2023/10/books/Jhumpa-Lahiris-Roman-Stories. Accessed 1 Feb. 2024.

Review of *Roman Stories*, by Jhumpa Lahiri. *Kirkus Reviews*, 13 July 2023, www.kirkusreviews.com/book-reviews/jhumpa-lahiri/roman-stories/. Accessed 1 Feb. 2024.

Review of *Roman Stories*, by Jhumpa Lahiri. *Publishers Weekly*, 28 July 2023, www.publishersweekly.com/9780593536322. Accessed 1 Feb. 2024.

Shankar, Avantika. "Jhumpa Lahiri's *Roman Stories* Is a Poetic Illustration of City Life in All Its Colors." Review of *Roman Stories*, by Jhumpa Lahiri. *Vogue*, 15 Oct. 2023, www.vogue.com/article/jhumpa-lahiri-roman-stories-review. Accessed 1 Feb. 2024.

Rough Sleepers
Dr. Jim O'Connell's Urgent Mission to Bring Healing to Homeless People

Author: Tracy Kidder (b. 1945)
Publisher: Random House (New York). 320 pp.
Type of work: Biography, medicine
Time: 1985–2022
Locale: Boston

Rough Sleepers *explores the storied career of Dr. Jim O'Connell, a Harvard Medical School graduate who founded Boston Health Care for the Homeless and led the program for almost forty years. Paired with the history of O'Connell's career, Tracy Kidder presents vivid descriptions of unhoused patients, giving the reader intimate and unromanticized portraits of these complex individuals and their life stories.*

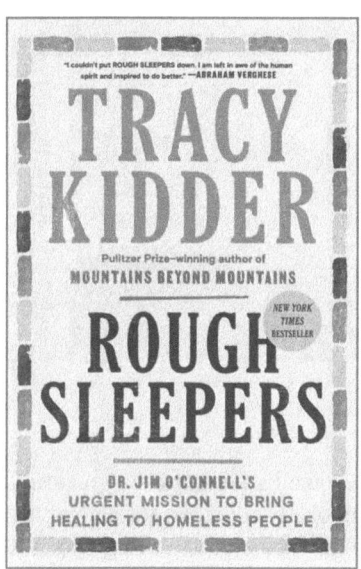

Courtesy Penguin Random House

Principal personages

JAMES "JIM" O'CONNELL, a.k.a. Dr. Jim, a doctor and founder of Boston's Health Care for the Homeless Program
ANTHONY "TONY" COLUMBO, a member of the unhoused community who forges a close relationship with him
BARBARA MCINNIS, one of his early mentors, a nurse at Boston's Pine Street clinic
DAVID, an unhoused former college professor under his care
HARRISON, an unhoused former college professor under his care

Tracy Kidder is a renowned Pulitzer Prize–winning writer of nonfiction. In previous books, he has tackled subjects that often have a humanitarian bent, such as *Mountains Beyond Mountains* (2003), about an American physician in Haiti, and *Strength in What Remains* (2009), about the Burundian refugee crisis. In *Rough Sleepers: Dr. Jim O'Connell's Urgent Mission to Bring Healing to Homeless People* (2023), Kidder explores the unhoused population through the lens of Dr. Jim O'Connell and the program he created in Boston in the mid-1980s. While parallels may be drawn between *Rough Sleepers* and Kidder's earlier works, reviewers noted that Kidder's later book stands alone, as O'Connell's life story and contributions lend *Rough Sleepers* its own unique character.

In 1985, Dr. Jim O'Connell was preparing to complete his medical residency at Massachusetts General Hospital in Boston with plans to head to a prestigious fellowship in oncology at Memorial Sloan Kettering Hospital in New York City. But, Tom

Tracy Kidder

Durant and John Potts, esteemed leaders and administrators at Mass General, asked him to set those goals aside for a year to help the hospital launch a new program called Health Care for the Homeless. One year rolled into two and, nearly four decades later, *Rough Sleepers* profiles O'Connell still hard at work at the helm of the Boston Health Care for the Homeless Program (a.k.a. "The Program"). The book chronicles the history of The Program, focusing on O'Connell in terms of professional leadership, his learned approach to practicing disaster medicine, and the qualities of his personality and professionalism that led him to develop such success with and passionate commitment to The Program. Interwoven with the discussion of O'Connell's life's work, Kidder introduces sensitive and thought-provoking profiles of select patients of O'Connell's. Perhaps the greatest amount of detail is given to Anthony "Tony" Columbo, a pseudonym for a complex and memorable patient treated by O'Connell for several of the years during which Kidder was shadowing the doctor for his research. The juxtaposition of O'Connell's career alongside portraits of his patients' lives allows Kidder to avoid solely presenting a heroic medical professional as a savior figure. *Rough Sleepers* is, in this way, an interwoven biography of a hard-working and highly impactful medical professional as well as an exploration of the motivation he found in the complex challenges and personalities of his patients over a career spanning four decades. Moreover, beyond these individual stories, *Rough Sleepers* provides a probing look into the complexities of corporate medicine, the failures of the social safety net in the United States, and the very real challenges of reducing the footprint of homelessness in cities across the country.

The primary focus of *Rough Sleepers* is on the exemplary program O'Connell has built. Kidder offers information about the history and development of The Program, beginning at its inception. O'Connell's early career was shaped by the outbreak of the AIDS epidemic, which ran rampant through the homeless community, while a portion of the research for the book was conducted during the COVID-19 pandemic beginning in 2020. In some ways, those watershed moments in public health can be seen as bookends to O'Connell's career. Although there is substantial information in *Rough Sleepers* about the full scope of O'Connell's career with The Program, Kidder's specific focus is on the years after he meets O'Connell in 2014. During this final phase of his career, O'Connell has opted to somewhat reduce his footprint, focusing his work on "The Street Team," a program that uses a medical support van and a fixed schedule of drop-in clinics to work with the most challenging portion of the unhoused population—those individuals who "stayed outside year-round" and "died at about ten times the normal rate" of the state's general adult population.

Throughout *Rough Sleepers*, then, the reader becomes acquainted with the complexities of treating and working with people who are perhaps the most difficult patients in the entire medical system. Indeed, numerous "rough sleeping" patients conceal facts from their medical team, including the realities of their various substance addictions. Many of these patients have had numerous dehumanizing and unpleasant encounters with the medical system, leading them to lose their trust in doctors and most other health professionals. Such patients simply cannot be successfully treated within a medical system that does not understand their backgrounds nor seek to work with the realities of their many physical and psychological challenges. O'Connell's framework offers an alternative approach to working with unhoused populations. Some have compared his work to the task of Sisyphus, the mythical Greek king forced to repeatedly push a boulder up a hill. Most unhoused patients will not, in fact, be successfully "treated" and obtain a long and healthy life in a stable home. Instead, the challenges recur, and the failures are many. However, there is strong evidence that the Street Team brings better prognoses and much greater dignity to its patients, offering a repeatable model for other contexts.

If O'Connell is a remarkable person, his patients are hauntingly memorable. *Rough Sleepers* opens with a poem titled "I Am," written by an unhoused US Army veteran and patient of the Street Team named Michael Frada. Frada's words ask the reader to recognize his complexity, citing multiple, contradictory aspects of his persona. The poem concludes by invoking his humanity: "If we should meet for a moment on my life's journey / Smile at me, talk to me, or simply be still / And know that I am." O'Connell's approach toward his patients is to forego judgment and to serve them with a sense of caring humanity. Kidder seems to ask the reader to take the same approach. Throughout the book, the stories of numerous patients are shared, including some of deceased patients who are recalled from the vivid memory of O'Connell. Among these, the stories of David and Harrison paint a particularly remarkable picture. Both claimed to be former college professors, and O'Connell, himself a former student of philosophy, recalls periodic occasions on which he would take the two individuals out for a meal to listen to their fascinating intellectual debates.

The central case study of *Rough Sleepers*, though, is that of Tony Columbo. Convicted at a young age of sexual assault, Columbo is unable to receive housing because of his criminal history. He suffers from substance abuse and from the post-traumatic stress and psychological damage of abuses he experienced as a child. He is also an incredibly resourceful and generally kind member of Boston's unhoused community. He protects women living on the street, defends various weak and vulnerable people in his community, and, during his periods off the street, even serves as an informal house manager for McInnis House, a recovery home associated with The Program. In one touching narrative, Kidder and O'Connell accompany Tony on his first (and, presumably, only) visit to the Boston Museum of Fine Arts, where he exhibits a deep connection with art, which he nonchalantly ties to his own Italian heritage. Tony's life is a tragedy, and his story can hardly be seen as an unmitigated medical success. Yet the recounting of Tony's life in the book represents a powerful acknowledgment of the value of The Program and its success in creating a sense of shared humanity and purpose for the unhoused community, often against great odds, including a broken system of social safety nets and medical care.

Kidder's book is not primarily directed at social change, but, nevertheless, the author does not shy away from critiques of corporate medicine and government policies that worsen the situation of homelessness in the United States. The presidency of Ronald Reagan is highlighted as a triggering force in the rise of homelessness in the United States. Similarly, the presidency of Donald Trump, which took place during Kidder's research, caused the specter of financial crisis, and threat of closure, for The Program. Mostly, though, the critiques are not aligned with one political party but focus instead on highlighting the issues in medical education and in policy approach to homelessness. One area of particular interest is the book's discussion of the solution of providing housing to the unhoused population, which yields mixed results. As O'Connell's years of data make clear, housing alone is not the solution. A rigorous support structure, many layers of training, and a robust social network are all necessary components to successfully move an individual from "rough sleeping" to regular housing. Further, the layers of expertise and efforts of the Street Team lay bare how impossible it is for an unhoused individual to navigate the complexities of the system on their own. The book makes clear that a better, more navigable, and supportive system will be the only viable route for reducing homelessness in American cities.

Reviews of *Rough Sleepers* tended to focus largely on two aspects of the book— its position within Kidder's oeuvre and the remarkable, even heroic, character of its protagonist. *Washington Post* critic Richard Just explained that a "pragmatic call to action is a through-line connecting much of Kidder's writing" and advised that readers who "might be tempted to skip this book based on the surface similarities" between it and Kidder's previous works, in particular *Mountains Beyond Mountains*, which also focuses on a heroic medical figure, would be making a mistake. Chris Hewitt expanded on the description of O'Connell in his review for the *Star Tribune*, writing that "the picture that emerges over the course of the absorbing, inspiring 'Rough Sleepers' is that O'Connell is not only one of the good guys but a good guy who is vigorous, self-critical and even funny." Some critics found fault with Kidder's reporting, noting that viewing the issue of the unhoused population from Dr. O'Connell's perspective can result in too big of a distance between the reader and those living on the streets. In his review for the *New York Times*, Wes Enzinna, referring to O'Connell's patient Tony, remarked that Kidder "never establishes the rapport with Tony that might enable him to probe deeply into key aspects of his experience." Even so, the figure of Dr. O'Connell shines bright, and, as Just remarked, "The one constant is that O'Connell offers treatment—and abundant kindness" to all of his homeless patients.

Author Biography

Tracy Kidder is the award-winning author of several books, including *The Soul of a New Machine* (1981), *Among Schoolchildren* (1989), *Home Town* (1999), *Mountains Beyond Mountains* (2003), and *Strength in What Remains* (2009). He has been the recipient of numerous literary awards, including the Pulitzer Prize (1982) and the National Book Award (1982).

Julia A. Sienkewicz, PhD

Review Sources

Enzinna, Wes. "Boston's 'Rough Sleepers' and the Doctor Who Treats Them." Review of *Rough Sleepers: Dr. Jim O'Connell's Urgent Mission to Bring Healing to Homeless People*, by Tracy Kidder. *The New York Times*, 16 Jan. 2023, www.nytimes.com/2023/01/16/books/review/rough-sleepers-tracy-kidder.html. Accessed 16 Oct. 2023.

Hewitt, Chris. Review of *Rough Sleepers: Dr. Jim O'Connell's Urgent Mission to Bring Healing to Homeless People*, by Tracy Kidder. *Star Tribune*, 13 Jan. 2023, www.startribune.com/review-rough-sleepers-by-tracy-kidder/600243198/. Accessed 16 Oct. 2023.

Just, Richard. "'Rough Sleepers' Follows a Doctor Devoted to the Homeless." Review of *Rough Sleepers: Dr. Jim O'Connell's Urgent Mission to Bring Healing to Homeless People*, by Tracy Kidder. *The Washington Post*, 15 Feb. 2023, www.washingtonpost.com/books/2023/02/15/rough-sleepers-tracy-kidder/. Accessed 16 Oct. 2023.

McAlpin, Heather. "'Just Give Love': One Man's Tireless Care for Homeless People." Review of *Rough Sleepers: Dr. Jim O'Connell's Urgent Mission to Bring Healing to Homeless People*, by Tracy Kidder. *The Christian Science Monitor*, 16 Jan. 2023, www.csmonitor.com/Books/Book-Reviews/2023/0116/Just-give-love-One-man-s-tireless-care-for-homeless-people. Accessed 16 Oct. 2023.

Smith, Erika D. "Column: It Shouldn't Take a Saint to Ease Homelessness. But Dr. Jim Tries in 'Rough Sleepers.'" Review of *Rough Sleepers: Dr. Jim O'Connell's Urgent Mission to Bring Healing to Homeless People*, by Tracy Kidder. *Los Angeles Times*, 11 Jan. 2023, www.latimes.com/entertainment-arts/books/story/2023-01-11/column-tracy-kidder-author-rough-sleepers-homelessness. Accessed 16 Oct. 2023.

Saints of the Household

Author: Ari Tison (b. 1995)
Publisher: Farrar, Straus and Giroux (New York). 320 pp.
Type of work: Novel
Time: Present
Locale: Minnesota

Saints of the Household *is a young adult novel about two teenaged brothers born of a Bribri mother and a father of Nordic descent. Told in alternating voices, the book follows the two as they navigate life in a small Minnesota town in the aftermath of a violent incident.*

Principal characters
JAY, a Bribri American teen
MAX, his brother, a gifted artist
NICOLE, their cousin
LUCA, their high school's star soccer player
FERNANDO, their maternal grandfather
MELODY, Max's love interest

In the earlier years of her career, Ari Tison was known predominantly for her poetry (which notably includes a piece in *Poetry* magazine's first-ever issue for children,) and for her short fiction, anthologized in such collections as *Our Shadows Have Claws*, a 2022 volume drawn from Latin American mythology. In those works, she introduced readers to the culture of the Bribri people, one of eight Indigenous Peoples in Costa Rica who live in largely matrilineal, agricultural-based communities in the country's Talamanca region.

The publication of her debut young adult novel, *Saints of the Household* (2023), introduced a wider audience to both the Bribri people and Tison's writing. The book began amassing honors soon after its publication. It was named among the best books of the year by the New York Public Library, Chicago Public Library, Amazon, *School Library Journal*, and *Kirkus Reviews*, among other such outlets; and won the Pura Belpré Award and Walter Dean Myers Award for Young Adult Literature.

The novel takes place not in Costa Rica, as might be expected for a tale so immersed in Bribri culture, but in Minnesota, where Jay and Max, the main characters, are growing up. Their mother is Bribri, and their father is a White man of Nordic descent. He has a familial connection to a Native American culture; his stepsister (the boys' aunt, Shelly) and step-nieces (their cousins, Tia and Nicole) are part of the Red Lake Nation of Ojibwe, based in Minnesota.

Tison herself grew up in that state and has explained to interviewers that while there are very few people of Bribri descent in the US, she feels a sense of connection with other people of Indigenous descent who have experienced colonialism and displacement. That type of connection is embodied in the character of Nicole, who has recently moved with her mother, a successful real estate agent, to a home not far from Jay and Max, and who is one of the only other Indigenous students in their small-town high school.

As the novel opens, the reader learns that Jay and Max have badly beaten up Luca, a popular and charismatic high school athlete who is dating the recently arrived Nicole. The brothers had chanced upon the young couple arguing and feared that Luca was becoming physically abusive to their cousin. As a result of that violent incident, the brothers are being treated like pariahs by their fellow students and are undergoing mandatory counseling.

Saints of the Household, which is told in alternating chapters by Jay and Max, examines the tangled ways violence, gender, generational trauma, and ethnicity are connected. Are Jay and Max truly as dangerous and violent as their mainly White classmates fear? Or was the fight with Luca an isolated occurrence? Are they following in the footsteps of their father, who has a long history of domestic violence? Or are they simply victims of their dysfunctional environment? Will they be able to transcend the abuses they have both suffered and committed?

Tison's sympathies are firmly with the brothers, and, in a broader sense, with the Bribri people, whom she depicts as an almost universally wise, gentle people, with a reverence for the natural world and tradition. In one vignette, Jay asserts: "Our people's stories can take months to tell. . . . Nearly everything has a story. The woodpeckers, the foxes, the butterflies." He relates the Bribri creation story, which involves a spirit, Sibökma, who travels from a negative plane in the spirit world in hope of discovering if peace and joy are attainable. Sibökma falls in love with a fellow spirit from a more positive plane, and their union results in the birth of Sibö the Creator, whose mission becomes to build the peaceful, joyful world his father envisioned.

The boys' maternal grandfather, Fernando, the only other major Indigenous male character in *Saints of the Household*, represents a strong role model for them. Jay tells us that when the elderly man visits, despite the chaos of everyday life in their household, "I can hear him humming a Bribri lullaby I recognize. Already the whole world sings of normalcy with Grandpa here. Even the bugs come out at night. They are singing and fighting all the time. For song's sake, for sex's sake, for death's sake, for life's sake. I don't know why I could never hear them from other springs before. How much of all this has been taken from us?"

By contrast, the sole reason for the unrest in the household is their father, who has made it impossible for Jay and Max to have any semblance of security or peace. They are unable to appreciate even something as simple as the nighttime sounds of insects because they must be constantly on guard, alert to how inebriated he is, his moods, and the likelihood that he will resort to physical abuse. The two have taken it upon themselves to protect their mother, making sure that one is always home when their father is around—a vow that requires juggling Jay's need to work at a local convenience store to supplement the family income and Max's desire to be off painting and spending time with Melody, a neighborhood girl to whom he is becoming increasingly attached. Counseled by his pastor, the boys' father attempts to change his ways from time to time, and that he is never fully successful highlights the failings of conventional Western religion in his sons' minds.

Despite his popularity, Luca, too, has a violent side that exhibits itself not just during that initial argument with Nicole but in small ways throughout the book. In one especially notable example, he flies into a rage while visiting the convenience store where Jay is working, banging on the plexiglass separating the cash register from patrons and shoving displays off the counter. Tison has explained to interviewers that she hopes the character will serve to remind her readers, particularly those in their formative years, that everyone has elements of good (in Luca's case, charisma and athleticism) and bad (his temper and propensity for violence) in their personality and that it takes concerted effort to ensure that the good triumphs.

The main female characters in *Saints of the Household* also embody something of a dichotomy in terms of how they are viewed by Bribri culture versus how their families treat them. On one hand, Tison stresses that the Bribri deeply respect women; reflecting on the fact that Sibö the Creator's mother was from a more positive spiritual plane than his father, Jay explains: "The women are the better of us, and our people know this." Readers are also forced to grapple with the idea that Max and Jay's mother remains in a physically abusive marriage and stays silent when their father begins beating them as well. Similarly, Nicole remains committed to maintaining a relationship with the handsome and magnetic Luca for much of the book, despite how poorly he treats her. Jay sees his own psyche as subject to conflicting internal impulses. "For thousands of years our people steadied our children into a light direction despite evil equally residing in us," he states. "I remember this with each dark gleam in our father's eye and each light gleam in our mother's." Max, too, feels this pull. In one section, he writes: "With every painting, / I learn / two skin tones, / one dark, / one light . . ."

Among the most striking features of *Saints of the Household* is its unusual format. Alternate sections of varying length are devoted to Jay, who relates his points of view in straightforward prose sentences, and Max, whose words are in the form of free verse, with no consistent meter or rhyme. Some entries use the technique of concrete poetry, in which the words on the page form a visual representation of an object; in one poem whose theme is alienation, for example, the words are printed in such a way that a torso-shaped blank space is left in the center of the page.

Tison has explained that after being introduced to the subject of ethnomathematics, the idea that different cultures have different, equally valid, ways of using mathematics, she began thinking about her own craft in mathematical terms. She thus eschewed the five-part pyramidal structure of much of Western literature, which involves an expository introduction that rises into a climax before the action begins its descent into a resolution (known as Freytag's Pyramid, after nineteenth-century German novelist and playwright Gustav Freytag). She chose instead what she saw as a more-balanced structure, in which each brother serves as a reflection of the other.

Critics were largely impressed, with most agreeing that Tison is an up-and-coming talent to watch and a knowledgeable guide to a culture that deserves to be better known and represented in literature. Calling *Saints of the Household* a "striking, assured debut exhibiting a measured pace and delicate writing," in a starred review for

Kirkus, the unnamed reviewer went on to write, "The author peels apart each brother's bruised psyche by ingeniously rotating among Jay's tense vignettes, Max's wistful verses, and Bribri cultural elements to underscore their anguished journey to reconciliation." In another starred review, *School Library Journal* reviewer Shelley M. Diaz praised Tison's "masterly economy of language—every word and even punctuation mark is chosen for a specific purpose." Diaz concluded, "Violence can be inherited but so can love and forgiveness. This vulnerable and magnetic tale of brotherhood belongs on every shelf." Ricki Ginsberg, the reviewer for the website *Unleashing Readers*, highly recommended the book, calling it "gorgeous" and asserting that it "will take your breath away." *Saints of the Household* is a strong debut from a young and talented writer, telling a compelling story through the lens of an under-represented culture to great effect.

Author Biography

Ari Tison is a Bribri writer whose poems and short pieces have been published in such outlets as *Rock and Sling* and *Yellow Medicine Review*. She is the recipient of a Vaunda Micheaux Nelson Award, given to a person of color or Indigenous writer showing exceptional promise. She works as a coordinator with the Minnesota Prison Writing Workshop to amplify under-represented voices and also teaches at Minnesota's Hamline University. *Saints of the Household* is her first novel.

Mari Rich

Review Sources

Diaz, Shelley M. Review of *Saints of the Household*, by Ari Tison. *School Library Journal*, 1 Mar. 2023, www.slj.com/review/saints-of-the-household. Accessed 14 Feb. 2024.

Ginsberg, Ricki. Review of *Saints of the Household*, by Ari Tison. *Unleashing Readers*, 31 Aug. 2023, www.unleashingreaders.com/26894. Accessed 14 Feb. 2024.

Review of *Saints of the Household*, by Ari Tison. *Kirkus Reviews*, 23 Dec. 2022, www.kirkusreviews.com/book-reviews/ari-tison/saints-of-the-household/. Accessed 14 Feb. 2024.

Saying It Loud
1966—The Year Black Power Challenged the Civil Rights Movement

Author: Mark Whitaker (b. 1957)
Publisher: Simon and Schuster (New York). Illustrated. 400 pp.
Type of work: Nonfiction
Time: 1966
Locale: United States

In chapters organized chronologically around core dates and events throughout 1966, Mark Whitaker traces the competing origins of the Black Power movement in Saying It Loud. *The book seeks to set an accurate historical course between contradictory first-person accounts and inflammatory journalistic coverage.* Saying It Loud *also probes the origins of the movement in intersection and conflict with the civil rights movement.*

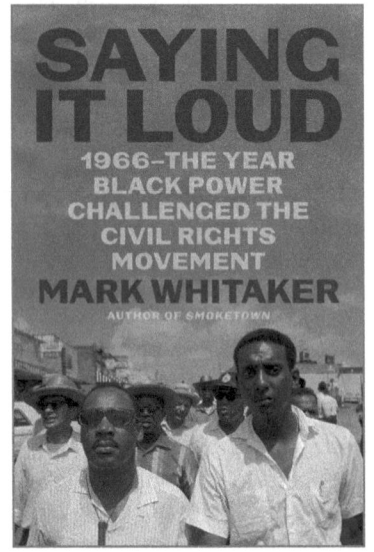

Principal personages
JULIAN BOND, a Student Nonviolent Coordinating Committee (SNCC) organizer and politician in Georgia
STOKELY CARMICHAEL, a civil rights leader and SNCC chair, credited with popularizing the slogan "Black Power"
MARTIN LUTHER KING JR., a famed civil rights leader committed to nonviolent protest
LYNDON B. JOHNSON, US president from 1963 to 1969, who signed the 1964 Civil Rights Act and 1965 Voting Rights Act into law
JOHN LEWIS, a civil rights leader and SNCC chair unseated by Carmichael; later, a member of Congress
JAMES MEREDITH, a civil rights leader shot by a White man while marching across Mississippi in June 1966
HUEY NEWTON, a cofounder of the Black Panther Party for Self-Defense
RONALD REAGAN, a movie star and politician who would benefit from White backlash in 1966 to win the governorship in California
BOBBY SEALE, a cofounder of the Black Panther Party for Self-Defense
MALCOM X, a prominent Black leader assassinated in 1965
SAMMY YOUNGE, a college student and voting rights activist in Alabama who was murdered in January 1966

In *Saying It Loud: 1966—The Year Black Power Challenged the Civil Rights Movement* journalist and author Mark Whitaker uses a probing, journalistic style to tease apart the complex events of a turbulent year, focusing with careful precision on the

Mark Whitaker

origins of the "Black Power" slogan and the larger movement that grew from it. In seventeen chapters, organized chronologically around specific dates in 1966, *Saying It Loud* follows civil rights leaders, voting rights advocates, and emerging influential voices in the Black community, as they sought to respond to prevalent issues and current events in 1966. Across the span of this single year, the slogan "Black Power" rose to the forefront of national consciousness after Stokely Carmichael was persuaded to use it at a rally in the Black neighborhood of Baptist Town in Greenwood, Mississippi. Earlier that year, Carmichael and other members of the Student Nonviolent Coordinating Committee (SNCC) had devised the "Black Panther Party" as the nickname and logo of the Lowndes County Freedom Organization as part of their efforts in voting rights advocacy in rural Alabama. Throughout the book, Whitaker seeks to not only find the origin points of these specific phrases, but to trace the complex, and often competing, currents by which these words became social and political concepts in the name of which individuals increasingly took action over the course of this flashpoint year.

While prying apart the knotted web of 1966, *Saying It Loud* looks both to the contexts in which the year's events unfolded and also to the long reverberations of these developments. Through the lens of 1966, Whitaker argues, we can understand the origins of the Black Lives Matter movement. He also presents the year as an important catalyst for a more widespread embrace of Black consciousness; an origin point for the academic field of Black studies and the founding of Black student unions (and other centers) on higher education campuses throughout the United States; and the moment in Kwanzaa was invented as part of a yearlong sequence of Black-centered holidays.

Within the larger historical exploration of the intersection of Black Power and civil rights activism, the book can be seen as pursuing three related themes, which Whitaker highlights as important formative vectors connecting 1966 to the contemporary Black Lives Matter movement. First among these is leadership, not by messiahs, but by prominent figures with exceptional charisma and vision. *Saying it Loud* offers an especially probing leadership profile of Carmichael, but also considers the promise and pitfalls of other early leaders in the Black Power movement. Carmichael concluded that the assassination of Malcolm X, while a driving force toward the movement that Carmichael spearheaded, also left its younger rank-and-file members without the vision and maturity needed to build a highly effective movement. Though less conclusively, Whitaker also considers the relationship between Carmichael and Rev. Martin Luther King Jr. in 1966. While the two had strong differences of opinion, Whitaker also identifies significant mutual respect and the foundation of a productive working relationship between them during the Meredith March, precipitated by the nonlethal shooting of civil rights activist James Meredith, who had set out on a peaceful one-man march across the state of Mississippi to encourage Black voter turnout.

A second, highly significant, vector that Whitaker evaluates is the "unending nightmare of violence against unarmed Black Americans, either committed or condoned by the police." Even though Whitaker's account spans only one year, the anti-Black violence throughout the book is significant. The first chapter recounts the horrific murder of Tuskegee Institute student Sammy Younge, while the seventh and eighth chapters focus on the Meredith March. These are just two, among many, incidents of murder, assault, bodily threats, wrongful incarceration, and verbal abuse that appear frequently over the course of 1966. Whitaker makes clear that the personalities, psyche, and decisions of Black leadership were all made and developed while living in the constant reality of such experiences. Whitaker's coverage of Carmichael in particular offers ample evidence of the impact of violence on his subsequent decisions. At the opening of 1966, Carmichael grieved the death of Younge, his friend and fellow voting-rights activist. Younge's death led Carmichael to briefly spiral into a nervous breakdown. Later, Carmichael's embrace of the "Black Power" slogan occurs on the same day that he has been wrongfully arrested and detained by Mississippi law enforcement officers who sought to suppress and harass participants in and leadership of the Meredith March. As he stepped onto the podium at the nighttime rally, Whitaker describes Carmichael as speaking "in a voice filled with anger not only at the infuriating events of the day but at all the indignities he had suffered and witnessed in five years of working in the South."

Lastly, Whitaker observes that both the first Black Power activists of 1966 and the contemporary Black Lives Matter movement leaders were motivated by disappointment in conventional politics. While King and other mature leaders of the Black community were more inclined toward patience and were more tolerant of a slower pace of progress, Carmichael and other younger leaders could no longer endure such half steps. They had good reason to be frustrated with partial commitments and frequent abandonment by White politicians, including those who appeared to be allies, like President Lyndon Johnson. Though Johnson had championed passage of the Civil Rights Act and Voting Rights Act, he participated in the political backlash against Black activists and moved to activate the FBI against Carmichael.

As noted in the subtitle of the book, the three themes of *Saying It Loud*—movement leadership, anti-Black violence, and Black disappointment in conventional politics—come together to tease out the interaction, and even confrontation, between the civil rights movement and the early Black Power movement. Whitaker considers the issue on several levels, but perhaps most significantly with respect to sharp differences on two questions, which he explores in great detail: whether violence was justified to protect Black lives and resist anti-Black violence; and whether White allies should play a role in the movement. Because both matters came to a head in 1966—with the foundation of the Black Panther Party for Self-Defense and with the expulsion of White staff from SNCC—the chronological approach and single-year focus of *Saying it Loud* enables him to convey the many differences of opinion and complex twists and turns through which these issues were approached. While he takes a nonjudgmental approach, his narrative seems to express some regret about the SNCC decision to expel White staffers from the organization.

Across the second half of the book, Whitaker traces the growing rejection of White efforts to work toward civil rights and integration and the increasing White backlash that led to political and social setbacks in the efforts of the civil rights movement. He draws a direct association between the actions and rhetoric of Carmichael (and other early advocates of the Black Power movement) and the political machinations of figures such as Ronald Reagan and George Wallace, who capitalized on sensational journalism and unclear statements by activists in order to foment White voters' rejection of progressive race policy at the polls.

Reviewers of *Saying It Loud* praised Whitaker's diligence and investigative approach, which led to revelations about both the individuals and the movements under consideration. Perhaps even more critical attention has been given, though, to the relevance of the research for understanding the origins of the Black Lives Matter movement and the maturation of the contemporary Black intellectual community.

Author Biography

Mark Whitaker is an award-winning journalist and the author of four books: *My Long Trip Home* (2011), *Bill Cosby: His Life and Times* (2014), *Smoketown: The Untold Story of the Other Great Black Renaissance* (2018), and *Saying It Loud* (2023). As the top editor of *Newsweek* from 1998 to 2006, he was first African American to lead a national newsweekly and was subsequently the Washington bureau chief for NBC News and managing editor of CNN Worldwide.

Julia A. Sienkewicz, PhD

Review Sources

Gross, Terry. "How Stokely Carmichael and the Black Panthers Changed the Civil Rights Movement." Review of *Saying It Loud: 1966—The Year Black Power Challenged the Civil Rights Movement*, by Mark Whitaker. *Fresh Air*, NPR, 8 Feb. 2023, www.npr.org/2023/02/08/1155093955/mark-whitaker-black-panthers-stokely-carmichael-civil-rights-saying-it-loud-1966. Accessed 15 Nov. 2023.

Nathans-Kelly, Steven. Review of *Saying It Loud: 1966—The Year Black Power Challenged the Civil Rights Movement*, by Mark Whitaker. *New York Journal of Books*, www.nyjournalofbooks.com/book-review/saying-it-loud-1966. Accessed 15 Nov. 2023.

Power-Greene, Ousmane. "Mark Whitaker's *Saying It Loud* Gives New Insight into the Black Power Movement." Review of *Saying It Loud: 1966—The Year Black Power Challenged the Civil Rights Movement*, by Mark Whitaker. *The Boston Globe*, 2 Feb. 2023, www.bostonglobe.com/2023/02/02/arts/mark-whitakers-saying-it-loud-1966-gives-new-insight-into-black-power-movement. Accessed 15 Nov. 2023.

Sullivan, Patricia. "With Black Power's Rise, a Turbulent Shift in the Civil Rights Movement." Review of *Saying It Loud: 1966—The Year Black Power Challenged the Civil Rights Movement*, by Mark Whitaker. *The Washington Post*, 16 Feb. 2023, www.washingtonpost.com/books/2023/02/16/black-power-book-1966-whitaker. Accessed 15 Nov. 2023.

Silver Nitrate

Author: Silvia Moreno-Garcia (b. 1981)
Publisher: Del Rey (New York). 336 pp.
Type of work: Novel
Time: 1993
Locale: Mexico City

Following a pair of film industry workers neglected by the business they love, Silvia Moreno-Garcia's novel Silver Nitrate *is both an homage to classic horror films and a chilling tale of the real occult terror that might be lurking nearby.*

Principal characters

MONTSERRAT CURIEL, a sound editor in the Mexico City film industry, often overlooked by her male counterparts
TRISTÁN ABASCAL, a former actor whose career was ruined by a car crash, and Montserrat's childhood friend and secret romantic interest
ABEL URUETA, an aged noir film director whose last film was never finished, which he believes has caused him to be cursed

Silver nitrate is an inorganic chemical compound that was used in film and photography up until the 1950s. The substance was combined with chemical salts and polyester to give it a gelatinous aspect that was eventually made into strips used to record film. This film stock, however, was extremely flammable, exploded easily, and was soon discarded in favor of a plastic base.

Bestselling author Silvia Moreno-Garcia's ninth novel takes the name of this chemical as its title, and uses it to examine the hidden powers of seemly innocuous objects like antique film stock. Moreno-Garcia is widely considered one of the more versatile writers of the fiction world, whose novels and short stories contain the influence of a number of genres, from horror to science fiction to classic noir and romance. While virtually all of Moreno-Garcia's works are set in Mexico, each new novel reveals another facet of the country and its past, with settings spanning late-1970s Baja California to present-day Mexico City, Jazz Age-era Yucatán Peninsula to a fictional world reminiscent of nineteenth-century Mexico. Nearly all of Moreno-Garcia's work contains a fantastical element, manifesting in such ways as vampire urban fantasy, as in the 2016 novel *Certain Dark Things*, or a romantic high fantasy novel of manners, such as *The Beautiful Ones* (2017), or, as in the case of *Gods of Jade and Shadow* (2019), a deep dive into Mayan mythology.

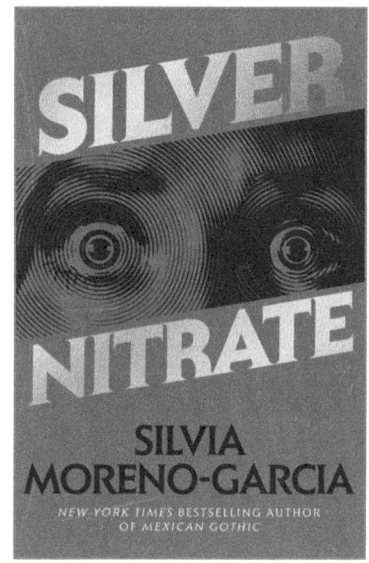

Silvia Moreno-Garcia

Moreno-Garcia first earned widespread recognition for her 2020 novel *Mexican Gothic*, an eerie horror mystery set in the 1950s, whose twisty plot conceals a number of imaginative reveals. The neo-gothic novel went on to win the Aurora, British Fantasy, and Locus Awards. Following that novel, Moreno-Garcia has produced a new novel at least every year; in 2022, she set a new benchmark with her novel *The Daughter of Dr. Moreau*, a Mexican and female-centered retelling of H. G. Wells' *The Island of Dr. Moreau* (1896).

Silver Nitrate (2023) rearranges the scenery once again by centering on Mexico City's struggling film culture of the 1990s. Moreno-Garcia shows a Mexico whose media production tends toward the repetitive and hackneyed, following an increase in capitalist and neoliberal rhetoric during the mid-twentieth century. The novel's protagonists, Montserrat and Tristán, whose narrative perspectives alternate throughout the novel, are in their late thirties, both victims of this economic and professional roller coaster that is the entertainment business—Tristán as a forgotten soap opera actor and Montserrat as part of the minority of underpaid female sound engineers. Though wildly different from each other—Montserrat, whose considers herself plain and nondescript, prefers the behind-the-scenes nature of her job to having a public presence, while the handsome Tristán is vain and always eager to be recognized—the two are childhood friends, having bonded over their devotion to film and its history.

"Montserrat had three loves," reads a line early on in the novel. "One was horror movies. The other was her car. The third was Tristán." The friendship is complicated by the fact that Montserrat has been nursing an apparently unrequited attraction to Tristán for years. Tristán, meanwhile, has been carrying his own emotional baggage. Ten years ago, his career atrophied after a disfiguring car accident that killed his then-girlfriend and costar, whose producer father subsequently slandered Tristán's name throughout the film business.

Despite the trying nature of their experiences in the industry, the protagonists have not left behind their obsession with film trivia. When they learn that Tristán's new neighbor is former noir film director Abel Urueta, both of them are eager to meet him and learn his secrets, particularly those of his unfinished final film, *Beyond the Yellow Door*, which was abandoned after a series of unlucky events plagued the filming crew. The truth of Urueta's last film, however, is darker and stranger than either Tristán or Montserrat bargained for.

Moreno-Garcia's novel follows Tristán and Montserrat on a perilous journey of the paranormal, a plot which combines cult horror, romance, and even World War II trivia. When Urueta asks the pair to help him finish the production of *Beyond the*

Yellow Door once and for all, things take a turn: Urueta, as it happens, hopes to finish the movie to break a curse that he believes was placed on him and the rest of the crew when they first began the project in 1961. The silver nitrate stock used for filming at the time, Urueta claims, actually contains a spell cast by Wilhelm Ewers, a Nazi occultist hoping to preserve the so-called Aryan race, by magic if necessary. After they agree to come to Urueta's aid, things begin looking up for the two friends for the first time in years. Montserrat is finally able to afford cancer treatment for her sister, and even considers producing her own film, while Tristán gets his first starring role in a decade. The forgotten Abel Urueta becomes a household name once again.

Soon after beginning work on the project, however, Tristán and Montserrat begin sensing the presence of dark ghostly figures around them, including Tristán's deceased girlfriend, Karina. Meanwhile, Montserrat must confront her feelings for her friend and continue to care for her sister, as Tristán reflects on his past tragedies and his flagging career. They decide to discover the dark secret behind what is happening to them before it is too late. Beyond the veneer of cult film references and technical jargon, *Silver Nitrate* is the story of two unlikely heroes battling overwhelming obstacles from both the tangible world and the spirit realm.

This is not the first time that Moreno-Garcia's work has used the fantasy genre to examine the hidden possibilities of the objects used in media production. Her first novel, *Signal to Noise* (2015), follows a music-obsessed teenager in the 1980s who discovers a way of using vinyl records to cast spells and improve her and her friends' lives. *Silver Nitrate* follows this earlier example by showing the reader what happens when a curse of racial supremacy is concealed in vintage film stock. In her novel, Moreno-Garcia reminds that the "forgotten" protagonists of early media, like Urueta himself, tend to stick around—along with the unresolved projects and lingering dreams that defined their careers.

Tristán and Montserrat have had the experience of living as minorities, both during their childhood and later in their field as adults. Montserrat, born into a dysfunctional family and frequently bullied for a physical disability, is a rare female member of the "boys' club" of sound engineers. Tristán, who also stood out as a child due to his small size and Lebanese background, is still reckoning with his guilt over Karina's death and his self-consciousness surrounding his own disfigurement a decade after the accident. From a gritty portrayal of the diversity that forms such a large part of Mexico City, to an eventual exploration of queerness within the film community, *Silver Nitrate* pulls back the curtain on a story of outcasts using the uncanny power of film to defeat the literal and figurative ghosts of their past.

Silver Nitrate received widespread praise, with reviewer Jason Heller for NPR highlighting Moreno-Garcia's nods at old film and horror references. Heller suggested that *Beyond the Yellow Door* was inspired by author H. P. Lovecraft's "Beyond the Wall of Sleep" (1919) and Robert W. Chambers' *The King in Yellow* (1895). Tristán's career-destroying accident, on the other hand, may be a reference to 1950s film star Montgomery Clift, whose disastrous car crash left him with physical trauma and a permanently altered career. Just as can be observed in the dissolution of the novel's titular silver substance, wrote Heller, "the careers, legacies and queerness of Tristán and Montserrat are being edited by the forces of neglect and erasure. . ." *Kirkus* also published a glowing review of the novel, praising its immersive and well-researched atmosphere, as well as its smooth assimilation of fictional details into real historical events. Miguel Salazar for the *New York Times* commended the novel's moments of "electrifying rhythm" and its "robust and haunting picture of 1990s Mexico City, its film scene hollowed out by neoliberal reforms and bad taste." At other times, however, wrote Salazar, the storytelling became unsubtle and predictable, with certain plot points "telegraphed from the beginning," with the narrative occasionally interrupted by dense historical detail. Meanwhile, Paula L. Woods for the *Los Angeles Times* praised *Silver Nitrate* for the ways in which it called upon and subsequently reinvented the classic tropes of the ghost story. As in her earlier novels, wrote Woods, Moreno-Garcia is an expert in both following and subverting the familiar patterns of genre narrative.

Author Biography
Silvia Moreno-Garcia, the author of a swathe of novels and several short story collections, is the winner of multiple science fiction and fantasy awards including the British Fantasy Award and the Pacific Northwest Book Award. Though best known for her multi-award-winning, breakthrough novel *Mexican Gothic* (2020), she also received widespread praise for her 2022 book, *The Daughter of Doctor Moreau*.

Maya Greenberg

Review Sources
Heller, Jason. "In 'Silver Nitrate,' a Cursed Film Propels 2 Childhood Friends to the Edges of Reality." Review of *Silver Nitrate*, by Silvia Moreno-Garcia. *NPR*, 19 July 2023, www.npr.org/2023/07/19/1187300629/silver-nitrate-review-silvia-moreno-garcia. Accessed 26 Oct. 2023.

Hubbard, Laura. Review of *Silver Nitrate*, by Silvia Moreno-Garcia. *BookPage*, Aug. 2023, www.bookpage.com/reviews/silver-nitrate/. Accessed 26 Oct. 2023.

Review of *Silver Nitrate*, by Silvia Moreno-Garcia. *Kirkus Reviews*, 24 May 2023, www.kirkusreviews.com/book-reviews/silvia-moreno-garcia/silver-nitrate/. Accessed 26 Oct. 2023.

Salazar, Miguel. "The Dark Magic Wrought by a Nazi Occultist and a Doomed Horror Film." Review of *Silver Nitrate*, by Silvia Moreno-Garcia. *The New York Times*, 17 July 2023, www.nytimes.com/2023/07/17/books/silvia-moreno-garcia-silver-nitrate.html/. Accessed 26 Oct. 2023.

Siciliano, Jana. Review of *Silver Nitrate*, by Silvia Moreno-Garcia. *Book Reporter*, 4 Aug. 2023, www.bookreporter.com/reviews/silver-nitrate. Accessed 26 Oct. 2023.

Woods, Paula L. "A Genre-hopping Novelist Reinvents the Ghost Story as a Mexico City Horror Film." Review of *Silver Nitrate*, by Silvia Moreno-Garcia. *Los Angeles Times*, 17 July 2023, www.latimes.com/entertainment-arts/books/story/2023-07-17/a-genre-hopping-novelist-reinvents-the-ghost-story-as-a-mexico-city-horror-film. Accessed 26 Oct. 2023.

Simon Sort of Says

Author: Erin Bow (b. 1972)
Publisher: Disney-Hyperion (Los Angeles). 320 pp.
Type of work: Novel
Time: Present day
Locale: Grin And Bear It, Nebraska

A heart-wrenching yet hopeful middle-grade novel, Simon Sort of Says *follows a young boy who moves to a deliberately isolated town in order to escape the past trauma of a school shooting, only to find that you can never completely evade the past, even in the most remote of places.*

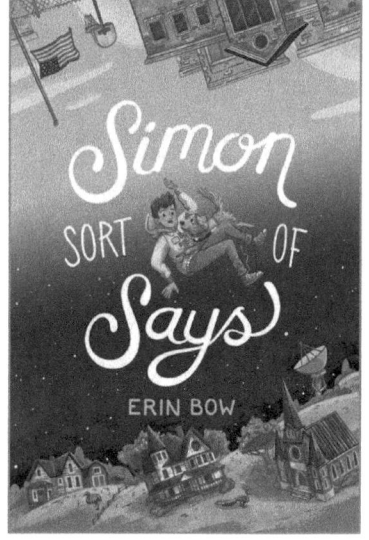

Principal characters

SIMON O'KEEFFE, a twelve-year-old boy who has recently moved to an eccentric Nebraskan town to escape the media following a tragedy at his old school

AGATE VAN DER ZWAAN, his classmate and best friend

KEVIN MATAPANG, his classmate and eventual close friend

MR. O'KEEFFE, his father, a Catholic deacon struggling to reconcile his faith with his son's trauma

MRS. O'KEEFFE, an undertaker whose own faith has been substantially shaken since Simon's experience

Numerous studies in the early 2020s found that the number of mass shootings in the United States increased sharply over the preceding decade, a trend reflected in heightened media coverage of such tragedies. As mass shootings have become more frequent, the intensity of the public debate over gun control has also increased, often adding a highly emotional element to social and political discussions. Some mass shooting survivors have become prominent activists against gun violence, leveraging the visibility of their own traumatic experience to raise awareness of the issue. However, many others very likely want nothing to do with the newfound media attention or responsibility that surviving a mass shooting can entail. While perhaps less widely known, the stories and needs of these survivors are just as important and worthy of respect, and serve as a reminder that people cope with trauma in varying ways.

It is in this context that award-winning YA novelist Erin Bow's *Simon Sort of Says* explores the story of an ordinary student who finds himself abruptly in the public spotlight against his will after a mass shooting incident at his school. Protagonist and narrator Simon O'Keeffe was just ten years old when he was discovered to be the only survivor of a shooting in his fifth-grade class at Eagle Crest Elementary, in a suburb

Erin Bow

of Omaha, Nebraska. In the wake of the tragedy, all he desired was to be left alone to lead a private life with his family. Instead, however, he was continually accosted by the news and social media, eventually becoming a familiar face online. For two years, he has asked himself why he, alone in his class, was spared. While the official reason for this becomes clear in the novel, Simon continues to grapple with his own "luck" at having survived, if luck is in fact what it was, as he inches toward his eventual recovery.

When the novel opens, Simon, now twelve, and his family have relocated from Omaha to a fictional town unique for its emu farms and its self-imposed isolation. Grin And Bear It, Nebraska, also known as GNB or the National Quiet Zone, is substantially populated by astronomers listening for signs of alien life. In order for their radio telescopes to avoid intercepting disruptive radio signals, the town has banned the use of most electronics and radiation devices—including radios, televisions, internet, cell phones, and even unshielded microwaves. While other children his age might be disappointed by this news, Simon is eager to live somewhere where no one knows about him or the tragedy that has defined the past two years of his life.

While *Simon Sort of Says* centers on weighty, difficult issues, it balances these with quirky humor. For example, when people ask Simon why his family came to the National Quiet Zone, he tells them that they were driven out by alpacas and relates a story that his dad, a Catholic deacon and liturgical director, was fired from his church after he forgot to ban alpacas from attending the church's blessing of the animals for the Feast of Saint Francis. Fortunately, another one of GNB's notable features is the "cathedral-size church . . . named for Saint Barbara, the patron saint of architects, explosives, and people in danger of a sudden death," which means that Simon's dad was able to find work in town amid scant job openings for liturgical directors elsewhere in the state. Simon's mother, who is an undertaker and can work anywhere, bought the town's funeral home, Slaughter and Sons.

As the O'Keeffes adjust to their new lives, they continue to experience the repercussions of trauma. Simon's experience remains the central focus, but Bow paints a nuanced picture of how such a devastating event can have a cascading effect on even those who were not directly involved. Themes of religious belief become especially important here. Through Simon's eyes, we see how his father finds his faith continually tested as he witnesses his son's post-traumatic stress disorder (PTSD) and social anxiety. That conflict eventually takes center stage when, later in the novel, Mr. O'Keeffe gives a sermon recognizing and naming Simon's many former fifth grade classmates who did not survive. Mrs. O'Keeffe's faith has also been deeply rattled by the family's ordeal.

Simon tries to adjust to seventh grade at his new school, GNB Upper, where he is grateful that none of his classmates have heard about the shooting. Hoping to start afresh and avoid mentioning the tragedy or his trauma, Simon attempts to build his reputation around some of the lighter, funnier reasons that the O'Keeffes left Omaha, such as the alpaca story. At first, this succeeds in helping Simon fit in without too many questions being asked. Simon even makes two new friends among his classmates fairly quickly: Agate van der Zwaan, a daughter of farmers and self-described autistic person who is deeply interested in disgusting fun facts and space signals; and Kevin Matapang, the sports-minded class clown trying to branch out beyond the limited expectations of his astronomer mother. But even the National Quiet Zone cannot stay completely silent, and eventually some covert web surfing brings to light the one secret that Simon hoped to keep hidden. This unwanted revisiting of the past adds another layer to his budding friendships, which he is forced to reconcile with those he lost, while leading the O'Keeffes to re-evaluate their relationship with the media and its relentless hunt for stories.

Bow's novel does not dwell only on trauma and heartbreak, however. At its core, *Simon Sort of Says* is a heartwarming story about the experience of starting over in a new place and welcoming newcomers into a unique community. The reader witnesses the personal growth of not just Simon, but also his parents, his friends, and their own families. The unique setting also contributes much to the gentler, funnier side of the narrative and characterization. Early on in the book, Simon finds that Agate's observation that GNB can be divided into two groups, "Team Science" and "Team Farm," is valid. Team Science consists of the astrophysicists who require the radio silence of the town to manage their telescopes; those on Team Farm are "homesteaders and other socks-with-sandals types" who moved to GNB for the less expensive, slower-paced experience of living off the land. Naturally, there is overlap—while Agate comes from a farming family, she seems more interested in using microwaves to create space signals from "aliens" in order to encourage the scientists to keep searching for distant signs of life, a project for which she immediately recruits Simon. Meanwhile, Kevin is far more drawn to football than to his mother's scientific pursuits, though he later ends up joining Simon and Agate on their mission.

Though the specter of Simon's past is always present during his experiences in his new home, very little of the book actually recounts the terrible details of the shooting, and virtually no details are given about the shooter. As might be expected from a novel for children and tweens, there is no on-page violence, and most of the novel's actual events have more to do with Simon's take on the everyday absurdity of living in GNB. Simon's father accidentally gives a squirrel the holy sacrament. A corpse mysteriously disappears from his mother's morgue. Meanwhile, Simon and his friends go to increasingly ridiculous lengths to fake alien signals so that the town's scientists do not "give up hope," as Agate puts it, to chaotic results. More than anything, Bow's novel is a guide for finding joy and humor in a violent world where children are not always safe. Even when the GNB community eventually finds out about Simon's notoriety as the sole survivor of the shooting at Eagle Crest Elementary, in part due to a well-meaning but misguided parent, the novel maintains its focus on the importance of compassion and friendship, rather than gory flashbacks. Though the author does not sugarcoat the ripple effects of gun violence on survivors and their loved ones—while sheltering in place during a tornado, Simon experiences a severe PTSD episode, and his GNB friends have trouble wrapping their minds around someone their age experiencing what he has—the novel reminds us that victims like Simon are not alone, and that the enduring power of friendship cannot be underestimated. Bow also includes a content warning in the novel's front matter as well as a list of mental health resources in the end matter.

Simon Sort of Says won several literary honors. It was longlisted for the National Book Award for Young People's Literature, named a 2024 American Library Association Newbery Honor Book, and received recognition as the School Library Journal Best Book of the Year. Bow also received near-unanimous acclaim for her novel from reviewers, who praised its ability to handle difficult subjects with both sensitivity and humor. Erin Entrada Kelly for the *New York Times* wrote that Bow's characters are "authentic, multidimensional and complex," and described the narrative as a "perfectly paced, layered novel that never speaks down to its readers and handles difficult situations with remarkable sensitivity." Kelly concluded, "Bow hits all the right chords and delivers a story that is funny, poignant and—most important—hopeful." An anonymous critic for *Kirkus Reviews* similarly called the novel "adroit, sensitive, horrifying, yet hilarious," writing that "Bow crafts an uproarious small-town comedy with a devastating tragedy at its core played out by a cast as memorable for its animals as its people." In a review for KMUW Radio, Suzanne Perez declared that "in a world of mass shootings and lockdown drills" *Simon Sort of Says* is as necessary for adult readers as for middle-graders: "Bow's deft treatment of the subject matter proves that middle-grade fiction isn't just for kids. We all need lessons on kindness, empathy, and the redemptive power of humor."

Author Biography

Erin Bow is the award-winning author of several novels for young people, including *Plain Kate* (2010), *Sorrow's Knot* (2013), *The Scorpion Rules* (2015), and *Stand on the Sky* (2019). Writing as Erin Noteboom, she has also published three collections of poetry, including *Ghost Maps: Poems for Carl Hruska* (2003) and *A Knife So Sharp Its Edge Cannot Be Seen* (2023).

Maya Greenberg

Review Sources

Entrada Kelly, Erin. "Lost (and Found) at Sea and in Space." Review of *Simon Sort of Says,* by Erin Bow. *The New York Times*, 19 May 2023, www.nytimes.com/2023/05/19/books/review/julia-and-the-shark-kiran-millwood-hargrave-simon-sort-of-says-erin-bow.html. Accessed 26 Jan. 2024.

Perez, Suzanne. "National Book Award nominee 'Simon Sort of Says' Finds Joy and Humor in a Violent World." Review of *Simon Sort of Says,* by Erin Bow. *KMUW,*

25 Sept. 2023, www.kmuw.org/podcast/book-review/2023-09-25/national-book-award-nominee-simon-sort-of-says-finds-joy-and-humor-in-a-violent-world. Accessed 26 Jan. 2024.

Review of *Simon Sort of Says,* by Erin Bow. *Kirkus Reviews*, 27 Sept. 2022, www.kirkusreviews.com/book-reviews/erin-bow/simon-sort-of-says/. Accessed 26 Jan. 2024.

The Six
The Untold Story of America's First Women Astronauts

Author: Loren Grush (b. ca. 1989)
Publisher: Scribner (New York). 432 pp.
Type of work: Biography, history, science
Time: 1960s to 1980s
Locales: California, Texas, and Florida

In The Six, *science journalist Loren Grush chronicles the experiences, struggles, and accomplishments of the first six American women to ever go to space.*

Principal personages
SALLY RIDE, the first American woman to go to space; an astrophysicist and former amateur tennis champion
JUDY RESNIK, the second American woman to go to space, an electrical engineer
KATHY SULLIVAN, the third American woman to go to space and the first to walk in space; a geologist and oceanographer
ANNA FISHER, a doctor, the fourth American woman to go to space and the first mother to do so
RHEA SEDDON, a surgeon, the fifth American woman to go to space
SHANNON LUCID, a biochemist, the sixth American woman to go to space
CAROLYN HUNTOON, a physiologist serving on the NASA astronaut selection panel

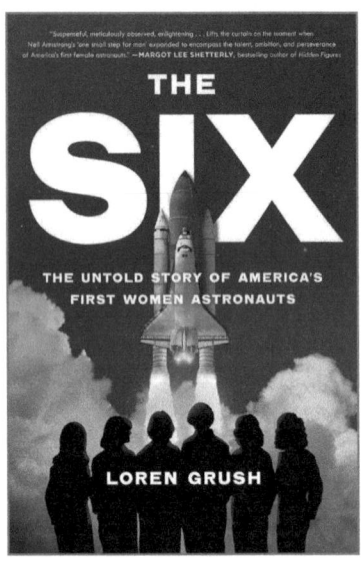

In the twenty-first century there has been a growing movement to recognize the contributions that women have made in science. Space science in particular is an area in which many activists, writers, and others have worked to illuminate the work of women throughout history. The trend received a mainstream boost with the success of the 2016 book and 2017 film *Hidden Figures*, about three African American women mathematicians who played a crucial role in NASA's achievement of spaceflight. In her debut book, *The Six* (2023), journalist Loren Grush picks up the mantle to chronicle another important chapter in the history of women at NASA by detailing the incredible lives of the first six American women to go to space.

The early chapters of Grush's book establish that these women successfully becoming astronauts was indeed historic—especially when considering the number of obstacles they were up against. NASA had a long-standing tradition of excluding women, as evidenced by the fact that from 1950 to 1960, women comprised only 1 percent of NASA engineers. When scientific studies conducted in the late 1950s and early 1960s suggested that women might be fare better in space than men in a number of respects, a series of tests were performed on potential female candidates. But this

Loren Grush

effort was met with resistance. In a disheartening excerpt from the book, Grush reports that a 1962 congressional subcommittee shut down the idea due in part to astronaut John Glenn stating, "The men go off and fight the wars and fly the airplanes and come back and help design and build and test them. The fact that women are not in this field is a fact of our social order." As *The Six* reveals, his was an attitude shared by many men in power at the time.

Yet this did not stop little girls from fantasizing about exploring outer space. One of the most compelling aspects of *The Six* is the way in which it chronicles the subjects' early years to demonstrate how becoming an astronaut had been a lifelong dream for several of them after witnessing the Space Race as children. Most were afraid to admit wanting to pursue such careers, however, because there was no indication that NASA would ever give the opportunity to women. The organization changed only after an African American employee named Ruth Bates Harris and two others took the initiative to compile a report in 1973 showing that its diversity and inclusion efforts had been a "near-total failure." When Harris was later fired for this, the media caught wind and suddenly NASA faced strong pressure to open its doors to people other than White men. In 1976 it began actively encouraging women and scientists, doctors, pilots, and engineers of color to apply its astronaut program.

While *The Six* highlights the importance of inclusion and diversity, it is never didactic. This is thanks largely to Grush's biographical angle to the story, focusing primarily on the women, their careers, and experiences. Their life stories prove inspirational, as each was a trailblazer in their own respect. By learning about how Anna Fisher and Rhea Seddon were among the very few women in their medical schools, for instance, readers will be reminded of how far gender equality really has come in most professions beyond NASA. The other women of the six were also anomalies in their fields, with Sally Ride being an astrophysicist, Judy Resnik an electrical engineer, Kathy Sullivan a geologist and oceanographer, and Shannon Lucid a biochemist.

Grush's decision to provide readers with a full picture of the lives of the Six at the time they joined NASA also means that she discusses the women's personal relationships and families. Her decision to do so demonstrates how important supportive partners can be in the fight for gender equality. The story of the relationship between Anna Fisher and her husband, Bill, proves especially compelling, as they had both applied to be astronauts but only she was initially accepted. He remained overwhelmingly supportive of her, however, and would become an astronaut himself years later. Several of the other women had partners as encouraging as Bill, including Sally Ride, who in 1983 became the first American woman to ever go to space. Although Ride was then married to fellow astronaut Steve Hawley, she would eventually spend more than two decades with her partner Tam O'Shaughnessy. Ride's queerness is explored at several points throughout *The Six*, making it a welcome addition to LBGTQ history books.

One of the most important aspects of *The Six* is the way in which it captures just how pervasive sexism still was in America in the late 1970s through the mid-1980s. The six women immediately became public spectacles in 1978 after they were selected by NASA from thousands of applicants. But few journalists at the time wanted to discuss the women's impressive professional backgrounds and credentials—they just wanted to know if the women would have sex with the male astronauts up in space. Beneath such questions was the belief system of a generation who could hardly imagine women doing anything besides being sexual or secretarial companions to men. As Grush reveals, the six women proved the sexist assumptions about their capabilities wrong by throwing themselves into their intense, often physically demanding training and work. They were also quick to stand up for both themselves and each other anytime they were met with disregard. For example, when someone in Mission Control remarked that Seddon was a good "seamstress" because she stitched something together while in space, Ride corrected them that in fact she was a "good surgeon." Additionally, a couple of the women continued their duties, training, and flying planes while pregnant.

The Six is, in many ways, a story about the importance of breaking societal conventions and blazing new trails even when doing so is terrifying. As Grush reveals, America's first female astronauts persevered even when it meant putting themselves in harm's way, whether it was psychological abuse from a misogynist press or the physical danger of their jobs. The reality of the latter issue comes into focus when the book arrives at the point in the story of the 1986 *Challenger* explosion with Judy Resnik aboard. Having devoted many early pages to Resnik's brilliant mind and intrepid spirit, the book succeeds in conveying what a tragedy her death was. It also demonstrates just how much the six were willing to put on the line in order to pursue their dreams while paving the way for other women to do the same. Many readers will be inspired by their accomplishments and sacrifices.

Although *The Six* tackles many heavy topics, it is often an entertaining read thanks to the many fascinating anecdotes Grush includes throughout its chapters. For example, prior to NASA recruiting the six, the only females that the United States had sent to space were Miss Baker, Arabella, and Anita—a monkey and two spiders. When it finally launched a nationwide campaign to recruit a more diverse hiring pool of astronauts in 1976, NASA hired actor Nichelle Nichols (best known for playing Lieutenant Uhura on the sci-fi show *Star Trek*) to lead the charge. Details about how NASA tested out its new space toilet for women by having some of the six drink enormous amounts of water before going for rides on a low-gravity aircraft nicknamed "the Vomit Comet" are also amusing.

Indeed, many critics remarked on how much they both enjoyed and learned from *The Six* in their reviews, most of which were positive. This sentiment was evident in Melissa L. Sevigny's review for the *New York Times* in which she stated, "The day-to-day work of the astronauts—surprisingly mundane—makes for fascinating reading.

The women test spacesuits, maneuver a robotic arm and work out the quirks of interacting with male colleagues who keep pinup calendars on their office doors. The spaceflights themselves contain plenty of drama and danger." Here, Sevigny demonstrates how *The Six* remains a highly engaging read throughout all the different aspects of the story that it covers, both on the ground and up in space.

The Six is not without its shortcomings, however. In its otherwise positive review, the critic for *Publishers Weekly* remarked that Grush is not always as strictly factual as she might have been, stating, "Unfortunately, the author sometimes resorts to dubious speculation, particularly in the re-creation of Resnik's mindset in the minutes before she died in the 1986 *Challenger* explosion." It is true that Grush's speculation here is a deviation from the mostly otherwise objective text, which may bother some readers. Many others, however, will feel that her decision to do so provided an extra layer of humanness that helps readers more fully feel the loss that resulted from the *Challenger* accident—an event that might otherwise come across old news.

Another criticism could be made that *The Six* sometimes feels as though it is just starting to skim the surface of these women's lives. Grush includes as much information about them as possible to make the central story about America's first female astronauts work, but it is easy to want details more about their careers, accomplishments, and day-to-day lives. Furthermore, Grush focuses primarily on four of the six: Sally Ride, Judy Resnik, Anna Fisher, and Rhea Seddon, making Kathy Sullivan and Shannon Lucid's story lines come across as mere sketches.

Despite these issues, however, *The Six* ultimately succeeds as a well-told piece of long-overdue history. As the critic for *Kirkus Reviews* concluded, "Grush has an important story to tell, and she tells it well. An inspiring story of the first American women to go into space, charting their own course for the horizon." For those who are interested in reading about women who successfully shattered glass ceilings and paved the way for women in STEM, *The Six* will not disappoint. Similarly, readers who love learning about NASA and spaceflight in general will also find much to enjoy in the book.

Author Biography

Loren Grush is a space reporter for *Bloomberg* and a former senior science reporter for *The Verge*. Her work has appeared in *Popular Science*, the *New York Times*, and *Nautilus Magazine*. *The Six: The Untold Story of America's First Women Astronauts* (2023) is her first book.

Emily E. Turner

Review Sources

Sevigny, Melissa L. "When the Portal to Space Travel Opened, 'The Six' Stepped Through." Review of *The Six: The Untold Story of America's First Women Astronauts*, by Loren Grush. *The New York Times*, 12 Sept. 2023, www.nytimes.com/2023/09/12/books/review/loren-grush-the-six-women-astronauts.html. Accessed 10 Jan. 2024.

Review of *The Six: The Untold Story of America's First Women Astronauts*, by Loren Grush. *Kirkus Reviews,* 31 May 2023, www.kirkusreviews.com/book-reviews/loren-grush/the-six-first-women-astronauts/. Accessed 10 Jan. 2024.

Review of *The Six: The Untold Story of America's First Women Astronauts*, by Loren Grush. *Publishers Weekly,* 26 June 2023, www.publishersweekly.com/9781982172800. Accessed 10 Jan. 2024.

The Slip
The New York City Street That Changed Art Forever

Author: Prudence Peiffer (b. ca. 1980)
Publisher: Harper (New York). Illustrated. 432 pp.
Type of work: Fine arts; history; biography
Time: Primarily 1956–67
Locales: Coenties Slip, New York City; Paris, France

Art historian Prudence Peiffer chronicles the lives of a group of artists who lived in the same New York City neighborhood during the 1950s and '60s, revealing a unique perspective on the postwar American art scene.

Principal personages

JACK YOUNGERMAN, an artist known for abstract and minimal paintings
DELPHINE SEYRIG, his wife, a French actor
ELLSWORTH KELLY, a painter, sculptor, and printmaker known for hard-edge painting
ROBERT INDIANA, a painter and sculptor whose work helped launch the pop art movement
AGNES MARTIN, an abstract painter known for watercolors and linear minimalism
LENORE TAWNEY, an artist who helped bring crafts such as weaving recognition as fine art
JAMES ROSENQUIST, a former billboard painter and founding member of the pop art movement

Early in the introduction to Prudence Peiffer's acclaimed debut book, *The Slip* (2023), she poses a challenge to the way art has historically been assessed and contextualized. She notes that artistic movements are typically categorized by the techniques and philosophies of a given era, and postwar American art in particular has often been cast as a series of distinct movements steadily emerging one after another as the cutting edge of creativity. But Peiffer asks, "What if we thought about groups in art history based instead on shared places? What if, rather than technique or style, it's a spirit of place that defines a crucial moment?" Here, the central thesis of *The Slip* comes into focus.

In its simplest description, *The Slip* is a biography of seven artists who all lived on the same street, Coenties Slip, in New York City at the same time during the 1950s and '60s. While their time on "the Slip" was relatively early in their careers, each would go on to be recognized as important figures in their own way. They were closely involved as friends, colleagues, and lovers, and all influenced each other's work—but, for the most part, they are normally associated with different artistic movements.

Prudence Peiffer

By considering these artists' lives and work together, connected by the unique conditions of a shared place, *The Slip* aims to flesh out an important chapter of art history from a new perspective.

After the introduction, Peiffer divides the book into four main chronological parts. Part 1, "Before," sets the stage for the eventual fateful grouping of artists. The first chapter presents a broad historical overview of Coenties Slip itself, from the first traces of people in the region, to the development of Lower Manhattan and streets named after the waterfront "slips" used to service ships from the 1600s on, to the neighborhood's appeal as a cheap spot for artists to rent by the 1940s. The second chapter introduces artists Jack Youngerman and Ellsworth Kelly as young men studying in Paris, France, in the late 1940s and early 1950s, absorbing crucial influences but also chafing against elements of the artistic mainstream. They become friends thanks to their shared obsession with color and creating art through an "economy of means" by distilling artistic expression into its simplest, most basic forms. It is also in Paris that Youngerman meets his eventual wife, Delphine Seyrig, a French actor.

That "French Prelude" leads directly to the book's core concern. In 1954, Kelly moved to New York City, where he eventually discovered the abandoned warehouse lofts on Coenties Slip were perfect for live-in art studios; although many did not have heat or running water, they were big and cheap and full of light. It was not long before other artists began to migrate there, including Youngerman, Seyrig, and their infant son. The remaining three sections of the book, then, are dedicated to following the career trajectories of Youngerman, Kelly, Seyrig, and four other artists they would become closely involved with at the Slip: Agnes Martin, Robert Indiana, Lenore Tawny, and James Rosenquist. Part 2 covers how they all ended up in New York City, with a chapter dedicated to each (Seyrig and Youngerman are combined). Part 3 focuses on the work they produced while living at the Slip, and part 4 examines what their legacies became after they left the neighborhood. By organizing the narrative into this clear four-part structure, Peiffer succeeds in making its sprawling cast's disparate styles, influences, and philosophies easier to follow.

One element that immediately stands out about the artists' colony that grew at the Slip in the 1950s is how different it was in composition compared to many prior groups or movements in American art—and particularly the then-dominant abstract expressionism scene—which tended to be "macho" in both their membership and subsequent perspective. Of the seven artists Peiffer focuses on, three are women. Peiffer also shows how other women had important influence on the group as well, as in the example of Betty Parsons, the gallerist who would help integrate the Slip residents to

New York's established arts community. Additionally, several of the artists and others in their orbit were openly gay or bisexual. (The romantic relationship between Kelly and Indiana earns notable coverage for its influence on the work of both.) Peiffer makes a strong case that with this diversity of gender and sexual orientation, the community subtly helped usher in a new understanding of who could "belong" in the art world.

Similarly, Peiffer emphasizes the group's diversity of artistic styles throughout *The Slip*. She successfully explains the different processes of each artist, how groundbreaking they were for their time, and the way in which their work would transform the art world. A central tenet of her argument is that the Coenties Slip artists arrived at a time when the American modern art scene was finally taking flight thanks to the success of abstract expressionism over the preceding decade, as represented by Jackson Pollock, Mark Rothko, and Willem de Kooning. In Peiffer's depiction, the Slip artists were in many ways like a rebellious sophomore class determined to subvert the ideas of their predecessors. Specifically, Youngerman and Kelly helped foster minimalism and the color field movement with their use of bold, simple shapes and hues. Many of their stylistic elements would also appear in pop art—a movement that Indiana and Rosenquist helped pioneer. But even within these classifications, Peiffer is attentive to each artist's particular style. For example, tapping into his background as an advertising artist and billboard painter, Rosenquist proved especially effective at capturing a sense of the nation's growing capitalist culture. Meanwhile, Indiana's incorporation of words into his imagery would also become a defining aspect of pop art.

While *The Slip* presents the female artists' contributions to the art world as being just as significant as those of their male counterparts, they also often prove to be more difficult to categorize. Martin's paintings, for example, helped launch the minimalism movement along with the work of Kelly and Youngerman. However, she used desaturated earth tones compared to their bright elementary school colors and considered herself an abstract expressionist in that she was more interested in using non-objective imagery to communicate spiritual truths. Tawney also crossed genres with her work and, in some ways, is the most obvious "outsider" of the group. Best known for fiber art and collage, she frequently used craft processes that the artworld establishment had long mostly dismissed as unsophisticated "women's work" for domestic spaces. Her innovative approach to the tradition of weaving, however, helped earn the craft the place and recognition it deserved as a fine art. Like Tawney, Seyrig also paved a new path for women in the art world. After becoming a movie star in the 1960s with works by some of the most acclaimed directors of the time, she decided to reject any roles that had been crafted by the male gaze. She would subsequently help launch the twentieth-century feminist film movement, working with noted directors like Chantal Akerman, with whom she made Jeanne Dielman, *23 quai du Commerce, 1080 Bruxelles* (1975)—now considered by many critics to be one of the best films ever made.

Beyond detailing these artists' lives and impact, *The Slip* also provides a fascinating look at how the landscape of New York City itself evolved over time and influenced the vital art being produced there. Indeed, Peiffer notes in the introduction that New York City is essentially another central character in the book and that the era of the Slip colony in the 1950s and '60s was "a pivotal time in its development." In this way, the book expands far beyond biography to include historical, geographical, economic, and sociological analysis. The long-term story of the Coenties Slip neighborhood becomes a microcosm of the city's and the country's broader arc, going through rapid development to become a key part of one of the busiest harbors in the US, witnessing earlier flourishes of art and culture, and going through cycles of urban decline and renewal. Such complex, far-ranging factors led to the Slip's cheap rents and relative isolation from the rest of New York's art scene by the 1950s, which in turn allowed the Coenties artists to create in a pure, uninterrupted way. Peiffer also makes a compelling case that this was one of the last times that such conditions were possible for artists in New York City, as further waves of change not only brought the physically destruction of much of the former Slip neighborhood, but also shifted the entire societal makeup of the city.

The Slip's insight into what life in New York City was like during this fruitful, important time in art was a common point of praise among the book's many positive reviews. For example, the critic for *Publishers Weekly* stated that "Peiffer vividly traces the community's genesis and makes a detailed and persuasive case for its influence on other 'alternative models to conventional city life.' It's a gratifying deep dive into New York City art history." Writing for *ArtReview*, Martin Herbert also highlighted how the multifaceted narrative serves as both a window into a much different time and a contemporary argument for the value of similar artistic communities in an affordable urban setting. "In the end, Peiffer is careful not to be too prescriptive, or despondent, concerning what form a 'collective solitude' of today might take, but she doesn't slide into lamentation," he noted. "*The Slip*, for all its immersion in a rebuilt past, nevertheless has a hopeful, toolkit feel: you leave wondering how and where such unseen but crucial communities might coalesce in the future."

Many critics also commended *The Slip* for its blend of thorough, well-researched history with an easily digestible, intimate tone. In a review for the *New York Times*, Walker Mimms pointed out that the book has a "strong oral history flavor," due in large part to the fact that Peiffer was able to conduct extensive interviews with Jack Youngerman before he became the last of the Coenties Slip artists to die, in 2020. Such perspective helps Peiffer offers behind-the-scenes details of the artists' personal lives alongside her bigger-picture themes, drawing in readers by humanizing her subjects but without ever coming across as exploitative or salacious. These personal touches include serious topics such as heartbreak and mental health struggles, but also many funny incidents, especially in the descriptions of ways the artists adapted to survive and get around the restrictions of their loft spaces. "As the artists found their voices in those drafty illegal lofts, the antics reached a sitcom level," Mimms noted, appreciating how the book is dotted with "rich art-world anecdotes and respectful gossip."

The result is a book that feels lively even as Peiffer's academic background largely sets the style and tone. It is worth noting that *The Slip* is still more a scholarly work of art history than a light read, but it will still appeal to a wide general audience. Anyone interested in learning more about twentieth-century American art or the history of New York City will likely find themselves rewarded by Peiffer's innovative and informative work.

Author Biography
Prudence Peiffer is a Harvard-educated art historian who has served as a senior editor of *Artforum* magazine and a managing editor at the Museum of Modern Art (MoMA) in New York City. She has written for publications including the *New York Times* and the *New York Review of Books*.

Emily E. Turner

Review Sources

Herbert, Martin. "*The Slip* Review: Not a Dead-End." Review of *The Slip*, by Prudence Peiffer. *ArtReview*, 29 Aug. 2023, artreview.com/the-slip-the-new-york-city-street-that-changed-american-art-forever-by-prudence-peiffer-harper-collins-review. Accessed 1 Feb. 2024.

Mimms, Walker. "At New York's Coenties Slip, an Artist Colony and a 'Rebellion.'" Review of *The Slip*, by Prudence Peiffer. *The New York Times*, 27 July 2023, www.nytimes.com/2023/07/27/books/review/the-slip-prudence-peiffer.html. Accessed 8 Nov. 2023.

Review of *The Slip*, by Prudence Peiffer. *Publishers Weekly*, 8 May 2023, www.publishersweekly.com/978-0-0630-9720-9. Accessed 8 Nov. 2023.

Small Mercies

Author: Dennis Lehane (b. 1965)
Publisher: Harper (New York). 320 pp.
Type of work: Novel
Time: 1974
Locale: South Boston, Massachusetts

Set against the backdrop of the South Boston riots protesting school busing, Small Mercies *is at once a taut crime novel and a harrowing study of a fractious time in American history.*

Principal characters
MARY PAT FENNESSY, a White working-class mother living in South Boston
JULES FENNESSY, her seventeen-year-old daughter
CALLIOPE WILLIAMSON, a.k.a. Dreamy, one of her coworkers, a Black mother from Mattapan
AUGUSTUS "AUGGIE" WILLIAMSON, Calliope's twenty-year-old son
MARTY BUTLER, a South Boston mobster, based on the real-life career criminal Whitey Bulger
BRIAN SHEA, one of Butler's criminal underlings
BOBBY COYNE, a police detective and Vietnam veteran
RONALD "RUM" COLLINS, her daughter's boyfriend
GEORGE DUNBAR, her son's former friend, a drug dealer
BRENDA MORELLO, her daughter's best friend
PEG MCAULIFFE, a.k.a. Little Peg, her niece and daughter's friend

Small Mercies is a taut and timely crime novel that unfolds against the backdrop of the White backlash against busing and desegregation in 1974 South Boston. As a native of the adjacent working-class neighborhood of Dorchester, which is situated between White South Boston and predominantly Black Roxbury, Lehane lived through this era as a child. He brilliantly channels the White resentment, bigotry, and clannishness that fueled a series of riots and protests against the court-ordered policy of busing Black students into South Boston's White schools. Deftly balancing foreground and background, Lehane creates a propulsive plotline that is entangled with and symbolic of the larger issues of racism and desegregation. The result is a compulsively readable crime story that both encapsulates a crisis from a bygone era and holds a mirror up to our own divided American society.

Lehane, having written more than a dozen novels, including the Kenzie and Gennaro detective series, is a master at crafting mysteries. As in so many of his works,

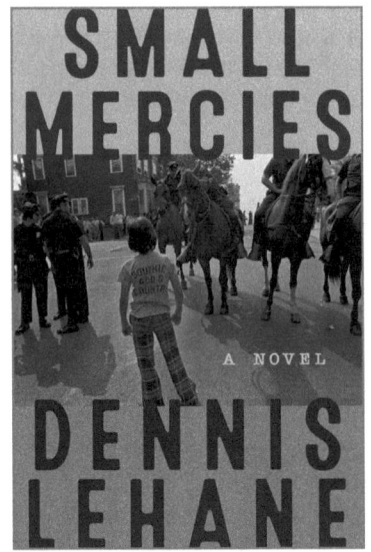

Dennis Lehane

disparate plotlines converge and offer revelations about each other. *Small Mercies* opens with a pair of seemingly unrelated incidents on a summer night in South Boston in 1974. First, a White teenager named Jules Fennessy fails to return home from an evening out with her friends. The next morning, the body of a young Black man named Auggie Williamson is found at a neighborhood train station under suspicious circumstances.

The engine that powers the novel's plot is the force of nature that is Jules's mother, Mary Pat Fennessy. A working-class, Irish American resident of South Boston, Mary Pat is determined to find her daughter or, failing that, to uncover the truth about her disappearance. Mary Pat's life is a difficult one: twice divorced, she lives in public housing, mourns her son who died of a heroin overdose, works two menial jobs, and drinks more than is good for her. Lehane is unflinching in his portrayal of the novel's protagonist, so much so that some readers may struggle to sympathize with her. Not only is Mary Pat frequently combative and belligerent in her relationship with her daughter, but she shares many of the assumptions and prejudices about Black people that are endemic to her neighborhood and culture. Lehane is interested in flawed people, not idealized heroes, and Mary Pat emerges as one of his most compelling protagonists. Despite being warned off—at first politely and then more bluntly—by thugs working for neighborhood crime boss Marty Butler, Mary Pat refuses to accept that her daughter is gone or that she would be best served by dropping the case. Once Mary Pat's fuse is lit, it is just a matter of time before she explodes. Part of what makes this novel such a page-turner is the reader's growing awe at the lengths to which the fearless Mary Pat is willing to go to find the truth or to take her revenge. As she cruises Southie in Bess—the battered but powerful green station wagon that comes to stand as a symbol for its driver—Mary Pat interrogates drug dealers at gunpoint, attacks or abducts lowlifes, and makes such a name for herself that she quickly becomes wanted both by the police and by the Southie mob. Lehane creates a ticking-clock dynamic, in which the reader and Mary Pat herself are aware that she is running out of time to find the truth and to keep herself alive and out of jail.

The second major plotline likewise involves a grieving mother, Calliope Williamson, trying to discover what happened to her child. When Auggie Williamson is found dead at a train station in Southie, White residents, including Mary Pat, immediately assume that the young Black man was in the neighborhood to sell drugs. This blame-the-victim response masks a terrible truth about who actually supplies drugs to Southie and about what happened to Auggie on the fateful night that he died and Jules disappeared. As Mary Pat uncovers the truth about how Auggie's and Jules's lives intersected at the train station, however, she also discovers the extent to which she has deluded herself about the experiences of Black families like Calliope's and the depths of racism in her own White community.

A strength of Lehane's novel lies in his portrayal of Calliope and her family as more than mere victims. In a deft narrative sleight-of-hand, Lehane eventually reveals how much of the readers' assumptions about Calliope have been filtered through the lens of Mary Pat's casual bigotry. A scene in which Mary Pat, out of a sense of largesse, attends Auggie's funeral, is one of the most surprising and riveting ones in the novel. While Calliope has far less time on the page than the vengeful Mary Pat, she plays a critical role both throughout the story and in its powerful denouement.

The twin cases of a dead Black youth and a missing White one attract the attention of compelling supporting characters on either side of the law. Marty Butler, a fictional version of the real-life Southie crime lord Whitey Bulger, is the novel's chief villain. Though he presents himself as a champion of the neighborhood and a preserver of the peace, Butler funnels drugs into Southie and is willing to take ruthless steps to maintain his criminal empire. Just as Bulger did in real life, the fictional Butler uses the busing ruling as a means for galvanizing White resentment and consolidating his power base in the neighborhood. Community members praise Butler for standing up for Southie, while Senator Ted Kennedy, who makes a cameo in a scene based on a real event, is spit upon by a mob of White protesters for defending integration. Butler is served by a host of henchmen, some two-dimensional and others more nuanced. Perhaps the most interesting of these is the enforcer Brian Shea, with whom Mary Pat had a dalliance in high school. To all outward appearances, Shea is a reasonable man who has both Mary Pat's and the neighborhood's best interests in mind; ultimately, though, he has sworn his allegiance to the hypocritical Butler. Part of Mary Pat's spiritual evolution is to recognize how hollow Shea's claims on her, as a classmate and neighbor, really are.

Another terrific character emerges to investigate Auggie's death: Boston police detective Bobby Coyne. A heroin user in recovery who is more interested in truth and justice than are most of his colleagues on the force, Coyne lives with his six adult siblings in the Dorchester house in which they were raised. Coyne's formidable sisters are a highlight of this book. Lehane's character-driven dialogue is so compelling that the scenes around the detective's dinner table are a delight to read. They advance the plot, as Coyne, with his sisters' help, talks through the connections between Auggie and Jules and puts together the pieces of the puzzle. Yet they also serve as a powerful counterpoint to the scheming of the Butler crew. Whereas Butler uses the language of community, family, and common culture as a mask for his criminal activities, Coyne's family shows the power of the real thing.

Dialogue has always been one of Lehane's strengths, as evidenced by his writing on the legendary HBO crime series *The Wire* and his many novels that have been turned into successful films. To compare Lehane's earliest novels, such as *A Drink Before the War* (1994), to this most recent one is to see an evolution of style, as exposition gradually cedes ground to conversation. This voice-driven storytelling allows Lehane to represent the words, thoughts, and attitudes of a working-class neighborhood of half a century ago. Indeed, the language and shibboleths of the community put themselves up for reexamination over the course of the novel. Several characters mouth the ubiquitous and seemingly innocuous phrase, "It is what it is." As the novel progresses, this refrain seems increasingly like a call to ignore injustices, to accept the status quo, and to numb oneself with alcohol and mindless distractions, rather than taking a hard look at why things in Southie really are the way they are. The triumph of Lehane's book is to allow characters to speak for themselves, offering a testament to how people once saw their world and to the divides that Americans still need to bridge today.

Small Mercies was largely lauded by critics. Writing for the *Washington Post*, Dennis Drabelle said, "Lehane's sociological precision gives 'Small Mercies' a gravitas seldom found in crime novels." Many critics noted that while it might be set fifty years ago, the novel serves as a powerful reflection of the issues of our own age. In the *New York Times*, J. Courtney Sullivan wrote that "Lehane masterfully conveys how the past shapes the present, lingering even after the players are gone." No reader should come away from this novel thinking of it as a period piece; it is, sadly, a message for our own time. Writing for NPR, Gabino Iglesias remarked, "The main element here is racism, and that makes it a relevant read today because, sadly, some of the discursive elements present in the story are still around." He noted that the novel's stark portrayal of the era may simply be too much for some readers to handle, since "it's hard to feel empathy for racist characters." For his own part, however, Iglesias saw it as "a call to action and an invitation to do better moving forward." Perhaps in part because of the vitriolic racism that the novel portrays, the blurbs on the back cover of Lehane's book carry praise from prominent novelists of color, with Jacqueline Woodson calling it "hilarious and heartbreaking, infuriating and unforgettable"; S. A. Cosby terming it "beautiful, brutal, lyrical and blisteringly honest"; and Junot Díaz asserting, "In the midst of our racial nightmare *Small Mercies* asks some of the only questions that matter: What's gonna change? When's it gonna change?"

In her comprehensive review for the *New Yorker*, Laura Miller critiqued an aspect of the novel's craft rather than its sociological import: the disconnect between Mary Pat's development as an avenger and her journey of self-revelation. Miller wrote, "She's meant to be scoured down by loss into an elemental, almost mythic personification of revenge . . . this notion meshes uneasily with the novel's other, more psychological tale of discovery: Mary Pat's growing and humbling recognition of her own racism and of the hatred festering all around her in Southie." This kind of disconnect may be endemic to the crime novel, as the author sometimes must choose between the exigencies of a plot-driven story and the more reflective nature of a character-driven one. Yet as Miller astutely pointed out, one-off novels have an advantage over series in this regard: unlike a detective in a recurring series, Mary Pat may be radically transformed by the end of her story.

Small Mercies is both compulsively readable and lingeringly profound, the rare book that straddles the line between genre and literary fiction. In honestly depicting the ugliness of a previous era and the devastating losses that arise from bigotry and misunderstanding, Lehane tells a story that is both entertaining and enlightening.

Author Biography
Dennis Lehane has published more than a dozen novels, including the bestsellers *Gone, Baby, Gone* (1998), *Mystic River* (2001), *Shutter Island* (2003), and *Live by Night* (2012). At least six of them were adapted for the big screen. He has also written for and produced television and film.

Matthew J. Bolton

Review Sources
Drabelle, Dennis. "Dennis Lehane's Masterful New Novel Revisits the Territory of Mystic River." Review of *Small Mercies*, by Dennis Lehane. *The Washington Post*, 21 Apr. 2023, www.washingtonpost.com/books/2023/04/21/dennis-lehane-small-mercies-review. Accessed 28 Nov. 2023.

Iglesias, Gabino. "Dennis Lehane's *Small Mercies* Is a Crime Thriller That Spotlights Rampant Racism." Review of *Small Mercies*, by Dennis Lehane. *NPR*, 28 Apr. 2023, www.npr.org/2023/04/28/1172426738/book-review-dennis-lehane-small-mercies. Accessed 28 Nov. 2023.

Miller, Laura. "A Dennis Lehane Novel Investigates Boston's White Race Riots." Review of *Small Mercies*, by Dennis Lehane. *The New Yorker*, 17 Apr. 2023, www.newyorker.com/magazine/2023/04/24/small-mercies-dennis-lehane-book-review. Accessed 28 Nov. 2023.

Sullivan, Courtney. "Dennis Lehane's Latest Depicts Boston's Desegregation Battles." Review of *Small Mercies*, by Dennis Lehane. *The New York Times*, 24 Apr. 2023, www.nytimes.com/2023/04/24/books/review/dennis-lehane-small-mercies.html. Accessed 28 Nov. 2023.

Soil
The Story of a Black Mother's Garden

Author: Camille T. Dungy (b. 1972)
Publisher: Simon and Schuster (New York). 336 pp. Illustrated.
Type of work: Memoir, nature, history
Time: Primarily nineteenth century–present day
Locales: Fort Collins, Colorado; San Francisco, California; New York, New York; Lynchburg, Virginia

Camille T. Dungy's memoir Soil: The Story of a Black Mother's Garden *connects societal issues such as racism, sexism, and climate change denial to the loving labor that goes into tending to a garden and family. Vivid scenes from Dungy's "prairie project" combine with careful examinations of historical wrongs to culminate in a surprising and exciting read.*

Principal characters

CAMILLE, the author, a poet, professor, and gardener
RAY, her husband, a fellow professor, and a bike rider
CALLIE, their daughter
MOM, her mother, a Fort Collins resident, close to her and her family
DAD, her father, who lives with her mother in Fort Collins
AUNT MARY, her mother's beloved lifelong friend and "chosen sister"
ANNE SPENCER, a well-known poet of the Harlem Renaissance, who lived in Virginia, where she carefully tended a well-maintained garden
JOHN MUIR, a Scottish-born, California-based naturalist, writer, and orchardist who explored much of the United States, including Alaska, and who is also remembered for racism and sexism
THOMAS NUTTALL, an English botanist and ornithologist, who spent more than three decades exploring the United States and naming many of the species he found

Camille T. Dungy's mind works in a pleasingly tangential way. A moment spent planting some native flowers leads to a meditation on the beneficial insects those plants will support, leading to a dive into thoughts about the history of the land where she now finds herself gardening.

The history of gardening and nature writing is long, stretching back centuries within the United States alone, and the tradition is filled with a rather homogenous group,

Camille T. Dungy

mostly White men. From records kept during the westward expansion of the early nineteenth century, to journals and texts written by such notables as Henry David Thoreau, to advocates for the natural world, such as Sierra Club founder John Muir, the story of America's wilderness has lacked diversity, if not eagerness for exploration. Dungy asks why that circle can't be expanded even further, not only to include people of color and other under-represented groups, but also mothers, a demographic that is sorely missing from the tradition. And why can't that exploration begin in one's own backyard? The result is a dizzying, exciting, sometimes messy memoir that reaches beyond simple observation and asks what it means to be a person in connection with the natural world in modern times and who came before to support the legacy we find ourselves with today.

Soil: The Story of a Black Mother's Garden starts simply, at the beginning of Dungy's desire to grow a garden. Dungy has decided that she will rewild a large portion of her suburban Fort Collins yard to support local wildlife and insects. She decides to do this in response to climate change, the insect apocalypse contributing to habitat collapse, and as a way to fuel hope in a world that often feels hopeless. The book begins vividly as she and her husband, Ray, struggle to pull a tarp over the heaps of soil and mulch that have been delivered to their home, one pile in their driveway, the other on their street. Their house sits on a lot that is one-fifth of an acre, and Dungy has designated a southern portion of the plot the "prairie project," into which she will plant species native or nonharmful to her section of the United States. This is a practice that has become increasingly popular in the 2010s and 2020s, particularly since the COVID-19 pandemic. This project, the reader learns, coincides with Dungy's award of a Guggenheim Fellowship, which will allow her to take a year off from teaching to work on a book of nature poetry. However, both of these projects—the book of poetry and prairie—are soon sidelined by the pandemic, during which she must homeschool her daughter while her husband continues at his full-time job at the university. This rather clear timeline is what gives Dungy the structure her story needs as she introduces the other topics up for discussion within its pages.

At top of mind for Dungy is the tradition of nature writing in the United States and the reality that people of color have largely been excluded from it. She notes many of the men listed above, but also many of the women who have been allowed to experience nature in solitude and write about it. Complicating her argument is the fact that she is a mother and also wants to understand why mothers have been largely excluded from this genre. Nature writer and naturalist Edward Abbey, a friend notes in a text exchange, was often out in the desert with his wife and children, but he omits them from his pages. John Muir once traveled with his wife into the wilderness but found the experience so bothersome—she did not share the same temperament as he while out of doors—that he never took her with him again. Dungy also turns to revered nature writer Annie Dillard, whose 1974 nonfiction book *Pilgrim at Tinker Creek* won the 1975 Pulitzer Prize for General Nonfiction, as an example of the privilege that came with being a White, then-childless writer. Dillard becomes both a beacon and repellent for Dungy through much of the book's middle sections, as Dungy grapples with her current reality of teaching a preteen daughter at home and the historical repression she has experienced in her life. Dillard, along with poet Mary Oliver, who is well-known for her nature writing, and writers Willa Cather and Sarah Orne Jewett are each held up as examples of women who seem to fall in line with the men of their time, foregoing traditional motherhood and reserving a solitary life for themselves.

Dungy's argument is muddled at times—why a woman must be seen as a mother in the first place is one question that comes to mind—but ultimately lays a foundation for her to discuss other women artists who were at the mercy of the racist practices of their times. For example, she is perplexed that Dillard, a White woman, is living during the entirety of *Pilgrim*, near Roanoke, Virginia, the site of major social unrest at the time, while the humanmade world rarely makes an appearance in the pages of *Pilgrim*. Its proximate location, however, provides Dungy the opportunity to discuss her time living and teaching in Lynchburg, Virginia, along with an exploration of the world of Harlem Renaissance poet Anne Spencer, who kept a home and garden in that southern city. Dungy, who is working on her own garden at the time, discusses the many plants found in Spencer's garden, along with a history of higher education and segregation in Virginia. A digression, perhaps, but Dungy's writing about the history and people of Lynchburg is captivating.

Most successful in Dungy's memoir are the moments when she writes closer to home. After the 2016 election, Dungy and her family fear for their safety, living for a time in their basement during a renovation and keeping their upstairs blinds closed. Dungy uses this moment to dig deeper into her relationships and their broader implications. For instance, she illustrates a break with a preacher, and ultimately, a church that she and her family called home, after a particularly insensitive sermon following the election. She describes a trip north to help spread the ashes of her beloved adoptive aunt Mary, who was a lifelong family friend and lived nearby in Fort Collins. The moments spent outside with Mary's family are both touching and grounding. Dungy later reflects on this moment as wildfires burn around her family's home. Though they never have to evacuate, the fire's proximity is unsettling and inspires Dungy to further invest herself in her garden. In other passages, she uses personal experiences such as a dispute with her homeowners' association over the visibility of a compost bin to illuminate the history of racial control over Black Americans' relationship to the land, from the time of slavery onward.

Toward the book's end, Dungy also speaks of the pain caused by the unjust deaths of many at the hands of the police and how she has had to prepare her daughter for this reality. A meditation on the life and death of Elijah McClain, a twenty-three-year-old Black man who was killed by police just an hour from Fort Collins in 2019, is juxtaposed against the story of the wildfires and a detailed description of the flowers she planted in his memory in her yard, brown tulips and daffodils.

Soil received mostly positive reviews before and upon its publication. *Soil* was also named one of the *Washington Post*'s ten noteworthy books in May. *Publishers Weekly*'s reviewer noted the poems that appear between chapters tie the collection together, writing, "Fans of Dungy's poetry will delight in her sparkling prose, and the wide-ranging meditations highlight the connections between land, freedom, and race. It's a lyrical and pensive take on what it means to put down roots." In a thoughtful review for the *Brooklyn Rail*, Victoria Richards praised Dungy's astute insights "that serve to expand our own internalized biases towards whom and what ideas belong in canonical environmental literature" and her awareness of "the privilege inherent in being able to imagine and write about the environment in a manner where one only thinks of oneself and has time to ponder in the 'wilderness.'" Even one of the more critical reviews, by *Kirkus Reviews*' anonymous critic, concluded, "While the threads don't always cohere neatly, they form a whole that reveals a remarkable mind in constant motion. Sometimes thorny but deeply felt, fluidly written, and never boring."

Author Biography

Camille T. Dungy is an award-winning poet and author who has received an Academy of American Poets Fellowship, an American Book Award, and a Guggenheim Fellowship, among many other honors. Her 2017 essay collection *Guidebook to Relative Strangers: Journeys into Race, Motherhood, and History* was shortlisted for the National Book Critics Circle Award. *Soil* is her sixth book.

Melynda Fuller

Review Sources

Bonhomme, Edna. "The Pleasure and Peril of Gardening while Black." Review of *Soil: The Story of a Black Mother's Garden*, by Camille Dungy. *The Nation*, 25 Oct. 2023, www.thenation.com/article/culture/camille-dungy-soil-review. Accessed 30 Nov. 2023.

Carrigan, Henry L., Jr. Review of *Soil: The Story of a Black Mother's Garden*, by Camille Dungy. *BookPage*, May 2023, www.bookpage.com/reviews/soil-camille-dungy-book-review. Accessed 30 Nov. 2023.

Golden, Renata. "Lessons in Quotidian Honesty." Review of *Soil: The Story of a Black Mother's Garden*, by Camille Dungy. *Terrain.org*, 15 Oct. 2023, www.terrain.org/2023/reviews-reads/soil. Accessed 30 Nov. 2023.

Richards, Victoria. Review of *Soil: The Story of a Black Mother's Garden*, by Camille Dungy. *The Brooklyn Rail*, 27 Apr. 2023, brooklynrail.org/2023/05/books/Camille-T-Dungys-Soil-The-Story-of-a-Black-Mothers-Garden. Accessed 30 Nov. 2023.

Review of *Soil: The Story of a Black Mother's Garden*, by Camille Dungy. *Kirkus Reviews*, 2 May 2023, www.kirkusreviews.com/book-reviews/camille-t-dungy/soil-dungy. Accessed 30 Nov. 2023.

Review of *Soil: The Story of a Black Mother's Garden*, by Camille Dungy. *Publishers Weekly*, www.publishersweekly.com/9781982195304. Accessed 30 Nov. 2023. Accessed 30 Nov. 2023.

A Spell of Good Things

Author: Ayọ̀bámi Adébáyọ̀
Publisher: Knopf (New York) pp. 352
Type of work: Novel
Time: Present
Locale: Nigeria

In Ayọ̀bámi Adébáyọ̀'s second novel, a local election entangles the fate of two Nigerian families from very different social classes.

Principal characters

Ẹ̀NIỌLÁ, a sixteen-year-old boy with big dreams for his future
BÙSỌ́LÁ, his little sister, a star student
BÀBÁ ẸNIỌLÁ, his depressed father
ÌYÁ ẸNIỌLÁ, his mother, who is struggling to keep their family afloat
AUNTY CARO, a local tailor who takes him on as an apprentice
WÚRÀỌLÁ, a young doctor engaged to be married
KÚNLÉ, Wúràọlá's abusive fiancé whose father is running for state governor
ÒTÚNBA, Wúràọlá's father, a wealthy businessman

When Nigerian author Ayọ̀bámi Adébáyọ̀ published her debut *Stay With Me* (2017), it was met with overwhelming acclaim. Not only did the novel receive the 9mobile Prize for Literature, but it also earned rave reviews for its story about a young, in-love Nigerian couple who are unable to have children and subsequently pushed into a polygamous marriage by their families. Many critics compared Adébáyọ̀ to compatriot novelists Chinua Achebe and Chimamanda Ngozi Adichie, while others praised the way she used a story ostensibly about a relationship to illustrate how Nigeria, despite all of its modernizations and progress, continues to be limited when it comes to women's rights.

In her long-awaited follow-up to *Stay With Me*, Adébáyọ̀ again provides readers with an intimate snapshot of contemporary Nigerian society and the social constraints that continue to entrap its people. While her sophomore novel *A Spell of Good Things* (2023) shares some themes with its predecessor, especially that of sexism, it differs in that its primary focus is on Nigeria's wealth inequality and how the nation's different socioeconomic classes essentially live in different worlds. To illustrate just how stark the difference between these worlds can be, Adébáyọ̀ chronicles the journeys of two characters from disparate backgrounds whose fates become tragically intertwined as the result of corrupt local politics, alternating back and forth between their storylines in the novel to compare and contrast their lives.

Ayọ̀bámi Adébáyọ̀

It is through the character of sixteen-year-old Ẹniọlá and his family that the struggles lower-middle class Nigerian families face are brought to light. The son of a schoolteacher, Ẹniọlá works as the apprentice to a local tailor and has big dreams for his future that involve him going to university one day. However, these dreams become out of reach when his father loses his teaching job and is unable to pay for his and his sister Bùsọ́lá's secondary school fees. Ẹniọlá's mother, Ìyá Ẹniọlá, does everything she can to come up with the school fees for her children, who are being beaten by their principal every day for not having it, but she is dyslexic and unable to read. As such, she resorts to picking through refuse to find pieces of trash that she can resell before taking to the streets with her children to beg for money. In addition to keeping a roof over her family's heads and food on the table, Ẹniọlá's mother's efforts are largely fueled by a determination to help her children one day achieve a better life, as private school is the only viable path towards university in Nigeria. When she eventually has enough to pay for the family's rent and half of the tuition fees, she must make the impossible choice of which of her two children "deserves" to go to school and, in turn, have a better life. Ultimately, Ẹniọlá and his family's strife demonstrate just how near-impossible upward mobility remains for many Nigerians despite the nation's steady economic growth in recent years. Their world is not a meritocracy nor does it pretend to be one—a myth like "the American Dream" does not exist there.

Meanwhile, the novel's other protagonist, Wúràọlá, provides readers with a look at what life is like for the upper echelon of Nigerian society. In addition to being the daughter of a wealthy businessman with political clout, Wúràọlá is a dedicated doctor and engaged to Kúnlé—the son of a professor running for state governor. In many ways, Wúràọlá appears to be the epitome of a modern, empowered Nigerian woman as she is well-educated, independent, and has a career. However, as Adébáyọ̀ quickly demonstrates, these feminist qualities are not enough to save even her from the pervasiveness of cultural sexism. At twenty-eight, Wúràọlá is considered rather "old" to be single and so there is enormous pressure for her to follow through with her marriage to Kúnlé—even when he starts to physically abuse her.

As Wúràọlá's relationship with Kúnlé demonstrates, *A Spell of Good Things* is as interested in the domestic problems its characters face as it is societal ones. This is especially true when it comes to the theme of mental health. Just as Wúràọlá struggles with whether or not she should leave her abusive fiancé when she loves him and their union is important to their families, Ẹniọlá's father is so incapacitated by depression that he can barely get out of bed, let alone look for another job. Here, Adébáyọ̀ demonstrates that there is a real lack of understanding in Nigeria when it comes to the issue of mental health. Ẹniọlá's mother recognizes that her husband is afflicted with some kind of illness that she does not know how to address and is gentle with him. However, other family members think he is just a lazy disgrace and that she should divorce him. So much of Bàbá Ẹniọlá's depression stems from the loss of his job and, in turn, his identity, masculinity, and self-respect. Through his character, Adébáyọ̀ offers an empathetic light on men similar to him while highlighting how mental health issues are another factor keeping working-class people down.

The idea that Ẹniọlá and Wúràọlá's families may live in different worlds but both struggle with serious problems rooted in Nigerian society becomes especially evident in the novel's final act. Adébáyọ̀ spends most of the narrative exploring each family's background and how they are dealing with their respective predicaments. And then, through a series of unexpected events, their lives intersect and become marred by a politician who is also running for state governor and willing to do whatever it takes to win. This politician becomes a symbol for Nigeria's political corruption and the way that it can hurt the rich and the poor alike. Beyond that, his character is demonstrative of the way that so many politicians understand how to manipulate their constituents and the political system to become untouchable.

A Spell of Good Things is not new in its examination of the issue of wealth disparity. While stories about the different lives that different socioeconomic classes lead are as old as the written tradition itself, what makes the novel unique is that it is not a story about the proletariat versus the bourgeoise. Adébáyọ̀ acknowledges that Wúràọlá's father, Ọ̀túnba, donates to political campaigns to grease the wheel for favorable business deals and sees donating to Kúnlé's father's run for office as an investment in his daughter's future. However, as a whole, Wúràọlá's family is not vilified or depicted as the blatant "enemy" of the poor. Wúràọlá may be extremely privileged, but she is also a dedicated doctor who tries to care for her patients as best she can despite a severely underfunded hospital system. Instead, a case can be made that if there is an antagonist in *A Spell of Good Things*, it is the corrupt, broken political system that continues to enable Nigeria's social and economic problems. It is this system that ends up hurting both Ẹniọlá and Wúràọlá in unspeakable ways suggesting that, in the end, it does not benefit anyone.

Since its publication, *A Spell of Good Things* has been met with overwhelmingly positive reviews. Many critics commended Adébáyọ̀'s ability to tell a such a compelling story about socioeconomic-political issues that also provided an even-handed perspective on its characters. In her review for the *New York Times* (5 Feb. 2023), Aamina Ahmad wrote, "In one sense, this story line offers little ambiguity; its villains are predictably corrupt, the cruelty of their methods operatic. But Adébáyọ̀ humanizes those sucked into the vortex of that power with a striking compassion—the characters' misjudgments and delusions are deeply and empathetically imagined, wholly alive." Here, Ahmad touches on the author's talent for creating characters that can engage in awful behavior but still feel real and relatable. These qualities are especially evident in Ẹniọlá, for example, who begins working as a thug to try and make money, and in his father who admires a former colleague who committed suicide after losing his job. *Publishers Weekly* touched on how well the novel depicted human nature in its review, stating, "As the characters are pushed to the brink, Adébáyọ̀ delivers a searing indictment of the country's corruption and gender inequalities. This packs a powerful punch."

A Spell of Good Things is not without its shortcomings and may not appeal to readers who prefer more plot-driven stories. It is important to note that a significant part of the novel is about the characters themselves, their backstories, and the circumstances they are facing. It is not until the very end that any type of "exciting" action begins to take place and the storylines come together. Fellow Nigerian fiction writer Esther Ifesinachi Okonkwo remarked on this in her review for *Southeast Review*, writing, "The novel rewards its patient reader."

It is true that a large part of what makes *A Spell of Good Things* engaging is the way in which it shines a light on how good, well-intentioned people like Ẹniọlá and Wúràọlá can find themselves in situations doing things they never thought possible because of forces larger than them. However, poverty, corruption, and sexism are not the only elements of Nigerian life that the novel presents to its readers. Another quality that makes *A Spell of Good Things* a worthwhile read is the way that it celebrates the richness of Nigerian culture—especially when it comes to the nation's food and different languages. As Ife Olatona writes in his review for the *Chicago Reader*, "Unapologetically Yoruba, an unmistakable Nigerian verisimilitude permeates the novel. Readers unfamiliar with tribal nuances in southwestern Nigeria get no glossaries, soggy transliterations, or italicizations of Nigerian contexts." Anyone who wants to better understand the many different facets that comprise contemporary Nigerian life will find *A Spell of Good Things* to be deeply rewarding. Those looking for a universal story about human nature will too.

Author Biography

Ayọ̀bámi Adébáyọ̀ is a Nigerian novelist. Her debut *Stay With Me* (2017) was the 9mobile Prize for Literature and the Prix Les Afriques. The recipient of the Future Awards Africa Prize for Arts and Culture in 2017, her second novel, *A Spell of Good Things*, was long-listed for the Booker Prize.

Emily E. Turner

Review Sources

Ahmad, Aamina. "A Novelist Bridges the Class Divide in Contemporary Nigeria." Review of *A Spell of Good Things*, by Ayọ̀bámi Adébáyọ̀. *The New York Times*, 5 Feb. 2023, www.nytimes.com/2023/02/05/books/review/ayobami-adebayo-a-spell-of-good-things.html. Accessed 3 Oct. 2023.

Okonkwo, Esther Ifesinachi. Review of *A Spell of Good Things*, by Ayọ̀bámi Adébáyọ̀. *Southeast Review*, 1 Aug. 2023, www.southeastreview.org/single-post/book-review-a-spell-of-good-things. Accessed 3 Oct. 2023.

Olatona, Ife. "An Expansive Nigerian Landscape in *A Spell of Good Things*." Review of *A Spell of Good Things*, by Ayọ̀bámi Adébáyọ̀. *The Chicago Reader*, 24 Feb.

2023, chireviewofbooks.com/2023/02/24/a-spell-of-good-things/. Accessed 3 Oct. 2023.

Review of *A Spell of Good Things*, by Ayọ̀bámi Adébáyọ̀. *Publishers Weekly*, 22 Nov. 2022, www.publishersweekly.com/9780525657644. Accessed 3 Oct. 2023.

Starling House

Author: Alix E. Harrow (b. 1989)
Illustrator: Rovina Cai (b. 1988)
Publisher: Tor Books (New York). Illustrated. 320 pp.
Type of work: Novel
Time: 2010s
Locale: Eden, Kentucky

Opal, a high school dropout and sole caretaker of her younger brother, Jasper, is plagued by nightmares involving Starling House—*a sinister place shrouded in mystery and the subject of many ghost stories. When she accepts a cleaning job from the house's warden, Opal is drawn into a real-life nightmare that threatens to tear apart not just her own life, but that of all the residents of the small coal town of Eden, Kentucky.*

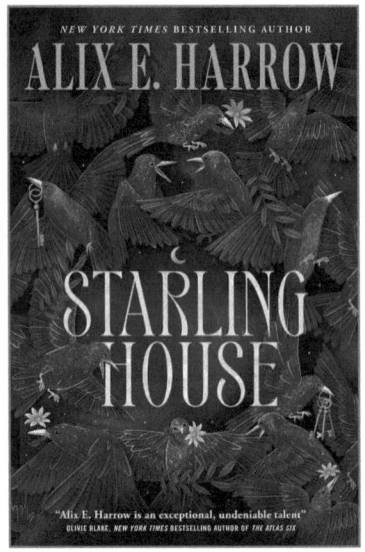

Principal characters

OPAL, a twenty-six-year-old high school dropout who struggles to provide for her younger brother after they are orphaned
JASPER, her sixteen-year-old brother
ARTHUR STARLING, the last warden of Starling House
BEV, the owner of the Garden of Eden Motel
CHARLOTTE, a town librarian
ELIZABETH BAINE, the Innovative Solutions Consulting Group's representative for Gravely Power
ELEANOR STARLING, a.k.a. E. Starling, the nineteenth-century children's author-illustrator who built Starling House

Starling House (2023) is Alix E. Harrow's third full-length novel. Known for writing award-winning speculative fiction, Harrow left her position teaching African and American history at Eastern Kentucky University following the success of her first two best-selling books, *The Ten Thousand Doors of January* (2019) and *The Once and Future Witches* (2020). Harrow's previous works feature themes of feminism and authenticity, and *Starling House* is no exception, although the tale—which Jenny Maattala, a reviewer for *Southern Review of Books*, described as an updated version of "Beauty and the Beast" or "The Labyrinth"—explores other topics, such as loneliness, grief, family, and home, as well.

Harrow's third novel begins with an introduction to Starling House as told in first person by Opal, the story's antihero. Orphaned at an early age, Opal has spent her

Alix E. Harrow

life scrounging a meager living to provide for her younger brother, Jasper, a gifted student whom she believes is destined for greater things than hourly shifts at Gravely Power, the local power plant. Living with Jasper in a rundown room at the Garden of Eden Motel, Opal works part-time at Tractor Supply and supplements her income by selling stolen goods and shoplifting basic necessities. When not scrambling to keep Jasper warm and fed, Opal is plagued by dreams of Starling House—the kind of place that locals believe is haunted and kids would "ding-dong-[ditch]" if they could get through the imposing wrought-iron gates. The gates are embellished with images of beasts that call to mind those featured in a children's book that Opal was obsessed with before her mother's untimely death. The book, *The Underland*, was written by Eleanor Starling, the woman responsible for building Starling House after her husband died on their wedding day. *The Underland* became something of a cult classic when Starling disappeared suddenly in 1886.

When Arthur Starling, the owner, or "warden," of Starling House offers Opal a job as a housekeeper, she takes it and sends the money she earns to a private school that has agreed to take Jasper the following year—if she can pay for it within three months. Once inside the house, Opal discovers that although it does not necessarily seem malevolent, it is something of a sentient being. Arthur, on the other hand, is a shady character—first sending her running from the house and telling her never to return, and then showing up with unexplained cuts and bruises following glimpses of him fighting unknown forces with a giant sword out on the house's front lawn.

What ensues is more gothic fiction than fantasy. A genre first created by Horace Walpole with his 1764 publication of *The Castle of Otranto*, the gothic novel typically features a bleak, oppressive landscape pervaded by a sense of horror and mystery. Eden, Kentucky—a small southern town that has fallen into poverty and disrepair after the shuttering of its coal mines—definitely qualifies as a gothic setting. The residents of Eden are subject to hard luck, and many find a tragic, early end, including several members of the Gravely family, owners of the town's coal mining and power company, who no longer reside in Eden but live in palatial homes outside the town's borders. While many blame the town's bad luck on the coal mines' residual effects, others blame Starling House and point to the tragedies that have befallen Eden since Eleanor Starling's unexpected arrival and mysterious departure.

In keeping with gothic genre conventions, Eden contains all its prior evils, including its history of slavery. Harrow, who grew up in Kentucky and worked there as an adult, does not shy away from Kentucky's complicated history, including the fact that it was built on the backs of enslaved people. By 1860—around the time the

Gravelys were building their fortune through slave labor—enslaved people made up approximately 20 percent of the state's population. The state's history of slavery has often been left out of the story of slavery in the South because its legislators assumed a policy of neutrality during the Civil War.

The house itself, in addition to being a main character in the story, is representative of yet another gothic horror element. Like the titular abode in Shirley Jackson's 1959 novel *The Haunting of Hill House*, Starling House seems to breathe on its own, causing feelings of unease and sometimes terror. Opal, however, makes peace with the moody house, speaking to it respectfully and asking it to provide protection on occasion. To Opal, Starling House feels like home. While others fear the old house, Opal is called to it, and when she cuts her hand on the old iron gate, it accepts her blood as an offering and willingly opens its doors to her.

Home and family are two underlying themes in *Starling House*, and Opal feels that she has missed out on both. Following the car accident that took her mother's life and made Opal solely responsible for her brother's welfare, Opal becomes cynical and battle-weary, hardened to the outside world. That world includes those who consider Opal to be family—Bev, the Garden of Eden motel's owner, who had an agreement with Opal's mother to let them have room 12 for free, and Charlotte, the town librarian. Opal is immune to both, seeing them only as a means to an end and considering herself alone in the world but doing just fine, thank you very much. Opal is loath to call room 12 "home" and has tunnel vision regarding her purpose in life: to get Jasper out of town as soon as possible and help him avoid her own dead-end fate.

With crooked teeth, a "mean smile," and distinctive red hair, readers are led to believe that Opal is not conventionally pretty. She is perpetually angry and grief-stricken. She lashes out at the world around her and has no remorse about taking what she needs to get by. While Opal becomes an unlikely heroine, she is not always likeable or moral. Neither is Eleanor, who becomes so obsessed with revenge that it harms the subsequent wardens of Starling House, anyone bearing the Gravely name, and the townspeople at large.

Harrow's feminist ideals are revealed in Opal's story and in Eleanor's. Both are filled with "female rage," which, as scholar W. Scott Poole pointed out to NPR's Kalyani Saxena, has been a recurring theme in gothic fiction written by women in the 2020s, when the Supreme Court's overturning of *Roe v. Wade* in 2022 and state abortion bans have turned back the clock on women's rights. In *Starling House*, Opal and Eleanor fight the patriarchy, big money, sexism, and more.

By contrast, Elizabeth Baine, a cold woman who earns a healthy living by threatening others to get what she wants on behalf of Gravely Power, appears to have no redeeming qualities. She becomes more sinister than the Beasts that emerge from Starling House to wreak havoc.

Starling House is not just a ghost story; it is a love story, one about many kinds of love. The most obvious relationship is the one that develops between Opal and Arthur. Initially sharing space grudgingly, while Opal cleans and Arthur spends his time brooding elsewhere, the two misfits are drawn together not only as romantic partners, but a team destined to break the cycle built around Starling House and its inhabitants.

Opal's other major relationships include the one she has with her brother—who, she comes to realize, needs her less than she needs him—and Bev and Charlotte, who really are mother figures to Opal although she fails to see them in such a light until it is almost too late. Finally, Opal carries her love for her deceased mother—a social outcast who barely scraped by but was willing to do anything for her children, including swallowing her pride—as overwhelming grief and not just a little bit of anger and resentment.

Harrow has a lyrical writing style full of metaphor and detail. She is a rule breaker who plays with tense and perspective—jumping between Opal's first-person narrative and Arthur's third person. The author incorporates footnotes throughout, which provide backstory and context. She creates a fictional Wikipedia page, to which Opal turns in her research on Eleanor Starling. Harrow also employs stories within the story—each set apart with a subhead and different font and each changing slightly with every retelling, framing the book's larger narrative. The addition of engaging illustrations by Australian fantasy artist Rovina Cai add to book's whimsical quality.

Critical reviews of *Starling House* have been overwhelmingly positive. The *New York Times*' Olivia Waite recommended the novel for the reader who wants "that Shirley Jackson creepy manor sauce drizzled over the small-town romance plot." Waite wrote that "Harrow has shuffled the familiar Gothic motifs like an adroit Vegas dealer"—namely, a catastrophic fire, a sinister company representative, and a "threatening and powerful" haunted house. NPR's Saxena reviewed the book's underlying themes, pointing to the author's use of gothic elements as a way to "process the ills of society," which, in this instance, include class, poverty, and historical trauma, as well as nods to climate change and environmental disasters. Maattala, writing for *Southern Review of Books*, called Harrow's writing "pristine and atmospheric," and claimed that, like Harrow's other novels, *Starling House* is "whimsical and tangible," and its words "illustrative." *Reactor*'s Natalie Zutter praised the novel as "undoubtedly [Harrow's] best work yet," and "a masterful meditation on the stories that make and unmake us," but also wished that the footnotes, which "immediately grab the reader's attention," had been incorporated throughout as they added a "strong dimension" to the book. Finally, *Locus*'s Gary K. Wolfe praised Harrow's use of place and the way Eden grounds what could have been a "traditionally claustrophobic haunted house" tale. Wolfe called Harrow's voice "sharply intelligent, defiant, and resourceful," writing that it "gives her fiction a consistent and consistently appealing tone."

Author Biography

Alix E. Harrow is the acclaimed author of the speculative-fiction novels *The Ten Thousand Doors of January* (2019), *The Once and Future Witches* (2020), and *Starling House* (2023), as well as the fractured-fairytale novellas *A Spindle Splintered* (2021) and *A Mirror Mended* (2022). Honors for her work include a 2019 Hugo Award for Best Short Story and the 2021 Robert Holdstock Award for Best Fantasy Novel.

Rovina Cai is an illustrator whose work has appeared in publications by Tor, DC Comics, and Hasbro, among others. She won World Fantasy Awards in 2019 and 2021,

Hugo Awards in 2021 and 2022, and the Children's Book Council of Australia Award for New Illustrator in 2019.

Diana C. Coe

Review Sources

Maattala, Jenny. "'Starling House': The Modern Gothic Fantasy You've Been Waiting For." Review of *Starling House*, by Alix E. Harrow. *Southern Review of Books*, 20 Nov. 2023, southernreviewofbooks.com/2023/11/20/starling-house-alix-e-harrow-review/. Accessed 10 Jan. 2023.

Saxena, Kalyani. "For Alex E. Harrow, Writing 'Starling House' Meant Telling a New Story of Kentucky." Review of *Starling House*, by Alix E. Harrow. *NPR*, 4 Oct. 2023, www.npr.org/2023/10/04/1203421254/book-review-alix-e-harrow-starling-house-gothic-fantasy-novel. Accessed 10 Jan. 2023.

Waite, Olivia. "Steaming-Hot Romance Novels for Frosty Winter Nights." Review of *Starling House*, by Alix E. Harrow. *The New York Times*, 2 Dec. 2023, www.nytimes.com/2023/12/01/books/review/new-romance-books.html. Accessed 10 Jan. 2023.

Wolfe, Gary K. "Gary K. Wolfe Reviews Starling House by Alix E. Harrow." Review of *Starling House*, by Alix E. Harrow. *Locus*, 31 Oct. 2023, locusmag.com/2023/10/gary-k-wolfe-reviews-starling-house-by-alix-e-harrow. Accessed 10 Jan. 2023.

Zutter, Natalie. "Alix E. Harrow's Multi-Genre *Starling House* Builds a Home Inside a Story." Review of *Starling House*, by Alix E. Harrow. *Tor.com*, 30 Oct. 2023, www.tor.com/2023/10/30/book-review-starling-house-by-alix-e-harrow. Accessed 10 Jan. 2023.

A Stranger in Your Own City
Travels in the Middle East's Long War

Author: Ghaith Abdul-Ahad (b. 1975)
Publisher: Knopf (New York). Illustrated. 432 pp.
Type of work: Biography, history
Time: 1980–2019
Locale: the Middle East (primarily Iraq)

Journalist Ghaith Abdul-Ahad chronicles the modern history of conflict, occupation, corruption, and war in Iraq—a history that resulted in a severely fragmented Baghdad, leaving the author to feel like an outsider in the city in which he was born.

Principal personages

GHAITH ABDUL-AHAD, a journalist and photographer documenting the war in his home country of Iraq
SADDAM HUSSEIN, president of Iraq from 1979–2003
NOURI AL-MALIKI, the leader of the Islamic Dawa Party who became Iraq's prime minister in 2006
HAMEED, a Sunni commander in the district of Tarmiya
HASSAN, a military surgeon and an old friend of Abdul-Ahad's
ABU SALEH, a young jihadist
WASSAN, a doctor in Mosul

The first chapter of *A Stranger in Your Own City: Travels in the Middle East's Long War* (2023) begins in 1980, when the author, Gaith Abdul-Ahad, was just five years old. The chapter is titled "My First War," detailing the first of many conflicts that he would bear witness to as an Iraqi citizen. Unlike most war memoirs—such as James Ashcroft's *Making a Killing* (2007) or Mark Owen's *No Easy Day* (2012)—*A Stranger in Your Own City* is not about the experiences of a combat soldier. Instead, it is Abdul-Ahad's firsthand account of life in a war-torn country, brutalized by dictatorship, sectarianism and civil war, foreign occupation, government corruption, and killings so common that they become a facet of everyday life.

By the time US forces ended Saddam Hussein's hold over Iraq in 2003, Abdul-Ahad was a military deserter working as an architect in Baghdad, the city that had always been his home. Shortly thereafter, he began working as a translator and fixer for foreign correspondents sent to cover the American occupation, ostensibly designed to rebuild Iraq following the thirteen years of UN sanctions that devastated the country's economy. Before long, Abdul-Ahad was reporting on the international armed conflict

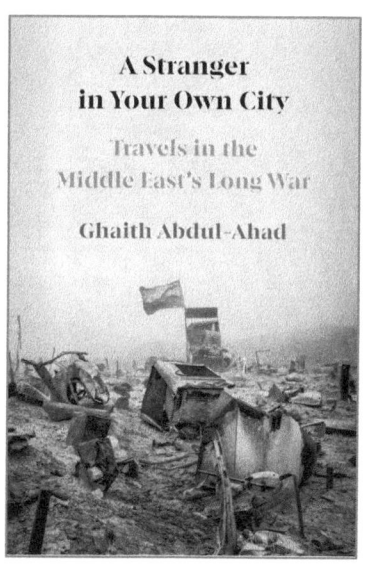

Ghaith Abdul-Ahad

between the US and Iraq as an insider. His status allowed him to document not just the death and destruction—first at the hands of American soldiers; then when sectarianism pitted Islamic factions against each other in civil war after civil war—but also to highlight the stories of the Iraqi people.

Some of these stories are simply snapshots: The old man who, in 2003, believed that the Americans would bring their tanks and electricity and turn his poverty-stricken neighborhood into heaven; Abu Karrar, an intelligence officer in the Mahdi army who kept a pistol tucked into his pants and felt he was providing a humanitarian service by killing Sunni Muslims; a seventeen-year-old Syrian boy named Osama who ran away from home to join the Free Syrian Army but who, by 2012, became disenchanted with the lack of organization and joined the jihadists in Iraq; a psychiatrist whose only method of treatment available for the scores of patients seeking refuge from war-induced depression is electroconvulsive therapy, delivered in a shabby back room in one of Baghdad's oldest neighborhoods; a young militiaman who became so enamored of the Iran-backed Hezbollah terrorist organization that he named his first son after its leader, Imad Mughniyah; and Um Tahseen, a woman who raises what's left of her family in a two-room brick house adorned with portraits of her four murdered sons. Other stories involve people whose lives are interwoven with the author's or who reappear time and again throughout his travels. For example, Hameed—introduced in his own self-titled chapter—is a senior rebel commander interested in the direction of a new constitution designed to give weight to the Sunni community. Abdul-Ahad relates how Hameed grew up in a lush village on the banks of the Tigris and completed a law degree in the late eighties. Although a once highly respected member of the Directorate of General Security, he became a "non-entity" in an Iraq shaped by the Americans.

The chapter titled "Hassan" introduces the reader to an old friend of the author's, a boy with whom he had gone through school. Years later, accompanied by a man with Sunni contacts and a driver who identified as Shia, Abdul-Ahad searched segregated Baghdad neighborhoods for Hassan and found that he had become a surgeon, working in a military hospital. A bitter man who had lost what little family he had left, Hassan was still a fervent supporter of Nouri al-Maliki, the controversial prime minister who resigned in 2014 following allegations of corruption and the encouragement of sectarian violence. Abdul-Ahad and his old friend meet several times throughout the years, often dining at upscale restaurants while the war rages around them—an irony not lost on the author. In another story, Abdul-Ahad introduces the reader to Abu Saleh, a young jihadist who grew up working farms along the Euphrates River. Following the American occupation, Saleh joined a small band of fighters, compelled by "the same xenophobic impulse that drove them to fight the foreigner." During the fall of Mosul, in 2014, the author meets Wassan, a doctor who struggled under the Islamic State (IS) mandate to provide treatment to only those who are loyal to the regime. She moved from "passive resisting to active rebellion" by treating other patients in secret, stashing tools and medicine at home where she performed operations and delivered babies on her dining room table.

Through these interviews and observations, Abdul-Ahad tells of the bigger picture of life in Iraq during a roughly twenty-year period following the fall of Hussein's Baath Party. He documents the unraveling of a country—its government, its economy, and the relationships between its people. The author takes the reader on a journey from the authoritarian regime of Saddam Hussein and the sectarianism that sprang up following the American occupation to the rise of jihadist organizations such as Al-Qaeda and the IS; and Iraq's second civil war.

In a departure from typical memoirs of Middle Eastern conflict, Abdul-Ahad decenters the West. Historic events such as the terrorist attacks of 9/11 and the death of Osama bin Laden, which an American reader would expect to be at the forefront of a book of this kind, are given only passing mention as they relate to the way Iraqis are perceived globally or the rise of jihadism. Instead, Abdul-Ahad focuses on how his country changed from one in which people of varying religions and sects lived together peacefully to one in which Christians were killed or exiled and Muslims were divided into Sunni or Shia, pitted against one another, and relegated to neighborhoods separated by cement walls, barbed wire, and military checkpoints.

With the occupation came death. Through the author's eyes, the reader becomes aware of just how Iraqis became inured to the bodies piling up in the streets, and the family members who were "disappeared." Abdul-Ahad spares sentimentality in his telling. He writes of the extremes taken by residents of Mosul who wished to evade torture by the IS: a man who confined his five sons to the attic for two years, causing the youngest two to lose the ability to speak; another who reclusively walled himself and his family into their home for safety. Yet some, like state-approved Sunnis, appreciated the new regime. As an example, the author spoke to a Mosul resident named Ahmad, who saw the IS as freedom, even as the "new State beheaded, tortured, and raped." Many chose to leave Iraq for Europe, following routes laid out on social media platforms like Facebook by helpful Kurds. Although Abdul-Ahad had tried and failed to emigrate in 1999, he documented the journeys of others in 2015. With the migration came human smugglers, profiteers who offered safe passage for tens of thousands of dollars. Corruption grew rampant and was equally evident among the many parties who vied for state money following the lean sanction years. While examples litter the book's many pages, the chapter devoted to "The State of Corruption" concludes with a quote from one of the author's friends regarding the IS-imposed cycle of kidnapping, torture, and bribery: "It's not about your guilt or innocence, but about how much money they can get out of you."

A Stranger in Your Own City is divided into five parts. The first, "The Leader Necessity and His Statue," details the years spent under the Baathist regime, led by Hussein. The second part, "The Collapse of the State and the First Civil War" describes the US-led occupation, along with the beginnings of sectarianism. Part three, "A New State," focuses on Maliki as prime minister. "In Between Two Wars" introduces the reader to the rise of jihadism and the Arab Spring, and the fifth and final part, "The Islamic State and Second Civil War," focuses on the fall of Mosul, the resistance of the people, and life in Iraq around 2018 and 2019. Throughout, the author's illustrations depict scenes described in the book's pages: an abandoned American tank, buildings laid waste by car bombings in Mosul, a dead body at a military checkpoint, and a young man in sweatpants and sneakers brandishing a machine gun.

The book was well received by critics across the globe, with many pointing to the author's use of sarcasm and detail to elevate his war reporting. Renad Mansour, writing for the *Guardian*—home of many of Abdul-Ahad's own journalistic pieces—praised the book for how it "shatters some of the assumptions held in Western capitals" about Iraq. Mansour points to the ways in which Abdul-Ahad teaches the rest of the world that the country's sectarian divisions did not spring from decades of Sunni–Shia hatred, but instead were "imposed on many Iraqis post-invasion by new rulers who came back to the country after decades in exile." Cyma Hibri, a reviewer for the *Conversation*, referred to *A Stranger in Your Own City* as a "'standout' war memoir" that helps to change the ways the media has covered the long years of conflict in Iraq, including the images and stories that "reduced the Iraqi population to a monolith." In Hibri's opinion—one shared by many—the book neither meanders nor does the reader get lost in the "frequent shifts in focus." Instead, Cibri argued, "its structure foregrounds what the book does best: unsettling the enduring myths about the origins of Iraq's never-ending crisis." *Financial Times* writer Charles Clover agreed, calling *A Stranger in Your Own City* an "excellent and haunting book." Like many critics, Clover points to the successful choice made by Abdul-Ahad to center the stories on his country's people, calling their "unrelenting agony" the "tragic inevitability of one dictatorship being replaced by another." Phil Klay, providing a review for the *Wall Street Journal*, said that Abdul-Ahad "delicately evokes the fears and hopes of a nation eager to be rid of Saddam but fearful of the consequences." The end result, Klay says, is a "powerful and beautifully written portrait of the soul and psychology of a nation reeling from one cataclysm to the next."

Author Biography

Ghaith Abdul-Ahad began writing for the *Guardian* in 2003, shortly after US-led coalition forces toppled the Baath Party in his homeland of Iraq. Since then, the journalist has won numerous awards including two Emmy Awards and the British Press Awards' Foreign Reporter of the Year in addition to being longlisted for the 2014 Orwell Prize. An accomplished photographer as well, Abdul-Ahad's images have been published in such major media outlets as the *Washington Post*, the *New York Times*, and the *Los Angeles Times*.

Diana C. Coe

Review Sources

Clover, Charles. "A Stranger in Your Own City—the Post-Invasion Agony of the Iraqi People." Review of *A Stranger in Your Own City: Travels in the Middle East's Long War*, by Ghaith Abdul-Ahad. *Financial Times*, 30 Mar. 2023, www.ft.com/content/8bf19627-c1bc-4907-bd82-c928e54a4e7a. Accessed 20 Feb. 2024.

Hibri, Cyma. "Iraqi Journalist Ghaith Abdul-Ahad Watched Saddam's Statue Topped in 2003. His 'Standout' War Memoir De-Centres the West." Review of *A Stranger in Your Own City: Travels in the Middle East's Long War*, by Ghaith Abdul-Ahad. *The Conversation*, 6 Aug. 2023, theconversation.com/iraqi-journalist-ghaith-abdul-ahad-watched-saddams-statue-topple-in-2003-his-standout-war-memoir-de-centres-the-west-203962. Accessed 20 Feb. 2024.

Klay, Phil. "'A Stranger in Your Own City' Review: Finding the Iraq Within." Review of *A Stranger in Your Own City: Travels in the Middle East's Long War*, by Ghaith Abdul-Ahad. *The Wall Street Journal*, 10 Mar. 2023, www.wsj.com/articles/a-stranger-in-your-own-city-review-finding-the-iraq-within-acd8ca93. Accessed 20 Feb. 2024.

Mansour, Renad. "A Stranger in Your Own City by Ghaith Abdul-Ahad Review—20 Years of Frustration and Fury in Iraq." Review of *A Stranger in Your Own City: Travels in the Middle East's Long War*, by Ghaith Abdul-Ahad. *The Guardian*, 19 Mar. 2023, www.theguardian.com/books/2023/mar/19/a-stranger-in-your-own-city-travels-in-middle-east-long-war-by-ghaith-abdul-ahad-review-charting-20-years-of-frustration-and-fury-in-iraq. Accessed 20 Feb. 2024.

suddenly we

Author: Evie Shockley (b. 1965)
Publisher: Wesleyan University Press (Middletown, CT). 112 pp.
Type of work: Poetry
Time: Present day
Locales: Memphis, Tennessee; Jersey City, New Jersey; Paris, France

Evie Shockley's poetry collection suddenly we, *a 2023 National Book Award finalist, seeks to understand what it means to exist in the world, today and in the past. Poems in the collection focus on the struggles and triumphs of historic characters, like Ida B. Wells, as placed alongside more exploratory pieces with an eye on the pandemic and post-pandemic life.*

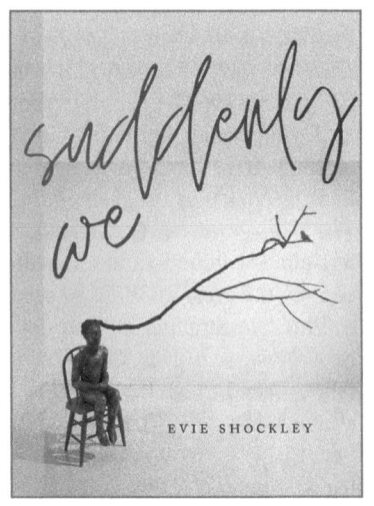

Principal characters

IDA B. WELLS, journalist and activist

CHERYL A. WALL, professor of English and literary critic

ALMA THOMAS, major painter of the twentieth century, known for bold colors, shapes, and patterns

CY TWOMBLY, American painter, sculptor, and photographer known best for works of abstract expressionism

Evie Shockley's poetry collection *suddenly we* is a book years in the making. Shockley, who has published several other collections of poetry in addition to criticism, spent much of the COVID-19 pandemic and the years leading up to it composing the pieces that would make up *suddenly we* without a theme or ending point in mind. But like her other collections, the collection found its voice and message through Black feminist expressions of place, time, identity, and representation. Enriching her poetry with various tools of the medium—experimental capitalization, playful and powerful breaks in words and line, wordplay that drives deeper into the core of her message—the final result is a collection that fits snugly into both Shockley's body of work and contemporary life.

Suddenly we is interested in the work of pronouns and the subjects they represent, specifically how "I" might turn into "us" or "we." The "we" of the book title shows up in four of the collection's section titles: "we :: becoming & going," "we :: uppity & down," "we :: indurate & out," and "we: adhere & there." Shockley immediately begins to play into the slipperiness of language with these headings that also give the collection its shape.

Evie Shockley

Before the reader gets to the poems, however, a series of epigraphs set the tone with quotes from Aretha Franklin, Alexis Pauline Gumbs, Nathanial Mackey, and Bernice Johnson Reagon. Franklin states, "we should believe, believe in each other's dreams," while Reagon's quote reads, "There is nowhere you can go and only be with people / who are like you. It's over. Give it up." The ebb and flow, push and pull of collective connection plays out between the first and last quote, with Gumbs meditating on hatred against Black women as a part of one's identity, while Mackey's focuses on the state of who a person is in relation to the harsh world around them. Each of the collection's following sections grapple with these issues in one way or another.

Like many poets, Shockley is interested in the intersection between writing and art, how artistic creation shapes existence and moves people closer to connecting. In line with this, she opens *suddenly we* with a series of poems titled "alma's arkestral vision (or, further out)." The pieces are inspired by Alma Thomas's 1972 painting *Starry Night and the Astronauts*, which she completed at the age of eighty. Thomas (1891–1978) found success as a representational painter for much of her long career and was the first Black woman to receive a solo exhibition at a major art museum. She began experimenting with abstraction in her seventies, particularly focused on themes of space exploration with many works referencing the Apollo moon missions. The painting in question brings to mind a vast night sky with a small island of red, orange, and yellow tiles stacked atop each other in the upper right-hand corner. The "alma's arkestral vision" poems, numbered one through nine, place the reader inside both Thomas's painting and Shockley's ekphrastic response.

The first poem in the series is a calligram, a form in which the words are arranged to create a picture of a thematically related image or word. Shockley uses the word *you*, lower case, forty-three times, along with a single instance of the word *me* to form the word *we*. The technique is powerful, as the reader begins to imagine how each individual might join together to create something more powerful, more lasting. The calligram also evokes the sense of floating above the Earth, how singular people, even buildings, begin to form a "we" as one moves further away from the surface. Other poems in the series evoke images of "blue snowflakes," sailing "the starry night," and "an astral-ark plotting movement." Language continuously evokes nautical images, giving the poems a sense of movement as Shockley waves her word play. She writes, "we row / will row / will have rhone," in the series' sixth poem. The eighth features the lines, "we are the sailors / we are the ship / we are the stars." The series culminates in another calligram, this time using the word *we* to create the letter *U*, which completes the words "unique" and "universe."

In the second section, "we :: becoming & going," Shockley's ekphrastic poem "Perched" responds to the collection's cover image of the sculpture *Blue Bird* (ca. 2003) by Alison Saar. Saar's sculpture depicts a young girl seated on a red chair; her thick braid is a tree branch, in which perches a wooden bird. Shockley writes, "if i must be hard, it will be as a tree, alive with change." Further along in this section, Shockley's "the beauties: third dimension" responds to images from artist Willie Cole's series *Beauties*, which were produced by flattening ironing boards and applying ink to them through an etching press. Cole named each image after a woman in his family or a historical figure, and Shockley repeats these names in each section of the poem. In a section titled "Carolina," Shockley writes, "you / wonder if you could bear all / that life has imprinted upon me. / well, no. but resilience may / be your inheritance, too."

In the poem "blues-elegy for cheryl," Shockley pays tribute to Dr. Cheryl A. Wall (1948–2020), one of the scholars who instituted African American literary traditions as an academic field of study in the 1970s and 80s. The imagery of the poem is more grounded and literal than many of the others in the series or the collection as a whole. Shockley writes, "she weeded our mothers' gardens with tender loving care / tended hurston & cade & Morrison (&&&!) all with loving care / our daughters won't have to search hard for the bounty there." Shockley takes a similar story-telling tone in "no car for colored [+] ladies (or, miss wells goes off [on] the rails)." Here, she recounts what Ida B. Wells accomplished by sitting in the (White) "ladies' car" during a train ride from Memphis, marking an early protest of segregation that made Wells a hero.

Shockley also joins a growing body of writers exploring what life felt like after the height of the COVID-19 pandemic and chronicles her experience during those years. One of the poems in the section "we :: adhere & there," "pantoum: 2020," tackles this theme directly. A pantoum is a poetic form in which lines are repeated in a pattern across quatrains. Shockley's poem is rich in imagery that evokes major social issues, including coyotes returning to quiet streets emptied of humans; essential workers being put in harm's way because of their jobs, whether in a hospital or grocery store; the racial justice protests of the summer of 2020 after the murder of George Floyd; and the politicization of mask-wearing that began after a few months into the pandemic. The poem's form is particularly powerful because it forces Shockley, and her readers, to revisit startling images and memories over and over. Earlier in the collection, in the poem "the lost track of time," Shockley writes of the pandemic's after effects, which have affected her sense of "dailiness" and time: "i've measured out my life in package deliveries and what's in bloom. the time is now thirteen boxes past peonies. if you can locate my whenabouts on a calendar, come get me."

Suddenly We was very well-received by critics, notably being named a finalist for the National Book Award. It also received starred reviews in outlets such as *Publishers Weekly* and *Library Journal*. The anonymous critic for *Publishers Weekly* wrote that the collection "is a welcome companion for that ride as it celebrates the collective, the 'we' that is vital to survival." Christopher Spaide for the Poetry Foundation wrote, "Amid its openhearted tributes, *suddenly we* puts Shockley's honed stylistic innovations on unmissable display. A lush biodiversity of forms, often in unprecedented variations." The *Los Angeles Review of Books* featured a collaborative review of *suddenly we* and Will Harris's *Brother Poem* by poets Victoria Chang and Dean Rader. Chang said of the collection, "Perhaps the play in Shockley's book is one of subversion or protest. I'm interested in how play doesn't diminish the subject matter in the work but supplements it," while Rader stated, "It is as if she is seeking community or connection through humor, sweetness, vulnerability. I get the sense in these poems that Shockley is dropping her—and asking us to drop our—guard." In a review for *ASAP Journal*, Sarah Jane Cervenak wrote, "There is a beautiful way that Shockley conceptually dwells ... with respect to a notion of 'we' that floats above and around a place, floats above or around words, and where connection is sensed even if the actual flight feeling is not easily shared."

Author Biography
Evie Shockley is an award-winning poet and scholar. Her poetry collections include *a half-red sea* (2006); *the new black* (2011), winner of the Hurston/Wright Legacy Award in Poetry; *semiautomatic* (2018), a Pulitzer Prize finalist and winner of the Hurston/Wright Legacy Award in Poetry. Her critical works include *Renegade Poetics: Black Aesthetics* and *Formal Innovation in African American Poetry* (2011).

Melynda Fuller

Review Sources
Cervenak, Sarah Jane. "The Page's Turn: Praise for Gayl Jones's *Butter*, Gabrielle Octavia Rucker's *Dereliction*, and Evie Shockley's *suddenly we*." Review of *suddenly we*, by Evie Shockley. *ASAP Journal: The Open-Access Platform of /Journal*, 6 Oct. 2023, asapjournal.com/the-pages-turn-praise-for-gayl-joness-butter-gabrielle-octavia-ruckers-dereliction-and-evie-shockleys-suddenly-we-sarah-jane-cervenak/. Accessed 22 Nov. 2023.

Chang, Victoria, and Dean Rader. "Two Roads: A Review-in-Dialogue of Will Harris's 'Brother Poem' and Evie Shockley's 'Suddenly We.'" *Los Angeles Review of Books*, 13 July 2023, lareviewofbooks.org/article/two-roads-a-review-in-dialogue-about-will-harriss-brother-poem-and-evie-shockleys-suddenly-we. Accessed 22 Nov. 2023.

Hoffert, Barbara. Review of *suddenly we*, by Evie Shockley. *Library Journal*, 1 Apr. 2023, www.libraryjournal.com/review/suddenly-we-2179085. Accessed 22 Nov. 2023.

Spaide, Christopher. Review of *suddenly we*, by Evie Shockley. *Poetry Foundation*, www.poetryfoundation.org/harriet-books/reviews/159859/suddenly-we. Accessed 21 Nov. 2023. Accessed 22 Nov. 2023.

Spring, Angela María. "On Poetry: April 2023." Review of *suddenly we*, by Evie Shockley. *Washington Independent Review of Books*, 26 Apr. 2023, www.washingtonindependentreviewofbooks.com/index.php/features/on-poetry-april-2023. Accessed 22 Nov. 2023.

Review of *suddenly we*, by Evie Shockley. *Publishers Weekly*, www.publishersweekly.com/9780819500236. Accessed 21 Nov. 2023. Accessed 22 Nov. 2023.

Symphony of Secrets

Author: Brendan Slocumb
Publisher: Anchor (New York). 448 pp.
Type of work: Novel
Time: 1918–1936; present day
Locales: New York City; Oxford, North Carolina

Interspersed between 1920s and present-day Manhattan, Symphony of Secrets *explores the enduring power of music connecting individuals across centuries, and the troubling erasure of diverse voices within the industry.*

Principal characters

FREDERIC DELANEY, a famous classical composer from the 1920s
JOSEPHINE REED, a musical savant and close confidant of Delaney
KEVIN "BERN" HENDRICKS, a music professor and Frederic Delaney expert
EBONI WASHINGTON, a friend of Bern and brilliant computer scientist
MALLORY DELANEY ROBERTS, a descendant of Delaney and head of the Delaney Foundation

For much of history, classical music was dominated by White male composers. Those who did not match that description, such as women and people of color, were excluded from the genre, and their contributions largely expunged from the annals of musical history. This systemic discrimination not only prevented the wider dissemination of these individuals' creative works but also deprived them of recognition for their talents. As a result, the industry remained perpetually homogeneous. Author Brendan Slocumb, a Black classical musician himself, strives to raise awareness for and nurture the skills of marginalized creatives, particularly those who have faced discrimination because of their race, gender, disability, or socioeconomic status. Released just a year after his debut work, *The Violin Conspiracy* (2022), Slocumb's *Symphony of Secrets* (2023) continues his dedicated pursuit to cultivate a more inclusive, representative classical genre, particularly by highlighting the contributions of Black musicians.

Symphony of Secrets, while framed as an enthralling mystery, deftly confronts the social inequities of past and present America, addressing prejudice in both classical music and higher education. The novel follows two distinct timelines set nearly one hundred years apart. In the present, the accomplished music professor Bern Hendricks is approached by a philanthropic organization, the Delaney Foundation, with a unique task: to decode and transcribe the long-lost symphony of the famous classical composer

Brendan Slocumb

Frederic Delaney. Bern is considered an expert on Delaney, having devoted his life to studying the composer's vast portfolio. But when Bern notices a cryptic symbol embedded in the lost opera, he recruits his former classmate and computer scientist, Eboni Washington, to assist him in deciphering the meaning of the peculiar "doodles" often found in Delaney's sheet music. Thus, a thrilling detective adventure ensues, with the duo zealously collaborating to crack Delaney's mysterious code. Through their intense research, they unearth the identity of Josephine Reed, a Black woman whom they theorize may have played a substantial, yet overlooked, role in Delaney's success.

Slocumb mirrors Bern and Eboni's crusade with a parallel timeline occurring in 1920s Manhattan, in which a young "Freddy" Delaney is struggling to secure employment as an untrained musician. Through New York City's vibrant jazz club scene, Delaney encounters Josephine, an Black woman with an astonishing ear for music who—in current terms would most likely be described as neurodivergent—is labeled by her contemporaries as "crazy." Driven by a mixture of pity and fascination, but mostly self-interest, Delaney befriends Josephine and the two begin to navigate newfound success in the burgeoning Manhattan music industry. The events of the past are intermixed frequently with the contemporary timeline, in which Bern and Eboni discover the complete erasure of Josephine's involvement with Delaney, and with it, her potential contributions to his musical accreditation. The pair soon realize that the famous composer's legacy is complicated by hidden truths, compelling them to bravely confront power and privilege to rectify past and present injustices.

Perhaps the most impressive aspect of Slocumb's sophomore novel is the encapsulation of diverse representation. Not only are three protagonists Black Americans, but the central character driving the plot of *Symphony of Secrets* is a neurodivergent woman. Throughout the book, Josephine's musical genius is often dismissed, primarily due to her introverted demeanor and jumbled manner of speaking. Her talents are further overlooked as her accessibility to power and resources is limited by her race and gender. While it could be argued that the portrayal of Josephine as a prodigy falls into the historic trope of depicting neurodivergent people exclusively as savants, Slocumb effectively dispels this cliché. The author ensures that Josephine emerges as a fully realized character with ambitions and flaws who significantly develops throughout the course of the story. Crucially, the author provides alternating perspectives throughout the novel, granting readers access into how Josephine perceives the world, her racing thoughts, and the broad spectrum of her emotions. For example, while Delaney views her as doting and naive, Josephine's point of view reveals her enterprising spirit and strong will. As the novel unfolds, Josephine encounters triumphs and challenges in the classical music industry of 1920s New York City, effectively dismissing the possibility of her being reduced to a one-dimensional depiction of neurodivergence.

In addition to presenting the discrepancies of how characters perceive one another versus themselves, the alternating timelines and perspectives serve as driving forces for the plot. The narrative structure steadily reveals critical details through Bern and Eboni's research, as well as the direct viewpoints of Josephine and Delaney, allowing for an exhilarating oscillation between suspense and action. The chapters, presented in large segments from each timeline, provide a methodical disclosure of information from the differing character point of view, ultimately culminating in an exploration of the complex legacy of Delaney's career. These separate timelines also often mirror each other in tone, particularly through the character's actions and emotions. For example, one scene from Bern's perspective describes his inner turmoil regarding his shifting view of Delaney, as he trembles "like a champagne glass about to overflow, about to slosh over with emotions." The following chapter morphs into Delaney's point of view as he grapples with his own burdens, describing his day as if he "were immersed in a dull roar, as if the world's sounds didn't quite penetrate." In employing this technique, Slocumb is able to maintain a harmonious narrative despite the frequent shifts in timelines and perspective.

The parallel structure also serves to underscore one of the themes of *Symphony of Secrets*; the similar injustice Bern, Eboni, and Josephine face because of their race and gender. Through the mirrored perspectives, Slocumb reveals a disheartening lack of progress toward inclusivity in both classical music and higher education. In the 1920s timeline, Josephine experiences a remarkable restriction of freedom despite her gifted abilities. Her lack of agency is starkly contrasted against Delaney, whose Whiteness allows him to navigate the industry effortlessly. His complexion, charm, and successful scores grant him privileged access to coveted venues and influential people, while Josephine remains powerless under his alleged protection.

Similarly, though Bern has earned a PhD and is recognized as the leading authority in his field, he frequently acknowledges throughout the novel several times when he felt a disadvantage due to his race. He often agonizes over his vernacular and clothing, always desiring the perception of a polished appearance when interacting with his White peers in higher education or with representatives of the Delaney Foundation. Crucially, Bern attributes his introduction to the classical genre to the Delaney Foundation and, by extension, his life's accomplishments. He is a "DF kid," having participated in an outreach program offered by the organization that supplied instruments to underprivileged youths. As a result of the initiative, Bern discovered his passion for classical music through which he founded a firm sense of identity. While Bern has devoted his life to studying Delaney and feels indebted to the Foundation, as he and Eboni unearth the details about Josephine and Delaney's relationship, he is not only confronted with White arrogance but how powerful entities utilize bigotry to protect their own interests.

Despite presenting a bleak commentary on the limited progress of social change in America, Slocumb conveys an uplifting central theme regarding the profound influence of music on people's lives. Through his various characters, he asserts the universality of music and the manifold methods by which it can impact individuals. In *Symphony of Secrets*, both Bern and Delaney are masters of the technicalities of compositions, such as the notes, chords, and stylistic differences. They use high-level language when describing songs or sounds and recognize the specific attributes of a piece that elicit an emotional reaction. In contrast, Josephine experiences music as a means to expel and imbue meaning in the way she is absorbing the world through sounds, interactions, and feelings. Though she is unable to express the technical aspects of songs, Josephine demonstrates a complex, visceral knowledge of melodies and the release they can evoke. With all three, Slocumb emphasizes the immense opportunities music can offer when one demonstrates passion and determination in their craft. Thus, while the characters range in their formalized training, they all embody a shared appreciation for the deep effect music has on their thoughts, emotions, and actions.

In his education, music, and literary careers, Slocumb has consistently striven to improve diversity by increasing the representation and celebration of marginalized groups in these spaces. In *Symphony of Secrets*, Slocumb creates a conduit for these communities in three of his main characters: Bern, Eboni, and Josephine. Those reviewing the novel praised the author's extensive inclusion of details to construct characters with distinctive personalities and ambitions. In his article for the *Washington Post*, Erik Gleibermann wrote, "Delaney, Bern and Eboni are all entertaining, but Josephine emerges as singularly intriguing." He specifically cited Slocumb's deft portrayal of her neurodiversity, particularly the sensory descriptions of her perception of the world in chapters written from her point of view.

Additionally, those reviewing *Symphony of Secrets* celebrated Slocumb's ability to incorporate his musical background not only through technical descriptions of compositions but also by employing a melodious style and structure throughout the novel. Critics found Slocumb's command of pacing and the novel's parallel plotlines to be masterful and compelling. Alyssa Cole, writing for the *New York Times*, described the structure of *Symphony of Secrets* as analogous to a thrilling piece of music, stating, "what makes the book sing is how it makes audible the chords that echo between present and past, coming together to create a consonant harmony." She also applauded the comparable lives of Josephine and Bern despite the two being separated by over a century. As described by Cole, the two face "demoralizing" experiences at the hands of White privilege, yet both maintain a resolute reserve of hope and pursuit of justice through this endless love and appreciation of music. Overall, reviews of *Symphony of Secrets* reveal Slocumb was successful in his intentions to celebrate and amplify those communities often underrepresented in the music industry.

Author Biography

Brendan Slocumb is an accomplished musician and educator. He earned several accolades for his teaching, including a Teacher of the Year in 2005, and has performed with several professional orchestras. His first novel, *The Violin Conspiracy*, was a Good Morning America Book Club Pick.

Annie Schwartz

Review Sources

Cole, Alyssa. "A Lost Opera Manuscript Discovered. A Century-Old Mystery Ignited." Review of *Symphony of Secrets*, by Brendan Slocumb. *The New York Times*, 18 Apr. 2023, www.nytimes.com/2023/04/18/books/review/symphony-of-secrets-brendan-slocumb.html. Accessed 25 Sept. 2023.

Gleibermann, Erik. "Brendan Slocumb's Latest Is As Rich and Suspenseful As 'The Violin Conspiracy.'" Review of *Symphony of Secrets*, by Brendan Slocumb. *The Washington Post*, 20 Apr. 2023, www.washingtonpost.com/books/2023/04/20/brendan-slocumb-symphony-thriller. Accessed 23 Sept. 2023.

Review of *Symphony of Secrets*, by Brendan Slocumb. *Kirkus Reviews*, 23 Feb. 2023, www.kirkusreviews.com/book-reviews/brendan-slocumb/symphony-of-secrets. Accessed 24 Sept. 2023.

Review of *Symphony of Secrets*, by Brendan Slocumb. *Publishers Weekly*, 2023, www.publishersweekly.com/9780593315446. Accessed 27 Sept. 2023.

Wallace, Julia. "Review: Thrilling Novel Filled With Music and Plot Twists." Review of *Symphony of Secrets*, by Brendan Slocumb. *The Ithacan*, 4 May 2023, theithacan.org/47691/life-culture/reviews/review-thrilling-novel-filled-with-music-and-plot-twists. Accessed 23 Sept. 2023.

Temple Folk

Author: Aaliyah Bilal (b. ca. 1982)
Publisher: Simon & Schuster (New York). 239 pp.
Type of work: Short fiction
Time: Twentieth and twenty-first centuries
Locale: United States

Aaliyah Bilal's debut short story collection, Temple Folk, *explores the lives of Black Muslims in the United States through carefully written stories that expose both the good and the bad experienced by members of the Nation of Islam community.*

Principal characters

SISTER MEMPHIS, a leader among the women of her temple, originally from Memphis
SISTER NORAH, a middle-aged widow taking care of her son, Hanif
HANIF, Sister Norah's son, who has developmental disabilities
HAROLD, a lawyer who has distanced himself from his home and the temple where he was raised
JAMES, a college acquaintance of Harold's who has run into trouble as an adult
IMANI, a high school senior exploring how she fits into the Black Muslim community
QADIRAH, the daughter of a famous preacher who has found a new life in a temple community
TAQWA, a young woman haunted by her dead father
JABRIL, Taqwa's free-spirited brother who was estranged from the family

When Yahdon Israel posted an unorthodox call for submissions on Instagram after being appointed senior editor at the prominent publishing company Simon & Schuster in 2021, Aaliyah Bilal, a self-taught writer who did not have an agent, took a chance and sent him a manuscript. The decision paid off, as Bilal landed a book deal that resulted in the publication of her debut short story collection, *Temple Folk*, in 2023 to widespread acclaim. The work caught the eye of Israel and soon many others in the literary world in large part because it focuses on a culture rarely portrayed in mainstream American fiction: Black Muslims in the United States, in particular those who belong to or were associated with the Nation of Islam, a religious movement that draws its ideology from the Islamic faith as well as political ideologies such as Black nationalism. Inspired by her grandparents, who were members of the Black Power movement and members of the Nation of Islam, Bilal took stories she had heard as a child and young adult and began to spin them into the ten pieces that make up the collection.

Aaliyah Bilal

Temple Folk is wide in its representation of Nation of Islam members. Many of the stories, like opener "Blue," the heartfelt and heartbreaking "Candy for Hanif," and the surprising "Nikkah," focus on the particular experiences of women within the temple community. Yet Bilal is careful to also interrogate the lives of men, children, and older adults who make up this diverse body of people. Life within the temple itself is often at the center of Bilal's narratives, but she also explores the Black Muslim experience in society at large. The realities of modern existence—including the ups and downs of online dating, the effects of poverty, the pitfalls and promises of crime, and the changing and complex ways in which people view themselves—provide interesting opportunities for the cast of characters as they maneuver their complicated daily lives. Bilal often asks what might happen to someone whose life takes a sudden turn.

Like many short story collections, *Temple Folk* includes a couple of keystone pieces. These include "Nikkah," in which the Qadirah, the daughter of a famous preacher, turns to the internet to find a match who feels as strongly about his Muslim faith as she does, and "Due North," a story about a young woman being haunted by her recently deceased father without reason. Appearing at the midway point and concluding the collection, respectively, these stories work to anchor *Temple Folk*'s many ideas and directions to Bilal's central concern, which is the struggle of people longing to find a true home in the world while staying true to themselves.

Bilal's strong focus on her characters' lives—both external and internal—is apparent even in stories that feature larger historical events occurring in the background. For example, in "Blue," the plot involves members of the Muslim Girls Training class taking a bus trip to Chicago to attend a celebration of Saviours' Day (a holiday commemorating the birthday of Nation of Islam founder Wallace Fard Muhammad). Contextual clues, and especially a piece of news that eventually reaches the group, places the action precisely in February 1975. But these touches mainly provide context, with the true heart of the story lying in the intimately realistic characterization. Helping to organize the group is Sister Memphis, a woman from Memphis, Tennessee, with a traumatic past. A trainee named Saundra arrives with a young child named Danielle in tow. Danielle is unruly, but Saundra insists she must come along on the trip. So, the child is assigned a seat next to the austere Memphis, who is certain she can keep the child in line. Once on the road, Memphis and Danielle begin to connect, and soon the child is nearly serene sitting next to her guardian for the ride. When the buses must stop at a truck stop along the way, a run-in with a drunken attendant casts a sinister shadow on the trip, with the man slurring his words as he throws racist jabs the women's way. This confrontation then escalates just as the women believe themselves to be clear from his path. This vividly drawn present world is intercut with flashbacks providing an in-depth look at Sister Memphis's early life.

Many of the stories feature a similar tone as characters face some kind of shift from relative certainty to the unknown. In a later entry called "Candy for Hanif," also focused on the women of a temple, in this case the women who run the temple's kitchen, the lives of four Sisters intertwine despite their different backgrounds. Sister Norah, the youngest and most recent addition to the temple kitchen, is raising her son, Hanif, who has developmental disabilities, after the death of her husband. Early in the story, Bilal reveals that several of the women were also prematurely widowed and are, somewhat ironically, leading better lives as a result. Sister Norah, however, is facing nothing but difficulty and tension as she tries to keep her adult son out of a group home and under her care. As the women go on a dinner cruise in thanks for their hard work in the kitchen, Sister Norah is left to ponder how things might be different while her three friends enjoy their night on the dancefloor.

This question of what life could be, and how it contrasts with reality, haunts many of the other characters in *Temple Folk* as well. For example, in "Janaza," Harold, a man who was raised within the Nation of Islam community but left as a young man, returns home following the death of his childhood temple's leader. Visiting the funeral home, he encounters James, a man he knew in college whose life took a very different turn. James, the reader learns, may be responsible for a double homicide—yet he stands before Harold and says nothing like that took place. James and Harold are forced to behold each other as grown, aging men whose lives were shaped by the foundations of their youth and consider alternative paths.

The collection's final story, "Due North," centers on its narrator, Taqwa, as she deals with other people pushing her to consider what a fuller life might look like. Taqwa, a young woman who lives strictly by the tenets of her Muslim faith, finds herself haunted following the death of her father. He appears to her as an apparition, eventually manifesting a physical body and taking residence in her home. Taqwa is not sure why her father has come back, but she keeps him at bay with images of women in lingerie and bathing suits, a strategy that seems to work. It is only when she discloses her father's secret visits to her brother, Jabril, who was long ago estranged from the family because of his parents' strict rule, that Taqwa's true desires in life come into clearer focus. Both her father, who tells her during one of his early hauntings that he misled her during his life, and her brother push her to see her true, beautiful nature. Bilal's story telling particularly shines in such moments, with a sensitivity of thought that informs the kinship between characters who are struggling to become their true selves.

Temple Folk was received significant critical acclaim, including nomination for the National Book Award for Fiction. The judges of the award, in a statement published on the National Book Foundation's website, noted that the collection "offers an intimate look into a community rarely explored in fiction, but it is the skill of debut author Aaliyah Bilal—and her rare gift for capturing the nuances of the human condition—that makes this short story collection one of the most important books of the year." The book also received a starred review from *Publishers Weekly*, with the anonymous critic concluding that "These singular stories offer great insight on a community underexplored in literature." The critic for *Kirkus Reviews* also praised Bilal's debut effort, calling it "beautifully thorough" and "well-balanced." However, they did note some points of critique, suggesting that "despite the many, many attributes that make up this fine collection, there is a sameness to the structure and style of narration in many of the stories, especially those that are voiced in first person. The narrators tend to resemble each other."

Other reviewers were also highly positive. The anonymous *New Yorker* reviewer highlighted that, "Built largely around vignettes, Bilal's stories depict characters who serve as sensitive guides to matters of apostasy, racial prejudice, and gender roles." *Temple Folk* was named a must-read book by *Time* magazine in 2023, with reviewer Shannon Carlin summing up the critical consensus that the book "offers a vivid and nuanced portrait of the Black Muslim experience" and characterizing it as "Bilal's love letter to her community."

Author Biography
Aaliyah Bilal's debut short story collection, *Temple Folk*, was published in 2023 and shortlisted for the National Book Award for fiction. Her writing has also appeared in publications such as *The Rumpus*, and *Michigan Quarterly Review*.

Melynda Fuller

Review Sources
Carlin, Shannon. "*Temple Folk*: 100 Must-Read Books of 2023." Review of *Temple Folk*, by Aaliyah Bilal. *Time*, 14 Nov. 2023, time.com/collection/must-read-books-2023/6332723/temple-folk/. Accessed 25 Jan. 2024.
Chisolm, Archuleta. "Book Review: *Temple Folk* Portrays the Lived Experiences of Black Muslims' Faith, Family, and Freedom." Review of *Temple Folk*, by Aaliyah Bilal. *Black Girl Nerds*, 29 June 2023, blackgirlnerds.com/book-review-temple-folk-portrays-the-lived-experiences-of-black-muslims-faith-family-and-freedom/. Accessed 25 Jan. 2024.
O'Neal, Sarah. Review of *Temple Folk*, by Aaliyah Bilal. *BookPage*, 7 Nov. 2023, www.bookpage.com/reviews/temple-folk-aaliyah-bilal-audiobook-review/. Accessed 25 Jan. 2024.
Review of *Temple Folk*, by Aaliyah Bilal. *Kirkus Reviews*, 4 July 2023, www.kirkusreviews.com/book-reviews/aaliyah-bilal/temple-folk/. Accessed 25 Jan. 2024.
Review of *Temple Folk*, by Aaliyah Bilal, et al. *The New Yorker*, 21 Aug. 2023, www.newyorker.com/magazine/2023/08/28/the-peacock-and-the-sparrow-temple-folk-schoenberg-and-brave-the-wild-river. Accessed 25 Jan. 2024.
Review of *Temple Folk*, by Aaliyah Bilal. *Publishers Weekly*, www.publishersweekly.com/9781668020289. Accessed 23 Jan. 2024.
"Temple Folk." *National Book Foundation*, 2023, www.nationalbook.org/books/temple-folk/. Accessed 16 Feb. 2024.

Tenacious Beasts
Wildlife Recoveries That Change How We Think about Animals

Author: Christopher J. Preston (b. ca. 1968)
Publisher: MIT Press (Cambridge, MA). 319 pp.
Type of work: Nature

In Tenacious Beasts: Wildlife Recoveries That Change How We Think about Animals, *Christopher J. Preston discusses efforts to increase the populations of select animal species and the lessons that can be learned from such resurgences.*

When writer and educator Christopher J. Preston moved to the United States in the 1990s, he was initially startled by the prevalence of wildlife, having spent little time around animals that were not pets during his early life in England. In subsequent decades, however, his experiences working in nature and observing interactions involving animals, humans, and the natural landscape gave Preston a more nuanced understanding of the relationships between human beings and wildlife—relationships that ultimately underly much of his 2023 book, *Tenacious Beasts: Wildlife Recoveries That Change How We Think about Animals*. Preston previously explored concepts related to wildlife recovery in his book *The Synthetic Age: Outdesigning Evolution, Resurrecting Species, and Reengineering Our World* (2018), which deals in part with the potential future use of technology to create artificial lifeforms or resurrect extinct organisms. In *Tenacious Beasts*, however, he details ongoing contemporary efforts to increase the populations of species that have been decimated or even pushed to the brink of extinction by factors including overhunting, the fur trade, dam building, competition from invasive species, and climate change.

Along the way, Preston chronicles both the past and present human actions that have contributed to some species' precarious positions and the actions scientists, lawmakers, Indigenous leaders, volunteer organizations, and others are taking to correct past wrongs and provide threatened animals with better chances of survival. He stresses that while the wildlife recoveries discussed in *Tenacious Beasts* are undoubtedly signs of progress, their success should not be taken as a signal that further efforts are unnecessary. "Animal populations are not out of danger," Preston writes near the start of the book. To the contrary, "their outlook remains dire." He likewise notes that his work specifically covers a select group of wildlife recoveries taking place in Europe and the US, the geographic regions with which he is most familiar; however, efforts to rejuvenate struggling animal populations are being carried out worldwide, and the insights gleaned from wildlife recoveries in the United States and Europe are likely also "available elsewhere."

Tenacious Beasts is divided into seven sections, and most sections include multiple chapters. Preston begins his discussion of wildlife recoveries and includes chapters dealing with the resurgence of wolf populations in the United States as well as in European countries such as Germany and the Netherlands. There are some key differences between the two recoveries: in the United States, for instance, wolves were deliberately transported to and reintroduced into targeted areas, while in Europe, the proximity of many countries has enabled wolves to cross national borders and claim new territories on their own. As Preston explains, wolves are not always welcomed by the human residents when they arrive in a new area; this stems from longstanding cultural narratives that depict wolves as frightening, villainous creatures prone to harming humans and from the real-life tendency of wolves to prey on sheep and other livestock. Successful efforts to combat societal opposition to wolves, then, often require not only public outreach initiatives designed to dispel old misconceptions but also tangible aid to farmers whose livelihoods would be harmed by predation. Preston calls attention to the work of volunteer organizations such as Germany's WikiWolves, which assists farmers by installing fences designed to protect sheep from roaming wolves. Organizations such as WikiWolves, Preston points out, provide material assistance but also help to forge connections between pro-wolf volunteers and anti-wolf farmers, the latter of whom may become less opposed to the presence of wolves in the region thanks to the volunteers' efforts.

Throughout the remainder of *Tenacious Beasts*, Preston delves into the recovery of a number of other species, including the American bison. As he explains, the decline in the US bison population was the result of excessive hunting but was also inextricably linked to the US government's suppression of Indigenous people amid the country's push for western expansion, as efforts to kill large numbers of bison were historically carried out both to interfere with Indigenous lifeways and to clear land for settlers, most of whom were White. Efforts to restore the US bison population, then, have a complex history and are complicated further by issues related to Indigenous sovereignty and land rights. In addition, Preston writes, many surviving bison are not genetically pure examples of the species. Rather, crossbreeding with cattle has left them with some cattle genes, and that fact has led some bison proponents to question whether many of the existing animals should truly be counted as bison in a wildlife-recovery context.

Christopher J. Preston
Courtesy MIT Press

One particularly fascinating phenomenon Preston brings to light throughout *Tenacious Beasts* is the manner in which some animal species help shape the landscapes in which they live and benefit the other wildlife around them. American bison, for instance, fertilize prairie soil with their waste and help plants to grow in that environment; these plants can then be eaten not only by the bison themselves but also by other animals, including pronghorn antelope. Beavers, the focus of another portion of the book, help to shape rivers and streams through the construction of natural dams that, unlike the dams built by humans, interfere minimally with fish migration patterns. By trapping water in a particular area, beaver dams likewise contribute to the overall health of the land surrounding the waterway, rendering it more habitable for insects, birds, and other creatures. Preston points out that on one notable occasion, researchers experimented with relocating beavers to an area of Washington that had recently experienced a wildfire and found that the beavers had a substantial impact on the restoration of the soil and plant life there. Efforts to improve the state of an ecosystem through the strategic introduction of a key animal also took place in the United Kingdom, where European bison were released into the Wilder Blean woodland in Kent, England. Unlike beaver, which had lived throughout North America prior to the arrival of European fur traders, European bison are not believed to be native to England, and their arrival in Kent was thus not a reintroduction but a new introduction that wildlife managers hoped would improve the woodland's soil and biodiversity.

While adding beavers or bison to a specific area can have substantial benefits for the overall ecosystem, the arrival or introduction of new species in regions they had not previously inhabited is not always beneficial to the animals already living there. Preston provides an example in the form of the barred owl. Previously found in the eastern portion of the US, barred owls moved west over the course of the twentieth century and began to settle in forests that were already home to smaller spotted owls, whose habitats and population had previously been threatened by deforestation. Proliferating in the forests, barred owls represented a new threat to the spotted owl population, and as a result, some wildlife managers were tasked with the controversial duty of killing barred owls to reduce their numbers and protect the spotted owls. That tactic, like others discussed at points throughout *Tenacious Beasts*, raises a host of ethical questions, and Preston considers multiple perspectives on that approach and the other complex ethical issues he considers. Indeed, one of the book's strengths is the presentation of multiple varied perspectives, and it was made possible in large part by Preston's extensive research and discussions with experienced individuals working in different wildlife-related fields. The endnotes and reference list provide further evidence of the author's thorough approach, while the portions of the book dealing with Preston's personal visits to some of the locales under discussion demonstrate his willingness to seek out firsthand knowledge.

Above all else, *Tenacious Beasts* promotes the idea that if more wildlife recoveries are to be successful, human societies must undergo a shift in the prevailing mindset about human-animal relationships. In the US, such a shift would require much of the population to reject not only the deeply influential views of early European colonizers, who believed the country's wildlife existed to be exploited, but also the beliefs of some later American conservationists, who thought that enforcing strict boundaries between nature and human society was the only way the natural world could be protected and who had little, if any, concern for Indigenous land rights or traditions when setting such boundaries. Rather than considering animals something to be either exploited or admired from afar, Preston argues, human beings must grow accustomed to living alongside a variety of wildlife, even when doing so requires them to make changes to their own lifestyles.

As Preston demonstrates, such a shift is already underway in some rural areas of Italy, where the resurgent Marsican bear population has required farmers to bear-proof their properties but has also inspired the creation and sale of bear-themed bread and wine. Beyond being essential to further recoveries, such a shift in mindset is particularly crucial because of the ongoing phenomenon of climate change, which Preston identifies as a major threat to many of the world's species. Continuing increases in global temperatures and the damage already done to animal populations around the world mean that changing the fate of threatened species will remain a challenging task in the years to come. However, the examples presented in *Tenacious Beasts* demonstrate that such change is possible—and worth the effort.

Tenacious Beasts: Wildlife Recoveries That Change How We Think about Animals received positive reviews from critics upon its publication. Reviewers widely appreciated Preston's nuanced approach to the book's subject matter and inclusion of diverging perspectives on the management of land and wildlife. In a review for the Royal Geographical Society's magazine, *Geographical*, Geordie Torr identified Preston as "an extremely engaging guide to the philosophical complexities of conservation." Jonathan Hahn, writing for the Sierra Club's *Sierra* magazine, wrote approvingly about the ways in which the author "unpacks and disavows some of our most common and problematic cultural conceptions of wild animals."

Critics, though cognizant of the hardships many animal species still face, likewise praised Preston's hope-inspiring discussion of successful wildlife recoveries. The anonymous reviewer for *Publishers Weekly* wrote that Preston came across as "clear-eyed about the need for meaningful change" even as he "mostly stays upbeat" and stated that the book "will hearten nature lovers." Writing for *Library Journal*, Catherine Lantz made a similar point and characterized *Tenacious Beasts* as "an excellent recommendation to readers searching for thoughtful but hopeful books on the future of nature." The book's relatively narrow geographical scope did receive some notice from reviewers; for example, the anonymous critic for *Kirkus* called attention to Preston's focus on wildlife recoveries in the US and Europe and added, "Conservationists are working hard in Africa and Asia, but there is apparently little to cheer about." However, that point did not detract from the *Kirkus* reviewer's appreciation of Preston's work, which they described as "a satisfying account of a dozen successes without minimizing the difficulties involved."

Author Biography
Christopher J. Preston is the author of *The Synthetic Age: Outdesigning Evolution, Resurrecting Species, and Reengineering Our World* (2018). He has also taught at the university level and worked as a professor of environmental philosophy at the University of Montana.

Joy Crelin

Review Sources
"Briefly Noted." Review of *In Memoriam*, by Alice Winn; *Rombo*, by Esther Kinsky; *Benjamin Banneker and Us*, by Rachel Jamison Webster; and *Tenacious Beasts*, by Christopher J. Preston. *The New Yorker*, 17 Apr. 2023, www.newyorker.com/magazine/2023/04/24/in-memoriam-rombo-benjamin-banneker-and-us-tenacious-beasts. Accessed 16 Jan. 2024.
Hahn, Jonathan. "The Tenacious Beasts That Don't Give Up." Review of *Tenacious Beasts*, by Christopher J. Preston. *Sierra*, 9 Apr. 2023, www.sierraclub.org/sierra/1-spring/books/tenacious-beasts-don-t-give-up-christopher-preston. Accessed 16 Jan. 2024.
Lantz, Catherine. Review of *Tenacious Beasts*, by Christopher J. Preston. *Library Journal*, 2 Dec. 2022, www.libraryjournal.com/review/tenacious-beasts-wildlife-recoveries-that-change-how-we-think-about-animals-2165333. Accessed 16 Jan. 2024.
Review of *Tenacious Beasts*, by Christopher J. Preston. *Kirkus Reviews*, 7 Nov. 2022, www.kirkusreviews.com/book-reviews/christopher-j-preston/tenacious-beasts/. Accessed 16 Jan. 2024.
Review of *Tenacious Beasts*, by Christopher J. Preston. *Publishers Weekly*, 16 Nov. 2022, www.publishersweekly.com/9780262047562. Accessed 16 Jan. 2024.
Torr, Geordie. "*Tenacious Beasts*: The Philosophical Complexities of Wildlife Conservation." Review of *Tenacious Beasts*, by Christopher J. Preston. *Geographical*, 30 Jan. 2023, geographical.co.uk/book-reviews/tenacious-beasts-review. Accessed 16 Jan. 2024.

The Terraformers

Author: Annalee Newitz (b. 1969)
Publisher: Tor (New York). Illustrated. 352 pp.
Type of work: Novel
Time: 59,006–60,610 CE
Locale: Planet Sask-E, a.k.a. Sasky

With a plot spanning more than a thousand years in a distant future, Annalee Newitz's ambitious novel The Terraformers *(2023) explores complex ethical challenges facing inhabitants of a planet purpose-built to be a paradise, offering both highly imaginative worldbuilding and insightful social commentary.*

Principal characters
DESTRY THOMAS, a ranger with the Environmental Rescue Team (ERT)
WHISTLE, her mount and helper, an intelligent flying moose
NIL TOM, her friend and fellow ranger
MISHA, her protégé
RONNIE DRAKE, the vice president of the planetary development company Verdance Corporation
SULFUR, a Archaean who works with Misha
SCRUBJAY, a sentient flying vehicle
MOOSE, a journalist cat person
CYLINDRA, an executive of the Emerald corporation

The concept of terraforming—a hypothesis that science could turn other planets or moons into Earthlike habitats for humans—has existed since the late nineteenth century. During the twentieth century, the idea became a staple of science fiction, including in works by esteemed authors such as Robert Heinlein, Arthur C. Clarke, Poul Anderson, Isaac Asimov, and Kim Stanley Robinson. Acclaimed journalist and novelist Annalee Newitz simultaneously builds on and reworks that tradition with *The Terraformers* (2023), a densely packed work of epic scope that projects many weighty twenty-first century social issues into the far future. As the title suggests, planetary engineering is a central concern, providing a backdrop for commentary on everything from environmentalism and urbanism to capitalism and posthumanism. Yet Newitz gives these serious themes a unique spin, tempering the broad scientific speculation and social critiques with rich characterization, plenty of humor, and a refreshing sense of optimism.

Annalee Newitz

The Terraformers is set on a planet named Sask-E (colloquially called "Sasky"), so far from Earth that the Sun appears as no more than a pinpoint of light even under powerful magnification. The setting is also distant in time: Part I of the book, "Settlers," opens in the year 59,006, while Parts II and III take place approximately 700 and 1,600 years later, respectively. Such an extensive timeline allows Newitz to not only introduce radically futuristic technology, biology, and more, but also imagine how those concepts themselves might evolve over many generations. And even the most outlandish elements are still grounded in science rather than pure fantasy; Newitz noted in interviews that they consulted extensively with an array of experts from materials scientists to geophysicists while developing the novel. The result is a blend of the familiar and the bizarre in classic sci-fi fashion.

Key parameters of Newitz's worldbuilding emerge throughout the narrative. There are no alien species, but humans—or more accurately, hominins—have expanded far beyond Earth and evolved considerably. In addition to Homo sapiens, who now enjoy lifespans of hundreds of years thanks to genetic and technological enhancement, there are even further genetically modified Homo diversus. Many animals have developed into more intelligent, person-like forms as well. Cooperation between humans and other life forms is a legacy of the so-called Great Bargain, an agreement reached many thousands of years ago to stave off ecological collapse through revolutionary forms of land management and agriculture. In some ways this has led to a utopian interplanetary civilization, with the Environmental Rescue Team (ERT) playing an important role in terraforming and sustainably managing other planets. But the pervasive influence of powerful corporations reveals major flaws in this idealistic view, as becomes apparent on Sask-E.

The entire planet of Sask-E is owned by the huge Verdance Corporation. The company has engineered it to attract investors and colonists interested in visiting or living on a world that recalls a pristine Earth of the Pleistocene Era. As Verdance's advertising notes, the terraforming of Sask-E has been 10,000 years in the making. Now it is nearing completion. The project is headed by Ronnie Drake, the H. diversus vice-president of Verdance, but the company has had relatively little direct presence on the planet since initiating its ecosystem development technology. Instead, as on other planets throughout the galaxy, a crew of ERT rangers has overseen the work of achieving the desired environmental balance.

One of these rangers, Destry Thomas, is the main protagonist of Part I. Destry is described as muscular, tanned, with gray-black hair and blue eyes, and more than five hundred years old. She is *H. sapiens*, but as usual was grown in a lab from heirloom genetic material and "decanted" rather than born. Created expressly to work on Sask-E, Destry is technically the property of Verdance, like everything else on the planet. She has multiple implanted sensors with which she connects to the local ecosystem to process data about current environmental conditions. Her mount—and work partner—is Whistle, a moose capable of flying and communicating with Destry through simple text messages.

The novel opens with Destry and Whistle discovering a person trespassing on Sask-E. The intruder turns out to be a *H. sapiens* remote—an avatar, an expensive toy controlled at a distance by someone offworld seeking to experience the planet's pristine conditions. The defiant remote claims that as a human he has a birthright to the Earth-like environment (hinting at some of the themes of land rights and anthropocentrism that Newitz will continue to develop). As part of her mission to protect the still-fragile ecosystem, Destry promptly destroys him and all evidence of his presence. However, she senses that the encounter might be the precursor to further trouble as Verdance prepares to open the planet to settlers and visitors.

In subsequent chapters, readers meet Destry's colleagues: her fellow ERT ranger and close friend Nil; his partner, Rocket, a sentient drone; Hellfire and Crisp, two cat-sized drones that share a consciousness; another Ranger named Long; and Long's mount, a moose named Midnight, in whom Whistle takes a romantic interest. Various aspects of the ERT creed are revealed, such as the motto: "We are not humans and animals. We are allies in the Great Bargain." A major tenet of the Great Bargain is the recognition that all living things want to survive, which is why killing is a last resort for ERT rangers. But it also becomes clear that Ronnie and other Verdance leaders are much more interested in profit than in remaining faithful to the Great Bargain.

The action of *The Terraformers* accelerates when an earthquake is detected at a volcano known as Spider Mountain and the ERT team is dispatched to investigate. There, they unexpectedly find a surviving community of *Homo archaea*—descendants of a population created to carry out work during an early phase of Sask-E terraforming but intended by Verdance to die off as the planet's atmosphere changed. Instead, the Archaeans adapted and developed an underground refuge known as Spider City. Long forgotten by Verdance, they now consider themselves wholly independent of the company. Destry and her fellow ERT members are sympathetic to Spider City residents (which include such diverse persons as naked mole rats and earthworms). However, Verdance wants to wipe them out, especially as the fact that Spider City has been self-governing for hundreds of years could legally threaten Sask-E's designation as a private planet. Destry ends up playing a key role in the ensuing conflict.

Part II of the novel, "Public Works," set hundreds of years later, sees new challenges emerging on Sask-E. Verdance still maintains influence on the planet but in diminished form, as it competes with other corporations such as Emerald, headed by executive Cylindra. These powers have helped develop numerous cities that are now beginning to feel the strains of growth. Misha, Destry's protégé and successor as ERT network analyst, has been ordered by the still-active Ronnie to create a public transit system to connect the planet's urban areas. Once again, however, the priorities of Verdance and other corporations do not necessarily align with the best interests of the world's inhabitants, and the actions of Misha and his allies bring fresh attention to various injustices.

The third and final part of the novel, "Gentrification," begins in the year 60,610. Clues are given about what happened on Earth eons ago to cause humans to seek alternative habitats in the first place and the founding of the first ERT. Meanwhile, the situation on Sask-E has changed radically yet again. The lead characters now are Scrubjay, a sentient train evolved from Misha's public transit system, and a cat person named Moose. But corporate malfeasance remains a problem, with Emerald violently destroying housing and discriminating against anyone who is not *H. sapiens*. A new revolution is in the air, especially as a crucial secret comes to light that offers new hope for the future of the planet and its increasingly diverse population.

Reception of *The Terraformers* was largely positive. In a starred review, *Publishers Weekly* hailed it as a "staggering feat of revolutionary imagination" that "feels like a new frontier in science fiction." Many critics praised the way Newitz takes many pressing contemporary issues and extrapolates them to a highly original fictional universe, offering incisive social commentary but never at the expense of an engaging narrative. For example, in his review for *Locus*, Gary K. Wolfe commended both the work's "refreshingly playful sensibility" and its "deeply serious critique of capitalism as a mechanism for environmental management." Wolfe concluded that the novel "entices with its brilliant and varied cast of human and nonhuman characters," ultimately presenting a "hopeful template that's a lot closer to home than all those distant light-years and centuries might at first suggest." Writing for *Scientific American*, Amy Brady agreed, noting that "The novel smartly argues that people—particularly when the term expands to include sentient forms far beyond human—might just be a planet's best resource."

Several reviewers did raise points of critique, however. In particular, some felt that the huge amount of time covered creates inherent storytelling challenges. For instance, writing for *Book and Film Globe*, Dan Friedman found that "Newitz struggles to keep narrative continuity across the final hundreds of years of the terraforming project." Similarly, as Mark Athitakis suggested for the *Los Angeles Times*, "because the book's three-part structure introduces a new set of characters each time, it's harder to feel invested in any one of them." These concerns are valid, and perhaps not all readers will connect with Newitz's ambitious vision. But many others will likely agree with Doug Johnstone's take in a review for *Big Issue* that *The Terraformers* is "Entertaining and thought-provoking in equal measure."

Author Biography
An experienced journalist, Annalee Newitz has written for *New Scientist*, the *New York Times*, the *Washington Post*, *Popular Science*, the *Atlantic*, the *New Yorker*, and many other outlets. Newitz debuted as a novelist with *Autonomous* (2017), which won the Lambda Award and was nominated for several other science fiction literary honors.

Jack Ewing

Review Sources

Athitakis, Mark. "In a New 'Galaxy Brain' Novel, It's AD 59,000—And We're Still Kind of a Mess." Review of *The Terraformers*, by Annalee Newitz. *Los Angeles Times*, 28 Jan. 2023, www.latimes.com/entertainment-arts/books/story/2023-01-28/in-a-new-galaxy-brain-novel-its-59-000-a-d-and-were-still-a-bit-of-a-mess. Accessed 24 Jan. 2024.

Brady, Amy. "If Future Humans Terraformed a New Earth, Could They Get It Right?" Review of *The Terraformers*, by Annalee Newitz. *Scientific American*, 1 Jan. 2023, www.scientificamerican.com/article/if-future-humans-terraformed-a-new-earth-could-they-get-it-right/. Accessed 10 Nov. 2023.

Di Filippo, Paul. "*The Terraformers* Is a Dazzling Look at the Distant Future." Review of *The Terraformers*, by Annalee Newitz. *The Washington Post*, 27 Jan. 2023, www.washingtonpost.com/books/2023/01/27/annalee-newitz-terraformers/. Accessed 23 Jan. 2024.

Friedman, Dan. "So Far Away, So Close." Review of *The Terraformers*, by Annalee Newitz. *Book and Film Globe*, 31 Jan., 2023, bookandfilmglobe.com/fiction/book-review-the-terraformers/. Accessed 10 Nov. 2023.

Johnstone, Doug. "*The Terraformers* Review: 'A Remarkable Piece of World Building.'" Review of *The Terraformers*, by Annalee Newitz. *Big Issue*, 11 Feb. 2023, bigissue.com/culture/books/the-terraformers-review-a-remarkable-piece-of-world-building/. Accessed 10 Nov. 2023.

Pickens, Chris. Review of *The Terraformers*, by Annalee Newitz. *BookPage*, 31 Jan. 2023, www.bookpage.com/reviews/the-terraformers/. Accessed 10 Nov. 2023.

Review of The Terraformers, by Annalee Newitz. *Publishers Weekly*, 26 Sept. 2023, www.publishersweekly.com/9781250228017. Accessed 24 Jan. 2024.

Wolfe, Gary K. Review of *The Terraformers*, by Annalee Newitz. *Locus*, 23 Feb. 2023, locusmag.com/2023/02/gary-k-wolfe-reviews-the-terraformers-by-annalee-newitz/. Accessed 10 Nov. 2023.

Thin Skin

Author: Jenn Shapland
Publisher: Pantheon (New York). 288 pp.
Type of work: Essays
Time: Present
Locales: The United States

*Thin Skin is a collection of essays about different topics, including racism, environmental concerns, late-stage capitalism, and post–*Roe v. Wade *motherhood that have come to define life in the 2020s.*

Principal personages

JENN SHAPLAND, author and narrator
CHELSEA, her partner
RACHEL CARSON, the scientist and writer who helped launch the environmentalist movement
DOROTHY FREEMAN, Carson's confidant
MARIAN NARANJO, an environmental activist and the founder of Honor Our Pueblo Existence

American writer Jenn Shapland first burst onto the literary scene in 2020 with her critically-acclaimed debut, *My Autobiography of Carson McCullers*. A memoir, it chronicles how discovering novelist Carson McCullers's queer love letters while working at the Harry Ransom Center in Texas led Shapland to come to terms with her own identity as a lesbian. The story of Shapland's hunt for further evidence of McCullers's sapphic relationships while learning new truths about herself along the way proved to be so powerful and well-written that *My Autobiography of Carson McCullers* became a National Book Award finalist.

In her sophomore book, Shapland's focus becomes wider and more eclectic. A collection of five essays, *Thin Skin* (2023) explores a variety of topics that shape modern life—from racism to the prevalence of environmental toxins and their impact on human health, the perils of late-stage capitalism, and the significance of motherhood in a world where *Roe v. Wade* is no longer supported by the Supreme Court.

Despite its broader focus and essay format, *Thin Skin* feels connected to its predecessor in several ways. For example, by blending history, research, and facts with Shapland's own stories, thoughts, and fears, the essay collection is also a very personal book and succeeds in filling some of the gaps in Shapland's life that *My Autobiography of Carson McCullers* left behind. Another noticeable commonality between *Thin Skin* and its predecessor is how it also celebrates a female writer whose sexual orientation has been downplayed, if not completely erased, by previous biographers. Just as

Jenn Shapland

she did for McCullers, Shapland shines a new light on both the work and sexuality of Rachel Carson—a scientist and writer whose books like *Silent Spring* (1962) were largely responsible for sparking the environmentalist movement.

As a reoccurring figure in *Thin Skin*, Carson helps make the essays feel interconnected and read more like a cohesive work than five separate vignettes. Shapland shifts the angles from which she examines Carson throughout the book to fit whatever topic she is discussing. When writing about toxic chemicals, for example, she details Carson's work studying nature, her call-to-action about the problem of pollution, and how she died of cancer that was possibly induced by whatever she was exposed to while doing her job. While discussing motherhood in "The Meaning of Life," Shapland brings up Carson again to reveal that becoming a surrogate mother to her nephew essentially ended the scientist's work.

More than anything, however, Shapland is focused on examining the obfuscated relationship between Carson and her best friend Dorothy Freeman, which many biographers have traditionally characterized as merely a friendship while others have challenged this narrative. Complicating this, nearly all of Carson's correspondence with Freeman was destroyed shortly before her death. As such, Shapland chronicles the few details that have survived over the years about Carson and Freeman's relationship and brings new ones to light, ultimately arguing that Carson had hidden her romantic relationship with Freeman out of fear that it would be weaponized against her by the chemical companies Carson was standing up to.

The overall tone and perspective of *Thin Skin* is largely established in its first essay, which is eponymously titled. This essay begins with Shapland discussing the lingering impact of the Manhattan Project in her newly adopted home of New Mexico or, more specifically, how testing the nuclear bomb there ultimately led to an enormous increase of cancer and health problems for residents living within proximity to the site—many of whom have been of Indigenous and Latino descent. Shapland then goes on to discuss the way that all manmade chemicals, toxins, and waste have come to threaten human health over the decades and that it is a problem that continues to be either ignored or misconstrued. While discussing the issue of toxicity, Shapland reveals that she has been diagnosed with "thin skin" by doctors and wonders if all her chronic health problems stem from the fact that she is more vulnerable to absorbing the harmful elements in her environment. Her dermatological diagnosis becomes a metaphor for the book's thematic engines like the increasing permeability of the world's boundaries and the fact that Shapland is a "thin skinned" sensitive person more likely to obsess about the world's bad things.

In many ways, the first essay's examination of environmental pollutants like nuclear and industrial waste successfully exemplifies *Thin Skin*'s central ideas. Although never directly asked, the question of whether or not human life on Earth has a future underlies most of the book's essays. This question is especially evident in "The Toomuchness," in which Shapland examines the unsustainability of consumerism and capitalism by detailing the way that shopping for material goods oppresses foreign workers by keeping them at impossibly low wages. In "The Meaning of Life," she focuses on the societal pressure put upon women to have children despite the planet's overpopulation and trajectory towards environmental disaster. Again and again, Shapland illustrates that humanity cannot continue operating on flawed logic and broken systems.

Although Shapland is quick to point out the serious problems of contemporary life, *Thin Skin* is not a gloomy book. This is largely thanks to the author's talent for explaining complex situations, events, and forces in such an intelligent, eye-opening way that often make the writing feel more like a galvanizing revelation than a depressing fact. This phenomenon becomes especially clear in "The Meaning of Life," in which she makes a compelling argument that women choosing not to have children is not a rejection of femininity but of the capitalist system that requires women to do the unpaid labor of raising the next generation's workforce. She goes on to reveal how the societal pressure to engage in motherhood has always been economically motivated for centuries and often takes the form of telling women there is something dangerously wrong with them for not wanting to be mothers as evidenced by the historical witch hunts of old that were often aimed at childless women or those who used forms of birth control and abortion.

A large part of what makes *Thin Skin* unique is Shapland's literary style. Many nonfiction essays operate as a deep dive into a singular topic, never straying too far from the point they are trying to make. Shapland's approach proves to be quite different as she starts with one idea and meanders into many unexpected, but relevant, others. Although her writing style reflects the fact that she has a PhD, in that it can come across as very academic in tone, analysis, and use of research, it also has a stream-of-consciousness quality that resembles the kind of unfiltered writing found in one's journal. Most of the essays are quite long and some are even divided into subsections that tackle different but related ideas. For example, the first essay goes from discussing the history of the Manhattan Project and its harmful legacy in its subsection entitled "This Downwind Thought" to "Safer," a section of the essay that discusses the impact of COVID-19, and then later to "The Toxic Donut," which is focused on Shapland's mother's cancer. The three of these as well as the other subsections all revolve around the idea of vulnerability to dangerous external forces.

Reception of *Thin Skin* has been positive, although not unanimously so. In her review for the *New York Times* (8 Sept. 2023), Noor Qasim wrote that the book was sometimes hamstringed by Shapland's self-awareness, especially when it came to the matter of her own privilege, stating, "At times her personal reflections feel overly constrained by a set of left-of-liberal, white anxieties, which Shapland attempts to interrogate yet cannot seem to move beyond (in a passage on 'self-care,' she describes 'an iceberg of white guilt: What right have I to take care of myself, my mind, my body, when mine is the body of the colonizer?')." Here, Qasim touches on the fact that Shapland's perspective is very much a product of demographical forces that have shaped her identity. In this way, for better or worse, *Thin Skin* can occasionally come across as a kind of snapshot of White millennial angst. Meanwhile, Qasim's criticism that Shapland interrogates her anxieties more than she moves beyond them is founded as Shapland as a writer has a tendency to ask more questions about what it means to have privilege than provide readers with answers.

This does not mean Shapland does not have any answers, however. Throughout the book, Shapland succeeds in providing brilliant new takes on problems that have plagued humanity for decades if not centuries. She may not always have a firm solution, but her thoughts on the matter are often inspiring and might lead readers to discovering their own. *Publishers Weekly* touched on this in their review (7 June 2023), stating, "It's hard not to marvel at how the author draws unexpected conclusions from a diverse array of anecdotes, illuminating the profound ways in which individuals and the world shape each other. This is a gem." *Kirkus Reviews* (5 May 2023) expressed a similar sentiment when they wrote, "Breathtaking in their sharp synthesis of a variety of ideas and experiences, Shapland's essays are a truth-telling balm for mind, body, and spirit."

Overall, *Thin Skin* may not be about uplifting topics but what it has to say is about them feels essential. Jessica Ferri touches on this in her review for the *Los Angeles Times* (15 Aug. 2023) when she writes, "Progressive thought and discussion can feel a lot like screaming into a tornado at best, preaching to the choir at worst. But books like 'Thin Skin' are important. They run on hope, which is perhaps the only capital left to those who would like to see the human race survive." Here, Ferri touches on the fact that throughout *Thin Skin* Shapland succeeds in reminding her readers that although most things are bad or in a state of crisis, they still have the ability to make choices in how they live now to ensure a better future for humanity.

Author Biography

Jenn Shapland is an American writer whose essays have been featured in the *New York Times, Guernica,* and *Tin House* and have earned her a Pushcart Prize. In addition to being a finalist for the 2020 National Book Award, her book *My Autobiography of Carson McCullers* won the 2021 Christian Gauss Award, Judy Grahn Award, and Lambda Literary Award.

Emily E. Turner

Review Sources

Ferri, Jessica. "What Did 'Oppenheimer' Leave Out of the Frame? This Book of Essays Will Help You Refocus." Review of *Thin Skin: Essays*, by Jenn Shapland. *The Los Angeles Times*, 15. Aug. 2023, www.latimes.com/entertainment-arts/books/story/2023-08-15/jenn-shaplands-essays-in-thin-skin-are-antidote-to-oppenheimer-film-omissions. Accessed 31 Jan. 2024.

Qasim, Noor. "Political Histories Refracted through a Personal Lens." Review of *Thin Skin: Essays*, by Jenn Shapland. *The New York Times*, 9 Sept. 2023, www.nytimes.com/2023/09/08/books/review/myriam-gurba-creep-jenn-shapland-thin-skin-wang-xiaobo-pleasure-of-thinking.html. Accessed 31 Jan. 2024.

Review of *Thin Skin: Essays*, by Jenn Shapland. *Kirkus Reviews*, 5 May 2023, www.kirkusreviews.com/book-reviews/jenn-shapland/thin-skin-shapland/. Accessed 31 Jan. 2024.

Review of *Thin Skin: Essays*, by Jenn Shapland. *Publishers Weekly,* 7 June 2023, www.publishersweekly.com/9780593317457. Accessed 31 Jan. 2024.

This Other Eden

Author: Paul Harding (b. 1967)
Publisher: W.W. Norton and Company (New York). 224 pp.
Type of work: Novel
Time: 1793; 1815; early 1900s
Locale: Apple Island, Maine

Paul Harding's third novel, This Other Eden, *follows the fate of a small colony of people who live on an isolated island off the coast of Maine. Inspired by true events that took place on Malaga Island, the story explores themes of racism and prejudice in the face of extreme poverty.*

Principal characters

ESTHER HONEY, great-granddaughter of Apple Island settlers Benjamin and Patience Honey
EHA HONEY, her son, who works as a carpenter
ETHAN HONEY, her grandson, a gifted artist
TABITHA AND CHARLOTTE HONEY, her granddaughters and Ethan's younger sisters
MATTHEW DIAMOND, a retired teacher and minister who comes to Apple Island every summer as part of a religious relief effort to teach the children and preach to the population
THEOPHILUS AND CANDACE LACK, cousins or siblings who live as spouses after being orphaned.
THE LARK CHILDREN, also known as Rabbit, Millie, Camper, and Duke; all are mostly nocturnal due to their very pale coloring
VIOLET AND IRIS MCDERMOTT, sisters who live in a grounded boat on Apple Island and run a laundry service for people on the mainland
ZACHARY HAND TO GOD PROVERBS, a former preacher who lives inside a tree in which he has created intricate carvings

American history is filled with moments of intense injustice spurred by classism, racism, and many other types of bigotry. Sometimes these moments are recognized and atoned for, other times, they are not. In *This Other Eden*, author Paul Harding focuses on one such moment that occurred off the coast of Maine in the early twentieth century. The novel centers on Apple Island, a stand-in for real life Malaga Island, which saw its inhabitants unjustly evicted to make room for gentrification. Harding lends this moment in history some true humanity, populating the island's landscape with families clinging to each other through intense poverty and pressure from the outside world

Paul Harding

to disappear. Like his debut, Pulitzer Prize–winning novel, *Tinkers* (2009), which gave voice to a dying man's inner monologue through lyric prose, *This Other Eden* takes a similar tone in voice and manner as Harding gently peels back the layers of his characters' lives and their doomed fate. By giving voice to families who the modern world might believe should not exist, and writing to the heart of human connection, Harding uses his novel to urge readers to question their own biases and bigotries and to try to understand how these flawed belief systems can have big impacts in the real world.

The Other Eden opens with a brief history lesson in how it came to be inhabited, namely by Benjamin Honey, a runaway enslaved person, and his wife, Patience, a White woman from Ireland. The moment provides the island with a legacy, as Benjamin's interest in apples and his work to build an orchard on the island are cataloged. When the reader first meets the Honeys' great granddaughter Esther, who is presented as something of a prophet, her son Eha, and her grandchildren, the weight of the family's history is already felt. It is also during that first chapter that Harding gives their provenance a biblical flair as Esther tells her grandchildren the story of a great flood that destroyed the island and its many apple trees when a hurricane blew through decades before. The story is meant to echo the biblical story of Noah and his arc, and the belief that he and his wife and children repopulated the world after emerging from their watercraft after thirty days of rain. Similarly, most of the inhabitants of Apple Island are related in some way. In some cases, as with Esther, Eha, and the Larks, the genetics have even redoubled over themselves. What follows this biblical retelling of the origins of the island's dwellers is a story of extreme gentrification and bigotry building up as eugenics becomes a favorite topic both domestically and abroad.

In the summer of 1912, retired schoolteacher and preacher Matthew Diamond arrives once again for his sessions teaching the children on the island. This summer, however, he brings a sense of foreboding that Esther can feel. This will be, the reader soon learns, the summer that the inhabitants of the island will be either institutionalized or expelled from the only place they have ever called home thanks to both squatters laws and eugenics, which have allowed local officials to deem many of the islands' people as unfit for society. The story, told in a series of four sections, draws out the daily lives of the island's citizens and the forward march of the state's move to get rid of them.

The structuring of the novel allows it to avoid monotony in moments when the story might reach that point. For example, the first lengthy section provides just enough room to introduce the characters and activities from their daily lives, like digging oysters and clams for dinner when they are lucky, Esther's moments sitting atop the bluff where her father is said to have committed suicide, and the Lark children's outings in the dark of the evening as everyone else is soundly in their homes. This first section also sets up the trajectory of each character's life following the decision to evict them by the state of Maine. Ethan, who is given a vivid inner and outer life, is singled out by Matthew, who believes the boy could pass for White and be a great artistic talent in a bigoted world. The following section shows how Ethan fares in a world that is not necessarily made for him, and subsequent sections show the painful experiences of his fellow islanders are laid bare.

Perhaps the most notable element of *This Other Eden* is Harding's rendering of the island. Harding, who grew up in Massachusetts, is a known nature-lover and frequently works lyrical meditations on the natural world into his work. Moments spent meditating on the night sky where the residents can see thousands of stars is echoed in a moment between Ethan a love interest Bridget when she tells him that she believes the chirps of crickets are actually coming from the lights in the sky. The Lark children, pale in every aspect of their appearance, mirror the frothy waves of the ocean that surrounds them. Esther, an old woman by this point, is in tune with the movement of the ocean around her as her chair rocks back and forth above its waters. Zachary Hand to God Proverbs creates a living embodiment of the religious tales that fill his mind in the flesh of a tree, a tree that he has essentially become a part of. These moments are relevant in that that make it all the more unbelievable that these people will be taken from a landscape they are so entirely a part of.

By contrast, when state officials land on the island's shore, they come with sharp instruments and shoes that are not made for this environment, and motives that even the island's stray-but-loved dogs easily pick up. The officials end up with soggy clothes as they stumble about the ocean's surf. The artistry employed to create this contrast is powerful and effective. It also sets Apple Island's residents up as something not altogether outside of nature—their huts become caves, their ragged clothes are sometimes described as being more similar to animal hides—once again creating an effective comparison. Outings spent picking berries and mushrooms on the mainland are described with delight and festivity that are not found in many other passages of the book.

While the lyricism of the novel is what gives it strength, Harding does at times stumble in his ability to create a coherent narrative with so many characters to keep in mind. For example, sisters Violet and Iris sometimes feel like afterthoughts, if only because they are treated equally to the other members of the island community in early pages and then set aside. Resident Annie Parker is mentioned in the beginning but barely shows up in the following pages until the story's end.

This Other Eden was largely celebrated by critics and received a starred review from *Publishers Weekly* ahead of publication. Their anonymous critic wrote that Harding, "suffuses deep feeling into this understated yet wrenching story inspired by an isolated mixed-raced community's forced resettlement in 1912 Maine." *The New York Times* featured a rave review by writer Danez Smith who said of the lyric story: "Harding has written a novel out of poetry and sunlight, violent history and tender remembering. The humans he has created are, thankfully, not flattened into props and gimmicks, which sometimes happens when writers work across time and difference; instead they pulse with aliveness, dreamlike but tangible, so real it could make you weep." Outlets including the *Guardian*, *NPR*, the *Washington Post*, and the *Sydney Morning Herald* also featured reviews of the novel which celebrated its achievements. For the *Washington Post*, critic Wendy Smith wrote, "Harding's finely wrought prose shows us a community that refuses to see itself through the judgmental eyes of others, a society composed of people who give their neighbors the same latitude to go their own way that they claim for themselves." The critic for the *Los Angeles Times*, Mark Athitakis, offered a dissenting take, writing, "*This Other Eden* is a short novel, but it's encumbered with all the symbolic import Harding strives to apply to it. At times, the book's language is charming in its elegance. Too often, though, it's fussed over, as if every syllable were held up with a jeweler's loupe and assessed for shine and heft."

In addition to its multitude of positive reviews, *This Other Eden* was shortlisted for the Booker Prize and was a finalist for the National Book Award for Fiction.

Author Biography

Paul Harding is the author of three novels: *Tinkers*, which won a Pulitzer Prize; *Enon*; and *This Other Eden*. He is the recipient of the PEN/Robert W. Bingham Prize and the Fernanda Pivano Award.

Melynda Fuller

Review Sources

Athitakis, Mark. "Paul Harding's Modest Debut Won a Surprise Pulitzer. His Third Novel Aims Too High." Review of *This Other Eden*, by Paul Harding. *Los Angeles Times*, 24 Jan. 2023, www.latimes.com/entertainment-arts/books/story/2023-01-24/paul-hardings-debut-tinkers-won-a-surprise-pulitzer-but-his-third-novel-aims-too-high. Accessed 26 Oct. 2023.

Chakraborty, Abhrajyoti. "This Other Eden by Paul Harding Review – a Novel That Impresses Time and Again." Review of *This Other Eden*, by Paul Harding. *The Guardian*, 7 Feb. 2023, www.theguardian.com/books/2023/feb/07/this-other-eden-by-paul-harding-review-a-novel-that-impresses-time-and-again. Accessed 26 Oct. 2023.

Smith, Danez. "In 'This Other Eden,' A Historical Tale of Paradise Lost." Review of *This Other Eden*, by Paul Harding. *The New York Times*, 24 Jan. 2023, www.nytimes.com/2023/01/24/books/review/this-other-eden-paul-harding.html. Accessed 26 Oct. 2023.

Smith, Wendy. "In 'This Other Eden,' an Island Refuge Is Destroyed by Good Intentions." Review of *This Other Eden*, by Paul Harding. *The Washington Post*, 25 Jan. 2023, www.washingtonpost.com/books/2023/01/24/paul-harding-this-other-eden/. Accessed 26 Oct. 2023.

Review of *This Other Eden*, by Paul Harding. *Publishers Weekly*, 10 Nov. 2022, www.publishersweekly.com/9781324036296. Accessed 25 Oct. 2023.

Thunderclap
A Memoir of Art and Life and Sudden Death

Author: Laura Cumming (b. 1961)
Publisher: Scribner (New York). 272 pp.
Type of work: Memoir; biography; fine arts
Time: 1600s to present
Locales: Delft and Amsterdam, Netherlands; London, England; Dunfermline, Scotland

Laura Cumming's Thunderclap *is a memoir recounting her father's life as an artist in Scotland, her own development as an art critic, and her avid appreciation for artists of the Dutch Golden Age, particularly a little-known artist from that period, Carel Fabritius.*

Principal personages
CAREL FABRITIUS, a Dutch painter
JAMES "JIMMY" CUMMING, the author's father, an artist in Scotland
REMBRANDT HARMENSZOON VAN RIJN, a Dutch master painter
JOHANNES VERMEER, a Dutch master painter

Art critic and *New York Times* best-selling author Laura Cumming's 2023 memoir, *Thunderclap: A Memoir of Art and Life and Sudden Death*, shares similarities with her previous memoir, *On Chapel Sands: The Mystery of My Mother's Disappearance as a Child* (2019). Both books focus on a parent-artist, and both combine memoir and art history. In *On Chapel Sands*, Cumming recounts her mother's abduction, in 1929 at the age of three, and gradually exposes a number of family secrets to explain her mother's disappearance and true parentage. In addition to this central story, Cumming mentions a number of artists and paintings, most notably *Landscape with the Fall of Icarus* (ca. 1558), attributed to Flemish painter Pieter Bruegel the Elder (ca. 1525–69), and she uses her incisive analysis of paintings and family photographs to further illuminate the story of her mother and help explain it.

Cumming has chosen a similar thematic structure for *Thunderclap*, focusing this time on her father, the Scottish artist James Cumming (1922–91), as well as her own childhood introduction to art and how the study of art became a lifelong passion. Cumming also delves into the life and art of the Dutch Golden Age painter Carel Fabritius (1622–54), about whom little is known. Fabritius was one of six to seven hundred artists in Holland who were active during the Golden Age of Dutch painting in the seventeenth century, but only a dozen or so of his paintings have survived. His contemporaries included better-known painters such as Rembrandt Harmenszoon

Laura Cumming

van Rijn (1606–69), whom he served as an apprentice, and Johannes Vermeer (1632–45), who owned three of his paintings and lived nearby. As Cummings tries to draw together a portrait of Fabritius and his work, she expertly weaves together her own awakening as an art critic, her father's life and ambitions as an artist, and her analysis and appreciation of the works of other Dutch Golden Age artists.

Cumming's title, *Thunderclap*, is a reference to the Delft Thunderclap, a gunpowder explosion in Delft in 1654 that took Fabritius's life at the height of his artistic powers and many other lives as well. The explosion also had far-reaching consequences since it demolished part of the city and could be heard and felt by people as far as seventy miles away.

Cumming begins the book with one of Fabritius's best-known paintings, *A View of Delft, with a Musical Instrument Seller's Stall* (1652), which she encountered for the first time in the National Gallery in London when she was in her early twenties. Cumming is so enchanted by the painting that she returns to it again and again, describing her visits as an ongoing pilgrimage to note and appreciate different details with each viewing. This experience, combined with a memorable childhood family trip to art museums in the Netherlands and her father's teachings on art, sparked her lifelong interest in Dutch Golden Age art and artists and a particular fascination with Fabritius.

Fabritius was a student of Rembrandt and a peer of Vermeer. Few specifics are known about Fabritius's studies with Rembrandt, however, and there is no documentation confirming that Fabritius and Vermeer ever met, despite living near each other in Delft and Vermeer having owned several of Fabritius's paintings and hung them in his home. At the very least, the two were aware of each other's existence and work. As Cumming describes and analyzes the lives and works of these Dutch painters, she counters the critical notion she learned in school that "Golden Age Dutch art was all about *things*," with its many still-life paintings of flowers, fruit, and streetscapes. Cumming believes Dutch Golden Age art is about much more than things, and her astute analysis of numerous sketches and paintings, such as Rembrandt's *Portrait of Saskia as a Bride* (1633) and Vermeer's *The Little Street* (ca. 1658), affirm her viewpoint. She exalts the works as having a "mysterious kind of beauty, a strangeness to arouse and disturb, an infinite and fathomless world." Over the course of the book, Cumming makes a strong case that there is much more depth and nuance in the work of Dutch Golden Age artists than had previously been asserted.

One of the highlights of *Thunderclap* is Cumming's writing style, which is elegant and accessible, even for those who may not have experience reading art criticism. When Cumming describes *The Goldfinch* (1654), one of Fabritius's last and most well-known paintings (and the one author Donna Tartt chose as the centerpiece for her 2013 Pulitzer Prize–winning novel of the same name), she describes the bird as if it were alive:

> The first sight of *The Goldfinch* is abrupt and austere. The little bird appears on its perch, so quick and alert, dark against the wall that receives its hovering shadow. One eye glistens as it turns its head out of profile towards you. You must not disturb the millisecond in which this winged creature looks straight at you, eye to eye, and yet of course it can never fly away. It takes a moment to notice the chain around its leg.

According to Cumming, the bird has such a strong personality that the reader sees his vibrancy and alertness before noticing the chain that binds him to the spot. Cumming prompts readers to notice the details of the painting, such as the way the bird simultaneously looks directly at the reader yet is aware he cannot escape. In the next few paragraphs, Cumming further describes how Fabritius creates tension in the painting with the bird's awareness of his predicament, and it is this tension and alertness that so mesmerize viewers of the painting.

While Cumming's writing style is justly praised for its luminosity, the organizational features usually included in many nonfiction books of this type are minimal in the hardcover edition, which may make it difficult for some readers to find information they wish to review later. Cumming provides a list of illustrations at the end of the book that references the many sketches and paintings discussed, but the hardcover edition lacks a table of contents, chapter titles, descriptive headings, and an index to easily locate discussions of artists, works, or subjects mentioned throughout the book. The book is organized into three large sections, labeled numerically, but the information in each section is organized by vignette rather than chronologically or by topic. Additionally, though the hardcover edition has been published with heavy, high-quality paper and high-resolution photographs, as befits a book that delves into detailed analysis of the featured paintings, some of the images are so small that it is difficult to see the details Cumming references in her discussions. When Cumming analyzes Fabritius's *A View of Delft, with a Musical Instrument Seller's Stall*, for example, she describes "the polished lute, the viola with its deep curlicues" that are challenging to see in a photograph that measures roughly two inches by four-and-a-half inches.

Most critics found much to admire in *Thunderclap*, particularly Cumming's vivid descriptions, her enthusiasm for and approach to the material, and her rich critical analysis of art and artists. A starred review from *Kirkus* praised the book for "moving reflections rendered in precise, radiant prose," and *Publishers Weekly* rated *Thunderclap* an "elegant and luminous work" in which "art lovers will be enthralled." Like other reviewers, Becca Rothfeld noted for the *Washington Post* that *Thunderclap* was "genre-spanning," and much more than a memoir, since it includes a significant amount of biography and art criticism.

Critics commended Cumming's ability to weave so many elements masterfully into one narrative, particularly the stories of her father and Fabritius. Despite living centuries apart, both artists were enigmatic; both sometimes struggled to support their families while creating their art; both died unexpectedly (Fabritius at age thirty-two from the accidental gunpowder explosion and James Cumming at age sixty-eight due to metastatic lung cancer); and both are mourned by the author. One critic, Stuart Kelly noted for *The Scotsman* that Cumming discusses Fabritius much more than her own father, and Kelly, as a Scot himself, would have liked more information and analysis on the work of James Cumming, an artist he was not aware of and whom he believes should be more widely known. Aside from this point, Kelly called the book "remarkable" and thought the stories Cumming wove through history, artist, and artwork were especially compelling. Kelly also appreciated Cumming's emphasis that art should be viewed in person in a museum or art gallery for the truest and most moving experience rather than relying on more passive ways of viewing art.

Cumming's *Thunderclap* conveys a deep appreciation for the art of her father, James Cumming, and the master painters of the Dutch Golden Age, and as the author also implies, this book is one way of keeping the art of both Fabritius and her father alive.

Author Biography

Laura Cumming is a widely acclaimed author of nonfiction and art history, including the award-winning, New York Times Best Seller *The Vanishing Velázquez* and *On Chapel Sands: The Mystery of My Mother's Disappearance as a Child* (2019), a National Book Critics Circle Award finalist. Cumming has been the art critic for the London-based *Observer* since 1999.

Marybeth Rua-Larsen

Review Sources

Conrad, Peter. "Thunderclap by Laura Cumming Review—a Visionary Examination of Dutch Golden Age Art." Review of *Thunderclap: A Memoir of Art and Life and Sudden Death*, by Laura Cumming. *The Guardian*, 23 July 2023, www.theguardian.com/books/2023/jul/23/thunderclap-a-memoir-of-art-and-life-and-sudden-death-laura-cumming-review-delft-explosion-dutch-fabritius-vermeer. Accessed 23 Jan. 2024.

Kelly, Stuart. "Book Review: Thunderclap: A Memoir of Art and Life and Sudden Death, by Laura Cumming." *The Scotsman*, 26 July 2023, www.scotsman.com/arts-and-culture/books/book-review-thunderclap-by-laura-cumming-4233200. Accessed 23 Jan. 2024.

Rothfeld, Becca. "'Thunderclap' Combines First-Rate Art History with Deeply Felt Memoir." Review of *Thunderclap: A Memoir of Art and Life and Sudden Death*, by Laura Cumming. *The Washington Post*, 28 June 2023, www.washingtonpost.com/books/2023/06/28/thunderclap-laura-cumming-review. Accessed 23 Jan. 2023.

Review of *Thunderclap: A Memoir of Art and Life and Sudden Death*, by Laura Cumming. *Kirkus Reviews*, 18 Apr. 2023, www.kirkusreviews.com/book-reviews/laura-cumming/thunderclap. Accessed 23 Jan. 2024.

Review of *Thunderclap: A Memoir of Art and Life and Sudden Death*, by Laura Cumming. *Publishers Weekly*, 11 Apr. 2023, www.publishersweekly.com/9781982181741. Accessed 23 Jan. 2024.

Yeazell, Ruth Bernard. "When Life Resembles a 17th-Century Dutch Painting." Review of *Thunderclap: A Memoir of Art and Life and Sudden Death*, by Laura Cumming. *The New York Times*, 9 July 2023, www.nytimes.com/2023/07/09/books/review/thunderclap-laura-cumming.html. Accessed 23 Jan. 2024.

Tom Lake

Author: Ann Patchett (b. 1963)
Publisher: Harper (New York). 320 pp.
Type of work: Novel
Time: 1988; 2020
Locales: Tom Lake, Michigan; Los Angeles; New York; Traverse City, Michigan

A masterclass in homespun storytelling, Tom Lake *follows a mother recounting her fleeting acting career to her grown daughters. Presented through a series of flashbacks interspersed with the present, the novel provides a profound commentary on love, family, and the decisions one makes in life.*

Principal characters
LARA KENISON, a former actor and the matriarch of the Nelson family
PETER DUKE, a famous actor and her brief love interest
JOE NELSON, her husband and lead operator of the family's cherry orchard
EMILY, the eldest Nelson daughter, slated to take over the family farm
MAISIE, the middle Nelson daughter, studying to be a veterinarian
NELL, the youngest Nelson daughter, an aspiring actor
PALLACE, the understudy for Lara in Our Town and an accomplished actor and dancer
SEBASTIAN, a prolific tennis player and Peter's brother

Tom Lake (2023) is the ninth novel by the acclaimed author Ann Patchett. Throughout her literary career, Patchett has firmly established herself as a powerful storyteller, with her works often characterized by lyrical language and in-depth explorations of family dynamics. To embody the metamorphosing nature of familial relationships, Patchett often elects to have her narratives span multiple decades, providing an expansive examination of people changing over time. Several of her works have been recognized as best sellers, and some have earned prestigious awards. Her fourth novel, *Bel Canto* (2001), received the PEN/Faulkner Award for Fiction, and *The Dutch House* (2019), which follows the lives of a brother and sister over many years, was a finalist for the 2020 Pulitzer Prize in Fiction.

In *Tom Lake*, Patchett flexes her customary style, with dual timelines revealing protagonists who grow over decades. The novel, initially set in 2020 during the beginning of the COVID-19 pandemic, follows Lara Kenison as she tells her three adult daughters, Emily, Maisie, and Nell, the story of the summer in the 1980s that she appeared in a production of Thornton Wilder's play *Our Town* alongside Peter Duke, an actor who

Ann Patchett
Courtesy HarperCollins; ©Emily Dorio

would go on to become famous. The daughters, forced to return to their family's cherry orchard due to the pandemic, are enthralled by their mother's brushes with celebrity and her fleeting romance with Duke. When the family learns of the actor's premature death, the three girls push to understand more about the summer he and Lara were together at the Tom Lake theater company. It quickly becomes apparent that while the three girls have previously been told bit and pieces about that time, the tale has never been told in its totality, and they are elated to get the intimate details of their mother's short-lived acting career and her first love.

Lara's retelling of her time at Tom Lake in the present is interspersed with flashbacks, beginning with her first role as the leading character, Emily, in *Our Town* in high school. Stories from the past, including Lara getting scouted for a Hollywood movie, auditioning for Broadway, and romancing Duke at Tom Lake, are delivered in small pieces before returning to the family at present. Both timelines unfold from Lara's first-person perspective, granting readers intimate access to her thoughts and emotions as she navigates Hollywood and the prestigious Tom Lake theater.

Lara is in her mid-twenties when cast in *Our Town*, balancing the confidence and naivety of newfound adulthood and budding success. Young Lara falls head over heels in love with the enigmatic Duke, who dazzles her with his sultry charm and star power. The crystalline lake and steamy summer months set an enchanting backdrop for their love affair as they spend their days acting, swimming, and playing tennis with Lara's understudy, Pallace, and Duke's brother, Sebastian. In these sections of the novel, Patchett creates a closed, pressurized environment, similar to that of a summer camp or boarding school, for her characters to form close bonds, exploring the complexities of friendship, love, and ambition during the formative years of their twenties. Every experience is tinged with intensity, for all the players seem to realize their time together is limited while simultaneously hoping it will last forever.

In the present timeline, the first-person perspective serves the unique purpose of showing readers when Lara withholds details of her past from her daughters. In this way, Patchett effectively addresses one of the key themes of *Tom Lake*—the mysterious lives of parents before their children. She acknowledges these individuals as whole people with pasts, dreams, and opinions instead of simply their role as fathers and mothers. Throughout the novel, Lara is peppered with questions from her inquisitive daughters. They interrupt each other, eagerly filling in missing details from the parts of the tale they know and asking probing questions when given new information. Lara handles these interruptions with patience, grace, and an unmistakable desire to share this significant part of her life with her offspring. Yet often, due to the first-person point of view, readers watch as Lara edits her story as she is telling it. She omits details, some seemingly meaningless, others that could potentially shake the foundation of the family. In these moments, sometimes Lara explains her reasoning for not sharing a piece of the story, and in others she avoids accountability entirely. The effect is one of authenticity, as there can be justification for making a certain decision or simply an instinctual reaction. Lara exhibits remarkable self-awareness and understanding of her audience, knowing exactly what to share with her daughters and husband and which memories to reserve for only herself.

This method of withholding is mirrored in Patchett's masterful writing style, specifically the narrative structure of *Tom Lake*. For the majority of the novel, she follows a steady, meandering pace reminiscent of a muggy summer. She then provides sporadic, profound revelations that incite direct connections between the past and present timelines. Most notably, the identity of Lara's husband, Joe, as well as the inspiration for their daughters' names, are divulged intermittently with a heartfelt impact. The effect highlights what is perhaps most central, theme of *Tom Lake*: that the meaningful discoveries of one's life are often made from a collection of small, simple moments. While it would seem to readers (and Lara's daughters) that her fiery affair with Duke and brief tenure in Hollywood would be Lara's most prized chapter in life, her commentary throughout the 2020 timelines proves otherwise. Validated by the occasional input from Joe in his calm demeanor, Lara provides sage insight into how the relationships and decisions she made during that period impacted her, rather than the heated romance and glint of fame.

At its core, *Tom Lake* operates on the straightforward premise of a mother telling her daughters a story from her past while they toil through the repetitive responsibilities of cherry farming. Patchett further reflects the concept of simplicity through her use of language and plot structure. Lara recounts the tale of her Tom Lake days while she and the family are completing basic daily activities, such as picking fruit from the trees, preparing and eating meals, and watching old movies. Through her perspective, the narrative frequently offers concise yet poignant commentary on the nature of life, love, and family, delivered in a completely unselfconscious manner. While Lara tackles difficult subjects with her family throughout the book, such as Emily's decision not to have children, there is an underlying tone of gratitude and unconditional love emanating from her. For example, when enjoying a moment of rest on the beach, Emily expresses that she wishes life could stay like this. Lara voices agreement, though thinking, "I know she means the temperature of the lake and I mean this summer, everyone home and together." She repeatedly stresses that life consists of both suffering and joy, and the two are each valid and necessary. Her wise, confident nature guides the core intention of the story, that while plans may go awry, it is still possible to feel immense appreciation for the realities of how life unfolds.

Patchett's thematic focus on finding the joy in simplicity can be seen as echoing some other literary works, including examples directly referenced in *Tom Lake*. As noted by several reviewers, she in many ways draws on Anton Chekhov's play *The Cherry Orchard* (1904), which as the title suggests is set against the same kind of place as much of Patchett's novel. Both Chekhov's work and *Tom Lake* also feature intimate explorations of family bonds. Continuing Patchett's playful self-awareness in her book, Duke blatantly references *The Cherry Orchard* when the group visits the idyllic homestead of one of their castmates.

Of course, Patchett even more prominently refers to *Our Town*, the 1938 play widely considered Thornton Wilder's masterpiece, as an integral part of Lara and Duke's backstory. That play operates on minimal decorum and strongly focuses on internal character performances. Lara, immediately identified by Patchett as a lover of literature as she reads the epic novel *Doctor Zhivago* (1957) in the opening scene, demonstrates a skilled comprehension of *Our Town*, engrossing herself entirely in the character of Emily. As *Tom Lake* unfolds, readers observe as Lara becomes aware of her acting limitations, musing that she is "a pretty girl who wasn't so much playing a part as she was right for the part she was playing." Ultimately, Patchett gleans a similar inspiration from *Our Town* as from *The Cherry Orchard* for her premise of happiness found in both the monumental moments and banalities of life.

Patchett's intention in composing a story praising an unremarkable life (even with characters that dabbled in fame) was noticed and commended by reviewers. *Tom Lake* received overwhelming praise for the central arc of Lara's wise reflection on her past decisions and her appreciation of motherhood. Many critics, such as Katy Waldman, writing for the *New Yorker*, found that they initially bristled at the novel's "determined positivity" but eventually celebrated the perceptive self-awareness Patchett conveys. They appreciated that the overall benevolent mood was reflected in the author's use of language, which brings to life the tranquil feeling of hot summer days. Alexandra Jacobs, in her review of the book for the *New York Times*, declared the blissful, mellow tone of the novel evokes a folksy, leisurely sensation, with Patchett "slyly needle-pointing her own pillowcase mottos" throughout the story, mainly through Lara's keen observations on life.

While *Tom Lake* was very well-received overall, some reviewers did raise a few criticisms. Though Patchett is generally known for her competency in handling alternating timelines, Rachel Cooke, in her review for the *Guardian*, expressed some aversion to Lara's ponderous retelling of her past—in some ways echoing the feelings of the three daughters in the novel, who urge Lara to skip to the zestier parts of her relationship with Duke. However, Cooke ultimately praised Patchett's calculated revelations throughout the book, stating, "the understanding comes, not in some soaring climax, but cumulatively, across many moments, each one brimful of the half glimpsed, the almost understood." This sentiment reflects the core of *Tom Lake*, that the fulfillment of life comes not from singular, pivotal events but the totality of all experiences, even those seemingly inconsequential, and in the delight and suffering endured.

Author Biography
Ann Patchett is an accomplished author of fiction, nonfiction, and children's books. She has earned several awards for her writing and owns an independent bookstore, Parnassus Books, in Nashville, Tennessee.

Annie Schwartz

Review Sources

Cooke, Rachel. "Tom Lake by Ann Patchett Review—a Lesson in How to Kiss and Tell." Review of *Tom Lake*, by Ann Patchett. *The Guardian*, 25 July 2023, www.theguardian.com/books/2023/jul/25/tom-lake-by-ann-patchett-review-a-lesson-in-how-to-kiss-and-tell. Accessed 9 Oct. 2023.

Jacobs, Alexandra. "'Tom Lake' Finds Ann Patchett in a Chekhovian Mood." Review of *Tom Lake*, by Ann Patchett. *The New York Times*, 30 July 2023, www.nytimes.com/2023/07/30/books/review/ann-patchett-tom-lake.html. Accessed 9 Oct. 2023.

Review of *Tom Lake*, by Ann Patchett. *Kirkus Reviews*, 24 Apr. 2023, www.kirkusreviews.com/book-reviews/ann-patchett/tom-lake-patchett. Accessed 9 Oct. 2023.

Waldman, Katy. "Ann Patchett's Pandemic Novel." Review of *Tom Lake*, by Ann Patchett. *The New Yorker*, 31 July 2023, www.newyorker.com/magazine/2023/08/07/tom-lake-ann-patchett-book-review. Accessed 9 Oct. 2023.

Tremor

Author: Teju Cole (b. 1975)
Publisher: Random House (New York). 239 pp.
Type of work: Novel
Time: Present day
Locales: United States; Lagos, Nigeria

Teju Cole's largely plotless novel offers a collage of shifting viewpoints and styles to reflect on such issues as art, race, and death.

Principal characters
TUNDE, a photographer and professor
SADAKO, his wife
TUNDE'S DECEASED FRIEND, referred to as "you"
LUCAS, the son of Tunde's deceased friend

In 2011 Nigerian American writer Teju Cole experienced breakout success with his novel *Open City*. That book details the wanderings and thoughts of its protagonist, Julius, a German Nigerian psychiatry student in New York. Julius is a restless, rootless young man, and as he traverses the New York streets he narrates his reflections on the city, which often involve him locating traces of history beneath the present-day surface. He contemplates such subjects as racism and slavery, his past life in Nigeria, and the differences between American and African cultures. Although Julius also travels abroad and meets many people in his wanderings, the novel is mostly plotless. Only toward the end, when a revelation about Julius' past arises and changes the reader's perception of the narrator, does plot emerge as a driving factor of the novel's story.

Open City was something of a sensation when it was published, earning critical plaudits, landing on multiple lists of the best books of 2011, and being named a finalist for the National Book Critics Circle Award for fiction. It was also emblematic of a bourgeoning trend at the time known as autofiction. That term refers to works that play with the tensions between fiction and nonfiction, featuring protagonists based on their authors and structures that are more essay-like than plot-driven, often concerned with the protagonist's efforts to write the very book that the audience is reading. A number of authors associated with autofiction, including Ben Lerner and Sheila Heti, came to prominence in the US during the 2010s. *Open City* differed slightly from the works of such authors, however, in that Julius was not meant to be taken as being Teju Cole, even if the two shared many similarities, and that this character was not a writer working on a book. Nonetheless, *Open City* was often held up as a stellar example of this suddenly popular genre.

Teju Cole

After releasing *Open City*, Cole put out several books of essays and photography, but did not return to fiction until the 2023 publication of the novel *Tremor*. Like *Open City*, *Tremor* partakes of the autofiction mode, but it also spins out into more experimental territory. As the novel opens the narrative sticks closely to the thoughts of the narrator, a Harvard professor named Tunde, who seems to more closely resemble Teju Cole, himself a professor at Harvard, than does *Open City*'s Julius. Tunde is also considerably less morally troubling than Julius, with no terrible secrets in his past and no dark thoughts that make the reader question his morality. Like Julius, he is cosmopolitan, a man with Nigerian roots living in the United States, but he does not exhibit the same restlessness as Cole's earlier protagonist. At the beginning of the novel, Tunde's biggest personal issue is his difficulties with his wife, Sadako, although even this subject is not lingered on at any great length. Another difference between *Tremor* and *Open City* is that the newer novel has third-person narration rather than first-person. This perspective creates some distance between author and character and asks the reader to reflect on this difference.

For the first four of the book's eight chapters, the novel follows Tunde's thoughts and reflections as he travels to Maine, teaches classes, and remembers his upbringing in Nigeria. These sections proceed in a manner somewhat similar to that of *Open City*, with Tunde's wanderings and daily activities triggering a succession of meditations. For example, at the beginning of the novel, Tunde and Sadako travel to Maine and visit an antique shop there. For sale at the shop is a *ci wara*, a headpiece used in ceremonies by the Bambara people of West Africa. This sets Tunde thinking about questions of authenticity, value, and provenance when it comes to African objects being sold in the US. He reflects on what makes these objects valuable to Westerners and the strangeness of the colonial marketplace.

At the same store, he also sees a sign commemorating the establishment of a homestead settlement and the killing of the White settler's family by a group of Native Americans. This leads Tunde to reflect on the ways that White people are privileged as protagonists in the history of relations between White people and Indigenous people. It also causes him to reflect with alarm on his own lack of feeling when he reads of this massacre. Although *Tremor* is not a book that involves considerable amounts of self-questioning on the part of its narrator, this is one moment where the narrator struggles with an essential inner conflict: the challenge of reconciling his cold historical understanding with his sense of human feeling.

Other parts of the first four chapters depict Tunde in various settings, including in a classroom where a student fuels Tunde's obsession with videos made by a convicted mass murderer. These videos trigger further reflections from Tunde on a variety of subjects, including death. The theme of death is further taken up by the introduction of another character, a dead friend of Tunde's that he thinks about on occasion; this friend is referred to only as "you." This introduction of the "you" prefigures the shifting perspectives of the book's second half.

Tunde's thoughts on racism, colonialism, and death are highly engaging and mark the book as being more about ideas than conventional narrative. Nonetheless, Cole is up to something a little different than what he did in *Open City*, and he is wary of sticking too closely to the narrator and authorial stand-in. Starting in chapter five, the book shifts gears, with each chapter reflecting a different perspective or style. Chapter five itself consists of the text of a lecture, presumably given by Tunde, in which he reflects on the representation of slavery in European art. But it is chapter six that perhaps represents the novel's boldest gambit. It is divided into twenty-four short sections, each lasting no more than a couple of pages and each told in the voice of a different resident of Lagos, Nigeria. These residents relate their experiences, the circumstances of their lives, and their daily travails. The sections are by turns humorous, eye-opening, and horrifying. The decision to turn the narrative over to these random voices is a daring one, but it pays off. While the earlier part of the novel is devoted closely to one person's point of view, the shift in chapter six allows the novel to fan out and take on a wider perspective. Tunde is a worldly person, someone who inhabits multiple cultures, but he is still just one person. By focusing on the voices of others, Cole transforms his book from a portrait of one globally minded character into a truly global novel.

After a short chapter that consists of a series of poetic descriptions of the narrator's return to Lagos, the book returns to Tunde's point of view for the final chapter. However, unlike the third-person narration of first four chapters, this section is narrated in the first person by Tunde. After the preceding three chapters, the return to Tunde's perspective is refreshing and the switch to first person is welcoming. It is as if the reader has returned to Tunde's familiar perspective after completing a global journey beyond the limits of Tunde's worldview, with the added comfort of hearing Tunde narrate in his own voice. With this shift the novel comes full circle, allowing readers to understand Tunde's thoughts and meditations in a wider context. These reflections are the product of a global experience on the narrator's part; since readers are able to experience a more global perspective due to the book's wide-ranging nature, they end up in a better position to appreciate Tunde's penetrating insights.

Tremor received largely positive reviews from critics and was named one of the top ten fiction books of 2023 by *Time* magazine. Writing for the *New York Times*, Brian Dillon called the book "the most sundry and vagrant of Cole's works to date," praising it for showing off the full range of the author's talents. For Dillon, *Tremor* demonstrates Cole's ability to work in a number of capacities: "novelist, essayist, critic, photographer, teacher." These sentiments were echoed by Tope Folarin, who reviewed the novel for the *Nation*. Folarin was especially impressed by the ways that Cole plays with narrative and the writer's decision to let readers draw their own conclusions. "This is an alluring novel," Folarin wrote, "almost hypnotic in its unstable relationship to narrative."

Tremor did draw some dissenting opinions, evident in Ryu Spaeth's review for *Vulture*. For Spaeth, the character of Tunde comes across as too morally pure. Unlike the tension Cole created with his complex character Julius in *Open City*, Tunde is defined by his "wish to be good," which Spaeth found to be a rather dull character trait and which he felt led to a series of "morose musings." Nonetheless, Spaeth still found much to enjoy in the book, particularly the chapter containing the collage of voices from Lagos.

Far more typical of the critical consensus was Julian Lucas's review for *The New Yorker*. Calling the book "a work of autofiction with the ambition of a systems novel," he found *Tremor* to be "an elegant and unsettling prose still-life." This combination of intimacy and ambition allows Cole's second novel to build on the basic set-up of his previous literary triumph and then push far beyond the original template.

Author Biography
A multifaceted scholar and professor at Harvard University, Teju Cole has published works across a range of genres, include fiction, essays, and photography. His writing has earned several major awards, including the Windham-Campbell Literature Prize, PEN/Hemingway Prize, and a Guggenheim Foundation Fellowship.

Andrew Schenker

Review Sources
Dillon, Brian. "For Teju Cole, Art Is a Lens on a History of Violence." Review of Tremor, by Teju Cole. *The New York Times*, 17 Oct. 2023, www.nytimes.com/2023/10/17/books/review/teju-cole-tremor.html. Accessed 29 Jan. 2024.
Folarin, Tope. "A Multitude of Selves." Review of *Tremor*, by Teju Cole. *The Nation*, 2 Oct. 2023, www.thenation.com/article/culture/teju-cole-tremor/. Accessed 29 Jan. 2024.
LeClair, Tom. Review of *Tremor*, by Teju Cole. *Open Letters Review*, 13 Oct. 2023, openlettersreview.com/posts/tremor-by-teju-cole. Accessed 29 Jan. 2024.
Lucas, Julian. "Teju Cole's New Novel Is Haunted by the Trespasses of Art." Review of *Tremor*, by Teju Cole. *The New Yorker*, 9 Oct. 2023, www.newyorker.com/magazine/2023/10/16/tremor-teju-cole-book-review. Accessed 29 Jan. 2024.
Spaeth, Ryu. "The Reluctant Cosmopolitan." Review of *Tremor*, by Teju Cole. *Vulture*, 19 Oct. 2023, www.vulture.com/article/teju-cole-tremor-book-review.html. Accessed 29 Jan. 2024.
Tepper, Anderson. "Teju Cole Knows His New Novel Resembles Autofiction. Please Don't Be Tempted." Review of *Tremor*, by Teju Cole. *The New York Times*, 16 Oct. 2023, www.nytimes.com/2023/10/16/books/teju-cole-tremor.html. Accessed 29 Jan. 2024.
Wood, James. "The Arrival of Enigmas." Review of *Open City*, by Teju Cole. *The New Yorker*, 20 Feb. 2011, www.newyorker.com/magazine/2011/02/28/the-arrival-of-enigmas. Accessed 30 Jan. 2024.

The 272
The Families Who Were Enslaved and Sold to Build the American Catholic Church

Author: Rachel L. Swarns (b. 1967)
Publisher: Random House (New York). Illustrated. 352 pp.
Type of work: History
Time: Primarily 1600s–1800s
Locales: Maryland and Louisiana

The 272 *is an in-depth exposé of how the American Catholic Church and Georgetown University were both originally funded by slavery and the slave trade.*

Principal personages
HARRY MAHONEY, an enslaved man to whom the Jesuits promised that his family would never be sold or split up
ANN JOICE, one of his ancestors, a Black indentured servant forced into slavery
ANNY MAHONEY JONES, one of his daughters, who was among the 272 people sold to save Georgetown
ARNOLD JONES, his son-in-law, Anny's husband, who managed to escape to freedom
LOUISA MAHONEY MASON, another of his daughters, known for her piety
THOMAS MULLEDY, the Georgetown president behind the sale of the 272 enslaved people
FATHER JOSEPH CARBERY, a priest overseeing the plantation where the Mahoneys were enslaved

On April 16, 2016, the *New York Times* published Rachel L. Swarns's groundbreaking piece about Georgetown University's efforts to reckon with the revelation that it had been saved from closing its doors in 1838 by the sale of 272 enslaved African Americans. Although Georgetown was not the first university to publicly acknowledge that it had benefited from slavery and the slave trade (Brown having been the first to do so in 2006), it would become the most well-known thanks to Swarns's article. In *The 272: The Families Who Were Enslaved to Build the American Catholic Church*, Swarns expands upon her initial report by further investigating the institutions and individuals involved in the 1838 sale. In turn, she brings to light additional details about the event while also providing a new perspective on the role that Christianity played in slavery.

The 272 covers many topics, but its primary focus is on how the American Catholic Church was able take root by exploiting the labor and lives of enslaved African Americans. As Swarns writes in the book's prologue, "Without the enslaved, the Catholic

Rachel L. Swarns

Church in the United States, as we know it today, would not exist." Most of the book is subsequently dedicated to this thesis, examining the way in which the church used slavery to fund expansion efforts in colonial America, such as missions, churches, and educational institutions like Georgetown.

To provide readers with a complete picture of how the church became involved in slavery, Swarns moves chronologically through the religion's history in British North America. This begins with the seventeenth-century arrival of Jesuits who had been granted twenty thousand acres of land in Maryland by Charles Calvert, Lord Baltimore—a prominent English Catholic creating a new territory for the British Crown. Many of the people used to settle the new territory were indentured servants from different backgrounds contracted to work until they had paid off their debts. Among them was Ann Joice, a Black woman who arrived in Maryland from England in 1646, eighteen years before the colony legalized slavery. By the end of her service, she was working on the tobacco plantation of a wealthy Catholic named Colonel Henry Darnall, a cousin of Calvert who refused to recognize that she was now entitled to her freedom. Darnall burned her indenture papers, leaving Joice with nothing to bequeath her descendants except her story of injustice, which would be passed down to the following generations. The story would become like an heirloom to her family (who later became known as the Mahoneys), influencing how they saw themselves in a world that constantly tried to degrade them. In 1791, Joice's descendants Charles and Patrick Mahoney petitioned the Maryland Court for their freedom, using the argument that they were descended from a free woman.

By following Joice's descendants over the next few generations, Swarns provides *The 272* with a unifying throughline for what could otherwise be a glut of disparate information. Furthermore, the book's focus on Joice's family humanizes the historical events it covers to ensure that the emotional weight of these events are felt instead of just appearing as facts on the page. Although Swarns approaches her subjects from an objective, journalistic perspective, she tries to fill in the blanks about what their experiences were like through indirect speculation. Often she accomplishes this by stating the details that are not known but possible. For example, when discussing how Charles Mahoney recounted in court how Joice had been imprisoned in a cellar for attempting to assert her freedom from Darnall, Swarns writes, "He did not say whether she screamed, pounded her fists against the walls, or wept in silence."

Running parallel to the Mahoney family in *The 272* is the storyline of Georgetown's founding and early years. Swarns recounts how "by the mid-1700s, the Jesuit order had become one of the largest enslavers in Maryland," both by inheriting enslaved people from wealthy parishioners and by purchasing them to work on their plantations. The profits from these Jesuit priest-run plantations would eventually be used to fund Georgetown, the nation's first Catholic college, which was founded in 1789. However, mismanagement of those properties and their profits over the years would become a continual problem for Georgetown, making the early years of its existence precarious. By the mid-1830s, the power-hungry Georgetown president, Thomas Mulledy, had decided to sell all the Jesuits' enslaved people to keep the university afloat.

The 272 examines slavery from a new angle, shining a light on horrific facets of the institution that often get ignored in lieu of its more obvious and violent evils. For example, the book focuses on how Christianity was used to justify enslaving other people as a way to "save their souls" in addition to generating the funds necessary to spread the religion further across the region. And while the Jesuit priests in Maryland were ostensibly less abusive than the enslavers running Southern plantations, they still had a degrading, paternalistic view of African Americans—believing them to be in need of their superior guidance. Furthermore, when news broke about the upcoming sale, many of the priests appeared more worried about whether the enslaved people could continue practicing Catholicism down South than that they would likely face horrific treatment by Southern plantation owners.

Throughout *The 272*, Swarns presents separating loved ones from each other as one of the greatest sins committed by Georgetown and the Jesuit priests running it. Beyond being a dehumanizing, abusive act, separating these families was the one thing the Jesuit priests had sought not do. Even the Mahoneys were not spared, and the Jesuits had formerly promised to their patriarch, Harry, that his family would never be sold nor separated after he helped them during the War of 1812. Like his ancestor Ann Joice, however, he would become the victim of another broken promise from White people as his daughters Anny and Bibiana were among the 272 sold. Sent to separate plantations in the South, they were unable to even find solace in each other's company.

Swarns chronicles all of the horrors and injustices that her subjects suffered with meticulous detail, but she also ensures that *The 272* is a book about African American resistance. Through the Mahoney family's story, she illustrates the different ways that enslaved people fought for their autonomy. While Ann Joice and Charles Mahoney tried to use legal contracts and the courts, their descendants implemented other methods for achieving control over their destinies. For Anny Mahoney's husband, Arnold, this meant escaping to freedom. Other members of the family, like Harry Mahoney, leveraged their ability to become reliable assets to the Jesuits in an effort to win their family more humane treatment. Later, Harry's daughter Louisa would try to protect her family like her father had by becoming an especially "industrious and virtuous" servant. She also became well-known among the priests for her piety, faith, and regular presence at church. Whether she truly found comfort in being a devoted Catholic or knew that acting as one would keep her family safe is unclear. Nonetheless, it was an act of self-determination that benefited her and her loved ones' status.

The power of the Mahoney family's resistance over the generations becomes clear in the parts of *The 272* in which Swarns reports on their present-day descendants—a number of whom are African American Catholics like her. In the decades that followed the 1838 sale, Mahoney descendants became scattered and lost touch with each other, but many continued to pass down the stories of their ancestors. Swarns's decision to include these stories in *The 272* became a point of praise for some critics reviewing the book: The historian Ana Lucia Araujo wrote for *The Washington Post*, "Through painstaking investigative work, she found, met and interviewed the descendants of the Mahoneys who still remember their family's harrowing past. Swarns makes full use of these oral histories to recount the Mahoneys' resistance, courage and resilience, which until now had been preserved only in the family's private circles." Araujo further underscored the triumph of Swarns centering Black experiences in *The 272* by highlighting how difficult it can be for researchers to even identify individuals among records that obscure their identities.

The thoroughness of Swarns's research is indeed one of the most admirable aspects of *The 272*, which is packed with details derived from an array of different historical documents. *Publishers Weekly* noted this in their starred review of the book, stating, "Swarns makes excellent use of archival sources to recreate the lives of the enslaved families and the circumstances of the sale, which was fiercely opposed by some Jesuit priests at the time." Arguably, Swarns's most resonant use of historic documents is that of the ledgers, sales contracts, and receipts she used to determine how much the Jesuits were making from slavery and the slave trade. The revelation that all 272 people were sold for an eventual total of $130,000 (approximately $4.5 million today) is a disturbing but necessary reminder of the way in which capitalism can so easily facilitate immoral actions, including the dehumanization of others.

Not all critics were wholly positive in their reviews of *The 272*, however. In a mostly encouraging review for the *New York Times*, historian David W. Blight also noted difficulty following the book's chronology at times and took issue with "Swarns remind[ing] us of the Jesuits' hypocrisy more than necessary; the entire book embodies that fact." His latter assessment, however, is a subjective one, as many readers will feel Swarns's repeated reminder that the Catholic Church enslaved other human beings is wholly necessary—something that should be shouted from the rooftops. Furthermore, Swarns does not utilize a one-note perspective on her subjects. Just as she highlights most of the Jesuits' hypocrisy, she is also quick to note those who, like Father Joseph Carbery, engaged in more moral behavior. The priest who oversaw St. Inigoes plantation, where many of the Mahoneys lived, Carbery treated the enslaved people there as tenant farmers who were allowed to raise and sell their own crops as long as they gave a portion back to the plantation. He also vehemently opposed the 1838 sale and, on the day when Mulledy's slave traders arrived, told the Mahoneys to run.

Ultimately, Swarns's decision to place narrative importance on the Mahoneys and people like Father Carbery makes *The 272* a hopeful read on a dire subject. This sense of hope is furthered by the book's sections on Georgetown's present-day efforts to atone for their participation in American slavery and the people who subsequently discovered their shared Mahoney ancestry thanks to her 2016 article. As she relays how these distant relatives are working with the university to find an appropriate form of justice for what happened to their ancestors, it becomes clear that nothing can ever truly make things right when it comes to slavery but there still is an opportunity to make things better for those who continue to be affected by its legacy. The book's revelation that some institutions and people are fighting for this becomes a heartening one.

Author Biography

Rachel L. Swarns is a *New York Times* contributor whose work focuses primarily on race, religion, and labor. An associate professor of journalism at New York University, she previously published *American Tapestry: The Story of the Black, White, and Multiracial Ancestors of Michelle Obama* (2012) and coauthored *Unseen: Unpublished Black History from the New York Times Photo Archives* (2017).

Emily E. Turner

Review Sources

Araujo, Ana Lucia. "An Intimate Account of the Enslaved People Sold to Save Georgetown." Review of *The 272*, by Rachel L. Swarns. *The Washington Post*, 13 July 2023, www.washingtonpost.com/books/2023/07/13/272-georgetown-rachel-swarns. Accessed 12 Feb. 2024.

Bordewich, Fergus M. "'The 272' Review: Slaves of Georgetown." Review of *The 272*, by Rachel L. Swarns. *The Wall Street Journal*, 28 July 2023, www.wsj.com/articles/the-272-review-slaves-of-georgetown-4d7cd74c. Accessed 15 Feb. 2024.

Review of *The 272*, by Rachel L. Swarns. *Publishers Weekly*, 17 Mar. 2023, www.publishersweekly.com/9780399590863. Accessed 12 Feb. 2024.

Wright, David W. "The Slave Sale That Saved—and Stained—Georgetown." Review of *The 272*, by Rachel L. Swarns. *The New York Times*, 28 June 2023, www.nytimes.com/2023/06/28/books/review/the-272-rachel-swarns.html. Accessed 12 Feb. 2024.

Valiant Women
The Extraordinary American Servicewomen Who Helped Win World War II

Author: Lena S. Andrews (b. ca. 1987)
Publisher: Mariner Books (New York). 368 pp.
Type of work: History
Time: 1940–48
Locales: United States, Europe, North Africa, and the Pacific

Andrews provides a detailed history of World War II, viewed from the perspective of American women who served with the armed forces, noting their contributions in supporting the United States' efforts to defeat Axis forces.

Principal personages

OVETA CULP HOBBY, the first director of the Women's Army Auxiliary Corps (WAAC, later renamed the Women's Army Corps [WAC])
MILDRED MCAFEE, the first director of the Women Accepted for Volunteer Emergency Service (WAVES)
DOROTHY STRATTON, the first director of the Coast Guard Women's Reserve (SPARS)
RUTH CHENEY STREETER, the first director of the US Marine Corps Women's Reserve (MCWR)
JACQUELINE "JACKIE" COCHRAN, head of the Women's Flying Training Detachment (WFTD) and, later, the Women's Airforce Service Pilots (WASPs)
NANCY HARKNESS LOVE, head of the Women's Auxiliary Ferrying Squadron (WAFS)
CHARITY ADAMS, head of the all-Black 6,888th Central Postal Battalion, a WAC unit serving in Europe

In 1940 and 1941, as the United States struggled to stay out of the armed conflict raging in Europe and the Pacific, American political leaders and military planners slowly came to the realization that were the nation forced to go to war, it might lack the "manpower" needed to field an army, navy, and marine corps capable of deploying overseas and fighting in sustained combat across multiple fronts for an extended time. Like all armies, the troops on the front line would need a support system to produce armaments and supplies and get them to the fighting forces. Additionally, modern warfare required substantial investment and personnel in areas such as communications and administration. Slowly, and reluctantly, President Franklin Roosevelt and his chief military advisers concluded that to win a future war, it would be necessary to enlist

Lena S. Andrews

the help of a hitherto untapped source of people power: America's women. Hence, shortly after the United States declared war on the Axis powers in December 1941, when the nation began calling up men to serve, concerted plans were developed to allow women to join the fight—in uniform.

The story of how the military recruited, trained, and deployed women during the years 1942 to 1945 is the principal focus of Lena S. Andrews's *Valiant Women: The Extraordinary American Servicewomen Who Helped Win World War II*. The book is exceptional in that Andrews successfully contextualizes the story of women's military service within the larger picture of global warfare. Deftly weaving together a concise history of the United States's progress toward victory in Europe and the Pacific with personal narratives of some of the women who took part in military operations, she achieves her principal goal in this study: to highlight the contributions women made directly to the war effort.

It was a given for the men making decisions about staffing the armed forces that were women to be recruited, they would serve only in supporting roles rather than combat duty—"release a man to fight," as the saying went. Even so, American leaders contemplated two major unknowns. First, would women serve if called upon? Second—and perhaps more troubling—would Americans stomach the idea of having young women subjected to the rigors of military life and the potential dangers faced by anyone in a combat zone?

As Andrews recounts with a sense of pride, the answer to the first was a resounding "yes." In fact, recruiters were faced with the happy problem of having a plethora of highly qualified young women eager to join the war effort. The idea of women serving in uniform, however, did not receive immediate, enthusiastic backing by military leaders, politicians, or the general public. Merely getting legislation through Congress and organizing women's units within the various services proved a herculean task. Much of *Valiant Women* is given over to explaining how those in favor of women's service overcame substantial problems to successfully employ women in the armed forces.

Andrews devotes chapters to the formation of each of the women's organizations that were authorized for the US Army (including the Army Air Forces), Navy, Marines, and Coast Guard following the United States' entry into the war. In these, her particular focus is on the women chosen to lead the groups. Andrews explains how Oveta Culp Hobby—the wife of a former Texas governor, publisher of the *Houston Post*, and head of a War Department public relations office—was hand-picked to organize the Women's Army Auxiliary Corps (WAAC). Mildred McAfee, chosen to lead the navy's auxiliary (WAVES), and Dorothy Stratton, first head of the Coast Guard's auxiliary (SPARS), came to their positions from academic administration. The first director of the Marine Corps Women Reserve, Ruth Streeter, was involved in aviation and civic affairs before donning the uniform.

The two women who eventually led competing air services came from the most radically different backgrounds. Jackie Cochran, founder of the Women's Flying Training Detachment, had grown up in poverty and become an entrepreneur. Nancy Harkness Love, who convinced Army Air Force leaders to allow women to fly for Air Transport Command, had received a high-society education and been a successful businessperson (and professional pilot) prior to her appointment. Their rivalry, which led eventually to Cochran's appointment as head of the combined Women's Airforce Service Pilots (WASPs), forms an interesting subtext in Andrews's larger narrative.

While each of these women may have come to their new positions from different circumstances, they found their tasks similar: recruiting qualified women (fortunately from a large pool of willing volunteers); organizing and training them both in basic knowledge of military service and in the many specialties in which they would be performing while in uniform; and perhaps most difficult, getting the political and military hierarchy to accept the fact that women could and would serve as well as men in positions to which they were assigned. However, the lack of or relatively low military rank given to these first directors proved a significant hindrance, as they were often ignored by generals and left out of important strategy sessions where they might have provided advice on how to use this new source of "manpower"—a term Andrews uses for its historical accuracy, despite its gender implications.

The institutional prejudices women leaders faced in Washington were mirrored in the communities where women in uniform trained and served. As Andrews explains, the gender and racial biases that characterized mid-twentieth-century US society affected most of the young women who volunteered for military service. Many Americans were skeptical about the value of having women in the armed forces, suggesting they might actually weaken the war effort, since women were perceived as being incapable of doing jobs normally performed by men. Some worried that the presence of young women close to young men preparing for combat would be an unwelcome distraction. Others simply could not accept the idea of having women involved in what was perceived as a man's world. Andrews catalogs numerous incidents when women were publicly humiliated, chastised, abused verbally—and on occasion physically— as they tried to perform their duties or enjoy their limited time off. The situation was even worse for Black women who volunteered. At the time, all military services were segregated, and Black troops regardless of gender were often subjected to the same racially motivated hatred that they experienced outside the service. Whisper campaigns about the character of women who volunteered for military duty abounded, usually alleging that only prostitutes or lesbians would find military life attractive. Adding to women's problems was the various services' difficulties in adapting uniforms and equipment for them. Worse, as Andrews recounts with some sense of outrage, women were on occasion issued outdated or defective equipment—or gear that may have been deliberately sabotaged, as in the case of women working with the Army Air Force— that placed their lives in danger.

Despite these drawbacks, between 1942 and 1945, more than 350,000 women served with distinction in a wide range of jobs. Not all were assigned to jobs in administration and health care, tasks already traditionally performed by women. Many were flyers who became cornerstones in the services' aviation-training programs and in units flying support missions. A number of others worked in maintenance. Some were illustrators, postal workers, or intelligence analysts. They did this work for modest wages and often with few of the benefits provided to men who served. In all branches except the US Navy, they were merely auxiliaries and hence ineligible for military pensions, insurance, or ongoing care for disabilities incurred while serving in uniform. As Andrews reminds her readers, the women who stepped forward to serve the nation during World War II were trailblazers in the reformation of the US military. Though they may have served only in supporting roles, some were often close to the front lines—and some ended up as prisoners of war. Their competency and their valor validated the prediction made by First Lady Eleanor Roosevelt shortly after the country entered the war: "Women are a weapon waiting to be used."

Andrews tells the story of these women with the skill of an accomplished researcher and an engaging style that makes readers feel like they are in conversation with some of the participants in the conflict. Not only is Andrews able to relate the personal stories of women serving during World War II with the progress of the conflict; she is also adept at balancing exciting narratives of those engaged in dangerous jobs with more sobering ones that bring out the personal toll that prejudice took on those who stepped forward to serve their country in its hour of need.

Andrews's accomplishments have not gone unnoticed. Deborah Hopkinson, in a starred review for *BookPage*, called *Valiant Women* a "vital, authoritative account of an almost-forgotten history" that deserves to be known by all Americans. *New York Journal of Books* critic Jerry Lenaberg, who found *Valiant Women* "compelling," said Andrews has done these veterans a great service in recording their achievements "so that a new generation can remember their contribution to saving the world from fascism and militarism." Another notable tribute came from Linda Weissgold, a former deputy director of the US Central Intelligence Agency. In a review for *The Cipher Brief*, Weissgold asserted Andrews's book "goes beyond being merely a recollection of noteworthy stories," inviting readers to view World War II "in a different way" and to "use that new perspective to understand that like WWII, the requirements of war in this modern era will stretch the capacity of even the largest and best prepared combatants." Viewed in that light, *Valiant Women* is not merely a reclamation project to assure that women's stories are captured and remembered; it is an important historical record of women's service to the nation in a time of crisis and a reminder that the contributions of all citizens are required to preserve a nation's way of life.

Author Biography
Lena Andrews earned a doctorate in political science at the Massachusetts Institute of Technology. She worked for the US Central Intelligence Agency, the RAND

Corporation, and the United States Institute for Peace before becoming an associate professor of public policy at the University of Maryland. *Valiant Women* is her first book.

Laurence W. Mazzeno

Review Sources

Hopkinson, Deborah. Review of *Valiant Women*, by Lena Andrews. *BookPage*, Aug. 2023, www.bookpage.com/reviews/valiant-women. Accessed 17 Nov. 2023.

Lenaberg, Jerry. Review of *Valiant Women*, by Lena Andrews. *New York Journal of Books*, www.nyjournalofbooks.com/book-review/valiant-women-untold-story. Accessed 17 Nov. 2023.

Statler, Chad E. Review of *Valiant Women*, by Lena Andrews. *Library Journal*, 1 July 2023, www.libraryjournal.com/review/valiant-women-the-untold-story-of-the-american-servicewomen-who-helped-win-world-war-ii-1797597. Accessed 17 Nov. 2023.

Review of *Valiant Women*, by Lena Andrews. *Kirkus Reviews*, 24 May 2023, www.kirkusreviews.com/book-reviews/lena-andrews-valiant-women. Accessed 17 Nov. 2023.

Review of *Valiant Women*, by Lena Andrews. *Publishers Weekly*, 10 May 2023, www.publishersweekly.com/9780063088337. Accessed 17 Nov. 2023.

Weissgold, Linda. "A Tribute to Valiant Women." *Cipher Brief*, 24 Oct. 2023, www.thecipherbrief.com/column-article/a-tribute-to-valiant-women. Accessed 17 Nov. 2023.

The Vaster Wilds

Author: Lauren Groff (b. 1978)
Publisher: Riverhead Books (New York). 272 pp.
Type of work: Novel
Time: Early 1600s
Locale: Jamestown, Virginia

A survivalist thriller, this historical fiction novel follows a girl from the lowest rungs of English society as she fights to stay alive amidst the inhospitable terrain of the seventeenth-century American wilderness.

Principal characters

THE GIRL, a.k.a. Zed or Lamentations Callat, a teenage servant who has run away from the English colony at Jamestown
THE MISTRESS, the wealthy woman who purchased her from a poorhouse when she was four
THE CHILD BESS, her charge, the mistress's beautiful daughter who has severe intellectual disabilities
THE MINISTER, the mistress's new husband who brings them all to the New World
KIT, the mistress's cruel son

Historically, man-versus-nature literature has consisted almost exclusively of stories by and about men. From Daniel Defoe's *Robinson Crusoe* (1719) to Herman Melville's *Moby-Dick* (1851) to Ernest Hemingway's *The Old Man and the Sea* (1952)—the genre has long been defined by male heroes using their intellect, courage, and physical strength to take on Earth's most dangerous elements and creatures. In this way, it reflects the pervasive underlying idea of antiquated history textbooks that great White men were exclusively responsible for the development of human civilization.

In *The Vaster Wilds* (2023), lauded American author Lauren Groff breaks free of such myopic tropes by chronicling the journey of an uneducated servant girl forced to survive in the wilderness of seventeenth-century Virginia on her own. The novel begins with the girl running away from the Jamestown colony during its infamous "starving time," the 1609–10 winter when most of its settlers were killed by disease, famine, or attacks by the Powhatan people. Although it is unclear what she is running from and why she has become a fugitive, the treacherousness of her circumstances are immediately evident. Alone in the darkened woods as snow and "needles of ice" fall from the night sky, she has not eaten in days and must get as far from the people chasing her as possible. This is no easy feat as the threat of death looms everywhere.

Lauren Groff

As such, much of *The Vaster Wilds*' plot is simply about the girl's efforts to stay alive. This proves to be extremely difficult as every new day arrives with the urgent need to find new shelter and more food in a barren winter landscape. By detailing the desperate measures the girl must resort to for sustenance, Groff successfully conveys just how challenging meeting such basic needs were for the first wave of Europeans who arrived in America. For example, at one point, the girl robs a squirrel's nest of its pink, furless babies to eat. At another, she eats grubs and then mushrooms that she knows might be poisonous but ultimately takes the risk of consuming them anyway. And when she is not getting sick from the things she consumes, she must worry about predators—both animal and human. In one of the novel's most disconcerting sequences, she encounters a Jesuit priest whose decades in isolation have led to both madness and an animalistic desire to strike her dead.

Although the details of the girl's journey across the Virginia wilderness are often unsettling, they are written in beautiful, poetic prose. To further ensure that her struggle does not feel too heavy or monotonous, Groff breaks up the present storyline with memories from the girl's past. These include glimpses of the events that preceded her fleeing Jamestown days earlier as well as flashbacks to her life back in England. Both sets of memories ultimately succeed in shining a light on just how barbaric English society was, though they considered themselves to be the civilizing force in the New World. Their barbarism is especially evident in the way that the girl was dehumanized throughout her life. Because she was impoverished and of low social status, her mistress deemed her unworthy of a real name, instead calling the girl "Zed" after her dead pet monkey, and used her as a footwarmer at the end of her bed. It is not until the mistress's second husband, a "honey-tongued minister," brings them all to the New World that the girl's treatment as chattel changes. There, famine and disease become equalizing forces within the community that allow her to claim her autonomy and, in turn, her destiny.

In many ways, the girl is a testament to Groff's ability to craft strong female protagonists who are not only compelling but also provide readers with insight into what life was like for women during different points in history—a subject that is often overlooked. It is a talent that Groff has demonstrated with her previous novel, *Matrix* (2021), in which she imagined the life of the twelfth-century poet Marie de France, about whom little is actually known despite her significant contributions to medieval literature. Like *Matrix*'s Marie de France, the girl in *The Vaster Wilds* also succeeds in illustrating the different ways that women have overcome the sexism they faced in patriarchal societies. Despite being uneducated and abused her entire life, the girl continually demonstrates the kind of brilliance and tenacity throughout the novel that most readers will find inspiring.

Beyond feminism, *The Vaster Wilds* also grapples with religion and faith. A large part of the girl's motivation to keep going, despite all the obstacles she faces, is her faith in God. However, the more time that she spends trying to survive on her own amid the danger and beauty of the wilderness, the more her Protestant beliefs evolve into a new form of panentheistic or mystic spirituality. In turn, her journey can be interpreted as a pilgrimage of sorts through which Groff presents a different take on the existence of God that feels as though it could be representative of her own beliefs.

The tone of *The Vaster Wilds* is best described as dark. The girl's odyssey is one of constant suffering as she faces one new threat after another with little reprieve. The intensity of her struggle is especially resonant thanks to the narrative's underlying atmosphere of realism, as everything she encounters comes across as well-researched and accurate to the time and place. This sense of realism is further amplified by Groff's refusal to gloss over the different types of bodily horrors that Europeans experienced in seventeenth-century America; from the boils of smallpox to gastrointestinal distress, she spares no details.

These prove especially harrowing as Groff refuses to cushion her narration with such common Western storytelling tropes as Deus ex machina; Indigenous people willing to befriend and help the White hero; or tidy, happily-ever-after endings. Yet, despite its painstaking dedication to realism, *The Vaster Wilds* is not a nihilistic book. Because the girl endures so much horror, the small, beautiful moments she occasionally experiences come across as especially important and worthwhile. Whether it is the love she feels for the mistress's daughter, the romance she experiences with a Dutch glassblower, the smell of an orange, or the wondrous beauty of the wilderness—all of these things fuel the girl's determination to keep going. In turn, Groff makes a compelling case that life's suffering can be endured by embracing the power of communing with other people and nature.

Upon its publication, *The Vaster Wilds* became a New York Times Best Seller and earned significant acclaim. For many critics, the novel's ambitiously original premise was a testament to why Groff was already a three-time National Book Award finalist. In her review of it for NPR's *Fresh Air*, Maureen Corrigan expressed this sentiment, stating, "She's such an evocative writer who always sets herself the challenge of doing something different: The domestic fiction of *Fates and Furies* was followed by the medieval historical fiction of the *Matrix*, which in turn is now followed by the eerie survival story of *The Vaster Wilds*." Expanding upon this point, a case can be made that fans of Groff's work will indeed enjoy that she is again taking them somewhere that they have never been with her before and that she accomplishes this with the same mastery of storytelling and prose that she has demonstrated throughout her bibliography.

Indeed, Groff's prose was another common point of praise among critics, many of whom were impressed with how she uses language and cadence in a way that accurately reflects how English people in the seventeenth century spoke. Constance Grady was especially effusive about this aspect of the novel in her review for *Vox*, stating,

"Groff's prose takes on a hallucinatory, feverish quality that pushes the tension high. Her pastiche of Elizabethan prose is playful and fluid, dense with alliteration and allusion.... Its rhythm is so quick and unfaltering that it becomes impossible to put the book down; the rat-a-tat-tat of each sentence just keeps carrying you along."

In addition to creating a propulsive narrative engine, Groff's prose also captures the beauty of the natural world impressively. This is exemplified when she describes the sight of the sky at one particular moment as "eternal churning blues and pales, and the lonely heap of cloud in the west, frothing and delicate and whipped and with silvery creases deepening to violet." In the hands of Groff, everything from grubs to rocks feels like miraculous creations.

Although most critics were favorable in their reviews, some felt that the novel lacked in its pacing and messaging. Corrigan called it a "marathon run of a plot" that was "kind of exhausting in its repetitiveness" and found herself longing for a more satisfying ending. Similarly, writing for the *Washington Post*, Ron Charles said that the narrative had "constant movement but little momentum, as though the girl were on a woodland treadmill," before ultimately concluding that she "runs and runs and runs untold miles, yet she ultimately arrives at a place wholly comfortable to us." Here, Charles alluded to the fact that the evolution of the girl's perspective throughout the novel hews closely to fairly mainstream ideas today of spirituality, colonialism, and Indigenous people. For some readers, this may feel like a jarringly contemporary left turn after Groff's dedication to historical accuracy and realism. For many others, however, it will provide a portal to the present moment through which the discoveries that the girl made during her journey four hundred years ago arrive as a meaningful, relevant message for today.

Author Biography

Bestselling author Lauren Groff has published several short story collections, including *Florida* (2018), as well as the novels *The Monsters of Templeton* (2008), *Arcadia* (2011), *Fates and Furies* (2015), and *Matrix* (2021). Three of her books have been shortlisted for the National Book Award, and Groff was the recipient of the 2018 Guggenheim Fellowship for Fiction.

Emily E. Turner

Review Sources

Charles, Ron. "Lauren Groff's 'Vaster Wilds' Is Light on Action, Heavy on Inspiration." Review of *The Vaster Wilds*, by Lauren Groff. *The Washington Post*, 7 Sept. 2023, www.washingtonpost.com/books/2023/09/07/lauren-groff-vaster-wilds. Accessed 18 Jan. 2024.

Corrigan, Maureen. "Lauren Groff's Survivalist Novel 'The Vaster Wilds' Will Test Your Endurance, Too." Review of *The Vaster Wilds*, by Lauren Groff. *Fresh Air*, NPR, 21 Sept. 2023, www.npr.org/2023/09/21/1199199765/lauren-groff-the-vaster-wilds-review. Accessed 18 Jan. 2024.

Grady, Constance. "The Book of the Year So Far Is Lauren Groff's The Vaster Wilds." Review of *The Vaster Wilds*, by Lauren Groff. *Vox*, 12 Sept. 2023, www.vox.com/culture/23840033/vaster-wilds-review-lauren-groff. Accessed 18 Jan. 2024.

Mozley, Fiona. "Lauren Groff's Latest Is a Lonely Novel of Hunger and Survival." Review of *The Vaster Wilds*, by Lauren Groff. *The New York Times*, 2024, www.nytimes.com/2023/09/08/books/review/lauren-groff-the-vaster-wilds.html. Accessed 18 Jan. 2024.

Vera Wong's Unsolicited Advice for Murderers

Author: Jesse Q. Sutanto
Publisher: Berkley (New York) 352 pp.
Type of work: Novel
Time: Present day
Locale: San Francisco, CA

Jesse Q. Sutanto's novel Vera Wong's Unsolicited Advice for Murderers *is a cozy mystery set in present-day San Francisco. Vera Wong is an empty-nester whose Chinatown tea shop has fallen on hard times. When a man mysteriously dies there one night, Vera is convinced he was murdered and begins to gather her cast of suspects. Told in vivid detail with a heavy dose of humor, this book provides a delightful read that is able to broach harder topics like loneliness and death while maintaining a lightness that serves its plot well.*

Principal characters

VERA WONG, a sixty-year-old tea shop owner often found minding other people's business
TILBERT "TILLY" WONG, her son, a lawyer
MARSHALL CHEN, a twenty-nine-year-old man found dead in her tea shop
JULIA CHEN, Marshall's widow; a photographer
EMMA CHEN, Marshall and Julia's two-year-old daughter
RIKI HERWANTO, a tech-wiz from Indonesia
SANA SINGH, a once-rising artist; the daughter of a famous author
OLIVER CHEN, Marshall's twin brother
OFFICERS GRAY AND HE, police officers investigating Marshall's death

Jesse Q. Sutanto's novel *Vera Wong's Unsolicited Advice for Murderers* is a lighthearted romp into the world of the eponymous tea shop owner and the cast of "suspects" she collects after a man is found dead and possibly murdered in her shop. The narrative is told in a series of chapters that alternate between Vera's perspective and chapters told from the perspective of each of the book's main characters. As each character narrates their chapter, the reader learns more about their backgrounds and how they were connected to Marshall. Exploring themes of loneliness, aging, family connections, and gentrification, *Vera Wong* packs a wealth of emotion and curiosity into a fast-paced plot. As the characters move through their home city of San Francisco, the reader is made to feel connected to them and to their city, understanding their motivations

Jesse Q. Sutanto

through a sharpened lens. A cozy mystery in every way, this novel does not shy away from heavy emotional scenes or themes, allowing the grace of its characters to guide the plot to its surprising ending.

As the novel opens, the reader is introduced to Vera Wong on a typical weekday morning as she prepares to open her shop, Vera Wang's World-Famous Teahouse—which she named for the famous fashion designer and teas that were famous in China but less so in the United States. Vera rises before the sun, texts her son, Tilly (short for Tilbert), about finding a girlfriend at work, and then descends the staircase from her apartment to the shop below, where she expects to greet just a handful of customers on a busy day. Instead, she finds a body lying in the middle of the shop's floor. The body turns out to be that of Marshall Chen, age twenty-nine.

The subsequent chapters introduce Vera's lineup of suspects. Marshall's wife, Julia, remembers the fight she had had with him the night before, when he claimed that he had made it big and did not need her anymore before leaving her and their young daughter, Emma. The following morning, Julia is wondering how she will cope in his absence when Officers Gray and Ha come by to tell her that her husband is dead and that a bag of ecstasy (MDMA) was found on his body, although they do not know what caused his death. As the officers leave Julia, Officer Gray notices the garbage bags by the door, which Julia had stuffed with Marshall's belongings after he left her.

The reader then meets tech wizard Riki and artist Sana in their own respective chapters, though their connections to Marshall are not made clear at first. Finally, the reader meets Oliver, Marshall's partially estranged twin brother, who gives everyone a fright when he shows up at the scene of the crime. In each case, Sutanto makes it clear that none of the suspects had kind or loving feelings for Marshall while he was alive. Though they do not appear to grieve his loss, his survivors grow closer to each other over the course of the book.

Sutanto's method of introducing each of the main characters by chapter not only creates a rewarding opportunity for the reader to get to know each of them, but also allows for a slow unraveling of the plot. While Vera does take up the bulk of the book's story line—it is her murder investigation, after all—Julia, Oliver, Riki, and Sana are each given room to express their feelings about Marshall's death and to also give clues into what might have been their own motives for killing him. Marshall constantly made Julia feel inferior, and he was often unkind to Emma as well. Sama was swindled by Marshall, as was Riki, and Oliver's lifelong tension with his brother also gives reason for suspicion. In interludes placed throughout the story, Vera adds to and subtracts from her suspect list, adding a dose of humor to a steadily rising tension among the characters.

One of the more profound and interesting themes explored in the novel is that of loneliness. It seems that each of the characters portrayed is experiencing some sort of isolation or loneliness and cannot quite find their place in the world. Vera is a widow who misses her husband every day. She also misses her son, who also lives in San Francisco but rarely has time for his mother, working long hours as a junior associate at a law firm and preferring to keep some distance from her. Vera's tea room, once a place that welcomed a host of customers, in no small part because of her well-curated selection of Chinese teas, now welcomes one older man, Alex, as a regular customer. Vera prepares tea for him each day and sends him home with small satchels of dried leaves for his wife, who has dementia. The interactions between Vera and Alex are particularly touching as each is hesitant to let the other know just how alone they feel.

Riki, the reader learns, is dealing with some heavy family drama as he tries to bring his highly gifted younger brother to the United States to attend a special school. Riki thus often feels it necessary to sacrifice in his daily and personal life and is constantly worried about his family in Indonesia. Sama has a difficult relationship with her mother, a famous writer who has sold millions of copies of her books, and as a result suffers from creative block and has also shut herself off from the world. Julia and Oliver were best friends in high school but had a falling out after Julia began to date Oliver's twin, Marshall. Since then, Julia and Oliver have both missed each other's company. Ironically, while Marshall isolated himself from each of these characters through his aggressive personality and hostile actions, after his death, they bond with each other over their shared trauma of having been involved with him. The latter part of the novel deals largely with how each of these characters comes to terms with their relationship with him and find strength and love within themselves.

One other important point of connection in the book is Vera's cooking. Sutanto clearly feels great love for Chinese cuisine and those who cook it, as Vera often travels with a thermoses of tea and tiffin towers full of meals she's spent hours cooking. She uses her food to get closer to her suspects and earn their trust, as when she prepares a feast that she takes to Julia's with Sama, Riki, and Oliver in tow. It is also at Julia's that she employs Emma as her kitchen helper, slowly bringing the young girl into herself. Humorous moments involving food occur at the police precinct where Vera has gone to give a reluctant Officer Gray an update on her case, though Vera is in no way being supported or encouraged by the police to investigate this case.

Vera Wong's Unsolicited Advice for Murderers was not widely reviewed upon its release, but the attention it received was positive. For the *Star Tribune*, Chris Hewitt wrote, "The title character in 'Vera Wong's Unsolicited Advice for Murderers' is like *Jane Austen*'s Emma if Emma were a believer in the healing powers of tea and if she actually knew what was best for everyone instead of incorrectly thinking she did." The novel received a starred review in *Library Journal*, which stated, "Sutanto excels at creating lovably flawed characters, the mystery has plenty of twists to keep readers guessing, and Vera's case notes at the end of some chapters add humor to the deductive process." The novel also received a starred review from *Publishers Weekly*, whose reviewer enjoyed its "engrossing plot, which is full of laugh out loud humor and heartfelt moments." The novel was also included in mystery roundups in the *Washington Post* and the *New York Times*.

Vera Wong's Unsolicited Advice for Murderers strikes a universal note with its characters, in particular, that readers and reviewers enjoyed. Like *Dial A for Aunties*, *Vera Wong* will further cement Sutanto's place as a writer for adults, and, even more so, as a go-to source for cozy mysteries.

Author Biography
Jesse Q. Sutanto grew up in Indonesia, Singapore, and England. She is an award-winning and best-selling author whose novels for adults include *Dial A for Aunties* (2021), which was awarded the Comedy Women in Print Prize and bought by Netflix; *Four Aunties and a Wedding* (2022); and *Vera Wong's Unsolicited Advice for Murderers* (2023), which was bought by Warner Brothers. She has also written the young-adult novels *The Obsession* (2021), *Well, That Was Unexpected* (2022), *Theo Tan and the Fox Spirit* (2022), and *Theo Tan and the Iron Fan* (2023).

Melynda Fuller

Review Sources
Draper, Tristan. Review of *Vera Wong's Unsolicited Advice for Murderers*, by Jesse Q. Sutanto. *Library Journal*, www.libraryjournal.com/review/vera-wongs-unsolicited-advice-for-murderers-1795145. Accessed 13 Oct. 2023.

Hewitt, Chris. "Review: Jesse Sutanto's 'Vera Wong's Unsolicited Advice for Murderers' an Irresistible Comic Creation." Review of *Vera Wong's Unsolicited Advice for Murderers*, by Jesse Q. Sutanto. *Star Tribune*, Star Tribune, 2 June 2023, www.startribune.com/review-vera-wong-is-an-irresistible-comic-creation-in-san-francisco-set-mystery/600279636/. Accessed 13 Oct. 2023.

Kelleher, Ella. "Book Review: Vera Wong's Unsolicited Advice for Murderers (2023) by Jesse Sutanto – a Wholesome Investigation of the Unconventional." Review of *Vera Wong's Unsolicited Advice for Murderers*, by Jesse Q. Sutanto. *Asia Media International*, 3 Aug. 2023, asiamedia.lmu.edu/2023/07/06/book-review-vera-wongs-unsolicited-advice-for-murderers-2023-by-jesse-sutanto-a-wholesome-investigation-of-the-unconventional/. Accessed 13 Oct. 2023.

Review of *Vera Wong's Unsolicited Advice for Murderers*, by Jesse Q. Sutanto. *Kirkus Reviews*, Berkley, 14 Mar. 2023, www.kirkusreviews.com/book-reviews/jesse-q-sutanto/vera-wongs-unsolicited-advice-for-murderers/. Accessed 13 Oct. 2023.

Review of *Vera Wong's Unsolicited Advice for Murderers*, by Jesse Q. Sutanto. *Publishers Weekly*, www.publishersweekly.com/9780593549223. Accessed 13 Oct. 2023.

Victory City

Author: Salman Rushdie (b. 1947)
Publisher: Random House (New York). 352 pp.
Type of work: Novel
Time: Fourteenth to sixteenth centuries
Locale: Bisnaga Empire, India

Rushdie's epic novel unfolds an alternate, mythological history of the real-life Vijayanagara Empire, which flourished for several centuries in southern India.

Principal characters

PAMPA KAMPANA, also known as Gangadevi, a poet, prophet, and three-time queen of Bisnaga
HUKKA SANGAMA, a cofounder of Bisnaga and its first king, based on a historical figure of the same name
BUKKA SANGAMA, his younger brother, cofounder of Bisnaga and its second king, based on a historical figure of the same name
VIDYASAGAR, a mystic and religious leader
ZERELDA LI, Pampa Kampana's descendent, a warrior
KRISHNADEVARAYA, the king of Bisnaga in the early sixteenth century

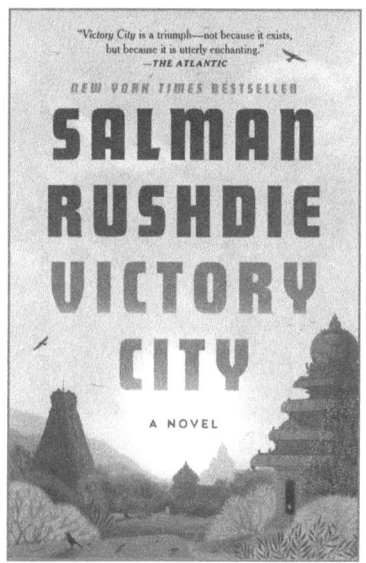

Across a storied, four-decade career, comprising over a dozen novels, Salman Rushdie has continually drawn on both magical elements and mythology to offer a surprising look at world history. In his acclaimed second novel, 1981's *Midnight Children*, for example, he retells the history of India from the time of the country's independence in 1947 forward, using numerous magical realist touches to show that history in a new light. The main character, Saleem Sinai, is one of hundreds of children born at midnight on the day of independence and these children are endowed with magical powers and can also communicate telepathically. The "midnight's children" form a kind of chorus that reflects on the tumultuous early history of India.

In more recent books, Rushdie has drawn on a wide array of background sources, from the *Thousand and One Nights* to *Don Quixote*, to bolster his explorations of both historical and present-day situations. In his latest novel, *Victory City*, Rushdie looks to the distant past, offering up a magic realist-laden reimagining of a real-life medieval Indian empire. The Vijayanagara Empire was established in southern India in 1336 and continued on for a few centuries, although it was effectively finished as a major power by 1565. In his novel, Rushdie spins an epic tale, chronicling the full history of the empire, which is referred to here as Bisnaga. Respecting the real history of the empire and including all the major real-life figures that defined that history, Rushdie also introduces fictional characters and situations, as well as numerous magical realist touches. The result is a fevered epic that uncovers and brings to vivid life an era of forgotten history. In applying magical realist techniques to the distant past, it serves as a worthy companion to *Midnight Children*'s similarly constructed take on more recent history.

Victory City begins with a framing device, which sets up the narrative as a found text. The narrator informs the reader that a "blind poet, miracle worker, and prophetess" named Pampa Kampana composed an epic poem in Sanskrit of twenty-four thousand verses, named the *Jayaparajaya*. On the last day of her 247-year life, he narrates, she buried the poem in a clay pot and sealed it. Only four and a half centuries later was the poem discovered. The narrator proposes to tell the story contained in her poem in his own language and the book that follows is his paraphrase of the *Jayaparajaya* and tells the multi-century history of Bisnaga.

Salman Rushdie

The fictional figure of Pampa Kampana stands as the book's main character, and she is a wholly original creation. Scarred by a childhood memory and endowed with magical powers, this visionary woman sets about shaping the course of history, attempting to bend the arc of that narrative toward justice while continually running up against the reality of human nature. When she was nine years old, Kampana witnessed her mother join many other women in killing themselves by plunging into a fire after the kingdom where they lived suffered military defeat. Shortly after, she is possessed by the goddess Pampa and endowed with special powers. Once she is endowed with these powers, she sets about creating a new empire, using a pair of real-life historical figures, Hukka and Bukka Sangama, as her instruments. The two former cowherds become the first two rulers of the nascent empire, but in the early days, Kampana is the main power behind Bisnaga. She creates all the people of the empire and whispers their backstories into their ears, endowing these newly hatched citizens with a fictional history that seems real to them.

After the experience of watching her mother and the other women self-immolate because of military defeat, Kampana sets about founding an empire that will be based on more humane and egalitarian principles. At first, Kampana's influence remains strong and Bisnaga becomes established as an enlightened empire where men and women hold equal powers and are equally capable of filling any jobs. Over the course of two and a half centuries, though, Kampana's influence wanes significantly, and she can no longer whisper to the empire's inhabitants to control their thinking. The result is a charged history that alternates between periods of religious oppression and those of more enlightened rule. As Rushdie spins out his epic century-spanning tale, he joins together real-life historical events, magical realist touches, and fanciful and occasionally humorous situations to tell the tale of one long ago dissipated empire.

In presenting several centuries of history in one volume, Rushdie allows the reader to see the ways that history often ebbs and flows depending on who is in charge. It is clear that in writing this historical book, Rushdie also has more contemporary politics in mind. After publishing his fourth novel, *The Satanic Verses*, in 1988, Rushdie became the subject of a fatwa issued by Iran's leader Ayatollah Khomeini calling for his death over the alleged blasphemy of the book against the religion of Islam. More recently, in 2022, an admirer of Khomeini viciously attacked Rushdie and nearly killed him. Throughout *Victory City* runs a thread of religious intolerance that sprouts up periodically depending on who is in charge of Bisnaga. During these periods of repression, anyone who follows a religion other than the preferred faith is subject to persecution and women are forced to assume a subservient role. Later in the book, two characters are forcibly blinded, an account of intolerance that eerily prefigures Rushdie's own partial blinding during the 2022 attack, which occurred after he had finished writing the book.

Victory City vividly evokes the consequences of repressive government, and one of the shocking things about the book is how quickly the government can change. One moment, a tolerant regime is in place, but then the ruler dies and suddenly everyone's freedoms are suddenly abridged and many fear for their lives. This nearly arbitrary nature of governing is one of the guiding forces of the book, and it may be eye-opening for readers who are used to more predictable, less volatile changes in government. But *Victory City* is not simply a despairing or cynical take on the question of governance and civilization. Although humanity is often presented as small-minded and power-hungry throughout the novel, there is also another thread of tolerance and openness. It is clear from the narration that Rushdie himself favors this latter form of government, and in the moments when it does triumph, he provides a picture of what enlightened governance might look like.

Throughout the novel, Rushdie's magical realist moments endow the story with a more mythical basis. For example, in one key moment, Kampana needs to escape from a tight situation and receives a feather that allows her to turn into a bird and fly away. The feather gives her the power to shift back and forth between bird and human three times, and she makes smart use of this feather throughout the novel, employing it in key situations. The introduction of the feather, as well as other magical realist touches, add a fanciful element to the story that is highly entertaining. They enliven what could otherwise have been a dry historical account. They also add some heft to the story. In Rushdie's telling, the Bisnaga Empire is not only significant for its historical interest, but because it is a magical, larger-than-life kingdom. By turning the empire into a mythical creation, by crafting a compelling set of characters both real-life and fictional, and by focusing on both micro- and macro-level details, Rushdie creates a vividly evoked world. His epic story of that world both serves a valuable historical purpose and, perhaps more importantly, a wonderful literary purpose as well.

Victory City received largely positive reviews from critics. Writing for *The Atlantic*, Judith Shulevitz summed up the critical consensus, calling the book a "triumph" and "utterly enchanting." She especially enjoyed the book's metafictional and political elements and the ways that Rushdie "plays adroitly" with these elements. Writing in the *New York Times*, Michael Gorra particularly praised Rushdie's "own generosity towards his predecessors, his consciousness of working within a great tradition." As Gorra pointed out, Rushdie has long drawn on a wide range of sources, historical, mythological, and literary, and in *Victory City*, he skillfully continues this tradition.

Not every critic was equally enamored with Rushdie's novel, however. Writing in *The Guardian*, Anthony Cummins found Rushdie's voice to be, by turns, "pulpy," "oddly corporate," and "inescapably stodgy" and Rushdie's magical realist world to be less fecund than in his past efforts. He concluded that the book constitutes a kind of "autopilot postmodernism en route to nowhere but platitudes about the power of words." Similarly, Gorra and Shulevitz, despite their overall praise, both found the book to be strangely "muted."

Nonetheless, these are dissenting voices for a book that met with heavy acclaim. More typical were the words of *Vogue* critic Avantika Shankar who found that Rushdie successfully "weaves historical fact with mythological fiction." She was particularly impressed by the multitudes the book contains, noting that the novel "is many things: a myth, an epic, a polemic parable, a real-world historical landscape flattened into a fable and embellished by fantasy." *Victory City* is another example of how a top-tier novelist can draw on a wide variety of materials and knit them into a powerful and multitudinous work. As Shankar notes, the book expertly uses its many modes in the service of a lively retelling of real-world history.

Author Biography

Salman Rushdie is the author of fifteen novels as well as many other books. He has won numerous awards, including the Booker Prize, the Whitbread Prize, and the PEN/Allen Foundation Literary Service Award. Born in Bombay (now Mumbai), India, he attended King's College, Cambridge in the United Kingdom.

Andrew Schenker

Review Sources

Cummins, Anthony. "A Knotty Chronicle of Intra-Dynastic Rivalry." Review of *Victory City*, by Salman Rushdie. *The Guardian*, 29 Jan. 2023, www.theguardian.com/books/2023/jan/29/victory-city-by-salman-rushdie-review-a-knotty-chronicle-of-intra-dynastic-rivalry. Accessed 5 Jan. 2024.

Gorra, Michael. "Salman Rushdie's Miracle City." Review of *Victory City*, by Salman Rushdie. *The New York Times*, 1 Feb. 2023, www.nytimes.com/2023/02/01/books/review/salman-rushdie-victory-city.html. Accessed 5 Jan. 2024.

Shankar, Avantika. "In *Victory City*, Salman Rushdie Deftly Weaves Historical Fact with Mythological Fiction." Review of *Victory City*, by Salman Rushdie. *Vogue*, 7

Feb. 2023, www.vogue.com/article/salman-rushdie-victory-city-review. Accessed 5 Jan. 2024.

Shulevitz, Judith. "The Miraculous Salman Rushdie." Review of *Victory City*, by Salman Rushdie. *The Atlantic*, vol. 331, no. 2, Mar. 2023, pp. 70–73. *EBSCOhost*, research.ebsco.com/linkprocessor/plink?id=1d7b9e35-51c9-31b1-9fca-8ca58df32bd0. Accessed 9 Jan. 2024.

The Wager
A Tale of Shipwreck, Mutiny and Murder

Author: David Grann (b. 1967)
Publisher: Doubleday. Illustrated. 352 pp.
Type of work: History
Time: 1740–46
Locales: England; Atlantic Ocean; Pacific Ocean; Wager Island; Brazil

In The Wager: A Tale of Shipwreck, Mutiny and Murder, *David Grann chronicles the wreck of an eighteenth-century British ship and the mutiny that followed, illuminating not only the gripping details of the event itself but also its broader historical and social implications.*

Principal personages
CAPTAIN DAVID CHEAP, captain of the Wager at the time of the shipwreck and mutiny
JOHN BULKELEY, the Wager's gunner and the leader of the mutiny against Cheap
JOHN BYRON, an aristocratic teenager serving as one of the Wager's midshipmen
LIEUTENANT ROBERT BAYNES, Cheap's second in command
COMMODORE GEORGE ANSON, officer tasked with leading the Wager's mission to capture a Spanish galleon

Journalist and longtime *New Yorker* writer David Grann established himself as a major voice in nonfiction, known for his compelling narrative style and attention to obscure but meaningful historical subjects, often with dark themes. His best-selling books include *The Lost City of Z* (2009), detailing a disastrous expedition to find a city in Brazilian rainforest; *Killers of the Flower Moon* (2017), about members of the Osage Nation who were murdered in the twentieth century for their oil holdings; and *The White Darkness* (2018), about British explorer Henry Worsley's twenty-first century attempt to walk across Antarctica. With his 2023 publication *The Wager: A Tale of Shipwreck, Mutiny and Murder*, Grann delves into a new realm, that of naval history. But it continues his signature blend of history, adventure, and true crime as it details the many unfortunate events experienced by the crew of the titular ship.

The narrative of *The Wager* takes place largely in the early 1740s, a period in which the British Empire was locked in an ongoing struggle with Spain. As rival imperial powers, the two empires had long competed for colonies and resources. By the time Grann focuses on, England and Spain were specifically engaged in a conflict known as the War of Jenkins' Ear, which had developed following allegations that

David Grann

Spanish forces had mistreated a captain named Robert Jenkins in an encounter during the prior decade. Amid that conflict, British naval leadership developed a plan to attack the Spanish-controlled city of Cartagena, on the Caribbean coast in present-day Colombia, as well as other Spanish targets on the Pacific coast in what is now Chile. Another key objective in the Pacific Ocean was to capture a famed Spanish treasure galleon bound for the Philippines.

While a large fleet would be sent to attack Cartagena, a smaller group of British Navy ships were tasked with making the notably dangerous journey to the Pacific. In addition to evading Spanish warships while crossing the Atlantic Ocean and journeying south, the vessels on this mission would need to sail around the southern tip of South America, known as Cape Horn, through a route known as the Drake Passage. The route was infamously hazardous for several reasons. As Grann vividly explains, the uniquely harsh weather conditions between the area of South America known as Patagonia and the northern coast of Antarctica presented extreme danger to any ship passing through. Furthermore, geological characteristics of the region, such as abrupt changes in the level of the seabed, could create immense waves capable of swamping even the British Navy's largest ships.

After several setbacks, in September 1740 a group of ships finally departed England for the Pacific mission under the command of Commodore George Anson. The vessels included the *Centurion*, the *Gloucester*, the *Pearl*, and the *Severn*, all men-of-war; the smaller ship the *Trial*; and the *Wager*, a former merchant ship that had been repurposed as a man-of-war. Much like the other ships in Anson's convoy, the *Wager* was plagued by hardships throughout the journey across the Atlantic. Outbreaks of typhus and scurvy killed many on board, thus substantially depleting the crews before the ships could even engage in battle. Such deaths also forced leadership changes across multiple ships in the convoy, and the *Wager* was no exception. Originally led by more experienced officers, the ship eventually came under the command of David Cheap, who had been first lieutenant under Anson on the *Centurion* and then briefly captained the *Trial* before moving to the *Wager*.

While Cheap and his remaining crew successfully sailed around Cape Horn, disaster soon struck. Having lost sight of the other ships in the convoy, the *Wager*'s crew attempted to navigate to a rendezvous point but misjudged their position, accidentally approaching an island. On May 14, 1741, the ship struck and became lodged on rocks offshore. Water began to enter the ship, forcing the crew to take refuge on land. There the survivors would remain for the next five months, struggling to build shelters, retrieve supplies from the wreck of their ship, locate food, and repair small boats in the hope of escaping what would become known as Wager Island.

A thoroughly researched work of nonfiction, *The Wager* is based in large part on eighteenth-century documents, including memoirs written by survivors of the shipwreck. Grann's use and explanation of specific source documents therefore sometimes reveals the fates of some of the *Wager*'s crew in advance. For instance, he draws extensively from a narrative written by John Byron, a teenage midshipman on the *Wager*, and notes early on that Byron will go on to become the grandfather of the famous poet Lord Byron (George Gordon Byron, the sixth Baron Byron). While this removes some of the element of surprise about who will survive the harrowing experiences that unfold throughout the book, it does not undermine the overall gripping suspense of the narrative. Indeed, the availability of writings by Byron, gunner John Bulkeley, and other survivors, as well as ship's logbooks, enables Grann to tell the story of the *Wager* in extraordinarily rich detail.

Notably, however, contemporary accounts of the *Wager*'s shipwreck and ensuing events often starkly contradicted each other. Another important aspect of Grann's narrative is illustrating just why the survivors' tales were so at odds. Here, the developments on Wager Island prove crucial. As food dwindled and tensions grew on the island, the survivors split into two primary groups, one of them loyal to Cheap and the other led primarily by Bulkeley. Cheap wanted to escape the island and continue the journey into the Pacific, hoping to reunite with Anson's other ships and carry out the planned missions against the Spanish. Bulkeley, however, believed that it would better to re-enter the Atlantic through the Strait of Magellan and sail to a Portuguese colony in what is now Brazil, where he hoped he and the remainder of the crew could arrange passage to England.

As *The Wager*'s subtitle suggests, the two factions could not come to an agreement—in October 1741, Bulkeley and his allies mutinied and departed the island in the repaired boats, leaving Cheap and his small group of supporters behind. While many in Bulkeley's party did not survive to return home, a number of the group did make it back to England, where their story became a media sensation. Some of them published books about their journey as means of gaining public support and validating their reasoning for abandoning Cheap, whose fate was then unknown.

Cheap, however, proved more resilient than expected, and his own eventual return to England put the facts of the incident in question. While Bulkeley and his group of survivors claimed that their actions were necessary, particularly in light of Cheap's murder of a young midshipman while on the island, Cheap himself claimed that that it was Bulkeley's group that was in the wrong and had committed the serious crime of mutiny. As Cheap was an officer, naval leadership was potentially more disposed to believe his account than that of a mere gunner. The resulting 1746 court-martial investigation was a high-stakes affair, as mutiny was considered a crime punishable by death.

Over the course of *The Wager*, Grann presents a compelling narrative that not only chronicles the events surrounding the shipwreck and mutiny but also delves into the earlier lives of the men involved and explores some of the ways in which the *Wager*'s story would influence later works of fiction and poetry. In addition to relying heavily on primary sources, he visited Wager Island in person during the process of writing the book, and his visceral descriptions of the island likely benefit from the firsthand knowledge of the landscape, weather, and surrounding oceanic conditions that he gained. *The Wager* also offers readers a greater understanding of the relevant geography through the inclusion of several maps depicting the areas discussed in the book. A selection of illustrations—including portraits of key individuals such as Cheap and a photograph of ship debris discovered by archaeologists in 2006—likewise provide visual context for curious readers. Grann concludes *The Wager* with an extensive set of endnotes as well as a bibliography that would likely prove useful to readers seeking to learn more about the topics at hand.

The Wager: A Tale of Shipwreck, Mutiny and Murder received much praise from critics, with *Guardian* reviewer Matthew Teague calling it "one of the finest nonfiction books I've ever read." The anonymous critic for *Publishers Weekly* described the book as "concise and riveting" and praised Grann's attention to detail and use of primary sources. The reviewer for *Kirkus Reviews*, which named *The Wager* one of the best books of 2023, described it as both "chilling" and "vibrant," and also noted that the work is set "in the context of European imperialism as much as the wrath of the sea." In a review for the *New York Times*, Jennifer Szalai praised the structure of the narrative as well as Grann's handling of the hardships the *Wager*'s crew faced, while *AP News* critic Michael Hill noted that Grann "manages to wring maximum drama out of the events and sketch out nuanced portraits of key players on the doomed ship. Writing for the *Washington Post*, Carl Hoffman did suggest that some of the book's principal figures "remain inaccessibly distant" to the reader, although he acknowledged that this was ultimately "a result of the limits of nonfiction grappling with 280-year-old events." Hoffman still expressed appreciation for the work as a whole, describing *The Wager* as "a tightly written, relentless, blow-by-blow account that is hard to put down."

Author Biography

A staff writer for *The New Yorker* since 2003, David Grann is the author of several books, including the New York Times Best Sellers *Killers of the Flower Moon* (2017) and *The Lost City of Z* (2009). The latter was a finalist for the National Book Award and won an Edgar Allen Poe Award.

Joy Crelin

Review Sources

Hill, Michael. "Review: A Harrowing Shipwreck and Mutiny in 'The Wager.'" Review of *The Wager*, by David Grann. *AP News*, 17 Apr. 2023, apnews.com/article/wager-david-grann-book-review-2d15209bb3a25c68ee579cd2bfc7275e. Accessed 15 Dec. 2023.

Hoffman, Carl. "Anything Can Go Wrong at Sea. On This Voyage, Everything Did." Review of *The Wager*, by David Grann. *The Washington Post*, 18 Apr. 2023, www.washingtonpost.com/books/2023/04/18/wager-david-grann-shipwreck-review/. Accessed 15 Dec. 2023.

Szalai, Jennifer. "With His Tale of Shipwreck, David Grann Is Steady as He Goes." Review of *The Wager,* by David Grann. *The New York Times*, 24 Apr. 2023, www.nytimes.com/2023/04/14/books/review/the-wager-david-grann.html. Accessed 15 Dec. 2023.

Teague, Matthew. "*The Wager* Review: David Grann's Magnificent Shipwreck Epic." *The Guardian*, 30 Apr. 2023, www.theguardian.com/books/2023/apr/29/the-wager-review-david-grann-shipwreck-epic. Accessed 15 Dec. 2023.

Review of *The Wager*, by David Grann. *Kirkus Reviews*, 10 Feb. 2023, www.kirkusreviews.com/book-reviews/david-grann/the-wager-shipwreck-mutiny/. Accessed 15 Dec. 2023.

Review of *The Wager*, by David Grann. *Publishers Weekly*, 28 Feb. 2023, www.publishersweekly.com/9780385534260. Accessed 15 Dec. 2023.

Warrior Girl Unearthed

Author: Angeline Boulley (b. 1965)
Publisher: Henry Holt (New York). 400 pp.
Type of work: Novel
Time: 2014
Locale: Sugar Island, Michigan

An Ojibwe Tribe's summer internship program, Kinomaage, takes sixteen-year-old identical twin sisters on a mysterious, life-changing adventure of cultural twists and turns that solidify their passion for their heritage and fuel their outrage over its appropriation and desecration.

Principal characters

PEARL MARY "PERRY" FIREKEEPER-BIRCH, the protagonist, a sixteen-year-old who is interning at the tribal museum
PAULINE FIREKEEPER-BIRCH, her identical twin sister
AUNTIE DAUNIS, their maternal aunt
POPS, their father
COOPER TURTLE, the tribal museum director
LUCAS CHIPPEWAY, their childhood friend, another summer intern
ERIK MILLER, a summer intern who just moved to town
SHENSE JACKSON, a summer intern and teen mom

Warrior Girl Unearthed is award-winning and best-selling author Angeline Boulley's follow up to her hit debut young adult novel, *Firekeeper's Daughter* (2021). Boulley's first novel follows an eighteen-year-old Daunis Fontaine as she is thrust into the middle of an FBI drug investigation into the Ojibwe reservation on Sugar Island near Sault Ste. Marie, Michigan, after the murder of her best friend. *Firekeeper's Daughter* received positive reviews not only for its thrilling story, but for Boulley's careful sharing of the Ojibwe culture from which she hails. *Warrior Girl Unearthed* is a companion novel to *Firekeeper's Daughter*, returning to the communities of Sugar Island and Sault Ste. Marie ten years after the events of *Firekeeper's Daughter*, and focusing on Daunis's teenage nieces. While it is not necessary to have read *Firekeeper's Daughter* to enjoy *Warrior Girl Unearthed*, the novel does reference events from the previous novel and features a cast of returning minor characters.

Boulley narrates *Warrior Girl Unearthed* through the voice of its witty, raucous, and outspoken teenage protagonist, Perry Firekeeper-Birch, the "not-as-smart" and "not-as-nice" twin sister of Pauline, the anxiety-prone overachiever. Despite being identical twins, the girls are opposites in personality and interests, although they share

Angeline Boulley

a love and respect for their ancestors and Anishinaabe culture. While Pauline is excited to begin her summer internship, Perry has planned a summer of relaxation and fishing, that is, until she gets into a car accident while avoiding a bear cub. Since the Jeep was gifted with safety stipulations to both siblings from their Aunt Daunis, Perry is forced to join Pauline in the Kinomaage program—an Ojibwe Tribe summer internship program for tribal teens and young adults to work within the Anishinaabe community and learn about their cultural heritage—until the damages are paid off.

Perry is assigned to intern at the Sugar Island Cultural Learning Center's tribal museum under director Cooper Turtle, whom the community has nicknamed Kooky Cooper. At first, Perry is committed to finding a way out of the internship, however, after Cooper brings her to the local college, Mackinac State College, to visit the remains of an Anishinaabe ancestor nicknamed Warrior Girl being held in its collection, Perry vows to help Cooper bring her home. At the same time, Boulley presents additional conflict as a series of tribal women go missing. Amidst the danger of a serial kidnapper targeting women and girls from her community, Perry works with Pauline, as well as their childhood friend Lucas Chippeway and fellow Kinomaage interns Erik Miller and Shense Jackson, to bring home not only Warrior Girl, but all of the ancestors in Mackinac State College's Native American collection.

Perry's primary journey centers around retrieving ancestors' remains and sacred artifacts from universities, museums, and other institutions. Boulley uses the Native American Graves Protection and Repatriation Act (NAGPRA) as a central focal point to highlight the tactics used by institutions to evade the law and as the springboard for Perry's response to the legal loopholes, stalling tactics, and hoarding behaviors she witnesses by those in charge of said institutions. Perry's choices occasionally put her in direct conflict with her internship supervisor, Cooper Turtle, who takes a more cautious and calculated approach to dealing with grave-robbing institutions. Besides the repatriation theme, Boulley does not shy away from other complex, painful issues, including hard-to-hear family secrets, racial identity, gender-based violence, and the plight of Missing and Murdered Indigenous Women (MMIW). As Boulley explains within the novel, search efforts for Indigenous women who go missing are often given fewer resources by regular police agencies, and so several characters take up the task of making sure those missing women are remembered and found. With storytelling dexterity, she confronts these topics seamlessly through the characters' lives that make up this captivating mystery.

Boulley tackles these contentious topics and issues in an up-close and personal way through the characters' lives in *Warrior Girl Unearthed* while eloquently demonstrating intergenerational family and community cohesion and contention through this fact-filled thriller. The author strikes a truth-telling tone immediately, opening the book with the quote, "When questioned by an anthropologist on what the Indians called America before the white man came, an Indian said simply, 'Ours,'" from Vine Deloria, Jr.'s *Custer Died for Your Sins: An Indian Manifesto*. Well-researched, an encyclopedia of facts about the legacy of colonialism and its generational impact on the lives of Native American communities is skillfully woven through Perry's adventurous summer internship. Conversations surrounding tribal politics, enrollment eligibility, tribal citizens, and blood quantum illustrate the burden of colonialism and its internalization by some.

Throughout the book, Perry's voice flows effortlessly between English and Ojibwemowin, authentically anchoring the story in her culture but also signaling her youth with interchanging English words and phrases like "hella," "hold up," and "dudes." The dialogue is exquisite, formidable, and engaging, keeping the reader on edge in the present while grappling with the past. The audio version of the book provides the reader with accurate pronunciation of Ojibwemowin words and phrases used, and the print version offers precise spelling. Perry's quick-witted humor, sarcasm, and double-entendres come through in either version of the novel and effectively remind the reader that she is a precocious teenager, wise beyond her years when it comes to living the traditions of her people. There are many instances in which her innocence and inexperience shine through equally. Boulley does an excellent job of reflecting Perry's (and Pauline's) vulnerabilities, challenges, and persistence as she balances reliance on her elders while asserting her agency and independence. The author's use of nicknames provides the reader with another layer of family and community intimacy and emotional context. For example, Perry calls her sister "Egg," their childhood friend Lucas calls Perry "Pear-Bear," and everybody in the community calls the Tribal Police Officer Sam Hill "What-The." The tribal museum director, Cooper Turtle, is known as "Kooky Cooper" in the community.

Warrior Girl Unearthed received overwhelmingly positive reviews from critics, including several starred reviews. In one such starred review, the anonymous reviewer for *Kirkus* described it as "a nuanced exploration of critical issues of cultural integrity" and praised Boulley for her "compellingly readable and deeply thought-provoking" characterizations. The *Kirkus* reviewer also marveled at the way Boulley, "sensitively and seamlessly weaves in discussions of colorism . . . , repatriation of cultural artifacts and human remains, Missing and Murdered Indigenous Women, and more." Jodi Kruse, writing for the American Library Association, also recognized the strength of Boulley's ability to skillfully craft an entertaining story while including serious themes in *Warrior Girl Unearthed*. She joined the chorus of other reviewers in noting how Boulley "seamlessly weaves the issue of Missing and Murdered Indigenous Women" and domestic abuse prosecution challenges into the story plot in a way that explicit messaging is not needed for readers to "feel the injury." Additionally, Kruse pointed out that the family and community dynamics in the story are universally appealing and "invite readers to feel the pain of the desecration of Indigenous people's ancestors in the name of 'science' on a much more visceral level." Kruse also praised Boulley for providing readers with a list of Repatriation Resources through Cooper's character, which she believes "further allows readers to judge the inequities for themselves." Kruse acknowledged *Warrior Girl Unearthed* as "a solid mystery/adventure that will appeal to fans of true crime and history."

In a review for *NPR*, Caitlyn Paxson, praised Boulley for knowing "how to construct a riveting, culturally focused thriller." Like Kruse, Paxson noted that the "book offers a very visceral view of what it might feel like to have your culture disrespected by the very people who claim to cherish history and culture." Consistent with other reviews, Paxson noted that the book is heavily character-driven and offered admiration of Perry's "formidable character who will not suffer fools and will not wait around for permission or salvation . . . making her a pleasure to spend time with." Despite her otherwise positive review, Paxson warned that some twists and turns "were born out of a pressure to make this somewhat quieter story reach the same levels of drama" as Boulley's first novel, *Firekeeper's Daughter*. Despite such critiques, however, most agreed that *Warrior Girl Unearthed* was a well-depicted story and further proved Boulley's place in young adult literature.

Author Biography

Angeline Boulley is an award-winning and best-selling author of young adult stories about her Ojibwe community. Her debut novel, *Firekeeper's Daughter* (2021), dominated the awards for young adult fiction, winning a Michael L. Printz Award, William C. Morris Award, Walter Dean Myers Award, and an American Indian Youth Literature Award.

Valandra, PhD

Review Sources

Castellitto, Linda M. Review of *Warrior Girl Unearthed*, by Angeline Boulley. *BookPage*, May 2023, www.bookpage.com/reviews/warrior-girl-unearthed-angeline-boulley-book-review/. Accessed 27 July 2023.

Kruse, Jodi. Review of *Warrior Girl Unearthed*, by Angeline Boulley. *American Library Association*, 24 July 2023, www.yalsa.ala.org/thehub/2023/07/24/best-fiction-for-young-adults-bfya2024-featured-review/. Accessed 27 July 2023.

Paxson, Caitlyn. "'Warrior Girl Unearthed' Revisits the 'Firekeeper's Daughter' Cast of Characters." Review of *Warrior Girl Unearthed*, by Angeline Boulley. *NPR*, 10 May 2023, www.npr.org/2023/05/10/1172699332/warrior-girl-unearthed-firekeepers-daughter-novel-angeline-boulley. Accessed 27 July 2023.

Review of *Warrior Girl Unearthed*, by Angeline Boulley. *Kirkus Reviews*, 13 Mar. 2023, www.kirkusreviews.com/book-reviews/angeline-boulley/warrior-girl-unearthed/. Accessed 10 May 2023.

Review of *Warrior Girl Unearthed*, by Angeline Boulley. *Publisher's Weekly*, 30 Mar. 2023, www.publishersweekly.com/9781250766588. Accessed 27 July 2023.

We Are All So Good At Smiling

Author: Amber McBride
Publisher: Feiwel and Friends (New York). 304 pp.
Type of work: Poetry, Novel
Time: Present day
Locale: Marsh Creek Lane

Whimsy is tired of being handled as if she is too fragile to survive. She does struggle with depression that her parents cannot understand, but her sadness is the result of a childhood trauma that she can barely remember and that her parents cannot remember at all. During a stay in a hospital, Whimsy meets Faerry, a boy who seems familiar.

Principal personages

WHIMSY, a troubled teen, a Conjurer
FAERRY, a troubled young man
COLE, Whimsy's older brother
TALE, Faerry's older sister
GRANDMA, Whimsy's deceased grandmother, a Conjurer

Amber McBride debuted as a novelist with her novel *Me (Moth)* in 2021. Told in poetic form, the novel follows Moth, an African American teen living with her aunt after the deaths of her parents and brother in a car accident. Moth struggles until she meets Sani, a Native American boy who has recently moved to her school district. As the two become friends, Moth's aunt suffers a breakdown of sorts, leaving the girl alone yet again, and Sani's stepfather's abuse escalates to a point where he can no longer stay. The two take a cross country trip to Sani's father's home. On the way, they learn more about each other and their respective heritages while stopping at various historical sites. The novel ends with a surprising twist that has been foreshadowed throughout.

We Are All So Good at Smiling introduces two African American teens, Whimsy (a Hoodoo Conjurer like her grandmother) and Faerry (a Fae boy). Both suffer from depression, which has resulted in self-harm, attempted suicide, clinical depression and hospitalization. They meet in the hospital but upon returning home, they find out their families are now neighbors. In addition to the struggles leading to their hospitalization, the pair face challenges at school, where they are bullied for both the mental illness issues and their race. As they become friends who can depend on each other, they learn that they have even more in common, including the loss of siblings ten years earlier, which they have glimpses of memory about but their parents seem to have completely forgotten. Through their new relationship, they promise to take care of each other,

Amber McBride

so when Faerry disappears in the forest at the end of their street, Whimsy knows she must go after him, even though she has avoided that area since she was a small child. Once she locates him in a hidden garden inside the forest, the two join forces to overcome the troubles of their past in a fantastic journey to hope.

Depression, as a form of mental illness, is both the major theme and the main conflict in the novel. Readers are introduced to Whimsy and Faerry in a hospital setting, where they are confined in an effort by their parents to keep them safe. Whimsy immediately explains that not only is Hoodoo real, but also magic, witches, fairy tales and Fae people. When Faerry enters the hospital, he confirms those ideas with his wings, which have wilted from his own depression. As the story unfolds, a prior connection between Whimsy, Faerry and their families is revealed, a forgotten link to a shared family trauma that has undermined their lives for years. Despite the difficult themes, the teens fight their way to a happier life as they learn to accept, work through, and move past the tragedy of their past.

McBride creates a hauntingly beautifully original fairy tale that intertwines legend and traditional fairy tales with a young-adult story. Through the use of magical realism, McBride integrates the reality of family trauma with Hoodoo, fairy tales, and legend. Pulling from a variety of cultures, she introduces characters such as Slavic folklore's Baba Yaga, as well as West Africa's Anansi the spider, and the Ewe people's Adze to illustrate the realm of mental anguish the teens traverse in their desire to heal. European fairy tale characters like Bluebeard, Snow White, and Hansel and Gretel are seamlessly intertwined with pop culture references to *The Wizard of Oz* (1939) and Disney's *The Little Mermaid* (1989). In addition, she personifies Sorrow as the monster who wants to devour their very essence. McBride's skill as a writer is further illustrated in the teens' poignant battle to overcome the loss of siblings and their parents' mistakenly damaging attempts to shelter them from the sadness that, ironically, sets the stage for their journey.

We Are All So Good at Smiling is written as a poetic novel full of magical realism. McBride starts the novel with a self-revealing note and dedication, where she talks about her own personal struggle with clinical depression and warns readers that the topics may be "triggering to some," so it "might not be the best book for you to read at this time." This is followed by a page titled "Narrator (Interlude)" where readers are given a skeletal outline of the story to come: forewarning the audience of "a Fairy Tale rarer than Middlemist's Red blooms—a Conjurer & a Fae soaked in sorrow," and a "Forest holding a Garden." That garden is the center of the depression that stops both main characters from being able to live life with joy. The novel closes with an Author's

Note that reminds teen readers that asking for help is not a weakness, and McBride offers websites and phone numbers where that help can be found.

The novel itself is separated into four sections. "Part One: The Wilting" contains a prologue and seven chapters; "Part Two: The Tears" contains chapters eight through sixteen; "Part Three: The Rebirth" contains only one chapter; and the novel concludes with "Epilogue: Happy Endings: Whimsy & Faerry," which also frames the story by including a section titled "Narrator (Interlude)." Each main Part starts with a foreshadowing poem about "The ancient Bennu bird of Egypt." In Part One, the Bennu bird "sat soundless in darkness— / alone, waiting & (perhaps) wilting." In Part Two, the poem about the Bennu bird is repeated and expanded to include, "then the Beenu bird's cry broke through the silence & darkness / & its cry decided creation / & light began to trickle in / slowly." Part Three of the novel adds a final stanza to the Bennu bird's tale. Each stanza reflects the stage in which the characters are in throughout the section.

The chapters also start with magical notes. In Part One, the chapters present an image found in tea leaves along with an explanation of the meaning behind that image. For instance, chapter three, "Stone Ridge High School," starts with "Tea Leaves: Kite" and the explanation "Usually signals a long trip / that will end well. / Imagine Me (Whimsy) a kite / with a hole / hurtling to the ground." The explanations often contain an ironic note (as seen in chapter three) or a warning, such as chapter five's "Tea Leaves: Arrow": Unpleasant news is coming, / generally, from the direction/ the arrow is pointing. / If there are many arrows / pointing in many directions— / hide."

McBride changes the chapter openings in Part Two. Here the author introduces specific times, plant names, and plant uses. Chapter eight, for example, is titled "Baba Yaga's House." Below the title is the time, 11:02 PM, and "Angelica Root: Hoodoo / Also known as the Holy Ghost Root, / often used for protection." The connections each flower represents in the middle section of the novel are dark with only a slight possibility of a positive meaning, while the connection made with the final flower in part three and the epilogue, the "High John the Conquer Root: Overcomes all obstacles" and "Daffodil: New beginnings / New chances. / New joy" provide a sense of hope in an otherwise difficult story. There are also several fun and helpful items at the end of the book, including sections titled "Glossary of Fairy Tales, Stories & Folklore," "Fairy Tales in This Story," and "Whimsy & Faerry's Playlist."

Reviews of the novel offered praise for McBride's poetry, her use of fairy tale and legend, as well as her ability to expertly handle difficult themes. Reviewer S. R. Toliver, writing for the *Horn Book Magazine*, noted the "lush free-verse poetry" which "creates a vibrant world teetering between the real and the magical." In her review for *Booklist*, Melanie Marshal further explained that McBride's writing, "weaves elements of fairy tale, fantasy, and hoodoo into stunning free-verse poetry." The *Kirkus Review* reinforced the positive response with the claim, "The choice of verse to tell this absorbing story is a strong one; readers are drawn along by the intense and vivid imagery, and the depictions of clinical depression, guilt, and grief are visceral." In relation to the themes, the anonymous reviewer for *Publishers Weekly* called the book "a dark, whimsical adventure that viscerally depicts experiences of clinical depression, generational trauma, racism, self-harm, suicidal ideation, and survivor's guilt." Toliver further pointed out that despite the weight of the content, McBride successfully reminds readers that "no one is alone," while Terry Hong for *School Library Journal* called the book "a healing balm for suffering souls." Reviewers also praised McBride's characterizations of the protagonists. For instance, Marshal stated, "Readers will revel in the depth of Whimsy and Faerry's relationship, all the while finding solace and relief in the calculated messiness of their search for wholeness."

Author Biography
Amber McBride is a writer and a professor of English at the University of Virginia. She has a bachelor's degree from James Madison University and an MFA from Emerson College. Her first novel, *Me (Moth)* was a finalist for the 2021 National Book Award for Young People's Literature.

Theresa Stowell

Review Sources
Hong, Terry. Review of *We Are All So Good at Smiling*, by Amber McBride. *School Library Journal*, Apr. 2023, p. 115. *Literary Reference Center Plus*, search.ebscohost.com/login.aspx?direct=true&db=lkh&AN=162689444&site=lrc-plus. Accessed 16 Oct. 2023.
Marshall, Melanie. Review of *We Are All So Good at Smiling*, by Amber McBride. *Booklist*, 1–15 Jan. 2023, p. 67. *Literary Reference Center Plus*, search.ebscohost.com/login.aspx?direct=true&db=lkh&AN=161198394&site=lrc-plus. Accessed 16 Oct. 2023.
Review of *We Are All So Good at Smiling*, by Amber McBride. *Kirkus Reviews*, 1 Nov. 2022, www.kirkusreviews.com/book-reviews/amber-mcbride/we-are-all-so-good-at-smiling/. Accessed 16 Oct. 2023.
Review of *We Are All So Good at Smiling*, by Amber McBride. *Publishers Weekly*, 17 Nov. 2022 www.publishersweekly.com/9781250780386. Accessed 16 Oct. 2023.
Toliver, S. R. Review of *We Are All So Good at Smiling*, by Amber McBride. *Horn Book Magazine*, Jan./Feb. 2023, pp. 87–88. *Literary Reference Center Plus*, search.ebscohost.com/login.aspx?direct=true&db=lkh&AN=160862880&site=lrc-plus. Accessed 16 Oct. 2023.

Wednesday's Child

Author: Yiyun Li (b. 1972)
Publisher: Farrar, Straus and Giroux (New York). 256 pp.
Type of work: Short fiction
Time: Late twentieth and early twenty-first centuries
Locales: Beijing, China; Amsterdam, Netherlands; Paris, France; San Francisco, California; New York City

Wednesday's Child, Yiyun Li's third short fiction collection, following A Thousand Years of Good Prayers (2005) and Gold Boy, Emerald Girl (2010), explores far-ranging yet subtle differences between various types of woe. (Content contains references to suicide.)

Principal characters

ROSALIE, mother of a child who died by suicide
AUNTIE MEI, a longtime live-in nanny for new mothers
NINA AND KATIE, best friends and frequent traveling companions
BELLA, naturalized US citizen born in China
BECKY, a governess, mother to a son with special needs
DR. EDWINA DITMUS, a retired entomologist
IDA, Edwina's carer
MIN, a mother of three, including twin daughters
NARANTUYAA, daughter of Mongolian parents who defected to the United States
SUCHEN, survivor of a teenage suicide pact
JIAYU, a woman whose teenaged son died by suicide

The title story and first entry in Yiyun Li's *Wednesday's Child* (2023) establishes the overarching theme of the short fiction collection, which consists of ten well-wrought stories and a novella: the subtle distinctions of emotional pain implied in the word "woe." This variety includes such concepts as grief, guilt, remorse, dread, misery and disappointment. The stories—all but one written in third-person, all from a feminine point of view, most involving Chinese American characters, and many touching on premature death, often because of suicide—were written and originally published in various outlets over a period of fourteen years. During this span, Li herself experienced a series of personal losses, including the deaths of four individuals who "live among these pages now," as she writes in the acknowledgments: her father, a close friend, her mentor, and her son, Vincent, who died by suicide at the age of sixteen.

Yiyun Li

Courtesy ©Bass Cannarsa, Agence Opale Li

"Wednesday's Child" concerns Rosalie, a woman who lives in North Carolina with her husband Dan. She is touring Europe by herself just as the COVID-19 pandemic is gaining speed. Meanwhile, Dan is in the process of renovating their sunroom back home. As the story opens Rosalie is at the railway terminal in Amsterdam, Netherlands, waiting for a connection to Brussels, Belgium. As an aspiring novelist, she writes down random thoughts in a notebook she keeps in her purse. She has jotted down lines from a nineteenth-century nursery rhyme: "Wednesday's child is full of woe / Thursday's child has far to go." Rosalie learns that all trains to Brussels have been canceled because of an incident in Rotterdam: a man walked in front of the train and was killed. This is an uncomfortable reminder that Rosalie's daughter, born on a Wednesday, had committed suicide on a Thursday just before her sixteenth birthday, by laying down on railroad tracks. Rosalie experiences guilt over her mother's observation that when a child dies by suicide, "you have to wonder what the parents did." She and her husband have learned that "a shared pain was simply that, a permanent presence of a permanent absence in their lives." Rosalie's feelings are reinforced by references to Hungarian writer Ágota Kristóf's The Notebook Trilogy, a saga of evil, conflict, and cruelty, and to Swiss writer Robert Walser (1878–1956), who spent the last twenty years of his life in an asylum for psychiatric patients.

"A Sheltered Woman" deals with a milder form of woe, regret. Auntie Mei, a "gold medal" live-in nanny for new mothers, has worked for many years for upscale families in California's Bay Area. Though she has helped with the early raising of 131 children—she keeps detailed notes about her clients, babies' names and birthdates—she has no offspring of her own. Her only husband died at age fifty-one of injuries received after being mugged by a gang of teens. As a widow late in life, she has lost the opportunity to be a birth mother. This brings on painful self-reflection: "She was getting older, more forgetful, yet she was also closer to comprehending the danger of being herself," Li writes.

"A Small Flame" involves anguish over the loss of identity. Protagonist Bella had a different name in China, her home country. Her new name appears on her US passport, her marriage licenses, and her two sets of divorce papers. Her birth name appears on the gravestones of her family, where she is listed as her parents' only child—her father was a diplomat, her mother an opera singer, and her maternal grandfather a member of the group that established the Chinese Soviet Republic in the 1930s. But the gravestones perpetuate a lie. Bella, an attractive child, was actually adopted, replacing another adopted girl who turned out to be deaf and mute and was sent away once her condition was discovered.

"A Flawless Silence" contrasts the traditional and the modern. Min, the mother of a grown son and twin daughters by her politically conservative husband Rich, regularly receives emails from a linguistics professor she met in Beijing when she was nineteen before moving to the US. At the time, she was considered by a matchmaker as a potential wife for one of the professor's three sons. Instead, she dated Rich—who grew up in a poor section of Beijing and long ago gave up his Chinese name—long-distance through letters and phone calls for eight months before they married. Rich has strong opinions: "Anyone who does not set his heart on getting rich should be ashamed of himself. Especially in America." He enjoys repeating a Chinese saying: "The longer a woman's hair is, the shorter her sight is." Rich, a supporter of politician Donald Trump, has purchased a bottle of expensive wine to share with friends celebrating the 2016 presidential election results, which Min considers breaking accidentally. Because she cannot bring herself to confront her husband, Min takes out her frustration on the linguistics professor by replying forcefully to his persistent electronic messages.

In "Let Mothers Doubt," Narantuyaa, a young woman of Mongolian ancestry whose parents defected to America, is in Paris, "because of one live man and two dead men." She counts animals depicted in artworks at the Louvre and counts angels at Montparnasse Cemetery as a kind of penance for her feelings of guilt. She was unable to protect her beloved younger brother Jullian, who died of an overdose while camping with friends. Borrowing the car of her married lover, Mark, to rush home after her parents insisted she come without telling her what happened to her brother, she drives through heavy fog and runs over the body of a man lying in the road.

The longest piece in the collection is the novella "Such Common Life." It contains two characters who enjoy verbally sparring: retired entomologist Dr. Edwina Ditmus and her carer, who changed her name from Xiangquan to Ida when she arrived in the United States seventeen years earlier. Edwina, who had ice skated every day before she severely injured herself in a fall on a staircase, benefits from Ida's traditional Chinese medical training, particularly acupressure. Edwina enjoys asking Ida a series of questions until Ida admits she has no answer.

The only story written in first-person, rather than third-person, is the final one, "All Will Be Well." The unnamed narrator, a teacher and mother of two children, frequently visits a hair salon run by Lily, a Chinese woman who grew up in Vietnam and loves to chat about her family.

Critical reception of *Wednesday's Child* was almost uniformly positive. *Financial Times* reviewer Nilanjana Roy called Li's collection "quiet, subtle and often agonisingly wrenching as Li explores the brittle fractures within the human heart," wherein "many of her characters are caught in mid-life, looking back at—or away from—the murk and griefs of the past." Michael Schaub, a reviewer for *NPR* agreed, noting that "The short stories in Li's book focus chiefly on people trying to put themselves together after some kind of loss, dealing with anguish that takes its time, rises from its dormancy at unexpected moments." Schaub highlighted Li's "gift for dialogue and her deep understanding of human connection," praising her "gorgeous prose and painstaking attention to detail," the factors that make "these stories so beautiful, so accomplished . . . by a writer at the top of her game." Writing for the *Guardian*, Sarah

Crown concentrated on Li's themes and techniques. "These haunting, harrowing tales are—without exception, and whether their characters are prepared to acknowledge it or not—full to the brim with woe." Crown further explained: "Rather than focusing on the significant, storylike event—the moment, as it were, of the bomb going off—these tales dwell instead on the unremarkable details of the lives people are obliged to on living afterwards, amid the wreckage."

One mildly critical voice was that of Ian J. Battaglia, writing for the *Chicago Review of Books*. While praising the author's "careful handling and delicate prose" surrounding the themes of death, suicide, and attempted suicide, that allows examination from different vantage points, Battaglia complained that Li's male characters "tend to serve more as antagonistic forces for her female protagonists." He also pointed out "a number of overly-contemporary elements, such as a few mentions of the COVID-19 pandemic and some anxiety about recent elections and Donald Trump," which he felt "[took] away from the near-timeless feel most of the stories have." Despite such critiques, overall *Wednesday's Child* offers sensitive, insightful consideration of difficult topics, making it a valuable read for many people.

Author Biography
Yiyun Li is the author of eleven books, including five novels, three story collections, and a memoir. The recipient of many honors, including a MacArthur Fellowship, a Guggenheim Foundation Fellowship, four PEN Awards, and a Windham-Campbell Prize, Li teaches creative writing at Princeton University, where she became director of the creative writing program in 2022.

Jack Ewing

Review Sources
Battaglia, Ian J. "The Lingering Pain of Grief in Yiyun Li's 'Wednesday's Child.'" Review of *Wednesday's Child*, by Yiyun Li. *Chicago Review of Books*, 13. Sept. 2023, chireviewofbooks.com/2023/09/13/the-lingering-pain-of-grief-in-yiyun-lis-wednesdays-child/. Accessed 8 Feb. 2024.
Blumberg-Kason, Susan. Review of *Wednesday's Child*, by Yiyun Li. *Asian Review of Books*, 1 Sept. 2023, asianreviewofbooks.com/content/wednesdays-child-by-yiyun-li/. Accessed 8 Feb. 2024.
Crown, Sarah. "Wednesday's Child by Yiyun Li Review—Motherhood as Loss." Review of *Wednesday's Child*, by Yiyun Li. *The Guardian*, 30 Sept. 2023, www.theguardian.com/books/2023/sep/30/wednesdays-child-by-yiyun-li-review-motherhood-as-loss. Accessed 8 Feb. 2024.
Cummins, Anthony. "Wednesday's Child by Yiyun Li Review—Dialogues with Death." Review of Wednesday's Child, by Yiyun Li. *The Guardian*, 24 Sept. 2023, www.theguardian.com/books/2023/sep/24/wednesdays-child-by-yiyun-li-review-dialogues-with-death. Accessed 8 Feb. 2024.

Roy, Nilanjana. "Wednesday's Child by Yiyun Li—Brittle Fractures of the Heart." Review of *Wednesday's Child*, by Yiyun Li. *Financial Times*, 5 Sept. 2023, www.ft.com/content/6e6a8c83-164a-4003-8611-0c5d485eb693. Accessed 8 Feb. 2024.

Schaub, Michael. "Wednesday's Child Deals in Life after Loss." Review of Wednesday's Child, by Yiyun Li. *NPR*, 7 Sept. 2023, www.npr.org/2023/09/07/1197601727/wednesdays-child-deals-in-life-after-loss. Accessed 8 Feb. 2024.

Review of *Wednesday's Child*, by Yiyun Li. *Kirkus Reviews*, 5 Sept. 2023, www.kirkusreviews.com/book-reviews/yiyun-li/wednesdays-child-li/. Accessed 8 Feb. 2024.

Wellness

Author: Nathan Hill (b. 1975)
Publisher: Alfred A. Knopf (New York). 624 pp.
Type of work: Novel
Time: 1990s–2010s
Locale: Chicago, Illinois

Wellness is a sprawling satiric novel that tellingly touches upon the absurdities of consumer culture, academia, diet and fitness trends, the art world, the internet, suburbia, and various other facets of modern life.

Principal characters
JACK BAKER, a photographer and adjunct art professor
ELIZABETH AUGUSTINE BAKER, his wife, a researcher
TOBY, his and Elizabeth's troubled school-aged son
BRANDIE, his wife's one-time friend
EVELYN, his free-spirited older sister
LAWRENCE, his conspiracy-obsessed father
BENJAMIN QUINCE, his friend, an art student who became a real estate developer

When Nathan Hill's debut novel, *The Nix*, was published in 2016, various critics dubbed him "Dickensian," "the Love Child of Thomas Pynchon and David Foster Wallace," and a new Jonathan Franzen because of his panoramic, intricately detailed narrative and evocatively drawn characters. That reputation is cemented by his sophomore effort, *Wellness*, which hit bookstore shelves—and bestseller lists—in the fall of 2023. As in *The Nix*, Hill examines several satire-worthy aspects of modern life in *Wellness*. The book takes its name from that of a clinic run by protagonist Elizabeth Baker, a researcher who explores why people fall for sham medical treatments—a field that her mentor has dubbed "placebo studies."

The reader first encounters Elizabeth as a college student in 1993. Newly arrived in Chicago, she is uncertain about her future path and has thus cobbled together a course schedule that includes cognitive psychology, behavioral economics, evolutionary biology, neuroscience, and, for fun, theater. She lives in an apartment building across the alleyway from Jack, a Midwesterner also newly arrived in the city. Jack, feeling like a fish out of water among his more cosmopolitan and wealthier peers, is studying at the Art Institute of Chicago and earning money by photographing up-and-coming bands in the grungy clubs of then-ungentrified Wicker Park neighborhood.

Nathan Hill

Each secretly observes the other across the alleyway, and Jack quickly becomes enamored of Elizabeth, projecting traits onto her on the basis of her clothing, reading habits, and apartment decor. "To say that he finds her beautiful is too simple," Hill writes. "She's exactly the kind of person—cultured, worldly—that he came to this frighteningly big city to find. The obvious flaw in the plan, he realizes now, is that a woman so cultured and worldly would never be interested in a guy as uncultured, as provincial, as backward and coarse as him." Yet the attraction, as it turns out, is mutual. Watching Jack painstakingly examine film negatives, smoke, and come home with increasingly elaborate tattoos, Elizabeth thinks, "He's exactly the kind of person—defiant, passionate—that she came to this remote city to find. The obvious flaw in the plan, she realizes now, is that a man so defiant and passionate would never be interested in a girl as conventional, as conformist, as dull and bourgeois as her." When the two finally meet at an indie-rock show, where Jack is photographing a band an overzealous and pretentious date has insisted Elizabeth must hear, they admit their feelings and fall into bed, remaining there all night, and on, and on, "for countless nights thereafter, for the rest of the year, and the next many winters, and all the baffling time to come."

Believing themselves to be soulmates, Elizabeth and Jack are stunned and disheartened to discover that by 2014 they have been beset by common discontents of average married couples: a lack of sexual desire and a constant low-grade annoyance with her husband on Elizabeth's part, and career woes and a seeming inability to understand his wife on Jack's. The Bakers fruitlessly seek solutions. Elizabeth is even willing to explore polyamory at the behest of another couple who purport to enjoy a closer relationship and better sex as a result. Elizabeth also pushes for a move to a yet-to-be built development in the suburbs, spearheaded by Jack's old friend Benjamin Quince, who has unabashedly become one of the gentrifiers they railed at in their youth. Enamored of the trendy idea of "dual master bedrooms," which the developer bills as a useful option for any busy, modern couple, since the setup allows both to avoid moving out should they file for divorce, she parrots the marketing material to Jack, touting it as a "forever home." (In one mordant passage, her elderly mentor cautions, "If you want the gods to really laugh at you, by all means call it *your forever home*.")

In truth, Elizabeth knows full well from first-hand experience that a house, no matter how grand, does not make for a stable or happy life. The reader learns in flashbacks that she is a scion of the wealthy Augustine family, whose ill-gotten gains stem from their underhanded dealings in railroads, textiles, and other industries. She summered in a hulking home called the Gables, whose fourth floor has gradually become inhabitable due to a growing colony of bats (and the attendant guano, which serves as a fitting metaphor for the clan's dysfunctional dynamic). Elizabeth has come to Chicago not just to attend school and find a boy like Jack but to escape her pathologically competitive and angry father and her vapid mother. For his part, Jack is also seeking escape from parents who blame him for not being a traditionally robust, sports-oriented midwestern boy and, later, for a tragic event involving his beloved older sister.

Given their difficult childhoods, Jack and Elizabeth are determined to give their son, Toby, as nurturing an upbringing as possible, but they are stymied by Toby's emotional outbursts and seeming inability to relate to other children; Hill does not explicitly label Toby as being on the autism spectrum, but any reader familiar with parenting literature will likely recognize some of the descriptions. (A fellow parent, Brandie, keeps a "quiet room" in her home, with calming colors and weighted blankets in the event of meltdowns.) Toby spends much of his time immersed in the game Minecraft. However, he is not the only character to fall into an online rabbit hole.

Hill cannily satirizes internet culture via the character of Lawrence, Jack's father. In his quest for "likes," Lawrence becomes involved in an insidious social media approval-seeking loop that draws him into conspiracy theory groups that oppose vaccines, traditional cancer treatments, and government control, among other things. While these passages are broadly drawn, such groups will be instantly recognizable to readers who have spent time on social media themselves. Groupthink of that sort is not reserved only for uneducated, tinfoil hat–wearing rubes in *Wellness*. Brandie, a quintessential suburban mom, runs a neighborhood group that fervently touts the power of positive thinking and the "law of attraction"—despite all evidence that those ideas have never worked for anyone in the group.

The main target of Hill's astute social commentary is the speed at which society adopts trends and our gullibility in believing whatever best serves our current desires. Jack, for example, at one point subscribes to something called "The System," which requires him to wear a monitor that records his blood oxygenation and lactic acid levels, UV exposure, and other physiological data (despite his lack of medical degree or ability to interpret it) in order to optimize his diet and exercise regime. Elizabeth herself is the proprietor of Wellness, an erstwhile clinic that once engaged in serious study to debunk fad diets and spurious medical cures but now actually peddles placebos, including a useless "love potion" that purports to help troubled couples—a cruel irony given Jack and Elizabeth's situation.

Many of the topics Hill describes do not seem like exaggerations, but rather accurate depictions of the more absurd aspects of life (at least for a certain demographic). This can be attributed in part to the extensive source material he drew upon in writing the story. Unusually for a novel, *Wellness* ends with an eight-page bibliography of the popular and academic sources that informed his descriptions of everything from Toby's picky eating to the efficacy of wearable health monitors.

Critics found much to admire in Hill's insights. Calling *Wellness* a "stunning novel about the stories that we tell about our lives and our loves, and how we sustain relationships throughout time," Michael Schaub opined in a review for *NPR*, "It's beyond remarkable, both funny and heartbreaking, sometimes on the same page." He took particular note of how Hill handles the malaise of modern American life, "an emptiness that we attempt to fill with *one simple lifestyle change* or *one revolutionary new product*, despite knowing subconsciously that it probably won't make much difference." Schaub deemed *Wellness* "a perfect novel for our age, filled with a deep awareness of the Internet-poisoned, marketing-driven engineered emptiness of modern times, but also a compassionate optimism about our ability to find and maintain love nonetheless."

More than one reviewer marveled at Hill's ability to hold readers' interest for some six hundred pages, especially in an era in which writers like Charles Dickens and George Eliot, known for their expansive books, are in exceptionally short supply. Daphne Merkin expressed this point in a positive review for the *Atlantic*, noting how "The book swarms with characters, ideas, and sociological evocations" and how Hill frequently digresses from its main romantic story line involving Jack and Elizabeth "to reflect on the art market, real estate, interior design, parenting, sex, and many other topics." The book was also lauded lavishly in *Kirkus Reviews*, whose critic drew a similar conclusion: "Hill romps through our soufflélike culture with a nice sendup of academic literature and broad jabs at memes ranging from organic food ('one-hundred-percent *bioavailable*') to progressive parenting, open marriage, and cult behavior ... while delivering a story that suggests that while love may not conquer all, it makes a good start." In delving into those myriad topics, Hill holds a mirror up to his readers and encourages them to reexamine their value systems, human relationships, and lives.

Author Biography

Nathan Hill burst onto the literary scene with the 2016 novel *The Nix*, which earned him rave reviews, a place on numerous best-of-the-year lists, and the Art Seidenbaum Award for First Fiction from the *Los Angeles Times*. He is a graduate of the University of Iowa and the University of Massachusetts.

Mari Rich

Review Sources

Athitakis, Mark. "Did Gen X Sell Out? In Nathan Hill's Stealthy New Satire, It's Way Worse Than That." Review of *Wellness*, by Nathan Hill. *Los Angeles Times*, 15 Sept. 2023, www.latimes.com/entertainment-arts/books/story/2023-09-15/did-gen-x-sell-out-in-nathan-hills-stealthy-satire-wellness-its-way-worse-than-that. Accessed 4 Jan. 2024.

Cline, Jake. "Oprah's Book Club Pick 'Wellness' Pokes Fun at Our Era of Mindfulness." Review of *Wellness*, by Nathan Hill. *The Washington Post*, 19 Sept. 2023, www.washingtonpost.com/books/2023/09/19/oprah-book-club-wellness-review/. Accessed 4 Jan. 2024.

Martin, Andrew. "Nathan Hill's *Wellness* Satirizes the Modern Condition—Kind Of." Review of *Wellness*, by Nathan Hill. *The New York Times*, 17 Sept. 2023, www.nytimes.com/2023/09/17/books/review/nathan-hill-wellness.html. Accessed 4 Jan. 2024.

Merkin, Daphne. "A Worthy Heir to David Foster Wallace and Thomas Pynchon." Review of *Wellness*, by Nathan Hill. *The Atlantic*, 17 Oct. 2023, www.theatlantic.com/books/archive/2023/10/wellness-nathan-hill/675657/. Accessed 4 Jan. 2024.

Schaub, Michael. "'Wellness' Is a Perfect Novel for Our Age, Its Profound Sadness Tempered with Humor." Review of *Wellness*, by Nathan Hill. *NPR*, 20 Sept. 2023, www.npr.org/2023/09/20/1200197882/book-review-nathan-hill-wellness. Accessed 4 Jan. 2024.

Review of *Wellness*, by Nathan Hill. *Kirkus Reviews*, 26 July 2023, www.kirkusreviews.com/book-reviews/nathan-hill/wellness-hill/. Accessed 4 Jan. 2024.

Western Lane

Author: Chetna Maroo
Publisher: Farrar, Straus and Giroux (New York). 151 pp.
Type of work: Novel
Time: 1980s
Locale: United Kingdom

Chetna Maroo's unique coming-of-age novel tells the story of an eleven-year-old Indian British girl who uses squash to cope with her mother's death.

Principal characters
GOPI, an eleven-year-old girl
KHUSH, her thirteen-year-old sister
MONA, her fifteen-year-old sister
PA, her father
PAVAN, her uncle
RANJAN, her aunt
GED, her friend

There are many different ways to cope with the loss of a loved one. Some people retreat into silence, while others take up a new activity to distract themselves from their grief. While many experts have put forth suggestions as to the best way to deal with the loss, there is no getting around the pain that the loved one's death creates and the sense of emptiness that ensues. While different strategies can help, only the passage of time can truly lessen the impact.

In Chetna Maroo's 2023 debut novel, a coming-of-age tale entitled *Western Lane*, the numerous members of a Jain Indian family living in England react differently to the loss of the mother, and their various coping strategies form the backbone of this subtle, effective book. Taking place immediately after the mother's death, the book is narrated by eleven-year-old Gopi, who is looking back from the present day at several key months in her young life during the 1980s. She lives with her father, an electrician, and two sisters, Khush, who is thirteen, and Mona, who is fifteen. Each member of the family copes with the mother's death in different ways; for example, Gopi's father, Pa, retreats into himself, neglecting both his job and his home responsibilities, while Mona picks up the slack and focuses on running the household. Hovering over the book is the threat that Pa will give in to the suggestion of his conservative sister-in-law, Ranjan, and send one of his daughters to live with Ranjan and her husband in Scotland, thus breaking up the family.

The one area in which Pa is able to focus is on the sport of squash. The sport has long been popular in the family and Pa's daughters have all played casually for years.

Chetna Maroo

Now, to take their minds off their grief, Pa begins seriously training his girls in the sport. Gopi, in particular, takes to the game and begins playing every day, while her sisters lose interest and eventually drop out. As Gopi trains for an upcoming tournament, Gopi befriends another player, a thirteen-year-old boy named Ged, with whom she strikes up a friendship shot through with romantic yearning.

Maroo devotes ample time to descriptions of the sport of squash as Gopi trains. These descriptions not only give a good sense of the action on the court, but they pay particular attention to the sensations that Gopi experiences as she plays. For example, early on in her training, Ged asks her why she plays squash. In her thoughts she expresses a vague but definite sense of her reasons for playing. "I thought of Pa," Gopi narrates, "and of being on the court with Pa watching, and of the feeling when I forgot about Pa and I was just moving or striking the ball, and then the feeling when I wasn't playing." Gopi does not say what those reasons are, but the reader gets a sense that she is thinking about both the ways that the game connects her to her father and the ways that it allows her to forget about him and the family's grief and just live in the moment. As Gopi continues reflecting, she thinks, "a game can seem endless," revealing that the real reason she plays squash is the sport's all-consuming quality. Ultimately, however, Gopi is not able to answer Ged's question out loud and simply tells her friend, "I don't know."

Indeed, in Maroo's quiet, subtle book, much is felt but left unsaid, and it is this gap between feeling and articulation that gives the book its melancholy charge. For example, it is clear that Gopi and Ged have romantic feelings for each other, but neither verbalizes these words aloud. In fact, Gopi does not even verbalize them explicitly in her narration, but she offers clues about her longing and her sadness when she is separated from Ged that the reader realizes her feelings are deeper than friendship. This sense of things left unsaid between characters also extends to Gopi's relationship with her father. They do not directly address Gopi's mother's death, preferring to devote most of their dialogue to discussions of squash. It is clear in the book that Pa is not processing his wife's death well; as he retreats further from his household and professional duties, the reader is able to see how this inability to verbalize his feelings is preventing him from moving on from his wife's death and resuming his place in the life of his family.

In addition to offering distraction and connection with her father, squash provides Gopi with an awareness of her body. One of the training exercises that she performs repeatedly with Pa is what is known as "ghosting." In this exercise, the player simulates the movement of the game without using the ball. Pa calls out to Gopi, telling her where an imaginary ball is hit, and she has to run to the spot and swing her racket. This exercise allows the player to pay closer attention to their footwork and other aspects of their fundamental game, without worrying about results. The more Gopi practices, the more she develops an understanding of her body. "I began to feel the physical pressure of the movements," she narrates, "and could predict where and when the pain in my body would come. Often, it only felt painful and difficult, but other times I had a rhythm, and then something more than a rhythm."

Because *Western Lane* is a coming-of-age story, passages like these invite the reader to interpret them as revealing more about Gopi than she is relating on the surface. Maroo is a subtle writer and she packs most of her lines with significant meaning, much of which may not be immediately apparent. Although the passage about ghosting in squash involves Gopi talking about her awareness of her body on the court, her narration also hints at a growing awareness of her body in a physical sense. As a person begins puberty, they inevitably notice their body in ways they have not before. Because Gopi's squash training coincides with her tentative romantic feelings for Ged, this awareness of her body suggests a nascent sexual awareness as well. Either way, Gopi's increasing sense of her own body indicates a growing independence. This is made clearer late in the book when she runs through a ghosting drill with her father and he refuses to call out directions, asking her to lead the drill all by herself.

Although Gopi is able to channel her grief over her mother's death and her frustration with the ensuing family situation onto the squash court, eventually she can only take so much. Maroo's book is conspicuously short on dramatic action, preferring to focus on the ways that people process or fail to process their feelings. Nonetheless, in a pivotal scene late in the novel, Gopi gives in to a moment of violent impulse on the squash court. Although this incident has significant consequences for Gopi, the incident itself is not lingered upon by the author or the characters. Maroo's handling of this scene shows her delicate touch, allowing the reader to see the burst of violence through the eyes of the narrator, who is herself disoriented, and then cutting to the response as everyone around her tries to restore calm.

This scene perfectly captures the dynamic that Gopi's family is attempting to maintain during trying times. Even as heavy feelings frequently rise to the surface, they are tamped back down in the name of preserving order. In *Western Lane*, grief makes everyone act in different ways; Maroo's achievement is showing how, despite everyone's efforts to ignore a tough situation, it cannot be fully avoided. As her novel reveals in sharp but subtle ways, grief is a transformative process and must be confronted. *Western Lane*'s shrewd observations about the grieving process and family dynamics in a coming-of-age novel makes it a valuable addition to the literature of both grieving and of growing up.

Western Lane received significant critical acclaim upon publication in 2023, eventually getting shortlisted for the prestigious Booker Prize. Writing for the *New York Times*, where Maroo's novel was named a notable book of the year, Ivy Pochoda found the book to be a "polished and disciplined debut." She praised Maroo's writing, noting that "the beauty of [the] novel lies in that unfolding, the narrative shaped as much by what is on the page as by what's left unsaid." These sentiments were echoed by Caleb Klaces for the *Guardian*, who felt that *Western Lane* "feels like the work of a writer who knows what they want to do, and who has the rare ability to do it." Klaces was especially impressed by Maroo's handling of the subtle ways that people communicate meaning, both verbally and nonverbally.

Klaces did argue that the novel contained some elements that could come across as formulaic, however, such as the fact that the narrative follows a familiar, "Hollywood"-style arc and introduces a love interest for Gopi. Nonetheless, Klaces concluded that Maroo deftly sidestepped these traps and remained in command of her art throughout. This sense of control, particularly for a first-time novelist, impressed many critics, including the anonymous reviewer for *Publishers Weekly*, who noted, "Maroo skillfully balances the drama of Gopi's upcoming squash tournament with the nuances of family drama." Highlighting Maroo's control and balance, the reviewer called the book a "compact and powerful debut" that "will invigorate readers."

Author Biography

Chetna Maroo first came to attention for stories she published in *The Paris Review*, *The Dublin Review*, and other prestigious publications. She received *The Paris Review*'s 2022 Plimpton Prize for Fiction. Prior to turning to writing full time, Maroo worked as an accountant. Her debut novel, *Western Lane*, was published in 2023.

Andrew Schenker

Review Sources

Klaces, Caleb. "A Tender Debut." Review of *Western Lane*, by Chetna Maroo. *The Guardian*, 26 Apr. 2023, www.theguardian.com/books/2023/apr/26/western-lane-by-chetna-maroo-review-a-tender-debut. Accessed 2 Jan. 2024.

Pochoda, Ivy. "*Western Lane* Finds Solace from Grief on the Squash Court." Review of *Western Lane*, by Chetna Maroo. *The New York Times*, 7 Feb. 2023, www.nytimes.com/2023/02/07/books/review/western-lane-chetna-maroo.html. Accessed 2 Jan. 2024.

Review of *Western Lane*, by Chetna Maroo. *Publishers Weekly*, 28 Nov. 2022, p. 28. *Literary Reference Center Plus*, search.ebscohost.com/login.aspx?direct=true&db=lkh&AN=160446785&site=lrc-plus. Accessed 2 Jan. 2024.

Weyward

Author: Emilia Hart
Publisher: St. Martin's Press (New York). 336 pp.
Type of work: Novel
Time: 1619, 1942, and 2019
Locale: Primarily Crows Beck and Orton Hall, Cumbria, England

Despite living in three very different time periods and worlds, three women are tied together through a powerful family connection to the natural world in this intricate novel. All three protagonists search for peace and enlightenment as they navigate womanhood, face trauma, and find themselves.

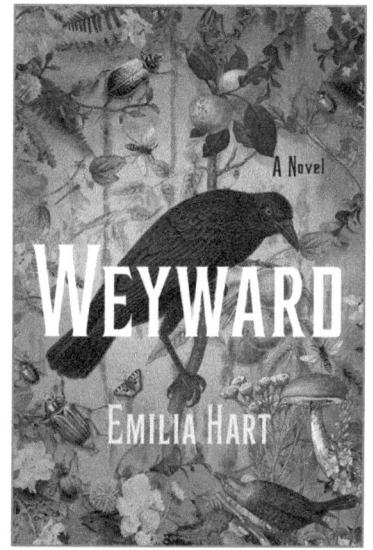

Principal characters

ALTHA WEYWARD, a healer accused of witchcraft
JENNET WEYWARD, her mother, a healer
GRACE METCALFE, also known as Grace Milburn, her childhood best friend, the daughter and later wife of yeomen farmers
ELIZABETH WEYWARD AYRES, her descendant
VIOLET AYRES, Elizabeth's daughter, a sheltered tomboy who longs to become a scientist
RUPERT AYRES, Ninth Viscount Kendall, Elizabeth's husband, Violet's controlling, distant father
COUSIN FREDERICK, Violet's cousin and love interest, a soldier
GRAHAM AYRES, Violet's younger brother
KATE AYRES, Violet's grandniece, Graham's granddaughter
SIMON, Kate's abusive partner

Weyward, the debut novel of British Australian writer Emilia Hart, is ambitious in both structure and theme. Jumping back and forth in time, it interweaves the stories of three women living in very different eras but linked to each other in important ways. Their experiences reveal that while society may have changed significantly over the centuries, patriarchy has remained persistent—as have creative forms of female resistance and self-realization. Hart skillfully balances the complex and often weighty narrative strands, drawing readers deep into the characters' lives and creating an engaging sense of mystery that propels the multiple story lines forward.

The novel is broken into three parts, with a varying number of chapters in each. Part 1 starts with a short prologue that introduces Altha, a young woman who has been

Emilia Hart

accused of witchcraft in 1619. This brief glimpse into Altha's life ends with a taunting cliffhanger about what will happen to the character. Chapter 1 then jumps forward four hundred years to 2019, when Kate, abused by her partner, escapes in secret to a new life. In chapter 2, the story shifts back in time again to introduce the third protagonist, Violet, in 1942. At sixteen years old, Violet wishes her father would allow her to attend school like her brother Graham.

Part 1 continues with nineteen chapters in total, alternating in a seemingly random way among the three women. Part 2 of the novel spans another twelve chapters, also alternating in focus but with a more organized pattern. This section begins with Violet, moves to Kate, and then to Altha, continuing this order until it concludes with a Violet chapter. Part 3 changes the focus and order of narration once again, with Violet's and Kate's stories largely taking precedence over Altha's history. Finally, the novel ends with an epilogue that is separate from the three main sections but more closely ties Violet's and Kate's lives together through a flashback.

As readers follow the life of each character, it soon becomes clear that the three intertwined stories all center on the struggles of women living in a patriarchal world. Indeed, this core concept emerges both through the specific plot details and through the broader themes to which Hart draws attention. For instance, Altha's story deals with witchcraft and the supernatural, but it also challenges readers to think about unconventional relationships and violence against women. Altha is the only child of a healer, Jennet Weyward, and from a young age learns of a special bond with the natural world that runs in the family. As a young woman, Altha travels around the village helping care for those who are pregnant or infirm. But when her best friend Grace's mother falls ill and Jennet cannot save her, the woman's husband banishes Jennet and Altha from his daughter's life. After Jennet dies and Grace is married off to a local farmer, Altha faces decisions that lead to persecution for witchcraft.

The legacy of gendered oppression continues in the other story lines. Generations later, Violet is born to Rupert and Elizabeth Weyward Ayres. Shortly after Violet's younger brother is born, Elizabeth disappears from the children's lives. Her death is shrouded in mystery. Growing up, Violet is both pampered and ignored. Though she has everything she needs financially—a home, food, clothing, and household servants to care for her—she lacks female guidance and parental love. As a result, the arrival of handsome Cousin Frederick proves both a temptation and a threat that the naïve girl cannot comprehend until too late. Banished from her father's home, ensconced in a rundown cottage once owned by her Weyward ancestors, Violet learns to rely on herself and her own surprising connection to nature.

Decades later still, Kate Ayres inherits the same cottage from her paternal great-aunt. She hides the inheritance from the man she has lived with for years, who has become so controlling and abusive that she cannot even leave the house without being spied on and punished. One night Kate decides she has had enough, packs a bag, and drives the seven hours to Weyward Cottage to start a new life.

In its focus on women grappling with inequality the novel is filled with examples of sexism and misogyny ranging from systemic discrimination to brutal violence, and readers may find these depictions quite disturbing. Several of the major characters experience abusive relationships and difficult reproductive choices. In many ways Kate's story is the most obvious and graphic example, as her boyfriend Simon regularly threatens, beats, and rapes her. Kate has a college degree and at one point had a rewarding job in the publishing world, but Simon has limited her self-esteem, her relationships with others, and her very existence so much that she long struggles to gather enough courage to leave him. Yet while this can make for difficult reading, it also allows Hart to ultimately showcase female strength and resilience, including the power of generational bonds. Importantly, it is Violet's will that gives Kate a crucial escape hatch in the form of the family cottage. Running away from Simon is still not easy, but Kate demonstrates her resolve to use the few resources she has left, including a cell phone she has kept secret. Even after leaving, Kate must continue to grapple with ongoing challenges related to Simon's abuse, but her gradual exploration of the home that is now hers leads to a vital connection with her family heritage and, like Altha and Violet before her, the life-saving power of nature.

The book's narrative structure also emphasizes that while Kate may be isolated, she is far from alone in facing such challenges. Her experiences are echoed and prefigured in other characters' circumstances throughout the book. One is beaten by her alcoholic partner for things beyond her control—such as a stillbirth and a miscarriage—and chooses to abort a third pregnancy rather than have that child live with the violence that has controlled her life. Another is seduced by an untrustworthy paramour and becomes a victim of rape, but then blamed and ostracized when a pregnancy is subsequently discovered. Lack of information about sexual matters does not stop her from ultimately finding a way to assert control, however. As that example shows, the novel suggests that while sexual violence may be recurrent throughout history, so are more hopeful forces, especially when backed by positive familial ties. Adding to this sense of recursion within the book is Hart's decisions to reuse surnames for characters in different story lines, suggesting continuity or repetition across time, extending through and beyond the Weyward descendance.

On one hand, *Weyward* presents as a historical novel that examines realistic social themes in three different centuries. But intertwined with the historical element is also a sense of magical realism that brings a touch of fantasy to the story. This is primarily expressed through the special connection the Weyward women have to nature, a form of magic that is much more subtle than typical in fantasy fiction. These powers are portrayed more as natural talents passed between generations, including an ability to communicate with animals. It informs the healing work of Altha and her mother, though it also complicates the misguided charges of witchcraft. Violet continues the tradition with a particular focus on the insect world, a childhood fascination that ultimately turns into a career when she becomes brave enough to seek her own path later in life. Kate's talents prove to be a combination of Altha's and Violet's, again reinforcing the idea of cross-generational ties and shared experiences regardless of era. Ultimately, the presence of these magical abilities adds lighter and more empowering aspects to each woman's story, helping to prevent the overall narrative from becoming overwhelmingly dark.

Together, the magical realism and strong moral themes lend an almost fairy tale–like quality to the novel. This can be seen as both a strength and a weakness. On one hand, it contributes to a unique and highly engaging tone that will surely resonate with many readers. On the other hand, Hart's characterizations can at times be overly simplistic: mothers are good, and fathers are either missing or prove to be selfish, evil-minded brutes. Indeed, as Sarah McCraw Crow noted in her review for *BookPage*, "Most of the novel's men are portrayed as unremittingly villainous, and some readers will wish for a little more complexity there." The loss of a mother's protection precipitates all manner of terrible events in the book. Positive sibling relationships are likewise few and far between—with Graham and Violet being the notable exception, and arguably the most well-drawn and dynamic.

Weyward was largely well received by critics, and it ranked as highly commended in the first novel category for the Caldonia Novel Award in 2021. A *Library Journal* review by Jane Jorgenson deemed the genre combination of magical realism and historical fiction "perfect" and recommended the book to admirers of Alice Hoffman's and Megan Giddings's speculative fiction. In a *Booklist* review, Bethany Latham pointed to the "well-realized" characterization and argued that Hart's real talent is shown "in its depiction of the terrifying way abusers spin their webs to ensnare their prey." Latham also lauded Hart for keeping up the tension and suspense, concluding, "The result is a tale of magic and female empowerment and an atmospheric, gripping read." The critics for *Kirkus Reviews* applauded the feminist aspects of the story, concluding, "Thoughtful and at times harrowing, this novel is a successful blend of historical fiction and modern feminism." Applauding *Weyward*'s subtle ecofeminism for the *Southern Review of Books*, Nicole Yurcaba noted, "The Weyward women's intimate connection with nature is a stark reminder of what humanity ultimately loses when environments are threatened and destroyed by humankind's follies." With such urgent social themes conveyed through page-turning prose, *Weyward* proves both a wondrous tale of womanhood and a riveting, timely thriller.

Author Biography
Emilia Hart studied English literature and law at the University of New South Wales and practiced as an attorney in Australia and England. She published works of short fiction before releasing *Weyward* as her debut novel.

Theresa L. Stowell, PhD

Review Sources

Crow, Sarah McCraw. Review of *Weyward*, by Emilia Hart." *BookPage*, Apr. 2023, www.bookpage.com/reviews/weyward-emilia-hart-book-review/. Accessed 26 Jan. 2024.

Jorgenson, Jane. "Reading beyond Conventions." Review of *Weyward*, by Emilia Hart. *Library Journal*, vol. 148, no. 2, Feb. 2023, pp. 40–42. *EBSCOhost*, search.ebscohost.com/login.aspx?direct=true&db=asn&AN=161458531&site=eds-live&scope=site. Accessed 23 Jan. 2024.

Latham, Bethany. Review of *Weyward*, by Emilia Hart. *Booklist*, vol. 119, nos. 9–10, Jan. 2023, p. 38. *EBSCOhost*, search.ebscohost.com/login.aspx?direct=true&db=lkh&AN=161198283&site=lrc-plus. Accessed 23 Jan. 2024.

Review of *Weyward*, by Emilia Hart. *Kirkus Reviews*, 15 Jan. 2023, vol. 91, no. 2. *EBSCOhost*, search.ebscohost.com/login.aspx?direct=true&db=lkh&AN=161253386&site=lrc-plus. Accessed 23 Jan. 2024.

Review of *Weyward*, by Emilia Hart. *Publishers Weekly*, vol. 270, no. 2, Jan. 2023, p. 45. *EBSCOhost*, search.ebscohost.com/login.aspx?direct=true&db=lkh&AN=161204165&site=lrc-plus. Accessed 23 Jan. 2024.

Yurcaba, Nicole. "Resilience through Generations in 'Weyward.'" Review of *Weyward*, by Emilia Hart. *Southern Review of Books*, 17 May 2023, southernreviewofbooks.com/2023/05/17/weyward-emilia-hart-review. Accessed 26 Jan. 2024.

Whalefall

Author: Daniel Kraus (b. 1975)
Publisher: MTV Books (New York).
   336 pp.
Type of work: Novel
Time: 2005–22
Locale: Monterey, California

While scuba diving off the Californian coast to find his father's remains, seventeen-year-old Jay Gardiner is swallowed by a sperm whale and has only an hour left of oxygen to escape in this thrilling work of fiction by Daniel Kraus.

Principal characters
JAY GARDINER, a teenage boy grappling with the aftermath of his estranged father's suicide
MITT GARDINER, his emotionally abusive father, a lifelong diver
ZARA GARDINER, his mother, who wants to reunite the family
EVA GARDINER, his older sister, a college student
NAN GARDINER, his oldest sister, a speech-language pathologist

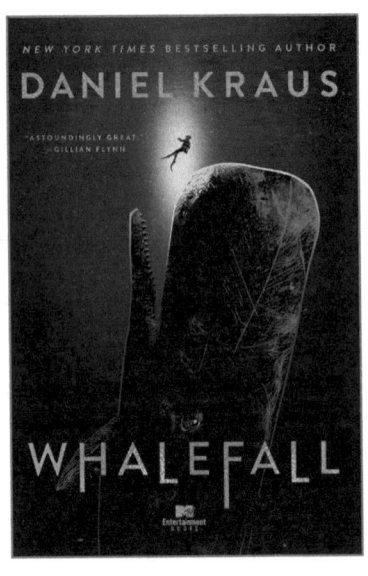

While men being swallowed by whales may seem an unlikely story, throughout history several iconic stories have been produced that feature just such a premise. The biblical story of Jonah and the whale is one example that has been important to those of Jewish and Christian faiths for millennia, while nineteenth-century Italian writer Carlo Collodi's novel *The Adventures of Pinocchio* (*Le avventure di Pinocchio*, 1883) became a well-known children's tale that ends with Pinocchio's father being consumed by a whale. With his 2023 novel, *Whalefall*, American author Daniel Kraus puts a new twist on the whale versus man proposition while also borrowing thematic elements from its predecessors.

At first glance, *Whalefall* appears to be an action thriller more in line with Kraus's previous works. After his breakout novel about grave robbers, *Rotters* (2011), Kraus made a name for himself by coauthoring books with film directors like Guillermo del Toro and George A. Romero—with whom he cowrote *The Shape of Water* (2018) and *The Living Dead* (2020), respectively. While the setup of *Whalefall* often feels as though it is intended to be a work of supernatural horror like much of the rest of the author's bibliography, Kraus has stated in interviews that he was inspired by a real news story of a pair of kayakers who were engulfed in the mouth of a humpback whale in 2020. The author wondered what would have happened if the whale had continued to swallow them, instead of spitting them back out as was the outcome in real life.

Daniel Kraus

After researching whether it was even possible for a whale to swallow a human, and learning that a sperm whale could indeed perform such an act, Kraus set about bringing the scenario to life through fiction.

Consequently, the tone of *Whalefall* is best described as a scientifically feasible monster story. While searching for his father's bones at the bottom of Monastery Bay, the novel's protagonist, seventeen-year-old Jay Gardiner, soon finds himself inside the stomach of an elderly male sperm whale. The details of how this happens and what then ensues all stay within the confines of reality. For example, because whales do not eat humans, Kraus makes the impetus for Jay's consumption an Architeuthis, or giant squid, which is one of the sperm whale's favorite foods. In the novel, the squid happens to grab Jay with its tentacles while it is being swallowed, thus dragging the boy along with it into the belly of the whale. The author's dedication to writing as realistically as possible quickly becomes further evident in his prose—especially in his descriptions of Jay's surroundings, as in the following passage: "First of all, he sees the stomach. An inch from his mask, hugging his fetal form. Pale pink folds bulleted by angry yellow ulcers, jiggling with the whale's sway, a coat of mucus gleaming in eerie neon light."

Indeed, a large part of what makes *Whalefall* a unique read is not that Kraus incorporates facts about marine biology, but rather that he uses them as the obstacles and opportunities of his hero's journey. At one point, a dead squid's beak is revealed to be as sharp and strong as an iron blade and subsequently becomes Jay's most precious tool, which he nicknames "beaky." At another, the sperm whale's capacity to make sounds louder than any living creature on Earth becomes Jay's biggest threat—even though it is intended to stun prey thirty feet away, the whale's echolocation is loud enough to crush every bone in Jay's body and begins to do just that. In this way, *Whalefall* becomes the ultimate story of man versus nature—a genre that became popularized with authors like Jack London and Herman Melville, the latter of which wrote another famous whale novel, *Moby Dick* (1851). In more recent decades, the man-versus-nature narrative has been defined by nonfiction books, such as Jon Krakauer's *Into the Wild* (1996) and *Between a Rock and a Hard Place* (2005) by Aron Ralston, many of which also were adapted into popular films.

Amidst *Whalefall*'s scientific accuracy is an emotional story about the grief of a son coming to terms with his relationship with his dead father. Mitt Gardiner was a tough-as-nails, alcoholic diver and sailor who hated modern life and tried to shape Jay into a specific image of what he believed a boy should be. Here, a loose comparison can be made to Geppetto, the father who carves his son, Pinocchio, out of wood. When other fathers were playing catch with their sons, Mitt was teaching Jay everything he knew about the sea while simultaneously degrading the qualities he saw as Jay's weaknesses. When Jay was fifteen, he could no longer take his father's emotional abuse and ran away from home, living at friends' houses while he finished high school. Their relationship became so tumultuous that when Jay learned that Mitt had been diagnosed with cancer, he refused to visit him in the hospital. In the end, he never got to make amends with his father, who ended up drowning himself before the cancer could kill him.

The exploration of Jay's grief is executed in a stylistically inventive way. Kraus alternates back and forth throughout the novel's chapters between the past and the present. By doing so, he provides insight into the formative events from Jay's childhood that inform what he is facing in the present. Some of these moments are the emotionally devastating ones that led to the grief that indirectly resulted in him ending up in the belly of a whale. Other moments are used to reveal times when Mitt taught Jay the exact knowledge he needs in the present to take another step toward his escape. The chapters themselves are quite short with some being only a page or even a single word long. Those set in the present are identified by their headings telling how much oxygen Jay has left in his tank, given in pounds per square inch (PSI). Kraus's decision to quickly move back and forth between truncated chapters, and with the regular reminder that Jay's PSI is dwindling, creates a thrilling, page-turning narrative of suspense.

If there is one deviation from the hyper-real, scientific world that Kraus has created in *Whalefall*, it is the voice that Jay begins to hear while fighting for his life inside of the whale. The author never clarifies who exactly is speaking to Jay's oxygen-deprived, methane-addled brain, leaving readers to wonder if it is the whale or Mitt or some combination of both. The whale itself seems to symbolize the way that Jay still feels consumed by his father. Like the whale, Mitt was a larger-than-life figure with immense power over Jay's well-being. He shaped Jay—both by teaching him everything he needed to know to survive the dangerous ocean waters and by crushing his self-worth. In this way, Jay's escape from the whale functions as a kind of metaphor for his need to break free from the complex guilt, pain, and grief he feels toward his father. While he recalls the knowledge and skills that his father taught him to try and escape the whale, he is simultaneously forced to come to terms with their relationship. Like Jonah in the biblical narrative of Jonah and the whale, Jay's story is one rooted in the theme of transformation.

Reception of *Whalefall* was overwhelmingly positive. In addition to the story's film rights quickly being snapped up, it received numerous celebratory reviews by critics—most of whom extolled Kraus's unique approach to blending science with storytelling. Sarah Lyall touched on this point in her review for the *New York Times*, stating, "I'm not one for slippery viscera, slimy effluvia, bits of dying squid or anything that suggests 'a sloshing basin of jelly,' all things that apparently feature in the inner workings of whales. But the technical descriptions of the undersea world, and the physicality of Jay's predicament, drowned out my squeamishness. I was absolutely gripped, unsure to the very end whether Jay would prevail." It is true that Kraus succeeds in the tightrope-like walk of keeping readers informed of the reality of both whale and other sea creatures' biology without ever becoming off-putting. In part, this is because he excels at making bodily functions visually striking and fascinating by employing poetic prose. However, as Lyall stated, it is also because the novel's propulsive sense of suspense never allows readers to linger on details that could otherwise be interpreted as gross. In a *Library Journal* review of *Whalefall*, Andrea Dyba also emphasized the novel's gripping storytelling, explaining "Jay's plight is viscerally intense and claustrophobic, even as he grapples with real and raw emotions." Similarly, a reviewer for *Publishers Weekly* concluded that the "deep-sea thrill ride will have readers on the edges of their seats."

Not all critics were unilaterally positive, however. In her piece for *America: The Jesuit Review*, Christine Lenahan wrote that "for Kraus's narrative to be effective, it requires an imaginative reader" and that "some elements of Jay's survival are difficult to grasp." Here, Lenahan raises an important point: *Whalefall* does indeed require readers to suspend their disbelief. Despite Kraus's dedication to scientific accuracy, it is occasionally difficult to ignore the impossibility of Jay's circumstances. The novel still works, however, as long as readers are willing to go along for the ride either as a work of horror, a scientific thought experiment, or even as a metaphoric exploration of grief. Overall, *Whalefall* blends and pushes the genres of horror and science fiction into new territory, proving that there is much more creative ground to tread even with well-worn narrative premises. Beyond that, the novel succeeds as an exciting thriller that is difficult to put down and is a welcome addition to the topic of father-son relationships and their emotional complexity.

Author Biography

Daniel Kraus is a *New York Times* best-selling horror and science fiction author. He is best known for collaborating on novelizations of horror film franchises with directors Guillermo del Toro and George A. Romero. He has two Odyssey Awards for his novels *Rotters* (2011) and *Scowler* (2013) and a Bram Stoker Award.

Emily E. Turner

Review Sources

Dyba, Andrea. Review of *Whalefall*, by Daniel Kraus. *Library Journal*, 1 May 2023, www.libraryjournal.com/review/whalefall-1796755. Accessed 1 Oct. 2023.

Lenahan, Christine. "In the Belly of the Beast: Daniel Kraus's Novel 'Whalefall' Considers the Power of Communion and Grief." Review of *Whalefall*, by Daniel Kraus. *America: The Jesuit Review*, 14 Sept. 2023, www.americamagazine.org/arts-culture/2023/09/14/review-whalefall-kraus-len-245974. Accessed 1 Oct. 2023.

Lyall, Sarah. "Swallowed by a Sperm Whale, and Mourning His Father." Review of *Whalefall*, by Daniel Kraus. *The New York Times*, 30 July 2023, www.nytimes.com/2023/07/30/books/review/daniel-kraus-whalefall.html. Accessed 1 Oct. 2023.

Review of *Whalefall*, by Daniel Kraus. *Publishers Weekly*, 22 May 2023, www.publishersweekly.com/9781665918169. Accessed 1 Oct. 2023.

What an Owl Knows
The New Science of the World's Most Enigmatic Birds

Author: Jennifer Ackerman (b. 1959)
Publisher: Penguin Press (New York). Illustrated. 352 pp.
Type of work: Nature, natural history

In What an Owl Knows: The New Science of the World's Most Enigmatic Birds, *Jennifer Ackerman explores contemporary research into the capabilities, biology, and behavior of the world's many owl species.*

A longtime nature writer, Jennifer Ackerman earned critical acclaim for *Chance in the House of Fate: A Natural History of Heredity* (2001), *The Genius of Birds* (2016), and *The Bird Way: A New Look at How Birds Talk, Work, Play, Parent, and Think* (2020), the latter of which was a finalist for the prestigious PEN/E.O. Wilson Literary Science Writing Award. In 2020, she began work on a new project in which she explored one specific category within the avian world, that of owls. The resulting book, 2023's *What an Owl Knows: The New Science of the World's Most Enigmatic Birds*, deals primarily with contemporary research concerning owls, including both recent scientific discoveries and ongoing research projects that, though promising, had yet to be completed as of Ackerman's writing. The text not only contains numerous enlightening insights into owl behavior, biology, migration patterns, and more, but is also interspersed with photographs of many of the different owl species Ackerman discusses, which help bring the birds on the page to life and showcase the remarkable diversity of species within the owl category.

Following a short preface, *What an Owl Knows* is divided into nine chapters, the first of which provides an introduction of sorts to the birds at the center of Ackerman's work. As she explains, about 260 individual species of owls are known to exist, and such birds live all over the world. The second chapter, "What It's Like to Be an Owl," explores the many adaptations that have enabled owls to become so widespread and to establish themselves as such effective predators. Those adaptations include the birds' specific arrangements of feathers and their proportionately large wings, which help them to fly quietly—though not, as Ackerman and the researchers she consulted point out, completely silently. Owls also tend to possess uncommonly good hearing that enables them to determine the location of prey animals even when such animals are underground or hiding under leaves, a skill that may be attributed in part to the asymmetrical placement of owls' ears. Some owls also possess notably sharp vision,

Jennifer Ackerman

and Ackerman provides a brief overview of research linking strong night vision in some owls to the makeup of the birds' retinas, which contain a greater proportion of rods than the retinas of other birds do.

Throughout *What an Owl Knows*, Ackerman discusses the many techniques human researchers use when attempting to locate and study owls. As she demonstrates, owl research incorporates a fascinating array of high-tech methods. Indeed, some technological advances have proven extremely beneficial for owl researchers; improvements to satellite tracking technology, for instance, have enabled some scientists to glean valuable data about migration patterns and nesting locations by placing small tracking devices on captured owls. Similarly, the development of smaller, more powerful cameras has allowed researchers to place cameras near owl nests and thus to collect valuable information about mating, egg laying, and the early lives of owl chicks, all of which would be difficult or impossible to observe in the wild without technological intervention. High-tech research strategies also include computer analysis of owl vocalizations, which can also be studied visually in the form of spectrograms.

At the same time, more traditional, low-tech methods remain essential to many owl researchers. The in-person, visual observation of owls remains a common strategy, as has the practice of mimicking owl sounds—or playing recordings of actual owl hoots—to draw owls out of hiding and potentially to lure them into traps for banding. One particularly intriguing strategy Ackerman discusses involves the use of a dog that has been specially trained to locate regurgitated owl pellets, which typically contain bones, fur, and other parts of prey animals that the owls cannot digest. Owl pellets are important to researchers for a number of reasons, including providing clear evidence of which kinds of animals a given owl has been consuming. In addition, the presence of owl pellets can indicate that owls themselves are present in a particular area and, if numerous pellets are found in one specific location, can help researchers find where an owl is nesting. As owls are often difficult to spot visually due to their natural camouflage, locating them through alternative means is often necessary, particularly when researchers are working to make an accurate count of an area's owl population.

What an Owl Knows takes a broad view of the avian world, considering regions as geographically and environmentally disparate as the Arctic Circle and Australia. While working on the book, Ackerman spent time with researchers in a variety of locales, including US states such as Montana and Virginia and countries such as Brazil and Italy. In addition to demonstrating the global reach of owls, Ackerman's travels abroad enabled her to gain firsthand knowledge of the differences that can arise between owls living in different regions, even when those owls ostensibly belong to the same species. A prime example of that phenomenon concerns the burrowing owl, a species that, by the early 2020s, was believed to encompass twenty-one living subspecies. As Ackerman learned while visiting Brazil, however, a population of burrowing owls living in the city of Maringá did not appear to "speak the same language as their relatives" in North America, as they did not respond as expected when played recorded vocalizations made by a burrowing owl from Oregon. That result and others proved intriguing to researchers, who sought to carry out further analysis of geographically disparate burrowing owl populations. By analyzing the genomes, behavior, and appearance of the owls, researchers sought to determine whether the world's different burrowing owl subspecies truly belonged to the same species or whether millennia of separation had led them to evolve into different species.

Later chapters of *What an Owl Knows* delve further into several major areas of study among owl researchers, including owl vocalizations, mating and the raising of chicks, and different species' approaches to nesting and migration. Ackerman describes a number of important findings in those areas, including research that has helped scientists gain a better understanding of the links between food scarcity and migration patterns in birds such as snowy owls, which tend to travel farther to breeding sites in years when the amount of available prey—lemmings, in the case of snowy owls—is insufficient.

Though dealing primarily with owls living in the wild, the book also includes discussion of owls raised and studied in captivity. In the United States, captive owls are typically taken in by rescue organizations after becoming injured; in other countries, however, it is legal to keep owls as pets, a practice criticized by some of the individuals discussed in the book. As Ackerman explains, the study of captive owls has raised questions about whether the birds' behavior and vocalizations would resemble those of owls living in the wild, particularly in the case of owls who had been raised by humans from early in life, and sparked further research into whether certain owl behaviors are inborn or learned. Ackerman explores beliefs about owls from around the world, explaining that some cultures associate owls with positive qualities such as wisdom, while others perceive them negatively or as omens of death. The ninth chapter of *What an Owl Knows* shares a title with the work as a whole and considers the topic of owl intelligence. Ackerman reports that the scientific consensus on the intelligence level of owls has evolved substantially over the years and that some contemporary researchers consider owls in general to possess a good deal of intelligence, albeit a specific avian form of intelligence that is not yet fully understood.

Ackerman concludes *What an Owl Knows* with an afterword, "Saving Owls," in which she describes threats that owl populations face, including habitat loss and cultural biases against owls. The majority of those threats are the result of human activity, including development and deforestation, although conflicts with other owl species have also proven detrimental to species such as the spotted owl. While some owls can and do survive in urban areas, as in the case of the burrowing owls Ackerman encountered in Brazil, the loss of suitable trees in which to nest remains a significant problem for many species. Habitat loss also has a negative effect on prey animal populations and can thus result in food scarcity for owls.

Much like nearly any book about wildlife in the twenty-first century, *What an Owl Knows* also grapples with the ongoing harms caused by climate change, which likewise contributes to habitat loss for owls via rising temperatures, droughts, severe storms, and wildfires. In light of such threats, Ackerman urges readers to do whatever they can to help owl populations survive and suggests a number of helpful actions based on her conversations with researchers, including inspecting trees for owl nests before having them cut down and allowing trees with hollows suitable for nesting to remain in place when possible. She also suggests that readers volunteer with research projects, noting that the public may be able to help with fieldwork and tasks such as banding and monitoring. Indeed, many of the researchers Ackerman interviewed work alongside volunteers, and some even began their engagement with owl research as volunteers themselves. Ultimately, *What an Owl Knows* demonstrates that protecting owls is a collaborative and exciting effort; learning more about the world's owl species will require contributions from researchers, volunteers, educators, and members of the public throughout the world.

The critical response to *What an Owl Knows: The New Science of the World's Most Enigmatic Birds* was positive, with reviewers widely praising Ackerman's informative and entertaining look into the world of owl research. In two separate starred reviews, the anonymous reviewer for *Publishers Weekly* described the book as a "masterful survey" that features "fascinating trivia on every page," while the *Kirkus Reviews* critic wrote that *What an Owl Knows* provides "fascinating food for thought for owl seekers" and is "sure to please any lover of immersive treks into the lives of birds." Simon Worrall, writing for the *Guardian*, described the book as "charming and deeply researched" and expressed particular appreciation for the work's eighth chapter, which deals with the owl's significance in different cultures. *New York Times* reviewer Jennifer Szalai noted Ackerman's enthusiasm for her subject, which she wrote could win over "even the avian-indifferent," and called attention to the book's illuminating selection of photographs and its extensive focus on researchers active in the field. Writing for the journal *Science*, Alan B. Franklin likewise commented approvingly on the book's focus on researchers, writing that Ackerman's work is "made all the more interesting by her decision to dive into the backgrounds of the scientists" studying the owls themselves.

Author Biography

Jennifer Ackerman is the award-winning author of several best-selling books, including *The Genius of Birds* (2016) and *The Bird Way* (2021). *What an Owl Knows* was a New York Times Notable Book of 2023 and won a 2023 National Outdoor Book Award in Outdoor Literature, among other honors.

Joy Crelin

Review Sources

Franklin, Alan B. "An Ode to Owls." Review of *What an Owl Knows*, by Jennifer Ackerman. *Science*, vol. 380, no. 6651, 2023, p. 1228, digitalcommons.unl.edu/cgi/viewcontent.cgi?article=3663&context=icwdm_usdanwrc. Accessed 16 Jan. 2024.

Review of *What an Owl Knows*, by Jennifer Ackerman. *Kirkus Reviews*, 20 Mar. 2023, www.kirkusreviews.com/book-reviews/jennifer-ackerman/what-an-owl-knows/. Accessed 16 Jan. 2024.

Review of *What an Owl Knows*, by Jennifer Ackerman. *Publishers Weekly*, 27 Mar. 2023, www.publishersweekly.com/9780593298886. Accessed 16 Jan. 2024.

Szalai, Jennifer. "A Book about Owls, in Which Each Species Is a Marvel." Review of *What an Owl Knows*, by Jennifer Ackerman. *The New York Times*, 14 June 2023, www.nytimes.com/2023/06/14/books/review/what-an-owl-knows-jennifer-ackerman.html. Accessed 16 Jan. 2024.

Wetzel, Corryn. "*What an Owl Knows* Review: Inside the World of This Mysterious Bird." Review of *What an Owl Knows*, by Jennifer Ackerman. *New Scientist*, 26 July 2023, www.newscientist.com/article/mg25934490-900-what-an-owl-knows-review-inside-the-world-of-this-mysterious-bird/. Accessed 16 Jan. 2024.

Worrall, Simon. "*What an Owl Knows* by Jennifer Ackerman Review." *The Guardian*, 29 June 2023, www.theguardian.com/books/2023/jun/29/what-an-owl-knows-by-jennifer-ackerman-review. Accessed 16 Jan. 2024.

When Crack Was King
A People's History of a Misunderstood Era

Author: Donovan X. Ramsey (b. 1987)
Publisher: One World (New York). 448 pp.
Type of work: History, sociology, current affairs
Time: 1965–the present day
Locales: New York; Los Angeles; Newark, New Jersey; Baltimore; Washington, DC

Alternating the in-depth stories of four individuals with historical and political background, journalist Donovan X. Ramsey paints a multifaceted portrait of the US crack epidemic of the 1980s and 1990s.

Principal personages
ELGIN SWIFT, a man who grew up in Yonkers, New York, during the height of the crack epidemic
LENNIE WOODLEY, a former crack addict and sex worker
KURT SCHMOKE, former mayor of Baltimore
SHAWN MCCRAY, community activist, basketball coach, and former drug dealer

In the 1980s and early 1990s, an epidemic of crack cocaine addiction hit American cities, disproportionately affecting Black Americans and other people of color. The prevalence of this highly addictive drug led to a generation of users whose lives essentially became ruined due to their use of the drug, as well as neighborhoods being torn apart by violence as dealers sought to stake out their territory. The epidemic, in turn, led to another wave of suffering for the communities most affected by the drug. As the government took a harsh response to the situation, focusing on criminalizing users rather than treating the epidemic as a health emergency, incarceration rates increased significantly, leaving communities decimated.

However a person looks at it, the epidemic was a dark time for the United States and particularly for Black American communities. According to journalist Donovan X. Ramsey, though, most people have traditionally looked at the epidemic incorrectly. In his 2023 book *When Crack Was King: A People's History of a Misunderstood Era*, he compellingly explains that the crack epidemic has often been viewed through a lens of demonization. Drawing on such stereotypes as the "crackhead" and the "superpredator," politicians and pundits have often sought to portray the people caught up in the epidemic, either as users or dealers, as subhuman individuals. This has allowed them to sell punitive measures to the American public that only made the situation worse. To this day, Ramsey illustrates poignantly, these images and stereotypes linger.

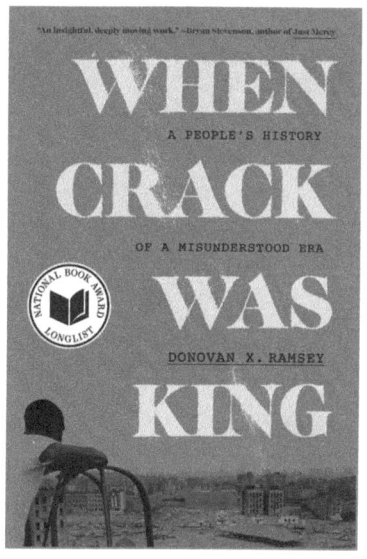

Donovan X. Ramsey

Ramsey's book is an intervention that aims to bring a wider understanding of the era to the reader. To do this, he divides his book between bigger-picture sections that provide historical background to the epidemic while detailing the official response and specific, personalized sections that follow four individuals whose lives became entwined with the epidemic in different ways. The result is a carefully woven tapestry that eloquently and seamlessly zooms in and out, providing a rich, comprehensive portrait of an era.

Ramsey's chapters dealing with the history leading up to the epidemic are especially eye-opening and allow the reader the full context necessary to understand the era. According to Ramsey, there were a variety of circumstances that helped account for the epidemic. On the supply side, the author explains how the government's focus on keeping heroin and marijuana out of the country, as well as their neglect in monitoring air trafficking, allowed international dealers like Pablo Escobar to fly in massive quantities of cocaine. Once dealers figured out how to cook the powder into a smokable, highly addictive rock form, known as "crack," the raw materials for an epidemic were in place.

At the same time, by the 1980s, many American cities had suffered from deindustrialization, with jobs that once sustained communities now no longer available. Black American communities were hit especially hard by this loss of jobs, and with many White people fleeing to the suburbs, these communities were often the subject of neglect by the authorities. This created desperate situations in many of these neighborhoods, where a lack of jobs and a lack of social services, exacerbated by the economic policies of the 1980s, led to a sense of desperation. Once crack was introduced to these neighborhoods, it provided a welcome escape to users. At the same time, it also presented a new economic opportunity for would-be dealers. As Ramsey explains in his typically nonjudgmental way, crack dealers were not creatures of pure evil as they were often portrayed in the press, but young people who were seizing the only chance to make money that was available to them.

If Ramsey does a good job explaining the background of the epidemic, it is the chapters dealing with the individuals affected by the epidemic that are at the heart of his book. He threads the stories of his four subjects throughout the book, doling out pieces of their story, chapter by chapter, and lining up their timelines with the historical chapters. These four subjects all have different relationships to the crack epidemic, and their stories show the different ways the epidemic affected communities. While Lennie Woodley's story is one of physical and sexual abuse as a child, leading to both a career as a sex worker and a heavy crack addiction, Shawn McCray's and Elgin Swift's find them working, somewhat reluctantly, as dealers. Finally, Ramsey tells the story of Kurt Schmoke, former mayor of Baltimore, whose efforts to combat the epidemic via a lenient policy of decriminalization met with mixed results.

Of the four subjects, Woodley's story is the most heartrending. Her childhood was spent in the 1960s and 1970s in South Los Angeles, in a Black American community. At first, she had a happy childhood, but her mother's behavior became increasingly erratic, leading to verbal and physical abuse. She also lived with her uncle, who was initially a confidante but soon began sexually abusing her. Before long, she discovered she could make a living as a sex worker by driving to a well-to-do White neighborhood and waiting until she was picked up by a man. After her first time having sex for money, while waiting for the bus, she met a man who gave her some cocaine. From there, her path was set as she became first a full-time sex worker and, later, once crack became easily available, an addict of that drug as well.

Woodley's story is particularly moving both because her life started out with plenty of promise and because it mirrors the decline of the Black American community where she grew up. She moved to the neighborhood from Florida when she was two and enjoyed her earliest years. Getting along with her family, she did well in school. Similarly, the neighborhood she lived in had a strong sense of community and was a good place to live for working-class Black Americans. During and immediately after World War II, many Black American people, including Woodley's uncle, had moved to the area and developed a thriving community. But just as her life took a negative turn due to her abuse, so did the fortunes of South Los Angeles soon change. Because of the departure of several factories and the lack of investment in the community, unemployment soon climbed and desperation sets in for many residents. When crack became widely available in the 1980s, it was only a matter of time before many people in the neighborhood, including Woodley, became hooked.

Woodley's story is filled with gruesome details, which Ramsey narrates subtly, making his point without giving in to lurid exposition or exploiting his subject. In general, he narrates the stories of his four subjects in a sympathetic voice that, while written in the third person, sticks very closely to their perspectives. It is easy to imagine the subjects telling Ramsey their stories in very similar terms to those in which he narrates them. These stories ultimately form the backbone of his ambitious book and, combined with the historical and political background, serve to craft a powerful portrait of an era that destroyed so many lives. Ramsey's book may not fully rewrite the common narrative of the crack epidemic, but it stands as an enlightening look at a time that too many people have failed to properly understand.

When Crack Was King, longlisted for the 2023 National Book Award for Nonfiction, received almost entirely positive reviews from critics. Writing for the *New York Times*, Jonathan Green was impressed by both Ramsey's ambition and his ability to cohesively pull together all of the book's threads. "Ramsey aims to give the story of the crack epidemic a human face while telling it from start to finish, a herculean task," Green wrote. "By and large he succeeds." Ilana Masad, reviewing the book for NPR, had a similar take. Calling the book "an excellent work of people-first journalism," she also praised the book for illustrating the ways that communities come together to help themselves in the face of adversity.

Some critics did have a few quibbles with the book. For example, Green felt that the book could have devoted more time to the homicide epidemic that resulted from the rise of crack cocaine. In his take, the narratives of the four main subjects tend a little too much toward uplift, at the expense of fully considering the consequences of some of their actions. Still, most critics had nothing but praise for *When Crack Was King*, applauding Ramsey's project for dispensing with damaging, perceived wisdom in favor of a fresh, more accurate perspective. Writing for the *Washington Post*, Zachary Siegel summed up this critical perspective, declaring that the book "is a master class in disrupting a stubborn narrative, a monumental feat for the fraught subject of addiction in Black communities."

By recasting the narrative, in both large-scale and intimate detail, Ramsey asks the reader to look anew at the era. Only by properly understanding this era, he argues, can politicians and other decision makers hope to avoid the negative lessons of the crack epidemic and make more humane decisions in the future. As Ramsey writes poignantly at the end of the book after describing a contemporary reality in which Black Americans still struggle against racial injustice as well as new challenges such as the COVID-19 pandemic, "If we fail to do this, to reckon with this history, we are doomed to repeat it."

Author Biography

Donovan X. Ramsey is a journalist whose work deals with race, identity, and power. His writing has featured in numerous publications, including the *New York Times*, *The Atlantic*, and the *Los Angeles Times*, where he worked as a staff reporter. *When Crack Was King* is his first book.

Andrew Schenker

Review Sources

Green, Jonathan. "Why Crack Became the 1980s 'Superdrug.'" Review of *When Crack Was King: A People's History of a Misunderstood Era*, by Donovan X. Ramsey. *The New York Times*, 11 July 2023, www.nytimes.com/2023/07/11/books/review/when-crack-was-king-donovan-ramsey.html. Accessed 17 Oct 2023.

Masad, Ilana. "*When Crack Was King* Follows Four People Who Lived through the Drug Epidemic." Review of *When Crack Was King: A People's History of a Misunderstood Era*, by Donovan X. Ramsey. *NPR*, 11 July 2023, www.npr.org/2023/07/11/1186750331/when-crack-was-king-follows-four-people-who-lived-through-the-drug-epidemic. Accessed 17 Oct 2023.

Siegel, Zachary. "Decades after the Crack Epidemic, We're Still Reckoning with Our Mistakes." Review of *When Crack Was King: A People's History of a Misunderstood Era*, by Donovan X. Ramsey. *The Washington Post*, 23 Aug 2023, www.washingtonpost.com/books/2023/08/23/crack-king-donovan-ramsey-review/. Accessed 17 Oct 2023.

White Cat, Black Dog

Author: Kelly Link (b. 1969)
Illustrator: Shaun Tan (b. 1974)
Publisher: Random House (New York). Illustrated. 272 pp.
Type of work: Short fiction
Time: Various
Locales: Various

In the short story collection White Cat, Black Dog, *acclaimed writer Kelly Link puts a modern, genre-blending spin on seven classic fairy tales.*

Principal characters
GARY, a middle-aged man who goes to incredible lengths to rescue his husband
PRINCE HAT, Gary's husband who has been kidnapped by the Queen of Hell
MIRANDA, a teenage seamstress in love with a ghost who only appears when it snows
ANAT, a young girl stuck on a small planet waiting for her parents to return
OSCAR, Anat's older brother, who takes care of her
ANDY, a graduate student getting paid to watch over a house with strange rules
SKINDER, the owner of the house where Andy is staying

For many critics, American author Kelly Link's work has always been difficult to pin down. She began her career writing stories for science-fiction and fantasy magazines in the 1990s before self-publishing her first collection, *Stranger Things Happen*, in 2001. In the years that followed, she gained a cult-like following thanks to her "slipstream" or "transrealism" literary style, which blends myriad genres to produce something completely new and different. Eventually, Link earned mainstream recognition for her radical approach to storytelling. Her 2016 short story collection *Get in Trouble* was a finalist for the Pulitzer Prize, and she was awarded a MacArthur "Genius" Grant in 2018.

While Link often included fairy tale influences in previous stories, these elements become the defining feature of the pieces in her 2023 collection *White Cat, Black Dog*. Each of the seven short stories in the book are each based on a specific folk story, clearly identified on their respective title pages. All of these source materials are Western in origin, but they are somewhat diverse within this scope, ranging from Brothers Grimm classics like "Hansel and Gretel" to the Scandinavian tale "East of the Sun, West of the Moon" and the Scottish ballad "Tam Lin." Yet readers do not need to be

Kelly Link

familiar with the original stories to appreciate the reinterpretations in *White Cat, Black Dog*, as most only loosely follow their inspirations.

Link's tendency to use the original fairy tales mainly as a jumping-off point for wider exploration is perhaps most evident in "The Game of Smash and Recovery," which is connected to "Hansel and Gretel." The story follows a young girl named Anat and her older brother Oscar, who live orbiting a small planet called Home that is also populated by alien vampires and more helpful creatures known as Handmaids. Written in third person, the narrative unfolds from the perspective of Anat, who knows little about her existence or the world around her except that her parents left when she was a baby but are supposed to be returning one day. In the meantime, Anat depends on Oscar to keep her safe. As they pass the time exploring the planet and playing a mysterious game, Anat begins to question what she has been told about who she is and what she and Oscar are doing on Home. While the story revolves around a brother and sister and deals with themes of trust and duplicity, little else is recognizable from the usual plot of "Hansel and Gretel." In this way, it illustrates just how unique and unpredictable Link's imagination can be, frequently taking readers into completely uncharted narrative territory.

Still, there are a few stories in the collection that do function more as relatively faithful retellings of the originals. The opening story, "The White Cat's Divorce," for example, stays quite true to its inspiration, Madame d'Aulnoy's French fairy tale "The White Cat," in its premise and many basic plot points. Both tell the tale of a powerful man who, seeking to delay handing down his fortune, tells his three sons that whichever of them finds him the smallest, most beautiful dog in all the land will be his heir. Undertaking this quest, the youngest son discovers a magical talking cat, who is happy to procure him a tiny dog and later help him fulfill further tasks set by his father. However, Link puts a playful, modern twist on the seventeenth-century template, turning d'Aulnoy's king into a narcissistic tech billionaire and the castle where his youngest son discovers the white cat into a marijuana greenhouse in Colorado. The result is witty satire of both fairy tale tropes and twenty-first century elites.

Humor continues to make regular appearances throughout *White Cat, Black Dog*. Link tends to execute this with a deadpan sensibility, often by simply highlighting the absurdity and selfishness of humans. For example, "Skinder's Veil" (an oblique take on the German fairy tale "Snow-White and Rose-Red") begins with graduate student Andy Sims struggling to write his dissertation in part because his roommate has recently found a girlfriend and made their apartment into a noisy lovers' den. Link relates this matter-of-factly, and writes, "Andy didn't begrudge any person's happiness, but was it possible that there could be such a thing as too much happiness?" Some of the collection's humor is also directly related to Link's embrace of standard fairy tale elements, from unexplained talking animals to more structural aspects such as rapid pacing and sudden endings. She makes particular use of arbitrarily important rules that the protagonist must follow; in "Skinder's Veil," Andy is given use of a cabin in the Vermont woods and told that he must allow whoever arrives at the back door inside without question but turn away the house's owner at the front door. Similarly, in "The Fox and the Lady," the teenaged Miranda can only see the ghost she is in love with if it snows—a rule she manages to get around by renting a snow machine.

Yet while there are many funny moments like these, the collection overall can hardly be categorized as purely comedic. There are many serious moments as well, and even the dry humor often has dark undercurrents. Like much of Link's previous work, then, *White Cat, Black Dog* can best be described as a blend of different genres and tones. These include magical realism, science fiction, fantasy, dystopia, and horror. Some of the stories themselves are more easily classified in specific genres than others. For instance, "The Game of Smash and Recovery" is certainly sci-fi with its interplanetary and technological focus, while "The White Road," in which a troupe of Shakespearean actors are being pursued by monsters while on the road in a post-apocalyptic America, fits under the umbrella of dystopian fiction. Many of the others, however, do not fit neatly into any category. It might be said that their defining characteristic is simply being strange, and it is a testament to Link's skill as a writer that this does not come across as gimmicky, but refreshingly interesting.

An illustrative example of this strangeness is "The Girl Who Did Not Know Fear," based on the similarly named folktale that traditionally features a male protagonist. Link's story is ostensibly about a professor who gets stuck in the city where she attended an academic conference because there are no flights home. She spends the next few days at the hotel, swimming in its pool at night as the urgency to get home to her wife and daughter steadily grows. When she finally gets on a plane, she gets caught up in an unsettling conversation with her seatmates and soon something begins to happen to her that completely undermines what readers might think the story was about all along. The steady sense of ominousness, dread, and unease found in "The Girl Who Did Not Know Fear" in many ways extends throughout the entirety of *White Cat, Black Dog*—these stories may be labeled as fairy tales but there are no typical "happily ever after" endings to be found.

In part, the book's unsettling atmosphere can be attributed to the themes that it explores. Death is a reoccurring motif, and is even personified in both "The White Cat's Divorce" and "Skinder's Veil." Fear is another frequent element across many of the stories. Taken as a collection, these works seem to reveal a preoccupation with middle age, loss, the passage of time, and solitude. Perhaps the story that best encapsulates this general tone and perspective is "Prince Hat Underground," inspired by "East of the Sun, West of the Moon." In it, the titular character suddenly disappears one day, which leads his partner, Gary, to go on perilous mission to try and bring him home. Link reveals that while Prince Hat has an unfaithful streak and has disappeared on Gary before, this time is different—he has been kidnapped by the Queen of Hell.

Gary's quest is often degrading and involves rats, snakes, and maggots. Yet he feels he has no choice because the alternative he can imagine is growing old and dying alone.

Reception of *White Cat, Black* dog was overwhelmingly positive. Many reviewers suggested that the book is further testament to Link being one of the best and most groundbreaking writers of her generation. The critic for *Kirkus Reviews* called the collection, "Enchanting, mesmerizing, brilliant work." Writing for *Vox*, Constance Grady noted, "Within these half-familiar story forms, Link's magic continually disrupts the ideas we think we have a solid grasp on. The worlds she builds are recognizable but fundamentally strange, other, not quite like anything you've ever seen before." Indeed, one of the most fascinating aspects of Link's fairy tales is how they break so many rules of both fiction writing and people's understanding of how life works that they rarely provide readers with easily decipherable conclusions. There are poignant emotional truths throughout the collection, but these often require dedicated effort and out-of-the-box thinking on the part of the reader. For some, this quality might be a deterrent, but many others will find it to be deeply rewarding. As Yvonne C. Garrett wrote in her review for the *Brooklyn Rail*, "I didn't want the spell to end and so, I will continue rereading this collection, discovering different details, different layers through each read. This is a truly well-wrought and magical work, rather than simple updates of fairy tales or fables, these stories have a chilling core and deep observations on modern life that we can all learn from."

Author Biography

Kelly Link is the author of several short-story collections, including *Stranger Things Have Happened* (2001), *Magic for Beginners* (2005), *Pretty Monsters* (2008), and *Get in Trouble* (2015). In addition to being a Pulitzer Prize finalist, she has received the Nebula Award, the Hugo Award, and the Bram Stoker Award. She is a co-founder of Small Beer Press.

Shaun Tan is an author and artist best known for his illustrations for children's books and young adult fiction. He won several awards for his graphic novel *The Arrival* (2006).

Emily E. Turner

Review Sources

Garrett, Yvonne. C. Review of *White Cat, Black Dog*, by Kelly Link. *The Brooklyn Rail*, Apr. 2023, brooklynrail.org/2023/04/books/Kelly-Links-White-Cat-Black-Dog. Accessed 9 Nov. 2023.

Grady, Constance. "Kelly Link Secures Her Crown as Queen of the Literary Fairy Tale." Review of *White Cat, Black Dog*, by Kelly Link. *Vox*, 10 Apr. 2023, www.vox.com/culture/23672639/white-cat-black-dog-kelly-link-review. Accessed 9 Nov. 2023.

Review of *White Cat, Black Dog*, by Kelly Link. *Kirkus Reviews*, 24 Jan. 2023, www.kirkusreviews.com/book-reviews/kelly-link/white-cat-black-dog/. Accessed 9 Nov. 2023.

The Wind Knows My Name

Author: Isabel Allende
Publisher: Ballantine Books (New York). 272 pp.
Translated from the Spanish by Frances Riddle
Type of work: Novel
Time: 1940–Present Day
Locales: San Francisco, California; Vienna, Austria; London, England; Nogales, Arizona

Isabel Allende's continent and generation spanning novel The Wind Knows My Name *explores the trauma of child separation, from the horrors of the lead up to World War II to US border policies that saw thousands of children taken from their parents.*

Principal characters

SAMUEL ADLER OR "BOGART," a young Austrian Jewish boy who flees the Nazi takeover of Europe
NADINE, Samuel's fiery wife
ANITA DIAZ, a young, blind Salvadoran girl who comes to the US with her mother after fleeing certain death at home
MARISOL, Anita's mother
LETICIA, a young Salvadoran woman who comes to the US as a child on her father's back after her family was killed in the El Mozote massacre
SELENA, a social worker representing separated children who aspires to become a lawyer.
FRANK, a young lawyer originally from Brooklyn who is a rising star in Los Angeles

Accomplished Chilean novelist Isabel Allende felt called to action over the family separation policies instituted at the US-Mexico border during the Trump administration that officially lasted from 2018 to 2021. She impelled her not-for-profit foundation to step in with support and worked on a novel that would chronicle the very real and personal trauma those policies created for many of the people impacted. That novel became *The Wind Knows My Name* (2023), which likens the US-Mexico border crisis to the sacrifices Jewish families made just prior to the outbreak of World War II, when activists organized the *Kindertransport*, a rescue effort that moved children from Nazi-occupied places in Europe and delivered them to safety elsewhere. Juxtaposing the outcome of one child saved by the *Kindertransport*, a young Austrian Jew named Samuel Adler, with the fate of a young blind Salvadoran girl named Anita Diaz

Isabel Allende

(who becomes separated from her mother at the US border in the present day after experiencing horror in her home country), the dots of history begin to connect. Allende adds additional layers to her novel by including a wide range of characters with diverse backgrounds, which allows their relationships to deepen the story and make it a universally relatable tale. Moments of violence and hopelessness are laid opposite real emotional connection and relationships that span continents and cultures. Allende delivers all of this with clear, precise prose that allows the experiences and emotions of her characters to shape the story and give new voice to some of the darkest moments in human history.

The Wind Knows My Name begins with two epigraphs: one, a quote from Antoine de Saint-Exupéry's *The Little Prince* (1943) stating in part, "Anything essential is invisible to the eyes." The other comes from Anita. Throughout the book Anita references traveling to an enchanted kingdom called Azabahar, where anyone can go if they know how to imagine and will be reunited with those people and animals who they miss most. She says of the kingdom, "It's even better than heaven, because you don't have to die to go there." These epigraphs set up some of the central tenets of the book, as many of its characters long for a place they cannot see but move blindly toward to make their lives or the lives of their children better. That place, one might suppose, is responsible for all their difficult decisions and hardships experienced. It offers a lasting hope for both the parents who have sacrificed to provide some sort of safety for their children and the children who have suffered tremendously and are often the pawns in a heartless political game.

Allende's novel is a masterful weaving of lives, beginning first with the Adler family as the Nazis are taking hold of the European continent. The chapter is written is such a way as to expose the very ordinary lives of these people. Samuel's father owns a pharmacy and the family lives in a nicely appointed apartment in a modest part of the city. The reader sees Samuel at his music lessons and his father at work, all against the backdrop of the growing hatred towards Jews throughout Nazi Germany. When the *Kristallnacht*, or night of broken glass, occurs in 1938, Samuel's father is captured and taken to a detention center and Samuel and his mother hide in a neighbor's apartment. Soon after, Samuel is on his way to England on a caravan with many other young Jewish children. His mother promises that they will be reunited as she kisses him goodbye, a luxury that Anita's mother, Marisol, does not experience.

The reader meets Leticia and her family in a similar way. Their day-to-day life living in El Mozote, El Salvador, is also quite ordinary. However, Leticia falls ill and her father must take her away to a nearby city to be treated. During this period, their village is destroyed by units of the Salvadoran Army's Atlácatl Battalion, which was trained by US advisers in the 1980s and later investigated by the United Nations for war crimes. Allende does not shy away from delving into the details of these events and questioning who else might be responsible for the terrors. This is particularly effective because of the ease of her prose—she allows the space required for heavy facts to be taken in. Similarly, when Anita and Marisol's story is told, the question of what makes a refugee is investigated. Marisol has taken Anita and fled to the US after being threatened and then shot by a man named Carlos Gómez. The reader realizes there is no way the pair could have stayed in the country and is presented with what happens when they reach the border: Anita is put into a child detention center, while Marisol is sent to Mexico where she is to await a hearing that will decide if she can enter the country. Soon after this happens, Marisol disappears. Characters Selena and Frank take on Anita's case, chasing every lead that might bring them closer to finding Marisol, including taking a trip to El Salvador where they meet Carlos as well as Anita's beloved grandmother.

The method in which each character is introduced in individual chapters allows for a more emotional investigation of both the family separation policy and how people from different conflicts and continents are treated. Samuel, though devastated by the loss of his family and abused in children's shelters, can build a stable life for himself; the only real instability often comes from his highly artistic and fiery wife Nadine. Equally, Leticia, though also from El Salvador like Marisol and Anita, can build a life for herself in San Francisco. Working as a cleaner, her path intersects with Samuel's, changing both of their lives and Anita's in the process. Because of the pacing and structure, when the novel's final revelations take place, the effect is even more impactful because of the various perspectives.

The Wind Knows My Name was widely hailed by critics and received a starred review ahead of its publication by *Publishers Weekly*, who called the book an "authentic and emotionally harrowing work." For the *New York Times*, author Lauren Fox wrote, "'The Wind Knows My Name' contains little of the magic that defined Allende's earlier novels. Instead, she turns her focus to the brutal details of government-sponsored violence and asks her reader to look closely at the devastation." The book was also reviewed by NPR, whose critic Marcela Davison Avilés noted that five decades into her career, Allende has imbued her storytelling with "lyrical romanticism" marked by "roads imposed by social and political turmoil." Aviles notes that the crux of 2023's civic discourse is found in two topics, immigration and identity, with a focus on "who belongs and who doesn't." She writes, "In Allende's version healing is possible, because empathy is a hopeful, albeit inconsistent, follower of migration." Though the book was widely well received, an anonymous reviewer for *Kirkus Reviews* noted that the book is written largely in exposition with characters that "never come to life." The critic notes, "Allende is too caught up in drawing historical and political parallels to imbue her characters with life."

Despite the family separation policy coming to an end in 2021 after Joe Biden won the 2020 presidential election, the ramifications of the policy are still evident: some statistics report that around one thousand children remained separated from their family. If Allende's story, with its parallel political storylines comparing the Nazi regime and its effects on marked children and adults to the Trump administration's border policies might sometimes feel a bit too neat, the shared bond between Samuel, whose life was forever marked by that solo train ride to England as a five-year-old boy, and Anita, who has to find her way in the world on her own, signifies the lasting sadness and trauma these events create, but also the hope one finds in human connection.

Author Biography

Isabel Allende is the author of many novels, including *The House of the Spirits* (1982), *Of Love and Shadows* (1984), and *Violeta* (2022). Her books have sold more than seventy million copies and have been translated into more than forty-two languages. She has received the Presidential Medal of Freedom, the Chilean National Prize for Literature, the Library of Congress Creative Achievement Award for Fiction, and the National Book Foundation Medal for Distinguished Contribution to American Letters, among many other honors.

Translator Frances Riddle's work includes English translations of several Spanish-language authors, including Isabel Allende, María Fernanda Ampuero, Sara Gallardo, Leila Guerriero, and Claudia Piñeiro. Riddle's translation of Piñeiro's *Elena Knows* was shortlisted for the International Booker Prize in 2022, and her translation of Allende's *Violeta* was a New York Times Best Seller.

Melynda Fuller

Review Sources

Avilés, Marcela Davison. "'The Wind Knows My Name' Is a Reference and a Refrain in the Search for Home." Review of *The Wind Knows My Name*, by Isabel Allende. Translated by Frances Riddle. *NPR*, 10 June 2023, www.npr.org/2023/06/10/1180103464/book-review-isabel-allende-novel-the-wind-knows-my-name. Accessed 28 Sept. 2023.

Fox, Lauren. "Isabel Allende Has a Message: History Repeats Itself." Review of *The Wind Knows My Name*, by Isabel Allende. Translated by Frances Riddle. *The New York Times*, 3 June 2023, www.nytimes.com/2023/06/03/books/review/the-wind-knows-my-name-isabel-allende.html. Accessed 28 Sept. 2023.

Francesca, Vanessa. "Ambitious and Moving, This Heartfelt Novel Is a True Gift." Review of *The Wind Knows My Name*, by Isabel Allende. Translated by Frances Riddle. *The Sydney Morning Herald*, 26 June 2023, www.smh.com.au/culture/books/allende-shows-her-compassion-in-a-novel-of-separation-and-tragedy-20230614-p5dgj3.html. Accessed 28 Sept. 2023.

Tanguay, Brian. Review of *The Wind Knows My Name*, by Isabel Allende. Translated by Frances Riddle. *The Santa Barbara Independent*, 18 Aug. 2023, www.independent.com/2023/08/18/book-review-the-wind-knows-my-name-by-isabel-allende/. Accessed 28 Sept. 2023.

Review of *The Wind Knows My Name*, by Isabel Allende. Translated by Frances Riddle. *Kirkus Reviews*, www.kirkusreviews.com/book-reviews/isabel-allende/the-wind-knows-my-name/. Accessed 26 Sept. 2023

Review of *The Wind Knows My Name*, by Isabel Allende. Translated by Frances Riddle. *Publishers Weekly*, 21 Mar. 2023, www.publishersweekly.com/9780593598108. Accessed 26 Sept. 2023.

"The Wind Knows My Name: Isabel Allende's Newest Novel Was Inspired by Family Separations at the U.S. Border." *Milwaukee Independent*, 16 June 2023, www.milwaukeeindependent.com/newswire/wind-knows-name-isabel-allendes-newest-novel-inspired-family-separations-u-s-border/. Accessed 26 Sept. 2023.

The Windeby Puzzle
History and Story

Author: Lois Lowry (b. 1937)
Publisher: Clarion Books (New York). Illustrated. 224 pp.
Type of work: Novel, history, memoir
Time: Iron Age to present
Locale: Northern Germany

In The Windeby Puzzle, *a unique blend of historical facts and fictional imaginings, Lowry enchants and educates young readers about teenage life during the Iron Age and the existence of bog people.*

Principal characters
ESTRILD, a teenage girl who lived during the Iron Age and who dreams of becoming a warrior
VARICK, her friend, a teenage boy who lived during the Iron Age

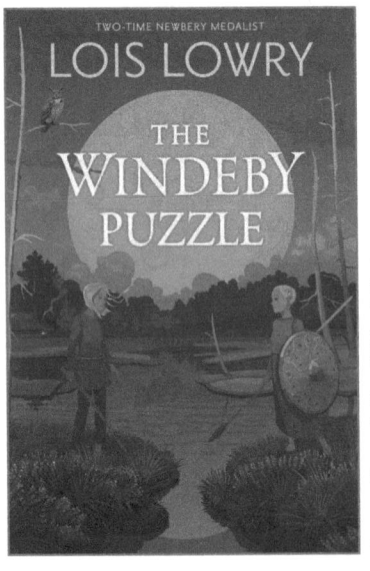

In *The Windeby Puzzle: History and Story*, revered children's writer Lois Lowry demonstrates that she remains an inventive and masterful writer late in her career, creating a unique book that effortlessly combines historical facts, historical fiction, and insight into her own writing process. While in most cases authors choose to clearly delineate one genre for their books, whether fiction, nonfiction, or memoir, Lowry here presents historical facts for background information and then brings those facts to life through fictional imaginings of what people at a particular time period—in this case, the Iron Age—might have experienced and makes those characters come alive. In the historical sections, Lowry also explains how and why stories are written as well as why she made the decisions she did as she put facts together and constructed characters. The result is an engaging book that educates, enchants, and offers insight into Lowry's writing process.

Lowry's inspiration for the book was her hope of solving the puzzle of the Windeby Girl. In 1952 in northern Germany on the Windeby Estate, workers uncovered the human remains of someone who was later determined to be a teenage girl, covered for centuries in a peat bog. Lowry explains that the specific organic makeup of peat, a particular kind of highly acidic soil that develops naturally in cold, swampy areas, preserves dead bodies unlike any other material because it keeps intact facial features, hair, and even fingernails. Peat bogs substantially slow down the decomposition of human bodies, and "bog bodies," as they are sometimes known, have been found before,

Lois Lowry — Courtesy HarperCollins Children's Books

such as the famous Koelbjerg Woman from approximately 8,000 BCE, among hundreds of others.

The Windeby Girl, however, is unlike most of the previously found bog bodies. For one, she does not appear to have died a violent death, as most of the others had, and for another, she was a young teenager and not an adult. With further examination, the Windeby Girl's remains were thought to be about two thousand years old, from what is known as the Iron Age (ca. 1200 BCE to 550 BCE), a time when iron tools and weapons were first developed but the Germanic tribes had yet to create written language; consequently, historians know little about the people who lived at this time. Thus, Lowry's impetus for writing *The Windeby Puzzle* was to solve a historical mystery of how the teenager might have died, but also to create a character, whom she named Estrild, that children and young teens could relate to, learn from, and understand, built on the available facts and Lowry's informed imagination.

There are five sections to *The Windeby Puzzle*. Sections 1, 3, and 5 delve into historical facts and Lowry's discussion of her writing process. Sections 2 and 4, which are significantly longer, are the fictional chapters that focus on Estrild, the Windeby Girl, and then Varick, Estrild's friend, and tell their stories vividly and believably.

Before Lowry begins Estrild's story, she reviews the research in the first historical section and speculates on how the Windeby Girl might have died. These causes included being some kind of ritual sacrifice, being punished for committing adultery, or becoming one of "those who disgrace their bodies [and] are drowned in miry swamps." All three reasons could explain an apparently nonviolent death, and Lowry also notes the importance of several details in the photograph of the Windeby Girl's body, which is included in the book. Of special significance is the detail that the Windeby Girl seemed to be blindfolded, as her eyes were covered with a woven ribbon or band, which eventually plays a key role in Estrild's story. Ultimately, Lowry decides on the third possible reason, of Estrild "disgrac[ing] her body" by trying to become a warrior, something only the males in her village are allowed to do. Lowry concedes later, in the second historical section, that her interpretation of Estrild's life is unlikely, and it is indeed a modern and feminist one, yet certainly one modern-day young woman and girls could relate to and be inspired by. Though unlikely in historical accuracy, Lowry's portrait of Estrild and her hopes and dreams of becoming a warrior are rendered realistically and with great heart.

Lowry is especially creative and adept at using known details of the Iron Age to place Estrild as a young woman in her village and describe what her life would have been like at that time, caring for her many younger siblings and helping her mother.

There would also be rigid gender roles, with women caring for their homes, children, and domesticated animals, and men and boys plowing in the fields and keeping their home and land safe from intruders. Because of her ambition to become a warrior, Estrild feels like an outsider, and she keeps her ambition from everyone except her friend Varick, who has his own struggles and ambitions. An orphan whose physical disability, a deeply curved spine, limits his ability to walk and work, Varick is nonetheless able to assist the local iron worker to forge swords and shields. He also has an affinity for birds and other animals and has studied their anatomy, and it is through this interest and Varick helping Estrild become a warrior like his father that he and Estrild build a friendship. At one point Varick gives Estrild a bird skeleton that she can hone into a clasp for her woven shawl, and she hopes she will find the time to work on it apart from doing her seemingly endless chores. Lowry found research on another bog person who had a clasp on her shawl made from bird bones, and she incorporated those details, as well as details about forging iron and life in an Iron Age village, into Estrild's story to create a colorful, historically accurate, and riveting tale.

After Estrild's story concludes, Lowry moves into the next historical section, where she discusses a dramatic revelation. New research by archeologist Dr. Heather Gill-Robinson determined that the Windeby Girl is really the sixteen-year-old Windeby Boy. Lowry astutely made this new information a part of her book. New technologies in DNA analysis and 3-D imaging had been developed since the Windeby bog body was discovered, and research conclusions were re-examined and updated. Rather than ignoring the new research and abandoning Estrild's story, Lowry wrote a second story on the Windeby Boy, elevating Varick from friend of Estrild to the protagonist in his own story. Lowry explained that the new research indicated the boy was ill, malnourished, and most likely died of natural causes. The "blindfold" over his eyes was not a blindfold but was most likely a headband that had fallen down to his eyes over time or while those 1952 workers on the Windeby Estate excavated his body. Lowry imagines, in Varick, a young man who is sickly and underfed and has few prospects because of his disability, but also someone who has a keen and questioning mind, especially in relation to animals and anatomy. His disability is evident, and he is ostracized because of it, but he finds some peace through his own proto-scientific research on animals and bones and his time in the forest. Lowry writes an equally vivid and poignant story for Varick, despite his short life.

Critics have overwhelmingly praised *The Windeby Puzzle*. Tracy Cronce, in a starred review for *School Library Journal*, called the book "expertly written and beautifully engaging." Cronce went on to conclude, "Readers will be transfixed with actual photographs and more than one explanation of this grim mystery." The photographs of the Windeby Girl and included illustrations, particularly of owls, contribute significantly to the reader's enjoyment of the book and their understanding of the science of bog people. Additionally, Marissa Moss, in the *New York Journal of Books*, deemed *The Windeby Puzzle* "ingenious" and stated that "we all have stories to tell, and Lowry provides a shining example of what a gift these stories can be." Reviewers especially admired how Lowry wove the three elements of historical facts, fiction, and discussion of her writing process together in a comprehensive yet effortless way. They also appreciated Lowry's discussion of her writing process and believed young readers would be equally fascinated. *New York Times* reviewer Laura Amy Schlitz summed up this perspective well, stating, "*The Windeby Puzzle* is structurally strange and beautifully crafted, zigzagging, as its subtitle announces, between history and story."

Surprisingly, most critics, with the exception of Schlitz, praised Estrild's story but neglected Varick's story and sometimes did not mention it at all. Possibly the feminist angle of Estrild wanting to be a warrior like her brothers and deceased uncle resonated more with reviewers than Varick's quieter, more introspective story, but Lowry tells both stories, while very different, with equal skill, weight, and tenderness. Varick's story is just as poignant as Estrild's story.

In telling Estrild's and Varick's stories, Lowry notably chooses to focus on their lives and not the imagined details of their deaths, believing that people live on after death when someone remembers them and writes their story. Estrild's and Varick's stories, and their history in the Iron Age, are memorable, and they live because Lois Lowry has told their story.

Author Biography

Lois Lowry, a best-selling and acclaimed author of children's literature, is a two-time winner of the Newbery Medal for her children's novels *Number the Stars* (1989) and *The Giver* (1993). She has written dozens of works of fiction, as well as several autobiographical books.

Marybeth Rua-Larsen

Review Sources

Cronce, Tracy. Review of *The Windeby Puzzle*, by Lois Lowry. *School Library Journal*, 1 Mar. 2023, www.slj.com/review/the-windeby-puzzle. Accessed 17 Jan. 2024.

Moss, Marissa. Review of *The Windeby Puzzle*, by Lois Lowry. *New York Journal of Books*, 14 Feb. 2023, www.nyjournalofbooks.com/book-review/windeby-puzzle-history-and-story. Accessed 17 Jan. 2024.

Schlitz, Laura Amy. "Lois Lowry Breathes New Life into a 2,000-Year-Old Child." Review of *The Windeby Puzzle*, by Lois Lowry. *The New York Times*, 10 Feb. 2023, www.nytimes.com/2023/02/10/books/review/lois-lowry-the-windeby-puzzle.html. Accessed 17 Jan. 2024.

Review of *The Windeby Puzzle*, by Lois Lowry. *Kirkus Reviews*, 14 Feb. 2023, www.kirkusreviews.com/book-reviews/lois-lowry/the-windeby-puzzle. Accessed 17 Jan. 2024.

Review of *The Windeby Puzzle*, by Lois Lowry. *Publishers Weekly*, 23 Nov. 2022, www.publishersweekly.com/9780358672500. Accessed 17 Jan. 2024.

Witness

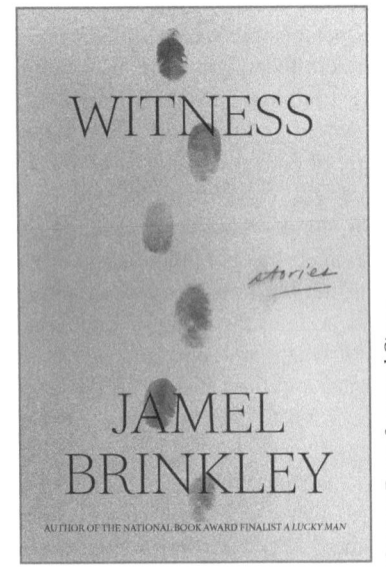

Author: Jamel Brinkley
Publisher: Farrar, Straus and Giroux (New York). 240 pp.
Type of work: Short fiction
Time: Present day
Locale: New York, New York

In this insightful collection of ten short stories, Jamel Brinkley explores the inherent tension that exists between observation and action in life.

Principal characters
REGINALD, a homeless man who gets a job as a volunteer at an animal sanctuary
SIMONE, a woman whose brother was killed by a White police officer
ANITA, a mother who wants to control her teenage daughter
DANDY, Anita's daughter, who has become increasingly hostile and unmanageable
GLORIA, a woman nearing retirement after almost forty years working at a hotel
BEVERLY, a young girl who loves dancing
SILAS, a young man living on his sister Bernice's couch
BERNICE, Silas' sister, who is suffering from symptoms the doctors keep ignoring

In 2018, writer Jamel Brinkley made his book-length debut with *A Lucky Man*, a collection of nine short stories united by their thematic exploration of the contemporary Black American male experience. The book was extremely well-received, winning multiple literary honors and becoming a finalist for several others, notably including the prestigious National Book Award. In his second collection, *Witness* (2023), Brinkley further demonstrates his talent in short fiction. With ten intimate stories that continue to highlight vividly realistic characters grappling with myriad challenges and small triumphs in their everyday lives, Brinkley solidifies his place as a rising literary star.

As with *A Lucky Man*, Brinkley focuses on life in New York City throughout *Witness*. While geographically restricted, the pieces reflect the city's vibrant diversity by featuring a wide range of characters and conflicts. The result is a group of stories that successfully achieves an overarching sense of connection even as each individual entry contains its own unique atmospheres, worldviews, and ideas. Indeed, moving from story to story within this collection becomes a journey through different literary styles, tones, and narrative points of view.

Jamel Brinkley (photo: Courtesy Farrar, Straus and Giroux; ©Daniele Molajoli)

The first story, "Blessed Deliverance," for example, uses both the fourth-person perspective of "we" and the first-person "I" to relay the experience of a boy in a group of five Brooklyn teenagers whose friendship is dwindling until they are reunited by the revelation that a homeless man they used to make fun of has started a job at a recently opened animal sanctuary in their neighborhood. To transport readers into the narrator's worldview, Brinkley deftly gives his prose an adolescent tone. In contrast, the later story "Sahar" has a much more neutral voice as it follows a woman nearing retirement named Gloria, who feels compelled to write letters on her phone to the person who delivers her takeout meals. Yet the main third-person omniscient narrative is broken up by the inclusion of Gloria's letters, which are written in first-person and clearly reflect someone who is lonely, frustrated, and questioning their place in the world.

Many of the challenges that the characters of *Witness* face prove especially compelling because they have timeless qualities and yet also touch on pressing contemporary issues. This dichotomy appears in the underlying theme in "Blessed Deliverance" of struggling with change: while time's ceaseless march forward is a perennial issue, the story's exploration of gentrification showcases a specific modern phenomenon. Similarly, "Sahar" combines Gloria's timeless desire for human connection and feeling like she matters with a critique of contemporary economic factors that can contribute to alienation. Without coming across as overly sentimental or didactic, Brinkley leverages enduring themes and emotions to communicate the gravity of modern problems—whether it is the erosion of community that accompanies gentrification or how today's gig economy undermines people's ability to survive both financially and spiritually.

In several stories, Brinkley turns this insightful method of social commentary to the issue of racial injustice, specifically against Black Americans. The short story "Comfort," for example, features a woman named Simone who is stuck in a cycle of self-destructive grief four years after her brother was killed by a White police officer. The title story, "Witness," provides a chilling look into the dangerous ubiquity of medical racism. While certainly grounded in twenty-first century racial issues, such stories also hint at the deep historical roots of racial injustice in America, making them all the more effective and reinforcing the understated power of Brinkley's literary approach.

One defining quality of many of the stories that comprise *Witness* is that they focus on small but pivotal moments in their characters' lives. In "Arrows," a man named Hasan finds himself arguing with his mother's ghost about moving his father into an assisted care facility and selling the family home to pay for it. In "The Happiest House on Union Street," a young girl named Beverly passes out while dancing, which causes new tensions between her father and uncle that have serious consequences for the Brooklyn brownstone they all share. In "The Let-Go," a young man spends an afternoon at a museum with a beautiful older woman who completely transforms his understanding of his father and childhood by offering new context. Like many masters of short fiction before him, Brinkley proves that high-concept premises are not necessary to make a story memorable, and sometimes examining everyday experiences to illustrate their significance within the big picture can create the most resonance.

Within these small but important moments, the stories of *Witness* are united by the thematic idea that people can either observe their lives unfolding or take action to set their own direction. Brinkley establishes this idea upfront by quoting the writer James Baldwin in the first of three epigraphs: "I was to discover that the line which separates a witness from an actor is a very thin line indeed; nevertheless, the line is real." This "thin line" comes into play in "Blessed Deliverance," for example. The narrator and his friends initially gawk at the man they used to mockingly call "Headass," literally and figuratively serving as passive observers. However, after the man is fired by his White employers and begins unleashing chaos on the neighborhood, the narrator steps forward to offer support, becoming, however slightly, an actor in his own life and the life of his community as it faces gentrification.

Brinkley also illustrates how people often struggle to be a true witness to their own lives, as doing so would threaten their positive self-image. In "Bystander," a devoted wife mother named Anita attempts to control her teenage daughter Dandy, who has been acting out by refusing to eat, picking fights with her, and engaging in online arguments about political issues. Anita does everything she thinks is right to try and help her daughter—which includes spying on her and forcing her to eat certain foods to get her to gain weight. However, when it turns out that Dandy's behavior is largely the effects of a serious health condition that Anita has exacerbated, she is forced to come face-to-face with the fact that, in many ways, she is a bad mother. This unwillingness to be a witness to one's own reality is shared by characters in several other stories as well, like Simone in "Comfort," who uses drinking, drugs, and sex to cope with her grief, or the narrator in "Bartow Station," who has found many ways to avoid confronting the trauma of his past. As Brinkley demonstrates, however, such avoidance can only go on for so long before dangerous consequences begin to erupt.

Reception of *Witness* was highly positive, with the collection named a best book of the year by numerous outlets including the *New York Times Book Review*, the *Los Angeles Times*, and NPR. It was also longlisted for the Joyce Carol Oates Prize and the Carnegie Medal for Excellence and made the shortlist for the Kirkus Prize, among other honors. Many critics hailed it as a worthy follow-up to *A Lucky Man* that further marked Brinkley as a writer in full command of the short-fiction medium. In his review for the *New York Times*, for example, Mateo Askaripour wrote, "Brinkley is a writer whose versatility knows no boundaries. He can make you laugh, cry, contemplate life's deepest questions, remember what it was like to be a child, and feel the warmth, or chill, of your own family history. Tapping into the sticky stuff of humanity, each story is a gift of the highest quality, reminding us that we are all both in the audience and on life's stage, even if we don't know it." Other reviewers agreed in praising

Brinkley's range and ability to transport readers into completely different experiences with each story, even given the fact that the pieces all take place in the same city at the same time within similar communities. Ultimately, he succeeds in demonstrating just how disparate and complex people's experiences can be no matter how their lives may appear to outsiders.

Another common point of praise among critics was for the well-crafted, unique characters that populate the pages of *Witness*, and in particular how many of them illuminate contemporary Black experience in nuanced ways. "Brinkley crafts unforgettable portraits, humming with barely restrained tension, of Black men and women exploring what it means to be part of families and communities that are awash in hope and disappointment alike," the reviewer for *Publishers Weekly* remarked. "These intimate vignettes have the power to move readers." Indeed, the rich characterization is a central strength of *Witness*, and for some readers the collection's wide cast may help the collection resonate even more than *A Lucky Man*, which focuses much more exclusively on male characters.

However, others may not feel that *Witness* quite reaches the same heights as its widely acclaimed predecessor. Such was the opinion of Houman Barekat, who wrote for the *Guardian* that while "*A Lucky Man* was an uncommonly subtle and poised debut, *Witness* is an accomplished but patchier effort." Barekat found Brinkley's messaging at times too heavy-handed, especially in the title story, and wished for more variety in approach to the theme of gentrification throughout the collection. Of course, such critiques may largely come down to personal taste. Notably, many other critics found "Witness" to be a standout story, as evidenced by the fact that it won an O. Henry Award in 2021 after its original publication in the *Paris Review*. Most readers will find *Witness* an exceptional effort thanks to Brinkley's ability to use deft, original storytelling as a vessel for powerful insights into the human condition.

Author Biography

Jamel Brinkley's acclaimed short fiction has appeared in the *Paris Review*, the *Yale Review*, and many other publications. His debut collection, *A Lucky Man* (2018), was a National Book Award finalist and received the Ernest J. Gaines Award for Literary Excellence, among other honors.

Emily E. Turner

Review Sources

Askaripour, Mateo. "What Does It Mean to Be a Witness?" Review of *Witness*, by Jamel Brinkley. *The New York Times*, 31 July 2023, www.nytimes.com/2023/07/31/books/review/witness-jamel-brinkley.html. Accessed 1 Jan. 2024.

Barekat, Houman. "Downbeat Tales of New York." Review of *Witness*, by Jamel Brinkley. *The Guardian*, 9 Aug. 2023, www.theguardian.com/books/2023/aug/09/witness-by-jamel-brinkley-review-downbeat-tales-of-new-york. Accessed 1 Jan. 2024.

Review of *Witness*, by Jamel Brinkley. *Kirkus Reviews*, 24 May 2023, www.kirkus-reviews.com/book-reviews/jamel-brinkley/witness-brinkley/. Accessed 10 Jan. 2024.

Review of *Witness*, by Jamel Brinkley. *Publishers Weekly*, 26 May 2023, www.publishersweekly.com/9780374607036. Accessed 10 Jan. 2024.

Women We Buried, Women We Burned

Author: Rachel Louise Snyder (b. ca. 1969)
Publisher: Bloomsbury (New York).
  Illustrated. 272 pp.
Type of work: Memoir
Time: 1977–present
Locales: Pittsburgh, Pennsylvania; Chicago, Illinois; Phnom Penh, Cambodia; London, England; Washington, DC

Rachel Louise Snyder's fourth book, Women We Buried, Women We Burned *(2023), tells how she became a journalist, activist, and author, and why she began specializing in reporting about domestic abuse and violence.*

Principal personages

RACHEL LOUISE SNYDER, the author and narrator
GAIL SNYDER, her deceased mother
RICHARD "DICK" SNYDER, her father
BARBARA SNYDER, her stepmother
DAVID, her older brother
JAZZ, her daughter
AARON AND HOLLY, her stepsiblings, Barbara's children from a prior marriage
JOHN-JOHN AND JOSHUA, her younger half-brothers, Richard and Barbara's children
ANN MAXWELL, her longtime friend and frequent world traveling companion

Memoirs, like Rachel Louise Snyder's *Women We Buried, Women We Burned* (2023), are similar in certain aspects to autobiographies. Both memoirs and autobiographies focus on a particular individual and are traditionally written by that person. Both are presumably honest in detailing the history of a life. Both often contain documentation to verify what is written (Snyder's memoir contains photos highlighting important points of her life). There are also differences between the two forms. Though an autobiography is usually a chronological record from birth onward, a memoir may start anywhere and deal with periods of time that are thematically significant to the author. Autobiographies are concerned mostly with facts, while memoirs deal with the author's feelings and opinions. Though the authors of both forms are subject to possible legal ramifications (defamation, invasion of privacy) for writing about real people in a less-than-flattering manner and risk personal consequences from family, friends and colleagues offended by secrets revealed, memoirs are usually not affected because feelings and opinions are not subject to lawsuits. In any event, Snyder's memoir, written in clear, compelling prose, is not afraid to name names.

Born to Gail, who was Jewish, and Richard, a Christian who had converted to Judaism to marry her, Snyder writes that both her parents "had been raised with a lackluster commitment to their respective religions" and celebrated both Jewish and Christian holidays and traditions as they raised Snyder and her older brother, David. When Snyder was eight, her mother died, age thirty-five, of breast cancer. While the death of a parent is distressing for a child, for Snyder, the experience was truly life-altering. As she writes: "Cancer took my mother. But religion would take my life." After her mother's death, "Judaism [was] summarily erased" from her family's household, and her father became a born-again Christian. Two years and one girlfriend later, he met another woman, Barbara, a divorcee with two children, at an evangelical revival. Barbara's children (given the pseudonyms Aaron and Holly) were near the ages of Snyder and her brother. The six-person family left Pittsburgh, the only place she had known, relocating to the Chicago area, where Richard and Barbara married.

Rachel Louise Snyder

The family was integrated into a fundamentalist Christian evangelical community, headed by Snyder's aunt and uncle, that was influenced by the teachings of motivational speaker Zig Ziglar and faith healer Kathryn Kuhlman. "These were the early days of American Evangelism," Snyder writes, "the movement that preached health and wealth as a birthright for the righteous."

Reluctantly, Snyder attended her aunt and uncle's religious school, Faith Center Christian Academy (FCCA) in Downers Grove, where she was taught by a system known as Personal Accelerated Christian Education, or PACE, which included academic subjects as well as theology. FCCA banned secular music and movies. Students were indoctrinated through such films as *A Thief in the Night*, the first installment in a 1970s evangelical Christian film series about the terrors associated with the lack of preparation for the rapture and the tribulation of the end times, when, according to doctrine, believers will be resurrected and nations will be judged in the aftermath. The film, which maintains that everything in the Bible is the actual truth, frightened Snyder.

Snyder bided her time, gaining strength and maturity before beginning her rebellion against what she considered intolerable conditions. When FCCA failed financially in the early 1980s and she, David, and Aaron transferred to Naperville North High School, she began acting out. She ran away from home several times. She took up smoking cigarettes and marijuana and experimented with drugs like LSD. She began drinking wine and listened to rock music in secret. She had sex with several different young men, including her stepsister's boyfriend, who assaulted her when she was underage. When she fell far behind in her studies, she was expelled from high school in her sophomore year.

In an effort to control the four oldest children, Richard (who had his own problems, including a tendency to make bad investments in dubious, get-rich-quick schemes, like multilevel marketers, California real estate, currency trading) imposed new rules. Snyder, her brother, and stepsiblings had specific curfews, strict orders about TV watching, household chores, church attendance, daily devotions, and other religious activities. When the four kids could not live up to their parents' expectations, they were forced to leave home. Richard and Barbara lined up four empty suitcases and told the children, "Pick one." Snyder took "the most colorful suitcase, a dark blue and maroon soft-bodied Samsonite."

Even in her early teens, Snyder proved to be resilient and resourceful, unafraid to try new, unfamiliar things. In survival mode, she began working menial jobs—restaurant server, receptionist, filing clerk—and living with acquaintances or coworkers, where she often witnessed incidents of domestic violence. She briefly attended Barbizon modeling school in New York City, where for a time she earned a living booking a garage band named White Lie into nightclubs. She created a promo pack (demo cassette tape, photographs, and bios of the band members), met in person with the most influential individual in the local industry, and cultivated other resources, obtaining a reference for every live-music venue and every music festival in the midwestern states. She learned how to improve her chances of profiting from the work as a successful band agent from a recording engineer named Frank, whom she ended up dating.

As Snyder aged—finally becoming adult enough to rent an apartment, sign a lease, apply for a credit card, open a checking account, and put utilities in her own name—she made better decisions. She earned her Graduate Educational Development (GED) diploma. With the aid of a Pell Grant and student loans, she graduated from college, then attended grad school. A turning point in her life came when her uncle Robert offered to pay half of her twelve-thousand-dollar Semester at Sea tuition, which enabled her to enroll in the program. To earn the other half, she tutored, answered want ads, cleaned apartments, and installed cable channels in Ohio motel chains. The opportunity to sail around the globe—visiting Japan, South Africa, India, Kenya, and China—was an unparalleled learning experience, which forever after ignited her desire to travel the world.

In the 2000s, after managing a squalid apartment building in Oak Park, Illinois, for six years, Snyder began publishing nonfiction, writing about such subjects as drug addiction, gender-based violence, racism, ageism, class warfare, natural disasters, human rights, conflict, and displacement. As an international reporter, she started traveling the globe with her friend Ann and received story assignments from publications such as the *Chicago Tribune*, *Glamour*, and *Seventeen*. She married a former British commando named Paul, lived several years with him in Phnom Penh, Cambodia, gave birth to a daughter in Bangkok, Thailand, and later divorced.

By 2016, Snyder had reconciled with her father and stepmother, and lived with them for a time in a situation that was eerily similar to her childhood experience.

Barbara, at sixty-eight, had been diagnosed with colorectal cancer and was dying, wasting away. Snyder, who helped pay for Barbara's treatment, observed, "This is cancer's real menace: that it attacks and then diverts your gaze. It adapts. It survives because it kills everything around it." Despite her sometimes difficult life, Snyder in the end managed to maintain a compassionate, forgiving perspective.

Reviewers were almost unanimous in their praise for *Women We Buried, Women We Burned,* using such terms as "riveting," "unsparing," "harrowing," and "exceptional." Jennifer Szalai for *The New York Times* made comments that were echoed by other critics: "Snyder would never succumb to the pretty idea that suffering makes a person stronger. What she does describe—vividly and powerfully—is how, instead of responding to relentless hardship by building a protective carapace against the world, she was determined to open herself up to possibility."

Katie Roiphe, writing for *The Washington Post*, called the memoir "absorbing," and complimented Snyder's approach: "Unlike many memoirists, she seems completely uninterested in self-mythologizing or reveling in her specialness. Though her childhood is unusually arduous, her writing is stripped of self-pity." Roiphe further attested to the author's skills: "Snyder seems to have obtained a kind of fruitful distance from childhood trauma, a serenity and perspective that few people achieve in their lifetime, which allows her to write very powerfully about these moments, to evoke them."

Rochelle Olson also praised the memoir and its author in her review for the *Star Tribune*, saying, "Snyder's memoir is as heartbreaking, wrenching and compelling as the stories of the victims in her eye-opening book on domestic violence." Norah Piehl, writing for *Book Reporter*, lauded the author's prose in as "a narrative whose style belies its depth" and commended Snyder for "commenting obliquely on how trauma is recapitulated and the countless ways in which male authority warps and erases women's stories and lived realities" in a way that is "subtle, even crafty."

Author Biography

A professor of creative writing and journalism at American University, Rachel Louise Snyder previously published *Fugitive Denim: A Moving Story of People and Pants in the Borderless World of Global Trade* (2009) and the award-winning *No Visible Bruises: What We Don't Know about Domestic Violence Can Kill Us* (2019). She also published a novel, *What We've Lost Is Nothing* (2020), and was a 2020–21 Guggenheim Fellow.

Jack Ewing

Review Sources

Kipp, Priscilla. Review of *Women We Buried, Women We Burned*, by Rachel Louise Snyder. *Book Page*, June 2023, www.bookpage.com/reviews/women-we-buried-women-we-burned-rachel-louise-snyder-book-review. Accessed 9 Feb. 2024.

Olson, Rochelle. "How a Journalist Recovered from Trauma to Raise Up Voices of the Vulnerable." Review of *Women We Buried, Women We Burned*, by Rachel Louise

Snyder. *Star Tribune*, 18 May 2023, www.startribune.com/review-how-a-journalist-recovered-from-trauma-to-raise-up-voices-of-the-vulnerable/600275935. Accessed 9 Feb. 2024.

Piehl, Norah. Review of *Women We Buried, Women We Burned*, by Rachel Louise Snyder. *Book Reporter*, 26 May 2023, www.bookreporter.com/reviews/women-we-buried-women-we-burned-a-memoir. Accessed 9 Feb. 2024.

Roiphe, Katie. "In *Women We Buried, Women We Burned*, Rachel Louise Snyder Recalls the Rage and Violence She Endured as a Child." Review of *Women We Buried, Women We Burned*, by Rachel Louis Snyder. *The Washington Post*, 23 May 2023, www.washingtonpost.com/books/2023/05/23/women-buried-women-burned-review. Accessed 24 Nov. 2023.

Szalai, Jennifer. "An Unsparing Memoir of Hardship Transmuted into Possibility." Review of *Women We Buried, Women We Burned*, by Rachel Louise Snyder. *The New York Times*, 24 May 2023, www.nytimes.com/2023/05/24/books/review/women-we-buried-women-we-burned-rachel-louise-snyder.html. Accessed 24 Nov. 2023.

Review of *Women We Buried, Women We Burned*, by Rachel Louis Snyder. *Kirkus Reviews*, 24 Feb. 2023, www.kirkusreviews.com/book-reviews/rachel-louise-snyder/women-we-buried-women-we-burned/. Accessed 24 Nov. 2023.

The Words That Remain

Author: Stênio Gardel (b. 1980)
First Published: *A Palavra Que Resta*, 2021, in Brazil
Translated from the Portuguese by Bruna Dantas Lobato
Publisher: New Vessel Press (New York). 153 pp.
Type of work: Novel
Time: Twentieth and twenty-first centuries
Locale: Brazil

Stênio Gardel's debut novel employ shifting narrative voices and a scrambled chronology to tell the powerful story of a Brazilian man's coming to terms with his sexuality.

Principal characters
RAIMUNDO GAUDÊNCIO DE FREITAS, a seamster living in Brazil
CÍCERO, his childhood friend and lover
DAMIÃO, his father
MARCINHA, his sister
DALBERTO, his uncle
SUZZANNÝ, his friend, a transgender sex worker

Stories about LGBTQ+ people growing up in homophobic and transphobic situations are often harrowing. Whether these narratives are drawn from real life or are the stuff of fiction, they often involve physical violence, parents disowning their own children, and other horrific situations. In books such as Judy Shephard's memoir *The Meaning of Matthew* (2009), in which she reflects on the hate-crime murder of her son, Matthew, in 1998, and Edmund White's novel *A Boy's Own Story* (1982), the brutal consequences of homophobia on individuals are probed.

Oftentimes, as these books make clear, these consequences include not only the more visible violence inflicted on LGBTQ+ people, but deep psychological trauma as well. Both of these consequences beset the protagonist of Brazilian writer Stênio Gardel's debut novel, *The Words That Remain*, first published in Portuguese as *A Palavra Que Resta* in 2021 and published in an English translation by Bruna Dantas Lobato in 2023. A gripping, psychologically astute book, the novel tells the story of Raimundo Gaudêncio de Freitas, a Brazilian man who has struggled throughout his life to come to terms with his sexuality, leading to a rift with his family and years of searching for his proper way in life. Raimundo experiences his share of homophobia

Stenio Gardel

throughout the book, but Gardel is more concerned with the psychological toll that all of this takes on his character.

The book begins in the present day but frequently jumps forward and backward in time, with the novel's scrambled chronology mirroring Raimundo's attempts to pull together the various jumbled threads of his life. At the start of the novel, Raimundo is learning to read and write. He is seventy-one years old, but because he came from a farm family in rural Brazil, he was not given the opportunity to become literate. The reason he is now learning to read is because for decades, he has been carrying around a letter from Cícero, his childhood friend and former lover. When the two were teenagers, they were caught having sex by Cícero's father and as a result, when Raimundo's father found out, Raimundo was beaten for weeks on end. At his mother's urging, Raimundo left home, but not before Cícero left him with a letter. Because he could not read and because he refused to allow anyone to read it to him, Raimundo carried around the letter for over fifty years without knowing its contents. Now, at the beginning of the novel, having finally accepted his identity as a gay man, Raimundo is determined to learn to read and finally discover the contents of the letter.

The novel jumps back and forth between the present, when Raimundo is taking reading lessons, and various moments in his past. Most of the book takes place in the past and tells the story of Raimundo's life. After leaving home, he works for many years unloading trucks, hoping desperately that his secret would not being uncovered, and finding sexual fulfillment only through going to pornographic theaters. His life changes when he meets a transgender sex worker named Suzzanný, who taunts Raimundo for his closeted homosexuality and in turn receives verbal and physical abuse from Raimundo. Eventually, the two become friends and even live together. With Suzzanný's help, Raimundo learns to accept his homosexuality, decides to change careers and become a seamster, and embarks on his quest to learn how to read.

Gardel is unsparing in his depictions of the physical violence that his characters undergo, but far more impressive is his understanding of the ways that homophobia perpetuates itself and the emotional toll it takes on its victims. In one early sequence, Raimundo learns that when his father, Damião, was a child, he learned that his own brother, Dalberto, was gay. Damião stood by his brother, but his own father, Raimundo's grandfather, was so full of hate toward Dalberto that there was little Damião could do to help him, leaving Damião deeply traumatized after his brother's death. Now that Damião has learned his own son is gay, he beats him mercilessly; however, as Raimundo and the reader come to understand, the motive for the beating is not simply hatred, but also fear. No one in the family's rural Brazilian community knows how to deal with a gay man, as this identity runs so counter to the prevailing macho ethos. In this sense, Raimundo's fear is typical of how the wider community feels; by beating his son, Damião hopes to "correct" what he views as a problem with his son and protect Raimundo from meeting a fate similar to Dalberto's.

This cycle of homophobic violence continues in Raimundo's encounters with Suzzanný. He first meets her when he is leaving a pornographic theater. Because Raimundo is closeted and because he can only express his sexuality in secret, he is filled with considerable shame. He is also worried that people will find out about his sexuality. Therefore, when Raimundo runs into Suzzanný and she taunts him, he showers transphobic abuse on her. As a person who lives openly as herself, she doubly shames the closeted Raimundo, and his shame and fear manifest themselves in more violence. This verbal violence soon turns to physical abuse when, during a later run-in, Raimundo begins kicking Suzzanný, and ultimately ends up taking her to the hospital. After having seen what the cycles of homophobia and transphobia can do to a person, Raimundo feels horrified at himself, and begins to change his ways.

Reflecting on what he has done to Suzzanný and the cycles of violence he is wrapped up in, Raimundo comes to an understanding of how he has been impacted by the vicious legacy of hatred. Mentally addressing Suzzanný, he muses, "Why did I do something that stupid, hit you like that? so much fear, this story of fear, wasn't it fear that raised my father's arm? He put this fear in me, it went from his arm through his belt and it entered my back, fear is my spine, it's what holds me up, and I'm using it to hurt others?" This is Raimundo's key realization and it sets him on a path of self-understanding and self-acceptance that allows him to undo the cycles of violence. Key to this journey is the influence of Suzzanný, who is one of the book's most sharply drawn characters. A haughty, confident, and generous woman, she is determined to live as herself regardless of the consequences. With such an example in front of him, Raimundo is able to find the courage to live as himself as well.

As the previous quotation makes clear, *The Words That Remain* often employs a stream-of-consciousness narration. Gardel writes in lyrical prose that often shifts between short, poetic sentences and rambling, searching passages in which Raimundo thinks through different situations. An experimental but controlled stylist, Gardel also switches seamlessly between first- and third-person narration; occasionally, Gardel even shifts between different characters' points-of-view in a single passage. While this literary experimentation could easily become burdensome or difficult to parse, Gardel's writing remains continually clear and his technique never overwhelms what is a relatively straightforward story. In fact, by allowing his audience into Raimundo's thoughts, Gardel allows readers to witness what is essentially an internal struggle unfold in real time. It is a generous gesture toward both the reader and Raimundo, whose full humanity comes across on the page. In Gardel's skillful hands, the psychological struggle of a closeted gay man, described in stream-of-consciousness passages, is as compelling as the outward struggle of a gay man in a homophobic society, which Gardel depicts in his clipped, poetic narrative style. These different literary modes match up perfectly with the different aspects of Raimundo's story, while the scrambled chronology perfectly mirrors its main character's disorientation and fractured identity.

That Raimundo is able to reassemble this identity shows that there is hope for all people, no matter what challenges society throws at them.

The Words That Remain, while not widely reviewed in the United States when it was published in translation in 2023, was uniformly praised by the American critics who covered it. Most notably, the book was awarded the prestigious National Book Award for translated literature, with the prize being awarded jointly to Gardel and Lobato, his translator. Reviewing the novel for *Reading in Translation*, Juliana Gaspar had plenty of praise for Gardel's novel. Gaspar's review focused on the power of language and the ways in which written language, whether Cícero's letter or the book itself, give voice to things that cannot be otherwise said. Complimenting the novel's treatment of all aspects of its character's sexual identity, Gaspar concluded, "*The Words That Remain* is not just a love story but an expression of queer desire, struggle, and resilience in spaces outside of romantic love."

An anonymous reviewer for *Publishers Weekly* provided one of the few other notable reviews of the book in the US and also thought highly of the novel. Calling the "wistful novel" an "auspicious debut" for the first-time novelist Gardel, the reviewer concluded that the work "introduces a worthy new voice." Indeed, Gardel's various achievements—his articulation of internalized homophobia and the desire to live an unfettered life, his command of language, and his perfect synching of language and feeling—is particularly impressive considering that he accomplished this in his first novel. An assured debut that did not make a huge impact upon first being published in English translation, it soon earned due recognition, both by the judges of the National Book Award and by the many readers who picked it up after the award significantly raised the novel's profile.

Author Biography

Stênio Gardel grew up in a rural section of Céara, a state in northeastern Brazil. He later lived in the state capital of Fortaleza and worked for the Regional Electoral Court. *The Words That Remain* is his first novel.

Bruna Dantas Lobato is a Brazilian novelist and translator working in the United States. Her previous translations include Caio Fernando Abreu's *Moldy Strawberries* (2022) which was longlisted for the PEN Translation Prize and won a PEN/Heim Grant, and Jeferson Tenório's *The Dark Side of Skin* (2024), which won an English PEN Translates Award.

Andrew Schenker

Review Sources

Gardel, Stênio. "The Voice of a Man Who Doesn't Know How to Write." Interview by David Martinez. *Air/Light Magazine*, Fall 2023, airlightmagazine.org/airlight/the-seventh-issue-of-air-light/stenio-gardel-interviewed-by-david-martinez/. Accessed 9 Jan. 2024.

Gaspar, Juliana. "Queer Struggle and Resilience in Stênio Gardel's *The Words That Remain*." Review of *The Words That Remain* by Stênio Gardel. *Reading in Translation*, 20 Feb. 2023, readingintranslation.com/2023/02/20/stenio-gardels-the-words-that-remain/. Accessed 9 Jan. 2024.

"The National Book Award Interviews: Bruna Dantas Lobato and Stênio Gardel." *Words Without Borders*, 3 Oct. 2023, wordswithoutborders.org/read/article/2023-10/the-national-book-award-interviews-bruna-dantas-lobato-and-stenio-gardel/. Accessed 9 Jan. 2024.

Review of *The Words That Remain* by Stênio Gardel. *Publishers Weekly*, Jan. 2023, www.publishersweekly.com/9781954404120. Accessed 9 Jan. 2024.

The World
A Family History of Humanity

Author: Simon Sebag Montefiore (b. 1965)
Publisher: Knopf (New York). 1,344 pp.
Type of work: History; biography
Time: Primarily ca. 2613 BCE–present

The World: A Family History of Humanity approaches the history of human civilization through the lens of lineages and dynasties, following power families across the globe from ca. 2613 BCE into the twenty-first century CE in a massive, yet concise, twenty-three-act tome.

Principal personages
NAPOLEON BONAPARTE, emperor of France
GENGHIS KHAN, a great warrior and conqueror of much of Asia
ADOLPH HITLER, leader of Nazi Germany
CLEOPATRA, Ancient Egyptian queen
CONSTANTINE, emperor of Rome who converted to Christianity
AUGUSTUS, formerly known as Octavian, the first emperor of Rome
JOHN F. KENNEDY, United States president
INDIRA GANDHI, third prime minister of India, daughter of its first prime minister
MOTECUHZOMA, emperor of the Mexica
MUHAMMAD BIN ABDULLAH, Arab religious and civic leader, the founder of Islam
AHOSU HOUEGBADJA, king of Dahomey, who sold thousands of enslaved people to European slave traders
GEORGE W. BUSH, United States president
MANIKONGO GARCIA, a Kongo ruler
XI JINPING, president of the People's Republic of China

Simon Sebag Montefiore's *The World: A Family History of Humanity* is a single massive tome, topping 1,300 pages, which offers readers a tour-de-force of the global history of humanity from the earliest civilizations to the twenty-first century. The book is organized around power families—think rulers of all stripes, oligarchs, and politicians—who have built spheres of influence, city-states, and empires across the span of human history. Montefiore presents the his approach as one that melds the genres of world history and biography. "World history often has themes, not people; biography has people, not themes," he notes, but he strives to provide both. *The World* offers the biography of dynasties and kingdoms, moving quickly across the individual characters in each family group in order to follow a larger arc of history. By telling the stories

Simon Sebag Montefiore

of family networks, Montefiore is able to follow the rise and fall of kingdoms, lineages, and movements in a focused, logical manner.

Montefiore, tipping his hat to Samuel Johnson, states that "every kingdom is a family and every family a little kingdom" and the family is the "essential unit of human existence" across every continent and span of time. He also asserts that the family-based approach has some distinct advantages. For example, it "makes it possible to pay more attention to the lives of women and children" and to present "a genuine world history, not unbalanced by excessive focus on Britain and Europe." Indeed, a strength of the book certainly lies in its attempt to present synchronous historical events across continents and to highlight themes of hybridity and interconnection across wide swaths of geography and civilizations that are often considered in isolation from one another.

The World is organized chronologically into twenty-three parts, which Montefiore labels "acts." The opening page of each act is labeled with its number and the world population over the years encompassed within it. Within each act, there are a varying number of sections, which could be considered chapters; a plurality of these are titled with dynastic names (such as the concluding "Trumps and Xis, Sauds, Assads and Kims"). Each section is divided further into finer-tuned moments or events, many of which, especially in the early historical periods, are given highly sexualized or violent heading titles (as in Act 3's "Who I Screw: Cleopatra, Caesar and Antony"). All of this adds up to a table of contents that runs to seventeen pages and is, perhaps, more provocative than the book itself. The globalized and interconnected nature of the text can be traced through these titles and headings. Notably, though, while Montefiore's efforts at creating a balanced world history are laudable, the table of contents makes clear that the balance of the work still tips toward Europe and the sections of North Africa and the Middle East that are most closely tied to Europe in their history.

The family organizing structure of *The World* is focused on dynasties and lineages of power—often beginning long before the most recognizable names among them appear, as Douglas Smith noted in a review for the *Wall Street Journal*. Montefiore does not apply a social history model to his discussion of family life, instead using family connections as a means to follow political and military history, infused with rivalry, jealousy, and large doses of violence and sex. From start to finish, the book presents a clear-eyed overview of how ambition, with its desire to gain and maintain power, has long been used to justify many of the most horrific acts of human history. The scale of such acts is sobering. How is the reader to come to terms with the assertion, based on recent DNA studies, that Genghis Khan may have raped so many women that he is "literally the father of Asia"? Although there are stories of love, whether sexual or parental, across the book, the role of love as a motivating force of human history and civilization is much less prominent in Montefiore's take on human action across history.

Readers will find little in this book about common families, except for the frequent mentions of enslavement, murder, rape, and other acts of violence that have supported the rise of various rulers across history. Thus, while Montefiore's narrative surely does include more focus on women and children than past generations of scholarship, it presents a view of history that is closely focused on the ambitions and agency of the elite classes across the world. The book remains firmly fixed in the halls, tents, and spheres of power. As massive as *The World* is, and as sweeping in its narrative, it therefore tells the story of only a privileged fraction of human civilization. As other reviewers have observed, an important aspect of Montefiore's narrative is his presentation of dynastic history in modern democratic nations as well as in monarchies, empires, and autocracies. In their own way, elite political families in democratic societies are just the next chapter in a long history of dynastic rule. Additionally, Montefiore points readers toward shadow powers such as "the unelected, invisible power of the despots of data," whose role is increasing in a digital civilization.

Montefiore seeks to avoid a presentist mode of history, in which knowledge of past events offers clarity of explanation and clairvoyance to the historian. He also asserts that he has set out to avoid telling the past as a means of speaking to present issues. Instead, he focuses on retelling many forgotten moments of human history, making use of primary sources to speak with the authentic voice of the past, and integrating lesser-known sources and narratives into the cast of characters and events that frequently appear in world history sources. This distinct approach to assembling history inevitably means that the integrative and interpretive thread across the sections of the book is limited. Readers can expect to find individual historical vignettes and personages within the book to be interesting and unfamiliar, but the overall feel of the text to be more encyclopedic than interpretive.

Given this context, it is notable that while Montefiore makes liberal use of footnotes, he offers only a single bibliographic paragraph at the end of the book as a window into his sources. In his acknowledgements, he lists a long line of specialists in different historical periods and places who offered feedback and corrections to his discussions of civilizations across time and the globe. The massive scale of the book, he asserts, precluded the possibility of including a complete bibliography. In his "Select Bibliography," Montefiore merely directs curious readers to his personal website, where a 140-page-long list of works consulted may be found, with some diligence. This unconventional format may rankle some of those interested to learn more about the myriad historical figures and civilizations that Montefiore introduces, but it does allow an opportunity to scrutinize and dig deeper into his sources.

The book concludes with Russia's invasion of Ukraine in the spring of 2022 and the subsequent war, a development that Montefiore reads as threatening to a longstanding world order. While the rest of the book is limited in its interpretive stance, the brief four-page conclusion is ominous. He writes, "The number of autocracies is surging, that of democracies ebbing," and reminds the reader that while "no empire nations have fought each other since 1945," eventually a war between such nations will break out. Still, despite the increased threat of destruction in war or through climate change, Montefiore sees hope for a continued long history of human civilization. He notes that while there is an "absence of great leaders . . . they are made by their opportunities," suggesting that new dynasties and solution-builders may rise to meet current and future challenges. And while he sees the balance of world power tipping toward autocracies, he also finds that "when [open societies] mobilize they are flexible, efficient and creative." Faced with a crisis of annihilation, he posits that autocratic leaders might have the motivation to enact proposed solutions and the absolute power to put them in motion.

The World has received largely positive reviews, with special attention paid to the global nature of the text and its engaging narrative vignettes across human civilization. Montefiore's focus on the dynastic nature of history, and the continued prominence of dynasties in democratic society, has been a point of special consideration for reviewers. Importantly, in engaging with Montefiore's approach, Maya Jasanoff reflected in a review for the *New Yorker* that nepotism has given operating structure to all classes of society throughout history; children have often followed the professions of their parents, whether these parents are world leaders or shoemakers. Yet, unlike Montefiore, she does not see dynastic power as a force that inevitably undermines democracy, but rather that "the family persists as a prime mediator of social, cultural, and financial opportunities" within democracies as in other forms of government.

Author Biography

Simon Sebag Montefiore is a prolific author who has published several historical-fiction novels for adults and seven other works of history and general nonfiction. He also cowrote an adventure series for young readers. He earned a doctorate at Cambridge University and became a fellow of the Royal Society of Literature.

Julia A. Sienkewicz, PhD

Review Sources

Jasanoff, Maya. "The History of Nepo Babies Is the History of Humanity." Review of *The World: A Family History of Humanity*, by Simone Sebag Montefiore. *The New Yorker*, 22 May 2023, www.newyorker.com/magazine/2023/05/29/the-world-a-family-history-of-humanity-simon-sebag-montefiore-book-review. Accessed 15 Jan. 2024.

Sempa, Francis P. Review of *The World: A Family History of Humanity*, by Simone Sebag Montefiore. *The New York Journal of Books*, www.nyjournalofbooks.com/book-review/world-family-history. Accessed 15 Jan. 2024.

Smith, Douglas. "*The World* Review: History Branched Out." Review of *The World: A Family History of Humanity*, by Simone Sebag Montefiore. *The Wall Street Journal*, 26 June 2023, www.wsj.com/articles/the-world-review-history-branched-out-4d18193a. Accessed 15 Jan. 2024.

Yacovissi, Jennifer Bort. Review of *The World: A Family History of Humanity*, by Simone Sebag Montefiore. *Washington Independent Review of Books*, 5 June 2023, www.washingtonindependentreviewofbooks.com/index.php/bookreview/the-world-a-family-history-of-humanity. Accessed 15 Jan. 2024.

Yellowface

Author: Rebecca F. Kuang (b. 1996)
Publisher: William Morrow (New York). 336 pp.
Type of work: Novel
Time: Present day
Locale: Washington, DC

Yellowface is a dark, thrilling satire about competition, greed, privilege, cultural appropriation, and tokenism in the publishing industry. It is the fifth book by Poppy War *trilogy author R. F. Kuang.*

Principal characters

JUNE HAYWARD, also known as Juniper Song, a White novelist in her twenties
ATHENA LIU, her friend, an extremely successful novelist of Chinese heritage
BRETT, her agent
DANIELLA, her editor
CANDICE LEE, a Korean American editorial assistant

R. F. Kuang has had the kind of career that many young writers dream about. Just as she was turning twenty years old, the rights to her first book sparked a bidding war among publishers. *The Poppy War* (2018), a fantasy novel that reimagined twentieth-century Chinese history, would go on to earn rave reviews from critics, with some even calling it the best book of the year. After completing the *Poppy War* trilogy in 2020, Kuang's star continued to rise when her standalone novel *Babel, or The Necessity of Violence: An Arcane History of the Oxford Translators' Revolution* (2022) debuted at number one on the New York Times Best Sellers list and won a prestigious Nebula Award. In just a few years, Kuang had gone from an unknown Georgetown University student to one of the most lauded fantasy writers in the United States.

According to Kuang's 2023 novel, *Yellowface*, however, such extraordinary literary success might not actually be a dream-come-true. A dark-satire thriller, *Yellowface* examines the dog-eat-dog world of publishing and the role that racial politics and social media have come to play in it. Through its twisted story, Kuang asks whether the increased demand for books by authors of color has actually made things better for racialized writers or just more complexly cutthroat.

To examine this question, Kuang sends readers into the mind of a memorably unsettling protagonist: June Hayward. A White woman in her late twenties whose debut novel flopped, June has never earned any real recognition for her writing, unlike her college acquaintance Athena Liu. While June cannot get her publisher to call her back,

R. F. Kuang

Courtesy R. F. Kuang; ©John Packman

Athena has enjoyed six-figure book deals for years, photo spreads in major magazines, and even a Netflix deal in the making. Everything comes easily to the beautiful, talented Athena, causing June to resent her so much that she wishes she would drop dead. And then Athena does just that—choking on a pancake right in front of June's eyes.

In many ways, *Yellowface* comes across as a modern-day parable. Athena's death leads to June making a kind of Faustian bargain that allows her to get everything she has ever wished for, but with dire consequences. More specifically, June decides to steal and take credit for the late author's manuscript about Chinese laborers during World War I. The book becomes a huge success and generates all the money, fame, and literary respect June always felt she deserved. It is not long, however, before her lies come back to haunt her.

While there is a classic, Brothers Grimm quality to June's karmic journey, the novel also feels very of-the-moment. This is largely because throughout the narrative Kuang leverages June's character to make sharp commentary on several issues that have shaped the dialogue surrounding literary culture in the 2010s and 2020s, like the mental health challenges authors face today because of "doom scrolling" and harassment on social media. Most importantly, June's character illustrates how many White writers have reacted to the increasing demand for stories written by and about members of marginalized communities. Behind June's horrible actions is the belief that she has been discriminated against in her literary career because she is a White woman. It is this deluded thinking that allows her to accept her White publisher's suggestion that June use her first and middle names as her penname, Juniper Song—which could be, and often is, mistaken as being Chinese. June's sense of being a victim who is owed success also drives her to try to sustain her lies rather than come clean.

Meanwhile, the character of Athena provides readers with insight into the challenges of being a contemporary Asian American Pacific Islander (AAPI) writer. In addition to experiencing the same type of online harassment and death threats as June, Athena was pigeonholed as a token Chinese author by publishers. This made her competitive with other AAPI writers who she saw as threats to her own success and therefore would refuse to help. Athena also knew that White publishers and readers wanted stories about Asian pain, so she would seek out people whose trauma she could use as material for her writing career. In this way, Kuang suggests that the publishing industry puts pressure on racialized writers to be exploitative in order to succeed.

Both Athena and June demonstrate Kuang's talent for crafting multifaceted characters capable of challenging readers' assumptions about who is good in this world and who is not. Athena might have seemed perfect on the outside, but she has also taken the tragic stories of other people and passed them off as her own original writing. In contrast, June is clearly a bad person in many ways, and yet, occasionally, she justifies her actions in ways that almost make sense. At one point, for example, she points out that she rewrote nearly the entirety of Athena's manuscript, so it was not really stealing. At another, June argues that stealing the manuscript was fair because Athena took something painful that happened to June in college and turned it into a short story.

The fact that June's logic can sometimes, sort of, make sense is a testament to how well *Yellowface* succeeds at the deceptive art of antihero storytelling. Throughout the novel, June relays her story with the relatable emotions of jealousy, insecurity, anxiety, and a desire to be understood in a first-person, present-tense narration. It becomes difficult for the reader not to feel invested in what will happen to her despite her despicable actions. In this way, June earns a place next to other manipulative literary characters like *Gone Girl*'s Amy Dunne and *Lolita*'s Humbert Humbert.

Readers who are looking for clear-cut answers on complex social issues may find *Yellowface* frustrating. Not only does Kuang avoid a typical hero one can root for, but she also paints an overall bleak picture of the publishing industry and society in general. None of the characters ever seem wholly interested in doing the right thing for the right reasons. Even those who catch on to June's wrongdoings and try to stop her seem more interested in the power and opportunities that come with vigilante justice than in actually improving the world at large. As such, the novel has a deeply cynical tone.

Arguably one of the most compelling questions that Kuang explores in the novel is that of who is allowed to tell which stories. While June's story might ostensibly be seen as a cautionary tale of why writers should "stay in their lane" by only writing stories about characters whose race and ethnicity match their own, the fact that Kuang, who was born in Guangzhou, China, and raised in Dallas, Texas, is writing about the experiences of a White woman suggests that perhaps the author does not actually believe this to be true. As such, astute readers might conclude that while perhaps June and Athena did not truly care about the World War I Chinese laborers that they wrote about, not all writers are simply exploiting others for the sake money and fame. Many, like Kuang, seek to try and understand the world from another person's perspective and spark important conversations among their readers along the way.

Critical reception of *Yellowface* has been quite divided. In his review for the *New York Times* Amal El-Mohtar argued that the attempt to make June into an unreliable narrator clashed with the book's "on-the-nose" social commentary. The novel "can't allow room for ambiguity or revelation without rushing in to fill that space," El-Mohtar wrote. "All its genre fluidity is in service of the same blunt frankness." However, one could counter that Kuang never presents June's character quite as a traditional unreliable narrator after all. Instead, June's narration has a kind of pathetic, confessional quality to it; she thinks of herself as the victim, but her attempts to justify her actions always fall short of being convincing. The manner in which she talks about her pettiness and insecurities is more like that of a flawed human being than a deft liar like the unreliable narrators Patrick Bateman from *American Psycho* or Amy Dunne from *Gone Girl*. An argument can be made that Kuang's decision to not make June into such a character was the better choice; often the scariest part about June is that sometimes her feelings, like her jealousy of Athena's success, can be very much relatable.

Another common criticism of *Yellowface* was that it tries to accomplish too much and therefore cannot help but fall short of its ambitions. As Reema Saleh's wrote for the *Chicago Review of Books*, "Yellowface has two missions—pushing cultural exploitation to its fictional limits and satirizing the state of the publishing industry in an internet era. Sometimes, the novel sacrifices the first mission for the second and becomes too obsessed with the online lives of books and authordom." Again, however, this critique ultimately comes down to individual preference and interpretation. For many readers, the amount of focus that Kuang puts on the toxic online culture that June and Athena had to deal with will feel appropriate.

Indeed, a case can be made that most of the criticisms directed toward *Yellowface* stem from the fact that it is a big swing—the novel is willing to wade into murky, uncomfortable topics. Yet for other reviewers, this is precisely what makes it such a compelling read. Lacy Baugher Milas touched on this in her review for *Paste Magazine*, stating, "It seems safe to say that R. F. Kuang's *Yellowface* is like no other book . . . It's addictive, shocking, compelling, ridiculous, and extremely fun to read by turns. It wrestles with hot-button topics in publishing surrounding race, classism, white privilege, and tokenism." Many readers are likely to agree with Milas that *Yellowface* succeeds as an exciting thriller. Even those who find problems with the plot will find the book difficult to put down, as Kuang ensures the narrative's pacing never slows and is rife with danger and cliff hangers. In a review for *NPR*, Keishel Williams summed up this perspective: "Kuang's first foray outside of fantasy is a well-executed, gripping, fast-paced novel about the nuances of the publishing world when an author is desperate enough to do anything for success. I was consistently at the edge of my seat until the very last page."

Yellowface is the kind of book that many will find fascinating thanks to its well-crafted storytelling and the incendiary topics it is willing to explore. It may not always say the things that readers want to hear, but the conversation it provokes is one that is highly worthwhile.

Author Biography

R. F. Kuang is a bestselling novelist best known for her *Poppy War* fantasy trilogy and the Locus and Nebula Award–winning book *Babel* (2022). As a Marshall Scholar, she earned a master of philosophy in Chinese studies from Cambridge University before going on to study Contemporary Chinese Studies at Oxford.

Emily E. Turner

Review Sources

El-Mohtar, Amal. "Her Novel Became a Best Seller. The Trouble: She Didn't Write It." Review of *Yellowface*, by R. F. Kuang. *The New York Times*, 16 May 2023, www.nytimes.com/2023/05/16/books/review/yellowface-rf-kuang.html. Accessed 9 Aug. 2023.

Milas, Lacy Baugher. "*Yellowface* Is an Addictive, Uncomfortable Evisceration of Modern Day Publishing." Review of *Yellowface*, by R. F. Kuang. *Paste Magazine*, 16 May 2023, www.pastemagazine.com/books/r-f-kuang/yellowface-review. Accessed 9 Aug. 2023.

Saleh, Reema. "The Specters of "Yellowface." Review of *Yellowface*, by R. F. Kuang. *The Chicago Review of Books*, 19 May 2023, chireviewofbooks.com/2023/05/19/yellowface-r-f-kuang/. Accessed 9 Aug. 2023.

Williams, Keishel. "*Yellowface* Takes White Privilege to a Sinister Level." *National Public Radio*, 15 May 2023, www.npr.org/2023/05/15/1175725398/r-f-kuang-novel-yellowface-takes-white-privilege-to-a-sinister-level. Accessed 9 Aug. 2023.

You Have to Be Prepared to Die Before You Can Begin to Live
Ten Weeks in Birmingham That Changed America

Author: Paul Kix
Publisher: Celadon Books (New York). 400 pp.
Type of work: History
Time: 1963
Locale: Birmingham, Alabama

Paul Kix provides an in-depth look at a pivotal ten-week period in which civil rights leaders staged an operation in segregated Birmingham, Alabama, in 1963.

Principal personages
MARTIN LUTHER KING JR., a minister and civil rights leader
FRED SHUTTLESWORTH, a fellow minister and civil rights activist
WYATT TEE WALKER, an executive director of the Southern Christian Leadership Conference (SCLC), a minister
JAMES BEVEL, a fellow minister and civil rights activist
THEOPHILUS EUGENE "BULL" CONNOR, the Birmingham commissioner of public safety
JOHN F. KENNEDY, the president of the United States
ROBERT F. KENNEDY, then the US attorney general

The civil rights movement was a long and varied period in American history. From the 1940s to the late 1960s, the movement was one of the most transformational moments in the country's ongoing narrative. Achieving major legislative gains such as the Civil Rights Act of 1964, which essentially ended the Jim Crow era in the South, the civil rights movement also transformed racial attitudes throughout the country and caused the United States to undergo a long-overdue, if incomplete, racial reckoning.

The term "civil rights movement," though, encompasses a wide variety of actions, involving both grassroots protests and official action at the highest levels of government. Over the decades that it lasted, thousands of leaders and activists staged dozens of protests throughout the South, while newspapers and television newscasts kept the citizens of the country updated, and governmental leaders considered what actions to take in response. While the movement is often portrayed as one unified series of actions, it actually encompasses a wide range of often unconnected, even contradictory, activities.

Because of both the movement's national importance and its long and varied nature, hundreds of books have been written that trace its history. While some books, like

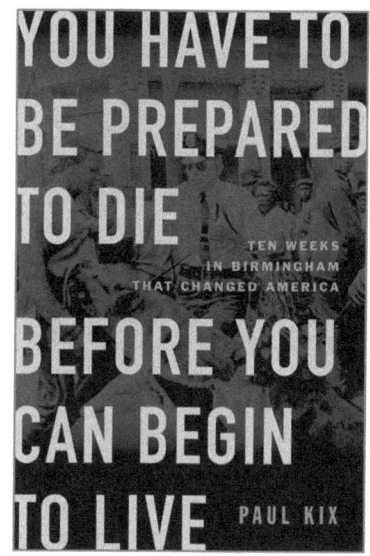

Paul Kix

Thomas C. Holt's *The Movement: The African American Struggle for Civil Rights* (2021), take a wider perspective, encompassing the whole history of the movement, most other books on the subject narrow their focus, zeroing in on a particular theme or event. Such is the case with Paul Kix's book *You Have to Be Prepared to Die Before You Can Begin to Live: Ten Weeks in Birmingham that Changed America* (2023), which confines its focus to Rev. Martin Luther King Jr.'s Birmingham campaign in the spring of 1963, only occasionally zooming out to take a look at the larger picture.

After a brief introduction, in which Kix, as the White husband of a Black woman raising biracial children, explains the personal importance of his project, he sets the reader down in Georgia, where civil rights leaders, including King, are planning a new action. At that moment, King and his organization, the Southern Christian Leadership Conference (SCLC), were reeling. Having recently undertaken an unsuccessful action in Albany, Georgia, King felt the urgent necessity to achieve a successful breakthrough. King's nonviolent approach relied on getting activists to peacefully violate local segregation laws and, in response, for local authorities to handle them violently. This approach was all about the optics, as they were staging these actions to win over the hearts and minds of both the average American watching at home and the politicians in Washington, DC, who they hoped to convince to pass civil rights legislation. In Albany, Georgia, though, the approach failed, as the city officials, wise to the SCLC's methods, peacefully arrested the protestors and quickly released them, not providing King with the dramatic results he needed.

At the meeting in Georgia, King unveiled his desperate follow-up plan—he would stage a similar action in what many thought was the most racist city in America: Birmingham, Alabama. Because of the virulent racism and brutality in that city, presided over by the White supremacist commissioner of public safety Bull Connor, activists had largely avoided the city. Now, King announced that the SCLC would target Birmingham directly. King—along with SCLC executive director Wyatt Tee Walker, who drew up the plans for "Project C," as it became known, and fellow activists James Bevel and Birmingham resident Fred Shuttlesworth—descended on the Alabama city ready to begin his boldest action yet.

Kix's book offers an in-depth, blow-by-blow account of the Birmingham campaign, with the majority of the book taking place over April and May 1963 in that city. Kix expertly tracks all the players as they organize, adjust their plans, and implement new plans in an attempt to gain national exposure and sympathy for their movement. As Kix chronicles, it was far from smooth sailing. When King and his compatriots arrived in Birmingham, for example, there was little enthusiasm among the locals for his plans. At this point in the movement, King, who was a national celebrity and was based in Atlanta, was often seen as a distant, imperious figure, given the derogatory nickname De Lawd by some in the movement. He had trouble winning over many of the locals, both because they distrusted him and his plan and because they did not want to lose their jobs.

The turning point in the campaign came, as Kix explains, when James Bevel, a headstrong and somewhat enigmatic minister and activist, came up with a new idea. If the adults in Birmingham were afraid to march, then he would enlist the children. After several weeks of recruiting, educating, and training the thousands of willing children and teenagers, the SCLC put this controversial plan in action, sending them out on peaceful marches, in defiance of Bull Connor's official rules. Eventually, the activists achieved the results they wanted, with Connor unleashing dogs and fire hoses on the children and revealing to a whole nation the moral rot of southern racism. This would lead the next year to the passage of the Civil Rights Act and the official end of the Jim Crow era in the South.

Kix's book is vividly written and brings to life each stage of the struggle in Birmingham. He provides the reader just enough background to understand the context of the actions being undertaken, but his focus remains relentlessly on the actions of the single campaign. This proves to be a smart approach, as Kix's attention to detail and his knack for lively and easily visualized description makes the reader feel the immediacy of the actions being undertaken.

In addition to giving the reader a sense of the more dramatic action unfolding in Birmingham, Kix also succeeds in conveying the mood of uncertainty. For much of the book, things are not going the way the civil rights leaders want them to go, and this frustration is also vividly evoked by the writing. Kix achieves this largely by grounding his narrative in the personalities of the major players involved, particularly the leaders of the movement. King, Walker, Bevel, and Shuttlesworth are all forceful personalities, each with his own take on the best way to achieve their goals. The four are often in conflict, and Kix's portrayal of this conflict gives a richness to what could otherwise be a simple blow-by-blow account of a historical action.

While Shuttlesworth and Bevel in particular emerge as fascinating personalities thanks to Kix's skill at character sketching, it is King who remains at the heart of the book. In one of the book's best sections, Kix steps back and traces the evolution of King's intellectual process. This rare moment of removal from the action occurs when King is arrested and taken to jail. It is during this incarceration that he writes his widely celebrated essay "Letter from Birmingham Jail" on a series of scraps that an associate then sneaks out of the building. In outlining the ideas that King puts forth in this essay, Kix provides a history of King's intellectual development, in particular noting the huge influence of both American religious philosopher Reinhold Niebuhr and Indian activist Mohandas Gandhi. Kix is effective in outlining the ways that King synthesizes these influences, as well as many others, into the searing and highly effective plea for justice that he had smuggled out of his confinement.

For the most part, though, Kix's narrative is limited to the moment at hand, and in that vein, it offers a vivid and detailed re-creation of a pivotal time in the nation's history. If anything, it ends too abruptly, with only a few pages dedicated to the aftermath of Birmingham, which shortchanges the tortured legislative history that separates Operation C from the passage of the Civil Rights Act. As a re-creation of history, though, Kix's book stands as a huge addition to the growing canon of books about the civil rights movement. That movement is so wide-ranging and various that a narrowing of focus is necessary, and Kix achieves that goal perfectly.

You Have to Be Prepared to Die Before You Can Begin to Live received largely positive reviews. Writing for the *New York Times*, historian Jefferson Cowie praised the book's character development and "edge-of-your-seat drama." He felt that "the richness of Kix's dramatis personae simply staggers," signaling out the many vivid figures Kix brings to life. In particular, he liked the chapters dealing with King at his most vulnerable, offering particular praise for the sections dealing with his writing of "Letter from Birmingham Jail." With Cowie's glowing notice, it is not surprising that *You Have to Be Prepared to Die Before You Can Begin to Live* made the paper's list of the 100 Notable Books of 2023.

Other outlets shared Cowie's praise, with *Publishers Weekly* and *Kirkus Reviews* each giving the book a starred review. The *Publishers Weekly* reviewer praised the book's "gripping, novelistic" approach, while the *Kirkus Reviews* writer called the volume "an eloquent contribution to the literature of civil rights and the ceaseless struggle to attain them." As that reviewer makes clear, the full goals of the civil rights movement have not been met, but as long as writers like Kix are around to remind readers of their importance, the efforts to achieve full equality will continue.

Author Biography

Paul Kix is a writer whose work has appeared in the *New Yorker*, the *Atlantic*, and numerous other magazines. He is the author of the bestselling book *The Saboteur*, which was optioned for a movie by DreamWorks.

Andrew Schenker

Review Sources

Cowie, Jefferson. "Martin Luther King Jr.'s High-Stakes Gamble in Birmingham." Review of *You Have to Be Prepared to Die Before You Can Begin to Live*, by Paul Kix. *The New York Times*, 8 June 2023, www.nytimes.com/2023/06/08/books/review/you-have-to-be-prepared-to-die-before-you-can-begin-to-live-paul-kix.html. Accessed 28 Nov. 2023.

Review of *You Have to Be Prepared to Die Before You Can Begin to Live*, by Paul Kix. *Kirkus Reviews*, www.kirkusreviews.com/book-reviews/paul-kix/you-have-to-be-prepared-to-die-before-you-can-begi/. Accessed 29 Nov. 2023.

Review of *You Have to Be Prepared to Die Before You Can Begin to Live*, by Paul Kix. *Publishers Weekly*, www.publishersweekly.com/9781250807694. Accessed 28 Nov. 2023.

You: The Story
A Writer's Guide to Craft through Memory

Author: Ruta Sepetys (b. 1967)
Publisher: Viking (New York). 224 pp.
Type of work: Miscellaneous

In You: The Story; A Writer's Guide to Craft through Memory, *best-selling novelist Ruta Sepetys introduces aspiring writers to the valuable creative inspiration they can glean from their own lives, from the lives of the people around them, and from history.*

In the years following the 2011 publication of her debut novel, *Between Shades of Gray*, author Ruta Sepetys established herself as a best-selling and award-winning author of novels that appealed both to young adult and adult readers. Specializing in historical fiction set during periods of social, political, and military unrest, she developed a reputation as a strong storyteller whose thoroughly researched, well-rendered narratives aptly capture the painful realities of those periods and the experiences of the people who survived them. At times, Sepetys drew inspiration from her own family history when developing her narratives. *Between Shades of Gray*, for instance, follows a Lithuanian teenager who struggles to survive after her family is sent to a Siberian labor camp—a fate shared by members of Sepetys's extended family during the 1940s. A Lithuanian refugee is similarly a principal character in the author's later novel *Salt to the Sea* (2016), and her experience in some ways reflects that of Sepetys's father and grandparents, who themselves became refugees during the same period. Other novels, including *Out of the Easy* (2013), *The Fountains of Silence* (2019), and *I Must Betray You* (2022), deal with different historical settings with which Sepetys has far less of a personal connection—1950s Louisiana, 1950s Spain, and 1980s Romania, respectively. However, they also demonstrate the engagement with history and memory characteristic of Sepetys's fiction.

With the 2023 publication *You: The Story; A Writer's Guide to Craft through Memory*, Sepetys explores and explains some of the storytelling techniques that have made her novels so effective and authentic, creating a writing guide that emphasizes the importance of drawing inspiration from one's memories and family history. As Sepetys's first major work of nonfiction—she had previously published short-form nonfiction in a variety of venues—*You: The Story* represents a significant departure from her body of work in terms of its genre and format. Its content and premise, however, are deeply fitting, and Sepetys herself is well suited to teach aspiring writers about the creative potential of their own lives.

Ruta Sepetys
Courtesy of Ruth Sepetys; ©Rachel Kinney Studios

Beginning *You: The Story* with a brief introduction, Sepetys provides an overview of the work's premise and clearly articulates the thesis of the book as a whole: "The secret to strong writing is embedded within your own experience." She emphasizes that she is not referring to the exclusive experience of the individual author; rather, a writer's experiences can encompass not only their personal experiences but also those of family, friends, and other people they encounter in life. Incorporating personal inspiration into a written work, she explains, grants it a greater degree of emotional authenticity, while "creating from nothing," she cautions, "results in a feeling of the same. Nothing." Sepetys also mentions her prior career in the music industry and several other personal details in the introduction, thus signaling the key role that personal anecdotes will play in *You: The Story* as the work progresses, and gives a brief summary of the book's structure and the components that make up its chapters.

Following the introduction, Sepetys begins her instruction with the chapter "Plot," in which she discusses the concept of plot structure and the questions that a writer might ask when setting a plot in motion. For instance, a writer might ask what inciting event sets the plot in motion, what conflict or layers of conflicts the characters will face, and what lessons the characters will learn about themselves. In keeping with the overall purpose of the book, Sepetys emphasizes the importance of drawing inspiration from one's own history and personal archive, which, she notes, may include diaries, receipts, photographs, and other ephemera. She also encourages the reader to think about people who have made positive or negative impacts in their lives, as "interesting plots are populated with interesting people." To that end, Sepetys shares information about her own immediate family in the "Plot" chapter, and her parents, in particular, become recurring figures throughout the remainder of the book.

In addition to setting the work in motion, the first chapter of *You: The Story* provides the first example of the format that will be used in each of the book's successive chapters. Each chapter is broken into several subsections—in the case of "Plot," they are "Personal Archives," "Curiosity," and "Conflict Layers"—that are then followed by a recap that briefly summarizes the key points discussed in the chapter. After each recap, Sepetys includes a selection of writing prompts based on the chapter's lessons, and she concludes each chapter with a subsection called "Stories to Uncover and Discover," which presents background information about several things or people mentioned in the chapter and asks the reader a question about each of them. The "Stories to Uncover and Discover" section has a dual purpose within the book. First, the section helps to familiarize readers with concepts or cultural references that may date to before their time; the section in the "Plot" chapter, for instance, provides information about union leader Jimmy Hoffa and the music genre of hair metal, both concepts that might be unfamiliar to readers born in the twenty-first century. As Sepetys explains in a later chapter, however, the questions included in each "Stories to Uncover and Discover" section likewise serve as simple research prompts and are designed to ease readers into the practice of performing historical and cultural research, a practice of great importance in the development of Sepetys's novels. Her tactic is a clever one, and it aptly underscores her assertions about the importance of research while also increasing the accessibility of the work for readers of all ages.

Throughout the next seven chapters—"Character Development," "Voice," "Perspective," "Setting," "Dialogue," "Research," and "Revision & Input"—Sepetys offers further insights into the elements that make up an effective narrative. In addition to major story elements such as setting, she places a great deal of emphasis on research, a key component of her work, as well as the revision process and the need to receive input on one's writing from others. Acknowledging that seeking out and accepting such input is often a daunting task, Sepetys discusses her own struggles with accepting feedback and recounts an incident in which she chose to ignore the feedback she received from her writing group and presented a manuscript to an editor despite her fellow group members' misgivings. The editor proceeded to point out problems with the manuscript as well, and Sepetys learned a valuable lesson about the importance of revision. In addition to emphasizing the need to repeatedly revise one's work, however, Sepetys stresses that it is important for a developing writer to recognize that a draft is simply a draft and thus does not need to be perfect. She also calls attention to the importance of taking time away from one's manuscript, as a degree of distance can often help writers view their work in new ways.

In addition to providing helpful advice to aspiring writers, *You: The Story* clearly demonstrates Sepetys's skill as a storyteller and showcases aspects of her personality and voice that do not always come through in her novels. While the Sepetys of novels such as *Between Shades of Gray* and *Salt to the Sea* and the Sepetys of *You: The Story* both display an acute understanding of emotions and of the complex, nuanced nature of human life, in the latter, the writer has a strong sense of humor that is evident throughout the book. The personal anecdotes she shares are often comedic and, at times, absurd, and they enable Sepetys to show a side of herself that may surprise readers more familiar with the brutal hardships characters face in many of her novels. Her less comedic stories are similarly compelling, and readers may wish they knew more about the fates of individuals such as Ten-Ten, an incarcerated woman Sepetys met through a mentorship program and from whom she learned a valuable lesson about perspective.

With the final chapter of *You: The Story*, "Courage," Sepetys encourages her readers to overcome any fears related to writing and the emotional reflection that will need to take place should they choose to follow her memory-focused approach. To assist writers in understanding and articulating emotions, the chapter also includes a list of more than 150 feelings that a person might experience, from abandoned or afraid to zany or zealous. Finally, Sepetys ends the book with a conclusion in which she asks aspiring writers another key question: "Instead of being trapped in our own experience and memories, could we use them to make the world less lonely for ourselves and others?" She refers back to her own experiences as a writer and recounts that the publication of *Between Shades of Gray* enabled her to connect with many readers of Lithuanian descent, including some who had personally experienced deportation or life in refugee camps during the mid-twentieth century, and even had brought her to the attention of a complete stranger who found letters pertaining to her family's time in Siberia. Sepetys emphasizes how meaningful those interactions were and stresses that those meetings would not have taken place if she had not set out to write such a personal novel. Concluding that personal memories and experiences are what make writers unique, she encourages her readers to set out on their own creative journeys of self-discovery.

You: The Story received positive reviews prior to and following its publication, with critics praising Sepetys's highly personal approach to teaching the craft of writing. In a starred review, a critic for *Kirkus Reviews* described Sepetys's approach as "sophisticated yet accessible" and noted that the work showcases "the dedication, hard work, and attention to detail that [Sepetys's] fiction is known for" as well as the author's "heart." Writing for *School Library Journal*, Kaitlin Malixi characterized Sepetys's many personal anecdotes as "endearing" and noted that such stories help Sepetys to "establish trust and connection with her readers." Malixi likewise praised the structure of the work, writing that *You: The Story*'s "scaffolding of questions and techniques, coupled with personal memories for context, offers an accessible and easily digestible approach." The tone of the work also inspired praise, with Lisa Denton of the *Chattanooga Times Free Press* calling attention to Sepetys's "warm, engaging and deeply honest" tone and describing the work as a whole as "magnanimous, witty and inspiring."

Some critics found the advice Sepetys gives aspiring writers to be somewhat basic in nature, however; the anonymous reviewer for *Publishers Weekly*, for instance, noted that her "advice largely follows prevailing wisdom" and will thus be best appreciated by inexperienced writers rather than those farther along in their journey as storytellers. Nevertheless, the *Publishers Weekly* reviewer appreciated the "bounty of writing prompts" featured within *You: The Story*, which they characterized as particularly relevant to the work's target audience.

Author Biography
Ruta Sepetys is the author of several historical novels for young adult readers, including *Between Shades of Gray* (2011), *Salt to the Sea* (2016), and *I Must Betray You* (2022).

Joy Crelin

Review Sources

Denton, Lisa. "Review: In 'You,' Award-Winning Author Ruta Sepetys Offers a Guide to the Craft of Writing." Review of *You: The Story; A Writer's Guide to Craft through Memory*, by Ruta Sepetys. *Chattanooga Times Free Press*, 17 June 2023, www.timesfreepress.com/news/2023/jun/17/review-in-you-award-winning-author-tfp/. Accessed 25 Sept. 2023.

Malixi, Kaitlin. Review of *You: The Story; A Writer's Guide to Craft through Memory*, by Ruta Sepetys. *School Library Journal*, 1 June 2023, www.slj.com/review/you-the-story-a-writers-guide-to-craft-through-memory. Accessed 25 Sept. 2023.

Review of *You: The Story; A Writer's Guide to Craft through Memory*, by Ruta Sepetys. *Kirkus Reviews*, 7 Feb. 2023, www.kirkusreviews.com/book-reviews/ruta-sepetys/you-sepetys/. Accessed 25 Sept. 2023.

Review of *You: The Story; A Writer's Guide to Craft through Memory*, by Ruta Sepetys. *Publishers Weekly*, 30 Mar. 2023, www.publishersweekly.com/9780593524381. Accessed 25 Sept. 2023.

Category Index

Autobiography
Family Style (Thien Pham), 160

Biography
The Art Thief (Michael Finkel), 35
August Wilson (Patti Hartigan), 40
The Exceptions (Kate Zernike), 149
Flee North (Scott Shane), 184
Impossible Escape (Steve Sheinkin), 291
King (Jonathan Eig), 306
Liliana's Invincible Summer (Cristina Rivera Garza), 339
Master Slave Husband Wife (Ilyon Woo), 362
Nearer My Freedom (Monica Edinger and Lesley Younge), 396
Rough Sleepers (Tracy Kidder), 489
The Six (Loren Grush), 512
The Slip (Prudence Peiffer), 517
A Stranger in Your Own City (Ghaith Abdul-Ahad), 541
Thunderclap (Laura Cumming), 578
The World (Simon Sebag Montefiore), 689

Criticism
Monsters (Claire Dederer), 372

Current Affairs
An Amerikan Family (Santi Elijah Holley), 30
Cobalt Red (Siddarth Kara), 93
The Deadline (Jill Lepore), 123
The Great Displacement (Jake Bittle), 211
Ordinary Notes (Christina Sharpe), 416
Poverty, by America (Matthew Desmond), 447

When Crack Was King (Donovan X. Ramsey), 657

Economics
Poverty, by America (Matthew Desmond), 447

Environment
Cobalt Red (Siddarth Kara), 93
Fire Weather (John Vaillant), 174
The Great Displacement (Jake Bittle), 211
The Parrot and the Igloo (David Lipsky), 433

Essays
The Half Known Life (Pico Iyer), 221
Our Migrant Souls (Héctor Tobar), 421
Quietly Hostile (Samantha Irby), 466
Thin Skin (Jenn Shapland), 569

Fine Arts
The Slip (Prudence Peiffer), 517
Thunderclap (Laura Cumming), 578

Graphic Nonfiction
Monstrous (Sarah Myer), 376

Graphic Novel
A First Time for Everything (Dan Santat), 179
Monica (Daniel Clowes), 367
Parachute Kids (Betty C. Tang), 429
Roaming (Jillian Tamaki and Mariko Tamaki), 479

History
American Ramble (Neil King Jr.), 25
An Amerikan Family (Santi Elijah Holley), 30

The Deadline (Jill Lepore), 123
A Fever in the Heartland (Timothy Egan), 169
Ghost of the Orphanage (Christine Kenneally), 206
I Saw Death Coming (Kidada E. Williams), 281
Impossible Escape (Steve Sheinkin), 291
Master Slave Husband Wife (Ilyon Woo), 362
More Than a Dream (Yohuru Williams and Michael G. Long), 381
Mott Street (Ava Chin), 391
Nearer My Freedom (Monica Edinger and Lesley Younge), 396
Ordinary Notes (Christina Sharpe), 416
The Rediscovery of America (Ned Blackhawk), 470
The Six (Loren Grush), 512
The Slip (Prudence Peiffer), 517
Soil (Camille T. Dungy), 527
A Stranger in Your Own City (Ghaith Abdul-Ahad), 541
The 272 (Rachel L. Swarns), 592
Valiant Women (Lena S. Andrews), 597
The Wager (David Grann), 616
When Crack Was King (Donovan X. Ramsey), 657
The Windeby Puzzle (Lois Lowry), 670
The World (Simon Sebag Montefiore), 689
You Have to Be Prepared to Die Before You Can Begin to Live (Paul Kix), 699

Horror
How to Sell a Haunted House (Grady Hendrix), 267

Law
The Deadline (Jill Lepore), 123

Literary Criticism
The Deadline (Jill Lepore), 123

Medicine
Rough Sleepers (Tracy Kidder), 489

Memoir
American Ramble (Neil King Jr.), 25
Family Style (Thien Pham), 160
A First Time for Everything (Dan Santat), 179
The Hard Parts (Oksana Masters with Cassidy Randall), 231
Liliana's Invincible Summer (Cristina Rivera Garza), 339
A Man of Two Faces (Viet Thanh Nguyen), 357
Monsters (Claire Dederer), 372
Mott Street (Ava Chin), 391
Ordinary Notes (Christina Sharpe), 416
Owner of a Lonely Heart (Beth Nguyen), 425
Soil (Camille T. Dungy), 527
Thunderclap (Laura Cumming), 578
The Windeby Puzzle (Lois Lowry), 670
Women We Buried, Women We Burned (Rachel Louise Snyder), 679

Miscellaneous
Big (Vashti Harrison), 60
You: The Story (Ruta Sepetys), 703

Natural History
What an Owl Knows (Jennifer Ackerman), 652

Nature
Soil (Camille T. Dungy), 527
Tenacious Beasts (Christopher J. Preston), 559
What an Owl Knows (Jennifer Ackerman), 652

CATEGORY INDEX

Nonfiction
Saying It Loud (Mark Whitaker), 498

Novel
The Adventures of Amina al-Sirafi (Shannon Chakraborty), 5
Age of Vice (Deepti Kapoor), 15
All the Sinners Bleed (S. A. Cosby), 20
The Bee Sting (Paul Murray), 45
The Berry Pickers (Amanda Peters), 50
Beyond the Door of No Return (David Diop), 55
Big Tree (Brian Selznick), 64
Biography of X (Catherine Lacey), 68
Birnam Wood (Eleanor Catton), 73
Blackouts (Justin Torres), 78
Bright Young Women (Jessica Knoll), 83
Chain-Gang All-Stars (Nana Kwame Adjei-Brenyah), 88
A Council of Dolls (Mona Susan Power), 98
The Covenant of Water (Abraham Verghese), 103
The Crane Husband (Kelly Barnhill), 108
Crook Manifesto (Colson Whitehead), 113
A Day of Fallen Night (Samantha Shannon), 118
The Devil of the Provinces (Juan Cárdenas), 128
Don't Fear the Reaper (Stephen Graham Jones), 136
Dust Child (Nguyễn Phan Quế Mai), 140
The End of Drum-Time (Hanna Pylväinen), 144
Family Lore (Elizabeth Acevedo), 155
The Ferryman (Justin Cronin), 165
The Fraud (Zadie Smith), 189
The Future (Naomi Alderman), 202
Greek Lessons (Han Kang), 216
Happiness Falls (Angie Kim), 226

The Heaven & Earth Grocery Store (James McBride), 236
Hell Bent (Leigh Bardugo), 241
Hello Beautiful (Ann Napolitano), 246
The House of Doors (Tan Twan Eng), 258
A House With Good Bones (T. Kingfisher (pseudonym of Ursula Vernon)), 263
Hula (Jasmin Iolani Hakes), 271
I Have Some Questions for You (Rebecca Makkai), 276
Imogen, Obviously (Becky Albertalli), 286
In the Lives of Puppets (TJ Klune), 296
Into the Light (Mark Oshiro), 301
Lady Tan's Circle of Women (Lisa See), 311
Land of Milk and Honey (C Pam Zhang), 316
The Last Animal (Ramona Ausubel), 321
The Last Tale of the Flower Bride (Roshani Chokshi), 325
Let Us Descend (Jesmyn Ward), 330
The Librarianist (Patrick deWitt), 334
Lone Women (Victor LaValle), 343
Loot (Tania James), 347
The Lost Year (Katherine Marsh), 352
The Most Secret Memory of Men (Mohamed Mbougar Sarr), 386
No One Prayed Over Their Graves (Khaled Khalifa), 401
North Woods (Daniel Mason), 406
Old God's Time (Sebastian Barry), 411
Pineapple Street (Jenny Jackson), 438
Pomegranate (Helen Elaine Lee), 443
Promise Boys (Nick Brooks), 452
Prophet Song (Paul Lynch), 461
Remember Us (Jacqueline Woodson), 475
Saints of the Household (Ari Tison), 494

Silver Nitrate (Silvia Moreno-Garcia), 503
Simon Sort of Says (Erin Bow), 507
Small Mercies (Dennis Lehane), 522
A Spell of Good Things (Ayọ̀bámi Adébáyọ̀), 531
Starling House (Alix E. Harrow), 536
Symphony of Secrets (Brendan Slocumb), 550
The Terraformers (Annalee Newitz), 564
This Other Eden (Paul Harding), 574
Tom Lake (Ann Patchett), 583
Tremor (Teju Cole), 588
The Vaster Wilds (Lauren Groff), 602
Vera Wong's Unsolicited Advice for Murderers (Jesse Q. Sutanto), 607
Victory City (Salman Rushdie), 611
Warrior Girl Unearthed (Angeline Boulley), 621
We Are All So Good At Smiling (Amber McBride), 625
Wellness (Nathan Hill), 634
Western Lane (Chetna Maroo), 639
Weyward (Emilia Hart), 643
Whalefall (Daniel Kraus), 648
The Wind Knows My Name (Isabel Allende), 665
The Windeby Puzzle (Lois Lowry), 670
The Words That Remain (Stênio Gardel), 684
Yellowface (Rebecca F. Kuang), 694

Poetry
Above Ground (Clint Smith), 1
The Diaspora Sonnets (Oliver de la Paz), 132
From From (Monica Youn), 194
From Unincorporated Territory [åmot] (Craig Santos Perez), 198

Nearer My Freedom (Monica Edinger and Lesley Younge), 396
Promises of Gold (José Olivarez), 457
suddenly we (Evie Shockley), 546
We Are All So Good At Smiling (Amber McBride), 625

Religion
The Half Known Life (Pico Iyer), 221

Science
The Exceptions (Kate Zernike), 149
The Parrot and the Igloo (David Lipsky), 433
The Six (Loren Grush), 512

Short fiction
After the Funeral and Other Stories (Tessa Hadley), 10
The Hive and the Honey (Paul Yoon), 250
Holler, Child (LaToya Watkins), 254
Roman Stories (Jhumpa Lahiri), 484
Temple Folk (Aaliyah Bilal), 555
Wednesday's Child (Yiyun Li), 629
White Cat, Black Dog (Kelly Link), 661
Witness (Jamel Brinkley), 674

Sociology
Poverty, by America (Matthew Desmond), 447
When Crack Was King (Donovan X. Ramsey), 657

Travel
American Ramble (Neil King Jr.), 25
The Half Known Life (Pico Iyer), 221

Title Index

Above Ground (Clint Smith), 1
The Adventures of Amina al-Sirafi (Shannon Chakraborty), 5
After the Funeral and Other Stories (Tessa Hadley), 10
Age of Vice (Deepti Kapoor), 15
All the Sinners Bleed (S. A. Cosby), 20
American Ramble (Neil King Jr.), 25
An Amerikan Family (Santi Elijah Holley), 30
The Art Thief (Michael Finkel), 35
August Wilson (Patti Hartigan), 40

The Bee Sting (Paul Murray), 45
The Berry Pickers (Amanda Peters), 50
Beyond the Door of No Return (David Diop), 55
Big (Vashti Harrison), 60
Big Tree (Brian Selznick), 64
Biography of X (Catherine Lacey), 68
Birnam Wood (Eleanor Catton), 73
Blackouts (Justin Torres), 78
Bright Young Women (Jessica Knoll), 83

Chain-Gang All-Stars (Nana Kwame Adjei-Brenyah), 88
Cobalt Red (Siddarth Kara), 93
A Council of Dolls (Mona Susan Power), 98
The Covenant of Water (Abraham Verghese), 103
The Crane Husband (Kelly Barnhill), 108
Crook Manifesto (Colson Whitehead), 113

A Day of Fallen Night (Samantha Shannon), 118
The Deadline (Jill Lepore), 123

The Devil of the Provinces (Juan Cárdenas), 128
The Diaspora Sonnets (Oliver de la Paz), 132
Don't Fear the Reaper (Stephen Graham Jones), 136
Dust Child (Nguyễn Phan Quế Mai), 140

The End of Drum-Time (Hanna Pylväinen), 144
The Exceptions (Kate Zernike), 149

Family Lore (Elizabeth Acevedo), 155
Family Style (Thien Pham), 160
The Ferryman (Justin Cronin), 165
A Fever in the Heartland (Timothy Egan), 169
Fire Weather (John Vaillant), 174
A First Time for Everything (Dan Santat), 179
Flee North (Scott Shane), 184
The Fraud (Zadie Smith), 189
From From (Monica Youn), 194
From Unincorporated Territory [åmot] (Craig Santos Perez), 198
The Future (Naomi Alderman), 202

Ghost of the Orphanage (Christine Kenneally), 206
The Great Displacement (Jake Bittle), 211
Greek Lessons (Han Kang), 216

The Half Known Life (Pico Iyer), 221
Happiness Falls (Angie Kim), 226
The Hard Parts (Oksana Masters with Cassidy Randall), 231
The Heaven & Earth Grocery Store (James McBride), 236

Hell Bent (Leigh Bardugo), 241
Hello Beautiful (Ann Napolitano), 246
The Hive and the Honey (Paul Yoon), 250
Holler, Child (LaToya Watkins), 254
The House of Doors (Tan Twan Eng), 258
A House With Good Bones (T. Kingfisher (pseudonym of Ursula Vernon)), 263
How to Sell a Haunted House (Grady Hendrix), 267
Hula (Jasmin Iolani Hakes), 271

I Have Some Questions for You (Rebecca Makkai), 276
I Saw Death Coming (Kidada E. Williams), 281
Imogen, Obviously (Becky Albertalli), 286
Impossible Escape (Steve Sheinkin), 291
In the Lives of Puppets (TJ Klune), 296
Into the Light (Mark Oshiro), 301

King (Jonathan Eig), 306

Lady Tan's Circle of Women (Lisa See), 311
Land of Milk and Honey (C Pam Zhang), 316
The Last Animal (Ramona Ausubel), 321
The Last Tale of the Flower Bride (Roshani Chokshi), 325
Let Us Descend (Jesmyn Ward), 330
The Librarianist (Patrick deWitt), 334
Liliana's Invincible Summer (Cristina Rivera Garza), 339
Lone Women (Victor LaValle), 343
Loot (Tania James), 347
The Lost Year (Katherine Marsh), 352

A Man of Two Faces (Viet Thanh Nguyen), 357
Master Slave Husband Wife (Ilyon Woo), 362
Monica (Daniel Clowes), 367
Monsters (Claire Dederer), 372
Monstrous (Sarah Myer), 376
More Than a Dream (Yohuru Williams and Michael G. Long), 381
The Most Secret Memory of Men (Mohamed Mbougar Sarr), 386
Mott Street (Ava Chin), 391

Nearer My Freedom (Monica Edinger and Lesley Younge), 396
No One Prayed Over Their Graves (Khaled Khalifa), 401
North Woods (Daniel Mason), 406

Old God's Time (Sebastian Barry), 411
Ordinary Notes (Christina Sharpe), 416
Our Migrant Souls (Héctor Tobar), 421
Owner of a Lonely Heart (Beth Nguyen), 425

Parachute Kids (Betty C. Tang), 429
The Parrot and the Igloo (David Lipsky), 433
Pineapple Street (Jenny Jackson), 438
Pomegranate (Helen Elaine Lee), 443
Poverty, by America (Matthew Desmond), 447
Promise Boys (Nick Brooks), 452
Promises of Gold (José Olivarez), 457
Prophet Song (Paul Lynch), 461

Quietly Hostile (Samantha Irby), 466

The Rediscovery of America (Ned Blackhawk), 470
Remember Us (Jacqueline Woodson), 475
Roaming (Jillian Tamaki and Mariko Tamaki), 479

TITLE INDEX

Roman Stories (Jhumpa Lahiri), 484
Rough Sleepers (Tracy Kidder), 489

Saints of the Household (Ari Tison), 494
Saying It Loud (Mark Whitaker), 498
Silver Nitrate (Silvia Moreno-Garcia), 503
Simon Sort of Says (Erin Bow), 507
The Six (Loren Grush), 512
The Slip (Prudence Peiffer), 517
Small Mercies (Dennis Lehane), 522
Soil (Camille T. Dungy), 527
A Spell of Good Things (Ayọ̀bámi Adébáyọ̀), 531
Starling House (Alix E. Harrow), 536
A Stranger in Your Own City (Ghaith Abdul-Ahad), 541
suddenly we (Evie Shockley), 546
Symphony of Secrets (Brendan Slocumb), 550

Temple Folk (Aaliyah Bilal), 555
Tenacious Beasts (Christopher J. Preston), 559
The Terraformers (Annalee Newitz), 564
Thin Skin (Jenn Shapland), 569
This Other Eden (Paul Harding), 574
Thunderclap (Laura Cumming), 578
Tom Lake (Ann Patchett), 583
Tremor (Teju Cole), 588
The 272 (Rachel L. Swarns), 592

Valiant Women (Lena S. Andrews), 597
The Vaster Wilds (Lauren Groff), 602

Vera Wong's Unsolicited Advice for Murderers (Jesse Q. Sutanto), 607
Victory City (Salman Rushdie), 611

The Wager (David Grann), 616
Warrior Girl Unearthed (Angeline Boulley), 621
We Are All So Good At Smiling (Amber McBride), 625
Wednesday's Child (Yiyun Li), 629
Wellness (Nathan Hill), 634
Western Lane (Chetna Maroo), 639
Weyward (Emilia Hart), 643
Whalefall (Daniel Kraus), 648
What an Owl Knows (Jennifer Ackerman), 652
When Crack Was King (Donovan X. Ramsey), 657
White Cat, Black Dog (Kelly Link), 661
The Wind Knows My Name (Isabel Allende), 665
The Windeby Puzzle (Lois Lowry), 670
Witness (Jamel Brinkley), 674
Women We Buried, Women We Burned (Rachel Louise Snyder), 679
The Words That Remain (Stênio Gardel), 684
The World (Simon Sebag Montefiore), 689

Yellowface (Rebecca F. Kuang), 694
You Have to Be Prepared to Die Before You Can Begin to Live (Paul Kix), 699
You: The Story (Ruta Sepetys), 703